French Tales of Vampires (Vol. 2)

FROM THE SAME PUBLISHER

Jean-Marc & Randy Lofficier. *The French Fantasy Treasury* (3 volumes)

Jean-Marc & Randy Lofficier. *French Tales of Alien Contacts*

Jean-Marc & Randy Lofficier. *French Tales of Cataclysms*

Jean-Marc & Randy Lofficier. *French Tales of Mad Scientists* (3 volumes)

Jean-Marc & Randy Lofficier. *French Tales of Vampires* (3 volumes)

Jean-Marc & Randy Lofficier. *Shadowmen: Heroes & Villains of French Pulp Fiction*

Jean-Marc & Randy Lofficier. *Shadowmen 2: Heroes & Villains of French Comics*

Brian Stableford. *Automata: The Imaginative Legacy of Jacques de Vaucanson*

Brian Stableford. *The Plurality of Imaginary Worlds: The Evolution of French* Roman Scientifique

Brian Stableford. *Tales of Enchantment and Disenchantment: A History of Faerie, with an Exemplary Anthology of Tales*

Brian Stableford. *Weird Fiction in France: A Showcase Anthology of its Origins and Development*

French Tales of Vampires (Vol. 2)

by
Paul Féval, Léon Gozlan
and **Etienne-Léon de Lamothe-Langon.**

translated, annotated and introduced by
Brian Stableford

A Black Coat Press Book

English adaptations
Etienne-Léon de Lamothe-Langon : The Virgin Vampire (1825)
Paul Féval : Knightshade (The Vampire Brothers) (1860)
Leon Gozlan: The Vampire of the Val-De-Grâce (1862)
Copyright © 2024 by Brian Stableford
Introductions Copyright © 2024 by Brian Stableford & Jean-Marc Lofficier.
Cover illustration Copyright © 2024 by Mike Hoffman.

TABLE OF CONTENTS

Introduction 7
Etienne-Léon de Lamothe-Langon: *The Virgin Vampire* 9
Afterword 169
Paul Féval: *The Vampire Brothers* 175
Léon Gozlan: *The Vampire of the Val-De-Grâce* 257

Introduction

The theme of the resurrection from the dead takes multiple aspects, but can be roughly grouped into three categories: ghosts, vampires and zombies, to use a terminology dear to the horror film fans.

A ghost is nothing more than a dead person who refuses to cross the threshold of death and persists in wanting to continue living, in a form that ranges from the ineffably ethereal to the grotesquely repulsive.

The ghosts in Oscar Wilde's *The Canterville Ghost* (1906), R. A, Dick's *The Ghost and Mrs. Muir* (1945), Alfred Adam's *Sylvie et le Fantôme* (1945) or Daniel Pennac's *Messieurs les Enfants* (1997) are *revenants*—the word defines the concept's underlying notion: sympathetic, funny and loving. In contrast, the specters from Shirley Jackson's *The Haunting of Hill House* (1959), Richard Matheson's *Hell House* (1971) or Peter Straub's *Ghost Story* (1979) are abominations whose evil existence is a threat to the physical, mental and spiritual survival of the protagonists.

From Casper, the friendly little ghostly child to the terrifying Spectre of DC Comics, from the love-struck revenants of Marcel Brion to those thirsting for revenge in the novels of Marc Agapit, the ghost is, to paraphrase Clausewitz, simply the continuation of life on another plane. The ghost only exists because it is attached to life and the living. If this connection is broken, the ghost no longer has any reason to exist and disappears into the afterlife, re-establishing the natural order of things. The ghost thus symbolizes a victory, alas all too ephemeral, over death.

The vampire, on the other hand, is an incarnated ghost, condemned to a parasitic existence—he sucks the blood of the living, or sometimes their "psychic energy", to feed him/herself and keep on living. This makes him not a revenant, like the ghost, but a superior form of life. The vampire is a dead person who refuses to be dead; he asserts that he is not dead, but "more-than-alive."

Like the ghost, the vampire is a myth with two faces: erotic and thanatological. The first category of vampires includes, to name but the most famous, John Polidori's Byronesque Lord Ruthven (*The Vampyre*, 1819), arguably the first vampire in popular literature, Sheridan Le Fanu's Carmilla (1871), Pierre Kast's Vampires of the Alfama (1975), Anne Rice's Lestat (1976) and Jean Rollin's two orphaned vampire girls (1993). The second category includes the famous Dracula by Bram Stoker (1897), and his even more monstrous cinematic alter-ego, Count Orlock from the film *Nosferatu* (1930), Barlow by Stephen King (1975) and all the various vampires fought today by Buffy, the endearing heroine of a 1997 TV series.

The moral ambiguity present in the literary treatment of the vampire, contrasting seduction and horror, is indicative of how the theme of survival after death is perceived by the surrounding culture. Is it a desirable dream or, on the contrary, a loathsome abomination? And what price must be paid for this survival? For the vampire is both superhuman and subhuman: a sexual predator yet impotent, a passionate romantic yet soulless, depending on the version... So many contradictions are embodied in the vampire myth. The vampire is our mirror of the afterlife, the embodiment of our choices.

The zombie, on the other hand, doesn't get the same preferential treatment. If the vampire is an "more-than-alive" creature, we could say that the zombie is a "less-than-alive" one. With the zombie, all moral ambiguity disappears. Any resurrection is an unnatural act, a sacrilege. Mary Shelley's Frankenstein's Monster (1818) is, of course, the prototype of the future zombie, especially in its film version: ponderous gait, hallucinated expression, raw savagery. It was cinema, more than literature, that gave the zombie its letters of nobility. From the classic film by Victor Halperin *White Zombie* (1932) to George Romero's *Night of the Living Dead* (1968), Lucio Fulci's *La Paura* (1980) and Sam Raimi's *The Evil Dead* (1982), and all their predecessors and successors, the zombie has become one of the pillars of horror cinema, successfully combining two taboos: that of death and that of cannibalism.

The simplicity of the zombie theme raises the question of the quasi-divine prohibition of resurrection. This notion is brilliantly evoked in W. W. Jacobs' short story *Monkey's Paw* (1902) in which a couple endowed with a magic talisman capable of granting three wishes prefer to send their resurrected son back to the grave from which he should never have emerged, rather than lay eyes on the abomination he has become.

The same theme can be found in Stephen King's *Pet Semetary* (1983) and Brigitte Aubert's *Ténèbres sur Jacksonville* (1994). The zombie is the final victory of death, presented as preferable to the horror of resurrection. The -only exception to this chorus of protests is Robert Silverberg's *Recalled to Life* (1958), in which the resurrection of the dead (limited to victims of recent accidents) is presented as an inevitable advance in medicine, without any other form of morality.

Jean-Marc & Randy Lofficier

Etienne-Léon de Lamothe-Langon: *The Virgin Vampire*

La Vampire, ou la vierge de Hongrie, *signed "Le B^{on} [i.e. the Baron] de Lamothe-Langon", was initially published in 1844 by three volumes by Madame Cardinal. The novel is primarily interesting as a significant contribution to early French vampire fiction; it is one of a group of works inspired by the widespread popularity of John William Polidori's novelette* The Vampyre *(1819),[1] which was rapidly translated into French because it was wrongly attributed, at first, to the immensely fashionable Lord Byron—a misattribution that its popularity and influence outlived.* La Vampire *represents a significant step in the elaboration and diversification of the literary image of the vampire. It is also of some interest, however, by virtue of its particular authorship; the Baron de Lamothe-Langon went on to become one of the best-selling writers in France during the 1830s, when he produced works of a highly distinctive and rather eccentric kind on a prodigious scale.*

The breakthrough work that boosted Lamothe-Langon's career to sudden and enormous success, and which remains in print to this day, was published under several different variants of its title during the author's lifetime, but it consists of six volumes, first issued in 1829-30, of the supposed memoirs of one of King Louis XV's mistresses, the Comtesse Du Barry. The Comtesse, who eventually perished on the guillotine during the Terror at the age of 50, had neglected to write her memoirs herself, so Lamothe-Langon did the job for her, mingling known historical fact with an abundance of highly imaginative and conspicuously salacious detail. Some bibliographies assert that the text he submitted was modified before publication by Amédée Pichot, possibly to remove some of the more blatant inaccuracies and inventions, and several of the later editions were modified by other hands for various reasons. As a dedicated professional, however, Lamothe-Langon immediately set out to capitalize on his success, and spent the next decade churning out fake memoirs by the dozen, many of which similarly featured royal mistresses and other "ladies of quality," but whose range extended to take in many other famous individuals, ranging from the Duc de Richelieu through various kings to Talleyrand and Napoléon Bonaparte (three times), not neglecting such fellow-fakers as Cagliostro and the Comte de Saint-Germain.

---

[1] Included in the Black Coat Press edition of *Lord Ruthven the Vampyre* (ISBN 9781932983104).

Nor did Lamothe-Langon limit his activities to faking memoirs; in 1829, he also published his Histoire de l'Inquisition en France *[History of the Inquisition in France], supposedly making extensive use of archives preserved in his native city, Toulouse—archives that did not actually exist. Until the fraud was discovered, many of the "facts" he recorded were widely repeated, especially in histories of witchcraft and Catharism—fields that still have not entirely recovered from the falsehoods he blithely incorporated into them. He had earlier written 459 articles for the* Biographie Toulousaine *(1823) and had published a* Biographie des préfets des 87 départements de la France, par un sous-préfet *(1826), as well as contributing articles to several other reference books, but the extent to which that work might be polluted by invention is unknown, because no one has ever cared enough to try to find out.*

Given that Lamothe-Langon made a career out of fantasizing other people's biographies, his own probably needs to be treated with a pinch of salt, at least insofar as the details contained in reference books can be traced back to him rather than to more objective sources. One contemporary bibliographical encyclopedia asserts that his original name was Langon, the "Lamothe" having been added belatedly as a hangover from the pseudonyms he used during the first phase of his literary career. The particule *in his name was earned rather than inherited; he obtained his barony by loyal service to the Empire, as a civil servant (although he did claim to have distinguished himself in battle in Italy while in administrative service there, and to have earned his ennoblement that way). If he owed his early success in life to his loyalty to the Napoleonic cause rather than his early literary endeavors, however, he owed his eventual literary career to the ruination that followed the Empire's collapse, when old Bonapartists fell out of fashion as instruments of state.*

The future Baron de Lamothe-Langon was born in Toulouse in 1786 and remained there until he was 20, when he went to Paris to make his fortune. His own accounts of his youth allege that he was a brilliant student who had already embarked on prolific literary endeavors before leaving his home town, but it was not until he reached Paris that he first reached print, initially trying to make his name as a poet. In that capacity, he published a number of Odes dedicated to various highly-placed personages, including members of Napoléon's family and the painter David, as well as a 130-verse account of Louis XVI dans sa prison (1808). He called himself Léon de La Motte for a while, and is mistakenly described as a "poète de Montpellier" in the Martyrologie littéraire *of 1816, which not only assumes that he is dead, but prints his self-penned epitaph.*

The Martyrologie littéraire *does note that the fictitious poet wrote prose as well, naming two works, but does not take the trouble to record the fact that he did so under a modified pseudonym, Léon de La Motte-Houdancourt—a blatant attempt to link his supposed descent to the famous Maréchal de France, Philippe de La Mothe-Houdancourt (1605-1657). Contemporary bibliographies credit him with three prose works published during the first phase of his ca-*

reer—Cinq chapitres de mon roman, ou les Rêves de ma cousine *(1808);* Clémence Isaure et les troubadours, précédé d'un Précis historique sur les troubadours et les jeux floraux *(1808); and* Gabriel, ou le Fanatisme *(1809)— without giving any further indication of what they contain. The title of the second is, however, reasonably informative; the Toulousian* Académie des Jeux Floraux *is the oldest literary society in the world, founded in 1323 by the Consistori del Gay Saber [The Society of the Gay Science, in Occitan, then the language of Provençal]. The "jeux floraux" [floral games] were—and still are— annual competitions in which prizes were awarded for poetry. Lamothe-Langon was appointed as one of the forty members of the Académie during the second phase of his literary career, and may well have been among its prize-winners before or during the first; "Léon de La Motte" appears to have fancied himself, or at least represented himself, as a modern troubadour.*

This brief initial phase of Lamothe-Langon's literary activity was, however, cut short when he began to obtain significant administrative posts, initially as a sous-préfet, in which capacity he returned to Toulouse in 1811, and then as préfet of the same city, before being transferred to various other locations. He was apparently still in possession of an administrative office in Carcassonne during the Hundred Days, having survived Napoléon's first exile in Elba, but following the subsequent confirmation of the Restoration in 1815, he was soon thrown out of the civil service entirely—at which point he went back home to Toulouse, and set out determinedly to make a living from his pen.

The earliest endeavor of the second phase of Lamothe-Langon's career that can now be traced back to him is the Gothic novel L'Hermite de la tombe mystérieuse, ou le Fantôme du vieux château *[The Hermit of the Mysterious Tomb; or, The Phantom of the Old Château] (1816)[2], which was originally misrepresented as a translation of a work by the popular English novelist Ann Radcliffe. If this was not the beginning of his career as a faker, it was at least the most conspicuous early evidence of the penchant. He reprinted the novel under his own name in 1822, when he corrected the spelling of the first term to* Ermite *(the H had presumably been included to make the work sound more English). It was followed by* Tête de mort, ou la Croix du Cimetière de Saint-Adrien *[The Death's-Head; or, The Cross of St. Adrian's Cemetery] (1817).*

His next novel, Les Mystères de la tour de Saint-Jean ou Les Chevaliers du Temple *[The Mysteries of St. John's Tower; or, The Knights Templar] (1819) was also passed off as a translation of English Gothic fiction, this time from the work of "Monk" (i.e. Matthew Gregory) Lewis. Again, he appears to have reprinted the work under his own name a few years later, as* Les Chevaliers du Temple—*that being the title given in the list recorded in* La Vampire—*although*

---

[2] Published by Black Coat Press as *The Mysterious Hermit of the Tomb* (ISBN 9781612277349).

the Bibliothèque Nationale catalogue does not include an edition with that title, or any edition of Tête de mort.

Lamothe-Langon published another novel in 1819, while he was still using the Lamotte-Houdancourt pseudonym, Maître Étienne, ou Les Fermiers et les châtelains *[Maître Étienne; or, Farmers and Chatelains]; it bears no subtitle might well have been the first of a series of novels whose later inclusions are mostly advertised as* romans de moeurs *[novels of manners]—which is to say, stories of contemporary life, supposedly illustrative of customs and folkways. Such novels were to become the author's major specialism during the 1820s, although their displacement of Gothic thrillers was gradual.*

The list of previous works included in La Vampire *does not include* La Spectre de la galerie du château d'Estalens, ou le Sauveur mystérieux *[The Specter of the Gallery of the Château d'Estalens; or, The Mysterious Rescuer] (1820, also described falsely as a translation from the English) or* Les Apparitions du château de Tarabel, ou le Protecteur invisible *[The Ghosts of the Château de Tarabel; or, The Invisible Protector] (1822), although both are credited to Lamothe-Langon in the BN catalogue, but it does include* Jean de Procida, ou les Vêpres Siciliennes, roman historique *[Jean de Procida; or, The Sicilian Vespers] (1822) and* Le Monastère des Frères noirs, ou l'Étendard de la mort *[The Monastery of the Black Friars; or, The Standard of Death] (1825), albeit without either subtitle. By this time, Lamothe-Langon had begun signing his books with the name he now used in real life, and had staked his claim to many of those issued earlier under other names.*

La Vampire *and* Le Monastère des Frères noirs *seem to have been Lamothe-Langon's final works in the Gothic vein for some while. The other books he published in 1825 were* Le 21 janvier, ou la Malédiction d'un père *[The Twenty-First of January; or, A Father's Curse],* Monsieur le préfet *[The Prefect] and* La Province à Paris, ou les Caquets d'une grande ville *[Provincialism in Paris, or Big City Gossip], all of which are presumably naturalistic—and perhaps, at least in the latter cases, autobiographically-influenced (the second title waxes lyrical on the subject of electoral fraud). He did go on to incorporate Gothic elements into the much later* Souvenirs d'un fantôme, chroniques d'un cimetière *[A Phantom's Memories; Chronicles of a Cemetery] (1838), which consists of fake memoirs in a more satirical vein, but* La Cloche du trépassé, ou Les Mystères du château de Beauvoir *[The Funeral Bell; or, The Mysteries of the Château de Beauvoir] (1839) may well have been an early work reaching print belatedly.*

Most of the novels Lamoth-Langon published in the late 1820s were subtitled romans de moeurs, *but the first thus advertised might be reckoned something of an anomaly, being* L'Espion de police *[The Police Spy] (1826). Although not a fake memoir itself, despite its pretensions to realism, it surely helped to inspire one of the most famous of all the fake memoirs of the period, Eugène Vidocq's* Mémoires *(1828), the author of which made extravagant* claims regarding his founding of the Sûreté—and thus became the godfather of the entire genre of crime fiction, cited by Edgar Allan Poe, Honoré de Balzac, Paul Féval and many other pioneers of honest fiction in that vein. It is not improbable that seeing his explicit work of fiction ripped off in this way helped to prompt Lamothe-Langon to demonstrate that he could play same game in a broader arena, having already begun to prepare the stage in La Cour d'un prince régnant ou Les Deux maîtresses *[The Court of a Reigning Prince; or The Two Mistresses] (1827)* and Le Chancelier et les censeurs *[The Chancellor and the Censors] (1828)*. The latter novel features Madame Du Barry as a central character, and contributed several incidents to her fake memoirs.

The other labeled romans de moeurs *of this period were* Le Grand seigneur et la pauvre fille *[The Nobleman and the Poor Girl] (1829)*, Le Ventru, ou Comme ils étaient naguère *[The Obese; or, How Things Were Before] (1829)*, Le Fournisseur et la Provençale *[The Tradesman and the Provençal Girl] (1830)* and Le Duc et le page *[The Duke and the Page-Boy] (1831)*. The sequence of titles presumably offers a fair indication of the direction the work in question followed, and the manner in which its interest in salacious material was developed. Given that Lamothe-Langon was also working on reference books and supposedly serious historical works during this period, the intensity of his production was remarkable even before he stepped it up by another gear in the 1830s.

How many prose works Lamothe-Langon produced in total is difficult to estimate, partly because he cited figures himself that are probably exaggerated, but there were at least 100. He also claimed to have written many more that remained unpublished, although that might also have been an exaggeration. What is certain, however—and perhaps odd—is that his production tailed off abruptly after 1840 and soon stopped entirely, even though he did not die until 1864. He therefore took no part in the spectacular boom in popular fiction that followed the feuilleton-based newspaper circulation wars of the late 1840s, although he would seem to have been ideally qualified to do so. Nor did he return to any conspicuous activity of any kind after Napoléon III's coup d'état in 1851, when old Bonapartists finally came back into fashion (although he was in his 60s by then, and might have blotted his copybook somewhat with his three faked memoirs of the first Emperor).

What became of Lamothe-Langon after 1840 remains something of a mystery; although he published a few more books, they might well have been written earlier; the novels L'Homme de la nuit, ou les mystères *[The Nocturnal Man; or, The Mysteries] (1842)* and La Dame de comptoir, ou une Princesse incognito *[The Lady at the Counter; or, The Princess in Disguise] (1844)* are more likely to have been leftovers than nostalgic revisitations of youthful pastures. The most probable explanation for his disappearance from the literary scene is that he simply figured that he had made enough money, and could finally throw away his quills, but his health might have deteriorated to the extent that he had no op-

*tion. There is an inevitable temptation to suspect something more exotically fit-
ting to a life of sustained deception, but there was always a prosaic figure behind the poseur, and it would not be inappropriate if he had reverted to mere
ordinariness long before his demise.*

    The sudden upsurge in French vampire fiction to which La Vampire *be-
longs had begun with a very loose dramatic adaptation of Polidori's story for
the Théâtre de la Porte-Saint-Martin, which premièred in 1820 as* Le Vampire.
*The play's principal author was probably Achille de Jouffroy, although Charles
Nodier and the theater's director, Jean Toussaint-Merle, also had a hand in it.[3]
Nodier also contributed an introduction to Cyprien Bérard's* Lord Ruthwen, ou
les Vampires *(1820)[4], which poses as a sequel to Polidori's work, although it is
actually a patchwork apparently strung together from various pre-existent mate-
rials, probably including at least one projected musical play (Bérard was the
manager of the Théâtre Vaudeville). Nodier went on to incorporate the theme of
vampirism into his hallucinatory fantasy* Smarra, ou les demons de la nuit
(1822; tr. as "Smarra; or, The Demons of the Night").[5]

    *Although Lamothe-Langon was undoubtedly jumping on a perceived
bandwagon, it seems highly probable that he had not had any opportunity to see
the Porte-Saint-Martin play, and might not have read any of the other prose
works cited. Nor is he likely to have been familiar with such foreign-language
poems as J. W. Goethe's "Die Braut von Korinth" (1797; tr. as "The Bride of
Corinth") or John Keats' "Lamia" (1820), both of which feature female vampires. What he definitely had read, however, is Dom Augustine Calmet's essay
on vampires in* Dissertations sur les apparitions des anges, des démons et Sur les
Revenants et Vampires de Hongrie, de Bohême, de Moravie et de Silesie *(1746),
from which he quotes extensively in his introduction. Given his character,
though, and the general tendency of writers to do their own thing rather than
slavishly copying models provided by others, it is not surprising that he decided
to pay little heed to the image of the vampire popularized by Calmet, and to in-
vent his own fakeloristic stereotype instead, which differs sharply from the images contained in actual folklore and the novel's immediate predecessors.*

    *Where Lamothe-Langon led, others were to follow, at least to the extent of
employing seductive female vampires in their prose fictions rather than imperious male ones. Théophile Gautier provided a more influential archetype in "La
Morte amoureuse" (1836; tr. under various titles, most frequently as "Clari-
monde"); Alexandre Dumas incorporated a tale of a female vampire into the
portmanteau work* Une Journée à Fontenay-aux-Roses *(1849; the vampire story*

---

[3] Included in our first volume.
[4] Published by Black Coat Press as *The Vampire Lord Ruthwen* (ISBN
9781612270043).
[5] Included in our first volume.

is sometimes reprinted separately as "La Dame blanche", and in English trans-
lation as "The Pale Lady"); the first of Pierre-Alexis Ponson du Terrail's three
novels featuring vampires was La Baronne trépassée *(1853);[6] and Paul Féval*
depicted a protagonist every bit as idiosyncratic as Lamothe-Langon's in his
own novel entitled La Vampire *(c.1856)[7]. Whether any of these writers took any*
inspiration from Lamothe-Langon's novel it is difficult to tell—none of them re-
produced any of his innovations—but Ponson and Féval, at least, probably knew
of its existence.

I shall leave detailed discussion of the contents of La Vampire *to an after-*
word, in order not to spoil the story for the reader, but it is probably worth not-
ing in advance that there is a sense in which Lamothe-Langon is guilty of
providing a mammoth spoiler himself, in choosing his title and providing a pref-
atory justification for it. If the novel were simply called Alinska, ou la vierge de
Hongrie *and had no preface, the experience of reading it would be markedly dif-*
ferent from the one obtained in the wake of the expectations created by the title
and the preface. Shorn of that supplementary material, the story would be deep-
ly ambiguous, at least to begin with, because Alinska's statements about herself,
and the mysterious events of the early chapters would pose a stern interpretative
challenge. As things stand, however, readers have no alternative but to start
from the fundamental assumption that Alinska really is a vampire, to interpret
everything she says and everything that happens around her in that light, and
thus to take a dim view of Raoul's and Edouard's obstinacy in refusing even to
admit the possibility the supernatural forces might be at work. Readers of this
translation will doubtless make up their own minds as to whether that prelimi-
nary revelation ought to be reckoned a mistake, and, if so, how dire a mistake it
was.

No matter what conclusion readers reach on that point, however, they will
hopefully be able to agree that the work is an intriguing one, largely because of
its originality. It offers us a female vampire who is certainly akin to others of her
imaginary kind, but also strikingly different, perhaps to the point of perversity.
The novel was a commercial exercise, probably written at speed, and certainly
made up as the author went along, with the aid of occasional hasty improvisa-
tions; nevertheless, it is far more fluent, as well as far more adventurous, than
Polidori's novelette or Bérard's sequel; if nothing else, it can be seen an inter-
esting forerunner of the techniques of popular fiction that were to be extrava-
gantly developed and refined in subsequent feuilleton fiction, but there is more
to it than that. It is not without literary merit as an item of dark Romantic fic-
tion, and the faint praise that Charles Nodier wasted on Bérard's damnable text

---

[6] Published by Black Coat Press as *The Vampire and the Devil's Son* (ISBN 9781932983555).
[7] Published by Black Coat Press as *The Vampire Countess* (ISBN 9780974071152).

could have been far more robustly applied to Lamothe-Langon's—which proba-
bly turned out better than its author had any reason to expect, and gives us some
cause for regret that he decided thereafter to exercise his talent for fantasy in a
very different fashion.

B.S.

Look here, Edmond, she said, 'tis me,
Who loved you once, whom you betrayed,
The one whose faithful amity
Lives on after the sin, delayed.
Étienne de Jouy
L'Ombre de Marguerite[8]

Dedication

A...

I have met you often in troubled times; in those moments, your heart has always responded to mine with the purest and most noble sentiment. I cannot repay you for so much soothing consolation, offered by disinterested amity to suffering amity, but accept this feeble testimony of my respect, my attachment and my gratitude

B. de Lamothe-Langon

Preface

We ought to begin by immediately offering an apology to the reader—if any is necessary—for the title that we thought it necessary to give our work, *La Vampire.* "Is that French?" we might be asked. "Don't we always speak of a male vampire? Don't dictionaries attribute the masculine gender to the word?" We do not disagree, but, as it is a woman who plays the role of the persecutor of the living in this romance, is it not appropriate to make the fact known? Would

---

[8] The original reference reads "M. de Jouy, *Rom. de Marguerite,*" *Rom.* being an abbreviation of *romance* [ballad]. The poem, whose title translates as "Marguerite's Shade," can be found in volume 17 of Jouy's *Oeuvres complètes,* with whose compilation Lamothe-Langon apparently assisted. The verse appears on the title-page of each of the original three volumes. I have had to improvise somewhat in order to reproduce the rhyme-scheme and scansion in this translation, but have preserved the meaning as closely as I could—a policy followed with respect to the four songs whose words are reproduced in the text.

Le Vampire have provided the necessary designation? It appeared to us that we might feminize the word without failing in the respect due to the language. We shall be pleased believe so if, in these humble pages, we have not committee any more grievous offense.

This is a subject as curious as any provided by the list of superstitions still existing in several parts of Europe. Vampires are principally renowned in Hungary, Moravia, Epirus[9] and the Greek islands. There, people firmly believe in the existence of these mysterious beings, belonging neither to death or to life and clinging nevertheless to both; of these cannibals of the tomb who, when the sepulchral stone covers them, acquire frightful appetites that they did not have before, and come forth to suck human blood in order to satisfy a frightful thirst, bringing terror and desolation to the very bosom of their families.

Vampires have been known since remote antiquity; it is not the modern era that has invented them. The ancients, in order to satisfy the appetite of the dead, placed tables laden with food and wine in cemeteries; evidence of that is found in a host of Greek and Latin authors. The early Christians conserved that custom, so that Saint Monica, the mother of the celebrated Bishop of Hippo,[10] wanted to continue it in Italy after the latter's death. Tertullian, in the introduction to his treatise *Resurrectio*,[11] reproaches the pagans for believing that the dead need to eat. In tombs in which both idolaters and Christians of the primitive Church rest, one does indeed find vessels of clay and glass containing the bones of quadrupeds and poultry, which can only have been offered to the deceased for their nourishment.

This opinion that cadavers still retain a portion of life has been deeply-rooted for a long time. It is still found today among almost all the peoples of the world; it has had, and still has, numerous partisans among intelligent individuals, who support it with documentary evidence.[12]

In modern times too, it has also been thought possible to certify the existence of Vampires. Here are a few examples that Dom Calmet reports on the subject in his treatise on the Apparitions and Revenants that plague Hungary:

"At the beginning of September 1737, an old man aged 62 died in the village of Kililova, three leagues from Gradiska. Three days after having been bur-

---

[9] Epirus was an ancient Greek kingdom south of Illyria and west of Macedonia.
[10] St. Augustine
[11] Presumably *De Resurrectione Carnis* [On the Resurrection of the Flesh].
[12] A section of text approximately 200 words long follows in which the author presumably cites a number of prestigious individuals who have believed in vampires, but the relevant pages—pp. xii-xiii—are missing from the *gallica* text; only the final reference, to the Roman Emperor Adrian, survives in part, along with a cautionary note by the author to the effect that "we cannot admit it without a more mature examination."

ied, he appeared by night to his son and asked him for something to eat; the latter having given him food, he ate it and disappeared. The next day, the son told his neighbors what had happened. That night, the father did not appear, but the following night he returned and asked for something to eat. It is not known whether his son gave him anything or not, but he was found dead in his bed the next day. That same day, five or six people in the village suddenly fell ill, and died one after the other shortly afterwards. The local constable or bailiff, informed of what had happened, sent a report to the tribunal in Belgrade, which sent two of its officers to the village with an executioner, to investigate the matter. The bailiff who had sent the report went to Gradiska in order to witness a fact of which he had so often heard mention. All the graves of the people who had died within the last six weeks were opened. When they came to that of the old man he was found with his eyes open and a ruddy complexion, breathing naturally, but motionless and dead—from which it was concluded that he was obviously a Vampire. The executioner plunged a stake into his heart; a pyre was built and the cadaver reduced to ashes...

"In 1729 or 1730, a certain infantryman, an inhabitant of Medreiga, was crushed by the collapse of a haywain. Thirty days after his death, four people died suddenly, and in the manner in which, according to the tradition of the region, those molested by Vampires die. It was then remembered that the individual in question, named Arnold Paul, had often recounted that, in the vicinity of Cassoura and on the frontiers of Turkish Serbia, he had been tormented by a Turkish Vampire (for it is also believed that those who have been passive Vampires during life become active after their death—which is to say that those who have been sucked suck in their turn) but that he had found a means of curing himself by eating earth from the Vampire's sepulcher and rubbing himself with the latter's blood. This precaution did not, however, prevent him from becoming one after his death, since he was exhumed forty days after his burial and his body was found to have all the marks of an arch-Vampire: his body was red; his hair, nails and beard had continued growing; and his veins were filled with fluid blood, which was leaking from all the parts of his body on to the shroud in which he was enveloped. The local bailiff, in the presence of whom the exhumation was carried out, who was an expert on vampirism, ordered a sharp stake to be plunged into the heart of the deceased Arnold Paul, according to custom, which traversed the body from front to back. The latter, it is said, uttered a frightful scream, as if he were still alive. When that had been done, the head was cut off and everything was burned...

"About fifteen years ago, while a soldier garrisoned in the home of a Slavic peasant on the Hungarian frontier was at table with his host, he saw a man come in who sat down to eat with them. The master of the house was strangely fearful, as was everyone else in the company. The soldier did not know what to make of it, not knowing what was going on. When the master of the house was found dead the next day, however, the soldier made enquiries; he was told that it was his host's father, dead and buried for ten years, who had come to sit down beside him, and had announced to him and caused his death.

"The soldier immediately informed his regiment, and the regiment passed on the information to the general staff, who commissioned the Count of Cabreras, a captain in the Alandetti infantry regiment, to investigate the matter. Having traveled to the place with other officers, a surgeon and a clerk, they took statements from all the people in the house, who attested, unanimously, that the revenant was the father of the tenant of the dwelling, and that everything the soldier had said and reported was the exact truth; this was confirmed by all the people in the village.

"In consequence, the corpse of that specter was extracted from the ground; it was found to be like that of a man who had just expired, and its blood similar to that of a living man. The Count of Cabreras cut off the head, and then returned it to the grave. He then obtained information about similar revenants, including a man thirty years dead, who had returned to his house on three occasions at meal times, and had sucked blood from the neck, on the first occasion of his brother, on the second of his son, and on the third of a manservant—and all three had died immediately thereafter.

"On the basis of this deposition, the commissary had the man's body disinterred, and found the corpse fluid, like the first, as that of a living man would have been. He ordered that a large nail be hammered into the temple, and then it was put back in the grave. He had a third burned, who had been buried for more than sixteen years, and had sucked the blood and caused the death of two of his sons. The commissary, having made his report to the general staff, was sent to the Emperor's court, who ordered that military officers, magistrates, surgeons and a few scholars be sent to examine the causes of these extraordinary events."

All Vampires, however, must conceded the palm of the horrible to another of whom the venerable Dom Calmet recounts the misdeeds, and especially the insolence. We shall conclude with this one, handing the floor to the Abbé de Sennones:

"A herdsman in the village of Blow, near the town of Shadan in Bohemia, appeared some time after his death and called on several people, who unfailingly died within the week. The peasants of Blow disinterred the herdsman's body and fixed it to the ground with a stake driven through the body. In that state, the man mocked those who subjected him to this treatment, telling them that he thanked them for giving him a stick with which to defend himself against dogs. That same night he rose again and frightened several people with his presence, suffocating more than he had killed before. He was then handed over to the executioner, who set him on a cart to transport him out of the village in order to be burned. The cadaver howled furiously, waving his hands and feet like a living man, and when he was pierced with stakes again, he uttered an exceedingly loud scream, and yielded a great quantity of very red blood. Finally, he was burned, and that execution put an end to the apparitions and infestations of the specter."

That is doubtless more than is necessary to inform the readers that Vampires, also known as Broucolaques, Upiers, Redivives, etc. have played for a long time, and perhaps still play, an important role on the world stage. The most enlightened centuries are not those in which there is less superstition. The human mind is always the same; it denies one object, and believes in another; skeptical as to the principal points of religion, it adopts the dreams of judiciary astrology and the card-tricks of fortune-tellers. Everything marches two abreast in the human brain, the astonishing receptacle of all that is most contradictory, the most bizarre contrasts and the most extraordinary conceptions.

Our rural regions contain a fundamentally credulous population, ever ready to adopt anything that appears to defy the common rules of life. The simplicity of the daily existence of peasants seems to create a need in them to launch their imagination into the boundless ocean of the fantastic. They obtain their recreation with chimeras and tales that excite and frighten them. Unable to dream of the grandeurs of which they are unaware, they replace them with terror, with which they amuse themselves. They have an abundance of practical superstitions, in which they find their consolation and their support. They populate old châteaux, profound caverns, silent forests and steep crags with a host of phantoms, spirits, fairies, witches and enchanters, which they set to work, and by means of which they explain all the events and causes to which their limited intelligence inevitably cannot find the key.

It is also among such people that mysterious tales thrive in which beings from another world, intelligences superior to humankind, take part. Vampires, for example, have never established their abode in large towns, in places where high society—that in possession of the best education and enlightenment—reigns; but they have shown themselves in remote areas, in distant villages, among isolated farmsteads; there, they can act without fear of being unmasked; they strike fear into weak and crude minds; and by such means, people who would throw off the yoke that weighs upon them if they were more enlightened are deluded. It is, moreover, convenient for certain interests that such prejudices exist. Permission has therefore been given to belief in vampires.

Why should we be surprised by that fact, anyway? So many clever men have believed in Vampires! Dom Calmet, for instance, had some inclination to admit their existence. For that reason, it is true, Voltaire mocked him. We, a sheep-like race, have blindly adopted the opinion of the latter and laugh at Vampires; even Lord Byron has been unable to alter our ideas on that subject. Oh well! Dear reader, we do not fear to say that the author of *Mérope* was wrong; the Benedictine had seen the matter clearly; we flatter ourselves that we can prove it to your without difficulty, simply by asking you to cast a glance at what is happening around us.

Are not the insatiable conquerors who are always at war, exhausting their states in consequence, Vampires drunk on our purest blood? Do we not incessantly encounter men avid for our sweat, who always think that the burdens with which they overwhelm us are light? Do you think that those wretches who wander through towns and the countryside to constrain the popular will with the lure of gain or the fear of suspicion are not real Vampires? And the man who, placed at a high rank, finding virtue in his path, stifles it with embroidered garments or strangles it with a silken ribbon—should we not call him a Vampire?

Do you think that the banker of a gambling house, where so many fortunes are swallowed up and such worthy reputations ruined, does not march in the foremost rank of Vampires? In the middle of Paris, in the busiest streets and the most obscure alleys, do we not find today, at night, Vampires who are sometimes adorned with all the charms of the beloved sex, no less possessed of depravity, avidity, vice and criminal inclination than their colleagues of the other world?

Finally, does not one see Vampires everywhere, some in priestly vestments and others in judicial togas? They can be seen wearing military uniform or administrative sashes. Their greatest concentration is to be found among tradesmen and entrepreneurs, the agents of the law and speculators, where they are present in large numbers; they can even be found in the ranks of physicians.

Chapter I

Misfortunes as undeserved as they were unexpected took Colonel Edouard Delmont away from his native land toward the end of 1815. Paris had given him birth, and he had wanted to live out his days in that capital of the world, but fortune had dictated otherwise. After the second return of the King, Edouard precipitately handed in his resignation and, his eyes bathed with tears that he had difficulty holding back, he informed his wife of the imperious necessity that obliged them to find an isolated plot of land where they might live in peace, far from Paris, and even far from Lyon, where she had been born.

This news was a blow to Madame Delmont, whose name was Hélène, but did not throw her into despair. She loved her husband and was loved tenderly in her turn; her children were sufficient to fill all the places in her heart; the cares of the household and the cultivation of the fine arts, wherever she might find herself, would employ in a pleasant manner such time as the sweet and sacred duties of motherhood left her. She did not indulge in any painful reflection, therefore, on listening to that unexpected speech; she scarcely questioned the colonel as to the reason for his prompt determination, only asking him one thing—whether some political fault had compromised his safety. Reassured on this point, and informed that failed speculations were the sole reason that rendered a retreat of some years necessary, she kissed her husband tenderly and swore that she would have no difficulty abandoning the tumult of Paris for the repose of solitude.

Delmont's haste to distance himself from the capital seemed extreme. He did not want to remain for the time necessary to sell his superb house; he asked a friend to take that responsibility, and the day after the one on which he had informed his wife of his decision, he left with her and their children, taking only a single domestic, without having said goodbye to the people who comprised the rather restricted circle of their acquaintances.

Once through the *barrière*, Edouard seemed to be relieved of an enormous weight. His gaze, which had been wandering hither and yon with an appearance of anxiety while he was still in the city, took on a more tranquil appearance when he found himself amid the fields. He seemed to be able to breathe freely and, squeezing his wife's hand warmly, he said: "Finally, we're out of that city of tumult and mire, the unique assembly-point of all the peoples of the universe; I'm glad to have crossed its limits, within which I can no longer suffer."

"Is it possible, my friend," his wife said to him, "that you can express yourself thus? Is Paris no longer your homeland? Has it lost, for you, the charm of which you once found so much therein? Have I not heard you talk about it with such enthusiasm? Is it no longer the same city? Must it displease you, because our situation has changed?"

"Yes," said the colonel, "I confess that I can no longer bear the sight of that which one enchanted me. The events that have succeeded one another with such rapidity—the profanation of the city that I regarded as sacred by the presence of enemies so frequently vanquished, the fury of contending parties reignited so violently, contrary opinions dividing the most closely-bound hearts—have all given me an aversion for my native soil. The magic of Paris no longer exists for me; it appears to my gaze merely as an ordinary city, and I feel that I could not bear to live in it at present."

"Be glad, then, that we are now leaving it. Can you, my friend, find in the city to which we are going, the peace that has been stolen from you here by so many painful memories?"

"What city do you mean?"

"The one in which we shall presumably live. He we are on the road south—where will our journey end? In Bordeaux, Toulouse, Tarbes, or Pau?"

"Alas, my dear Hélène," the colonel replied, with some embarrassment, "I fear that I must constrain you to complete the sacrifice entirely. Do you think that I can leave Paris to go to live in another city, in the midst of an ever-unwelcome racket and agitation? That I can consent to stay in one of those places where numerous crowds constantly form, where those strangers arrive every day whose business or restless curiosity brings them to every part of France? No, no—I feel that in my position, I need less noise. Be kind enough not to complain about my tyrannical resolution; I want to find an isolated rural region in which nothing can remind me of the past, and especially not put me in its presence..."

At this point, a swift blush colored Delmont's handsome face. He stopped in mid-sentence, and looked at Hélène with an indefinable expression, in which several dolorous sentiments were combined.

Hélène might perhaps have been alarmed had she thought that secret causes lay behind Delmont's profound chagrin. She knew, however, how much the misfortunes of France had oppressed him, and how his love for his family had caused him to bear impatiently the loss of a considerable fraction of their wealth—which would not permit him to give his children the brilliant education that he had planned for them. She knew, too, how much affection he had for her; she feared his regret at removing her from society and the worldly pleasures the doubtless believed to be dear to her, so, without digging any deeper, she stopped at the appearance.

Squeezing her husband's hand, she said: "Don't worry. The memory of Paris won't disturb me. No matter where we end up, I shall still have you; our children are with us; my harp is following us; my paint-brushes are in that case. What can I regret? What will prevent me from being happy?"

"What! The countryside, in all its solitude, doesn't frighten you, my beloved?"

"It would, if I found myself far away from the three individuals who are dear to me, but with them, my life will always be full. I shall never see anything beyond the circle of my most tender affections!"

"Oh, from what torment you have freed me! For I believe that you're sincere, my love; I have no doubt that your words express the sentiments of your heart. Well, I'll admit to you that I need to get away from the tumult that surrounds us. Only the calm of the desert will suit my soul; it's therefore necessary, in order to find tranquility, for me to find a haven that can shelter me from the internal tempest, not close enough to a city for any torment to each us, but not too far away for us to be unable to procure the pleasures of civilization and the assistance that the health of Eugène and Juliette might require." Those were the names of their children, who were both still very young.

"Well, Edouard, where do you hope to find this retreat?"

"Not far from Toulouse."

"I don't think you've ever lived in that city during your adventurous travels. Do you have relatives there? Have you already determined the place where we'll live?"

"No, in truth, I don't know where we're going; I'm leaving everything to chance in that regard. I'm drawn to Toulouse simply because I'm completely unknown there, so my trail will be lost and no one will come looking for me...for the sight of people is odious to me now. Oh, how I'd like to lose my memory, dear Hélène, how I'd love to have only ever lived for you!"

These tender words, which should have charmed Madame Delmont, actually provoked a contrary sentiment in her heart. The tone in which her husband had pronounced them seemed a bitter reproach, addressed to himself; at that moment his features bore the imprint of that agitation of the soul which tells a clear-sighted observer more than a long speech. Hélène, although long married, loved her husband as she had on their wedding day. No jealous impulse had ever arisen in her heart, because Delmont's constant attention had proved to her that she alone occupied his thoughts entirely—but that calm could occasionally be troubled.

Hélène had never wanted to dwell on her husband's life before the moment when they had met for the first time. She knew that a young and handsome military man must have had gallant adventures, but at the same time, she liked to believe that the rapidity with which the French armies had moved around Europe had not permitted those comprising them to engage in long intrigues, and to deliver themselves to sentiments that are dangerous when prolonged. On that point, therefore, Hélène as exempt from anxiety—and yet, as the colonel was speaking, a fatal thought led her to think that some ancient intrigue might perhaps be playing a considerable part in a journey that had the appearance of a precipitate flight.

Whatever ideas Madame Delomont had in this regard, she was careful not to express them; she even sought to suppress them, by starting a conversation on the history of the region that would soon be their home, whose renown was Europe-wide.

"The excitement of the parties in that part of France is of no importance to us," said the colonel. "We aren't going there to take part in shady intrigues and unjust vengeances. We're going in search of peace and quiet. We'll fulfill all the duties of citizenship there; we'll obey the laws and prevent any complaint. It would be deplorable if, while being so careful of our conduct, it could nevertheless as a pretext for the inquisitors of thought. In an isolated house the middle of the countryside, though, who will make demands on us? Have no worries on that score, my friend; prudence will save us from all peril."

The children, bored by a conversation in which they could not take part, interrupted it at this point with a host of questions about the places they were passing through. Delmont, amused by their babbling, hastened to satisfy them, while his wife, busy trying to decipher in his features what was going on in his soul, was still unable to divine the cause of the sporadic sardonic laughter and muscle contractions that gave a peculiar character to the colonel's handsome and noble physiognomy. She had too much perspicacity to attribute that deep-seated emotion to any mere reverse of fortune; the colonel's was large enough for the loss of a part of his wealth to affect him to such a degree.

The more Hélène tried to penetrate the mystery, the less success she had. In the meantime, her charming face was shaded by a melancholy gloom. Delmont did not take long to notice that, and, attributing the appearance to chagrin occasioned by their departure from Paris, he tried to make the cloud disappear by means of the most affectionate attentions.

It did not take long for him to succeed. Hélène, touched by her husband's concern, no longer wanted to lose herself in vain conjectures; she abandoned any attempt to plumb the past, and, entirely devoted to her present situation, enjoyed the pure joy of being in the company of her husband and children.

It is in that perfect situation that anxieties and chagrins ought to disappear. What a balm it pours over life's pains, and how trivial the latter become when conjugal love aids paternal love in banishing from the heart the cruel anxieties that disturb it!

Chapter II

When he arrived in Toulouse, Colonel Delmont lost no time in searching for the retreat he was in such haste to discover. He consulted a notary in order to find out whether he could rent or buy a country house deep in farmland, far from main roads, and yet within reach of the city.

Hazard favored him. The owner of the Château de R***, situated in the middle of one of the most fertile regions in Languedoc, not far from Toulouse, did not live in that ancient edifice. He had sought hard to find a lover of rural life, but in vain; none had yet appeared. He was, therefore, amenable to Delmont's proposal. The latter, informed that the manor was for rent, had been to see it and had come back delighted with its situation, which was all that he could desire.

As soon as the lease was signed the colonel left Toulouse with his family. He set out for R***, having the items of furniture necessary for his new establishment sent after him. They were simple but comfortable; elegance replaced a luxury that was scarcely in harmony with the simple beauties of nature. They were brought by a former sergeant in Delmont's regiment named Raoul, a brave soldier who owed his life to the colonel, and who, on reentering civilian life with him, had wanted to share his lot, serving him not so much in the capacity of a domestic servant as of a man entirely devoted to his fortune. A cook hired in Toulouse and a maid-of-all-work completed the Delmont household. Hélène and her husband having renounced all ostentation, it could no longer exercise the slightest attraction upon them.

The first days after their arrival in the countryside went by with the normal bustle of a new existence. It was necessary to be self-sufficient, so to speak. Workmen were scarce or incompetent; the interior decoration relied entirely on the skill of the colonel and Raoul. They were the ones who hung the wallpaper, set up the mirrors, arranged the furniture and assembled the beds. Their hands, accustomed to handle weapons, were able to use the tools of industry skillfully.

For her part, Hélène was not idle. She took care of everything relating to linen and household items. She did not neglect anything—and the two spouses worked side by side, adding charm to the passing moments with outpourings of affection and the joy of complete confidence. In the midst of these light tasks, however, a rapid memory occasionally darkened the colonel's brow; an involuntary shiver, immediately suppressed, advertised the presence of a hidden anguish in his soul. More than once, Hélène had to turn away in order not to put Delmont in the painful position of perceiving that she was disturbed by whatever was agitating him.

More often, however, he seemed calm. The presence of his children delighted him; he loved their youthful play, in which he often took part. Sometimes his flute occupied his time; at other times, accompanied by a hunting dog, he wandered the numerous hills that dotted the landscape. Then, deep in a woody thicket, he would stop at the foot of an oak, fold his arms across his chest, and abandon himself to reveries that lasted for hours on end. Only dusk or the passing of a few agricultural laborers returned him to his senses; then he would slap his forehead violently, and take the homeward path at a rapid stride.

The dwelling was situated on a high ridge, which overlooked all its surroundings. To the north, the view, gliding over vast low-lying hills, was limited by the villages of Mercilla and Vigoulet, which stood out on the horizon, while the valleys were shared between fertile lands cultivated with care, artificial meadows and a few clumps of trees—the remains of the immense forest that had once covered the entire region.

To the east, the eye found a multitude of hillsides, whose westward slopes were all gentle, charged with hamlets and country houses, among which, not far from the château, the ancient fief of Souterrène could be distinguished, still ornamented by two square towers built at opposite corners and two round towers at the other extremities. Only the central building still existed, and found itself standing after several centuries, while the long-demolished wings had given way to the riches of agriculture and a vegetation whose abundance testified to the fertility of the soil. A few cottages were grouped there in a rather extensive space, forming the nucleus of the commune. On a hilltop stood the simple church and the curé's house, more modest still.

To the south, a few spaced-out heights hid the course of the Ariège; villages of huddled rural edifices and a rather large wood gave the panorama a varied physiognomy. The beauty of that landscape, however, gave precedence to the one presented in the west. There, in the middle of an immense plain, the Garonne followed its rapid course; the countryside, fundamentally rich and intensively cultivated, presented at a distance the form of an endless garden strewn with numerous fabrications: hamlets, villages, and even fair-sized towns. The azure of the sky was reflected by the pure waves of the Guyenne, light mists rising up at times from the bosom of the waters, outlining their contours and rising toward the heavens like the incense that the people of that beautiful region burn in honor of the Eternal.

The Château de R***, built in the reign of Louis XIII, had lost all its interior magnificence. It formed a square, the middle of which enclosed a courtyard, and consisted of several vast apartments deprived of their original splendor. None of the original furniture remained; the tapestries had vanished; the doors were in a poor state; the windows had neither panes not shutters and were almost all boarded up, advertising the fact that the building had been long forgotten by its masters.

The gardens had similarly ceased to exist, fields of wheat advancing as far as the walls, and the moat that had once defended the approaches had been almost entirely filled in. Only the fugitive remains of a few pathways could still be found in a nearby wood. The vigorous vegetation that the gardener's shears no longer contained had invaded almost the entire area, extending over pathways once maintained with care, while the trunks of half-pruned trees and rampant brambles opposed their multiple obstacles everywhere to anyone wishing to stroll along the aligned routes where nature was completing its victory over artifice with every passing day.

It was in this desolate habitation that the Delmont family had taken up residence. There was a great deal to do in order to render even a small part of it habitable, but by dint of effort, everything was arranged for the best. A number of rooms were restored, in succession; they seemed like a camp retrenched in the middle of a ruined city.

If Madame Delmont had only possessed the futile tastes of society, she would have been unhappy in that place. No society was available to her there; the neighbors who might have been around her dwelling only came to the country during the summer, all of them living in Toulouse. For six months of the year, no one would have dared to risk visiting areas that were difficult to reach through the mud of the Lauraguais. As we have said, however, Hélène found precious resources within herself. Music, painting, and the choice of the finest literary works that human genius had presented to humankind, charmed her leisure with the various distractions they could provide.

Sometimes, she reproduced on canvas the various aspects of the earth and sky that struck her eyes; sometimes she played the harmonious songs of contemporary musician on her harp—the ballads of Alvimare, the nocturnes of Blangini, the pastorals of Dugazon.[13] Finally, she shed sweet tears with Racine, witnessed the marvels of the creation of the universe with Milton, and wandered in a world of enchantment with Ariosto. Sometimes, more serious reading occupied her leisure time. Pascal showed her human miseries or the folly of partisan-

---

[13] Pierre d'Alvimare (1772-1839), Felice Blangini (1781-1841) and Gustave Dugazon, the son of the famous actress Louise Lefebvre (who married into the celebrated Gourgand family, the members of which all used Dugazon as their stage name).

ship; in Bossuet she saw the grandeur of religion, which she learned to love in the eloquent pages of the Swan of Cambrai.[14]

A year went by without any extraordinary event introducing variety into the simple and monotonous life of the Delmont family. The more time passed, the more the colonel recovered his tranquility; it was untroubled by the slight fits of ill-temper that had formerly pursued him. He was entirely calm; no unwelcome memory seemed to be agitating him.

Secretly, Hélène, who watched out for such disturbances, in order to dispel them when possible, was glad of the change. Her spouse's absences were less frequent; he did not seek them with the same tenacity as before the restfulness of the woods or the agitation of the hunt. He remained with his wife and children, supervising the education of the latter, and, to distract himself, cultivated a few rare plants that he had procured in Toulouse.

Winter, which was without charm in that region, was nevertheless unable to inspire in Hélène and Delmont the desire to leave; they were able to amuse themselves—and when the waters of heaven had soaked the rich clay that forms the soil of that part of France, so that it became impossible to go out walking, the château's vast hall was transformed into a gymnastic arena, in which the father and children devoted themselves to salutary amusements good for the health of the body. Long and frank bursts of laughter resonated beneath the long-mute ceilings. The hours, usefully and pleasantly employed, went by rapidly, without anyone paying any heed to the rain bought by the westerly wind, which was falling in torrents and making the roof reverberate.

The evenings were employed in perusing instructive collections of engravings. Sometimes, a tale narrated by Hélène assembled around her a couple of avidly attentive listeners, their gazes fixed and mouths open, who found it full of interest. Delmont took delight in contemplating that charming tableau, and said to himself more than ever: *Oh, they have cause for complaint who have never experienced the happiness that cannot leave any bitter regret behind!* He wished for nothing more; his heart was full—and to complete his felicity, the sometimes-dolorous past disappeared entirely from his memory.

Several more months passed in that seductive calm. Toward the middle of August, however, a letter that Delmont received cast him into a strange perplexity.

He had a sister, who was married to a magistrate in the city of Nantes. Reciprocal errors by the spouses, both young and both perhaps slaves of their passions, had led to unpleasant scenes, the number of which increased by the day. A mutual friend of the unfortunates, fearful of an explosion that seemed inevitable,

---

[14] Jacques-Bénigne Bossuet's *Sermons* had a tremendous reputation for eloquence; *Le Cygne de Cambrai* [the Swan of Cambrai] was the nickname gave to the Abbé Fénélon, another 17th century religious writer of monumental reputation.

thought that it was his duty to alert Delmont to what was happening. He urged him to lose no time in coming to Nantes; only his presence, the colonel was advised, could return harmony to a household that was half torn apart.

This annoying confidence upset Delmont considerably. It would be painful to tear himself away from happiness in order to go back into the social environment that he had fled forever. At the same time, his heart reproached him for his indifference toward his younger sister, with respect to whom he had been obliged to replace their father. He felt that his advice might be very useful to her; it might perhaps stop her in the middle of the frantic course into which she had inconsiderately launched herself.

On the other hand, it would be necessary to leave his wife and children for an indeterminate time; the sacrifice was extreme, so he hesitated for some time. Before making up his mind, he attempted by way of correspondence to speak to the sentiments of Madame Lemorin—that was his sister's name—but vain representations could not prevail where tumultuous passions had raised their voices. In the replies they sent, the two spouses blamed one another, and would not consider reconciliation.

Finally, their quarrels became envenomed to such a point that Delmont's sister felt forced to leave the communal residence and withdraw to the country, to the home of a friend.

Chapter III

On learning this last news, the colonel hesitated no longer. He reproached himself for delaying his departure, and accepted some of the blame for the fault that had been committed. It was necessary to remedy it without delay, and after having asked Hélène's advice—which was in conformity with his own opinion—he took the road to Toulouse, knowing that the city offered him raid means of transport that would take him to Nantes.

He went on his own, leaving the honest and valorous Raoul—whom he could regard as another self with respect to the interests of his family—with his wife and children, to protect their safety.

Hélène needed courage to support the separation, which was the first, but, sealing off her pain, she only showed that portion of it that it was impossible for her to suppress.

"Oh, my love," she said, shedding tears, "hurry back. It's only now that this place will appear to me as a complete solitude; I shall lonely as soon as I can no longer see you."

Delmont tried to pour some consolation into Hélène's sensitive soul. The month of September was coming to an end; he promised her that he would return in December at the latest, and that she could rely on his affection to ensure that he would bring that date forward if it proved possible for him to do so. How vain consolations are at a time of departure, though! The present grief is crushing; one cannot see or feel anything else. The future is disenchanted; hope loses all its energy; one only experiences the tortures of the moment.

The first days that followed Delmont's departure left Hélène in complete apathy. Her mind, afflicted by a thousand sinister ideas, became susceptible to the most superstitious dreads. It was not without a secret horror that she now climbed the château's staircase or went through the great hall. The imagination, always so active in seeking that which frightens us, redoubled its enthusiasm to throw terror into Hélène's soul. The most trivial thing sufficed to make her shiver; she sometimes stopped, trembling, thinking that she had heard a strange noise, or closed her eyes for fear of some sinister apparition. The company of her children was insufficient to reassure her during the evenings that were already lengthening. She summoned Raoul; she asked for Germaine, the cook—a good woman, but very susceptible to believing everything that weak and uneducated minds imagine. She kept them with her for hours at a time, under the pretext of giving them instructions or asking them for accounts of the tasks she had entrusted to them.

The countryside was certainly solitary, and, the houses being far apart, nothing could check the curious investigation of the lower classes of society. There is a host of circumstances whose details are of interest to them; they take account of the most ordinary events. The slightest action seems important to them, the most trivial statement attracts careful comment. Everything becomes rapidly known; the field of conjectures grows with an incredible facility, and the most dangerous gossip often emerges from mouths to which the casual observer would scarcely attribute the gift of speech.

The advent of the Delmonts in the neighborhood had intrigued the village tribe greatly. What exaggerated tales had been made up about them! What ridiculous fables had been bandied about! But time had gone by; public malignity cannot always be occupied with the same material. After fifteen months, the Delmont family seemed to have been naturalized in the locality; no one took any further notice of them except to chat about mundane details, and people even associated with them willingly—stable-hands with Raoul, parlormaids with Germaine—tellingly them voluntarily what they had learned at the church door on Sunday, in the fields of neighboring communes on other days, or in the occasional gatherings occasioned by field-work.

When they found the time, Raoul and Germaine liked to tell Madame Delmont what they had heard. She bushed internally at the bizarre pleasure she obtained in listening to them, but, in her husband's absence, she needed distraction, and no matter what subjects were discussed in front of her, she preferred that to the isolation in which she spent her days.

Delmont had already been absent from the château for a week when Germaine presented herself, after nightfall, with such a self-important air that Hélène did not doubt that she had some remarkable news to tell her. She was not mistaken.

As soon as the good woman had sat down next to the lamp that was illuminating the evening's work, she said: "Well, Madame, we'll no longer be alone here now; the neighborhood's becoming populous; strangers abound here—and if it continues, according to the blacksmith, it will be necessary to ask the Prefect to establish a market every Monday in the Place de R***."

"My God!" replied Madame Delmont, surprised by this speech. "Who are these numerous inhabitants that have recently established themselves in the commune?"

"To tell the truth, Madame, no one knows as yet—but that will come. There's already Monsieur le Colonel Delmont and his family, and now a woman whose history no one knows, who has just acquired the little house at the bottom of the next hill, in the middle of the wood."

"She's chosen a very isolated dwelling; she must be very courageous, or have a good many people to keep her company, to live in that house without fear."

"That's what the whole village says—and yet she's alone, absolutely alone, for one can't count one old manservant, so pale and decrepit that she's less reminiscent of a living person than an inhabitant of the other world. As for the lady, it's said that she's pretty, although she has a very extraordinary manner. I can't be sure of that, for I haven't seen her, but next Sunday, I'll have to be very ill to miss mass. It's impossible that the lady won't come, and then I can get a look at her, so as to be able to give you a good description, if it so happens that you don't cast your eyes in her direction."

"I don't doubt, Germaine, the care you'll take to do your best to observe her, but until then, what are people saying about her? Do they know the reason that has led her to come to a place that is so disagreeable in the winter? Is she from Toulouse? Is she a widow or has she a husband?"

"All these questions have already been put to her domestic, without anyone being able to obtain a single satisfactory response. People are convinced that he's a surly, and even dishonest, individual. Do you know what he replies? *Yes, no, perhaps—that's none of your business*...and with that, he immediately pays for his purchases and goes away, without saying any more than if he were a block of wood. All that people have been able to ascertain is that they weren't born in France. They have a bizarre accent, and between themselves they use a foreign language. Perhaps they're English heretics, who've left their accursed country, where it's said that the sun never shines for an entire day, where vines never ripen and fig-trees have never been able to grow."

"Well, if the lady is English, she won't go to church, and you won't see her on Sunday at your ease."

"Is that possible? Oh, the evil people, who don't hear holy mass; they ought to be burned alive. Perhaps they're Huguenots? There you go! Vile *par-*

paillots![15] But no, it can't be—the lady's a good Christian, and she won't shun the church like an excommunicate."

"Has she been in the neighborhood for a long time?" Hélène went on, already experiencing a desire to encounter in the stranger a society that might introduce some variety into the monotonous march of her ordinary life.

"She arrived on the very day of Monsieur Delmont's departure. She came into Paul the shepherd's hut and asked him whether there was any house to rent or buy in the vicinity. Paul, who isn't malicious, told her that the Gerlot brothers wanted to sell the little house in the wood; she went in search of them right away, made a deal with them, and slept in her new acquisition that same night. As Paul and the Gerlots are sly, they made a mystery of the affair at first, doubtless wanting to keep the high price they exacted from the poor lady a secret— but everything comes out in the end; we found out what had happened, and I wasn't the last to hear about it. It's only an hour since the bell-ringer's wife came to tell me about it, and I would have thought myself remiss in my duty if I hadn't come right away to pass it on to Madame."

Hélène thanked Germaine for her good intentions with a nod of the head, and promised not to neglect to make the newcomer's acquaintance.

While the two women were chatting in this manner, Raoul kept silent, shaking his head from time to time. That gesture and his taciturnity surprised Madame Delmont, who asked him whether he had any reason to be suspicious of the unknown lady.

"Upon my faith, Madame," he said, "I don't see anything very satisfactory in her appearance here. A young woman, said to be pretty, comes with a single domestic to shut herself up in an isolated house—does that seem appropriate? Where is her husband? Has she no family? Is she not an adventuress? I've seen many of these mysterious princesses following the regiment, who avoid people's eyes and take care to hide themselves away as soon as they've found a dupe. Then they appear in daylight, flaunting their luxury and their immorality—and when the orange is sucked dry, they disappear like the will-o'-the-wisps we sometimes see in the valleys surrounding the château."

"I can, indeed, believe that," Hélène replied, "in a large city, one might encounter those unfortunate creatures who, in order to trade upon their charms more advantageously, attempt to pique curiosity by means of the darkness with which they surround themselves—but what would one of them be doing in R***, my good Raoul? Who is the rich individual that she wishes to seduce? I see no one around us but united families, who will be leaving the countryside in a few days until next summer. Are we not in one of those disastrous epochs in which great misfortunes lead to desperate resolutions? Might not this lady feel some shame at appearing in society in a manner inferior to the rank she once oc-

---

[15] The author inserts a footnote here to explain that in Languedoc, protestants are known as *parpaillots*.

cupied? The place of her retreat seems to me to speak for her. Is it in the middle of a wood, far from any road, that a modern siren would establish her lair? Wouldn't she seek instead to be closer to locations frequented by travelers? Come on, Raoul—less mistrust, I beg you. Let's not think ill of our neighbor without having good reasons to do so."

Raoul did not reply, but he did not seem convinced. The past served as his book; he thought that he was able to read fluently there everything that might happen in the future.

The next day was a remarkably beautiful one. Toward sunset, the children went out of the house, accompanied by Raoul, and their course took them into the pathways of the woods that extended from the château over the two neighboring hills and a part of the valleys encircling them.

Madame Delmont, being slightly indisposed, did not extend her walk as far; she went down toward the hamlet and chatted to the villagers she met, whose vintage seemed to have excellent prospects.

Everywhere, she heard talk of the stranger; the latter's presence piqued collective curiosity; people kept track of all her movements; it was known that she emerged from her abode at dusk to walk in the surrounding area, but that she rarely showed herself while the sun shone; she spent her days in an upstairs room into which no one had penetrated. Her aged domestic took care of all household matters; he was taciturn, though, and his face was always surly; he refused all conversation and constantly maintained a silence that did not suit the avid curiosity of the local housewives.

The more details Hélène was told about the unknown woman, the firmer became her intention to seek her out. With all her excellent qualities, Madame Delmont was still a daughter of our common mother. Nevertheless, she hid her secret desire beneath a complete indifference, and when night had covered the skies she went back up to the château, followed by Germaine, who had come to meet her.

As soon as the children saw her, they ran to her excitedly. "Oh, Mama, dear Mama!" the cried, both at once. "We've seen the beautiful mysterious lady. We've spoken to her, and she gave us crowns of flowers. Oh, how good she is, and how pretty too!"

These childish words and this unexpected encounter excited Madame Delmont's curiosity even more keenly. "Come on, children," she said to them, "don't both speak at the same time. Let one of you tell me what happened—and if there's a mistake, the other can remember what's been forgotten."

This proposition was very reasonable, but it presented great difficulties in being put into execution. Juliette, full of enthusiasm and generosity, did not seem disposed to give way to her brother—who, for his part, claimed his right as the eldest to be the narrator of the great adventure.

A serious dispute ensued. Hélène tried to bring about a reconciliation, but her efforts were futile. Juliette wanted to speak and Eugène did not want to shut up. The mother was finally forced to exert her authority; a dictatorial order commanded her daughter to be silent. The latter then put on a sulky expression and ran into a corner of the room to hide her pretty face, certifying that her brother might make mistakes, but that she would certainly not open her mouth to correct them.

Proud of the mark of distinction that his mother had granted him, Eugène thanked her for it with a gracious smile, and, standing before her, began his story.

"I had a desire, my dear Mama, to go down into the nearby valley, and I begged Raoul to take us, in order to collect the hyacinths that grow in the fields there. He agreed, and we had only been there for a few moments when Juliette, who can never keep still, ran toward the woods."

"That's not true, Monsieur!" cried Juliette, irritated by her brother's accusation. "I was following a green and blue damsel-fly, and you know it." The mischievous girl continued: "You'll get nothing exact out of Eugène, Mama, and I'll tell you what happened—because, after all, I'm the one the lady spoke to first."

"I ordered you to keep silent as long as Eugène didn't go wrong," Madame Delmont replied, softly but gravely. "I'm holding to my initial decision. Don't make me tell you a third time."

The curtness of this speech, not at all in harmony with the great affection that Hélène had for her loving daughter, caused the latter such distress that she dissolved in tears and, putting her arms around her mother's neck, began to weep bitterly.

Hélène recognized then that she had been too severe, and without saying anything, she caressed her daughter's beautiful blonde hair with her hand, and placed a soft kiss on her alabaster forehead, to which serenity was not long delayed in returning after that pledge of peace.

Meanwhile, Eugène continued his story. He explained that the foreign lady had appeared to his surprised gaze when he went to fetch his sister, who was lost in a thicket; that he had found her holding the lady's hand; and that the latter had joined in their games—although, the child went on, it seemed that she did not much like gaiety. She was serious, even while seeking diversion, and the long bursts of laughter that Juliette did not spare when she was amused seemed to make her shiver.

"She treated us with a rare generosity. Raoul tried in vain to bring us back; she continually retained us. She always had a few more flowers to add to the crowns she was weaving. She's very dexterous, I swear, my dear Mama, and yet she always wears a glove on her left hand, which must be a hindrance. Juliette tried, innocently, to take it off, but she forbade it forcefully, and gave her a look at the same time that frightened my sister and me, imprinted as it was with some chagrin that I don't feel capable of explaining to you."

This story was confirmed in every point by the little girl, who hastened to speak in her turn. She added a host of details. She told her mother that, at the moment when she had plunged into the thicket, she had suddenly found the pretty lady beside her, as if she had emerged from a nearby tree.

"I couldn't help being frightened at first," Juliette went on. "She saw that, and it distressed her. She came to me smiling, and her gracious words soon reassured me. She didn't ask me any questions, as people who see me for the first time usually do. She talked about the pleasures of the countryside, her desire to be my friend. She didn't say a word about you and Papa."

Raoul, questioned in his turn, confirmed everything the children said, but a profound anxiety seemed to be spread across his face. He tried to hide it but it burst forth regardless, and Madame Delmont could not help being struck by it.

"Well, Raoul," she said to him, "you're not as charmed by the foreign lady as Eugène and his sister. Are you maintaining your suspicion, or did you, perchance, recognize her?"

"Me, recognize her, Madame!" the soldier exclaimed, his face suddenly covered by an extreme pallor. "I can't see that anything in my conduct could have led you to form such a conjecture. I don't know the person at all, but I persist nevertheless in thinking that her coming to this place is too mysterious to signify anything good. If my advice isn't to be disdained, you won't permit your children to have any contact with her. As for allowing her set foot in the château, you can do as you wish—but if I were in your shoes, I wouldn't let her through the first courtyard."

"To act with so much rigor in her regard," Hélène replied, "I'd need to be certain that it was inappropriate for me to associate with her—which I might perhaps soon discover. But since you've seen her today for the first time, and the antipathy she inspires in you has no solid foundation, I can act as circumstances suggest—firmly committed, however, my dear Raoul, to regulate my conduct according to your advice, if you have any information about this lady that proves to you that I am running some risk in receiving her, in the event that she decides to pay me a visit, as neighborhood gives her the right to do."

On hearing Madame Delmont express herself with so much generosity, Raoul seemed momentarily uncertain as to what he ought to say, but his indecision came to a sudden end. In a firm voice, he assured her that his anxieties arose only from precaution, that the lady was not known to him in any fashion, and that his mistress had every right to act according to her will and her whim.

Hélène was familiar with the soldier's noble honesty, and when he expressed himself in these terms, she no longer suspected what he said. She attributed his insinuation to the natural mistrust of those who have seen a great deal: evil has been manifest before them in all its forms, so they always fear to encounter it when the slightest apparent sign presents itself. It is only in a sheltered life that the soul abandons itself to a confidence that nothing has deceived; only the company of human beings can teach fear of them.

Chapter IV

In affirming to Madame Delmont that the foreigner was unknown to him, however, Raoul had knowingly lied. He could not have forgotten those exceedingly remarkable features. He knew how worthy they appeared of inspiring affectionate attachment, and shivered at an encounter that seemed to promise cruel storms for the future.

In those circumstances, though, ought he to poison the tranquility that his worthy mistress was enjoying? Was it necessary to ignite the devouring flames of jealousy in her heart?

There are, unfortunately, occasions in life when it is indispensable to keep silent about the truth—when it is necessary to make a pact with deception, in order to avoid violent harm. One of them had presented itself now, and Raoul reluctantly sacrificed his natural honesty. He kept quiet about what he knew—but how desperate he was to see the evening end, in order to be free to retire to his room and reflect calmly on what he ought to do in this painful position.

At the same time, his prudence caused him to understand how important it was not to reveal what was troubling his soul. The suspicions recently aroused in Madame Delmont's bosom might lead to strange realities. He had to summon up all his energy, therefore, and, while watching over her carefully, he had to master his facial expressions, in which Hélène would not be able to read the indifference of everyday life.

Finally collecting himself, when eleven o'clock chimed on the landing clock, he hastened to sit down at the desk that was in his bedroom and wrote to tell his master what had happened:

How surprised you will be, Colonel, when you learn that Alinska is now living in R***, and that she is the château's nearest neighbor! What is she doing in this locality, after such a long lapse of time? What is her intention? I can't tell you anything about that. She didn't recognize me—at least, when she saw me, she didn't give me the slightest hint that would allow me to deduce it. Give me your orders and I will carry them out immediately. Would you like to see her again, and obtain an interview with her to find out what she intends? Or would you prefer that Madame and your children leave the locality immediately? That departure would perhaps be the most appropriate course; you will never be happy or tranquil as long as that unfortunate Hungarian woman exists—or, at least, as long as she is able to pursue you with her presence and her reproaches.

As he finished writing those last words, Raoul shivered, for he thought he had heard the rustle of a woman's dress behind him and felt the breath of someone leaning over his head to read what he had written. The illusion was so perfect that he did not doubt that Madame Delmont was there. Desperately confused by such a circumstance, at first he dared not raise his eyes or turn his head—but after a minute had gone by in that distressing situation, no further sound having reached his ear, he looked round and realized that he was mistaken. There was no one in the room, where a profound silence reigned, only interrupted at intervals by the cry of a solitary osprey perched on one of the château's towers.

That certainty caused him an infinite joy. He hastened to seal the letter, and after having carefully locked his door, he tried to go to sleep. For a long time yet, however, he was unable to savor the restorative balm; he could not get the mysterious Alinska out of his head, and, in his resentment against her, the honest soldier swore aloud, as he used to do when training recruits that had been sent to his company. By virtue of seeking to forget himself, however, he achieved it; his eyelids, weary of long wakefulness, finally closed, and the man within him no longer existed, save for his nocturnal relationship with the celestial intelligences.

Dawn almost always found Raoul awake in anticipation. This time, he failed in his usual custom, and the sun had already appeared above the hills of Coronsac when the former sergeant-major awoke with a start, still surprised by his profound torpor. The field-work must already have begun, and he had not presided over its commencement.

Ashamed of his failure, for which he alone would reproach himself, he hastened to get up, and ran to the farm to see whether the laborers had arrived. He had only taken a few steps outside the château when he suddenly remembered that he had left the important letter to his master on his desk. He judged that prudence did not permit him to leave it lying around like that, so he immediately went back in to get it, intending to give it to a day-laborer in order that he might put it into the post in Toulouse.

The letter was no longer where Raoul had left it. Torn into a hundred pieces, it was strewn on the floor of the room! That sight, as surprising as it was sinister, drew a vehement exclamation from Raoul, and soon led him to exceedingly painful reflections.

Who could have torn up the letter? Who had gone into his abode so promptly, to act with such audacity? Could it be Madame Delmont, Germaine or the girl who tended the poultry? Those were the only three people who could be up at this hour. He remembered that Jeannette, the last-cited, had gone out of the château before him. Germaine, busy in the kitchen with household chores that took up all her time, could not have left her work. The windows of their mistress's apartment, carefully shuttered, indicated that she was still in bed.

Exceedingly troubled by such an extraordinary incident, he was unable to recommence the destroyed letter. He carefully gathered up all the pieces, which he burned in the nearby fireplace, and went out utterly confused by what had just happened, to which he could not assign any satisfactory cause.

The day had gone by before Raoul's mind had recovered its usual disposition. Although he was convinced that Madame Delmont was not the perpetrator of the outrage committed in his room, he was still embarrassed the first time he found himself in her presence. Trying to control himself, he tried to read Hélène's features, but nothing in particular was evident there. She was calm, and gave no indication that any unexpected discovery had disturbed her tranquility.

More astonished than ever, Raoul lost himself in vague conjectures. He was distressed when the children proposed that he should take them on a walk that evening—when, they said, they hoped to see their new friend again. He wanted to refuse, but Madame Delmont was present, and before he could say anything, she had already agreed. He was no longer able to make his sentiments known; prudence, in any case, told him how important it was not to give rise to any anxiety in the soul of his colonel's wife. He therefore suppressed a gesture of impatience that escaped him, and slowly went down the hill, as his young companions desired.

Scarcely had they entered the little meadow when the Hungarian woman Alinska emerged inopportunely from the wood. She was carrying a mallet, two balls and a beautiful doll, intended for the children. As soon as they had seen their new friend they ran toward her, and Juliette—the bolder of the two—did not hesitate to throw herself into her arms. That innocent action seemed to disturb her; she took a step backwards, and looked at the foolish girl with an expression so somber and peculiarly sinister that the courageous Raoul stood there in confusion. But that first impulse did not last; a slight smile came to animate the foreigner's features, and she distributed the presents she had brought with a charming grace.

Enchanted with the mallet and balls, Eugène ran to a nearby road to try them out. Juliette, happy at the sight of her doll, asked permission from the lady of the wood to collect flowers to decorate its dress, bosom and forehead. The foreigner raised no opposition to that. She drew away slightly, however, and when she saw that the children were busy with their new amusements, she drew nearer to the sergeant-major.

The latter, leaning on a poplar planted in the meadow, remembered the past anxiously; he feared that new storms might trouble his colonel's rest. He was not content, but he did not know what to do to ward off impending disaster. Utterly self-absorbed, he had not heard the lady approaching him when he was snatched from his reverie by the sound of a voice that was familiar to him, but which, at that moment, had a certain hoarseness and solemnity, apt to disturb anyone who heard it.

"Well, Raoul," she said to him, "what have I done to you to set you against me forever? Will your unjust aversion never cease to pursue me with the same rigor?"

Surprised to the highest degree by such questioning, the soldier raised his eyes, stood aside from the tree that was supporting him, and seemed reluctant to reply. Making an effort to collect himself, however, he said "What do you want, Alinska? Why have you abandoned your homeland? What are you looking for in the depths of France? Has time no empire over you? Do you think that you are still as you were in your youth? If so, I pity you—or rather, I deplore the folly that is carrying you away."

"Time," the foreigner replied, in the most solemn tone possible, "no longer has any hold over me; there is a period of existence when its empire ceases, when sentiments become as inalterable as eternity, of which they are an integral part. Have no fear of my presence; it's not my will that directs me. I no longer belong to myself; I have a cruel, imperious master who commands my every step. My past wound still bleeds, and time, as you call it, has lost the right to scar it over."

"Why cling to futile hopes?" Raoul replied. "It's all over between you and the colonel. Perhaps he did wrong, but he can no longer think about that. It's already several years since he married a wife worthy of his affection. Do you intend to trouble the peace of the household? Will vengeance lead you to break the heart of the woman who has given him her hand?"

"Could he do that, Raoul? Was it your master's prerogative to give himself freely? Was it not with the blood in his veins that he signed the promise never to go to the altar with anyone but me? Do you not know that, you who have just brought up the past, which will be reanimated in its entirety to crush the perfidious individual that you are supporting? Was I less beautiful than our new mistress? Was I less virtuous? Did crime ever undo the white veil protecting my face? What have I done wrong? Was it in returning love for love, abandoning myself without reserve to a sentiment I believed to be sincere? Have I gone back on the promise that I signed with my own blood in my turn? Is it not still in Edouard's power? Is he legitimately married, according to Heaven's law? What are my misdeeds? Let him enumerate them; he will search in vain to oppose me with them, while I can strike him down by presenting the mass of his own to him."

While speaking thus, the beautiful foreigner did not seem to belong to this world at all. Her form, tall and slender at the same time, the vague uncertainty bursting forth in her gaze, and the marks of indignation imprinted in her features—which gave her mouth a terrible expression—might have allowed her to be mistaken for one of the redoubtable intelligences that serve as intermediaries between humankind and the divinity, which the latter sometimes invests with a portion of his omnipotence for the punishment of human perversity.

Raoul could not sustain the scrutiny of her staring eyes, which seemed to be pursuing his thoughts into the remotest crannies of his soul. He admitted, internally, his master's wrongdoing—but in his view, that wrongdoing was irreparable. The years appeared to have sanctioned it; the colonel's marriage was indissoluble; and Alinska, in spite of the justice of her claims, had to renounce her demand that they be met—so he tried to make her understand that by means of his response.

The foreigner listened to him with a disdainful smile, but without interruption, without manifesting any surprise or discontent. Perhaps he was already flattering himself that he had convinced her of the pointlessness of the step she had taken, when she stopped him by placing her right hand on his shoulder.

That gesture, made with a kind of negligence, nevertheless produced a surprising effect. At the place where Alinska had touched him, he felt an extraordinary commotion; he seemed to pass rapidly into the heart of an ardent furnace, then into an ocean of ice—but the sensation disappeared as soon as the hand that had given birth to it was withdrawn.

"And have I given him back his promise?" said Alinska, tranquilly, without responding to the arguments that had just been put to her. "Will he be able to show it to me?"

"What does it matter whether he has it or not? It is no longer able to regulate his destiny. Whether it is in his hands or yours, what use is it? The tribunals will pay no heed to it."

"It might be, frivolous Frenchman, that the human law of your land does not punish that kind of perjury, but there are incorruptible judges outside this world; they have received it, have recorded it in their tablet of eternal bronze; it is to them that I have addressed myself to obtain justice, and I believe that I might expect their equity."

"Upon my faith, Alinska," said Raoul—who, scarcely occupied with venerable matters of religion, saw nothing in life but the present moment—"you've waited a long time to see that justice executed. Believe me, you'd best go back to your homeland, to your family. Be persuaded that the colonel, in exchange for that promise, for whose return he will ask you, will not hesitate to give you everything he can, to help you enjoy a peaceful existence."

"That is no longer in his power," said the foreigner, in a tone more solemn still. "I no longer have any family; the entire Earth is my new homeland; it is to her bosom that I have confided Edouard's promise. And as for the advantages that you offer me in his name, I have no need of them; I have a considerable portion at my disposal—and if you would care to promise not to send word to your master that I am here, I will promise in my turn to outbid the demands that you might make on his fortune." Taking am extremely well-stuffed purse from her girdle, she went on: "Here, take this, as an advance on what you shall have later."

Alinska's bizarre words left the soldier completely nonplussed. He knew that the Hungarian woman, the daughter of simple villagers, was certainly not rich, but now she was offering him proof of an extreme opulence. That was not calculated to reassure him, but at least she was flattering herself in her turn to think that she could seduce him. Raoul's hand made no move toward Alinska's; he did not dart any covetous glance at the gift she was offering him.

"I too, Alinska, have more than I need," he replied. "Thank you for your generous offer; it could not tempt me if I had any intention of sending word to my master that I had seen you."

"You have that intention, liar," she replied, swiftly. "You've already tried to put it into action."

That direct attack, and the insult addressed to him—for which a person of a different sex would have paid in blood—threw Raoul into an inconceivable perplexity. He hesitated as to whether to let his anger burst forth or try to hide it, but the force of his character carried him away, and he cried, resentfully: "Give thanks to your dress, which protects you from my vengeance. And what title do you merit, imprudent woman, who do not hesitate to introduce yourself into someone else's house in order to spy on the actions of its inhabitants? You're abroad early, it seems to me, but be certain that it will be a long time before you can get into the Château de R*** without my knowing it."

Another smile, whose significance was indeterminable, was Alinska's only direct response; she seemed disdainful of the soldier's attack. Suddenly assuming a dignified attitude, however, which contrasted with the simplicity of her manners and costume, she said: "Remember, Raoul, that you have played an active part in my misfortunes. Now that they're complete, don't throw yourself blindly on to a road that might lead you to ruin. Believe me, remaining neutral in the struggle that might develop is the only mean to shield yourself from the gusts of the imminent tempest."

There was an extraordinary gleam in her eyes as she finished. She made a gesture whose significance was terrible, and drew away at a rapid pace, following a path that soon hid her from any gaze, without paying any heed to the voices of the little children—who, wearying of their playthings, were coming back in order to talk to her.

Raoul, confused by the scene that had just been played out, and entirely preoccupied with the future misfortunes that he anticipated, stayed motionless in the same spot for some time.

Eugène finally drew him out of his reverie. "Can you hear the thunder rumbling in that thick cloud, Raoul," he said. "Look—see how beautiful the lightning flashes are. There's definitely going to be a storm."

"A storm!" Raoul exclaimed. "Is her prediction coming true already?"

As he pronounced these words, he looked up at the sky and saw an enormous mass of vapors toward the west, over the Garonne, which emitted livid lightning bolts from time to time, while the rumble of thunder was repeated all around by echoes.

Prudence did not permit the excursion to be prolonged; he took his young friends by the hand and, choosing the quickest and most direct path, went straight back to the château, which he reached before the rain began to fall.

Chapter V

Madame Delmont, who had been watching the storm gather for some time through the drawing-room windows, had already become anxious about the prolongation of her children's walk. She had been unable to master her impatience, and, emerging from the château, went toward the woods in order to meet them as soon as possible.

She did not have far to go; she soon heard the laughter of the petulant Juliette and she saw the dear creatures, who had met the pretty lady again, running toward her with the presents the latter had given them. The mallet, the balls and the richly-dressed doll were all shown to her urgently. Madame Delmont was a mother, and, in consequence, already favorably impressed by the woman who loved creatures so precious to her affection. She asked what the foreigner had said.

"Oh, she didn't speak to us for very long this time," the little girl replied. "She never stopped talking to Raoul—and it seemed to me that she got very angry with him."

This inopportune revelation upset all the plans the sergeant-major had made. He immediately envisaged the perils of a denial, which Madame Delmont would probably not believe. In consequence, he made his decision, and in spite of a keen regret at plunging deeper into deceit, he did not wait to be interrogated. As soon as a gesture from Hélène had sent the children away he said; "I was right, Madame, not to trust that unknown woman. Be sure that that she has not come to R*** without some dangerous plan. She interrogated me for an entire hour, never ceasing to ask questions about your family and all our neighbors. She wanted to know everything: everyone's age, status and occupation. She never let up, and her investigation was truly wearying. I tried at first to avoid her indiscreet questions, but she was not to be held at bay; she returned to the charge. One question followed one another without delay, like relay fire. I soon got tired of it. I gathered my platoon, and with a vigorous charge I routed her. My resistance shocked her, and she effected her retreat in a bad mood."

This discourse, interspersed with military terms, made Madame Delmont smile. The foreigner's interrogations did not seem to her to be as blameworthy as Raoul represented them. It seemed quite natural that, if she intended to live in the locality, she should seek information about its inhabitants. "I hope, my dear Raoul," she said, "that your replies were not disagreeable. It's necessary to respect ladies, and a military man, most of all, should only speak to them politely."

"That's all right for officers," Raoul replied, "but those of us who don't enjoy their privileges don't think it necessary to imitate their gallantry."

After these words, deliberately voiced in an abrupt tone, he took leave of his mistress, who was similarly not sorry to terminate a conversation that had no objective. She went back to her children, while a violent wind got up and large drops of water began to fall.

Madame Delmont had no fear of the sound of thunder, nor had her children, but Germaine and Jeannette were terrified. They came to their mistress, as if in search of a refuge, which she did not refuse them.

Raoul who was now at liberty, went to his room. Certain of not being disturbed, he started once again to write to the colonel, in spite of an involuntary disturbance that sometimes afflicted his heart.

Meanwhile, the storm increased in violence, its winds battling one another forcefully in the vast plans of the atmosphere. They seemed in their fury to shake the solid foundations of the château. Mingled with the booming of the thunder and the shrill whistling of the wind, Raoul occasionally heard sounds like plaintive voices; he heard whispers in his ears that seemed to be formed by familiar voices. Several times, he could not help pausing, but soon, ashamed of his weakness, he took up the thread of his thoughts, and by supper-time the letter was finished.

Not wishing to take the risk of exposing himself to Alinska's endeavors, and mistrustful of one of the two women in Madame Delmont's service, he put the letter into a casket, which he placed at the back of his cupboard, and, taking the keys to both with him, he left the room more contentedly, sure that his deposit was safe.

The storm was still howling; it had become even more furious as the rain slackened. Germaine and Jeannette were still numb with fear; the children, weary of waiting for the evening meal, were asleep on a sofa and Hélène was reading Abbé Richard's voyage to Italy.[16]

Raoul's arrival reanimated the two maidservants, both of whom decided to return to their posts. The delayed supper was eventually served.

Toward midnight the sky cleared, the clouds accumulating over the hills of Lauraguais, and clam gradually returned to nature. Raoul had seen the disturbance of the weather with some pleasure; he knew that when the ground was soaked, it would not be possible to go out walking for several days. He hoped that something might happen in that interval that would break the new link formed between his master's children and the Hungarian woman Alinska. He even imagined that a reply from the colonel might give another direction to the family's communal life.

Occupied with these ideas, which were tormenting him, the brave soldier did not sleep much. The new day had not dawned when he was already up and about. Searching for his keys, he opened the cupboard and the casket in order to take out the letter that he wanted to send to Toulouse without delay. He found it

---

[16] Abbé Richard's *Description historique et critique de l'Italie* (1766) is another of the reputedly improving works by churchmen of which Hélène seems to be so fond.

by feel, without seeing it, darkness still reigning. He placed it in his coat pocket and went downstairs to summon the peasant he wanted to serve as is messenger.

Before the latter arrived, a few moments went by. The wan first light gave way to a redder dawn; bright light illuminated the landscape and nature, refreshed by the previous day's tempest, displayed the brilliance of its radiant and varied adornment.

It was at that moment that the day-laborer Mathieu appeared before Raoul; the latter asked him to set off immediately for the city in order to put an urgent letter in the post. As he gave that order he took the missive out of the refuge where he had placed it and looked at it, as was his habit, to check the seal.

Unparalleled surprise! The paper was covered with large drops of blood, which scarcely permitted the address to be read!

This bizarre circumstance drew a cry from the disconcerted soldier. He could scarcely believe his eyes. He stood still, turning the letter over and over, without succeeding in coming to terms with such a strange incident. He turned out his pocket hurriedly; there was nothing staining it, and no trace of blood was detectable therein.

Then, making his decision, he went back into the château, went back to his room and took out the casket in which the letter had been locked—but it too retained no trace of the stain who existence had alarmed the courageous Raoul.

Without losing any time, over, he hastened to recommence the letter for a third time. He shortened it, but that rendered it more expressive. As soon as he had finished it, he gave it to the messenger, and as an extra precaution, he made the decision to accompany him as far as the limits of the commune of Castanet.

Raoul was brave, but he could not help feeling a certain superstitious dread. He remembered anxiously the doubtless-exaggerated tales that he had heard in Hungary while he was living there in the company of his regiment, about the extended power of perverse humans who, to the detriment of their souls, had made a pact with the perpetual enemy of our salvation. He recalled, with a superstitious terror, everything that he had been told about that matter— and the two incidents that he had just witnessed led him to fear that Alinska might have a fraction of a magic wand, which had surely been divided between several of her compatriots.

The soldier did not take long, however, to put these thoughts out of his mind. *I'm being stupid*, he said to himself, *believing in such nonsense. In Hungary they're barbarians, but in France the Devil has lost his rights, or has handed on his skill to prestidigitators, as the colonel calls them. They work for him and perhaps Mademoiselle Alinska is merely a clever trickster. She'd better watch out, though; if I catch her at it, she'll have a hard time.*

He left it at that, and a visit he paid to a bottle of old rum, kept on a corner of his mantelpiece, completed the reassurance of his mind. He promised himself to redouble his vigilance, and to discover by some means how he Hungarian woman was able to take action in the château. Then he went back to his usual work, hoping for a prompt reply from the colonel.

The profound solitude in which the Delmont family lived was not so entire that it was uninterrupted by a few visits made to the château by the neighbors living in the surrounding houses. They were always received with equal politeness. Hélène even took pleasure in seeing them, especially since her husband's absence. She needed a stronger dose of distraction then, and found it in her relationship with the strangers.

It was not, therefore, with surprise that at about two o'clock in the afternoon of that same day she saw a country gentleman coming into the drawing-room. He was a former master of waterways and forests who had emigrated in order to do as everyone else was doing, but had found, ten leagues from the frontier, that he had done enough for glory and honor and had come back in a hurry to find in France the easy life that he missed so much, and which Germany did not offer. Thanks to his docility in bending to the will of all governments, he had spent twenty years of revolution in almost perfect tranquility. He had been obliged, it is true, to wear the red bonnet with the Jacobins, applaud the outrages of the 18th of Fructidor, approve of the events of the 18th of Brumaire, give his vote to the lifelong consulate, and for the elevation of Napoléon Bonaparte to emperor; he had joined the allies of the 16th of April 1814; had signed, scribbling his name as best he could, with no flourish, the famous *Acte additionel*, and had taken his heroism so far as to pack his trunk to send it to Gand when the news of the disaster at Waterloo had reached his ears.[17]

In spite of his oscillations, the worthy gentleman nevertheless talked about his devotion to the dynasty of the legitimate kings, his hatred for the Charter and the purity of his chivalric affections; and if some resentful individual reminded him about the fatal bonnet he had donned, he proudly claimed that, having taken care to choose the color puce as a background, it could not reasonably be claimed that he had adopted the livery of the Jacobins.

This individual, fundamentally the most decent fellow in the world, lived in a beautiful house in the commune of Merville. He spent his life in the fields, in which he labored with his walking-stick; he was his own rural policeman and displayed an enthusiastic enmity toward the birds of the air, which he pursued by throwing stones at them with a rare vehemence. He had once dined in Tou-

---

[17] The dates to which this page refers are some of those on which the government of France suddenly took a new direction. 18 Fructidor, an V (4 September 1797) saw the *coup d'état* in which members of the Directoire seized power. 18 Brumaire, an VIII (9 November 1799) was the day on which Napoléon, having returned from Egypt, abolished the Directoire. On 16 April 1814 the so-called "Senatorial Constitution" was put in place, on the eve of Napoléon's exile to Elba; the *Acte additionnel* was the reformed constitution with which Napoléon replaced it on his return therefrom.

louse with the Prefect and from that moment on had entered into complete opposition to his mayor. He was the latter's despair, pestering him unremittingly with unjustified complaints and motiveless denunciations. He wanted his properties to be sacred, and under the empire of the Civil Code he was seen relentlessly demanding the execution of the laws of feudality. He was, moreover, a great visitor, an intrepid trencherman and an inexhaustible drinker. He refused neither a visit to a château nor a collusion in a modest farm. He read the *Écho du Midi*, without refusing to cast a glance over *Le Constitutionnel* when he encountered that rag in the home of some local black-hat.

As soon as he entered Madame Delmont's home, Monsieur Berneval, a tiresome complimenter, exhausted all of what he called "the protocol of the old court." He praised, in addition, the pleasantness of the Château de R***, the purity of the sky and the fertility of the soil. He slipped in a word about the negligence of the local magistrates, who were not multiplying their reports, and on the losses occasioned to him by malevolent magpies.

When these important subjects had been exhausted, he went on: "Well, Madame, you have a friendly neighbor—I don't know why I say friendly, for she has treated me with disheartening rigor. Informed only last Tuesday of the presence in the canton of a beautiful foreigner, whose charms were praised by the voice of the public, I thought it my duty, as a French chevalier and to give her a high opinion of our gentlefolk, to pay her a prompt visit that might prove my enthusiasm to get along with her.

"Yesterday, therefore, neglecting an expertise that I was employing to determine the quantity of plums that the domestic pigs of one of my neighbors had eaten in my grounds, to my detriment, I headed for the house in the wood, with my umbrella under my arm, because it's necessary not to put one's trust in the weather or in people.

"I arrived; the door was closed. That didn't surprise me; it's appropriate to be master in one's own home. I knocked lightly; it was opened. I was about to go in when a genuine phantom presented itself and barred my passage. Imagine the tallest of human beings, and certainly the thinnest, with the face like a gin-trap and the eyes of an owl—an appearance more reminiscent of an inhabitant of the other world than a citizen of this one, harsh in speech, stiff in gesture, with poisonous breath.

"'What do you want?' he asked me, without saying *Monsieur*, as is customary.

"That abrupt question surprised me somewhat. Nevertheless, as a noble soldier in the army of Condé is not easily put off, I said to him: 'I am a gentleman of the neighborhood who is hastening to present his respects to your mistress, and who requests the honor of being introduced to her presence.'

"That polite response gave me some right to believe that I would be admitted immediately; my error was great as you shall soon see. That new Cerberus, without paying any heed to my manners—which, I dare to presume, reproduce those of the old court—said: 'I can't let you in. My mistress, constantly occupied, has no time to devote to socializing. She did not come here is search of society, and there is no point in presenting yourself here a second time.'

"Without awaiting my reply, the vulgar individual took a step back and set the barrier of the door between us, slamming it noisily. I cannot describe my chagrin. I withdrew, indignant at such bad form, and I intend to visit all my neighbors, to warn them of the fate that awaits them if they attempt to fulfill the duties demanded by convention."

This narrative amused Madame Delmont, who promised herself privately not to expose herself to such a reception, no matter how desirous she was to make the acquaintance of the mysterious stranger. She imagined that she might be fortunate enough to meet her during one of the walks she took with her children, and in the meantime, she protested against the incivility of the domestic—kindly adding that Monsieur Berneval must certainly have been unknown to him, for she could not imagine that, if he had known to whom he had the honor of speaking, he would have been so boorish.

The compliment almost consoled the former master of waterways and forests for his misadventure. In order to forget it, he hastened to talk about the politics of the new era, which were important enough to have the right to occupy the attention of all Frenchmen.

Madame Delmont knew that on that subject it was sufficient to let him talk, and that he made his exit delightedly from houses in which he had been heard without distraction. The worthy fellow credited himself with having divined everything; the secrets of courts were unveiled to him; he directed the course of affairs, and predicted an imminent change of administration—something that, in France, one can prognosticate at any moment without requiring any devotion to the study of witchcraft.

When that vast subject was exhausted, he passed on to new ground, reporting the latest stock prices in the Toulouse market, declaring that if he was not given a curé soon he was going to leave the commune, complaining of the insolence of poachers, and slipping in a few words on the excavation of a field from which he expected excellent results. These very important matters were listened to with an appearance of interest that charmed him. He quit Madame Delmont enchanted by her, especially when he compared her to the unsociable foreigner, and when he left the château he went to the home of a vicomte to sing her praises.

"That's all very well," was the reply he received, "but what family does she come from? Before the revolution, my dear, she and her husband were not riding in the King's carriages, and in consequence, can only be honest bourgeois, which is nothing much."

Chapter VI

Sunday finally arrived, keenly anticipated by everyone who hoped to content their curiosity on the subject of the beautiful foreigner at the church. Madame Delmont, very scrupulous in fulfilling her duties as a Christian, had been determined not to miss the opportunity; she was one of the first to take her place in the holy edifice, in order that she might witness the entrance of the woman she wanted to see.

Time went by, and she did not appear. The procession took place and the mass was sung in great pomp, but no inhabitant of the isolated house was present. That caused an extreme surprise. The most bizarre conjectures were advanced, and among the housewives of the commune it was decided that the lady was either ill or a Huguenot—from which a sentiment of malevolence arose against her. The refusal that she seemed to be making to deliver herself to their avid gaze was held against her.

Only Raoul was pleased by this circumstance. The tenacity of the mud had interrupted the excursions of the colonel's children; they no longer went out of the château, and gradually lost the memory of their beautiful friend. If their youth effaced their memory so promptly, however, the mystery woman was not forgotten by Madame Delmont. The latter had an absolute desire to see her, and waited impatiently for the moment when firmer ground would permit the recommencement of her accustomed walks.

The following Tuesday, her wish was granted; the warmth of the sun had dried up the moisture, and the day was fine. Raoul, occupied with the preparations for the grape-harvest, had gone to Aureville in order to confer with a barrel-maker. Hélène took advantage of the opportunity to go out with Eugène and Juliette, and it was toward the little meadow in the valley that she directed their steps.

A peculiar sentiment, whose cause was unknown to her, caused her to feel a singular oppression; her heart seemed to be laden with an enormous weight; she had difficulty breathing, and her entire body was prey to a general malaise. At the same time, by virtue of a physical depression, her mind lacked vivacity; it lapsed into a melancholy reverie that she tried in vain to banish. The enthusiastic gaiety of her children made no appeal to hers, and twice she felt tears forming in her eyes that no real pain had caused.

It was in this condition that she slowly went down the hill, attributing the disturbance in her soul and senses to the vague anxiety that always agitates us when we seek to unravel something unknown to us, when our ideas are lost in a confusion dangerous to our reason.

Having arrived in the meadow, Madame Delmont, refraining from darting curious glances her and there, sat down at the foot of the Italian poplar against which Raoul had earlier leaned; a natural seat formed by an abrupt rise in the grassy ground offered an inviting resting-place. Hélène took some embroidery out of her bag and set to work, while she gave the two children the liberating signal that authorized them to begin playing. They did not delay the resumption of their merry games.

They had been playing for a quarter of an hour when the light and silvery sounds of a harp became audible close at hand.

Surprised by this novel circumstance, Madame Delmont hastened to recall her children with a silent gesture, before they were able to pay any attention to the sound. She told them to be very quiet, made them sit down beside her, and listened avidly to the various tunes that the hidden musician was playing.

First, there were a few slow and almost monotonous preludes, which gradually gave way to less solemn tones. Soon, they were succeeded by a ritornello full of expression and vehemence, and a soft but nevertheless veiled voice intoned a singular ballad:[18]

> Can a day so radiantly bright,
> This cool valley and its pure stream,
> Not cause my eyes to alight?
> My heart is alone in a dream!
> From vain happiness I have fled,
> Having sought constancy therein;
> When I knew I had been misled,
> My hope was replaced by chagrin.
>
> In vain I seek slumberous respite.
> From my weary pupils it flees;
> No release for me in the night;
> Time itself has given me release;
> Rapidly it flees, but in vain;
> While I wait to be taken in hand,
> My torment is renewed again
> And hope is beyond my command.

---

[18] The text entitles this song *Point d'esperance* [No Hope] and subtitles it *Romance* [ballad], adding a footnote to record that it has been set to music by Mlle. Adèle Sendrier. The score in question is included in the text, and the book's prefatory material alleges that the music to all the text's songs—all of which carry similar footnotes—has also been published separately, but Mlle. Sendrier is not to be found in the catalogue of the Bibliothèque Nationale and the name scores no hits at all on Google or *gallica*. The lady in question might be the novel's mysterious dedicatee, but given Lamothe-Langon's track record, one is bound to suspect that she might be a figment of his imagination.

In the refuge of the damp tomb
I have tried to attain whole sleep,
Further punishment was my doom,
The rape of my dust in the deep.
I live but I do not exist,
Beginning a day without end;
In death I can never desist
Or find peace or hope to amend.

We can only describe in a very imperfect manner the sensations that agitated Hélène while that balled lasted. She listened with a secret shiver; she could not doubt that the person singing it was unhappy, for Misfortune, when it speaks, has particular inflections in the voice that are not the same as those of which the child of Prosperity makes use. Something continually reveals that daughter of pain, and to divine her presence one does not always need to see her.

That belief, however, far from cooling Madame Delmont's ardor, made her all the more eager to meet the foreigner.

A means to attain that end was suddenly offered to her; she was no longer restraining the enthusiasm of Eugène and Juliette, who had both recognized their friend's voice and were impatient to run to her. They did so as soon as it was possible, and found her in a clearing nearby, where she was sitting on the trunk of an old tree that had been recently felled. She was holding a small, simply-decorated harp, which she was still playing, although one of her hands remained constantly gloved.

She seemed delighted to see the children again, and called to her domestic, who was a short distance away. He came to collect the instrument, which she handed to him.

When that was done, the Hungarian woman asked her favorite, Juliette, what game she wanted to play. The little girl, already full of mischief, had made a plan to lead the foreigner to her mother; she took care not to say that she was close by, but contented herself with saying that she loved to run, and was sure that her friend could not catch her if she would give her three or four strides start.

Alinska accepted this challenge. Juliette fled; she was hotly pursued, but directed her course toward the place where Madame Delmont was—who was concealed in that direction by the thickness of the tree and an eglantine bush beside it. The little girl suddenly hurled herself into her mother's arms, and the Hungarian woman, taken by surprise, stopped just as she was about to seize her, and stood still on the spot from which she had seen Hélène.

The latter, delighted with the service that hazard had rendered her, got to her feet precipitately and took two steps toward the foreigner, while her investigative gaze looked her up and down.

Alinska had a fine figure; her graceful contours only had the curvature necessary to ensure their beauty; the outline of her face traced a perfect oval; her mouth was small, her nose straight, her eyes large; above her open forehead rose her superb hair, whose ebony shone beneath the golden net that retained a multitude of tresses; a few, escaping, fell gracefully to her shoulders.

In sum, Alinska was beautiful—and yet it was not her charms that created the most vivid impression; there was something incomprehensible in all her features, indefinable in its implications, which one could not weary of examining without ever succeeding in deciding whether it was procured by pleasure or an altogether extraordinary terror. The whiteness of her skin was extreme; bright colors embellished it. Nevertheless, there were earthen hues in the mix, gray tints that sometimes obliterated all of its harmony.

The freshness of her lips could not have been compared to the first rosebud born on the banks of the Eridan[19] on a clear, warm April morning; one might have wanted to admire the incessantly, but convulsive movements, a smile imprinted with infernal malice and awkward contractions of the cheek-muscles caused one to think that the foreigner's soul was not at all calm, and that, in spite of her efforts, she could not tame the violence of her passions or the bitterness of her memories.

But what could one say for certain about her eyes? What expression might serve to explain the odious mixture of celestial sweetness and redoubtable vivacity? Sometimes the fires of life set fire to them; sometimes, bleak and toneless, they remained inanimate in frightful stagnation; one could not look at them for an entire minute without recognizing they passed almost instantaneously from the activity of existence to the complete inertia of death; they were not reminiscent of anything that exists, while nevertheless not displaying the complete triumph of death, but an unparalleled combination of the two, an amalgam of the most extreme contrasts—in such a way that the person looking at them could not imagine ever having encountered anything similar.

A white woolen dress, garnished with black ribbons, tailored in a fashion unknown in France, and a black Cashmere shawl formed her costume; it was simple, but in harmony with its wearer.

After a rapid summary examination of the Hungarian woman, which left her in the indecision we have just described—and which she did not want to prolong any further, seeing that the other had no intention of speaking and was not going to move—Hélène thought it appropriate to initiate conversation with thanks for the kindness with which she had undertaken to contribute to the amusements of her son and daughter.

While listening to this speech, Alinska's pale face colored slightly. Her bizarre eyes emitted a flash that was reflected in those of her interlocutor, and she spoke in her turn.

---

[19] Eridan is an ancient name of the river Po.

"It's Madame Delmont, then, that I have the honor of seeing. She will pardon me if I have not introduced myself to her, but, being in search of complete solitude, only coming to the neighborhood in order to devote myself ardently to a project whose importance was the one thing that could transport me from my last dwelling, I did not want any distractions, whose cost I could fully appreciate. I am only here for a short while; I shall scarcely have time to fulfill my duty. My hours are limited, and those that I can devote to my pleasures are not numerous."

"I regret, Madame," Hélène replied, "not being able to enjoy your society; it would, I presume, be pleasant."

"Beware of believing that!" exclaimed the Hungarian woman, as if moved by an impulse she could not control. "Don't desire my presence; despair, tears and death follow in its wake."

A glance darted by Madame Delmont at the unknown woman's dress gave her the key to that enigma of sorts. She had no doubt that death had stolen a number of individuals dear to the lady, and that her reply had been wrung from the regrets that must be breaking her heart. She hastened to reply that it was not by avoiding all human contact that one could encounter the easement of pain, but that it was necessary to seek the consolations of which one might be in need in society.

"You're mistaken." The foreigner replied. "There are epochs in life after which an inflexible hand raises barriers that one can no longer push back, termini where all human progress stops, and beyond which once only encounters a definitively determined fate. I no longer have any easement to attain; my destiny henceforth will be as stable as the eternity of which it is a part."

The excitement of these statements, uncommon in everyday life, confirmed Madame Delmont's initial impression. She remained convinced that violent chagrins had troubled the young woman's life, and perhaps even disturbed her reason. In consequence, her pity increased, and, wanting to win the other over, she put out her hand to take hers—the one that was gloved.

Alinska saw the movement and took a step back in order to prevent its completion. "What are you doing?" she said, more impetuously still. "Do not, feeble mortal, run to meet the fate that is in store for you. Do you realize that, by touching me, you would be making a pact with matter, that you would be engaging with death?"

From that moment on, Madame Delmont no longer had any doubt that the foreigner was mentally ill; she tried to distract her by changing the subject. "If the company of reasonable people displeases you so much," she said, "at least these children who are listening to us seem to have found favor in your eyes."

"They have found favor in my eyes, you say!" Alinska replied, in her cavernous voice. "What favor! I don't advise them to be proud of it; it's more akin to the respite that an executioner accords his victim, during the time that he is preparing the instruments of torture with which he must afflict him."

These words were so sinister that Madame Delmont, struck by a sudden dread, made a movement as if to pull the children away.

Then a smile full of innocence strayed over Alinska's lips, and her eyes softened. "Oh, forgive me, Madame," she said. "Forgive me for frightening you—but there are moments when, entirely preoccupied with the past and the future, I no longer belong to the present. Insensate things escape my lips, which cannot retain them in spite of my efforts, and my inanimate heart cannot suppress without rebellion the only sentiment that it can possibly contain."

"I shall respect the dolor that is consuming you, Madame, and will content myself with praying for its disappearance—and if the sight of my children offends you, I shall forbid them to come near any place where you are."

"Believe me, take care to protect these children of which you are so proud. Some cruel malady, some destructive poison—what do I know?—a thousand sinister causes might separate you from them. Watch over them, without letting them out of your sight. They are so young, their constitution so frail, that they might soon cost you bitter tears."

She concluded, and an unparalleled aberration burst forth once again in her eyes. Her graceful mouth contracted horribly; her features lost their color, and it seemed to be not so much a woman as a disfigured cadaver that Hélène was looking at.

The latter would have liked to terminate that painful scene, but a sentiment of compassion still controlled her; she feared, in going away, leaving an individual devoid of help whose woeful madness seemed complete. "Aren't you suffering too much at present to continue your walk?" she said. "Would you permit me to take you back to the place where you're living?"

"Me, suffering! Set aside that error—I don't know what suffering is, for I'm now in my habitual state of mind. It must seem unpleasant to you; I don't know whether it pleases me or is odious to me, but it distresses you, so let's try to forget it. Come on—what she we talk about now? I wasn't born to delve into the higher sciences, but at present I find myself at the source of knowledge; I have drawn the curtain of human ignorance away from my eyes, and I can explain to you what humans don't understand."

These words advertised a continuation of the hallucination that was distressing to hear. Hélène tried once again to bring the foreigner's mind back to less confused ideas, and gradually succeeded.

Alinska seemed to recover herself; she was soon chatting about ordinary subjects in a simple fashion. Hélène could tell that she was not deprived of education, although there was something crude and semi-savage in her manners, which bore the imprint of a rather haphazard upbringing. She did not say anything revealing about herself, however, although the strangeness of her accent raised the suspicion that she had not been born in France, but that Germany was her homeland.

Madame Delmont conjectured that, having been the victim of a passionate and unfortunate love affair, the other had lost a part the celestial intelligence constituting that which we call reason; in consequence, she found it natural that the old man, to whose care the foreign woman had doubtless been confided, kept her in her retreat, far from human commerce. Thus she explained the mystery that had initially piqued her curiosity so sharply.

The conversation turned to music. Madame Delmont, who played the harp successfully herself, tried to give her new acquaintance the praise that she merited, although it was modestly refused. Even in that modest reserve, however, there was an indefinable sentiment of indifference and profound insouciance. The stranger spoke of her talent as if it were someone else's. Nothing astonished or engrossed her. She seemed totally uninterested in everything that charms, or at least absorbs the human mind—which was disturbing. It was not egotism; it was a cold carelessness, a disgust for everything so entire that, without sharing it, Hélène was pained by the manner in which it was displayed.

Is she a woman or a statue? Hélène wondered. *Is it only for the sake of dolor that she clings to humanity?*

In the end, the sun, sinking behind the heights of Old Toulouse, left the valleys plunged in the misty gloom that precedes the darkness of the night. The children, weary of amusing themselves without anyone taking part in their games, were the first to ask to return to the château.

"Yes," said Alinska, "the hour of retreat is approaching; all that is corporeal is in quest of repose; it will not be long before the atmosphere is inhabited by superior intelligences. Adieu, Madame; I wish I had never met you; our conversation will inspire me with exceedingly keen regrets for a long time." She concluded, and withdrew precipitately, as if drawn by a profound emotion.

Madame Delmont, still well-disposed toward the unknown woman, was pleased to construe these remarks as a mark of her benevolence. She regretted being unable to live for others a little more, and she retraced her steps to her home in the company of her children. Satisfied now by having seem the stranger freely, and perhaps flattering herself that she had divined the cause of her chagrin and the motive for her retreat, she mentioned the meeting casually to Raoul.

The faithful servant, who had made his decision as to what ought to happen as soon as the imminently-expected letter from the colonel arrived, showed no surprise as he listened to Madame Delmont's story. He was only desirous of knowing whether Alinska had cast any disturbance into the former's soul—but he could not detect any, and was obliged to conclude that the Hungarian woman had been discreet, for no cloud troubled the serenity of his mistress's face.

Chapter VII

The next day, the children talked about going to the meadow again. Raoul, instructed to take them there, reluctantly obeyed. To his great contentment, however, Alinska did not appear. The day after, her absence was continued.

That day was the one on which Edouard's reply should have reached the sergeant-major. He waited with great impatience for the return of the messenger, who was in no hurry to come. It was already getting dark when the man knocked at the door of the château.

"The letters! Quickly, the letters!" Raoul demanded. "I thought you were never going to bring them, damn it!"

"Letters?" the functionary replied. "You're mistaken, Monsieur Raoul—there's only one. Here it is—I hope it's the one you want."

Raoul seized it hurriedly, held it up to the lamp he was holding, and examined the address. It was definitely from the colonel, but it bore Madame Delmont's name.

A dagger-thrust could not have struck Raoul more painfully than the absence of the letter for which he was hoping. He no longer knew what to do. His colonel's negligence in replying to him seemed inconceivable. He turned the missive that had been given to him over and over in his hands. Sometimes, he wondered whether his former commanding officer had made a mistake in addressing it, and that the letter was for him. He dared not make sure of that, though. He was trembling as he took it to his mistress.

Madame Delmont, aware of the worthy non-commissioned officer's attachment to her husband, was accustomed to read him long excerpts from the dispatches she received, when they did not include personal details. She did not depart from her custom in this instance, and informed the confused listener that the colonel was very well, but that he could not fix a date for his return, as yet. The spouses he was trying to reunite were extremely annoyed with one another; he could not imagine bringing them together without great efforts, but he, Edouard, was exercising all his skill to return them to their initial mutual affection. He concluded by asking his wife to give his regards to Raoul, and to complain on his behalf of the silence the soldier was maintaining in his regard, even though he had promised to write to him, in order to give him news of what was happening in the fields.

The last part of the letter struck home too directly for the military man to contain himself. "By Roland's moustache!" he exclaimed. "That's a reproach I don't deserve! Is it my fault if what I send to the colonel doesn't reach him? I gave him all the information he's asking for, on the same day that Madame wrote the letter to which this one is the reply. Oh, Monsieur Messenger, I'll give you the slap on your back you deserve!"

Madame Delmont, alarmed by the anger bursting forth in Raoul's features, was about to try to calm him down when the latter suddenly stopped.

"Oh, wretch that I am," he said. "If the letter has been lost, it's not that poor devil's fault. Mistrusting him, without any reason, I told him to bring me a receipt from the postmaster in Toulouse, and he brought it back to me in good order. Come on—I'm losing my head!"

Hélène, who had no suspicion of the importance that Raoul attributed, with good reason, to the loss of his letter, gave no further thought to the incident. Joyful that she had received news from her husband, she experienced no other anxiety than that of the forced prolongation of the colonel's absence. She went back to her apartment, while the former soldier went back to his room.

The latter's intention as to begin another letter, to depart at daybreak, and to serve as his own messenger to the post office—for he went so far, in his chagrin, to suspect the probity of the counter-clerk. Determined to follow that plan, which ought to have reassured him, he opened his cupboard and his casket in order to take out the paper and ink he needed. Then, by the light of his lamp, which cast a rather feeble illumination, he perceived a packet whose form the thought he recognized.

It was his letter, as he had written it, with a few drops of blood soiling it— and an uncertain or tremulous hand had written on the envelope: *Your correspondence in futile; Edouard will never receive a line from you if you mention anything but that which concerns the interests of his farm.*

More than once, Raoul had found himself face-to-face with fiery mouths vomiting forth death in a hundred thousand ways; the saber of an enemy hussar had often been suspended above his head—and yet, he had never experienced in any encounter of that sort a terror similar to the one that froze his heart now.

Mechanically, he scanned his surroundings with a terrified gaze, as if he expected to see some hideous form rise up before his eyes. He passed his hand over his forehead several times to wipe away trickling droplets of sweat; otherwise, he remained motionless, as if he were under the spell of some fascination.

The more he thought about what had happened, the more he lost himself in vain conjectures. Sometimes, he wanted to doubt the evidence, to believe himself abused by a painful dream—but the letter was there, just as he had handed it to his messenger, and he was able to read the clerk's receipt repeatedly; the latter was undoubtedly the real guilty party. In that case, however, a new difficulty presented itself. How had the missive been so promptly returned to R***? Who possessed the three keys to his room, his cupboard and his casket? Where was the traitor within the house? Ought he to look among the workers or among the maidservants?

Raoul became lost in the chaos of reflections; he saw insoluble difficulties everywhere—and yet, through all of it, there was an incontestable reality that defied all the calculations of human prudence. More than ever, he—who scarcely believed in another life, such was the dearth of his education—was almost forced to admit the existence of being intermediate between creatures and the Creator. In his moments of weakness, he reverted to cursing the power of the magicians of Hungary, of whom he had heard so much talk during his sojourn in that realm.

There was no lack of terrifying substance in those tales—including the terrible Vampires, those larvae of Christianity which, according to the accounts of an entire nation, abandon the tombs from which the dead ought no longer to emerge in order to wander the earth of which they are the filth and the horror; which, in the dark of the night, go forth to seek in the veins of some unfortunate whose blood they suck, the foundation of a frightful existence that is not entirely life but is nevertheless far from death.

More frequently, though, Raoul rejected such superstitions as gross errors and reverted to more natural and plausible suspicions. It was intrigue and treason that he feared, and he promised himself that he would keep watch with sufficient attention to catch the person, male or female, who must have lent assistance to the Hungarian woman Alinska.

Before commencing that kind of warfare, however, which was scarcely in harmony with his frank and open character, he formed an intention to go and see once more the enemy whose light infantry he had to fight. He promised himself that he would go down to the little wood the following day—and that idea allowed him a few hours of sleep in the calm of the night.

He got up even more convinced of the necessity of talking to the foreigner, and when he thought that he might be admitted to her home he took the path to the manor in which she lived.

When he arrived there, the door was closed. He knocked, but no one answered. He knocked a second time, more forcefully, but the interior silence remained unbroken. The longer he waited, the more progress his impatience made. He started hammering for a third time without obtaining any more success.

What should he do? Was the house abandoned, or did no one want to open the door to him? Should he abandon his siege, or continue it with more enthusiasm the following day?

While he hesitated as to which course to take, he heard a slight sound close at hand. He turned round promptly, and found himself face to face with Alinska's old servant. The latter individual was extremely tall; his cranium, devoid of hair, had been exposed to the vagaries of the atmosphere for a long time; a frightful pallor reigned over his emaciated face. His eyes, their gleam half-extinct, were motionless, no longer swiveling beneath their icy lids. The sound of his voice was both halting and hoarse, and a noxious breath escaped his mouth, in which only a few teeth could be glimpsed. A coat woven in coarse cloth covered the gigantic individual. Everything about him advertised the lassitude of an excessively-prolonged existence, and a scorn for everything that might please ordinary humans.

"Hello, friend," said Raoul, on seeing him, unintimidated by his unpleasant exterior. "Has your mistress already gone out? Is she roaming the fields turning little birds out of their nests?"

"What gives you the right to ask me such a question, friend?" the domestic replied. "Do we know one another well enough to speak to one another with so much familiarity?"

The tone of this reply was not encouraging. In spite of his self-confidence, Raoul felt somewhat at a loss. Nevertheless, not wanting to seem defeated before hostilities had even begun, he spoke in his turn.

"Come on, grandfather, don't get annoyed. I've come to speak to your mistress. I knock deafeningly, but no gives any sign of life. You come up behind me on tiptoe and I question you—all that seems to me quite natural, and you needn't act the gendarme like that. Are you, by chance, one of those people who find it easier to get annoyed than give a straight answer? Your quarrelsome attitude makes me suspect so."

"If you knew me, *friend*," replied the old man, emphasizing the final word, "You'd easily see that there can be nothing in common between you and me. You're following your path, but mine terminated a long time ago. Not that I'll suffer any insult or threat in consequence—but I hope we won't get to that point, for you'd soon be finished with me. What do you want with my mistress, since that's what she is? I can give her your message as easily as you can."

"No thank you, *friend*," Raoul replied, extremely annoyed by the brisk manner in which he was being treated by a individual whose status he did not believe to be superior to his own. "My business with Alinska was can have no intermediary. It's probable that you know a part of it, and that perhaps you've played your part in the game of find-the-lady that brought me here—but it doesn't please me to take you into my confidence in my turn. I don't want to talk to anyone but the Hungarian woman, do you hear?"

"I hear—but that won't make me any more inclined to do as you wish. The Hungarian woman, as you're pleased to call her, has nothing to discuss with you, so go away. As you seem to be a military man, make what you all an *about turn*, and be off with you."

"Do you know, old man, that to make me retreat requires a more numerous artillery?"

"We'll find some, then," said the domestic, calmly—and before Raul had any suspicion of what he was going to do, he launched himself forward, grabbed him one-handed, with such extraordinary force that he lifted him off the ground, in spite of the ex-sergeant's efforts, and carried him some distance to a nearby path.

Oh, how Raoul regretted at that moment not having brought his sword, which would have served him to take a prompt revenge for an action that dishonored him in his own eyes! But that steel, the weapon of his courage, could no longer defend him, and his coarse adversary had snatched away the walking-stick that he might have used. No auxiliary means revealed itself to his attentive gaze. The soil in that region, and throughout Lauraguais, is of such a nature that one can often walk for a league without encountering a single pebble; it is composed of nothing but compact and supremely fertile clay.

How could he leave that offense unpunished, though? Rage did not blind the Sergeant-Major. He sensed that it would be impossible for him to fight the old man hand-to-hand—who was only an old man in appearance, for his muscular strength was superior to that of the most vigorous men that Raoul had ever encountered. To challenge him to a duel was all that he could do; so, with a voice half-stifled by an impetuous surge, he made a sudden appeal to his bravery.

The foreigner, who had not lost his imperturbable tranquility that reigned over his face in the meantime, looked at him without any more emotion.

"What do you want from me?" he said. "Is it for me to make use of weapons other than those employed just now to take you down a peg? Don't flatter yourself. I don't fight duels; I defend myself, and exterminate on the spot anyone who has no fear of insulting me. You seemed to know me. Go on your way, feeble child of audacity and vanity, and don't come back to a place from which I might not let you leave."

The ferocious tone in which these words were pronounced, the death-threatening gesture that accompanied them, and the homicidal flame that was suddenly burning in the old man's eyes had a significance so easy to divine that Raoul, in spite of his proven courage, stood there nonplussed.

He was still hesitating as to whether to repeat his challenge when the door of the house opened and Alinska, clad in a black dress that lent a strange expression to her physiognomy, suddenly appeared.

"Well, Ladislas," she said to her domestic, "you're always forgetting that I've forbidden you to give in to the violence of your character. Can it be that you still preserve a portion of human folly? Ought you to insult those who want to converse with me?"

As his mistress was speaking, the old man suddenly shivered, but his impassive face displayed neither respect nor confusion. Only an atrocious smile brushed his lips; he made no reply, but he drew away and went back into the manor at a slow pace, as if he had not been the principal actor in the rather extraordinary scene that had just been played out.

Alinska's presence was what Raoul wanted most of all at that moment. It was to talk to her that he had come down from the château, and the brutal manners of the porter had left him little hope of fulfilling his desire. He was therefore glad to see the Hungarian woman, ready to listen to him, so he no longer hesitated as to whether to take the path that would convey him back to the house. As he approached, however, he could not suppress the expression of his discontent, on the subject of the insulting manner with which he had been treated.

"To be sure, Alinska," he said, "your jailer—for that's the name he merits, ought to return abundant thanks to Providence for the fact that the King of France judged it appropriate to relieve me of a certain piece of iron that hardly ever left my side while I was in Hungary. If he had acted then with the insolence he showed just now, I would have insinuated a few inches of steel through his ugly breast, of which he would have given you news. Be patient, though—he won't always find me deprived, and I swear that, one of these mornings, he'll have to settle the account that he's just opened with me."

"Come now, Raoul," the Hungarian woman replied. "Don't pay any more heed to that unpleasant incident. Ladislas undoubtedly has his faults, but yours are no less; you provoked him with your insistence; judging only by the appearances of his age, you thought it would be easy to bend him to your will; that error was soon cleared up. Forget what happened—believe me, you can do no better for your peace of mind. Everything you try will rebound on your own head, and your vengeance will crush you."

"That's easy to say, but a soldier doesn't allow himself to be led like a recruit; I've passed the age of conscription, and I'll never tolerate an insult. Besides, have I reason to be any more satisfied with the mistress than the valet? Don't we have something to discuss, you and me? Aren't you playing the role of trickster with regard to me? Is that polite? Should I tolerate the fact that you've come here, firstly, to insult me, personally and by means of your hirelings, and then, consequently, to disturb the peace of my colonel's family?"

"I don't know what superior power is driving you to your destruction, Raoul," Alinska replied, coldly. "How can you dare to come to me in order to complain? Which of us has committed the greater sins in respect of one another? Wasn't it you, wretch, who were the principal agent of my ruination, in my father's house? Don't you remember that disastrous epoch when, to serve the guilty projects of the colonel, you never ceased talking to me about his perfidious affection? Weren't you always by my side, seeking to lead my reason astray and deceive my virtue? Wretched tempter? First cause of my misfortune! It ill behooves you to raise an arrogant voice and claim that I have done you any wrong! Get out of my sight, if you value your life, petty worm born of mud, which I should already have crushed underfoot!"

"Damn it, Alinska, how you go on! You don't mince your words, and if I had any desire to think myself a gentleman, you'd make me remember in spite of myself that I was born a good Bourbonnais peasant—but your birth was no more illustrious. Your father cultivated good vineyards, it's true, but I never heard it said that he was descended from the noble houses of Esterhazy or Palfrey."

"You're mistaken, Raoul, or you're trying to trick me. It isn't to dispute with you the hazards of destiny that I'm manifesting a just scorn for you. You have a complaint against me, you dared to say. I've reminded you of the past, to let you judge for yourself which of us is the greater, the veritable, criminal."

"That's nothing—I don't recall anything that happened so many years ago. Anyway, if you were credulous, don't blame anyone but yourself. What's important to me, and what I won't permit, is that anyone should discover my secrets, should put their hands on my correspondence and, finally, procure sly intelligence in the house of my benefactors."

Alinska did not reply; she gave Raoul a stare painted with a remarkable malignity, like the triumph of a certain vengeance.

"I repeat," he continued, "that I'm tired of your intrigues and conjuring tricks. You've now prevented two letters from leaving—for who, other than you, could have done that? I don't know what mean you employed to attain your end, but be warned that if I catch any of your accomplices in the act, his collusion won't go any further; I'll settle the arrears of our debt on his back."

"You'd do that, even with respect to old Ladislas!" said Alinska, accompanying that malign mockery with a smile that redoubled its bitterness.

"Oh, a thousand thunders! Let him come—him in preference to any other; I still have a loaded gun, with which I'll make him amply familiar, and against which the strength of his fist will be insufficient."

"For the last time, Raoul, I tell you that you're marching with great strides toward your imminent destruction."

"And you, Alinska, toward the conclusion of your criminal activities. I won't tolerate them any longer; if a third letter doesn't reach the colonel, we'll see whether the magistrates will render us any justice."

"Fool! What complaint will you make? On what plausible foundation can you establish your accusation? Will you hold me responsible for your insanity? Who will you persuade to believe that I can put obstacles between you and your master? If you complain, you'll become everyone's laughing-stock, and I'll be partly satisfied. Feeble plaything of the one to whom you speak, you won't take the insolent audacity of your speech any further."

"You can say whatever you please to me, Alinska. I admit that I've done wrong in your regard, if it really is wrong to bring together a young and elegant soldier and a pretty girl. In God's name, though, forget the past and let me alone!"

"I've promised to let you be, and I've even offered you rewards if you promise not to let Edouard know that I'm here. Why are you so obstinate in refusing me such a simple thing? Let him come back; let me talk to him for the last time. His happiness, his tranquility and his very existence all depend on our conversation. In any case, you'll struggle in vain against me. To vanquish you, I'll employ means that you cannot foresee. Tremble, above all, if a single word escapes you that makes me known to the fortunate rival who has taken my place with Edouard; your indiscretion would cost you your life. Yes, Raoul, I would immediately destroy you."

As she pronounced these final words, Alinska made a gesture so impetuous that a part of her garment tore, and Raoul was able to perceive beneath it, on the

Hungarian woman's left breast, a wound from which a few drops of blood had leaked.

The involuntary shiver that agitated his body at that sinister sight did not pass unnoticed by his interlocutrice; she divined its cause without difficulty, and sought to repair the disorder of her dress with her hand.

For his part, Raoul stood there in confusion, feeling a sudden pity rising in his soul. "Oh, what have you done, unhappy girl?" he exclaimed. "Can you, in that state, indulge in a dangerous passion? Go back into your house, quickly—your wound has reopened; you don't realize the peril you're in."

"What peril are you talking about? I no longer know any on earth?"

"But your blood is flowing; the dressing must have come away—don't lose any time replacing it. If you need my help, don't hesitate to accept it."

"Don't worry about me—my blood can't flow, for I no longer have any blood; it was drained to the last drop a long time ago. There's no shortage of that which replaces it—I know where to renew it. Let it flow, without paying any heed to it."

As he listened to these bizarre words, Raoul, like Madame Delmont, did not doubt that the Hungarian woman's misfortunes must have weakened her reason. All the anger that he had felt against her disappeared. Immediately, he sought to bring her back, by means of gentleness, to a calmer state of mind, and came forward to take her in his arms and sustain her. Then he noticed that a frightful pallor was already covering her face.

"Don't come any closer!" she cried, in a hoarse and feeble voice. "Don't touch me! Run away, instead—you must not see what is going to happen. Ladislas! Ladislas! Come to me, or I shall not be able to carry the mission you have confided to me to its conclusion."

Ladislas heard that appeal. He emerged from the house just in time to catch Alinska, who let herself fall into his arms, semi-conscious. The old man, having examined her momentarily, looked around wildly, and without speaking, made a gesture, as if to order Raoul to go away.

The latter did not seem inclined to obey him, but a sudden reflection caused him to decide to do so. He feared that he might perhaps cause the foreign woman's death by his obstinacy. Directed by that motive, he went back along the path and climbed the hill.

At a turning of the path that bought him almost opposite the place where Alinska was lying on the grass, he thought he might be able to see what was happening there. He saw, or thought he saw, the old servant lean over her to pour a red liquid into her mouth. At the same time, though, a violent blow to the head that Raoul received knocked him down.

He got up swiftly, to confront the enemy who had truck him, but there was no one nearby. He was obliged to attribute his fall to the unexpected impact of some tree-branch, for he was passing through a wood.

His curiosity led him to look for a second time at what the people he had left in the meadow were doing. They were no longer visible.

That disappearance plunged him into a singular astonishment. Entirely immersed in various and painful reflections, he went back to the château, saying to himself: *May it please destiny that everything here takes a more natural appearance! I don't like what I've seen, and I wish I were able to penetrate the mystery that surrounds us.*

Chapter VIII

The profound retreat in which the foreigner continued to live gradually ceased to excite public curiosity; one cannot always be occupied with the same subject, and in R***, as in the bosom of the most populous city, the march of the human mind does not change direction. Already, there was scarcely any mention of the inhabitants of the isolated house, when a new event, striking the attention of the villagers more forcefully, caused them to forget all about Alinska and her domestic.

There was a young woman in the commune, brilliant in health and strength, who was, as much by virtue of her charms as her fortune, the target of all the young men of the region. Every time Paschale appeared at a fête, a circle of rustic admirers immediately formed around her, who lavished upon her, in their own fashion, the adorations that lovers address to beauty everywhere.

For a long time, Paschale remained indifferent; she received the homage, but did not select out any on those who lavished it. Finally, however, a farmer from the commune of Montbrun succeeded in touching the heart of the indifferent beauty.

The proclamation of Paschale's choice irritated the self-respect of all those who should have lost hope. Furious threats resounded from all directions against the fortunate seducer, and several pacts, it was said, were made in order to raise obstacles to a union that had rendered so many disdained lovers desperate.

Tranquil in the midst of the general emotion, the fortunate couple prepared to tie the matrimonial knot. They were not waiting for anything else, in order to get married, but the return of the mayor—who, for the time being, was not resident in R***. His deputy was also absent, and the delay this caused, if it pleased Farmer Merlet's rivals, plunged him into a keen impatience. However, as the municipal officers of a commune cannot always be away, the time of their return was imminent. They were due to return on a Saturday evening, and the following day, before mass, the civil ceremony was to be preceded by the celebration of the holy union.

The Saturday in question was the same day that Raoul had chosen to pay the visit of the Hungarian woman whose results had been so unsatisfactory from his viewpoint. He had been invited to Paschale's wedding, and had to leave at daybreak the following day to meet the husband's friends in order, either to rejoice together or to ward off any furious interventions that ill-tempered rivals might attempt.

After supper, Raoul went to his room, still preoccupied with what he had seen during the day. The colossal strength of the old domestic was incessantly present in his mind, and he seemed to see blood running from the wound that Alinska had showed him.

While he buried himself in a series of thoughts that preyed on his mind painfully, he looked around the room distractedly. His eyes suddenly paused on a single object, and he uttered an exclamation. His gun—the one he had threatened to use on the Hungarian woman's agents—was damaged, and he was astonished to see that its barrel had been broken into several pieces.

At this unexpected blow, which seemed to him to be beyond the range of human strength, he was gripped by a glacial chill. He remained in the same position for some time, with his mouth open, his hand extended and his body leaning forward.

This absolutely surpassed the extent of his perspicacity; he was not longer able to assign any natural cause to it. In his involuntary terror he almost swore to himself not to interfere any further with anything concerning Alinska, recognizing that to it required a power superior to the feeble means that he possessed to compete with her successfully.

A considerable time went by before he was able to get to sleep. He shuddered at every nocturnal sound that reached his ears. Utterly dejected, he retained none of his usual energy, and entered, by virtue of his weakness, into the class of human beings whose pusillanimity he had so often scorned.

Fatigue finally threw him into a torpor, which was followed by a kind of lethargy—for it was seven o'clock in the morning when he was awakened by the sound of someone knocking urgently on his door.

Then Raoul remembered the wedding to which he had been invited, and thought that someone had come to look for him in order to go to it. He got up, ashamed of his sloth. When he opened the door, he recognized one of his friends from the village, and was struck by the dolorous alarm painted on his face. He was about to ask him the cause but the other anticipated him.

"Oh, Monsieur Raoul," he said, in a halting voice, "what a horrible catastrophe occurred last night! Paschale is dead, dreadfully murdered!"

"What are you saying, Mathurin? Who has committed this atrocious crime? You're making my shiver by telling me..."

"It's only too true, alas! But no one knows the murderer's name. He got into her bedroom, and bled her from four veins—and yet, by a particularity that has astonished everyone, there's no longer any blood in the victim's corpse. Only a few small droplets were found on the bedclothes..."

"No blood!" Raoul cried in consternation. "No blood! O Heaven! The horrors of Hungary are being renewed in France!"

After these few words he stopped, perhaps annoyed at having pronounced them—but the harm that he would rather have avoided was done. The villager Mathurin, his curiosity piqued, insistently demanded an explanation of a statement that he did not understand.

Raoul tried in vain to steer the conversation away, by demanding further details of the night's event, but his companion was not to be put off. After having told what he knew, he resumed his demand to know what had happened in Hungary. He was so persistent in his questions that it was necessary to satisfy him, or fall out with him.

"Upon my faith, my dear chap," Raul said, "you're giving me no more time to draw breath than the Black Hussars did in a rout that, thank God, soon changed into a total victory on the day of the battle of Jena. Since you want to know what took place a long way away, listen carefully—and if you're scared tonight, don't blame me.

"You know that Hungary is a vast country, extending from the extremity of Germany to the Turkish frontier. The people of its rural areas are only half-civilized; they are more closely related to beasts than to humans, properly speaking. They spend their lives in a kind of slavery, to which we would have difficulty becoming accustomed—but if they remain submissive to their masters while they're in this world, they take their revenge when they're covered with six feet of earth. Some of them, after being interred in their coffins and laid in the grave, rise up in the cold winter nights, with the assistance of the one that Monsieur le Curé calls the Devil, and return to earth, to the misfortune of the living.

"These beings, which are neither dead or alive, go into the homes of their friends and relatives, to their detriment. They lie down next to them and, opening the veins of their victims, they suck the blood that they need to sustain their odious existence, unrelentingly. After each day's end, from midnight to one o'clock in the morning, they continue this abominable operation, until the moment when all the stolen blood leads to the victim's death. Often, they address themselves to several people at once, and bringing mourning to different families at the same time.

"As soon as one of these demons, which are called Vampires in the region, is released in a village, one no longer hears talk of anything but terrible events. Mourning and destruction accompany them; every inhabitant dreads, on his own behalf and that of his family, the visitation of these enemies of humankind. Priests are summoned, but their exorcisms are unsuccessful; the Vampire continues its ravages regardless.

"Only one means remains of deliverance; it's necessary to seek out the body in the ground, which initially seems inanimate, but is soon observed to be alarmingly plump, with its cheeks strangely colored and its mouth crimson, still stained with the blood on which it has fed. Then one takes the detestable monster out of its coffin; its hands, head and feet are cut off, but there will be no effect until a sharpened stake pierces its heart—from which a torrent of bloody matter with emerge, accompanied by a terrible cry, which announced that life is finally escaping the homicidal corpse. Then, the ceremony is terminated by throwing the disgusting remains on a fire. The locality then becomes tranquil again, until the moment when a new Vampire rises from its coffin.

"What I've just told you, Mathurin, is the testimony of an entire nation, on which this execrable scourge has weighed for centuries, all the more terrible because vampirism appears to propagate itself. People who fall victim to these demons often become vampires themselves. The plague affects men and women alike—and I would never finish if I told you everything I learned in Hungary about the subject, or all that I've read in a book that Colonel Delmont bought during his last trip to Toulouse."

Raoul could have spoken for longer without his auditor thinking of interrupting him. The latter was listening with grim attention. Not a word was lost; he retained them all, and was already attributing the unexpected death of young Paschale to the horror of vampirism.

"Lord Jesus!" he exclaimed. "Are such things possible? I'm sorry I asked you about them, Raoul, although they've given me enlightenment I never had before. Thank God, in this land we've only encountered fays[20] and spellcasters. There are a few revenants from time to time, but they only occupy themselves with scaring the living, moving the furniture in a house, tormenting shepherds or flocks in the fold, and pigeons in lofts, as sometimes happens in Souterrène or R*** . But to feed on blood! It's enough to make one die of fright just thinking about it. Poor Paschale! It's a vampire that has stolen you from this world. Come on, there's no doubt about it."

In spite of his secret belief, Raoul advised Mathurin to attribute a more plausible cause to the poor bride-to-be's death—but the peasant was too avid to spread the new enlightenment that had just been gifted to him to abandon the idea.

"Everything you've said," he went on, "is sound—but it's no less true that there's vampirism in this. I want to publish the matter at high mass, if there isn't a better opportunity to do so beforehand, in order to pray to God that he might lift this scourge from us. But who among us could play that infamous role? That's a point that needs clarification, and I'm going to leave you now, in order to consult the elders of the parish."

Raoul's efforts to alter this determination were utterly wasted.

---

[20] The original text renders this word (presumably in Occitan) as *faés*, but adds a French translation (*fées*) in brackets. The word is conventionally rendered into English as "fairies," except in the context of Arthurian legend, where its singular signifies "enchantress" (as in Morgan le Fay). It is presumably the latter meaning that is intended here.

Mathurin went away precipitately, almost consoled with respect to the recent misfortune by the thought that he might be able to identify its cause. Scarcely had he reached the tree in front of the church door that he hastened to tell his tale to the first villagers he met. The marvelous nature of his story easily impressed ignorant souls over which superstition has so much empire.

Suddenly, several groups formed, each one adding its conjectures and creations to what had been learned here and there. No one had any doubt as to the existence of these corporeal demons, the history of which they were learning for the first time, and it was unanimously resolved, albeit with unequivocal signs of fear, that a vampire was to be found among the people of R***.

Opinions varied as to the name of the deceased to which this abomination was attributed. Here, the conversations became more mysterious; people feared that, by clearly identifying the individual they had in mind, they might attract the hatred of the family. The lives of all the recently deceased were reviewed, and all the remembered evidence of their malice and bad qualities cited. One enthusiast exclaimed that the Vampire must be among those who were dutiful churchgoers, especially those who prayed for souls in purgatory, and this terrible intimation encountered no contradiction.

One old woman, however, shaking her head, did not hesitate to say: "Don't you recall that *colporteur* who was so infatuated with Paschale? You know that she effused him, scornfully, and that the poor young man went back to Tarbes, his home town, saying that he was going there to find death. Well, since that time we've had no more news of him, and it's surely him who's come back from the other world to carry out last night's atrocity."

This speech, made with assurance, seemed to the villagers to be the natural explanation of an alarming prodigy. It was unanimously decided that the colporteur, doubtless deceased, was the real guilty party, and as they went their separate ways people promised, in turn, to pray for his soul, and to pass on any news they might obtain on the subject.

From that moment on, however, there was no more talk of the foreign woman and her eccentricities. People thought of nothing but the Vampire, to which they attributed the most singular enterprises. Every morning a new story circulated; some had seen, by moonlight, a white figure emerge from the cemetery and walk rapidly toward the village of Pechabou. Others affirmed that, a long time before first light, they had perceived a hideous form among the trees ornamenting the fish-ponds of Souterrène, which had moved without touching the ground and visibly swaying, and had disappeared in a flash of white light that had momentarily illuminated the crests of nearby hills. One person, who could not sleep, had distinctly heard a muffled noise at the door of his dwelling, as if someone were trying to force a way in. Another had felt himself embraced in his bed by a cold and sticky corpse, of which he had rid himself with a fervent prayer and the promise he had made to give two dozen eggs and a pair of chickens to Saint Lizier, the protector of the region.

These narratives, augmented by those who collected hem, spread universal terror far and wide, and for a long time, when darkness covered the hemisphere, the peasants consulted themselves repeatedly before venturing alone into the steep pathways of the commune.

Raoul, the original author of this new dread, did not share in it entirely. He was preoccupied with another concern: that of finding out, in a definite manner, the connection that the Hungarian woman had been able to establish with the château. He subjected to a minute secret surveillance, first the two serving women, and then all the farm-workers. He kept watch on their most trivial movements; he remained hidden for hours in a dark corner of his room, in order to catch whoever it was who was able to get into it.

His measures were uncrowned by any success. He could not, with any justice, direct his suspicions at any of the château's inhabitants; their conduct was so regular, so exempt from any singularity, that he was constrained to admit to himself, reluctantly, their complete and utter innocence.

Far from ceasing his research, however, he turned it in another direction. He knew that old châteaux almost always include unknown subterranean workings, secret passages that might serve to hide dark deeds. So, in order to obtain tranquility on this point too, he undertook a general inspection of the places in question, under the pretext of checking the solidity of the walls, in the company of a skilled mason whom he went to Castenet, the canton's capital, expressly to find. They spent two days together sounding the wall panels and floorboards and taping all the thick walls—and everywhere that a hollow sound advertised the presence of some cavity, they paused to discover what might be hidden there.

The strictness of this search finally gave them cognizance of a corridor opening in a corner of one of the ground-floor rooms, which descended deep into the ground via an exceedingly narrow stairway, in a north-easterly direction. On discovering this subterranean passage, especially given the route it seemed to follow, Raoul believed that he had found the route by which someone could obtain entry to the château.

Followed by his companion, each of them carrying a lantern, he attempted to follow it to its full extent. After advancing for about a hundred paces, however, they were halted by masses of rocks that seemed to have no exit. Having tried to establish whether the obstacle might be destroyed, the resistance that it opposed to their implements convinced them of the futility of their enterprise.

They returned to the château, but Raul was not content until he had closed the interior opening of the passage with chalk and sand—for it seemed dangerous to him, because it appeared to communicate with the isolated house in the wood, which, before the Revolution, had still belonged to the Seigneur de R***, only having been detached from the principal habitation during the unfortunate epoch of our political disasters.

Raoul, more satisfied, even though he had discovered nothing definite, imagined that he had thwarted the plans of the enemy of his repose, and he settled his account with the workman without a murmur, and without haggling.

Chapter IX

The time of the grape-harvest arrived; it succeeded in interrupting the relationship that had been established between the colonel's children and the unhappy Alinska. The activity and gaiety spread through the region by the grape-picking attracted all the young couple's attention. They followed the work of the pickers with interest, and they too, armed with a pair of secateurs and a basket proportionate to their strength, lent their assistance to the stripping of a grape-vine.

Madame Delmont, gladdened by their childish joy, and looking forward hopefully to her husband's return, followed Eugène and Juliette around, smiling. She too had lost some of the curiosity inspired in her by the madness of her neighbor—except that, from time to time, she smiled at the anger of Monsieur de Berneval, who had not yet forgotten the rude reception with which his kind attentions to the mistress of the isolated house had been greeted.

That worthy gentleman never missed an opportunity to bring the conversation round to that point, and by means of the story, intermingled with comical expressions, he amused, either the company that Madame Delmont received in her home, or more frequently, that gathered in the home of a family whose house was situated some distance from the château, on the road that led to the church. Pleasures and amusements were enjoyed there; a numerous Toulousian society came almost every Sunday to increase the number of those assembled there.

A continual gaiety presided over these meetings, sometimes augmented by humorous conjuring tricks invented and performed by a young advocate who, only appearing in count rarely, loved to make his clients laugh. Sometimes, an impetuous military man recounted stories of his adventures, or attempted feats of strength that did not always succeed. Music, over which the master of the house presided, added a further charm to the soirées; the melodious voice of his wife and the talent of a few amateurs contributed to it, while a witty conversation was sustained on the side by a doctor, as amiable in society as he was savant in respect of his patients, and by a young woman whose intelligence and precious qualities won her many friends.

On many occasions, the circle was amused by the slightly outré pretentions of a few pretty women. They played proverbs[21] and charades, or listened to the complaints of some boston-player who divided his time between paying court to

---

[21] Improvising mimes to illustrate proverbs was once popular parlor game, similar to charades.

ladies and quarreling with his fellow-players.[22] Recitations of verse were made by an author whose dramatic works had been dormant for years in the files of the Théâtre-Français, and who put people in drawing-rooms to sleep while waiting for them to emerge. In sum, they sought any and all means of passing the time, and succeeded without difficulty.

In spite of her love of retreat, Madame Delmont liked to descend upon these friendly neighbors. She played her part in the various diversions, and, as she delighted in singing and playing the harp, with considerable talent, she was not an idle member of the company.

October came to an end; the second day of November, consecrated to prayers for the dead, was about to begin.[23] The atmosphere was calm and the church bell was distinctly audible, repeating a dolorous knell. In the drawing-room whose ordinary society we have just described, the guests were about to go their separate ways in search of sleep when, almost at the same time, a bright light rose up from the depths of a valley situated to the north-west, illuminating the surroundings, and the bell, abandoning its sinister tolling, suddenly began to sound an ominous alarm.

A general silence reigned in the room where people had been laughing a moment before. They listened anxiously. Soon, a general cry went up: "Fire!" There was a fire somewhere, consuming a haystack or devouring a house.

Suddenly, they ran to the windows and looked out into the countryside, toward the point where the flames had been ignited.

Madame Delmont was the first to guess the truth. "If I'm not mistaken," she said, "it's the house where the foreign woman is lodged that is on fire."

She was right; her assertion was confirmed by the general opinion. Men ran out hastily to lend assistance where it was needed, while the women of the group, less bold, were still speculating as to what was happening. In the midst of this commotion, Hélène slipped out. She was followed by Raoul, who was waiting for her, and never ceased repeating on the way that she was wrong to want to go to the fire herself—but she hastened her stride, not wanting to listen to these unwelcome representations, entirely under the sway of the noblest humanity.

When she approached the theater of the conflagration, it was with anguish that she contemplated its disastrous progress. No hope remained of saving the house. The rapid flames had enveloped every part of it; clinging to ceilings, they launched themselves through the windows. They overshot the roof, which they covered in its entirety. A few villagers brought their good will in vain; there was

---

[22] Boston is a four-handed card-game akin to whist.

[23] All Souls' Day, or the Day of the Dead, celebrated on November 2, follows All Saint's Day, or Hallowmas, celebrated on November 1 in the Christian calendar; the final day of October, nowadys known as Hallowe'en, was not widely regarded as an occasion of any particular significance in 1825.

nothing to be done. They could only stand by woefully, watching the destruction of the manor.

When Madame Delmont arrived, she tried urgently to discover what had become of the foreign woman. She found her, by the horrid light of the fire, some distance from the house, standing on a mound, enveloped by a sheet that gave her the fearful aspect of an incensed shade. Her face was pale, her eyes haggard, and no expression animated them.

It was not obvious, on looking at her, whence that calm, that complete insensibility, came. People were wandering around her, approaching her to sympathize or console her; she made no reply, and everything addressed to her, she met with grim silence. Only the arrival of Madame Delmont was able to extract her from this stupor; she recognized her, for a horrible smile suddenly brushed her lips, but only to pass with lightning rapidity—then Alinska seemed to fall back into her mysterious reverie.

"Madame," Hélène said to her, in a penetrating tone, "I have until now respected your wishes, in leaving you to your solitary reveries; but now that misfortune has fallen upon you with a new determination, permit me to beg you to accompany me to the château. You have no hope of being able to continue to live in this dwelling, which will soon cease to exist. Accept a refuge offered to you with the utmost sincerity."

Listening to Madame Delmont, Alinska seemed to emerge entirely from her reverie, and even sought to give her somber physiognomy an agreeable expression. Without attempting a initial refusal, she accepted the generous offer that had been made to her. She told Hélène that at about midnight, the fire in the kitchen hearth, doubtless not completely extinguished, had reignited. A few sparks, she assumed, had set fire to a number of hemp sandals placed under a cupboard, and soon afterwards, the blaze had become evident.

"I was scarcely able to throw my purse and jewelry and a few clothes out of my bedroom window; then I ran down the staircase, which was already alight, and tried to find a refuge far enough away not to feel the effect of the flames. But I don't see my poor servant—what's become of him?"

"I saw him take the road to the hamlet," Madame Delmont replied, trying to hide the truth that she anticipated. "But you can't stay here, Madame; it's a cold night and you're not dressed. That bed-sheet can't preserve you from the impressions of the air. Follow me, and you'll find a refuge that I'm only too glad to offer you."

Alinska repeated her thanks. The men from the gathering who had come with Hélène each volunteered to take a part of the Hungarian woman's meager luggage, and all of them, charmed to be able to make her acquaintance at last, climbed the hill to the château with her.

Raoul, to whom we have temporarily neglected to pay attention, was plunged in an unparalleled confusion. He could not get used to the idea that Alinska was going to be living under the same roof as his mistress; he was already anticipating the scene that would be played out when the colonel returned. A peculiar presentiment caused him to fear the most terrible catastrophes, and twice, yielding to his first impulse, he opened his mouth to reveal the terrible truth to Madame Delmont, in order to make her aware of what kind of serpent she was nursing in her bosom—but both times, frightened by the consequences of such a confidence, whose danger he fully appreciated, he retained the secret that his heart wanted to let out.

A triumphant glance that his enemy darted at him completed his despair—but he promised himself that he would watch her so closely that she would not have the complete liberty to set in motion all the plans that she doubtless had in mind. In order not to lose sight of her, he too silently accompanied the group that was moving away.

The peasants who remained at the burning house would discover, an hour later, beneath the charred debris, the remains of a horribly mutilated cadaver, scarred by the fire and already attained by corruption. It gave off a noxious odor. The head had completely lost its form; nothing about it was any longer recognizable. As they found the corpse not far from the debris of a bed, however, they did not hesitate to assume that it was the body of the foreign woman's domestic—all the more so because, from that moment on, the man never showed his face in the village again.

The villagers were initially surprised by the promptitude with which he decomposed after his sad end, and promised to come back as soon as it was light to give him a decent burial—but that pious project was never accomplished. A considerable section of the wall, to which a few fragments of wood were still clinging, collapsed almost immediately upon the place where that hideous flesh and bones lay; the flames, flaring up again violently, did not take long to consume them, and nothing then remained of the individual but a feeble memory, which was soon effaced from human recollection.

Meanwhile, the company of which Alinska was a part arrived at the château. Impatient to go to sleep, Madame Delmont urged the foreign woman to go to bed immediately. Germaine came forward, and tried to remove the veils enveloping Alinska, but she was swiftly thrust back by the latter, who asked the favor of remaining alone for a while in the room. The expression of severe urgency with which she made this request forbade those with her any thought of opposition.

She was, therefore, left alone for several minutes, as she wished. As soon as they were convinced that she had gone to bed, they returned, bringing her some broth and other refreshments. She refused them obstinately, declaring that, in her present condition, it was impossible for her to eat anything—and when one of the ladies in the group insisted that she must at least drink a glass of warm wine, she pushed the beverage away with a gesture of her left hand—which, Madame Delmont observed, was still gloved.

That discovery surprised her, but she had another cause for astonishment when Germaine, on removing the sheets in which the foreigner had wrapped herself, discovered that they were moist with blood.

"You're wounded, Madame," said Hélène, anxiously. "Why won't you let us give you the attention that the accident urgently requires? Why refuse such a natural thing? Favorable chance, in the midst of your misfortune, has determined that among these gentleman assembled here we possess a skillful medical practitioner, whose merit is not limited to the city of Toulouse. Let him give you his care—the pallor covering your face testifies that you have need of it."

"No, Madame, no!" cried the foreigner, with a very peculiar appearance of fear to which it was difficult to attribute any just cause. "I don't want that; I'm not asking for any help. It's true that I'm wounded, but I have been for a long time. The harm that I was able to inflict on myself is complete; henceforth, I have nothing more to fear—and at the price of an entire life, if it is permitted for me to recommence it, I would not want to expose my bloody scar to any gaze. Believe that I can take care of myself. Grant me, if you will, a moment alone with my reflections; reassure your alarmed generosity. The danger that is most to be feared is not mine."

There was in the voice that pronounced these words such a mixture of sensibility, insouciance and even irony, that everyone listening experienced a shudder. They did not, however, think that they could oppose a desire so firmly expressed any longer, and after having lit a night-light and placed a hand-bell next to the bed, they retired in silence, going elsewhere to formulate excited conjectures relative to the singular mystery with which the young woman perpetually covered herself.

Madame Delmont invited the company to take the refreshments that the foreigner had refused; they were accepted gratefully, and the conversation only terminated at daybreak. Everyone then beat a retreat, but those who were staying in the vicinity said that they would return before long to obtain news of the unfortunate victim of the fire.

The latter got up late, and no one dared go into her room before having heard her walking about. Then Madame Delmont, after knocking softly on the door, received an invitation to come in. She found that the foreigner had already got up and put on a black dress, which emphasized the extreme pallor of her face.

News of the death of the old domestic Ladislas had reached the château. Madame Delmont did not think it possible to keep it from the stranger, but, at the same time, feared causing her too much emotion, thinking that there had been a reciprocal sentiment of affection between the two mysterious beings. In consequence, and in order not to hurry that which it was necessary to communicate, she sought to prepare Alinska for it. It was a futile effort however; at the first word she pronounced, the other had guessed, and a tranquil indifference painted in the features was the Hungarian woman's response. She seemed insensible to the story, not allowing the slightest sign to show of the commonplace human compassion caused by catastrophes that are always painful to envisage.

Such strange conduct increased Madame Delmont's surprise; by the changes that overtook her expression she revealed the extent of the effect it had on her.

Alinska noticed that, and, as if she wanted to repair her fault, said: "I astonish you, Madame, and you're forming a low opinion of me. Perhaps I ought to show more sensitivity, and exhibit my regrets on learning of the death of poor Ladislas, but I know how little such sterile marks of interest meant to him. No relationship linked me to him; both having emerged from the same refuge, we came together out of necessity. The will of the absolute master has separated us—well, it will not take long to reunite us again, and that will not be temporarily, but forever. Why should I shed tears? There are no longer any beneath my eyelids; they have been dried up by woe. I have shed too many in the course of my mortal life. Now that I exist, because I can no longer lie in the tomb, in spite of my keen desire to join that cold dwelling, should I occupy myself with that which does not affect me? No, no—one sole object animates me; I am inclined toward a single objective. When that is attained, I shall leave, with no more joy than pain, the body in which I cannot suffer."

Alinska could have spoken for longer with Madame Delmont thinking of interrupting. There was always something so incomprehensible and so incoherent in everything the young woman said, that it was impossible to decide whether it was necessary to pity her or fear her. Words escaped from her mouth in a monotonous tone, which almost always destroyed the effect that they might have produced; the motionless fixity of her gaze rendered it alien to her own conversation. In sum, everything about her was outside the ordinary rule, and she had no model or copy anywhere.

That bizarre discourse was so astonishing to its listener that Hélène could make no reply to it. She changed the subject, and asked whether her guest would care for a little nourishment. Alinska nodded her head affirmatively, and the mistress of the château went out to order the junior maidservant to bring the food that had been prepared in advance.

The children waited impatiently for the moment when they might be admitted to the presence of the woman who had testified to her friendship toward them. More than once, Juliette had already shown her mischievous face in the gap left by the incompletely-closed door. As no one appeared to be paying any attention to them, they kept quiet, but at the sight of the breakfast they became bolder and went into the room almost tumultuously.

Alinska greeted them with a smile that she tried to render benevolent; a sudden blush colored her face, which contracted simultaneously, as if she had taken a violent blow to the heart. Neither Eugène nor his sister noticed it; they were chattering hurriedly about the previous night's event, and the little boy was already manifesting a precocious sensitivity, which might one day trouble his life, if Providence had a long career reserved for him.

Madame Delmont, proud of her children, lavished the most affectionate caresses on them. They could not tear themselves away from her arms. Meanwhile, the Hungarian woman, doubtless agitated by a bitter memory, slyly darted glances full of disdain, or a profound anger, at the charming group. Often, to hide what she was feeling, she hid her head in her hands, one of which was always gloved, and for long intervals she seemed to be buried in profound reflections.

Chapter X

In an era that was now somewhat remote, the French armies had planted their banners on the towers of the city of Vienna. That abode of Caesars, courageously defended against the Turks, had been unable to put up any resistance to us on more than one occasion, and no human blood ran beneath its walls. The Leader who commanded a multitude of brave men was pursuing, in 1805, the course of his glorious enterprise, and advancing into Hungary. Several squadrons were successively taking possession of various villages, after having fought a number of battles against a bellicose population.

Among the officers employed in this part of the expedition, Captain Edouard Delmont was neither the least brave nor the least reckless. His ebullient courage often led him into perilous enterprises, but he counted them as trivial even though they offered renown to be acquired. Fortune, which loves to crown audacity, almost always supported him. Finally, however, the inconstant Dame, without abandoning him entirely, ceased to serve him as usual, and Captain Delmont fell on the battlefield, his body pierced by a bullet, just as his enemies were retreating.

Close at hand at this time was the watchful soldier Raoul, a brave man who was attached to him by bonds of gratitude. He saw his commanding officer fall in the crowd, but far from abandoning him, he ran toward him, and aided by his companions, transported him to a nearby house, inhabited by a family of farmers who enjoyed a certain ease. The arrival of a wounded officer was, for the Hungarian who welcomed him, a safeguard against the excesses of the soldiery, whose value they appreciated. The head of the household, a respectable old man, hastened to offer him the best room and to provide all the help that he could.

A surgeon was called. After taking off the superficial clothing, he decided that the wound was not mortal, but that it would be slow to heal.

Delmont spent nearly a fortnight in almost complete unconsciousness; he scarcely heard the sounds that were made around his bed, and his constantly-closed eyes did not permit him to recognize the affectionate cares that were lavished on him. Among the people who watched over the conservation of his existence, he would doubtless have identified, if his strength had left him full use of his senses, a young woman: the farmer's daughter, as distinguished by her admirable beauty as her air of innocence. Touched by a pity whose cause she could not yet determine, she spent entire days prowling around the invalid— who, in spite of an extreme pallor, bore in his features everything charming and attractive, be it their extreme perfection or a vivacity that suffering tempered but could not entirely extinguish.

Alinska continually found pretexts to come into the room, from which she was sometimes banished. She spent long hours there, almost constantly employed in a contemplation whose consequences might easily become dangerous. As soon as the officers who were Delmont's friends, or the soldiers of his company, came in search of news, however, the ingenuous girl, ashamed of being caught there, escaped as nimbly as a hind of the Carpathian Mountains, and waited for the unwelcome visitors to leave before going back.

Delmont's first gazes rested upon that terrestrial angel—and how could one contemplate her for any length of time without admiring her? He did not know the means, so he found it simpler to surrender to the sentiment that carried him away. He soon needed a confidant, in order to talk at his leisure about the person occupying his thoughts. Raoul was chosen, and, proud of that distinction, he hastened to merit it, seeking opportunities to talk to Alinska about the brilliant qualities of is commander—without, however, knowing exactly what the handsome officer's thoughts on the subject were.

Raoul's tales rendered the young woman singularly attentive. She listened to stories of gigantic battles, in which French bravery had stood out so advantageously; she followed Delmont through incessantly-renewed perils; she shivered every time they threatened to reach him. Then her attention was redoubled; she went pale and blushed by turns; her respiration became labored; and when the story was concluded by a success that was not bought at the cost of any wound, she raised her expressive eyes to the heavens, offering a thousand thanks to Providence.

In the calm of the night, as in the midst of the day's labors, she was occupied by one sole thought: the handsome and valiant captain was never absent from her imagination, nor her heart. The more time passed, the deeper the dart was embedded. Already she was experiencing all the deliria of love, although the object of her affection had not yet caused her to hear its language.

Delmont could not remain long under that restriction, which suited neither his profession nor his character. He finally explained, and was heard out without difficulty. Alinska was at that age when mistrust causes no anxiety; she loved forcefully, and it seemed natural to be cherished in the same way. She was oblivious to differences in rank or fortune; her beloved was young and handsome, everything else seemed immaterial to her—and for her, the future could not be other than a happy prolongation of the present.

In the midst of these vehement transports, however, she kept herself as pure as virtue itself; no culpable thought sullied her candor, and Delmont, astonished to find such passion combined with such complete innocence, did not seek to profane it. The more he saw of Alinska, the more his affection for her increased. He took that to the extreme, and one evening, after an entire day spent in the most delightful pleasures, he pierced his arm with a sharp dagger, and in blood drawn from the slight wound he wrote a promise of marriage, which he confided to the loyalty of his friend. Impressed by this action, she hastened to do likewise. The double pact, according to the ancient custom of the country, was deposited for five nights under the stone of a sepulcher, and from then on, the engagement was ratified in Heaven.

No one doubts, in Hungary, that by such an act, two lovers are irrevocably bound to one another; any union that is not contracted between the two of them cannot be happy. Eventually, a female virgin affianced in that fashion may rise from the tomb that covers her after her death, in order to torment, in the fashion of a Vampire, the perfidious man who has abandoned her. Delmont, a stranger to the land, was unaware of these superstitious details. He had no fear of the future, for it seemed to him to be impossible that he could ever forget Alinska.

Weeks and months went by. The peace treaty was signed. Already there were muffled rumors announcing a new war, and Captain Delmont's regiment advanced into northern Germany. The latter's wound had healed, but he prolonged his convalescence; love led him to become hard of hearing with respect to the voice of duty. An imperative order from the colonel, however, dissipated the enchantment of the new Renaud;[24] it was necessary either to leave Alinska or be dishonored.

The battle was terrible; glory nevertheless won the day. After having vanquished his own weakness, Delmont had still to combat that of his beloved. He reassured her with the most solemn oaths; he promised to come back to ratify at the foot of the altar the sacred pact that they had sworn together, and the only delay for which he asked was that necessitated by the new war—a year at the most. Finally, Alinska, unconsoled but reconciled to patience, contented to his disastrous departure.

"Edouard," she cried, at that heartbreaking moment, "I am yours for life, as you belong to me in perpetuity; I can only be liberated from my oath by our marriage, and you must be united with me before the funeral shroud covers us forever."

Delmont, charmed to find a means of reassuring her, repeated her forceful words. He left—and after that, he never saw Alinska again.

For a long time, he remained faithful to her; but the fatal absence produced its usual effect. The Hungarian woman gradually became a matter of indiffer-

---

[24] In a famous episode of Torquato Tasso's 16th century epic *Gerusalemma liberata*, whose French translation was enormously popular in the 19th century, Rinaldo (Renaud in the translation) is beguiled by the enchantress Armida, who retains him as a willing captive in an enchanted garden.

ence to him; he no longer recalled the promises that he had made, and his marriage to Hélène completed the destruction in his soul of the memory of his previous inclination.

Not that it was possible for him to break with her entirely; Alinska wrote to him punctiliously; she suffered a delay that seemed interminable with impatience, but nevertheless still hoped. She understood that the caprices of the French emperor were sending his legions to the various parts of Europe; she imagined, albeit with difficulty, that Delmont was not yet free to conclude his marriage while the fate of arms retained him in the depths of Spain, as he gave her to believe.

Finally, however, Providence broke the instrument that it had used against the nations, and peace, briefly troubled after its birth, soon returned to the Earth. That moment, enchanting for Alinska, promised her the happiness that she had always desired so ardently. Her letters became more urgent; she had no trepidation in telling Delmont that if he did not come to find her in Hungary, she would not hesitate to hasten to him in Paris.

Edouard, who had been promoted to colonel and had married Hélène, shuddered as he read that letter, which might be the prelude to a long series of misfortunes. He took a desperate step, and steeled himself to confess the frightful truth to his unfortunate lover.

With inexpressible anxiety he awaited a reply, from which he had everything to fear. She did not leave him in suspense. He received it, and a few moments later, he went to find his wife. Pretending that their fortune had suffered a loss, he told her that it was necessary to leave Paris and find a distant refuge. After that, he did not dare to cast another glance over that letter, and in a new moment of terror he took the decision to destroy it—with the result that no one would ever know what could have led him to make such a desperate resolution.

Chapter XI

Let us pass on now to a time nearer to the one at which we stopped, in order to tell the reader a story indispensable to the clarification of facts that might fill volumes.[25]

---

[25] This opening paragraph suggests that Lamothe-Langon had intended to insert another episode here before returning to his interrupted story, perhaps describing Alinska's suicide. He might simply have changed his mind and returned immediately to the frame narrative instead, without bothering to remove the lead-in, but the unusual brevity of the previous chapter might indicate that he did include such an episode in the manuscript, but that it was subsequently removed, either by him or his editor, and the stray sentence moved, inappropriately, to the next chapter.

It will be remembered that the Hungarian woman was living in the Château de R***, and that her presence in that abode could only be an evil augury for the Delmont family. Raoul, familiar with all the details of the story of which we have only given a brief summary, had vast objects of dread, and bemoaned the fact that he could neither confide them to anyone, nor send word to the colonel. But if Alinska, while still distant, had been able to prevent him from corresponding with the latter, how much easier it would be for her now.

Tormented by this thought, he prayed for the return of the master of the house, hoping that his presence, if it led to an explosion impossible to avoid, would nevertheless convince Alinska to seek another abode elsewhere. Driven by a thousand various sentiments, he thought it his duty to go to her, in order that he might, by talking to her, find out what her plans might be.

Already, several of the commune's property-owners had come to offer their services to the foreigner, perhaps impelled less by the desire to oblige her than the desire to see her at close range and satisfy their avid curiosity. They were all thwarted in their purpose. She refused to see anyone, asking Madame Delmont, with a fervor that was not usual in her, not to allow her retreat to be disturbed. She expressed her desire with such insistence that Hélène would have been in violation lo the laws of hospitality had she not honored then. She told the members of the circle that met in her drawing-room that it was futile to persist in forming any liaison with the foreigner, for she was absolutely adamant that she did not want to see anyone, not excepting the most important people in the commune. It was necessary to renounce an interview that promised the most piquant results.

The deputy mayor observed, laughing, that he would have the right nevertheless to demand to see the beautiful unknown's passport. As he had no knowledge, however, of her being placed in any category requiring supervision, nor on any list of suspects, and she had not been signaled out by the police, he would not overstep the bounds of his duty in her regard.

Monsieur Berneval was less reasonable; he affirmed that if he had the honor of being mayor, or even deputy, he would submit the lady to the hazards of an interrogation, which he would conduct as he wished. At this speech, a general clamor rose up against what was termed uncivil curiosity, and a few of the women present declared that if he continued to talk like that, they would no longer accord him the title of French *chevalier*, which he was so proud of meriting by birth as much as by his manners.

While the drawing-room was cheerfully occupied with Alinska, however, following the constant custom of society, whose sensibility is almost always conventional, Raoul, taking advantage of the moment when his mistress was occupied, boldly introduced himself into the Hungarian woman's room.

The latter was sitting next to a window. Young Eugène was balanced on her knees, looking at an illustrated book, and his companion, deeply immersed in meditation, was nevertheless looking at him with an expression that was not benevolent. One might, at the same time, have observed a singular indecision, which seemed to be combating the ferocity of a firmly interrupted resolution.

The sound of Raoul's footsteps having extracted Alinska from her reverie, she immediately changed the expression on her face, resuming her usual one of perfect indifference. The sergeant-major came forward, offering a rather curt bow that was not returned. Unintimidated by that impoliteness, however, he launched the attack as he had planned it.

"Well, Alinska," he said, "here you are, finally introduced into a house that prudence should not have let you enter, and which you ought to have avoided, for your own peace of mind and that of a respectable family. What are your plans now? Would you like to import dolor and conflict, as the price of the shelter you have been granted? Don't you think, since you obviously want to see the colonel one last time, that it would be more convenient to go and wait for the moment of his return in Toulouse?"

"It seems to me, Raoul, that in important circumstances, it's not from enemies that one ought to take advice; in any case, you're not fortunate in the advice you give. Didn't you tell me before to allow myself to be softened by the love of the most perfidious of men? You knew him, though; you knew how fickle he was—but that didn't stop you from urging me to my doom. What guarantee so I have that there is no such deceit in your present advice?"

"If I made mistakes, they were the produce of my age rather than my heart, whereas now, I am guided..."

"I no longer believe the words of men; I cannot deviate from the path that has been traced for me. I am in this house; I shall remain here until the hour when everything is finished for me, and I shall go to find the eternal torments that await me."

"If you have never committed any sin, what have you to fear?"

"It's not with you," replied the Hungarian woman, an in exceedingly grim tone, "that I shall debate that point. I'm tired of listening to you, and tired of answering you; your presence is unwelcome; I'm impatient to be free of it."

"I'm sorry to cause you displeasure, but if my appearance irritates me, don't imagine that you'll lose sight of it while you're in the château. Before coming here you already had such good spies here that I took it upon myself to catch them, and to keep watch day and night to make sure that nothing happened contrary to the tranquility that resided here until the moment when you appeared in the locality."

"Truly, Raoul, your vigilance will be very necessary, and you will harvest abundant fruit therefrom. Don't you fear that your conduct might eventually push me too far? Ought you to offer me the insult of expressing a mistrust to my face of which I am the object? Feeble obstacle to my desires, you would soon cease to oppose them if I no longer wanted to consent to see you incessantly casting an anxious eye over my every move. Be assured, you who speak to me with such audacity, that you will leave the château before I do."

"I don't doubt that my presence is a hindrance to you, but it would be easier for you to corrupt simple villagers than to rob me of the confidence of my masters. Neither of them will lend an ear to your calumnies, and if I wished, another hour would not pass without you receiving an order to go elsewhere to seek another shelter. I only have to say the word..."

"But you will not pronounce it; you appreciate the consequences only too well. Believe me, Raoul, if Madame Delmont's happiness is dear to you, leave her to spend in peace the days that remain to her. I don't want to give her a fatal enlightenment, save as a last resort, and if her existence is poisoned she will have no one to blame but you."

"But after all, what do you want? On what is your hope founded?"

"Of hope, I have none; I can no longer have any; I know that my fate is determined. No matter—there remains a duty for me to fulfill, orders for me to carry out. They would once have broken my heart; my soul would not have hesitated to rebel against their atrocious rigor, but that does not matter now, when all is regulated for it, when it can read the depths of the future fluently; it can no longer be agitated by the sentiments that once filled it."

"By my grandfather's saber, Alinska, I'm listening to you but I can no longer understand you. Certainly, when you were in your own country, it wasn't necessary for me to think hard about everything you said. Now your words are so obscure that I've racked my brains and still can't understand them. Speak to me without confusion. One might think that you've spent the years during which we lost sight of you reading the works of certain contemporary authors who chatter like magpies and never explain anything. You'd only have to write with exclamation marks to convince me that you're learned in their school."

In pronouncing these final words, Raoul was only his master's parrot; he was repeating what he had heard several times, and wanted, by means of that language, to impart a little humor to a conversation that Alinska did not have the artistry to render agreeable. He felt, as he talked to her, afflicted by a tendency to melancholy, for which he could not determine the reason. He did not like what the Hungarian woman had said to him; through the mystery in which she enveloped herself, he glimpsed something tenebrous and sinister, which frightened him somehow. He felt like a laborer tracking the course of a black cloud, uncertain as to whether it might blow over or unleash a destructive flail upon the field in which his hopes of fortune are founded.

Raoul had set himself not to fear the threat that had been made against him, but it had descended into the depths of his heart to strike him sharply. He knew the weaknesses of the colonel's better than anyone; he knew that, although full of bravery and energy on the battlefield, he abandoned himself easily in everyday life to the impressions that people wanted to make on him. Many men are like that, only deploying their firmness of mind in one arena.

Perhaps Alinska divined what Raoul was thinking, for she was gazing at him with an extreme malignity. A smile of triumph wandered over her lips, and she toyed with the book that Eugène had abandoned when he withdrew, when the soldier came into the apartment. She was in no hurry to reply, however, and a long pause succeeded the heat of the attack.

It was Raoul who broke it. "I can see," he said, with an appearance of ill-disguised resentment, "that I flattered myself in vain that I could make you see reason, or succeed in such an appeal to a person of your sex, so I promise not to try again. But if you persist in pursuing the accomplishment of a plan whose objectives escape me, never forget the generosity with which you have been welcomed at the Château de R***. Don't make us repent of the hospitality that has been accorded to you here."

These few words, simply spoken, caused a vivid blush to rise momentarily to the Hungarian woman's pale face. That color soon disappeared, and she replied, calmly: "Whatever reproach might be addressed to me, and whatever my subsequent conduct might be, did the man who was received with delight in my father's modest dwelling hesitate to import despair and death thereto?"

That vigorous reply, which struck the target so sharply, covered Raoul in sudden confusion. He felt all the justice of the reproach, and, incapable of silencing his conscience, which recalled the vision of his past conduct to his eyes, and simultaneously moved by the solemn tone in which Alinska had expressed herself, he shuddered.

Endeavoring to hide his disturbance from her, he said: "Come on—what is past no longer exists; the sins of others do not excuse our own, and further evil does not repair that which has been done."

Alinska made no reply; she contented herself with a gesture that advertised her desire to be alone—and Raoul, who feared that Madame Delmont might find him there, made the decision to retreat, while promising himself to clarify the intentions of the person he could only envisage as an enemy of the household.

When it had been conclusively proven that the foreigner was refusing to receive the visitors that curiosity attracted to her, the Château de R*** became solitary again. People only thought at increasingly long intervals about the mysterious beauty it contained, and the fire was forgotten as soon as its consequences could no longer provide fuel for conversation.

Madame Delmont, who would have found herself in absolute seclusion after the departure of her neighbors, was not displeased that Alinska was prolonging her sojourn. It was not, undoubtedly, a very pleasant society; her habitual melancholy, the silence she maintained when she was not asked questions, the brevity of her answers and, even more so, the indefinable air of her physiognomy, were not attractive. She sang, it is true, with style, and accompanied herself on the harp; but it was while she was shut up in her room that she devoted herself to those pastimes. An invincible timidity, she said, did not permit her to play in front of anyone else.

It required repeated supplications for Madame Delmont to persuade the foreigner to allow her to enjoy a talent that was truly remarkable. One evening, however, after strong insistence, she consented to touch the sonorous instrument—but that was with singular preliminaries. She had the light of the astral lamp hidden beneath a hood of green cloth and she retreated into a dark corner of the room, behind a screen. Then she commenced a song whose extraordinary words were in harmony with the tune that accompanied them.[26]

> The star of the night, midway through her course,
> Illuminates the plain with its wan light;
> On the bank of the stream far from its source,
> A pale, anguished pilgrim directs his sight
> Into the distance, seeking a safe place
> To rest his chagrin and his weary head.
> An impure spirit is matching his pace,
> The luckless pilgrim is to be misled.
>
> The malign goblin arrives at his side
> Swiftly carried on a delicate wing;
> It presents itself, its nature belied,
> In the guise of a shepherd wont to sing.
> "Worthy traveler," he says, with a smile,
> "Come to the house where my father resides,
> "Wait in peace for the dawn a little while,
> "To color the sky with easterly guides."
>
> The deadly seductiveness of this speech,
> And the innocent tone of its making.
> Deceived the pilgrim's imaginative reach
> Who fell into the trap of its faking;
> A precipice opened before his feet;
> He tottered thereon, and his death was cruel.
> Feeble mortals, do not thrust the deceit
> Of beauty that calls with the voice of a jewel.

If Madame Delmont had expected to obtain the pure satisfaction to which the culture of artistry ought to give birth, she was strangely disappointed when the harp ceased to make itself heard. The music chosen by Alinska was so bi-

---

[26] The text gives the title of this piece as *Le Voyageur et le lutin* [The Traveler and the Goblin] and describes it as a *nocturne*. Again, Mlle. Sendrier's score is reproduced, but I cannot tell whether it is capable of delivering the effect of which the text boasts.

zarre, and imparted such painful emotions to the heart, that, far from giving pleasure, it inspired a vague melancholy. Twice, a tear escaped Hélène's eyes, and, entirely immersed in her dolorous emotion, she could not bring herself to compliment Alinska on the piece she had just played.

"Oh, Madame," she said, "you will think me very strange, but it would be impossible for me to hide the hurt you've just caused my heart; that is doubtless the triumph for which you aimed on this occasion. I'd be most obliged to you if, changing the mood, you would care to revive my ailing spirits with some barca-role."

The foreigner made no reply; she simply resumed her seat and, taking up the harp again, played brilliant variations of the same tune that had just produced such a disagreeable effect. That was not exactly what Hélène had wanted, but she nevertheless had to be content with it. She promised herself not to ask such a person again, either to play music or to do anything else that might lead her to display talents whose effects were so peculiar.

From that moment on, Alinska's unsociability seemed to increase. She only emerged from her room at meal times; she sat down at the table, where she scarcely took enough nourishment to sustain her existence. She was vainly urged to eat more, obstinately refusing the best dishes, contenting herself with a little meat, which she sucked—for she appeared not to like vegetables at all. The peace that she enjoyed in her apartment was only interrupted by the daily visits made by the children. She was always good to them, and full of kindness; she flattered them, and spoke to the tenderly—but sometimes, she looked at them with an indefinable expression.

In the two weeks that she had been living in the château, her conduct had been consistent. Raoul, who watched her every move constantly, had been unable to discover anything suspect. He got up at all hours of the night, but in vain; he discovered nothing disadvantageous to her—and so, reluctantly, he began to believe that he had misjudged her, and relaxed his constant vigilance.

At that time, Eugène began to experience a few symptoms of ill-health that made his mother anxious. The child did not complain of anything in particular, and yet the color was visible disappearing from his cheeks and he was getting thinner. He became extremely weak, walked with difficulty, and could not tolerate daylight. At the same time, his attachment to the foreigner increased in its intensity. He could not bear to leave her; he gave vent to violent fits of anger if anyone sought to separate him from his friend; he wandered around her incessantly, in a manner that was both anxious and satisfied, and spent hours on end lying in her arms.

These demonstrations of affection were viewed with indifference by Alinska. Her attitude to the child was the same as to all the other members of the household—which is to say, excessively cold. She did not reject him; she consented to keep him company, but she seemed insensitive to his attentions. She even avoided looking at him, or did so listlessly, with a gaze deprived of all expression. She consented to care for him, though, encouraging him to take the mild medicine that he was given—and at those moments, if she was unobserved, she brought a sardonic smile to her lips that manifested neither concern not pity.

Madame Delmont wrote letter after letter to her husband to tell him about the depressed state into which their son had fallen. She made him party to her anxieties, and begged him to terminate an absence that was becoming too painful. She had already told him about what had happened in the neighborhood— the burning of the isolated house—and that it was in the château that the unfortunate foreigner had found a retreat.

In his replies, Delmont shared Hélène' anguish. He promised not to delay setting forth; everything led him to hope for an imminent reconciliation between his sister and her husband; the moment their reunion had been effected, he would leave immediately. He had paid little attention to the story of the fire, only mentioning it in passing, and lending his entire approval to his wife's conduct in that circumstance. He terminated his missives with ardent expressions of his wish that dear Eugène would recover his health.

Heaven, however, did not seem disposed to grant the father's wishes. The child continued to lose his strength and the freshness of his complexion. His breathing was already awkward, and his vacillating head continually fell on to his shoulder in spite of his attempts to maintain it in its natural position.

This fatal change threw Madame Delmont into consternation. She was partly reassured by the skill of a doctor who lived in a neighboring commune, who came every day to observe the progress of the singular malady. He could not make any positive diagnosis; the child was succumbing to an emaciation whose cause was unknown. He seemed to be suffering, but retained in the midst of his weakness an appetite that increased in proportion to the disease; he often complained of having a hunger that he had difficulty in satisfying. It was in the morning, especially, when he had not yet got out of bed that the need to eat made itself felt in him most keenly. He demanded the most substantial nourishment then, and swallowed it as if he had spent several days without being able to satisfy his imperious appetite.

In these symptoms, the doctor thought at one time that he recognized the presence of a tapeworm, which would have explained the voracious hunger that was consuming the poor child, but more attentive observations presented contrary appearances, which no longer permitted him to sustain his initial opinion. He kept his embarrassment secret, in order not to complete the fear of a mother who was already sufficiently alarmed. He pretended to believe that a tapeworm as the sole cause of the illness, and showed himself full of hope, although he saw no means of curing the condition.

Alinska rarely left her little friend's side. She listened to the doctor's questions and Madame Delmont's plaints without ever intervening in the conversation. She only became animated when it was necessary to give the child some remedy, when she used her influence on him to make him do what was required of him. Eugène smiled at her thankfully, taking her ungloved hand and promising to be good, if Alinska would promise not to leave him.

"Come on, my friend," she said to him. "Have no fear on that score; I am too closely identified with your being to consent to be separated from you. I shall not abandon you until the fatal terminus by which everything on earth is released."

These affectionate words lost all their value for those who heard them, because of the dryness with which they were pronounced. The Hungarian woman rarely put any expression into what she said, or did. One might have thought, most of the time, one examining her actions, that she was not so much a living creature as an animate automaton, solely obedient to the impulse of springs that moved her relentlessly in a uniform manner.

Such coldness sometimes excited a sight impulse of anger in Hélène's soul, but it was soon suppressed when she remembered that the unfortunate creature's mind had doubtless been weakened by some great misfortune. That reason alone had prevented her from asking the questions that one would normally ask of someone introduced into a household. She knew, from Alinska herself, that the latter's sojourn in the south of France had to be limited. Alinska had made her a semi-confidence, with the result that Madame Delmont had decided to wait for the return of spring before making a definite decision on the subject of the foreigner.

Now, fully occupied with her son's health, she was pleased to see that he liked having Alinska close at hand. It was a gentle distraction for him, while his habitual weakness did not give him the liberty to participate in the tumultuous games of his sister and the children of the farm. The further he advanced in life, the more the sources that ought to have alimented him dried up. Soon, it was no longer possible for him even to leave his room, and it was not without fatigue that he tried from time to time to take a few steps.

The worthy Raoul, who also cherished Eugène beyond all expression, was manifestly inconsolable at the sight of the malady that was devouring him. Once, without saying anything to his mistress, he went to Toulouse and brought back a physician he believed to have more science than the one whose daily cares were lavished on the child—but his hopes of obtaining a much-desired cure by this means proved vain. The artful man's response, after he had examined the patient, brought a new desolation to the former soldier's soul.

The treatment was perfectly suitable to an illness whose cause was unknown. One could add to these words a prescription for different drugs, but it would make no difference to the results; they would remain the same—and to expert eyes, it was the final evidence that Eugène was slowly progressing toward the grave.

This cruel certainty finally penetrated Raoul's heart. He had no doubt that Providence intended to take away that angel of sweetness, and his despair was extreme. He was doubtless carried away by it, for, in one of those moments of delirium when the soul abandons itself to the strangest conceptions, he imagined that poor Eugène was being poisoned, and that the Hungarian woman was the perpetrator of that abominable crime.

That thought, the first time it occurred to him, froze the blood in his veins. He was immediately ashamed of it, but then it returned to mind once again, and established itself therein, no longer letting him breathe. It haunted him incessantly, troubling his every waking moment; he struggled in vain against its implausibility.

He saw Alinska showing Eugène all the affection of which she was capable; she never left his side, and it seemed horrible to Raoul to suspect that she was only behaving thus in order to keep closer watch on the progress of the venomous substance, and to make sure that he did not take anything that would frustrate its effect. Suspended between a thousand confused conjectures, he sought a means of clarifying or obliterating his suspicions.

Chapter XII

The dolor that Madame Delmont was experiencing often caused her to implore divine protection. She went to the parish church piously, every day, to hear the mass celebrated in that holy place. She asked the Mother of the afflicted for help that she no longer dared to expect from humans. Every time she yielded to the appeal of her maternal dread, she made the reflection that the impassive foreigner gave any thought to the accomplishment of her pious duties.

Several Sundays had already gone by, and she remained constantly at the château. That indifference, hardly natural in a person who seemed well brought-up, caused Madame Delmont some pain. One day, when the bell sounded the summons to mass, the latter asked the Hungarian woman whether she would not like to come to church and join her prayers to those of the faithful.

"To church!" exclaimed Alinska. "Me, go to church! No, Madame, I can't; it's not permitted for me to go."

"Eh! Why would you be banished from the place to which all Christians are admitted? Have you committed some sin that has called down the thunderbolt of excommunication upon you? For unless that's the case, I cannot see why you would be prohibited."

"I am," the foreigner replied, in a grave one, "neither heretic not excommunicated. I have placed myself in a particular situation, and I have appeared before the sanctuary of the God of Truth for the last time. Since then, my efforts to climb up there again have been futile. If I tried to go, the angels would be there to prevent it."

There was such mysterious meaning in that statement that Madame Delmont, quite astonished, immediately formed the only conjecture by which it could be naturally explained. She judged that the young woman had undoubtedly contracted, at the foot of the altar, either a marriage that she had profaned, or, perhaps, a vow of reclusion to which she had been unfaithful. Not wishing to press her further on this point, for fear that her mind might go further astray, she ended the conversation and left, and did not ask Alinska to go with her again.

Meanwhile, Raoul, entirely possessed by his fateful idea, was desolate at being unable to find any solid support for it. His surveillance was vain, and Eugène was dying, without any remedy recalling him to life. Already his weakness was such that he no longer left his bed, and every night, his mother, Raoul and Germaine took turns to watch over him.

The moment that seemed the most critical was that when a visible improvement seemed to offer some hope of seeing him return to life. The assiduous cares that had doubtless been lavished upon him during the quiet of the nights restored a little strength to his emaciated body. His eyes were reanimated, and a hint of redness was already beginning to spread over his hollow cheeks. Joy erupted in the château.

Only Alinska remained insensible. The observant gaze of Raoul, who never lost sight of her, detected a change in her, opposite to that in the child; she lost a little of her plumpness. A sinister anxiety settled on her forehead, which became pale; her gait was abrupt, as if hampered; she often raised her hand to the scar that she had on the left side of her body, pressing it violently, as if she were trying to stop the vital principle escaping through that exit.

Twice, Raul caught her contemplating the young victim with the attention of a ferocious impatience; a gesture of frightful import doubtless expressed her thought. Raoul could not divine it, but he had seen enough to remain convinced that it was necessary for the Hungarian woman to leave the château the next day, or the child would be finished.

There were certainly no more grounds for hesitation. He promised himself to act prudently, but to say enough to Madame Delmont to ensure that she would lose no time demanding that Alinska go to see shelter elsewhere, because it was inappropriate for her to continue her sojourn in the château.

In the meantime, darkness fell. Madame Delmont, overcome by fatigue—for she had been watching over her son personally for several days—felt an imperious need to go to sleep. She was about to designate one of the women in her service to take her place beside the invalid when the Hungarian woman, informed of her intention, asked for her preference, claiming that it would give her great pleasure to lavish her benevolent cares on her young friend. She employed the most expressive terms, and showed such a strong desire to fulfill the role, that Madame Delmont thought that she ought not to refuse. It was, in any case, the first time she would take the night shift; until then she had not offered, and no one had dared to suggest it.

The matter was immediately settled, and Germaine, doubtless by virtue of forgetfulness, did not take the news to Raoul. The latter, when it was time to go to bed, was unaware of the changing of the guard that had occurred, and he got into bed convinced that his colonel's son would sleep under the vigilance of the most affectionate of mothers.

Scarcely had he gone to bed, however, when a host of painful thoughts assailed him. Slept ok possession of his senses momentarily, but procured him no rest. He was tormented by bizarre dreams, which agitated him to the highest degree.

At one time, he thought he was walking through the woods that bordered the gardens of the Château de R***; suddenly, a gang of brigands appeared before him, and, after a fierce combat, left him dying on the ground.

At another time, a memory of the distant past transported him to Hungary and the house of Alinska's father. On the threshold he saw a coffin covered by a black and white cloth, ornamented with a crowd of lilies and white carnations. A company of young women surrounded the funeral emblem. A priest appeared, and the procession took the road to the village cemetery. There, the coffin, stripped of its sad ornaments, was deposited in a ready-dug grave. The people drew away, after having cursed the French and their fatal gallantry. Impelled and directed by a superior power, Raoul was the only one who was unable, in spite of his efforts, to leave the field of final rest.

Confined to the ground that he trod regretfully, he saw the daylight disappear and darkness replace it; the moon rose slowly from the edge of the horizon, while the soldier tried to free himself from the power directing his steps. Finally, the star of cold light reached its zenith, whence it projected its rays on to the patch of earth enclosed the newly-deposited coffin.

Suddenly, the dust is thrown hither and yon by an impetuous wind, which whirls furiously, and a figure veiled by the shroud that covered it emerges from the hollow of the funereal shelter. It takes flight through the air, and Raoul is granted the power to follow it.

It traverses immense spaces rapidly, still accompanied by the terrified soldier, before their journey reaches its terminus. The reanimated cadaver eventually comes to a dwelling set in the countryside. Raoul recognizes the Château de R***, and shudders at what was about to happen. His mysterious companion, whose face he cannot see, detaches an entirely fleshless hand from the shroud in which it is wrapped, and knocks violently on the door, which is immediately opened. At the same time, the figure turns toward the soldier, and displays to his surprised gaze the angry face of Alinska.

A dream so horrible cannot last any longer. Raoul wakes up, bathed in sweat, at the height of his terror. He scarcely dares open his eyes in the midst of the profound darkness that surrounds him.

Everything that has just occupied him imprints a terror in his soul from which his natural bravery cannot preserve him. It seems to him that Heaven has just communicated a terrible enlightenment to him, from which he must now profit. All the tricks that astonished him are now explained; it is in the grave that Alinska has obtained the power that surprises him. He thought that he had to contend with a woman led astray by violent passion, but it is an infernal Intelligence that he must combat.

He finally yields to superstition, and grants more credence to the instigation of a dream than to everything that reason can inspire to reassure him. While he abandons himself to the delirium of his imagination, he recalls that Madame Delmont is occupied in watching over her son that very night. Without being obsessed by the demon that she has welcomed, she can listen to the important revelations that Raoul needs to make to her. Perhaps Alinska, plunged into a mortal torpor, will be unable interpose herself between him and the mother of the sacrilegious female's first victim.

That idea strikes him; he immediately leaps out of bed, dresses himself hastily, and is about to open his door when, all of a sudden, a new idea stops him in his tracks. He shivers at the thought of going without weapons through the vast rooms of the château, in which it is possible that a Vampire is wandering at this very moment.

He forgets that a human being is impotent against that which is not subject to the laws of nature, and searches by means of the moonlight that is shining through his window for his pistols, which he always keeps near at hand, loaded. Equipped with this means of defense, confident in the purity of his intentions, he finally emerges from his room, heading toward that of the sick boy, in which he expects to encounter his colonel's wife.

Still fearful that the slightest sound might wake Alinska from her lethargic slumber, he advances slowly, cautiously holding his breath, trembling at the thought that he might be heard. He has already climbed the great staircase, and reached the main hall, and nothing fearful has shown itself.

He arrives at the drawing-room, which he similarly traverses without any troublesome encounter, and he is already about to open the door of the room where Madame Delmont is beside her son... but at that moment he thinks that perhaps he is asleep, and that by appearing unexpectedly in her presence, he might cause her a moment of involuntary fright.

To determine whether she is asleep or awake, he puts his eye to the key-hole and looks into the apartment.

What a surprise! It is not Hélène that he sees, but the inexplicable Alinska. She is walking back and forth slowly; she seems, nevertheless, to be agitated by impatience. Sometimes she looks at the bed in which the child is asleep, sometimes at the moon, which is continuing its advance in a cloudless sky...

The château clock chimes one o'clock in the morning...

Then Alinska's face is altered; a frightful joy contracts her features. Precipitately, she takes off the glove that conceals her left hand and suddenly falls upon the bed. She places her fetid mouth on the pure mouth of the child, and seems to drink long draughts of blood, which she aspires from the unfortunate creature's lungs.

That is too much for Raoul. It might cost him his life, but he cannot bear that horrible spectacle. He draws a pistol, which he immediately cocks; he opens the door precipitately, and launches himself toward the monster whose crimes he wants to punish.

"I know what you are now!" he cries. "Go back to Hell, soil the earth no longer with your presence!"

So saying, and without calculating the consequences of his action, he pulls the trigger. The shot is fired, Alinska is hit—but, more promptly than an eagle surprised on its eyrie by an audacious hunter, she throws herself down on the bed that she has profaned.

"To me!" she says. "Death, to me! Don't flatter yourself, wretch. It's you who'll bury my secret with the end of your existence."

A pointed dagger glitters in her hand. Vainly, Raoul fires his second shot, which misses its mark, only striking the wall. The murderous blade, directed at his breast, pierces his heart—and Raoul, not even having the time to utter a sigh, falls to the floor, without life accompanying him there.

Chapter XIII

The repeated sound of the two firearms echoed through the château, immediately sowing an inexpressible terror there. The farm laborers, some of whom were sleeping in the château, had not yet gone to bed because of a journey they had to make to Toulouse, the preparations for which they were organizing. They spread out into the various apartments, while a woman opened the main door to call for help, either from the other farm-workers or the neighbors.

Madame Delmont, who had gone to sleep in spite of her anxiety, was awakened with a start by the first pistol-shot, which she sought to interpret as one of those nocturnal noises which, snatching us from sleep, seem to us to be a hundred times more extensive than they really are. The second made itself heard almost immediately, however, and she formed only one conjecture: that brigands had got into the château and that the brave Raoul was doubtless fighting them.

After that first thought, the second was devoted to her son; it gave her the courage to get up precipitately, and, without thinking about the danger to which she might be exposing herself, she went to the room where the object of her most pressing solicitude was to be found.

What a frightful spectacle struck her eyes when, by the moonlight shining through a wide-open window and the wan gleam of a night-light, she perceived two bloody bodies lying on the floor, and recognized Raoul and the foreign woman. Uttering a scream of horror then, she ran to the child's bed and hastened to take that feeble creature in her arms. It was in vain, however, that she sought to recall him from the sleep that seemed to have overwhelmed him. She could not do it, because Eugène would not cease to sleep until the uncertain moment of the eternal awakening. That dolorous certainty completed Hélène's plunge into a cruel despair; she fell more than half-unconscious beside the cadavers that were already filling that desolate space.

Shortly after that catastrophic moment, the farm-workers and the two maidservants arrived, armed with agricultural implements they had picked up. They saw a silken ladder firmly attached to the windowsill; they found Raoul and Alinska both bathed in their own blood, giving no further sign of life. Further away, they perceived Madame Delmont, who was still breathing, lying beside the sad remains of her son.

That horrible scene brought a perfectly natural terror into the souls of those who beheld it. The murderers could not be far away, but they might have taken flight already, by means of the ladder. On the one hand, they hastened to lavish hasty cares upon Madame Delmont, and, on the other, to continue the search of the château they had already begun.

It did not take long for the number of witnesses to increase; neighbors ran from all directions, with the local magistrates at their head. The most extensive investigations produced no result, however; no trace was found in the château to indicate the presence of thieves. The certainty was then acquired that, justly frightened by the pistol shots that had been fired, they had not delayed in taking flight. People set out in their pursuit; the neighboring countryside was arched, even before daybreak, but nothing was found. It was imagined that they were hiding from the punishment that such crimes merited.

Toward morning, Hélène seemed to come round; her overwhelmed senses were gradually reanimated, and her first exclamation was to ask for her son, her dear Eugène. A lady who had come running at the news of the event tried to bring some consolation to a heart broken by grief; her delicate attentions were fruitless for the moment. The afflicted mother called for her son, and did not want to listen.

Alas, the poor child could no longer hear her; he too had been a victim of that terrible night. He had succumbed unexpectedly, when a cure seemed assured.

Hélène had seen him dead, but nevertheless rejected that fatal verity; doubt seemed to her to be preferable to a realty that robbed her of all hope.

In the meantime, two newcomers arrived at the château: firstly, the doctor, and secondly, Colonel Delmont. The first had been sent for on the magistrates' orders, to draw up the death certificates required by law. The second, having finally reconciled his sister and brother-in-law, had lost no time in coming to seek his reward for that good deed in the embraces of his family. How far he was from expecting the catastrophe that he was about to witness! He thought that is presence would bring delight to the château, but it was an exceedingly cruel blow that he received when one of the public functionaries took him aside and revealed to him the misfortunes that had just fallen upon the house.

Delmont was a father; he had all the associated sentiments. Overwhelmed by the disastrous story he was told, he did not seek to hide his profound grief. At the same time, though, he demanded to see his wife, in order to mingle his tears with those that she must be shedding.

We shall not describe the heartbreaking scene of their meeting, the touching regrets that they both expressed. It was very difficult to take them away from the body of their son, which they could not bring themselves to leave. The sight of Juliette, far from calming them, further augmented the explosion of a just sensibility, and from the very beginning, the best thing to do was to abandon them to one another, time alone being able to soothe their regrets.

In the midst of the chagrin that the colonel experienced at the loss of his son Eugène, he did not forget that of the faithful Raoul. So many years spent together, so many perils run simultaneously, and services reciprocally rendered to one another, had left a sad memory in Edouard's soul. He asked the surgeon who had come to offer his care, not to neglect anything that might keep the brave soldier alive, but no hope could be entertained on that subject. The homicidal blade had struck the center of the heart too directly for anything to be able to recall the unfortunate to life.

It was the same with the young lady, who had similarly been the victim of the murderers; the bullet had entered her breast and emerged from her back; a double wound announced that her death was certain; nothing remained but to administer the last rites.

Delmont, consternated by such a report, did not ask to see the inanimate remains. He went back to his wife's room after having asked the public functionary to stand in for him in the duties that it was necessary to fulfill, but wanting the body of Eugène, who did not seem to have suffered a violent death, to be conserved until the following day. This time, he was given a favorable response, and they proceeded with the removal of the other two corpses. Raoul's was taken to the room that he had previously occupied; the foreigner's was taken to a room downstairs that was organized for the purpose as best they could.

The double burial was due to take place at four o'clock in the afternoon. The parish priest, who was returning from another commune, which he also served, was about to go into the church to put on his vestments, and the bell was already tolling the funeral knell, when thick clouds that had invaded the sky shortly before burst with an unparalleled din. Lightning flashes followed one another in quick succession, mingled with torrents of water.

A frightful combat was engaged between the violent *vent de Sers* and the *vent d'Autan*,[27] the impetuosity of which is similar. Those two fierce rivals disturbed the country; enormous whirlwinds of leaves, harvest debris, earth and even heavier substances, carried everywhere, smashed into roofs that were sag-

---

[27] In the south of France, the westerly wind known as the *vent de Sers*, which usually brings rain, and the dry but blustery south-easterly *vent d'Autan* are routinely contrasted and regarded as rivals, although they hardly ever blow simultaneously.

ging under the weight of the storm, and in the universal cataclysm, one might have thought that a new Deluge was extending its waters over that part of France, the elevated position of which should have protected it from such inundations.

In the midst of the oaring of the tempest, several villagers believed that they heard raucous and terrible voices uttering sinister clamors. They had no doubt that evil spirits, distributed in the clouds, were rejoicing in the crime that had just soiled the country. Perhaps, they thought, the murdered individuals were not in a state of grace, and their souls, ejected by Heaven, were wandering around their bodies, into which they were trying in vain to return.

The commotion agitating nature did not calm down until the night was well-advanced. While it lasted, it was impossible to think of holding the funeral ceremony; any imprudent individual who dared to expose himself by quitting whatever refuge that he had been fortunate to find would have been risking death. It was therefore necessary to postpone it until the following day, and that caused no little pain to the inhabitants of the château.

Only Madame Delmont was untroubled by it; the son that she would never see again enchained all the faculties of her soul. She too seemed only to be clinging to life by virtue of the hope of soon leaving it. Her husband was with her, obliged to overcome her anguish in order to soothe his own. He showed her their daughter, whose beauty, at that solemn moment, was heightened by the tears she was shedding. He implored her to have more resignation to the will of Providence.

Vain efforts! Hélène heard him, but paid no heed to him; she could only see one thing: that her son had been taken from her forever.

While this scene of desolation as prolonged in the family's apartment, in which thick darkness had reigned for some time, its density augmented by the blackness of the clouds, the peasants of R***, of both sexes, who were to maintain vigil over the dead, met in the kitchen of the château and made preparations for their sad duty by surrendering to the pleasures of the table. Wine circulated in large bottles of black glass, and they drank to the health of the honorable company. From time to time, the insensitivity of that social class allowed some coarse joke to escape, bringing involuntary laughter to the lips of its hearers, who soon quelled the outbursts, whose cause contrasted too strongly with the mourning with which the house was filled.

The conversation did not dry up, however; it changed its subject often, but always came back to the evens of the previous night.

"Look," said Germaine, "at what becomes of us—that poor Raoul, yesterday so sprightly, today lying dead in the next room!"

"And do you think that his soul, which you do not mention," said a decrepit old woman whose sinister gaze made the village children tremble when it alighted upon them, "is now at peace? Ha! Having died without confession, like a ewe whose throat has been cut! Will it leave us tranquil? Will it not come back to torment us on Christmas Eve, because it is suffering itself?"

"That's just like you. Mère Pernot," replied a laborer. "You wouldn't be content if you missed an opportunity to frighten us. Why should brave Raoul, who was always good to us during his life, come to harass us now that he's dead?"

"With his sins unconfessed?"

"Do you know that? Are you sure of the contrary? Besides, he fulfilled all his duties; he was standing next to me at mass last Sunday."

"Marvelous, Nicolas, for Raoul—but did the young lady who lives nearby go to mass? Did she ever let us know what her religion was? God's wrath had already manifested itself against her: the burning of the house that she had bought, her domestic burned before her eyes. She didn't heed any of those warnings, and she perished, while doubtless promising herself a long life She tried to reckon with death—extreme folly! She's there, and we're here!"

"And we're drinking to her health," replied a local miller, whose colossal build and extraordinary strength were objects of public admiration. "Let's hope that she's content in her grave and won't rise up from it."

At this point, a stifled groan was heard. All the villagers started in surprise; fear appeared in more than one face, and the man who had just spoken showed no less pusillanimity.

Midnight chimed on the staircase clock, and they heard the strokes echoing in the silence.

"Who would have sighed?" one of interlocutors finally asked.

"The young lady, perhaps," the old woman resumed. "She wanted to thank the four-maker for the good wishes he expressed for her health."

"Come on, Mère Pernot," said the miller. "No bad jokes. Let's leave things as they are and not go back over the past."

A second groan reached the company's ears, and they all uttered simultaneous cries of fright and confusion.

"Holy Virgin, protect us!" exclaimed Germaine. "That came from the room where the corpse of the lady is lying. My God! Who will have courage enough to go and make sure of it?"

None of those present responded to this appeal. Meanwhile, the voice was heard for a third time, in a manner so distinct that it was necessary to yield to the evidence. Terror then took hold of the bewildered company.

They hastened to get away from so fearful a place and several went to the château door while others made the decision to go and wake the surgeon—who had not wanted to leave Madame Delmont until she was calmer—and told him what had happened.

To begin with, he accused their fear of having given rise to the incident. On the multiple assurances he received as to the reality of the fact, however, he did not hesitate to get up from his bed, on which he had thrown himself fully clothed, and go down to the room from which the sounds that had caused the scare were coming.

Delmont, who was not asleep, having heard an extraordinary tumult, was curious as to its cause. Perceiving that his wife, succumbing to the excess of her weakness, had fallen sleep, he set off for the staircase, where he encountered the doctor, about to go down. As they descended the stairs, the latter told him that a terror doubtless born of panic had frightened all those who were maintaining the nocturnal vigil.

Neither of them, listening to the storm that was still rumbling outside, doubted that the whistling of the unleashed winds had been mistaken for lugubrious groans by the superstitious villagers, ever ready to attribute miraculous origins to the simplest occurrences. They continued their march and, followed by the crowd that was not yet reassured, reached the room where the foreigner's body had been placed, which was illuminated by several lamps.

As they crossed the threshold, there was a further groan; it was no longer permissible to doubt that it had emerged from the bier itself. The majority of the rural contingent immediately resumed its flight, but its braver members stayed when they heard the colonel and the doctor exclaim, simultaneously: "The poor woman's still alive! Oh, we must save her from the horror of her situation!"

Hastily, they drew nearer to the coffin in which Alinska was lying. They lifted her up gently, and, without removing her shroud, carefully transported her to the room she had previously occupied.

During the journey, the doctor placed his hand on the hearted of the resuscitated woman, and confirmed that it had resumed beating, albeit very faintly. Immeasurably confounded by such a phenomenon, he swore to devote all his skill to the woman who had returned to life from the very arms of death. He asked the colonel to remove the linen with which the young beauty's head was covered.

Delmont obeyed. He examined the utterly discolored featured with an avid curiosity—and his surprise was extreme when the charming visage proved to him that it was the unfortunate and passionate Alinska that he was holding in his arms!

An exclamation escaped his lips. That would have acquainted an enlightened observer as to his state of mind, but the doctor, utterly absorbed in his reflections, was paying scant attention; he attributed it to the colonel's sensitivity without suspecting the truth. Delmont, moreover, wanted to hide it from the watchers; he suppressed the host of emotions that were assailing him, and, although he was disconcerted by the inconceivable and dolorous events that were afflicting him from every direction, his facial expression was no more distressed than before his discovery.

The doctor asked the laborers to leave, wanting to be left alone with the women—who, emboldened as soon as the imaginary peril was averted, claimed the right to care for a person of their own sex. The colonel left the apartment himself—but before leaving, he went to the physician and, in a transport that he could not master, implored him to employ all the resources of his profession to bring the unfortunate woman back from the doors of the tomb into which she had just descended.

"Have no fear, Colonel," the doctor replied. "I am determined to conclude successfully a cure that has presented itself in a marvelous aspect. Medical art, perhaps, will be able to do a great deal; believe however, that greatest of scientific prodigies are the prerogative of Nature; she alone can bring about such astonishing returns. I would have sworn that the pistol-shot had killed the young woman on the spot; all the symptoms of animation had disappeared. If she survives, I shall regard it less as a cure than a resurrection, the cause of which will be forever hidden from us."

After hearing these words, which gave him some hope, Delmont went away slowly, no longer knowing what to think, so confused was his mind. He returned to his wife, who was still enjoying the unhealthy rest of a lethargic sleep.

How dolorous her awakening would be! How would she feel, on hearing the news of the foreign woman's return to life, while her son had not been subject to a similar phenomenon?

Chapter XIV

Among all the events that had disturbed the life of Colonel Delmont, the appearance of the Hungarian woman Alinska in the depths of France and in the Château de R*** was undoubtedly the most surprising.

The energetic character of the young woman, whom he had mistreated, and her extreme amorous passion, of which she gave him the most striking evidence by her presence, imported emotions into his heart of which he still could not take account.

It was not solely to reproach him for his perjury that she had traversed so many countries; she must want more, and he shuddered to think of the painful scenes she had prepared for him. On the other hand, and by one of those eccentricities so commonplace in the human mind, the man who would have been delighted never to see the woman again, now dreaded the prospect of losing her, and would have given a substantial fraction of his fortune to have the assurance that she would recover her health. He told himself that he wanted to have at least one more conversation with her; that it was necessary for him to hear from her own lips the story of everything that she had had to do to reach R***. Thus, under the mask of simple curiosity, Delmont disguised from himself the new presence of a dangerous sentiment.

While he was occupied with all these things, however, he promised himself to bury them in his bosom, and never to light the flame of jealousy in Hélène's soul by confidences whose dangerous effect he could appreciate. He resolved to treat Alinska as a stranger, to the extent that it was possible, unless, by some imprudence, the latter obliged him to make a belated revelation.

In the meantime, his anxiety did not permit him to remain at ease. The death of his beloved son, and that of Raoul, to whom he was so firmly attached, procured further anguish whose bitterness was extreme. In the former instance, he saw the object of his paternal affections and hopes disappear; in the latter, he lost a friend whose affection had been indubitable and who would have been a useful confidant in the present circumstances. It was, therefore, entirely natural that he should mingle his grief with that of his wife, and that, by her side, he should be apprehensive of the daylight that would soon return.

One fatal concern still troubled him: he did not want to know, and above all, did not want his wife to divine, the cruel moment that would remove the remains of their child forever. It was with a continual shudder that the slightest unexpected noise reached his ears. He trembled then, and hugged his wife involuntarily, as if to announce to her the consummation of their misfortune.

Thanks to the cares of an officious neighbor and those of the sensitive parish priest, a profound silence presided over the removal of the bodies, which took place at daybreak. The funeral ceremony only commenced at a considerable distance from the château, and the *vent de Sers*, which was blowing impetuously, bore the funeral chants and the mortuary knell away in the opposite direction.

Madame Delmont had formed the dolorous intention of seeing the remains of her son one more time, but when she asked for them they were already at rest in the holy ground, and the intensity of her despair increased when it became certain that nothing of her Eugène remained to her any longer but a heart-rending memory.

Entirely occupied in bringing to this grief, which he shared vehemently, consolations that he had difficulty finding in his own heart, the colonel almost forgot that Alinska was close at hand. It was not until the day was well-advanced that he thought if asking Monsieur Mélervant—that was the doctor's name—for news of her.

The doctor had come to find him. "I've already told you," he said, "that there's something inexplicable in the matter of this young woman, for which I've sought in vain to account. Never has any return to life been so unexpected. Will she live, though? I still can't be sure. The wound is very dangerous, and another, which must seemingly have extended all the way to the heart, must already have put her existence in imminent danger."

"Another wound, you say? You surprise me, doctor. I thought I heard, on my arrival, that the young woman had been struck by a single pistol-shot."

"I didn't say that the wound was recent. It was opened some time ago by a trenchant instrument; far from having scarred over, it's still bloody. It has a peculiar character, which, I admit, lies beyond my meager knowledge. In any other individual, it would suggest to me an urgent peril, and yet it seems that the lady has been freely fulfilling all the functions of life for a long time without being hindered by a wound that should have consigned her to the grave. She certainly cannot complain about the admirable constitution with which nature has endowed her. She has another rather peculiar feature: her left hand is covered by a glove, made from very thick hide. I tried to cut it off, in order to render the unfortunate woman full freedom of movement, but as soon as I touched it, her arm was subject to an unparalleled agitation, and the hand, open at first, closed with so much force that I was unable to accomplish my intention."

"Everything that you have told me, Doctor, causes me considerable surprise. Don't be repelled, I implore you; think how imperiously humanity commands us to take care of this unfortunate woman. Besides, she alone can enlighten us as to the details of everything that happened on that disastrous night; perhaps we'll be able to obtain useful information from her that will enable us to catch the wretches whose crime, fruitless for them, has nevertheless been so fatal for us."

"Your insistence is unnecessary, Colonel. In addition to the accomplishment of the duty to which I am submissive in embracing my profession, I shall not hide from you the fact that the woman inspires a keen interest in me. The rare perfection of her form and the beauty of her face have, I admit while blushing, cast an unparalleled disturbance into my senses. I would like, in rendering life to her, to obtain more than gratitude. Why does that confession disturb you? Does it seem reprehensible?"

"Who, me, doctor? What right would I have to blame you? It merely seems to me that everything that is happening within us and around us is now extraordinary. Here you are, in love with someone whom you did not know yesterday—and it's while she belongs are to death than life that she has already made your conquest. What will happen when she combines those physical advantages with the more attractive mental qualities that she must doubtless possess?"

"Permit me to say to you, Colonel, that you're treating this matter very lightly. I don't understand your frivolity."

"Oh! Forgive my agitation, my dear Doctor—I don't know what I'm doing, grief has annihilated my faculties to such an extent. You're making me realize that my speech is reflecting the confusion of my soul. In my situation, alas, whose torment you cannot fully appreciate, it's permissible to seem to be ignoring the rules of politeness—which, I flatter myself, I do not neglect at other times."

Far from contradicting what it was trying to say, this speech, by virtue of the incoherence of the statements comprising it, gave the doctor unequivocal proof that the colonel, still overwhelmed by grief, had not entirely recovered the exercise of his intelligence. He did not suspect that a secret cause, a rapid impulse of jealousy, had made Delmont speak.

The latter, ashamed of having momentarily forgotten his resolution and almost given Mélervant the opportunity to read his thoughts, preferred to let him believe that the excess of affliction had partly robbed him of his mental rectitude. He was not entirely satisfied until he was able to read in his interlocutor's eyes the proof that the latter attributed the strange carelessness of his words to the recent loss he had suffered. Reassured on this point, he changed the subject, and asked the physician not to leave the château except for an extreme emergency, so long as the wounded lady and Madame Delmont had need of his presence.

"This place," Mélervant said, "will henceforth by my headquarters, until further notice. I swear to you that I shall only leave it temporarily, and solely in the case that an unexpected accident imperiously demands my presence elsewhere. Have no fear—I know the duty I owe to such misfortunes."

Then Delmont asked whether he might be admitted to the foreign woman's presence, in order to pay her the visit that convention demanded.

"You are free to do so, Monsieur, but our compliments will be addressed, for some time yet, to an almost-inanimate body. The lady will remain unconscious for a fortnight, at least. The loss of blood she has suffered will maintain her in that weakness, and we ought to be glad if she is able to answer our questions when a month has elapsed after the date of incident."

"We must be patient until then," the colonel replied, in a tone that he tried to render indifferent. "It will be you, Doctor, who will guide us in what we have to do. Needless to say, I am investing you with the most absolute authority in this matter."

Mélervant replied to this politeness with a simple nod of the head.

Suddenly, the door to Madame Delmont's room opened and Germaine appeared, announcing that her mistress had just fainted. At this distressing news, the two men concluded their conversation in order to hasten to the duties to which sentiment summoned them.

For several days, Madame Delmont repeatedly suffered these fits of weakness, occasioned by the excess of the grief that she was nurturing. Nothing could any longer distract her; entirely possessed by a single thought, she resisted everything opposed to it.

Alinska was destined to deceive all the doctor's calculations. Her health was re-established in less time than he had predicted, and he was not the one who had the joy of being the first to hear the beautiful individual speak.

A week after the disastrous event, Delmont, who had already come to the Hungarian woman's room several times to obtain news of her, found the nurse anxious that her breakfast had not arrived. He thought he should offer to let her go in search of it, while he promised to watch over the invalid, promising not to leave before she returned.

The nurse, charmed by such kindness, and perhaps fearing that the colonel might take it back, took him at his word and left immediately.

At first, Delmont, left alone in the presence of the important object of his first love, stood motionless beside Alinska's bed, and soon abandoned himself to a dolorous reverie, while contemplating that wan complexion, those hollow cheeks and those firmly-closed eyes. The Hungarian woman's immobility was complete. Only a sight respiration proved that she was still clinging to life by a feeble thread.

"Poor creature!" Delmont whispered. "Is this how I have to see you again, and to which your fatal affection has led you?"

A sigh, escaping from Alinska's lips, reached the colonel's ears, procuring a painful sensation. He leaned closer. Soon, he saw the eyelids that he was examining so intently flutter, almost undetectably. Her eyes, gleaming at last, turned toward him. At the same time, a red flush covered Alinska's face, and her mouth pronounced Edouard's name.

"Alinska!" the colonel said in his turn, almost suffocated by the violence of the sensation he experienced. "Do you recognize me? Oh, what an object of horror I ought to be to you!"

"Do you love me, Edouard?"

At that unexpected question, which it was not easy to answer, Delmont stood as if petrified. His tongue was ready to pronounce a reassuring word, but his reason—perhaps the truth—held back that which was about to escape him. All he could do was cover his face with his hands, and he maintained a profound silence.

"Edouard, my cruel and dear friend, do you want to give me the death that I have escaped?"

Oh, how frightful it seemed to the man to whom that reproach was addressed not to reassure the unfortunate woman, who seemed to have been reborn in order to find him again, at the very moment when existence had returned the full reality of the chagrin that had been weighing on his heart for a long time! On the other hand, could Delmont maintain a fatal hope with a deliberate lie? Was he not Hélène's husband? Was his affection for her not founded on esteem and virtue?

All these thoughts, and a thousand other sentiments, battled within him. He was still in doubt when a stifled sigh attracted his attention imperiously. He hesitated no longer in directing his gaze at Alinska; he recognized, fearfully, that she had just fallen unconscious again. The transient color was no longer in her cheeks, and her eyelids were lowered again.

Dreading that he might have delivered the fatal blow to the wretched creature, the colonel launched himself impetuously out of the room, shouting loudly for the doctor and the household staff. They all came running, full of alarm. He told them that the foreigner, who had initially seemed to recover her senses and who had even pronounced a few words, had soon fallen back into a prostration that might be very dangerous.

"She spoke, you say!" cried the doctor. "She spoke! Are you quite sure? That seems impossible, Monsieur. If it's really true though, I can no longer be sure of anything regarding that indefinable being."

101

Having recovered from his initial seizure, Delmont assured the surgeon that the invalid had said something like: "Where am I? Who's there?" That was not how she had expressed herself, of course, but the colonel was careful not to reveal the distressing truth.

Mélervant found that Alinska had a pronounced fever. He did not hide the fact that the danger was presenting itself in a sinister form, and that the foreigner must have experienced a revolution whose consequences might become deadly.

At these words, Delmont felt an internal thunderbolt strike him. Fearing that he might be unable to control his poignant emotions, he hastened to withdraw, and went into the great hall, where he walked back and forth for more than an hour, without daring either to go back to his wife or to return to the room where Alinska might be about to render her last sigh.

Oh, how sharply he reproached himself, at that moment, for the errors of his youth, and the unpardonable sin that he had committed in seeking to ignite in the frank and sensitive Alinska a flame that would have such cruel results! He had been thoughtless then; he believed that love disappeared as easily as it arose; he had not known that the passion in question, ordinarily so frail, becomes eternal when it acts on certain personalities. He had obtained the proof of that in Alinska's constancy; nothing had been able to distract her from her affection. Distance, absence, bad behavior had slid over her heart without cooling it, and it still conserved all the delirium of the passion that had intoxicated it before. What torments, and what combats had prepared that fever of the soul!

He saw the future through a frightful cloud, and abandoned himself to his destiny. Was he not equally tormented by the rivalry of sorts that seemed ready to arise between him and the doctor? The latter, still young, might contrive, by is qualities and the grace of his face and figure, to inspire a tender attachment. He would pursue Alinska; perhaps he would even ask the colonel to speak on his behalf—and Delmont felt incapable of doing so.

As we have said, the Hungarian woman, deceiving all probability, continued to make rapid progress toward her cure. Scarcely twenty days had gone by, and she was already able to sit up in bed, say a few words and respond to brief questions addressed to her—but she was not in any state to undertake the narration of the events of the night that had been so disastrous for her.

At that point, Madame Delmont had only made one attempt to see her. The sight of the foreigner reminded her so sharply of Eugène's death that, on entering Alinska's room, she lost the use of her senses and required more than an hour to recover. Abundant tears soothed her anguish temporarily, and after a silent visit she returned to her apartment.

Although deprived of the society of the mistress of the house, Alinska was not alone. Mélervant was glad to stay with her, to the extent that his occupation permitted. Delmont, drawn by an irresistible sentiment, often came to see her, although he swore to himself every day that he would make his visits less frequent—but he arranged things in such a manner as never to be alone with her;

he feared a second confrontation, which might have led to results as troublesome as the first.

The Hungarian woman had already tried in vain, several times, to send away the unwelcome witnesses; her efforts had not been crowned with success. Delmont was careful not to be caught out, and he always withdrew at any moment when he might have been left alone with the victim of ill-starred love.

At such decisive moments, an extreme resentment burst forth in Alinska's expression, ordinarily so impassive. She sought by her gaze to retain beside her the man who dreaded the just bitterness of her reproaches; and whenever she saw him draw away, she abandoned herself to an anger that anyone remaining in the room had to suffer, and which sometimes even fell upon the doctor.

The latter, ever more infatuated with the foreigner, bore these outbursts—of whose cause he had no suspicion—with a rare patience, attributing them solely to the violence of physical pain. He tried, by means of caring words and deeds, to restore calm to an agitated soul. He declared that excitement and anger were greatly to be feared in such situations, and that one could only hope to be cured by complete mental calm. A mocking smile was almost always the response that this kind of threat provoked; then Alinska seemed to treat him with the disdainful superiority adopted by those who think they know better toward the person they suspect of inferiority.

Mélervant endured these caprices with admirable patience. He awaited a reward that, in his view, would compensate him for all that he had suffered.

After two weeks, just as winter was beginning to weigh upon the countryside, Alinska declared that she was able to get up. In response to this statement, the doctor uttered what were almost cries of despair. He assured the invalid that her weakness was still too extreme to allow her to satisfy her desire; that she ought to be patient at least until the new year; and that whatever vigor Alinska's constitution might have recovered, he would not answer for a relapse if she did not reign herself to remaining in bed.

She made no reply, as had been her invariable habit throughout her illness when anyone said anything to her that she did not like. When the doctor had gone, though, she asked the nurse to go to the parlor to fetch a fruit she wanted—and as soon as she was alone, she hastened to get dressed.

The nurse's surprise, when she returned, as great; she lamented the boldness with which Alinska had ignored the doctor's prescription, and threatened her with the latter's severe indignation if he did not find her in bed when he returned.

That threat did not frighten its addressee. After having taken a few steps around the room, she sent word to Madame Delmont, asking whether the latter would consent to receive her.

Chapter XV

Madame Delmont, and her husband even more so, were far from expecting to see Alinska appear before them. Fearing that her impatience might lead her to abuse her health, instead of yielding to her desire, they both went to her room.

"What are you doing, Madame?" Hélène said, as they went in. "Is this how docile you are to the instructions of our doctor? He has prescribed a more prolonged retreat for you, and here you are, without his authorization, seeking liberty therefrom."

"I have the highest opinion of the doctor's talents," Alinska replied, "but I believe that medicine has its limits, beyond which it no longer has the faculty of perceiving anything. Our friend, as I am glad to call him, judges my condition according to what he has seen before in circumstances that seem to him to be similar—but everything about me must deceive him; I enjoy an extraordinary existence. I cannot die completely, and you have proof of that. Must I then, when I feel my strength increasing, submit to advice that can only prolong my convalescence? I feel well; I want to act in consequence."

Since she had first welcomed the foreigner to the château, Madame Delmont had learned that it was futile to contest her will; in the present instance, she did not try. She contented herself with telling her that she ought to know, better than anyone else, what she could do, and the prudence would doubtless always be her guide.

The colonel maintained a profound silence. It was almost as if we were seeing Alinska again for the first time; he contemplated, with bleak compassion, the ravages that misfortune and suffering had inflicted on that beautiful face.

The young Hungarian woman had lost the bright coloration of her charms; her eyes seemed inanimate—and yet she still merited the attraction of gazes, and the inspiration of love. She still had her rich figure, the regularity of her features, and the grace embellishing the whole—and, more than all of that, a physiognomy imprinted with a profound melancholy. It displayed the anguish of her soul, inspiring a constant need to soothe her woes, to render her the happiness for which she had been created.

For her part, Alinska treated the colonel with that cool politeness which announces that the person we are addressing is unknown to us. She controlled her own sentiments, in order that they should not burst forth involuntarily. When she was certain, however, that an indifferent witness could not catch her, however, her gaze became animated; it launched bitter reproaches at Delmont, or sometimes seemed to say: come back, and all will be forgiven.

He understood these mysterious advances all too clearly; he thought, however, that he could withstand them, recklessly forgetting that it is necessary, in order to overcome perils of that sort, not to confront them but to flee them. Lovers, who imagine that a chain long since broken cannot be reconnected, you will be conclusively undeceived in your expectation; two hearts that have loved one another, and which find one another again, are almost always reunited.

While these individuals were engaged in benevolent conversation, the doctor came back from the journey he had been obliged to make to the commune of Falgarde. Already, since arriving to the château, he had been told what scant attention the foreigner had paid to his strict advice. He came to pick a fight, but his anger disappeared completely when he saw her in a condition that proved, in a positive manner, her complete well-being.

"I see, Madame," he nevertheless said to her, "that my cares are no longer useful to you; henceforth, you alone have the right to guide yourself. You have freed yourself from my authority—may you have nothing to regret!"

"Why do you want me to have no further recourse to your rare talents, Monsieur?" she replied. "They will always be necessary, when nature abandons me. Believe that my strength has now returned completely. My heart, which breathes more freely in recovering it energy, is filled as before with the gratitude that you inspire therein. Permit it to offer you a feeble mark thereof, and don't insult it by refusing."

As she concluded this speech, Alinska picked up from a table a superb diamond ring, of very considerable value. She presented it to the doctor—who, taken completely by surprise, did not know what he ought to do. He would have preferred to refuse a gift that he thought excessive in relation to his care, and he would have liked the young beauty to discharge her debt to him in another way, but Alinska was so imposing when she sought to distance herself from the appearance of familiarity, that he only refused the valuable gift half-heartedly. She pressed him again, with so much grace and perseverance, that he was forced to give in. Sighing, he took the ring, placed it on his finger, and could not help making it known to the colonel, by means of a glance, that this was not the manner in which he had wanted Alinska to recognize the care he had lavished upon her.

Madame Delmont was impatient for the revelation to be made of everything that had happened on the frightful night whose memory would only perish with her. At the same time, she felt incapable of listening to the sad details. Not wishing, however, to delay the story expected of the foreigner, she got up from her chair and, having repeated her compliments on the subject of Alinska's fortunate cure, left her along with the colonel and the doctor, who were charged with receiving her declarations.

Alinska shivered when a demand was made of her on that subject; they could see in her face how reluctant she was to have to turn her attention to the disagreeable matter. She remained silent momentarily, either to collect herself or in the hope that the question might not be repeated. She was disappointed; Delmont renewed the request, in an unsteady voice.

Even more emotional, Alinska turned her beautiful eyes—which took on an expression that they did not usually exhibit—toward the colonel, apparently disposed to obey him. "Madame Delmont," she began, "exhausted by fatigue, had asked me to watch in her stead the dear and unfortunate child that she has lost..."

At this point, the colonel uttered a bitter sigh. Disturbed, Alinska stopped, and a dolorous expression rapidly contracted her features. She hesitated before going on, but finally, gathering her resolve, she continued.

"I could not refuse that generous lady anything, and in spite of my reluctance, of which I could take no account—and which was, in the event, to prove justified—I agreed to spend the night with poor Eugène. At about midnight, sleep—which had rarely closed my eyelids for some years—assailed me with so much force that, struggling in vain against it, I realized that I had to yield to it. I leaned my head against the back of an armchair and my eyelids closed in a matter of seconds. I cannot tell you anything about what happened between that moment and the one in which I was abruptly awakened by a distinct noise.

"I opened my eyes and, by the light of the Moon, I saw four armed men in the room, who were coming toward me. Terror did not permit me to raise the alarm by calling for help. One of them took me by the arm; another advanced toward the child's bed. Then the door of the room opened violently. Raoul suddenly appeared. Two pistol-shots were fired. Could I tell by whom? I don't know. The second hit me, and I fell, thinking that I would never get up again.

"The brigands had undoubtedly got in through the window, for I heard my nurse say that a rope ladder had been found hanging down to the foot of the wall. I can't confirm that myself; I only saw the murderers and the death for which they had certainly destined me. It is equally impossible for me to be sure of the exact cause of your son's death. Was that the moment that he died? Did his fear bring it forward? Alas, he is unable to tell you, and no mortal knows the secret of his death."

Thus Alinska told the story, and no one could contest its veracity. She alone had survived; those who could have contradicted her, and perhaps known better, had been forever exiled from the earth, where crime and lies too often triumph over honesty and virtue.

Such feeble enlightenments did not offer any clarification. No trace had been found of the murderers, in spite of the most active searches. They had, however, been seen. An unequivocal witness had confirmed their appearance; the dead Raoul and a half-dead woman were certain proof that a horrible crime had been committed; a helpless child had been another deplorable victim of it.

Delmont and Mélervant lost themselves in reflection, while Alinska fell back into her customary impassivity. She expressed the desire to her interlocutors to be left alone for a while—in order, she said, to give her weakened senses an opportunity to recover from the mental shock that her story had just caused her to experience. Such a desire was an order, which Delmont and the doctor obeyed. They left immediately, and both went to inform Madame Delmont of what they had just been told.

The latter was largely unaffected by the story. It told her nothing about her son; the mystery of his unexpected death remained unclarified. The rest scarcely mattered to her; she saw nothing in it but a commonplace attack by brigands, which, without being crowned by success, had nevertheless been bloody.

From that moment on, Alinska resumed the course of her everyday life. Almost always shut in her room, she generally only showed herself at meal times, but after dinner, she sometimes consented to spend the evening with the family. Her conversation then was grave and melancholy; she seemed to have entirely forgotten her passion for the colonel and the words she had pronounced during their first interview. She was an incomprehensible being, who was, in sum, motivated by the most delirious affection, although a complete indifference was painted on all her features!

On observing this conduct, Delmont became less vigilant every day in avoiding an encounter that the Hungarian woman no longer seemed to desire. He went as far as to imagine that the terrible shock that Alinska's mind had experienced, and the blood that she had lost, might have extinguished the flames in her heart while her vital principle was being renewed. Such an effect, produced by such a cause, would have been very fortunate for him.

On the other hand, he sometimes forgot himself to the extent of contemplating with too much interest the charming features that love had once engraved in his memory. He compared them, involuntarily, in their imposing and energetic vivacity, to the calmer and perhaps more delicate features of the virtuous Hélène, and the latter lost all that the others were able to gain. Delmont was a man, and, like all his sex, he possessed a portion of the deadly propensity that bears us imperiously, less toward gentle and modest beauties, but toward those which deploy, in order to tempt us, the impetuosity of a firm character. Self-regard, in those circumstances, often comes to the aid of an exaggerated sentiment; it is flattered by the efforts that are made to please it; perhaps it over-values them, while almost disdaining a simple and natural affection that does not lend itself to disorderly impulses.

For Delmont, Alinska had quit her family and homeland; to cherish him, she had vanquished the effects of absence and forgotten his blameworthy behavior. She presented her attractions and passionate sentiments boldly, while Hélène, having tranquilly collected her husband's homage, had surrendered her hand to him—and since their union had been concluded had, it is true, shown herself affectionate, but without getting carried away, without delirium.

The two rivals were, therefore, contending for the same heart with unequal weapons. Could the victory be in doubt? We do not think so. The rights of duty are very weak, when they are not sustained by the vivacity of an ardent love.

All the horrors of winter were then in full force. Sometimes, rain rendered the roads impassable; sometimes, the icy blast of the north wind froze the sodden ground, and permitted excursions. Then the colonel recovered his liking for heroic amusement; he went to hunt swift hares or the birds of the air—which, in that inhospitable season, had difficulty finding shelter in the trees denuded of their leaves, and nourishment that heavy frosts prevented them from taking in the fields.

One morning, when rime covered the ground, the Sun rose in all its customary pomp. A little light mist, spread through the hollows of the valleys, brightened their tenebrous masses; they rose into the air, and the gentle breeze was sufficient to dissipate them. Edouard thought that the occasion was favorable to try out a superb hunting-dog that he had previously purchased, and, without informing Madame Delmont or Alinska, he went out early, rifle in hand, and directed his steps toward the hill that rose up to Mervilla.

The game, continually pursued by numerous enemies, disappeared into that region every day. In order to encounter a few specimens, Delmont was obliged to cover a considerable amount of terrain. He passed successively though the communes of Péchabou, Pompertusat, Deymes and Montbrun, and returned via Coronsac.

Finally, wearied by a prolonged march, which had nevertheless been fruitless, he paused to rest for a while before returning to the château, to which the hour fixed for dinner was calling him.

Not far away, on the slope of a steep hill, nature has placed fairly extensive reservoirs on three separate planes, alimented by a fecund spring whose source never dried up. Beautiful trees—a few Italian poplars, centenarian oaks and Oriental willows, and a host of saplings—decorate the place in question, which, by virtue of its situation, its coolness and the shade with which it is covered when springtime reanimates nature, offers a delightful refuge to a weary traveler, friends who enjoy being together, and lovers happy to hide there from the gazes of unwelcome company. The view one has from that spot is quite extensive; it takes in fertile and woody ridges, is animated by numerous habitations and is encircled by a vast horizon, the angular snow-covered peaks of the Pyrenees.

At the present moment, the Viviers,[28] as they are named in the locality, had lost a significant part of their amenities; the universal mourning-dress of winter was triumphant here, as it was everywhere else in the region; only a few vigorous brambles and the evergreen ivy ornamented them with their various garlands. A few benches, hollowed out in an inconsistent rock, offered a comfortable seat to Delmont. He took advantage of it and, leaning on the butt of his rifle, fell into a profound reverie, whose charm was enhanced by the monotonous and continuous sound of a spring, which, passing through a conduit in the wood, tumbled from the upper basin into the middle one.

A thousand thoughts assailed Edouard in turn, but in the midst of their conflict, those that related to the time of his early youth did not take long to eclipse all the others. He saw himself still in the foothills of the cold mountains of Hungary; he remembered that, during the rigors of one long winter, he had often

---

[28] A *vivier* is a fish-pond.

roamed snow-covered landscapes in the company of a woman who had then seemed to him to be an angel.

At that moment, his memory brought to mind the words of a ballad that he had composed for Alinska, in those happy times when a transient jealousy sometimes stirs the heart of the most cherished lover. Ceding to the desire to repeat it in its entirety, he raised his voice and sang, almost without being aware of it.[29]

No, no, I'm beloved no more
You've no more affection for me;
Of the dream I had formed before
Your caprice had destroyed the glee;
To deceive love shocked to the core,
Believe me, requires no fine key
No, no, I'm beloved no more
You've no more affection for me.

You no longer feel when away
The fear born of separation;
When I come back to you to stay
No love's in your alienation.
Coldly you've told me the score;
Another has stolen your amity
No, no, I'm beloved no more
You've no more affection for me.

Your eyes paint naught but rejection,
No longer a smile on your face;
Your gaze does not change direction
When I speak or stare into space.
Your heart has no longer in store
Delight or caresses, I see
No, no, I'm beloved no more
You've no more affection for me.

He had just concluded the final couplet, and did not yet appear to have emerged from his reverie, when he was suddenly snatched therefrom by the sound made by a few clods of earth falling into the waters of the pond. He raised his head to discover the cause, and it was not without an extreme emotion that he saw Alinska, about whom he had just been thinking so forcefully, coming

---

[29] The title attached to this piece in the text simply reproduces its first line, and the subtitle confirms its identification as a ballad. Again, the music is appended.

down a little stairway turning round the basin, decorated with a rustic wooden balustrade, which terminated near the seat on which Delmont was sitting.

The colonel could only avoid the Hungarian woman by making his escape through the fields, which he could not do without violating all the rules of propriety. He was incapable of acting thus; even so, he was anxious as to the consequences of this meeting, whose dangers he appreciated in full.

Unable to master his initial surprise, he got up precipitately, while the young beauty, perhaps experiencing sentiments similar to his own, stopped on a bridge set in the middle of the path. Resting her hand on the frail balustrade, she seemed to lose the use of her senses.

They stood like that for some time, in one another's presence, uncertain as to what to do. Alinska, however, resumed her progress, after making a violent gesture as if to give herself the courage she lacked. Coming down the last few steps, she came to confront Delmont.

Chapter XVI

"Do I inspire you with some fatal desire to draw away from me?" she said, her voice oppressed. "Can you not look at me without dread? Has it been necessary for me to rely on hazard to find myself in your company?"

Thus attacked, Edouard felt compelled to reply, but at the same time, he feared not being able to restrict his words with an appropriate moderation, and the discomfort of his situation seemed to be extreme.

"Alas," he replied, "is it appropriate for us to be in one another's company? Have not events, which obliterate all determination, separated us forever? Should I have expected to see you again in this extremity of France, Alinska, when the bonds that united us have been violently severed?"

"And by whom, Edouard, was that done? Is it me, or you, who ought to merit that reproach? Time alone has passed between us. My feeble attractions might have disappeared, but my heart has not changed. You are acquiring the sad proof of it at this moment; it ought to be crushing you."

"I have no need of your presence, Alinska, to address reproaches to me that I have addressed to myself for a long time. The errors of my youth present themselves to my gaze in the blackest colors. I know how you were deceived, and my conscience continually retraces the image of the past. But what can we do now? Present circumstances cannot cease to exist. Our situation is painful; we have no alternative, however, but to support it courageously; that is what destiny commands."

"You're explaining yourself, Edouard, in a very obscure manner. Speak to me frankly; let me find no awkwardness in your replies or our person; tell me what you think and I'll express myself with a similar honesty."

"How would it be possible for me to untangle what is in my heart? Should I, even if I could? Am I not constrained by imperious bonds? Do they not command me? Be more generous than me, Alinska; make the necessary sacrifice voluntarily. Forget me, if you can..."

"You're right to employ doubt in treating that important point. I'm like you, Edouard; I too have my weaknesses, perhaps my errors. You have not hesitated to abandon me, to offer to another the faith that you had pledged to me; I could not triumph over my sentiments, even when their futility was manifest. I know that my presence is unwelcome to you, but I cannot go away. I know that no hope remains to me, and yet I am content to cherish a vain chimera. Why do you expect me to be superior to you? That which you were unable to conserve for me, I feel incapable of stealing from you."

"What you say, Alinska, redoubles my profound despair. I would give my life for it not to be the case—for you to savor the pleasures of existence in peace, tranquil and therefore happy."

"There are, Edouard," Alinska replied, with a sinister expression, "wishes that can no longer be granted. There is no longer any peace and happiness on earth for me. No more shall I recover it when I go to lie down in the last abode—and it's you alone that I ought to blame for that cruel misfortune. You would give your life for me, you say? That sacrifice is not in your power. Do you not belong to me already? Is that not written in your own blood?"

"I don't deny that I gave you the monument of my love. But what resource can that vain script, which my conduct has belied, offer to you now? Our laws do not recognize it, and my union is indissoluble."

"Your laws! Always your laws! Will I never hear talk of anything else? What do the formalities that men have chosen to consecrate matter to me? They are futile, in spite of their apparent gravity; they are, above all, as transient as those who have instituted them. I have no wish to descend to reproaching you for your perjury before the tribunals of your homeland; I would do better to heed that of the incorruptible Being who does not makes decisions based on words, but on the cases themselves. He it was you recognized as your natural judge when you sealed the promise not to take any other woman than your Alinska. Tremble, wretch, lest He punish you for your perjury. Do you know all the means that He might use to strike you directly in the heart?"

"Calm down, poor Alinska. Don't get carried away. Since I can no longer offer you my hand, suffer that a purer sentiment replace an impetuous affection. You can no longer be my lover; be my friend. Content yourself with that sacred title, that it might link us together again by a chain that, less brilliant that that of love, will certainly be more durable."

The Hungarian woman seemed to have powerful objections to make to the colonel, but her somber physiognomy suddenly took on a more indifferent expression.

"Friendship, you say! Cold amity is all that Edouard can offer me in return for so many years of affection and suffering! I must either go away, to receive a few icy letters from afar, which will drive me to despair, or remain in his house, and there, witness to another's happiness, deliver myself to a continual torture! The choice is cruel. It is, nevertheless, impossible for me to demand another condition. Insensate that I was, a little while ago, when, hidden behind those trees. I heard a voice that went to my heart, repeating a song and words that I have not forgotten!"

"They must have given you proof that you have often been present in my thoughts, and that I remember, with bitter melancholy, times that were so happy for me. But Alinska, I beg you, save yourself, and save me from my despair. Make an effort of self-control, and don't seek to avenge yourself, although you warned me of that determination in that last and virulent letter..."

"Don't worry, Edouard; since the day when I wrote it, my ideas have taken a different course. It will not be by human means that I shall seek my vengeance; I can wait for certain superior events. Today, it depends less on my will than that of the punisher of all perjuries. I would even like to be able to renounce it, but any wishes I might form on that score would be futile; He will not retract the judgment that he has delivered."

The imposing tone that the young woman adopted in pronouncing these words inspired a sudden terror in Delmont. Accustomed, however, like all his peers, to treat affairs of the heart with excessive lightness, he felt at that moment that, if Providence was not conspicuous in its role as the protector of abandoned lovers, at least it commanded the punishment of their seducers with the perpetual reproaches of conscience.

Struck by an unexpected blow, Delmont tried to react against it, and, extending his hand to Alinska, he said: "I hope that our Creator will pardon my offense, if you will first be generous enough to forget it. Don't reject the hand I'm offering you like that, with cold disdain. Let's sign a peace treaty. Prove to me that you will be faithful to your promise, and that the tranquility my wife enjoys will not be troubled by you."

"And you, Edouard, are you able to pronounce the word *faithful* without shame? Can you tell me why I should be more faithful than you? After having broken the most sacred oaths, can you, who perhaps believe that you are a man of honor, ever believe that others might show more loyalty? Or have you descended so low in your own esteem that you're constrained to have a better opinion of others than of yourself? Anyway, I ask you, what does your wife's tranquility matter to me? Have you not destroyed mine? I shall seek to be superior to you in every respect; I shall only torment you. If I cannot vanquish myself completely, I shall show you no pity: you have treated me with such deliberate cruelty!"

The bitterness of this response completed the colonel's dejection; it seemed unbearable to hear, and yet was exempt from any exaggeration. In his despair, he paid no heed to the passing of time—that the sun had already reached the rim of the horizon, and that, in consequence, he ought to return to the château. Entirely preoccupied with his present situation, nothing could distract him from it.

Agitated as she was, Alinska thought of it on his behalf. "It's time for the evening meal," she said. "You can't continue hunting any longer without causing alarm to the woman whose tranquility is so dear to you. Follow that path—it will take you directly to the chateau. I'll go this way, over the crest of the hill. Farewell, Edouard; I have nothing more to say to you—but I dread the wrath of Heaven on your behalf!"

With these words, and without pausing any longer, Alinska went back up the little stairway carved into the hillside, and her rapid stride soon hid her from Delmont's gaze.

When he reached the top of the hill himself he searched with an anxious eye for the tracks of the woman who had been born to occupy his entire life.

It took him a considerable time to reach his home; the light was just disappearing when he arrived. The Hungarian woman had already returned; the colonel found her sitting beside Hélène, seemingly totally absorbed in her needlework.

The evening went by silently. Time had not yet deadened Madame Delmont's grief, having been unable to gain any purchase on her. She was almost always to be seen in constant immobility, holding a book whose pages she never turned, or inundating an item of embroidery with her tears. A bleak melancholy had taken possession of her; it was only briefly that, recovering the exercise of her consciousness, she testified to her husband that he was still dear to her.

She never allowed her daughter to be apart from her. If Juliette, carried away by her natural impetuosity, occasionally forgot her mother's instruction, the latter, launching herself out of the room in tears, shouted for her loudly, only seeming reassured when the child came back. She examined Juliette's cheerful face for hours on end; it seemed to her that the little girl was already infected by the deadly malady that had carried off her son; then her despair knew no bounds. The doctor gave her his most forceful assurances regarding her daughter's health, but in vain; he only succeeded imperfectly in suspending the anguish, which was reborn on the slightest pretext.

Edouard, distressed by the sight of such sadness, felt that it redoubled his own, and was afraid to leave his wife alone for a moment. On the other hand, he experienced in her presence all the torments of a sensitive soul violently racked. He saw that his wife, entirely occupied with Juliette did not perceive that she herself, by virtue of such excitement, was undermining her own vital principle. Already, a sinister pallor had appeared on her cheeks; her eyes were becoming hollow, and her labored breathing often became hoarse, as if she were being attacked by that frightful malady which never pauses in its murderous progress.

The following day, Mélervant came to the château. He arrived at the same time as the fastidious Monsieur Berneval.

The latter, still driven by his unquiet curiosity, was waiting very impatiently for the moment when he was finally encounter the mysterious foreigner, whose history seemed so intriguing, in Madame Delmont's drawing-room. He had already come several times, but Alinska had never offered herself to his sight. He no longer expected to see her, but, with great joy, he saw her sitting to the left of the fireplace, holding Juliette on her knees.

Monsieur Berneval was not noted for conventional tact. Accustomed to living in the country, with peasants to whom he thought himself far superior, he was unaware of the social delicacies that are the prerogative of well brought-up individuals. Proud of his status, which might perhaps have been contestable, he was humble before those that he supposed to be above him, and brazenly rude to others. As soon as he had taken his place by the heath, he hastened to address the conventional compliments to Madame Delmont, and then turned to Alinska.

"Madame," he said to her, "although perhaps that title is inappropriate, for it's possible that you're not married, it's not my fault if I have not fulfilled my obligations earlier. I appeared at your door some time ago, and your manservant, may Heaven forgive him, refused to introduce me to your presence, with a very strange rudeness. Truly, I am almost tempted to rejoice in the fire that devoured our property, since it is to that circumstance that I owe the honor of paying court to you."

This strange manner of expression did not please any of those who heard it. Alinska, to whom the speech was addressed, not seeing any direct question therein, continued to maintain silence, while the doctor, intending to render assistance, hastened to ask her for news of her health. She opened her mouth then, gave a brief reply on that subject.

Monsieur Berneval, undiscouraged by the discontent that he could have read, had he so wished, on every face, turned to Mélervant. "Well, savant Doctor, you're rich in a privilege that I don't possess—that of making this beautiful lady talk."

"It's true that she replies to me, but I owe that to the question I asked—the only one that well-born people may address to someone they don't know."

"I've been told, my dear chap," the gentleman riposted, "that you're fanatically devoted to liberalism; and you're not holding back in my presence. What, then, I pray, is a well-born person, if I do not count in their number?"

In spite of the icy severity of Alinska's brow, and her usual impassivity, she could not help smiling on listening to these words, while Madame Delmont shrugged her shoulders and the colonel prudently suppressed the reply that he was about to make to Monsieur Berneval before it reached his lips.

The latter, observing the surgeon's silence, thought he had won "hands down," according to one of his own favorite expressions when he recounted his disputes with villagers. He pursued the course of his insignificant chatter, recounting once again the quarrel he had had with one of his neighbors about whom he had sent an official denunciation to the Prefect of the département.

"And what wrong had he done to the authority," Mélervant asked, "for you to have taken such a step, in a dispute which is entirely the province of the Justice of the Peace?"

"A fine question to ask me, Monsieur Aesculapius! A man who dares stand up to a person of my rank can only be a Jacobin of the first water—and that alone proves how dangerous his way of seeing is."

Delmont, hastening to change the subject again, asked Monsieur Berneval whether it was true that the parish was finally to have a curé all to itself."

"Yes, Colonel," he replied. "I dined last Saturday with Monseigneur the Archbishop. That savant and modest prelate, who deigns to honor me with an entirely particular benevolence, gave me an assurance that, before long, our church will end a widowhood that has lasted too long."

Madame Delmont then joined in the conversation, to ask whether the name of the new curé was known."

"No, Madame, I don't know it," the gentleman replied. "All that I can tell you is that his praiseworthy qualities include his conciliatory spirit and his firmness of character. It's said that he's very learned, and that, although a foreigner, he will suit the parish perfectly. I'm eager to see him in our midst; I hope that his preaching will inspire more submission in the village folk; that he will prove to them how superior we are to them; and that, above all, he will seek to cure the superstitions that are deeply-rooted among the people, even while, in other matters, their incredulity increases."

"You astonish me, Monsieur," the doctor said, "when you speak thus. You, an enemy of superstitions! I thought them close relatives of the general run of prejudices."

"I don't know what you mean by that, my dear chap. I don't like superstitions because they deflect the peasants from their duty. Since those imbeciles have got it into their heads that there are Vampires in the commune, they don't want to step out of their houses by night."

"Vampires, here!" exclaimed Delmont. "Vampires! Is that execrable deceit being propagated in R***? Who can have brought the hideous fables of Greece and Hungary here?"

As he finished speaking, the colonel could not help looking at Alinska. He saw that she was upset. Her features were distraught, expressing an unparalleled horror; she had opened her mouth slightly; her eyes were fixed—and by virtue of a rapid impulse, immediately suppressed, she seemed to have intended to get up and leave.

A prompt reflection gave the colonel the probable key to the painful astonishment that Alinska had experienced. It was impossible that a daughter of Hungary did not believe in the reality of Vampires; she had talked to him about them on several occasions. She had told him stories about them, each more marvelous than the last. The mere mention of Vampires imposed a constant terror on all the people of that country. Ought he to be surprised by the effect that it had had on Alinska when she had been reminded, in such an unexpected manner, of a superstition that had occupied her through all the phases of her life?

Edouard would dearly have liked, out of consideration for her, to change the subject again, but that was no longer possible. Monsieur Berneval was charmed by the opportunity to reply to the question that had just been put to him.

"It was a wretch who no longer exists. The person to whom we owe the fear now spread through the locality was your domestic Raoul. He told his friends the story of these demons avid for human blood, with regard to the singular death of a peasant girl in the neighborhood. From that moment on, fear has reigned here; one is no longer obeyed after the sun has ceased to shine. The women only go out at daybreak, and the men, during the hours of darkness, have a great deal of difficulty venturing into the fields." The narrator addressed himself to Alinska to continue: "For God's sake Madame, don't manifest a dread similar to that of that population of idiots; you're too intelligent to believe in such a folly. These demons, these Boucolatres, these Vampires, only ever existed in the imagination of the man who first took it into his head to talk about them."

At his point the Hungarian woman directed a stare at Monsieur de Berneval so lugubrious, accompanied by a smile so frightful, that, in spite of his self-assurance, he stopped in mid-speech, nonplussed, losing along with his words the desire to talk, which had never left him before.

The doctor, having no knowledge of what Monsieur Delmont might know, was able to address the matter in his turn. He made fun of the hideous dreams to which Hungary and the Greek islands gave birth. He challenged Vampires to come and trouble the sleep of a courageous man—and would have continued that badinage if expressive and repeated signals addressed to him by the colonel had not interrupted him.

A moment of silence followed. Then Madame Delmont, speaking in her turn, said: "Why reject all these mysterious creatures so obstinately? No matter how atrocious they may be, can we know all of the means that Providence employs to afflict us? Vampires might exist; perhaps it is to a monster of that species that I owe the unexpected death of my son..."

Suddenly, a piercing scream escaped the foreigner. She rose to her feet impetuously, tried to take a step forward, and fell to the floor, deprived of consciousness...

Chapter XVII

The company assembled in the Château de R*** was justly alarmed, at first, by the beautiful foreigner's collapse. While the insensitive Berneval lost himself in vain conjectures as to the cause that had provoked it, Madame Delmont, her husband and the doctor hastened to help Alinska.

For a long time she seemed insensible to all their attentions; one might have thought that, in consequence of a violent shock, her soul had abandoned its carnal dwelling.

Delmont took advantage of this prolonged delay to reply to the gentleman. "I have traveled throughout Europe with the French armies, Monsieur," he said. "I have studied the customs and languages of the populations we have conquered; in consequence, either I am much mistaken, or this lady was born in Hungary. Given that, she must be imbued with all the prejudices and superstitions of her homeland. The conversation, turned to a subject perpetually redoubtable for her compatriots, will doubtless have reminded her of her childhood, and that, combined with the weakness of her health, must have produced the unconsciousness from which we are having so much trouble extracting her."

This explanation seemed sufficient to those who heard it. Berneval remarked that a Hungarian woman must know the method by which Tokay wine was made, and promised himself to ask her for information on that subject, in order to get a better yield from his own vineyard, whose produce was excellent. No one responded to this ridiculous proposal.

As Alinska was not coming round, Mélervant proposed that she be taken to her room. He and the colonel, accompanied by Madame Delmont, carried her to her bed, where she remained cold and motionless for a long time.

Eventually, she uttered a profound sigh, and, looking at those surrounding her, asked in a faint voice why she was in her present state, as if she did not know the cause.

"An extreme weakness," Mélervant replied, "the inevitable result of the blood that you have lost, will rob you from time to time of the use of your senses. You are not taking enough care of your health, Madame, and perhaps counting too recklessly on your constitution. You must conserve your strength, and from now on must be less disobedient to our advice."

"Is that what made me faint, Doctor? Wasn't someone taking about Vampires? Who dared to lift the mysterious veil with which Heaven covers the accomplishment of its terrible will?"

"Don't think about those dark ideas anymore," the colonel replied. "The imprudence that reminded you of them will not be repeated. In changing climate, you ought to change your habits. Here, no one believes in that which causes constant terror elsewhere. Enjoy the purity of our heavens; forget the dismal imagery that yours sometimes presents. Forgive me if I take the liberty of speaking to you thus if, lifting the veil with which you appear to like to cover yourself, I mention the place that gave you birth. You are Hungarian—don't hide it from us. We respect the reasons that lead you to dwell among us, but don't imagine that you can be anonymous to one of the former warriors who followed the glorious flag of France throughout Europe."

Alinska made no reply to what Delmont said. She maintained a somber silence, which convinced Hélène and the doctor that the colonel had guessed the truth. All three withdrew, when the Hungarian woman had assured them that she felt the need to rest for a while.

They went back to the drawing-room. Berneval was still there. Still indiscreet; he pestered them with annoying questions, to which they barely made any reply. He finally withdrew, delighted to know what country the foreigner came from, and promising to communicate that important discovery to all his neighbors.

When he had gone, Mélervant, after a momentary hesitation, addressed himself to the two spouses first, and then to Madame Delmont in particular. "I don't quite know," he said, "how to tell you about the sentiment that is dominating my soul, but your generosity toward me reassures me, and I flatter myself that you will support me in what I need to do to accomplish my desires. I'm thirty-four years old, with an honest fortune, and a profession that augments my wealth. Bachelorhood in no longer agreeable to me, especially since I have been able to make the acquaintance of the charming woman to whom you have given shelter. She is a foreigner; misfortunes, perhaps a sin that she is expiating by means of a regrettable exile, have doubtless brought her into our midst. I would like to ameliorate her fate by offering her my hand, if she will deign to accept it—and I thought that I ought, before saying anything to her, to address myself frankly to you, in the hope that Madame Delmont, to spare me the shame of a refusal, might try to discover the lovely lady's intentions, especially the dispositions that she might have in regard to me."

Delmont was too disturbed by such a confidence to take it upon himself to answer immediately. He left that to his wife, who, both good and prudent, while approving of the choice that the doctor had made, advised him not to declare himself before having learned the foreign woman's history, in a definite manner. By too much haste, she suggested, he might give himself cause for subsequent regret, when the effervescence of passion had diminished.

"Believe, Madame," he replied, "that I have already made, at least in part, the reflections that you are endeavoring to inspire. Specifically, I have learned from the former owner of the burned house that he sold the house and its dependant land for a sum of fifty-five thousand francs. The house has gone, but the fields are still there, and in this country, you know that they count for almost everything in such purchases, while mere dwellings count for very little. The lady, you have also told me, possesses valuable jewelry; a considerable sum in gold was saved from the fire, for which you have provided a temporary repository.

"These visible resources, the talents that the foreigner possesses, and her manners—noble, if a trifle bizarre—already declare that she does not belong to the unworthy class of women seeking to speculate on their charms. Since she has been here she has lived in absolute seclusion; she has obstinately refused all the advances made to her; your neighbors, in spite of their persistence in being drawn toward her, have scarcely been able to catch a glimpse of her in your home. They comprise a numerous society, however, and adventuresses never refuse an opportunity to show themselves in such circumstances, where they might easily encounter some prey.

"Now, might she be the victim of an imprudent passion? Might she have wanted to conceal, far from her homeland, the consequences of a youthful error? To that, I won't reply negatively—but the time that must have gone by since then, and the austerity of her present conduct, both serve to excuse it. I shall not occupy myself with the past, provided that she will make it known to you without mystery. I will go even further: I don't want to know. It will be sufficient for me, Madame, that you are informed about it, and I shall lead her to the altar if you assure me that she is worthy to bear the name of an honest man."

Touched by Mélervant's frankness, and the confidence he had in her, Madame Delmont promised to leave no stone unturned in order to satisfy his desires. The colonel, feeling that it would be appropriate for him to say something in his turn, found it difficult nevertheless to stammer a few words, and soon fell back into silence, after having certified yet again that the beautiful Alinska must hail from Hungary.

When this conversation finished, it was late. The doctor had to leave early the next morning for the commune of Clermont, where an invalid required his care. They separated, in order to go to bed. Nevertheless, they did not do so without thinking further about the subject that interested them all.

Delmont could not go to sleep; he was too agitated to be able to close his eyelids placidly. He was almost certain that Alinska would reject the proposal that was about to be made to her, but he feared that the young woman's impetuous nature might yet get the better of her, and that she might say something, or make some desperate resolution, that could trouble the tranquility of the household.

While he was abandoning himself to that reverie, he thought he heard a faint sound of footsteps coming from his wife's room, which was next to his own. At first he listened, to make sure that he was not mistaken—but when the noise continued, he feared that Hélène might be in distress.

He immediately got up, and went to the connecting door, treading softly. He was about to open it when he was suddenly struck in the face by a hand that he felt but could not see. The force of the slap threw him back toward his bed. He leaned on it for a few minutes, having lost his breath.

As soon as he had recovered from the shock, he threw himself precipitately toward his épée, which he always kept close at hand, and then, lit his lamp with the aid of a phosphorus match. He carefully examined the room, expecting to find the audacious individual who had struck him, and who must undoubtedly be a malefactor.

The colonel's search was fruitless. The door to the corridor was carefully locked from the inside, as were the windows. He found no cause for alarm—and when he went into his wife's room, he saw that she was sleeping deeply, albeit in a troubled manner. He did not want to wake her, but nevertheless made a search of the room.

Discovering nothing, he was force to conclude that he was mistaken, and that a sudden rush of blood had been the cause of his disturbance. He went back into his room.

Dawn broke while he was still awake. It appeared that they day would be fine; he was glad of that. Not wanting to stay to be a witness to the conversation between his wife and Alinska, he decided to go out hunting immediately, before anyone else in the house was awake.

Madame Delmont learned at breakfast that her husband would not be there to assist her; she was not annoyed by that. She was anxious to know the destiny of the Hungarian woman, and promised herself to embark upon that quest immediately after the morning meal.

Alinska appeared when the church bell had summoned her. A bleak sadness was engraved on her face, which was not as pale as usual. She thanked her hostess emotionally for the care she had given to her the previous evening.

"I ought," she continued, "to blush for my weakness, but it is one of those subjects that I cannot hear discussed without experiencing an invincible horror. We cannot easily rid ourselves of everything that strikes us in our childhood; humans, in the course of their lives, are almost always enslaved by the first impressions that their education makes upon them."

Madame Delmont only replied by means of the customary polite remarks; she did not want to explain what she had to say in front of Juliette. When breakfast was over, however—to everyone's great astonishment—she asked Germaine to take the little girl away until she sent an instruction to bring her back.

The two ladies then went into the drawing-room. Alinska, taking her embroidery to a chair by the fireplace, promptly set to work, and her companion, in order to maintain appearances, although she felt embarrassed, took up the first book she fund and pretended to read it attentively.

It was, however, necessary to explain. The doctor would return at dinner time, impatient to know his destiny, and it would be necessary to give him a definite response.

"Well, my dear Alinska," Madame Delmont said, finally, not without having hesitated, "will you always be the best but most mysterious of creatures? Will you never care to tell us what powerful motives have taken you away from your homeland? Will you maintain an eternal silence of that subject, which makes your friends anxious? You're looking at me in astonishment—perhaps my questions offend you? Believe that they're dictated by a sincere affection."

"I don't doubt that, Madame, and I excuse them because I know you—but if you have granted me our benevolence until now without enquiring as to whom I am, why do I not deserve that you will always have the same confidence in my regard? Have I recently shown myself to you in a more unfavorable light? Has some calumny been raised against my life? It's sufficiently retired, alas, not to give rise to the most active malignity."

"It's not a matter of anything disagreeable; no one has said anything that might trouble you—but do you think you can be beautiful with impunity? No one attempts to discover the lot of an ordinary woman; she is allowed to pass unperceived—while you, Alinska, strike the eye too vividly to be viewed with indifference. You have doubtless agitated more than one heart, and in that number there are some who would like to get closer to you, to obtain the gift of your heart. Those, you must admit, have some interest in knowing who you are, to discover whether you are free—in sum, whether any previous engagement might prevent you from disposing of your hand."

A melancholy smile preceded on the Hungarian woman's lips the reply that she was about to make. She seemed to meditate momentarily; then she raised the head that she had bowed over her work and gazed at Madame Delmont with an expression of severe indifference.

"If the knowledge of my lot pertains to my present situation, I can explain it without any need to say anything that might agitate the other party. I am free, Madame, but nevertheless, I do not belong to myself. I have given my heart; I no longer have the right to take it back. I am separated by the whole of existence from the man I love to excess; I can never be joined to him by the bonds consecrated by the Church. My oppressed soul is under the dependency of a superior power. I am Hungarian—or, to put it better, I now belong to the common earth. Don't ask me anymore; you have learned everything that I can tell you. Try to forget even that."

"I could doubtless be content with such an explanation, obscure as it is, but I cannot offer you the certainty that others will be satisfied by it. No one will want to listen to me if I cannot be precise. At any rate, permit me to talk to you in the language of reason. You are far from your homeland, alone and independent; you cannot, you say, ever hope to be united with the man you have chosen. What do you expect to do in a foreign land? Will there not come a time when, abandoned to the chill of age, you feel the need of a friend? Perhaps you would like to return to your own country? Events have raised obstacles to that, which you might not be able to overcome. You will then repent of the refusal that you do not hesitate to make now."

"I realize, Madame, all that my present condition would be painful for a woman who finds herself in one of the ordinary situations of life, but mine is placed in a special category; it does not resemble any of the cases that are routinely reproduced. I seem isolated to you—well, believe that I have no anxiety about my future fate; it has been settled for some years, and cannot change. I am describing a circle traced by an all-powerful being, from which I cannot escape. You think that I might need support; be undeceived—I would never consent to accept any. Tell the one on whose behalf you are speaking to me to forget that I am in the world, to abandon any hope, and, above all, to extinguish a love that might be fatal to him. The madman! He does not know that whoever loves me must receive death...

"You're shuddering, Madame. Oh, if only it were permissible for me to tell you my dire history—then you would know a veritable horror, the one that my situation would inspire in you. Nevertheless, I take the God I fear as my witness that I have never had to blush at my actions; they were always avowed by the purest virtue, and if I have done harm to myself, at least no reproach paved the way for that dolorous moment. Desist, I beg you, from pressing me any further; let me envelop myself in mystery. I ask nothing of human beings; I would not wish to obtain anything on earth but the peace of the grave, and that is refused me."

After these final words, Alinska expressed all her despair in a sinister glance, got up from the chair in which she was sitting and, taking her leave of Madame Delmont, went to her room.

Strange person! Hélène thought, watching her draw away. *Inexplicable creature! Who is she? What has she done? Why has she come to this country? What am I saying? Should I complain? Does she not have grief enough? Should she seem blameworthy to me solely because she refuses to satisfy my curiosity? Her story must be very interesting, though. It's impossible that the poor thing has not drunk deep draughts from the cup of misfortune.*

Madame Delmont's monologue ended there. She set to work, after having her daughter brought back, and remained plunged in her reflections until the arrival of her husband and the doctor, who appeared together.

"My poor friend," said the mistress of the house to Mélervant, "you are unfortunate. You have been refused, without leaving you the slightest hope—not because your merit is doubted, but for the sole reason that the heart of the unsociable foreigner is too full of an unknown sentiment for it to be possible to admit any other. I won't repeat the bizarre conversation I had with the Hungarian beauty; suffice it to say that she told me nothing, and that you are out of luck."

Far from being content with these words, the doctor insisted on receiving a more ample explanation. Madame Delmont tried to avoid that in vain; she was obliged to render a full account of what had been said, and he slightest expressions revealed by Alinska. The colonel was no less interested to hear the story of the conversation that we have reported above.

"My self-esteem," said Mélervant, then, "is fully sheltered in that circumstance; I understand that the Cruel One feels an affection that can never be satisfied. A great disappointment in love has certainly caused her to leave her homeland; the blow is hard but I shan't imitate her. Since she doesn't want to be my wife, I shall try to remain her friend."

"There," said the colonel, finally breaking his long silence, "speaks a reasonable man. No more sighs, believe me; affect a profound indifference, and perhaps the less you think about her, the more you will see that soul, now so haughty, take pity on you."

The doctor, although keenly distressed, did his best to conceal the condition of his heart. He did not abandon himself to the sentiment that inflamed him, for he too knew the full value of time; he found relief in confiding himself to that old man, who gives a new face, and the care of his dearest interests, to everything.

At dinner time, Alinska sent word that, feeling slightly indisposed, she would eat in her room. They thought at first that this was an excuse, to avoid meeting the doctor, but Germaine, who served her, declared that she was extremely pale and seemed violently agitated.

Chapter XVIII

The following day, Alinska, emerging from her retreat, appeared not to retain any memory of the conversation she had had with Madame Delmont. Mélervant was still at the château; she treated him as usual, without displaying anything particular in her behavior in his regard. If she showed herself indifferent to the doctor, however, it was not the same with respect to Edouard. Several times she looked at him with an expression of discontent and anger that almost made him afraid. She adopted a manner that was abrupt and familiar at the same time, which might have encouraged the deduction that they were not strangers to one another, if the other two members of the company had not been convinced that the Hungarian woman's reason was occasionally weak.

The colonel, on the other hand, who knew the truth, was nervous of this new caprice. The dearer Alinska became to him again, the more he did not want anyone to perceive it. He was worried about his wife, whose jealousy might be awakened by some imprudence. For his own part, he tried to reach an understanding; he implored Alinska with his gaze to be careful, to keep the promise she had made—but his efforts and gestures were futile; she continued her strategy regardless.

In the meantime, a messenger came to find the doctor to summon him urgently to the aid of a neighbor who was dying of apoplexy. At the same time, Madame Delmont needed to go to her room, and the enemies found themselves alone together.

"Don't you remember the promise you gave me?" the colonel immediately said to the Hungarian woman.

"You've forgotten," she replied, "what your heart promised me. Once again, O most untrustworthy of men, do you dare to reproach me for betraying my oaths? I shall adopt in your regard whatever conduct I please—but this is not the place for us to make reproaches. I need to talk to you; it's absolutely necessary."

"When?"

"Tonight, at midnight."

"Where?"

"In the great hall. No one will interrupt us there."

"What do you want from me?"

"You'll find out."

"What if someone catches us?"

"Don't worry."

"It might turn out badly."

"Will you come?"

"I'm afraid."

"Tremble, if I wait for you in vain."

Madame Delmont came back then, and put an end to the rapid conversation, which had taken place in whispers. She arrived so unexpectedly that her husband seemed disturbed by it, and she glimpsed a gesture that might have explained many things to her, had she not felt completely secure.

Never, since Alinska's arrival in the château, had the latter seemed in a better mood. She emerged from her everyday melancholy, and was almost cheerful. Her efforts succeeded in drawing a half-smile from Hélène—the first to brush her lips since she had been mourning the death of her son.

Far from sharing Alinska's gaiety, Delmont became ever more somber and sad as the sun sank into the west. He scarcely opened his mouth all through dinner; a vague anxiety was agitating him, and he dared not look either at Alinska or his wife. The meeting to which he had to go worried him intensely; he feared that, by some stroke of ill-luck, he might be found in conversation with the Hungarian woman at that hour. He knew how difficult it is to prevent domestics gossiping indiscreetly, and knew that the peace of his household might depend on the revelation of that detail.

Eventually, everyone retired to their rooms. Madame Delmont, who had seemed depressed for a week and often complained of a general weakness in all her limbs, which fatigued her greatly, was the first to go to bed. She soon sent Germaine away, telling her to go to bed too.

Delmont had also gone to his room, but instead of getting undressed he sat down in an armchair and, trembling like a criminal about to commit a further bad deed, he waited without impatience for the appointed hour to chime.

In such a situation, everything hurts and everything causes anxiety; the night goes by too quickly for the desires of such individuals. He would have like to slow the march of time, but the latter, regular in its course, marched at a steady pace; it sounded, in passing, the hour of midnight, and continued to draw away as it does incessantly. When the twelfth stroke had resounded, Delmont got up, with a sigh. Without taking a lamp, he made his way to the great hall, where Alinska was to come to meet him.

The total darkness that reigned in the vast room, the sharp cold that penetrated through the ill-fitting windows, and the fear of being discovered combined to make Delmont shiver as he had never shivered when facing five hundred fiery mouths, vomiting death in the motionless position that his duty had assigned to him. Then, however, he had been at peace with his heart; nothing troubled him; his conscience had been tranquil. Now he was at odds with himself, obedient to the orders of a woman who could no longer contribute to his happiness, and who might destroy it instead.

On the other hand, was it possible for him to refuse her? Had he not to fear that, by virtue of the natural violence of her character, she might publicly reveal the fatal secret they held in common? Delmont thought that he ought to do everything possible to restrain an insensate lover.

She did not take long to appear. She came in by the door to the staircase, dressed in white, half-veiled beneath an immense black shawl that gave her the sinister appearance of a specter—which was not belied by her listless gaze or the extreme pallor of her face. She was carrying a lamp, which she hurriedly placed on the floor when she recognized the colonel. Advancing toward him with the appearance of a melancholy contentment, she told him how glad she was that he was so punctual in the rendezvous.

"I shall always hasten to Alinska when she wishes to see me, especially since she has given me an assurance..."

"Edouard, I beg you, stop reminding me of a promise that is costing me too much to keep. Must I disguise myself incessantly? Can I not struggle against you with all the advantages of my position, when I see you searching for means to be rid of me—when you support the extravagant pretensions that were unhesitatingly communicated to me this morning?"

"Believe me, Alinska, I suffered as much as you when they were made known to me; it was already unbearable for me to suspect them—but what could I do but keep silent and let you take care of it? I hoped...I knew, I mean...that your reply would be negative, and since then, I've had an assurance that you will not be harassed again."

At these last words, a gleam of joy shone in Alinska's eyes.

"You hoped, you say! Oh, why can I not conceive any hope in my turn? I am the witness to a happiness that is odious to me, which I shall never taste. It is necessary that I tear myself away from a place that has become intolerable to me. I have seen you; I have consummated my misfortune; nothing remains but for me to go away."

"You're leaving, Alinska! You! Oh, what an insult you'll offer to our friendship!"

"To your friendship! Edouard, I don't care about offending that. Whatever I may have said, I didn't ask you for it, even when you offered it to me sincerely. My lot is sufficient, and I am bound to it."

She paused, then continued with a smile imprinted with an infernal malignity: "My departure, in freeing you from my presence, will render you the calm that it has stolen from you. You will no longer shiver, as you do when I show myself to you or when I speak to you; you will no longer be distracted from the love inspired in you by the woman you preferred to me."

At this point, a glance darted by Alinska at the physiognomy of her listener proved to her that she was mistaken in her complaint—but she was careful not to reveal what she had glimpsed.

"You are free to stay or go; I don't even know whether I ought not to beg you to take the latter course—but be persuaded that my heart does not demand your absence. It would be content to be near to you, if it did not fear you more; it senses more than ever how seductive you are, and henceforth, I would like to involve you in all my projects of prosperity."

"Eh? What place would you give me? In what role close to you would it be permissible for me to appear? You don't answer; what ought I to infer from that silence?"

"It explains my embarrassment. What can I say to you to make you content? The ties that bind me are indissoluble."

"Yes, indissoluble, like everything in human nature, as in everything that exists…until death."

There was such a mysterious meaning in the one in which these final words were pronounced, such an atrocious expressiveness, that Delmont shuddered and took a step back, immediately looking into Alinska's eyes—but he saw, by the feeble light that illuminated them, that they were filled with the peculiar indifference that almost always animated them. No torment showed in the young woman's countenance; everything about her was in such discord with what the sound of her voice alone appeared to be implying, that Delmont was on the point of believing that his ears had been deceived. He even sought to persuade himself of it, and gave no evidence of his secret distress.

A moment of silence ensued. Alinska did not seem disposed to break it. Edouard continued to reflect on what had just happened. They both seemed to have too much to say to begin the interrogation again. That mute game had to come to an end, however.

It was the Hungarian woman who was the first to resume speaking. "You're thinking very profoundly, Edouard," she said. "Are you occupied with the past or making plans for the future?"

"No, I'm not directing my gaze forwards or backwards; only the present is agitating me. I see nothing but you, and it casts me into an inexplicable confusion, unable to bring so many opposed sentiments into accord."

"Don't protest when I tell you that your weakness is known to me. You're incapable of making a decision; you don't know what you want, and I don't know why fortune linked my firm soul with yours, which has never been able to stiffen itself against difficulty."

"Oh everything is permitted to you, Alinska, and I authorize you to humiliate me in any manner—but if you could examine what is happening in my heart…if you were in my shoes, I'd like to know how you'd get out of it."

126

"After some reflection, my resolution would soon be made; I would consider the various possibilities presented to me, I would choose, and from then on I would advance boldly along the route mapped out for me."

"And if that route took you away from the path of virtue—if it led you to crime or error?"

"I would not leave the path I had taken, once it had appeared to me to be preferable; indecision is the worst of evils. But in your situation, have you really taken account of what is embarrassing you? Do you know for certain where evil lies and where virtue lies? Are the risks not equal on either side? For instance, were you not mine before belonging to another? Since when have new rights effaced the priority of old ones?"

"Alinska! What are you saying? What are you asking of me?"

"All or nothing, Edouard—you're shivering! You're not worthy to listen to me."

"What! I have given myself to a woman to whom I can't address any reproach! And to separate myself from a child!"

"All or nothing, I repeat; what are you complaining about, when I'm giving you a free choice; when I'm leaving you in the situation you're in, contenting myself with pointing out two ways that offer themselves to get you out of it?"

"What trap are you weaving for me, enchantress? No, Alinska, although I might be tempted by the first woman who gave me love, I will never consent to stigmatize myself in the eyes of the world, by abandoning the virtuous being that I have voluntarily surrounded with my well-deserved affection. I am, I must, be hers for as long as she lives..."

"Undoubtedly, you cannot run away without staining yourself, and your reputation is precious to me, but to hear you, one might think that the woman were not mortal, or that she has made a pact with eternity."

"Alinska, you're making me shiver; I don't want to listen to you. Perhaps you don't even understand the force of your expressions."

A sinister smile was the Hungarian woman's only response, and in her eyes, which she fixed upon the colonel's, she expressed all the profundity of her thought, in such a manner as to dispel any doubts that the other might form.

"No, no—a hundred times no. I will not add that crime to all my sins, You horrify me, barbarian!"

"Yes, I know—you were less guilty when you broke my heart; when, by your conduct and your shameful letter, you guided the dagger that struck me..."—as she spoke these swords she drew aside her clothing, and displayed the open wound on her body, which was still bloody—"...when my father and mother, in their despair, found their only refuge in death. No, undoubtedly, that was not a sin. Edouard was then, and still is, the most innocent and virtuous of men. It's me who is a vile creature—but the Inferno is set between us, and it knows rascality; I remit the judgment of our dispute thereto."

"Oh, despair! Oh, frantic Alinska! To what harsh extremity have you driven yourself? What? Your blood has flowed, and it was you who spilled it! What? By that action you have robbed your respectable parents of life!"

"Not me, Edouard, not me; I count for nothing in that fatal catastrophe. It is you, and you alone, who determined it. I was the instrument of which you made use to annihilate an entire family; it has disappeared from the earth, and yet you will sleep peacefully, or your sleep will only be troubled by the horror that I shall cause you henceforth. Adieu, artisan of all my miseries, enemy who has stolen from me irredeemably my share in the heavens at which I no longer dare gaze, who has consummated my eternal damnation!"

"You're overwhelming me; I'm annihilated; I scarcely know whether I still belong to existence. But why despair? My sins are very great, but I hope nevertheless for their remission; and you, whom the delirium of a fatal passion has led astray, can believe that by repentance that you may still..."

"Repentance!" cried the Hungarian woman, letting slip a burst of frightful laughter that disturbed the profound peace of the night. "Repentance! There is no longer any for me; I don't know where to find it. I've left it in my thatched cottage, with the rest of my human sentiments. I have taken my course; it is now impossible for me to recover all that I have left behind me. Nothing else remains to me but to pursue my course: I know already what recompense awaits me at the end of my journey; I have even tasted a portion of its ineffable sweetness."

The bitterness and somber irony displayed in this speech, and the indefinable tone in which it was pronounced, threw the colonel into an unprecedented confusion. He saw before him a woman embellished with all the charms of youth and beauty, who might yet furnish a long career, but who was giving way under the burden of remorse. Her reason, weakened by misfortunes, and by the prejudices of her childhood, presented nothing but torments in her future.

She was exaggerating the mass of her errors, and doubtless believed that she owed Providence a much greater debt than the one she really had to settle; but she was no less unfortunate for that, because it is not on the actual mass of our misfortunes that the vulgar judge the weight of our suffering, but the manner in which we bear them. Our first enemy is ourselves; a brilliant imagination lightens violent chagrin; a melancholy imagination renders troubles that seem light to others frightful and destructive.

It was on this basis that Delmont estimated everything dolorous that was in the soul of his victim. Moved by an affectionate pity, under which a gentler sentiment was hidden at present, he no longer had but one thought: that of consoling Alinska, of trying first to restore her tranquility and then to lead her to happiness. He drew nearer to her, and tried to grasp the hand that Alinska always kept covered with his own. That gesture, whose objective she divined, caused her to shiver. She took a step backwards.

"No, no, Edouard, don't test me any further—I've revealed all my weakness to you; I've even given way, in speaking to you, to a hectic transport at which I blush now. It only remains for me to terminate this conversation, to remind you of the motive that brought me to see you. I can no longer stay in this place; I need to leave without delay. Don't think of opposing my resolution; it is irrevocable. I shall leave the château as soon as it's light. I'll occupy myself with the repair of the house that was consumed by fire; I was told two days ago that I can move back into it. I'll go back into it, doubtless never to re-emerge. As for you, there's nothing to keep you here any longer. It was to avoid me that you quit the pleasures of the capital of France—go freely to taste its delights again; I won't pursue you with my presence. I set you free, and from this moment on I liberate you from all the terrors I have caused you."

"I can't consent to what you intend to do. Wait for a while longer before leaving us. Must you go to a newly-constructed house in the middle of winter? Perhaps you don't know how much there is to fear from damp walls."

"For you, perhaps, but not for me. I've found much damper ones in another dwelling, and yet you see me here. My part is done; a plausible reason that I shall establish in advance will eliminate the possibility of anyone suspecting the true cause; I'll pretend to fear the doctor's importunities, to have more than ever an urgent need for retreat. When a little time has gone by, no one will give me another thought."

The colonel, keenly afflicted by this determination, and also remembering the ominous ideas that a few indiscreet words spoken by the Hungarian woman had put into his mind, tried to weaken her resolve, but she was inflexible. Weary of supplications to which she no longer wanted to yield, she ran to her lamp, picked it up, and suddenly withdrew, without listening to the insistences that he was urgently addressing to her. The colonel, in his turn, went back to his room—but it was not sleep that he encountered in his bed.

Chapter XIX

At breakfast time, Alinska appeared in the dining room as usual. The calmness of her countenance and the indifferent expression of her gaze gave Madame Delmont no suspicion of the resolution she had made. Even the colonel was deceived; Alinska's arrival was a pleasant surprise—he feared that she might already have taken flight—and he conceived the hope that perhaps she had postponed her departure if not renounced it entirely.

She seemed as equable as ever; she talked about the needlework she intended to do between meals, without any reference to what she had said the previous night. She went into the drawing-room, sat down with her sewing, and proceeded to work with her habitual extreme attention. In the meantime, a peasant having come to ask for Monsieur Delmont, the latter went to his study, where he always dealt with business matters.

As soon as he had gone, Alinska got up and went out, as if to go to her room, without giving any reason for her departure. Madame Delmont knew how the slightest question was capable of displeasing her, so she never asked her any.

An hour went by, and the Hungarian woman did not return. When he came back in, Edouard noticed her absence and asked his wife what had become of her.

"She left shortly after you, my friend. I assumed that she was going in quest of some material that she didn't have to hand, but some time has gone by since she left, and she hasn't come back."

This simple and natural reply caused a keen despair to its listener. He saw the truth then, and realized how wrong he had been to think that Alinska had postponed the accomplishment of her plan until a later date—for he did not doubt that she had left the château. Seeking to overcome the emotion whose appearance he dreaded, however, he affected an indifference that certainly could not have been in his heart, still hoping, but dreading the imminent confirmation of his fear. He did not have to wait long for that confirmation. After a brief interval, the new domestic who had replaced Raoul appeared in the drawing-room carrying a letter, which he handed to Madame Delmont. It was from Alinska, whose handwriting they saw for the first time.

I must, Madame, wrote the unfortunate woman, *offer you excuses for the abrupt manner in which I have separated myself from you. I have returned to my former residence, ashamed of having caused you so much embarrassment and full of gratitude for your generosity. Why is it not permissible for me to give you proof of it? An unparalleled fatality always drives me to act against my own will; it is a constant, horrible torture for me. I have found nothing in you but the most perfect kindness, and yet it will be necessary...forgive my aberration, which does not leave me the free exercise of my moral faculties. I cannot do what I want but, much to my distress, only what I can. I would have liked to remain in your château, but it would then have been frequently necessary to see a man whose sentiments for me constrain avoidance; it would have been unjust to deprive you of his visits. It has thus been necessary for me to make my decision. I am now at home; I have returned here with all my desire for the most absolute retreat; I shall only break it when I can come, without fear of any unwelcome encounter, to assure you myself of everything that I am expressing only feebly.*

Following these words, and the signature, which simply bore the name Alinska, there were a few polite words for the colonel.

"That, I must say," said Madame Delmont, having read the letter aloud, "Is a very strange way of leaving us. Everything about that woman is truly bizarre and mysterious. Can you imagine that she is retiring, in the middle of winter, to a newly-built house whose plaster cannot yet have lost its unhealthy emanations, to flee a man that a single word would have constrained? We'll need to send on her clothes; doubtless she won't have taken them, in order to deceive us more effectively."

Delmont tried to stammer a reply that would seem indifferent, but had difficulty in doing so. Fortunately for him, Madame Delmont, still preoccupied with her own idea, was ringing for Germaine.

The latter, when she appeared, hastened to tell her what she already knew. She added, however that at the same time that the foreign woman's letter had arrived at the château, a cart had come to collect the lady's trunk and effects.

The colonel ordered that they should be delivered immediately, and, glad to have found a pretext for leaving, he went out, saying that he would supervise the removal of the various objects that the Hungarian woman required. Once free, he was able to breathe more easily, and although his body was in the château, his soul and thoughts were wandering in imaginary spaces.

Alinska's unexpected departure provided new fuel for the curiosity of the local inhabitants. Monsieur Berneval, who did not like the lovely lady, was the first to spread malign suggestions as to the reasons that had necessitated the retreat. Human malevolence, when it is aimed at a target, knocks at so many doors that it often encounters the true one. It was in accordance with the invariable way of things that the housewives of the neighborhood attributed the event in question to Madame Delmont's jealousy, which must have suddenly flared up.

Fortunately, these rumors did not get past the ground floor of the château; they did not reach its masters. Only the doctor had knowledge of them, and although he was well disposed toward the colonel, he was still to full of his own infatuation to receive such a communication indifferently. He recalled a host of details to which he had paid no heed at the time, which now furnished him with a beam of enlightenment. Nevertheless, as a prudent man, he refrained from making anyone else party to his discoveries; he preferred to explain himself to the colonel on that matter, in all frankness, at the first opportunity he found.

In the same period, Madame Delmont's health deteriorated visibly. Her heart, still broken since the death of young Eugène, had doubtless enclosed the greater portion of her grief. Such a retention, corrupting her life at its source, had completely overwhelmed it. Most of all, she experienced an extreme difficulty in breathing. She lost all her strength, and gradually fell into an emaciation that might prove fatal.

The doctor, a man of genuine merit, studied perspicaciously the symptoms of a malady that presented the same appearances of the one that has caused Madame Delmont's son to perish. An extreme exhaustion, a continual need to eat, slight but permanent sweating—everything was reproduced in a similar fashion.

Without being aware of the peril that menaced her, Hélène became dejected and melancholy. She drew nearer to her husband; she seemed to love him even more, at the moment when she was perhaps about to leave him forever.

For his part, Delmont was far from believing in so imminent a danger. Troubled in al his affections by Alinska's conduct, perceiving fearfully that the young woman was reacquiring an ascendancy over him whose consequences he feared, he wanted to hide from himself, and avoided delving too deeply into what was happening in his soul.

Sometimes he was glad that Alinska had gone; he imagined that it ensured the tranquility of his life. Sometimes he longed for the foreigner's return; it seemed to him that since her departure, the Château de R*** was no longer anything but a vast solitude. He often went into the room that Alinska had occupied, and imagined seeing her there again; he sat in the armchair that she had used, fondled the curtains of the bed where she had slept, and, parading a melancholy gaze over the furniture, substituted for the absence of the person who had inhabited that space the illusions of an active imagination, following in its disorderly progress the caprices of a tormented heart.

More than once, a noble sentiment brought the man thus led astray back to the true requirements of his duty. Then, ashamed of his weakness, rejecting a delirium that dishonored him, it was in the company of his wife and daughter that he came in search of purer ideas. He demanded of himself whether Hélène was not the same person who, for years, had led him to happiness, and by what fault she could have been diminished in his eyes. Nothing in her conduct, as in her virtues, had been lacking; she still possessed all the attractions with which he had once been so infatuated, and whose triumph had so often charmed his pride.

At such moments, the image of Alinska gradually faded away, disappearing almost insensibly from his thoughts; she no longer appeared there as anything but a light cloud that would not take long to be entirely effaced. But those hours of reason became rapid themselves, promptly followed by renewals of extravagance and folly. Alinska, adorned by the omnipotent attraction that invests an object no longer possessed, returned victoriously to replace herself in a soul that had banished her with regret.

In order to excuse himself with respect to his conscience, Edouard observed that the beautiful creature had been his first love; that it was by an anterior and solemn oath that he had bound himself to her; that the indissoluble bonds had attached him to her, and that those contracted subsequently could not have the same force as the first. Yielding then to his renascent passion, increased by all the impetuosity that it was able to acquire by virtue of the obstacles opposed to it, he appealed to Alinska, calling her his beloved—and then by degrees, fell into a somber apathy from which he only emerged blushing.

These conflicts, incessantly renewed, were devouring his soul. He was in permanent opposition to himself, and sought to dissimulate that internal disturbance—but in the calm of the night, or when a rapid excursion had take him far away from the bounds of the château, when he found himself alone in a wood stripped of its verdure, when he abandoned himself to his reveries, he expressed the violence of his thoughts in the energy of his movements. One might have thought, on seeing him struggling with himself, that, like Milton's Lucifer, he was insulting the majesty of the Sun.[30]

Several days went by while he lived in this permanent anguish. Madame Delmont's sufferings increased in parallel. She had not been able, as she desired, to go to Alinska's new dwelling. The latter, ever solitary, had not returned to the château; she contented herself with enquiring from time to time, from the minister or a peasant, of her friend's state of health.

Mélervant, by contrast, showed himself often; he sought, as we have said, an opportunity to talk to the colonel, and then devoted all his care to Madame Delmont, who appeared to be declining in a manifest manner. He multiplied his questions, in order to discover the primary cause of the illness, which only displayed itself in its effects. The responses he received were, by virtue of their ambiguity, far from satisfactory.

Delmont, in agreement with him on this point, urged his wife to recall everything she had done, no matter how distant, that might have been injurious to her.

"I can't recall anything," she said. "I don't know why I'm suffering to this extent. You can see, my friend, that I am succumbing just as my son did, and to a similar catastrophe."

"What are you saying, Madame?" said the doctor, interrupting her. "Your dolorous infection has nothing in common with that of your son. Above all beware of getting such an idea into your head; that would suffice to aggravate your condition."

Far from seeming to be deceived, Madame Delmont replied with a melancholy smile, which was evidence in itself of the extent to which her morale had been affected. "I know that you're trying to deceive me on that point; I would appear unreasonable if I explained my thinking entirely, but I'm not mistaken. I know what I have; I sense what is happening to me."

"That speech, Madame," Mélervant replied, "tells us that you're holding back something that you ought to keep secret from us. That's not good; such a resolution might have dangerous consequences. Don't blush at anything; be persuaded that human weakness, taken to excess, can only seem ridiculous in the bizarre schemes it can produce, especially when illness leaves the soul less energy. Whatever idea has struck you, or error in which you are complicit, you would do yourself a great service by revealing it to us. You might perhaps put me on the path what will lead me to giving you back your health—we might finally learn which is the more agitated: your body or your imagination."

For a long time, Hélène stubbornly refused to make known her own opinion of her condition. Delmont, greatly disturbed by this circumstance, in which he was beginning to see her wasting away, joined forces with the doctor. His pleas were so insistent that Hélène, no longer daring to resist, confessed that a

---

[30] The reference is to Satan's soliloquy in Book IV of *Paradise Lost*.

singular thought had be troubling her unrelentingly, but declared at the same time that she would never be able to explain it to anyone but her husband, and only then under the express condition that he would not reveal it to anyone else.

Although this compromise was not all that the doctor desired, he was forced to agree to it. He retired immediately, having made a promise never to question the colonel as to what was about to be confided to him, and agreed to come back the following day, because his presence was not reassuring to Madame Delmont.

When the latter found herself alone with her husband, she hid her head in her hands, seemingly in fear of being interrogated.

He too was hesitant to do so, afraid that his wife would confess to him that she had had some knowledge, either of his past love for the Hungarian woman, or the unfortunate flame that fatal circumstances had reignited. He had to say something, however, and, speaking in a faint voice he asked Hélène if she would care to deposit the promised confidence in his bosom.

"Oh, Delmont," she said, "how can I ever resolve myself to tell you such a thing? And how will you treat me when you know the secret of my folly?"

"Always with amity—for I cannot believe that, in your blackest vapors, you doubt my attachment."

"Eh? Why, Edouard, would I doubt you? It's not to matters of that sort that I have devoted my reveries; I'm pursued by an odious vision. Oh, how ridiculous I shall appear to you!"

"No, no, Hélène, have no fear," Delmont said, with extreme contentment, when he acquired the certainty that his own conduct was not suspect.

"Well, my friend, be it weakness or be it superstition, it seems to me that I am pursued by night, unrelentingly, by a horrible demon—by a monster—which, couched on my heart, aspires into its infernal mouth the blood that runs in my veins. In sum, a Vampire is tormenting me. Be certain of it; it's the one that has already caused the death of my son, and that of a village girl of the commune."

"Be serious, Hélène! Are you not trying to mingle a little humor with the confidence I'm expecting? Is it not inherent in that inconceivable revelation?"

"I knew that you would make fun of me—that mockery would reply to me confession—but it does not matter what you think, when I have the fatal certainty of the obsession of which I complain.

"It's not a recurrent dream that I have every night; the sting of the pain and the crushing weight of the Entity snatch me from my sleep, but a power superior to my resistance suppresses all my movements, closes my eyelids and overcomes al the efforts I make to escape it. I scream in vain; the sound dies in my throat before reaching my lips; I feel overwhelmed; the substance of my life gradually disappears; frightful dreams torment me when the malign Spirit has quit me, unless I experience an wakefulness a thousand times more painful.

"I realize how absurd this must sound to you, to what extreme you will think my reason has been driven. To all of that I can only oppose two things: I am convinced of what I am saying, and my malady remains unknown, while it is making rapid progress."

"The more you say to me, Hélène, the more my astonishment increases. I don't know what to say to you about such a matter. Don't you feel that you're the victim of an unfortunate illusion? Your agitated blood is laboring, your digestion is difficult; nightmares, with whose effects you are familiar, are playing a tiresome role in your malady—but that's all. Don't add to your real sufferings those, more dangerous still, of a stricken imagination. I won't seek to prove to you how impossible it is that your fears are real. Providence has never permitted the laws of nature to be inverted in such an atrocious manner; it's almost blasphemous to believe in such horrors. You need distraction; this place is no longer suitable for you. Tomorrow we must go to Toulouse, where we'll stay until you're completely cured."

"No, Edouard, I won't consent to leave the château. I beg you to continue to reside here; a cause that is all too dear attaches me to it."

"It can only remind you of a painful memory. It was not our birthplace. Let's go instead to Lyon, your homeland, or anywhere you like. It's necessary that the sight of new things makes you forget those that render you melancholy."

"I don't want to go away; if I go elsewhere, they won't be able to bury my remains next to those of my son."

This poignant reply, which was accompanied by a torrent of tears, broke Delmont's heart. Violently moved, he mingled his tears with those of his wife. Nevertheless, he did not give in to her desire; he made the most of powerful arguments to persuade her to move, and in the end, by dint of pleading, he obtained her consent to spend a fortnight in Toulouse.

At the same time, she exacted a promise from him that after that time, whatever the state of her health might be, he would bring her back to the château. The colonel made that promise without difficulty, fully persuaded that, if the malady got worse, Hélène would not demand the literal fulfillment of the pact.

In spite of the penchant that brought him back to his first passion, Delmont retained a veritable love for his wife. She had become even more dear to him at that moment, when her mind seemed so painfully stricken. He too had his share of excitement, and, entirely devoted to his duty, he forgot that he was about to go away from Alinska. When it eventually presented itself to his heart, however, that thought was unable to change his determination; he considered himself obliged to make that sacrifice.

Perhaps he thought that the woman whose love had covered so much distance, and overcome so many difficulties, in order to reunite her with him, would not be stopped by a distance of approximately two hours. We do not affirm that that was what he thought, but a man's heart is so constructed that it would be insane to imagine that it is possible to bring light into all its depths.

Chapter XX

The next day, while Madame Delmont saw preparations being made for the departure, she seemed to repent of the commitment she had made the day before. Renewing her insistence with regard to her husband, she would have liked him to renounce his determination, but such pleas were futile. Whatever Delmont's secret sentiments might have been, he knew full well what he had to do; he had to remain firm in his demand, and the supplications of a wife already exhausted by illness would cease when it was absolutely necessary to get under way.

Before then, Hélène wrote a note to Alinska, to tell her that she, her daughter and he colonel were going to spend two weeks in Toulouse, that the decision had been take too abruptly to be communicated to her in advance, but that if it were possible for her to visit, they would be delighted to see her—and that a room would be reserved for her in whatever apartment they chose.

The doctor, to whom a message had been sent at an early hour, arrived just as the family was about to climb into the carriage. The colonel, taking him to one side, only had time to tell him, without going into detail, that because Madame Delmont was troubled by frightful panic terrors, he had thought it necessary to distract her, in order to dispel the vapors in question—and that, in order to accomplish that, he was taking her into the midst of the tumult of a large city for a while.

In spite of the doctor's distress at the departure of his friends, and the desire he was nursing to have a conversation with Delmont on the subject of the foreign woman, he could not disapprove of the project. He promised effortlessly to come to Toulouse frequently, and, having done that, he withdrew.

Hard frosts had rendered the local roads practicable. The travelers were able to follow the road that climbed up to Mervilla, went through the commune of Auzeville and joined the highway nor far from the village of Saint-Agne. Two strong horses took them rapidly to the Auberge du Grand Soleil in Toulouse; there they took temporary refuge until the evening, when the colonel, who had searched the city, finally found an apartment of the sort he wanted. It was situated in the Rue des Cordeliers, almost directly opposite the church of the former monastery. It had a large garden, and the purity of the air there was such that it seemed to the Delmont family that they had not lost anything in exchanging it for that of the country.

That same night, they went to bed in their new abode. The colonel had placed his own bed in his wife's room.

"You see," he said to her, laughing, "that I can come to your aid; here I am beside you, with my épée, my pistols, and all my former arsenal of war, in order to fight advantageously with the demon that has been obsessing you. I hope, nevertheless, not to have any need to do battle with it, for it cannot have followed us here. Specters and evil spirits do not have permission to wander in cities; they can only haunt old châteaux."

That humor went completely to waste. Madame Delmont's brow was not unfurrowed; she remained somber and silent; the illness that had afflicted her had made too much progress in her heart. She went to bed early.

The colonel stayed up much longer and, when he got into bed in his turn, he was surprised by the extreme exhaustion in which he found himself. As soon as he had laid his head on the pillow, sleep closed his eyes.

He woke up at daybreak, and as he heard his wife, who was turning over to find a more comfortable position, he asked her how she had spent the night.

"Still in the same manner," she replied. "I've changed my habitation, but not my torture. Continue to laugh at me, but the cruel Vampire has not abandoned me; it has become more atrocious, more avid for my blood."

This reply troubled Edouard, by giving him the sad conviction that his wife was so ill as to be unable to experience any relief. Too well-educated to admit such fancies, he was obliged to believe that Hélène had surrendered to a fatal hallucination that must have disturbed her sanity. He promised himself not to neglect anything to restore it. He even determined to constrain her to go out into the world, to see the sights, hoping to vanquish, on the pretext of restoring her health, all the objections that might be raised by a mother inconsolable at the loss of her son. For the moment, thinking that he ought to remain silent, he made no reply to what she had said to him.

They got up, and as the weather was fine, he asked her whether she would like to attempt a tour of the city—not on foot, because she was too weak to be able to walk far, but in a carriage, which would not tire her out as much.

Madame Delmont had already reached the stage of emaciation that renders people indifferent to everything that had occupied them when their body and soul were better disposed. She understood the pleasure that her consent would give to her husband, and she agreed, although she was as incurious as she could be with regard to that distraction.

They went out after breakfast, accompanied by their daughter. First they went to visit the Hôtel-de-Ville, pompously decorated with the name of "the Capitol"; they were interested to see the room in which a busts of a few of the city's illustrious men were gathered, and the one in which the *Académie des Jeux Floraux* holds its special meetings, presided over by the white marble statue of Clémence Isaure, the founder of that celebrated institution. Our travelers then cast a glance over the new Allée d'Angoulême, the construction-site of the Château-d'Eau situated at one extremity of the city, which was to give it the fountains it had always lacked—remarkable works due to Monsieur de Bellegarde, mayor of Toulouse, whose economical and paternal administration has merited the gratitude of his co-citizens.[31]

The Museum was also an object of Monsieur and Madame's curiosity. They had both been born in cities where the arts are successfully cherished and cultivated; they knew enough about drawing and painting to give worthy appreciation to the fine images they had before their eyes. They were particularly struck by those due to the brush of a Toulousian artist almost unknown in the rest of France, but who was nevertheless placed, by virtue of the vivacity of his genius and the passion of his compositions, among our most skillful masters. Antoine Rivalz, superior to his renown, has left works that will render his name immortal.[32]

The part of the Museum devoted to antiquities and monuments of the Middle Ages held Delmont's gaze; the loved that sector of science. He noticed a beautiful arrangement of curious objects that completely surrounded a vast cloister, embellished in the center by an Elysian garden. He asked the who had placed these various pieces, and was no longer astonished by the taste of the man who had presided over their classification when he heard the name of Alexandre du Mege, a savant archeologist and distinguished writer.[33]

Dinner time brought the Delmont family back to their lodgings. Involuntarily Hélène had been amused by the variety of the things that had successively passed before her eyes. She seemed much better. She ate with a hearty appetite, and the colonel even saw a faint color return to her pallid cheeks. At that consoling sight he felt full of hope. Entirely devoted to his duty, he distanced himself from ideas that would have seemed criminal; he even tried to forget an imperious sentiment, triumphant in his efforts when he attempted to reject it more forcefully.

---

[31] Toulouse actually owed its *Château d'eau* [water tower] to Charles Laganne, who left the city 50,000 francs for that purpose in his will; although he died in 1789, construction was not begun until 1822, when Guillaume Bellegarde was indeed the mayor; it was completed in 1828 and decommissioned in 1870. Bellegarde obtained the *particule* in his name in the same way that Lamothe-Langon did, being granted a barony under the Empire.

[32] The reputation of the Toulousian artist Antoine Rivalz (1677-1735) actually made little or no progress throughout the nineteenth century, but a revival of interest in his work began in the 1940s.

[33] Alexandre Dumege, or du Mege (1780-1862) did go on acquire a considerable, but not untainted, reputation as a pioneer of regional archaeology in the South of France. Lamothe-Langon knew him well, and the two of them collaborated in the production of the *Biographie Toulousaine* (1823); presumably, Lamothe-Langon could not have known in 1825 that Dumege would become embroiled in scandals regarding the alleged faking of antiquities, but the two men obviously had a lot in common.

Nightfall brought the time to go to bed. In order to try to give more courage to his wife, Delmont asked her for permission to set himself beside her. Hélène agreed. He promised to stay awake for as long as he could, in order that his presence might disconcert the monster that she feared.

He had made a reckless promise, though; shortly after going to bed, sleep came to attack him with all its gentleness. Delmont struggled in vain; he had to concede defeat and his eyes closed in spite of his efforts.

On awakening, he felt a sharp pain originating in his heart. He touched that part of his body; it was also painful, as if from the effect of a violent pressure. He turned toward the lamp, which was still burning, and his surprise was considerable when he recognized on his skin the imprint of five fingers, marked by yellow and black traces. He decided initially that the pressure had been exerted by Hélène's hand, and simultaneously drew the conclusion that he must have been profoundly unconscious, since he had not been woken up when he had been pressed thus.

At the same time, Hélène emerged from her lethargy. She said nothing specific to her husband about what she had felt during the night, but her silence explained well enough that her situation had not ameliorated, and that she was still under the empire of the fascination that was consuming her. It was, therefore, all the more urgent to strive to cure her.

They went out together at the customary hour; they visited churches and public monuments, and then visited two physicians whose insights they wanted to exploit. One of them, a member of several scientific societies and the secretary of the one most closely related to his profession, was better placed than anyone else to undertake a cure dependent on human science; his talents inspired a confidence augmented by his politeness, his intelligence and the fluency of his elocution. He was already known to the two spouses, who had met him at R*** in the home of one of their neighbors; they implored his help, and received the assurance that nothing would be neglected in answering their desires. While pronouncing thee words, however, he had already seen human attentions were helpless to reanimate strength in a body in which life was becoming extinct; his science did not blind him to that. He thought it his duty, however not to pas an immediate sentence of death.

Delmont, deceived by what had just been said to him, conceived a hope that did not take long to vanish. The next day, Hélène was incapable of leaving her room. She received a visit there from their friend Mélervant, who had come to Toulouse expressly to spend the day with the husband and wife. A single glance darted at the latter gave him, too, the conviction that she had reached the final period of her existence, and that she might expire at any moment. He hesitated at first as to what he ought to do; then his skillful colleague came in and accompanied him to the invalid's bedside. They both observed the disease, which was increasing with so much rapidity, for some time. Their conclusion was the same. They estimated that Madame Delmont might lived for another week, and decided that it was appropriate to warn the husband about the loss that he was on the brink of suffering.

That disagreeable commission naturally fell to Mélervant, who had known the colonel for some time; he asked to speak to him for a moment, and made the painful truth known to him.

That cruel revelation plunged Delmont into bitter grief. He wanted to oppose doubt to the most certain probability, and on the point of being separated from his wife, he felt all the attachment that she had once inspired him reborn. Overwhelmed by his despair, it seemed frightful to him to let Hélène know how precarious her situation was. Being unable to make any decision in that regard, he brought the doctor to her and, placing himself where she could no longer see him, abandoned himself to his pain.

In a faint voice, Madame Delmont asked the doctor whether he had seen the Hungarian woman, or had any news of her.

"As for seeing her, Madame," he replied, "that's impossible, for she never comes out of her house, which remains constantly closed to all those who present themselves there. Can you imagine that Monsieur Berneval did not fear to show his face there, in spite of the experience the past had given him?"

"He was no more fortunate at the second attempt?"

"It was entirely similar to the first. She discouraged him to such an extent that, when I met him yesterday to the Falgarde road, he assured me that *that woman*, as his sovereign scorn named her, was not fit for polite company, since she had not been able to tolerate his."

This anecdote amused its hearer.

"As for us," said Hélène, "we've been more fortunate; she has kept us informed. I've received several gracious messages from her. The strange creature! Young and beautiful, what a life she has adopted! She might indeed be better placed in solitude than in society, for she makes little effort to succeed. Always cold, always indifferent, rarely moved, and more; at times, she seems more like a machine set in motion than a human being. I can't explain what ascendancy she has over me, but since she left us, I miss her; it seems to me that in the final hours of my life it would be pleasant to have a person of my own sex with me, who would be able to understand me, and who might be willing, after my death, to take responsibility for watching over my daughter."

This speech, pronounced in a faint voice, terrified those who heard it. Delmont, moved by an impulse he could not suppress, rose from his armchair impetuously and came to seize Hélène's hand, while stammering consolations and a few hopeful words belied by the somber expression of his face.

Mélervant, more accustomed to such scenes, while experiencing a profound emotion, thought he ought to take advantage of the circumstance to urge Madame Delmont to seek the help of religion. She was pious, but since her arrival in Toulouse she had not thought of fulfilling her duties, believing that she had time to resume them when she had returned to the country.

"You are doing yourself a great deal of harm, Madame," he said to her, "in filing your imagination with lugubrious ideas. I wish that you had enough confidence in me to facilitate the means of changing our opinion as to the state of your health, but since you refuse to believe me, why not consult one of those pious ecclesiastics accustomed to attending sick-beds? Perhaps he could reassure you better than I can. Would you be content to converse with such a man?"

A dolorous smile preceded Hélène's response, announcing that she had not been deceived by the doctor's proposal. "You've anticipated my desire," she told him. "I was about to ask my husband to summon a priest; I feel that henceforth, I shall have more need of his help than that of your amiable amity; his science begins to take effect at the moment when the art of medicine can do no more. At the same time, however, I repeat my original desire; I would like to see the young foreigner again, and would like her to consent to remain with me for some time."

This desire, expressed in a tone that showed how much Hélène desired its accomplishment, greatly surprised the two witnesses. Delmont was even more alarmed by it than the doctor. He sensed the peril for himself of finding himself with Alinska again, at a solemn moment when he feared that her presence might distract him from his sacred duties. On the other hand, he did not know how to refuse such a thing to his dying wife, who, alone and as if lost in a land that was not her own, would necessarily lack a host of particular cares that could only be rendered by a person of her own sex, whose habits brought them closer to her. His embarrassment and indecision prevented him from answering immediately.

Madame Delmont, astonished by the silence that he did not break, asked him whether the desire she had formed was reprehensible, and whether he perceived some great obstacle to its fulfillment.

That question brought the colonel out of his reverie. He hastened to reply that, if he had not explained himself immediately, it was for fear of the apprehension he had that the eccentric Hungarian might refuse to yield to any solicitations that were addressed to her. "But since," he added, "your absolute desire is that she should come, try to write a few lines to her, to which I will also join my pleas, and we'll send our domestic right away, with the carriage—which will, I hope, bring her back."

In saying this, Delmont tried with extreme attention to suppress the vocal inflections that might have revealed his inner agitation; in particular, he feared the perspicacity of the doctor. In the present circumstances, he would not, for all the happiness in the world, have wanted his secret to burst forth to prejudiced eyes. In spite of his efforts, he could not hide his emotion completely, but that did not surprise the doctor at all; he attributed it to the disturbance his friend must be feeling.

Madame Delmont trued to write an urgent note, expressing to Alinska how glad she would be if she came. It took her nearly an hour to write a few lines, so she ceded her pen to her husband as soon as he asked for it, in order to add the following sentences:

Yes, Madame, we request this act of your generosity. Whatever resolutions you might have taken, they ought to yield to the urgent pleas we are addressing to you. Come back to us. Madame Delmont desires your presence; I invoke it too. As there are cases in life when one must go beyond all that has been regulated, I repeat once more: come; give us proof of our benevolence. A refusal would prove that you have broken with us entirely, and what has my wife done to merit that rigor?

When Delmont had finished writing, and giving instructions to the domestic, the doctor—who knew Toulouse—went out in search of a minister of peace and consolation, who might support Madame Delmont on the painful path that remained for her to travel in order to make her exit from life.

He found the ecclesiastic who could fulfill his objective better than any other in the first pastor of one of the great parishes of the city. This venerable curé, although already advanced in age, still possessed all the ardent fire of charity. Amiable in his pious vigor, indulgent toward sins that were only the fruit of error, he did not portray the Divinity as ever-terrible, ever-wrathful; he represented him as accessible to repentance, and merciful to hearts gone astray. His unctuous and persuasive eloquence had a very particular charm; he spoke like a master blessing the golden and silver flowers that poets obtained for their productions in the annual ceremony; he spoke like a father, either on the throne of truth or the seat of penitence.

It was to him that the doctor went. He described Madame Delmont's critical situation, the need she had for the guidance of an enlightened priest, and by repeated urging contrived to vanquish his reluctance to go in search of a new lamb outside his own sheepfold. He promised to come early the next day to the place to which he had been summoned, and the doctor transmitted this welcome assurance to those who were awaiting his return anxiously.

From that moment on, Hélène seemed more tranquil.

They could not imagine what particular sentiment drew her to Alinska—what the mysterious link might be between those two creatures who, in the normal course of affairs, would have been separated by everything that sets hearts apart and breaks affections. On the contrary, Madame Delmont wanted to see the Hungarian woman again; that whim, taken to the point of excitement, was doubtless one of the consequences of her singular malady. Was it not a matter of summoning to her side the serpent that was to devour her?

Chapter XXI

Anxiety was running high in the Delmont family. In spite of the urgent solicitations that had been addressed to her, they did not know whether Alinska would consent to come to Toulouse. The doctor, called by his professional duties to the country, set off at sunset without having seen the indifferent beauty.

It was eight o'clock in the evening when the carriage, which had had left at midday, arrived at the door of the house. At the sound it made the colonel got up and, taking a lamp, went rapidly downstairs, not so much to meet the foreigner, if she was there, as not to reveal the agitation he was experiencing to his wife.

As he set foot on the peristyle, he saw a woman enveloped in a large black shawl advancing toward him at a slow pace, and such that he was initially taken aback, as if he had seen a supernatural apparition. His disturbance was soon further augmented, however, when he noticed by the light of his lamp the frightful pallor spread over Alinska's face. It was her—or, rather, it was a specter, so haggard were her eyes, so distraught her features. She seemed at that moment to be a hundred times nearer to the grave than Madame Delmont, whose life was nevertheless reaching its final terminus.

Confused by what he saw, the colonel could not bring himself to pronounce the customary words that politeness demanded of him. He remained immobile, contemplating the ravages that such a short space of time had produced in Alinska's features. The latter, with a grim smile, perceived his astonishment.

"Here I am," she said to him. "You summoned me; don't imagine now that you can constrain me to go when you wish."

These bitter words, vehemently pronounced, were only heard by the man to whom they were addressed. He shivered, but, eventually seeking to recover his courage, he replied with an appearance of gallantry that won him a thunderous glare by way of response.

When they arrived in Madame Delmont's room the latter, at the sight of the Hungarian woman—who appeared to be dying, as she was—shed a few tears. At the same time, she extended her hand to her in a friendly manner. "How good you are," she said, "to have answered my prayer! But permit me to ask why you too have not come to the city in search of the help that you appear to need?"

"The external condition of my person," the foreigner replied, "has led you into error. I am not in a different situation from the one I was in a month or two ago. It would be difficult for me to be better or worse. My features seem disordered to you, my pallor frightens you; all that, Madame, originates from the distress into which I was thrown by your letter and the orders it contained. You know how necessary retreat is to me; it has been very difficult for me to extract myself from it, but when I am begged in a certain manner, I no longer have the right to refuse. You wanted me; I am here; are you sure that you will find in me the assistance that you need?"

These somewhat disobliging words had an unpleasant effect on Madame Delmont, who could not make out their true meaning. A little reflection reminded her of Alinska's known character; she also recalled the customary strangeness of all her manners, and realized that it was necessary not to take offense at anything she did, for she did not do anything as everyone else did. Hélène had need of company; she was accustomed to hers; ought she complain about finding her with all her eccentricities and unsocial habits?

Meanwhile, Alinska, in spite of her apparent ill-humor, caressed little Juliette, who, before going to bed, complimented her on her arrival in her naïve fashion. Alinska leaned over to kiss her, and made that movement with such affection that she found herself reconciled in consequence with the pretty child's mother.

As for Delmont, who was incapable of saying anything, he was plunged into a profound reverie, not daring to look at either his wife or Alinska, sometimes envisaging a future that only showed itself to him enveloped by the most sinister vapors.

The next day, Madame Delmont declared that she had spent night more cruel than all those that had preceded it. It was easy to judge that from the expression of fatigue and dolor on her emaciated face. Her weakness was visibly getting worse, and the last threads of her life would perhaps soon be broken.

She seemed anxious at not having seen the arrival of the priest she was expecting. At that moment, Germaine announced him; the colonel went into the drawing-room to welcome him and Alinska, uttering a cry of fright, suddenly escaped through a hidden door and retired to the room allocated to her.

If there is anything in human life worthy of admiration, it is the sight of a venerable priest bringing holy consolation to a suffering or unfortunate individual at the fatal hour that arrives dissipate all human illusions. He is not then a feeble mortal; he is a god in the full force of his power. He turns the gaze of the sufferer toward the undeceptive hopes of a world where everyone is equal, where virtue, clad here in the rags of poverty, sits on a throne similar to the one destined for a king who has lived well.

They are strangely mistaken whose prejudices fear these interludes, these effusions which seem to them the infallible forerunners of death. Where is the man whose energy is sufficiently vehement for him not to experience any terror, and dread for the future, in that solemn instant? Will it, then, augment the horror to hear a consoling voice that calms your anguish by promising you eternal happiness, bough at the mere price of a sincere repentance? Will it not rather be a keen satisfaction to finish thus with life, completely reassured as to what awaits you in the new existence that the immortality of our soul does not permit us to refuse?

If the aid of religion has such a power with respect to a person tormented by remorse, with how much gentleness does it present itself to someone who has never deviated from the path of righteousness!

As her end approached, Madame Delmont, whose career had been spent in the exercise of solid virtues, and whose only regrets were for those she was leaving in this world, was untroubled by any fear for the future. If, one the one hand, it was painful for her to abandon her husband and daughter, on the other, she retained the well-founded hope that they would one day be reunited with her, and, at the same time, she possessed complete certainty that her son was already waiting. She poured into the bosom of the venerable ecclesiastic the trivial faults for which she reproached herself; they were pardoned without difficulty, and mysterious and efficacious words, in reconciling her with the Creator of all, gave her the assurance that she would take her place among the chosen.

Nevertheless, while talking to her about her future happiness, the pious curé set aside the thought that she must renounce the earth entirely, and made her glimpse the possibility that she might get better if Providence deemed it necessary. He told her about so many sick people who had returned to health when the grave had opened before them, and so many unexpected miracles of that sort, that Madame Delmont, without being entirely reassured, was calmer when he left, promising that he would return that evening, and the next day, if she wished.

When he had gone, the colonel came back into his wife's room. He too tried to reassure her troubled mind—but at that moment, Madame Delmont, still in the fervor of prayer, was uninterested in any but celestial conversation.

She was extracted from her contemplation by one of the Toulousian doctors, who came to see her then. He found her no weaker than during his previous visit; he prescribed a fortifying potion, of which he expected the best effects.

Delmont noticed that Alinska had not reappeared; he ran to her room and knocked lightly on the door.

"Who is it?" Alinska asked. "What do you want?"

"I've come," replied a voice only too well known to her, "to ask you to come back to Madame Delmont."

"Is she alone?" she said, opening the door. "Is he no longer there—the redoubtable man the sight of whom it is not permitted to me to sustain?"

"Who are you talking about?"

"Who am I talking about! The priest—yes, him. It's impossible for me, since I left Hungary, to be in the presence of one of his kind. An eternal barrier separates us. They have finished with me; I have nothing more to ask of them on earth."

Touched by his unfortunate friend's superstitious terrors, which he attributed to the attempt she had made to kill herself, the colonel did not continue the conversation. He contented himself with replying that the strangers had all gone.

"I'll come with you then," Alinska said. "But Edouard, I beg you, if you don't want to witness the most frightful spectacle promise me never to let me encounter one of the Lord's priests—that you will make arrangements to be able to let me out of our wife's room before her confessor comes. It's the least you can do for me, alas!"

This speech, pronounced in a tremulous voice, augmented the colonel's pity. He immediately made the promise Alinska had requested, and returned with her to Madame Delmont.

The latter seemed to be glad to see them together; she smiled at them kindly. Then, escaping a moment's silence, she said to then: "Listen, both of you. People are trying to deceive me about my condition; I might be able to deceive myself while the sun shines, but the deadly night does not take long to exhaust me."

Alinska shivered, doubtless involuntarily

"I know where I'm going," Hélène continued. "A little while longer, and my mortal course will reach its end. I have no more orders to give; I can no longer address anything but prayers. Pay attention to mine; fulfill them, I implore you—and I shall carry into death the certainty that my final desires will not be refused."

"Oh, my love," the colonel said, excitedly, unconstrained by Alinska's presence, "don't allow yourself to be so depressed. You'll live, for the benefit of your family, and you will carry out your desires yourself."

"One of them, Edouard, cannot be carried out by me, since it concerns my mortal remains; it is to you that I leave that obligation, in which you will not fail. After my death, I want to rest alongside my son, who has preceded me there; it's in the cemetery in R*** that my body must be buried; any other ground would seem foreign to me. That's absolutely necessary to me."

Sighs and a few sincere tears deprived Delmont of the power to respond. Pressing his wife's hand in his own, however, he gave her the certainty, by that mute testimony, that he would conform to her wishes. She made no further insistence, and turned to the pale-faced and distraught Alinska, who was watching and listening to what was happening in horrified silence.

"As for you, Madame, consent to watch over my daughter for a while; you have seemed to treat her with amity; give her your care until the moment when you interests demand that you leave this country, so that I shall still have, when I let her go, the consoling proof that she will not pass from the care of a mother to that of a woman indifferent to her happiness..."

A sharp cry, of inexpressible anguish, escaped Alinska at that moment. Covering her face with both hands, she let herself fall into an armchair, and seemed to succumb to the weight of a gruel dolor. Far from assuring Hélène that she would comply with her desires, she kept silent, incapable for the moment of expressing and making known whatever it was that was oppressing her.

Delmont, alarmed to see her in such a state, nevertheless did not dare to fly to her aid, lest he reveal something of his sentiment—and what a shock he had received himself on hearing Hélène order her secret rival, so to speak, to replace her in the most sacred of her duties! He saw in all of this an irresistible chain of mysterious causation that, in spite of his resolution, was bringing him closer to

Alinska. He dared not penetrate the depths of the future, and sought instead to enclose himself completely in his present grief.

As the silence maintained by Alinska extended, Madame Delmont thought that she ought to renew her plea. Then the Hungarian woman suddenly rose to her feet, and turned her eyes, full of somber fire, toward the heavens. "That is your will, O Providence—is it for me to struggle against you? Yes, I accept what you make this unfortunate woman propose to me; yes, I shall be her daughter's guardian until death."

In spite of the contentment that this promise ought to have caused Madame Delmont, the bitter tone in which it was pronounced pierced her sharply. She saw something fatal in that word *death*, so unfortunately placed at the end of the sentence—but she dared not make known what troubled her then; she only hastened to say, as if to avert the premonition: "At least, don't leave my Juliette until you have handed her over to the wife her father has chosen."

A disdainful smile was doubtless all that Alinska could find to express her acquiescence, for she did not say a word; soon, in fact, she asked for permission to withdraw, and her absence was prolonged until the hour when the pious curé came to make the visit he had promised.

Five or six days then went by, during which Madame Delmont continued to grow weaker. All the resources of medical art were lavished on her in vain; they could not battle advantageously against a terrible and hidden cause that was leading rapidly to total destruction.

Every night, her husband watched over her, with a nurse accustomed to that kind of service; and by a very singular coincidence, every night, at the same time, fatigue plunged the colonel and the nurse into a lethargic sleep. Every morning, Hélène complained of a greater degree of exhaustion, and secretly, to her husband, she accused the insatiable demon that was drinking her blood drop by drop.

Driven to despair by seeing the unfortunate woman's reason incessantly going astray in this manner, Delmont was no longer able to combat her fantasy; he only responded to it with sad sighs.

Throughout this time, Alinska did not communicate her secret thoughts to her former lover by any word or glance. She treated him as if he had never known him before. She lavished urgent cares on Madame Delmont; she scarcely left her room as long as the daylight lasted, but returned to her own at nightfall and did not show herself until the following day. She never offered to watch over her friend by night; it seemed that such an act of devotion was beyond her strength.

Delmont respected her caprices; he enclosed himself in his despair, thinking only of giving Hélène proofs of his affection, without wondering whether he might, by means of those demonstrations of affection, be breaking the Hungarian woman's heart.

Their friend the doctor came to Toulouse from time to time. He no longer importuned the grim Alinska with his sighs, which seemed to be intolerable to her. He devoted all his attention to Hélène's malady, the fatal moment of which he fixed during his final visit.

His prescience was not incorrect. The sacraments of the church has already completed the sanctification of Madame Delmont's soul when she died, almost unconsciously, just as a new day dawned whose end she would not see.

The colonel was not with her at that moment; he had gone back to his own apartment, where the ecclesiastic, who had spent almost all night praying in that of the dying woman, was preparing him for the eternal separation that had just taken place.

We shall not seek to retrace the details of all the heart-rending emotions that assailed Delmont when he discovered the truth. Removed several times from beside his wife's inanimate body by Mélervant, who never left him, it was only while hugging his tearful daughter that he listened, not to unwelcome consolations but the voice of necessity, which ordered him to submit to a misfortune that was henceforth irreparable.

For as long as that fatal day lasted, Alinska did not put in an appearance; nothing was seen of her, either beside grieving husband, or the child whom she had promised to serve as mother. At nightfall, the doctor believed that he had the right, by virtue of that dolorous circumstance, to go to her room, where she might perhaps be in need of help. He knocked on the door, and when he received an invitation he went into the room.

Wrapped in her black shawl, Alinska was sitting by the fireplace. Her head was resting on a table and her whole face was hidden by the folds of the shawl. She listened to what Mélervant said without seeking to look at him. She replied in a weak but calm voice that she did not need anything, and that she could not show herself, because solitude was an absolute necessity for her in such a circumstance, but that she would keep the promise she had made. In consequence, she would go back to the Château de R*** the next day, separately from the rest of the family, where she would await the arrival of the daughter she was to protect.

The doctor, who had expected a different reply, was surprised that Alinska did not want to accompany her friend's remains. Maintaining silence as to what he thought about that, however, he contented himself with asking whether it was necessary to procure her a carriage in which make the journey.

"Thank you again," Alinska replied, still without wanting to look at him, "but I've already taken the measures that will ensure my return to the château. I'll leave early; it will be impossible for me to attend the distressing ceremony that must take place."

She fell silent. Her constant immobility commanded the doctor to withdraw.

He did so, ever more astonished by the young woman's eccentricity. He repeated what she had said to Delmont, and the latter was glad that Alinska's presence would not distract him from the sentiments that ought to be his sole occupation.

Several days went by before he received the necessary permissions from the civil and religious authorities to transport Madame Delmont's corpse to the cemetery of the commune of R***. During that time, the colonel never left the room in which his wife had expired. He yielded to a profound melancholy, from which people sought in vain to distract him.

He had learned that a carriage had come to collect Alinska at daybreak and that she had set off immediately. He felt somewhat relieved by that departure, for the sight of the Hungarian woman caused him to experience such a particular emotion that it robbed him of the faculty of devoting himself freely to his regrets.

Finally, he was able to leave Toulouse himself. He took his daughter with him, and they both followed the funeral procession, the lugubrious hymns of which plunged him into a bitter despair. The new curé of R*** ended the ceremony, and the unfortunate mother found her last refuge beside the son whose death had perhaps occasioned her own.

Let us draw a veil over the details of that gloomy event.

Chapter XXII

Delmont, who had to summon up all his strength to get through the funereal ceremonies with which the church surrounds the moments that render to the earth a body whose material elements were formed therefrom, came away from the parish church supported by his friend the doctor.

He did not want to climb into a carriage to complete the short journey that he had to make to the château, and, immersed in a deep grief, he hid his face from the gaze of the crowd attracted by the unusual pomp, veiling it with the folds of a cloak. Every step he took retraced a memory of the woman from whom he was separated forever.

His emotion increased in vehemence when he entered the dwelling in which, for some time, his soul had savored the happiness of peace and contentment. He went upstairs quickly, as if to escape his black ideas. When he hugged his daughter, he was on the point of asking her where her mother was, so troubled was the exercise of his reason.

The doctor, who, by virtue of his profession, often had similar scenes before his eyes, tried to cut this one short by asking Germaine to take Juliette to the room prepared for her, where the foreign lady doubtless ought to be waiting for her

Alinska's name, unexpectedly pronounced, awoke a new sentiment in the colonel's heart. Mélervant, who had not acted without a particular motive in speaking it, wanted to know what effect it would have on his friend. A rapid reflection, however, saved Delmont from the trap of sorts that had been extended for him; he felt that it was more necessary than ever, in such circumstances, not to be found out. Controlling himself, he appeared to listen indifferently to that which made one of the fibers of his sensitivity vibrate.

That attack having been unsuccessful, the doctor did not attempt another. He feared that he had chosen his time badly, and decided that if he wanted to assure himself as to the colonel's sentiments, he would have to launch a new assault at a moment when it might be attempted with more success.

There was doubtless little generosity in this conduct, but where is the man who can rise above himself when he fears some peril to his most tender affections? Mélervant was in love; he feared, with apparent reason, that a fortunate rival had been placed between himself and the woman he wanted to obtain. Where is the man who, in his position, could impose silence on his anxiety in order not to be lacking in social etiquette? It would be difficult but find one; such ways of thought are not natural; nature ordinarily abandons itself more easily to the penchants that passions inspire.

The doctor would have been incapable of doing the colonel any harm, or seeing to inspire any jealousy or mistrust in him, but, heedless of the fact that he was acting slyly, he was able to want to read his thoughts accurately. He had promised to remain that château all day; he kept his word.

When it was time for the evening meal, Alinska, who had not yet appeared, sent word to the colonel that she would stay in her room, and that it might be several days before the state of her health would permit her to come and sit down at the communal table.

This announcement, while annoying the doctor, who was in a hurry to find opportunities to see his ingrate beauty, gladdened Delmont; the latter knew the extent of his own weakness, and feared the sight of Alinska, all the more so now that death had smashed the barrier raised between the two lovers. In his situation in which he found himself, he knew how unfitting any other expression than that of regret would be. Full of respect for the requirements of his duty and tender affection for the wife he had lost, he desired to flee all opportunities that might lead to him revealing himself to be less that he ought to be.

Spring reanimated nature then, and produced lovely days in scant rapport with the colonel's somber sadness. Everywhere, as the sap rose, new life shone; the trees recovered their foliage, the meadows were covered with radiant flowers and the air was warm and perfumed. In the depths of the rejuvenated thickets the birds called to one another, about to recommence their amours, and the sweet song of the nightingale was already captivating the ears of weary voyagers and hunters hidden in the bushes waiting for a hare to pass close to their fortress.

At that time, when everything is coming back to life, humans cannot remain alone in profound torpor; for them too, one might think that a new life is beginning; the blood seethes more impetuously in their veins; a secret languor, an imperious need, transports them to the most tender affections; they doubtless love in every season of the year, but in this one they are not so much yielding to penchants of the soul as to the imperious will of the senses; the sharpest grief is diminished by the effervescence that the determination of nature imposes on the body.

Involuntarily, Delmont experienced the vague agitations that we have just painted with broad strokes, which he was able to experience in full, down to the slightest detail.

A month had gone by, and Alinska maintained in the Château de R*** the profound retreat that she had already observed while she lived in the isolated house. Her chamber was inaccessible to everyone but the domestics who served her. Only Juliette was admitted into that forbidden interior; but the child, whose character refused melancholy, preferring running around the garden with companions of her own age, under the supervision of Germaine, who never left her. Thus, outside the hours when Juliette had to come to study, Alinska remained alone, and did not appear disposed to break the vow that she had doubtless made.

More than once, Delmont was surprised to experience resentment at this conduct. To begin with, he had feared the danger of finding himself in the presence of his lover, but now he reproached her for her obstinacy in staying away—and the more she seemed to want to avoid him, the more impatient he became, contrarily, to see her.

Whatever his desires were in that matter, however, he dared not reveal them as yet. He spent his days sadly, reading or wandering the countryside. His excursions often took him for his favorite walk, which extended as far as the village of Lacroix on the banks of the Ariège. He liked going up to the top of a hill that offered pleasant views in all directions, where an immense vista unfolded before him toward the east, at which the eye never tired of gazing.

Delmont often liked to rest in front of the door of the abandoned church of the village of Falgarde. There, seated on a stone that had once belonged to some sepulcher, he admired the richness of the surrounding landscape, and the striking contrast between the ruins of the edifice that was covering him with its shadow and the animated life presented by the nearby cottages.

In the former, everything was bleak and silent; the bells that had summoned the faithful to prayer were long broken and no longer ran; the hand of time had struck all the walls of the church; they were crumbling in several placed, while a few fragments of armorial black bands still remained on their linings, testimony to a pride impotent to perpetuate itself even in the hardest marble and the most compact bronzes.

In the latter, laborers whom the love of money or the needs of their families rendered hard-working were relentlessly occupied in the cultivation of fields or looking after their animals; shouts and amusing songs announced the presence of human beings; activity was observable everywhere; the background was replete with oxen drawing ploughs, peasants sowing grain, completed the animation of the scene.

As the colonel's thoughts retreated to the place where he was sitting, however, the sounds gradually died away in his ears. Absolute calm reigned in the cemetery beneath his feet, and that funeral silence, which only the birds in the heavens failed to respect, imported melancholy emotions into his soul by reminding him, involuntarily, of the double loss that he had recently sustained.

When his memories besieged him too poignantly, he got up precipitately and resumed his route, seeking the necessary distraction in the contemplation of new objects.

Mélervant, weary, for his part, of no longer seeing the Hungarian woman, finally formed the resolution to explain himself frankly to the colonel—whose sentiments, as we have said several times, he suspected. He wanted to know exactly what relationship might exist between the latter and the foreigner, in order to regulate in consequence the determination that he ought to adopt for the future. Several times, however, he was thwarted by particular circumstances that did not permit him to come to the château when he wanted, or which caused him to encounter there one of the neighbors in front of whom he could not appropriately raise the subject.

Although he had no suspicion of this resolution, Delmont was no longer as open with his friend since his situation with regard to Alinska had changed. By virtue of the effect of Madame Delmont's death, the doctor had become his rival. His rival! That was something he blushed to confess to himself, and yet his heart, involuntarily, as concerned by it. A vague dread caused him to fear the entreaties that Mélervant might make of him; his delicacy blushed at the mystery with which it was necessary to envelop his sentiments, lest they put him in a difficult situation—which would arise as soon as the doctor decided to talk to him about his constant passion.

Thus tormented, Delmont was rarely able to sleep. Often, when the other inhabitants of the château had long since surrendered to the sweetness of rest, he was awake in his room, seeking, by means of assiduous reading to escape the pain brought on by his reflections. He sought means to distract himself in vain, however; the image of Alinska and the memory of Hélène rendered him inattentive, and his eyes mechanically scanned words that were not engraved on his memory.

One night, when he was tormented more than ever by painful thoughts, he wearied of his inaction; to temper the ardor of his blood, he tried to leave his room, intending to go to the château's great hall, to walk around and soothe his distress. He picked up the lamp by which he had been reading and, going through various rooms, arrived at his destination. He placed the lamp of the mantelpiece of the old fireplace and, by the pale light it spread, wandered around, striding rapidly through the barely-dissipated gloom.

He had not been there long when the door of the room situated in the direction of the main staircase was agitated. Delmont stopped. Soon, the door, forcefully shoved, rotated on its hinges, and Alinska appeared...

The colonel scarcely recognized her, so much did the black veils in which she was enveloped confuse her, at a distance, with the darkness that the lamp could only penetrate with difficulty. The pallor of her face stood out all the more, however; she seemed no longer to have a human form and, as some kind of horrible apparition, she advanced alone into the middle of the room.

Delmont's impetuous imagination represented her momentarily as winged, and dripping with blood. That vision disappeared with lightning rapidity, but nevertheless terrified the person it had struck.

Without manifesting and surprise at the sight of her lover, whom she had recognized at first glance, Alinska stopped in her tracks and supported herself on the back of an old armchair, as if she had suddenly felt dizzy.

For his part, Delmont, although considerably more emotional, immediately went to the young Hungarian woman. "Finally," he said, "I can see you again, and it's in the same place, at the same hour, where you came to tell me that you were going away. How bizarre this meeting is! Do I really owe it to chance?"

"It's possible that chance plays a role in this for you," Alinska replied, still in her customary melancholy tone, "but I come to breathe in this room ever night, and I see can only see an encounter that had to take place sooner or later."

"What! You come here every night, Alinska, you say? By what charm are you attracted to a room which, by virtue of its size and disorder, can only inspire unpleasant ideas when daylight doesn't illuminate it?"

"The splendors of the sun and the funereal appearance of shadows are of no consequence to me, Edouard. I laugh at everything that intimidates my sex; I delight in terror and can only take pleasure, by virtue of the fatality of my destiny, in the midst of what the mass of human beings fears or detests."

"Alas! Will you never change? Will you never return to less somber ideas? The past, whose memory is so painful at first, loses its anguish in becoming distant. The course of events often leads inevitably to a soothing of pains that seemed the most durable. Are those effects not tangible in the depths of your heart?"

"No—they slide through it, but never stop there. You talk to me about the past, but I have no knowledge of it; the present is everything to me. It is fixed above my head; I cannot retreat into life, no more can I advance into the future. I am stationary in the midst of human revolutions, and the hope that even the most wretched conserve—that which promises an end to their misery—is absolutely foreign to me. What do you expect, Delmont? You have determined Alinska's fate; don't be astonished if it remains unaltered."

"The more I listen to you, cruel friend, the more your inexplicable words rend my heart. What is this boundless despair to which you have abandoned yourself? Are you the only person in the world who can have no hope in the future? Oh, get a grip on yourself; imagine once again that your situation might change. Fortune will not always be contrary..."

"Can fortune, Edouard," Alinska said, sharply, "bring back from the grave your promise, which I have buried there?"

"My promise, you say?"

"Yes—the one that you signed with your blood, which binds you to me irrevocably."

"Is this the moment to remind me of it? Whatever my secret sentiments might be, do you not see the garments I wear? Don't you remember the dolorous event that recently took place?"

"I know that you, who claim to want me to be happy, have never hesitated to inflict a further wound on my soul. I know that you have deceived me shamefully; that is the only past action that I recall—the one that crushes you, which you will always bemoan."

"I wanted to see you again, Alinska; I didn't anticipate that I would present myself to your eyes only so that I might hear your reproaches. How unjust you are, and how little you know me!"

A glint of joy shone in the Hungarian woman's bleak eyes, and her lips held back words that were about to escape. A brief silence followed; it was not without sweetness for her. A serenity that had not appeared on her brow for a long time was about to reappear there, when a sudden thought broke the spell instantaneously. Alinska's gaze filled with a grim expression; she put her hand to her heart, as if to suppress its dolorous beat.

"And I too, Edouard, experienced an imperious need to be together again. It seemed to me that by seeing one another, we could take ourselves back to a distant and happy time. Do you feel the same? Is it possible that you might present yourself to me as you were then, now that your unfortunate friend no longer posses any of her former charm?"

"I loved the virtues of your soul as much as your physical charms then. Time might have stolen a tiny fraction of your attractions, but what could it do to the precious qualities against which its devouring scythe had to be blunted?"

"I have no reply to make to you here and now; my voice cannot make itself heard, so overwhelmed is it by frightful anguish. All that I can tell you is that my body is as it was then, that you alone have occupied all the faculties of my soul, and that the void in which I now am has nothing terrestrial about it. This disgust is the child of eternity. Adieu; it's necessary that I go away. Don't prolong any further a conversation that can only cause us pain; mutually enlightened as to our sentiments, let's wait for whatever Providence decides. Oh, how heavy the task is with which my wrath has charged me!"

"Yes, like you I think that we have nothing more to communicate to one another. Let's let time go by; we shall meet again one day, when it will be possible for use to be together again, and then..."

"And then we shall march together directly to the tomb, which must serve as our nuptial bed..."

"What a horrible prediction! Alinska, you are the most cruel of women! Can you perceive nothing in the future but a coffin?"

Alinska did not reply; she left precipitately—and as she went up the stairs she allowed a few bursts of laughter to escape, which bore such an imprint of horror that Delmont, as if frozen by fear, thought he heard the frightful gaiety of an infernal power.

"Poor girl," he said, "she too has her share of the hallucination brought by great misfortune. Her eccentricities have distorted an amiable character, but she is more interesting by virtue of her misfortunes than any other woman would be in the wake of continual prosperity. Perhaps she will come back entirely to more accurate ideas; perhaps she will be freed from the cause that has reduced her to this wretched state."

As he concluded these words, which his agitation had prompted him to pronounce aloud, he thought he heard a profound sigh behind him. He turned around promptly, and in the darkest part of the hall he perceived, confusedly, a white-clad figure holding a child by the hand, which was going into the drawing-room with the boy...

In spite of his courage, Delmont shivered at the sight of this strange apparition. His imagination had even dressed it with features that reminded him of dear and accusing memories.

He hesitated as to what to do, but soon, seizing his lamp, he went into the drawing-room.

He found it empty; he alone troubled its silence, by virtue of his precipitate pace. He said seen, though, had seen...

He went back to his room, bathed with sweat and racked by remorse.

Chapter XXIII

Delmont did not try to go to sleep; he remained immersed in cruel thoughts, and continued walking at a precipitate pace for the rest of the night, sometimes looking out of a widow he had opened at the effect produced by the moonlight on the vast landscape that extended around him.

In vain he tried to doubt the reality of the vision that had struck his sight; all the circumstances finally combined to give him the assurance that he had not been the victim of a deceptive illusion.

Dawn finally arrived. Calmer then, Delmont felt the almost-invincible horror that had chilled him during the reign of night's shadows diminishing within him; his refreshed blood flowed more smoothly, and his heart ceased to beat with the violence that had scarcely left him able to breathe.

Every morning, when she got up, little Juliette came to kiss her father; for him it was a pleasure mingled with bitterness, but of which he would not consent to deprive himself. That day, the child appeared at the customary time, but her face, usually cheerful, was darkened, and an extreme pallor could be seen spreading over her features.

"Are you ill, my darling?" Delmont asked her, anxiously.

"No, Father," she replied, "but I didn't have a good night."

"What prevented you from sleeping? Was it some imposition—which Germaine claims that you carry out marvelously?"

"Oh, Papa, I'd tell you if I hadn't been forbidden to talk to you about it."

"Perhaps I ought to stop my questions there; nevertheless, I'm curious to know the cause of our insomnia. It must have some importance, for your face doesn't have the beautiful colors that normally ornament it."

"You won't weep if I tell you the truth?"

"I hope I have enough strength to overcome my initial impulse, if your story is tragic," Delmont replied, pretending to smile—although an ominous presentiment was already raising a surge of fear in his soul.

"Well, Eugène and my kind mother came to visit me. They stayed on either side of my bed almost all night—in order to defend me, they said, against the ferocity of the demon that had killed them, and would come to drink my blood. They frightened me at first, but afterwards I felt much better. Eugène seemed so happy! My mother looked at me so lovingly! They promised me not to lose sight of me again, and they left at daybreak, assuring me that from now on, I had nothing more to fear. They talked to me about many things—but would you believe that they never pronounced your name, even though I told them how much you wept. They shook their heads and smiled, without replying."

The child could have continued her frightful narration for much longer, without her father thinking of interrupting her. Mute with confusion, stricken to the utmost depths of his being by the most heart-rending effects of fear, horror and despair, he remained motionless in his armchair, as if he had already received a mortal blow. The inconceivable rapport between what he had seen and what his daughter had told him plunged him into an abyss of reflections from which he could not make up his mind to emerge. Attained for the first time by superstitious terror, he found himself under the empire of prejudices.

Meanwhile, the seconds went by. Juliette was still standing in front of him waiting for his reply. He finally contrived to break the silence, and in an emotional voice, he thanked her for what she had told him.

"You should," he said, "regard that dream as a blessing from God. He wanted to let you know that your mother and brother are watching over you from the heights of Heaven, to defend you against the demon, or, to put it better, from sin. That's the explanation of what they said."

"Oh, Papa, I wasn't asleep when they came. They came in through the door of my room that opens into the drawing-room. They didn't say anything to me about sin, but only an evil spirit that want to kill us all, and which they called a Vampire. I know what that is, because poor Raoul, before he died, often told us the story of that evil race. I can repeat it without forgetting a single word: Vampires or Boucolatres..."

"I know it better than you do, my darling. Those are tales that she should have spared you—which, taking over your imagination, must have troubled you during the night. Believe me, forget your dream; people will make fun of you if you repeat it; you'll be taken for a frightened little girl, and people might well accuse you of lying if you claim not to have been asleep. Personally, I don't doubt your veracity; you thought you saw something that can only have been an illusion; I beg you, above all, not to say anything about these things to Alinska. You'll give her a great deal of pain—and me too, if you forget my prohibition."

"Don't worry about that; I knew already that I mustn't say anything. Eugène has given me firm instructions; he says that she's my mortal enemy..."

This new blow struck the target at which it was aimed. Delmont got up immediately, to try to pull himself together, dismissing his daughter in order not to hear anything else that might add to his torments. He could not understand how many bizarre items had been gathered in the same place, or by what fatality the errors of a dream had taken on all the forms of truth.

Alas, he knew only too well that a stepmother is almost always the enemy of children she has not conceived. The colonel's own father had married for a second time, and his entire youth had been poisoned by daily quarrels, unjust accusations and attempts made to turn the author of his days against him, or to steal the better part of the latter's wealth. For the first time, he thought of the wrong he would do his daughter if he ever took another wife, and paternal affection raised a new conflict in his heart.

At breakfast time, it was not without a sharp surprise that he saw Alinska come into the dining-room. She appeared to want to seem content, but an extreme resentment nevertheless pierced her feigned joy. She looked at Juliette with a somber expression of repressed anger, but only not let it show when Delmont was not looking at her face. She joked about the long retreat she had maintained, promising not to lock away her distress henceforth, but to try to distract herself from it.

She showed off her wit so advantageously, and appeared so graceful and charming, that the colonel, initially on his guard, did not take long to yield to the influence she desired to have on him.

The past, if not forgotten, was at least pushed away. Edouard no longer saw any but the Alinska of the early days of heir reciprocal passion, and his enchantment reached its peak when, taking up the harp that she had not interrogated for a long time, she sang the following ballad with exquisite taste, which Delmont had heard before, and which expressed a part of what the Hungarian woman did not want to confess. It also depicted the embarrassment of her situation in the presence of a handsome officer who, placed far above her by fortune, did not appear to be destined to lower himself far enough to respond to her love.[34]

It is said that once in one's life
That love's ardors must be suffered
That pleasure is followed by strife
Before happiness can be offered.
    Hungarian maid
    Don't be dismayed,
I dread the hurt you praise that way.
    In my retreat
    I am complete,
And pure joy's worth more for delay.

Is it true the in that tenderness
Is descending into my heart?
I feel a fatal drunkenness
I'm vanquished by the Frenchman's art
    Hungarian maid
    Alone, afraid
May God free me from sentiment!
    Seduction's goal
    Inflames the soul
But leads at last to dire torment.

Yes, in love with no defender
 I lose repose and gaiety
You, whose gaze is soft and tender
Can I trust your sincerity?
    Hungarian maid
    Has not displayed
A Frenchwoman's wit or charm.
    Her innocence
    And continence
Will delight you or cause her harm.

As the beautiful foreigner completed the final couplet of her song, the doctor, who was not expected, arrived at the château. Surprised to hear harmonious sounds, which perhaps ought not to have resounded yet under vaults that the décor of mourning had not abandoned, he stopped as he entered the hall, and a

---

[34] This song, titled "The Poor [female] Hungarian" is subtitled as a *romance*/ballad.

mirror placed opposite the doorway allowed him to observe what was happening.

Mélervant had come with the intention of discussing the subject of Alinska with the colonel, but what he saw at that moment dispensed with the necessity of embarking on a futile conversation. Delmont's rapture, the Hungarian woman's gaze, the accord—so easy to recognize—between two hearts that share the same sentiment: all of that provided proof that a love older than he could have believed united those two individuals.

Horrible suspicions were suddenly born in his heart, but he rejected them immediately and was ashamed of them. He could not doubt the colonel's honesty—but the somber and grim Alinska did not inspire the same confidence.

Mysteries then became clear to him, the depths of which made him tremble. Nevertheless, he thought it appropriate to show himself, and he went into the drawing-room just as the enchanted colonel was asking Alinska to sing another ballad. His presence appeared to annoy the Hungarian woman, who, after the initial compliments, abandoned the company and returned to her room.

Delmont, tormented by that retreat—which left him, so to speak, in the doctor's power—would have liked some visit to interrupt the tiresome tête-à-tête, but no one came, not even Monsieur Berneval, who usually came every day to play chess with the colonel.

The latter's embarrassment was visible; it inspired a sort of pity in his interlocutor—who, in order to put an end to it, abruptly launched his attack.

"Monsieur Delmont," he said, "you are a man of honor; I believe I have the right to your esteem. Will you please reply to a single question that I need to ask you? There is nothing hostile about it; it will merely serve to regulate my subsequent conduct. Did you know the beautiful foreigner who has agitated my heart for some time before she appeared in this commune for the first time?"

"Doctor," the colonel replied, heatedly, "if anyone else were to interrogate me, I would maintain a profound silence in his regard, but I know how culpable I am toward you, and I can only repair my fault by total frankness. Alinska was the first woman who gave me her love. I was then in her homeland; I could not overcome her virtue. Nevertheless, I forgot her, after having made her the most solemn promises. She did not renounce me; she followed me to France, discovered me in this remote part of the kingdom, and came to join me here without informing me of the fact. So long as my unfortunate wife's life lasted, I did not encourage her passion in any manner. That is the whole truth; I swear by the decorations for bravery that I wear that the facts I have just told you are exact."

"That's sufficient, colonel; I ask no more. Perhaps, though, you might have taken me into your confidence sooner."

"How could I, my friend? Are other people's secrets entirely ours? Could I dispose of Alinska's? I have only revealed it to you, and you will not confide it to anyone else."

"Adieu, Monsieur Delmont. May you be happy! May the time to come not allow you to regret the past!"

After these words, Mélervant left, in spite of the colonel's efforts to persuade him to stay for dinner.

"No, permit me to go; I don't want my presence to disturb the foreigner's sentiments. She would feel awkward; I would not be comfortable. Adieu again; accept, I repeat, my good wishes for your happiness."

Everything in what the doctor said was doubtless natural and polite; nevertheless, Delmont believed that he recognized therein a suggestion of reproach that he resented. He retrained himself, however, attributing any possible bitterness in his friend's conduct, given the circumstances, to the disappointment of unrequited love.

Several weeks went by after this conversation, during which Delmont, gradually abandoning himself to the penchant of his soul, rendered the Hungarian maid sovereign mistress of his heart for a second time.

The latter sometimes seemed gladdened by this sentiment, but sometimes fell back into her grim melancholy. The greater the empire she obtained over her former lover, the more she delivered herself to extreme caprices. In particular, she began to manifest an extreme aversion to young Juliette; one might have thought that the sight of the child caused her a secret pain. She sought in vain to hide or overcome that singular antipathy, but she could not do it; it became evident in all her actions and was painted in her every expression.

Delmont could not ignore it for long; he expressed his surprise, and even his discontent.

"Oh, Edouard," the foreigner replied, "I reproach myself more than you can imagine. I know how unjust my hatred for that amiable creature is, but can one command the impulses of one's heart? I want to reign alone in yours, and everything that serves to remind you of another in unbearable to me. Time, I assure you, will render me more reasonable; but today, I cannot triumph over myself. In loving you more than ever, I have resumed my human weakness. Have pity on me; endure some of the pain that had besieged me since your fatal abandonment."

This speech, and shrewdly-shed tears, calmed the colonel's agitation. He felt obliged to remove a constant subject of involuntary chagrin from the sight of the woman who had subjugated him, and, without informing Alinska, he sent Juliette to a boarding-school run by nuns of the Maltese Order in Toulouse, telling himself that his separation from his daughter would only be temporary. Providence decided otherwise.

The inexplicable Alinska suffered cruel distress at Juliette's departure. "Sending her away from your house," she said to the colonel, "is constraining me to depart myself. It was for her sake that I was here; she is no longer here; what entitlement do I have to remain?"

"That which would be the most dear to me, Alinska," her lover replied, tenderly. "That which I would already have liked to offer you, if the severe laws of propriety had not prevented me. You were to be mine when my folly placed a barrier between us that would have been insurmountable. Providence has seen fit to raise it; will you refuse me that which would once have rendered you happy?"

Alinska must certainly have expected such a declaration; nevertheless, she remained confounded while Delmont spoke. A thousand various sentiments were stirring in her soul; she experienced the emotions of hope and despair simultaneously; she saw the moment approaching that would determine her existence; she knew where the cruel mission that she was about to fulfill must lead; she ought to have had nothing in her heart but vengeance, but the love that triumphs over everything that exists on earth usurped a share of the beat that Hell had excited.

Pale and oppressed, Alinska shivered at the reply she was about to make. In vain, the absolute power that commanded her acted imperiously upon her; by virtue of her senses she still belonged to the earth, and had in consequence the possibility of fighting, if not successfully, at least stubbornly.

Thus, making an effort, she cried: "No, Edouard, no, don't talk to me about a ceremony to which I once attached all the felicity of my existence. Can I be yours now, when I do not belong to myself? Besides, where are your pretentions taking you? Feeble child of humankind, what union are you proposing? Shall I prostrate myself at the foot of the altar that has rejected me? I've already told you—banished from the Lord's temples by a terrible malediction, I would not dare to cross the redoubtable threshold. You would believe it to be open to us, but I would see an exterminating angel there, which would escape your mortal sight. You love me, you say? Well, give me proof of it, by not importuning me again. I believe in your affection; that must suffice—it is not permissible for you to doubt mine."

"And it's because it speaks so poignantly to me heart that I want to be sure of it. Cruel friend, recover now the entire exercise of your reason; don't forge phantoms. Even an incomplete suicide is doubtless a crime before the Divinity, but if there is no sin that repentance cannot efface, why should yours be pursued by an inflexible rigor?"

"That is how humans are! One is delirious every time one speaks of them of things they cannot understand, or tells them a truth that they cannot unveil. Do you not understand that the moment you expect to complete our common felicity would be that of our eternal separation? And that separation fills me with horror. Here, we can remain together; down there"—she lowered her voice as she continued—"would each take an opposite route. What will the priest say before whom I shall present myself?"

"Will he possess the gift of divination? Will he know in R*** what sin your love caused you to commit in Hungary?"

"Edouard, God marked the forehead of the fratricide Cain with a terrible mark; I bear an equally formidable sign on mine; you cannot see it, but he would perceive it, and then it would be necessary to say adieu to you forever, for there is here, as in Hungary, consecrated ground ever-ready to receive bodies that must dissolve.

"Poor girl! How I pity you! You're misled by the prejudices of your education; thus, by virtue of a chimerical dread, you oppose our common happiness. If you fear the rigors of the church, though, would you be equally afraid of a union consecrated by the civil authorities?"

"Oh, that wouldn't matter—no sacred hand would touch my own."

At these words, which Delmont heard it home joy, he nevertheless darted an involuntary glance at the black glove covering Alinska's hand, which she never took off. That eccentricity inspired a sudden curiosity in him, but he was careful not to reveal it, postponing its contentment to another time.

"So you consent to belong to me, at least in the human manner? I don't ask for any more now; later, you will complete your condescension to my wishes, and then..."

A melancholy smile, and a shake of the head that signified a persistence in the refusal, were the Hungarian woman's only response. Delmont did not seem to pay any heed to it; he would leave everything to time and the power of his affection.

Chapter XXIV

Before conducting Alinska to the civil registry, Delmont let a few months go by. His first passion, violently reignited, would not permit him to appreciate the impropriety of that overly hasty step, but a confused sentiment of duty retained him against his will. His wife's virtues had inspired the most complete admiration in the inhabitants of the commune; the Hungarian woman's eccentricities, by an opposite effect, repelled them; it was to be feared that, informed of the union that he had contracted with her, they might make free with those insults disguised by the name of amusement by which a second marriage is stigmatized from the start in small towns and rural areas.

Nevertheless, Delmont could not hesitate forever; he had to make a decision, and he eventually decided to speak privately to the district's senior magistrate. The latter, surprised by the confidence, did not reveal how much it pained him. His duty was limited, in such circumstances, to fulfilling the legal formalities. He stayed strictly within the bounds of his obligation, and promised, in order to avoid a public outcry, to come to the château to perform the nuptial ceremony.

Having taken care of that, Delmont, driven by a power active within him, wanted to persuade Alinska to become his wife entirely, and without mentioning it to her, or giving her any grounds for suspicion, he conferred on this important point with the parish priest, who promised to do everything he could to facilitate the religious union of the two lovers.

The colonel, full of frankness and honesty, did not hesitate to take him fully into his confidence. He told him about the desperate attempt that Alinska had made on her own life, the religious terrors that she was experiencing in consequence, how she feared to enter a church, from which it seemed to her that divine wrath would expel her, the fear that ministers of religion inspired in her, and the necessity of exercising caution with respect to a woman weakened by misfortune and prejudices.

Fortunately, the curé was not one of those men who, confined by their paltry ideas to the center of a narrow circle, did not know how to get out of it. More enlightened and better educated as to everything that he had the right to do, he thought that for a greater good—that of avoiding scandal—it would be permissible for him to deviate from the ordinary rules, since by following them, there would be a danger that they would be promptly violated. He regarded the young woman's fear, and the remorse she experienced for her blameworthy action, as sufficiently satisfactory to the laws of the church; he saw in her repentance all that as necessary to replace, at least temporarily, the desired revelation at the tribunal of penitence. In consequence, he saw no difficulty in promising to come to the chapel of the château at midnight to bless the marriage of Alinska and the colonel, after the civil officer had done what he had to do.

Delighted with having obtained this important concession, Delmont went back to his lover and, approaching her excitedly, told her that they would be irrevocably united that very evening. A sudden blush covered the young foreigner's cheeks, but at the same time, a cloud of sadness spread within her eyes. She trembled from head to toe, and had to lean against a nearby table.

"Already, Edouard!" she said. "Already! You're in a great hurry! Can you not suffer our happiness to be prolonged for a little longer?"

"Is it destroying it to secure it forever? Will our union, solemnly approved, lose all its sweetness, by virtue of the fact that it can no longer be broken?"

"You think so, insane as you are! You're like all mortals; you can only see the present; the future has no impact upon you, unless your imagination embellishes it."

"And mine is made at this moment. Why do you remain plunged in this melancholy, which absorbs the faculties of our soul? What did you come to seek of me, if not the hope of our being united? Did you not claim me, as belonging to you? I recognize your right; I am now delivering myself; will you reject your property?"

"Oh, as to being mine, that point cannot be contested. The promise traced in your blood is a pledge more assured than all these ceremonies, to which I am indifferent. Satisfied by seeing you, however, I dread the hour that will give me frightful rights over you. Oh, Edouard, if you believe me, go beg the magistrate not to come in answer to your prayer; you have no suspicion of all the misfortunes that await you, if you bind yourself irrevocably to me."

So saying, she ran away from Delmont impetuously, and went to seek a retreat in her apartment that he dared not disturb. He remained confused by what he had just heard. He wondered exactly what point of exasperation Alinska's delirium might reach when she found herself in the presence of the minister of altars, but he no longer had time to take another course; the boat was launched, and must reach a port.

Two witnesses being indispensable to contract a legitimate union, whether before the civil registrar or the parish priest, Delmont chose his domestic and the château's farmer; he had them close at hand, and was certain of finding them at the requisite moment. In consequence, there was no danger that, having been notified in advance, some indiscreet revelation on their part might awaken public malignity—which already, suspecting what was about to happen, threatening to spread; the effects of which the colonel dreaded.

Immediately after his marriage, he intended to climb into his carriage to take his new wife first to Toulouse and then to Paris, where he would take up residence henceforth. Living in R*** now seemed intolerable to him, recalling too many cruel memories, which were an inexhaustible subject of chagrin and confusion.

Darkness finally arrived. Alinska, still shut up in her room, had manifested the desire not to emerge therefrom until the last minute. Delmont, agitated by everything that can excite a human heart, wandered back and forth, unable to settle anywhere.

An impetuous westerly wind was blowing just then; it penetrated the château, and by its various whistlings sometimes imitated the plaints of a soul in torment and sometimes burst of infernal laughter. It blasted the windows, which rattled continually, and shook the interior doors, causing them to render a lugubrious murmur. Its fury was such that the colonel's soul eventually felt a kind of terror. He experienced a fit that was not one of joy, and more than once he was on the point of capitulation, and of agreeing with Alinska that the hour of a desired union might nevertheless not be that of happiness.

In one of the aimless excursions that he made to the heart of the château, he drew near to the room where his domestics and farm-laborers were. They were talking among themselves about the order he had given that he carriage be should be ready at midnight. Some were surprised that he wanted to go out so late, others were trying to guess what the purpose of the unexpected journey might be.

"It doesn't surprise me," said one of the farmers. "We've known for some time that the colonel doesn't spend his nights peacefully, so it's more agreeable for him to go out at such times than to stay in his bed waiting for the frightful visits he receives."

"What are you saying, Pierre?" exclaimed Jeannette, in a voice already imprinted with fear. "What visits do you mean?"

"Those that Monsieur's wife does not fail to make, since she died. The bell-ringer and Monsieur le Curé, it's said, and Pernot's mother, who makes no mystery of it, have seen our former mistress emerge from the tomb on several occasions, call to her young son, who similarly comes forth, and both take the path to the château."

"That's an abominable lie," said the colonel's domestic—who, having been brought up in a big city, gave less credence to such superstitions.

"Don't get upset, Monsieur Gervais," Pierre replied. "It's not good for you. Anyway, perhaps it won't be long before you see what others have seen. It seems to me that tonight will have its marvels, like the preceding ones, for the apparition will take place, according to every indication, at the same time. I've just come back from looking for pigeons in Souterrène; well, I met Mère Pernot on the way.

"'Pierre, my lad,' she said to me, 'you're going to the château; if you take my advice, you'll say your prayers tonight; add a *De profundis* and two *Pater nosters*, for strange things are happening in that place. Those who roam by night, without fear of evildoers and wild beasts, have woken up sooner than usual; the wind that's blowing as never before has doubtless summoned them, and I've just seen them going by a few moments ago. They're marching more swiftly than usual, as if they fear arriving too late.'"

It would have required superhuman strength for Delmont not to be gripped as he listened to that strange story. His consternated senses robbed him of a part of his energy, and, afraid to hear the continuation of the conversation, he went away slowly and went upstairs.

He was already at the height of the first landing when, during one of the calm intervals left by the wind, he heard a slight noise behind him, which appeared to be that of labored breathing. He stopped abruptly and turned round...

Two white figures went past him rapidly, and were lost in the darkness...

He had seen them, and thought that he had recognized them. His knees buckled beneath him; it was impossible for him to overcome his terror, and, falling on to a step, he stayed there for some time, utterly immobile, prey to all the anguish of a heart-rending horror.

A confused noise of voices extracted him from that state of collapse; he recognized that of the municipal official. He got up immediately and, trying to disguise his fear, went down to meet the man he had been waiting for so impatiently a few minutes earlier.

The first words that the newcomer addressed to him were an enquiry as to the state of his health, so distraught was his expression. Delmont replied evasively, and took the magistrate to the drawing-room, where he left him temporarily in order to go tell Alinska that he had arrived.

It was necessary for him to go into the north-facing wing to reach the Hungarian woman's apartment. Delmont had had lamps lit in the preceding rooms, but nevertheless, as he went through them, he scarcely dared raise his eyes, so expectant was he that they would be struck by some sinister apparition, and so many strange sounds did he think he was hearing that did not originate from the tempest.

Alinska shuddered on seeing him and again when he had explained himself. She darted a glance at him in which so many sensations were painted that it would be impossible to describe them.

She had taken off her mourning-dress; a white dress, devoid of ornamentation, adorned her elegant figure; a simple pearl necklace and a single orange-blossom placed in her hair were the only decorations she permitted herself. She was beautiful, if that is possible when features take on several different expressions, almost painful to behold, at the same time.

Her mouth was pinched, in order not to offer the appearance of the sardonic smile that was habitually settled there; her eyes, almost always icy, were shining with an extraordinary gleam, which was not that of pleasure and contentment. Nothing, however, veiled the richness of her contours, the elegance of her figure or the majesty of her stride. Alinska was made to inspire keen desires, especially when the obscurity of the location only permitted her mobile and somber physiognomy to be seen imperfectly.

Delmont had to repeat his entreaties several times before she could be persuaded to go with him. She hesitated incessantly; she wanted to put off the moment he desired. Her speech was incoherent, all of it manifesting a continual fear of losing happiness and the very moment that they hoped to secure it. Her resistance came to an end, however; she seemed to make a powerful effort and, raising her arms and eyes to the heavens, she seemed either to be making certain of her compulsion or imploring a forgiveness that she did not hope to obtain.

The alerted witnesses were already in the room when the two lovers made their entrance. At the sight of them, and that of the magistrate, Alinska became more distressed, but responded modestly nevertheless to the compliment that the latter addressed to her. He began the ceremony immediately, and Delmont was irrevocably united with the Hungarian woman.

Meanwhile, the storm redoubled it fury, seeming to batter the walls of the château with a particular vehemence. The magistrate, in a hurry to leave, refused Delmont's pleas to stay until the following day. He addressed some trivial compliments to the new wife, who received them silently, and eventually left, accompanied by the two witnesses, who went to wait in another room until they were recalled.

Gervais, the domestic, had received his master's orders; he was to introduce the curé into the chapel, take the farmer there, and then come to find the colonel, under the pretext of receiving instructions before going to bed, announcing by his presence that the curé was ready.

Alinska, left alone with Delmont, did not seem more reassured. Her oppressed bosom was forcefully agitated; her movements seemed inhibited; her eyes wandered at hazard. Moreover, every time her husband came near her, she was seized by a convulsive shudder, her pallor increased further and her arms reached out as if to push away the man who seemed nevertheless to cherish her with such perfect ardor.

Delmont perceived the extraordinary battles that Alinska's heart was fighting against an unknown cause. He suffered on her behalf; he hoped that time and a more complete intimacy would eventually return her to her natural state. He tried, by soft words, to inspire less terror in her, to bring her back to the calm that had abandoned her, but his efforts were in vain.

The Hungarian woman's distress remained the same; incoherent words emerged from her mouth, sometimes expressing the impetuous delirium of love and sometimes predicting sinister vengeances; they invoked the pity of Heaven and repelled the punishments of Hell.

That situation was too painful to last for long. It reminded the colonel, in an overly distressing manner, of what had troubled him a little while before. Then midnight chimed, and Gervais appeared in the room. At the sight of him, Delmont came to Alinska.

"Come on, my love—a little more courage and it will all be over; we have to leave before one o'clock, and we have one more thing to do. We need to go into another room."

"Is it one," Alinska replied, in a lugubrious one, "in which I might find rest? Can you find me one, Edouard, into which that fatal woman will not pursue me?"

"What woman?" Delmont exclaimed, sharply. "Who are you talking about?"

"Eh? Don't you know? Hasn't she offered herself to your sight? What can she want with me, with that child who walks with her? Is it my fault if they aren't three? Why is she opposed to the entire completion of my mission? She knows that we shall never be together again; she will live on high, while I suffer down below."

"In the name of my love, Alinska, recover your senses. You're making me the unhappiest of men. What do you want? What's wrong with you?"

"I'm thirsty, very thirsty!"

"That can be satisfied."

"It's not refreshments I'm asking for! I need blood! Blood! Yours, Edouard!"

"Oh, unfortunate friend, has your reason abandoned you thus? Come back to yourself; forget the past; remember that we are one, that a career of happiness can commence for us."

"In three steps I shall cross it, and will I not find at the end the cold coffin in which I have already lain?"

"I'm no longer listening to you. Come—one last duty remains for us to fulfill."

Passing his arm around Alinska's waist, he drew her rapidly toward the chapel, while she uttered shrill screams that mingled with the roars of the tempest.

"Edouard! Edouard! Twice you will give me death: are you weary already of your poor companion? Don't you want her to breathe the coolness of morning's first light? Must I be separated from you forever?"

"That's not my intention, Alinska. On the contrary, I want to render our bonds more indissoluble; I want nothing on Earth to be able to separate us."

"Death! Oh death! How bitter it is! And you, my Edouard, must you also die? Yes, you are mine, you have solemnly given yourself to me again, and my terrible mission will soon be accomplished."

In the midst of the furies of this inexplicable delirium, the colonel finally reached the chapel, carrying rather than leading the semiconscious Hungarian woman. A more terrible cry escaped her when the illuminated altar and the priest, in ceremonial vestments, offered themselves to her sight.

"O Providence!" she said, weeping. "O destiny! For the first time, I yield to your ascendancy, and my ruination is certain."

Meanwhile, Delmont, almost using force, constrains her to kneel. She is no longer resisting; she is sobbing, shedding tears; her features, already tormented, complete their decomposition, and the palpitations of her bosom are interrupted. Alinska no longer seems to be hanging on to existence by a slender thread, perhaps about to break.

The ceremony continues; the nuptial ring has been blessed; the priest gives it to the husband in order that he might place it on his wife's finger.

The latter's hand is gloved, as we have observed several times; the colonel, by a swift effort, removes the glove before Alinska can raise any obstacle—and the hideous fleshless hand of a skeleton strikes his gaze, and that of the confused priest...

A simultaneous exclamation escapes all the witnesses to that horrible spectacle.

The minister of the Lord takes a step back. "Demon," he says, "in the name of God the Creator, I command you to make yourself known..."

That order could no longer be executed. The Hungarian woman's cadaver had just fallen to the floor, and floods of impure and corrupted blood poured from three reopened wounds.

Afterword
A Brief Note on the Theodicy of La Vampire

La Vampire *is an exception to the general run of vampire fiction, which is, for the most part, relentlessly secularized. Even though the trappings of religion continued to be cited in many of the vampire stories that followed this one, and not without effect, they became essentially gutless. Nowhere is this more obvious than in Gautier's* "La Morte amoureuse," *in which a young priest falls victim to a seductive female vampire. In that story too, a terminal exorcism works, but it is no victory of sanctity, for the damage has already been done and the protagonist has been sundered from Heaven forever. In the conventions of vampire imagery established by Bram Stoker and passed on to the cinema, the holy cross often retains its efficacy as a means of repelling vampires, but it is on a par with cloves of garlic; it works, after the fashion of mosquito-repellent, seemingly because of some contingent property rather than because it has any real force of divine authority behind it.*

In the previous French vampire novel that cynically attempted to cash in on the particular fashionability of Polidori's "The Vampyre," *Bérard's* Lord Ruthwen, ou les Vampires, *the author only pays the merest lip-service to the religious context of the story. There, the question is briefly raised in conversation as to why vampires have the Lord's permission to roam the earth, destroying the innocent on a lavish scale, but the answer suggested is blatantly unsatisfactory. That novel does introduce a female revenant, called a vampire although she does not hunger for blood, as an auxiliary to the quest to destroy the murderous male vampire, and that amendment is credited to Heaven, but no explanation is asked for or offered as to why she alone is allowed to return to Earth in order to assist in the pursuit of her murderer, whose other victims lie idle in their graves.*

The simple fact is that there is no ready specific explanation, in theological terms, for the activity of predatory vampires of the Ruthven/Dracula variety or their female equivalents. The only recourse anyone seeking such an explanation could have is to general arguments of theodicy, simply adding vampires to the catalogue of evils that somehow persist in spite of God's goodness, whether spearheaded by the active malevolence of the Devil or the haphazard incompetence of nature and chance. Most vampire fiction simply ignores the problem, or takes its solution for granted, and wisely so, for it would otherwise get in the way. La Vampire *is, however, different. It is much more aware of its religious context than any quasi-naturalistic one, and that awareness eventually accepts a particular theodicy quite distinct from those routinely encountered in Christian philosophy.*

This incorporation might be entirely accidental; La Vampire *bears all the hallmarks of a novel written as the author went along, and the incoherency resulting from its changes of direction strongly suggests that the author was never entirely clear in his own mind what was going on or exactly what lay behind it. Much is left unexplained—especially the hasty improvisations that the author introduced when he got into difficulties, the most blatant of which is the ladder that arbitrarily appears, dangling from Eugène's bedroom window, in order to supply Alinska with a (woefully unconvincing) means of avoiding responsibility for Raoul's murder. Whether the metaphysical schema underlying the novel was planned or not, however, it remains interesting, not only because it is unique in the subgenre of vampire fiction, but also because it is not without a certain admirable flamboyance.*

What marks Alinska out as foreigner in the ranks of female vampires, and those of vampires in general, is that she is not a predator in her own right. She is a mere instrument of a higher power, more puppet than actor. She might have volunteered for that service to begin with, but she certainly becomes extremely unwilling in the course of the plot, and direly distraught with respect to her inability to escape. Although she certainly knows that she is dead and irredeemably damned, it is not entirely clear that she is conscious of being a vampire, and she does not seem to be fully aware of her responsibility for the deaths of Eugène and Hélène. Although she is physically present when Eugène dies, apparently having somehow sucked blood from his body via his mouth, she does not seem to be physically present during the slow draining of Hélène; although there is one oblique suggestion that her phantom alter ego has wings, there is no suggestion that she undergoes a physical metamorphosis into some bat-like creature in order to gain access to her second victim. Nor is it entirely clear—in spite of the fact that Ladislas once appears to pour liquid blood into her mouth in order to revive her when she faints, and poor Paschale is drained via manifest cuts to feed her hunger—that there is any actual transfer of material substance during her Hélène's long depletion.

Whatever is actually going on during Alinska's vampiric activities, however, there is no doubt that it is not only reluctant but actually contradictory to her conscious desires. However avid she was to avenge herself on Edouard when she was first given her "mission," that avidity is eventually overridden by other emotions. By virtue of this fact, she is far more a victim than her own victims, whose places in Heaven are guaranteed. Unlike them, she knows that there is no hope for her own salvation, and that the only possible amelioration of her fate she can achieve is to delay the completion of her mission by determined but painful procrastination—a procrastination that the lust-driven Edouard opposes with all his might, ironically unaware of the evil he is doing.

There is, of course, nothing unusual about the literary representation of vampires as instruments of the Devil, working in dogged opposition to a good God, and La Vampire *makes a few half-hearted gestures in that direction, but they are soon abandoned. The originality of* La Vampire *lies in the fact that it gradually becomes obvious—and, indeed, explicit—that Alinska is obviously working directly for God, as an instrument of Divine Wrath. The Devil is occasionally mentioned in the text, albeit obliquely, and there are more direct references to demons and to Hell, but any Devil that could exist within the overall moral and metaphysical schema of the novel would be no Miltonian Satan, but a mere instrument, with little seniority over poor Alinska. In the world-view of the novel, God does not shirk His own dirty work, and he does it with a Will.*

Within the metaphysical schema of La Vampire, *the question tentatively asked and left unanswered by Bérard, as to why God allows evildoing vampires to persecute the innocent, simply does not arise. Here, vampires are not evil, and any persecution that is going on is the work of God. The innocents drained of their blood are not victims at all, because—from God's viewpoint—death is merely a commutation of their sentence of life, and by taking them into Heaven sooner rather than later he is doing them a favor. It is true that Hélène's grieving for Eugène looks more like a punishment than a trial by ordeal, at least to a naïve eye unused to the Divinity's mysterious ways, but within the conceptual framework of the novel, the only individuals who are actually being formally punished are Edouard and Alinska, the former for breaking a sacred vow, the latter for killing herself.*

The reader, of course, can have no sympathy at all for Edouard, who does not have an ounce of moral fiber in him, in spite of all his protestations and posturing; he is essentially fickle, driven by the kind of lust that requires continual visual stimulus for its sustenance, and ever-willing to make hypocritical promises. It is not merely his refusal to believe in vampires that reveals his fundamental lack of imagination. That does not, however, make him into the villain of the piece; he is merely a victim of his own pusillanimity.

On the other hand, the reader surely ought to sympathize with Alinska, whose one and only sin was a matter of fervent impulse—the same fervor, at source, that would not permit her to break her own oath. There is an appalling tyranny in the Divine Judgment that will not offer her even the possibility of redemption, no matter how repentant she becomes or how virtuously she strives to behave. If there is one thing that Edouard is definitely right about (and there are a few contenders) it is his observation that it would be horribly unfair if Alinska were—as she seems to be—the only creature in God's creation who is forbidden any possibility of forgiveness. Alinska is not merely a victim, but a victim of a truly terrible cruelty.

Given these judgments, it is obvious that the novel has only one real villain, and that is God. Edouard is feeble, but that is all; if he is damned for it, as he presumably is, even that smacks of overkill. Perhaps Alinska is weak too—or was at the moment when she recklessly plunged a dagger into her breast—but her eternal and irrevocable damnation is way over the top by reference to any conceivable scale of justice. If she is a monster, she is not a self-made monster;

her monstrousness has been inflicted upon her. The only veritable and voluntary monster in the plot is the God who dictates the fates of Edouard, Alinska and their secondary victims: a vile individual who is not merely immune to sympathy for the objects of his implacable wrath, but also seems to be taking something of a sadistic delight in their torture, which inevitably overflows into the torment of the secondary victims of vampirism. One can hardly doubt that His Hell will be a horrid place to be, but one is surely bound to worry, too, about the quality of His Heaven.

There are, of course, other victims of God's plan for vampiric vengeance. The most enigmatic of them is Ladislas, who really has no business being in the plot, once the author has decided that he is not the Devil, and is summarily dispatched therefrom when the author realizes the fact. We are not told whether he is a vampire himself or merely a minion, but either way, he is definitely dead, and has been ripped arbitrarily from his grave in order to serve as Alinska's helper. Even if that represents a brief reprieve from Hell, he does not seem to be enjoying himself, so we must assume that he too is suffering from the effects of his Creator's iron whim. He is presumably the unsubtle murderer who kills Paschale, since he is the one who seems deal in brute force and bottled blood rather than phantom presence and mysterious sucking, but he is obviously acting under irresistible orders rather than exercising his own free will; what is not at all obvious is why that particular crime is necessary at all, given that Alinska seems perfectly able to take care of herself, and the ready availability of other potential victims, including such conspicuous wastes of space as M. Berneval.

Raoul is a more obvious victim, not just because he too is summarily removed from the plot when his work teasing revelations from Alinska and filling in the back-story is done, but because he is punished for trying to do good—to guard and protect his master and his family from harm. We are not told what happens to him after his death, but it seems probable that he does not go to Heaven; he certainly does not return therefrom with Madame Delmont and Eugène to continue his good work on Juliette's behalf. It seems a trifle unfair, therefore, to force Alinska to stab him—but not, of course, out of keeping with God's general conduct within the universe of the novel.

Given that God, or possibly Alinska, has no trouble at all in providing an ad hoc ladder and an open window to produce the illusion of intruding bandits, He or she could presumably have generated actual bandits with equal ease, so that the old soldier could have gone down fighting—but that would have been a kindness, and there are not many of those going spare in this fictional universe (allowing Juliette to survive as an orphan is a dubious one at best). In fairness, the transposition of the narrative into the present tense during Raoul's final dream, and the retention of that tense after his apparent opening, did leave temporarily open the possibility that what he sees in Eugène's room is entirely hallucinatory, and that there really were murderous intruders—but that possibility *ceased to seem remotely tenable once the narrative voice has told us that Alinska's account of what happened is a lie.*

Another puzzle that arises in retrospective consideration of Raoul's role in the plot is why God and Alinska are so keen to prevent him from sending word to his master that Alinska is in R***. Given that she is there to take her revenge on Edouard, it might seem that the sooner she can get started, the better. She seems, briefly to be afraid that if he learns of her presence he will not come back, but will flee instead, but that is surely irrelevant; given that she found him once, she could presumably do so again. Even if it were a matter of serious concern, the method employed to prevent it seems odd. It is obviously no particular hardship for God—or His puppet, Alinska's phantom alter ego—to keep intercepting his letters and dripping blood all over them, but it seems a strangely finicky way of achieving a goal that, if it really were important, could surely be accomplished in a simpler and more direct way. The underlying purpose of the procrastination—apart, that is, from spinning out the wordage of the story— might be to allow Alinska to install herself in the château before Edouard gets back from his mission of dubious mercy, but if so, that too could have been achieved more directly, and without the intervention of any murderous arson, had God decided to act more directly. Presumably, this is simply one more example of the mysterious ways in which God is generally presumed to work, for reasons unfathomable go mere humans.

Some readers might feel, of course, that I am being a bit unfair to Lamothe-Langon here, that he probably did not mean to make God look as bad as he eventually does, and might even be horrified to discover, with the aid of critical hindsight, that he had. He might well have been unconscious of what he was doing—but that does not affect the fact that he did it, and we all know full well that it is the things we do unthinkingly that reveal our true character, which even those of us who do not lead lives of calculated deceit always tend to keep under polite wraps. Some readers might even feel that this analysis of the book's innate perversity does it no favors, but I would disagree; it is precisely the story's magnificent quirkiness that makes it striking, original and worth reading. Although it is certainly not God that we have to thank for that, He has played his part, as a helpless puppet of His true master within the morally-ordered universe of the text—and if the author of a Gothic novel is not entitled to operate Him in those time-hallowed mysterious ways, who is?

B.S,

Paul Féval: *The Vampire Brothers*

Le Chevalier Ténèbre *was the second of three novels by Paul Féval which touch on the subject of vampirism, although the notion is a less prominent feature therein than it had been in* La Vampire *(1856; tr. as The Vampire Countess)[35] or was again to be in* La Ville-Vampire *(tr. as Vampire City)[36], which was written in 1867 although it did not appear in book form until 1875.* Le Chevalier Ténèbre *also appeared in book form for the first time in 1875, but it had been serialized in* Le Musée des Familles *in 1860.*

Féval was at the height of his fame in 1860, having scored his greatest success three years earlier with Le Bossu *(The Hunchback)[37], which seemed to its readers to be pioneering a new kind of fiction that eventually came to be called the "roman de cape et d'épée" (novel of cloak and sword).* Le Bossu *was not a particularly original novel in terms of its content, much of which echoed the work Féval had already done in his capacity as a prolific feuilletonist–i.e. a writer of popular serial fiction–before his career was interrupted in 1854 by health problems, and had been second-hand even then, borrowed from more successful writers he was regularly commissioned to imitate, Alexandre Dumas and Eugène Sue. What was new, however, was the tone of the story, which clearly reflects the new spirit with which Féval had been inspired following his recovery from illness and his marriage to his doctor's daughter, Françoise Penoyée.*

By virtue of its fabular and metafictional qualities, Le Bossu *is, in some ways, a very modern book–and its modernity reflects the fact that while Féval was participating with his fellow feuilletonists in the discovery and invention of the strategies and techniques of popular fiction, he was doing so in a self-conscious and intellectually interested manner. He was, in fact, quite fascinated by the mechanics, politics and psychology of story-telling, and by the teasing intricacies of the relationship between authors and audiences.* Le Bossu *displays these fascinations indirectly and implicitly, but they are the heart of its cavalier attitude to its own subject-matter. The temptation to make such issues manifest and address them more explicitly must, however, have been strong–and that is presumably why Féval elected to exploit his new marketability by writing a fabulation about fabulation, a metafiction of unprecedented convolution:* Le Chevalier Ténèbre.

---

[35] To be included in our Volume 3.

[36] Included in our Volume 1.

[37] Published by Black Coat Press as *The Hunchback* (ISBN 9781649320667).

Le Chevalier Ténèbre *displays some of Féval's weaknesses as conspicuously as it displays his main strengths, but it is undoubtedly one of the most interesting works in Féval's canon, and one whose substance is echoed in many half-hidden corners of the contemporary popular fiction marketplace. The novelist and critic Edmond Jaloux (1878-1949), one of Féval's many slightly-grudging admirers, opined that* Le Chevalier Ténèbre *would be a masterpiece of the fantastic if it were not written in "the drab and mock-pathetic language of the 19th century."*

It seems highly probable that Le Chevalier Ténèbre *was, like most serial novels of the period, made up as the writer went along, and by no means improbable that its author had no idea when he began it how long it would be allowed to run. (Popular romans feuilletons were extrapolated according to editorial command while those that failed to catch on were sometimes ruthlessly cut short.) It is, therefore, quite possible that the wayward course, peculiar structure and hurried finale of the narrative are largely matters of chance and circumstance—but, whether they were planned in advance or not, they have a definite propriety as well as a certain charm. The novella is, after all, explicitly written according to the "Galland formula."*[38]

Le Chevalier Ténèbre *is not the first roman feuilleton to have been planned according to that formula, and Féval must have been conscious of the irony of the fact that it suffered exactly the same fate as its most obvious predecessor and model, Alexandre Dumas'* Les Mille et Un Fantômes *(1849; A Thousand and One Phantoms). Indeed, he must have been conscious of a double symmetry, in that his earlier novel* La Vampire *had similarly mirrored the progress of the series begun with Dumas'* Joseph Balsamo *(1846-48; tr. as Memoirs of a Physician).*

Just as Dumas had tried to find a more acceptable framework for supernatural fiction by employing the Galland formula and making the stories exemplary fictions told by and to urbane modern Parisians, so Le Chevalier Ténèbre *sets out to represent its horror stories as stories told for the sake of thrilling a sophisticated audience—but Féval already knew that* Les Mille et Un Fantômes *had been strangled in its cradle after a bare handful of nights.*[39] *It is, therefore,*

---

[38] Antoine Galland (1646-1715) was the Orientalist made famous by his early 18th-century translation of the Arabian Nights. That book established Scheherazade as the symbolic figurehead of all serial fiction, whose life would be forfeit if she were ever to let her husband retire to his bed without wanting to know what happened next.

[39] Most of the completed text was reissued in two volumes as *Une Journée à Fontenay-aux-Roses* (1849; lit. A Day in Fontenay, tr. as Horror at Fontenoy, Sphere, 1965) and *La Femme au Colliers de Velours* (1849; lit. The Woman with the Velvet Necklace, tr. as The Pale Lady or The White Lady), which contains the eponymous, oft-reprinted vampire story.

quite possible that Le Chevalier Ténèbre *was actually planned to seem as if it had been interrupted and hurriedly aborted, by way of peculiar homage to Dumas. Whether that is true or not, it certainly set out from the very beginning to add one complication that Dumas had not: the storytellers who play Scheherazade in Féval's narrative, tell stories whose characters not only tell stories themselves, but continually resurface in their own stories as archetypal villains, masters of deception and disguise. This is no mere metafiction, but metametafiction, which leads the reader into an inescapable maze of infinite regress. The nested sequence of pretenses quickly becomes absurd, but its very absurdity is a commentary on the nature and seductive appeal of popular fiction. Perhaps it is "written in the drab and mock-pathetic language of the 19th century," but it is, in its own defiantly peculiar way, a masterpiece of the fantastic.*

The tale of the brothers Ténèbre's exploits as undead monsters, petty criminals and ingenious story-tellers is so steadfast in its refusal to decide whether its supernatural apparatus is to be taken literally, metaphorically, or merely as a joke, that the drunken progress and hasty conclusion of the novella leave a great many pertinent questions unanswered–but that kind of playfulness is not at all inappropriate to the type of narrative it is, or to the time in which it was written. It is a story which continually raises questions about the terms on which storytellers may legitimately approach their audiences, and the way in which they manipulate those audiences, all the while exemplifying its own conclusions in its own approaches and manipulations. The narrative is full of nudges and winks, which seek–with a blithe disingenuousness that is actually rather ingenious–to establish that the reader is an active conspirator in the spinning of the story as well as a hapless victim of the spin.

The opening scene of Le Chevalier Ténèbre *is drawn from actual history, and it is populated by a cast of characters who include two of the most important men of their era. The story is carefully and specifically dated, all its events taking place in the 1820s. Everything described therein–in Hungary as in Paris–had been obliterated by 1860, from which vantage-point the narrative voice is speaking. Féval chose to begin his story on the eve of the destruction of the social world featured in its chief setting by a corrosive process whose key event was the "July Revolution" of 1830.*

The characters in the novella are, of course, unaware of what is soon to befall them, and their inability to respond to the obvious warnings contained in the tale of the brothers Ténèbre is a metaphorical reflection of their inability to see the real warning signs by which they must have been surrounded. The fundamental essence of the story is the tragically naive confidence of its exemplary characters in the aristocratic order re-established by the Bourbon Restoration in the wake of Napoleon's second defeat.

Although we have long grown used to speaking of the French Revolution, meaning the one that took place in 1789, Paul Féval and his contemporaries did not think in those terms. The July Revolution of 1830 seemed highly significant to Féval not merely because he had actually lived through it, but because he believed that in casually overturning the ambitions of the Restoration it had put the final nail in the coffin of royal hegemony. In 1860, Féval was actually living under what is nowadays called the Second Empire, set up by Napoleon III in 1852; like the characters in his novella, he had no way of knowing that it was doomed to be obliterated ten years later by France's humiliating defeat in the Franco-Prussian War of 1870.

In Féval's view, 1830 had been the year in which a new kind of darkness descended upon Europe; while enlightenment had banished the phantoms of old–including, in the observations of the novella's opening chapter, the dead who were reputed to rise from their graves along the banks of the Seine to haunt Paris–it had not contrived to deter a protean and proletarian class of irrepressible brigands, which operated on a world stage and would not rest until all the world's aristocratic treasuries had been looted and all the world's aristocratic bloodlines drained to extinction. This is the political subtext of Le Chevalier Ténèbre, *which remains raw and sore in spite of all the novella's garish good humor and casual absurdity.*

B.S.

I. One of Archbishop de Quélen's Soirées

Dinner had been taken at the Château de Conflans, the home of His Grace the Archbishop of Paris. It was not merely a priests' banquet; there were women present. Along the river bank on the road to Charenton, white dresses could be seen among the green lawns.

I don't know why that part of the Parisian countryside seems so sad. Are they not charming, those meadows where the Marne arrives to marry its waters with those of the Seine? Wine is gaiety, it is said; how is it that the ocean of wine that floods the town of Bercy does not enliven those heart-rending pastures in the slightest? Bacchus, whose praises are sung by our drunken poets, is there–can he not brighten up those mournful horizons? The Seine cannot contrive a smile while passing between them; the very trees seem sad. Ivry is sullen and sulky on one bank; on the other the park–which is so beautiful, in spite of the dismal pleasure-gardens on its edge, that its lawns should extend gloriously in the sunlight–is sulky and sullen behind its grey walls, at whose gate two sickly lions devoid of spirit or courage wrestle two boars which yawn as they defend themselves.

It is an exit. Parisian storytellers and chroniclers find the melancholy zone which starts at Charenton and extends as far as Bicêtre an ideal setting for their werewolves, brigands and phantoms. That flat country was a little less ugly in the past than it is today but it had a worse reputation in those days. As your aged uncles will tell you, nights thereabouts were full of horrors. Sabbaths were held–big ones–not far from the present site of Ivry railway station; the cemetery of the same name had not a single grave whose stone could keep it sealed, whether it was made of modern plaster or ancient cement. All the marble tombstones would raise themselves up at midnight, and whenever the darkness was briefly penetrated by the faint rays of the veiled moon, a long procession of the emergent dead could be seen to move slowly and silently upriver towards the monasteries of Vitry.

Archbishop de Quélen, as everyone knows, was not only a very eminent prelate but a perfect gentleman. His generosity towards the poor, an established historical fact, restrained his taste for luxurious and grandiose display, but his aristocratic heritage would not permit him to shut himself off from society. His receptions were carefully planned, especially those involving his closest friends. All shades of Royalist opinion would find an open and level field there, providing a lively opposition to the Restoration government in the very bosom of the House of Lords.

The events of our story took place in 1825; the Archbishop was then in his late forties, at the very height of his power as a primate of the Church of France and as a politician. In order that the glory surrounding him should lack for nothing, the Academy had also opened its doors to him.

This prelate—whose home some miserable wretches, who insulted the genuine people in taking the name of "the people," came to burn the day after the Revolution of July 1830—followed a well-known custom. He had made it a rule that after each of his receptions he would distribute to the poor a sum equal to the cost of his feast. I have heard it said by men who have never given anything to anyone that he would have done better to give twice as much and not receive visitors at all—well, perhaps. It would be necessary, in order to put together a jury capable of judging these good souls, to take immediate exception to all incapacity, all envy and all hatred. That would be hard work, and the preliminary hearing for the selection of the jury could take a long time. I said "perhaps" because although it is good to give, to do good is often better, because the eventual result is greater. The Lord Bishop de Quélen's feasts were productive, from the viewpoint of his benevolence. They rarely ended without misfortune having deducted its tithe from their serious and noble pleasures.

That was not all, however; Archbishop de Quélen also had another custom of which the Faubourg Saint-Germain and the court sometimes complained bitterly. He was a committed patron, always surrounded by an army of protégés, and he fought for these protégés with a courage that was as meritorious as it was redoubtable. His banquets were the peaceful tournaments where he broke lances on behalf of youth ardent to succeed, or old age eager to return after injury to the battle of life. I could name men in the highest places who would have good cause to remember the feasts of the Lord Bishop de Quélen.

It was an evening in September, in the same year that had seen the coronation of Charles X and the prodigious enthusiasm of Paris for the prince that Paris would, so soon afterwards, condemn to death in his absence. The weather was stormy and oppressively warm. Although night had begun to fall–dinner had been served at three o'clock, as was the fashion of the time–no one thought of going back indoors. The park was a welcome refuge from the torrid heat. The shade of the tall trees was fairly cool, and a light breeze blew fitfully from the low and ponderous river, trying to stir their leaves. The majority of the guests had come together again in the vast hall of verdure that was then the pride of the district, although the railway line to Lyon has since destroyed it. The Archbishop, who was by birth the Comte de Quélen, was originally of Breton descent; he belonged to the family that descended from the ducal houses of Aiguillon, Chaulnes and La Vauguyon; he was related to the Chateaubriants, the Rohans, the Dreuxes, the Guébriants, the La Bourdonnayes, the Coislins and the Goulaines. The gathering of all these names at the château, that evening, might have been a reunion of the general staff of François de Bretagne, or the court of Duchess Anne [40].

Such is the mysterious power of certain places that within that brilliant circle, in the glades where important theological questions had been debated from the days of François de Harlay, founder of the Château de Conflans, to those of the His Lordship de Talleyrand-Périgord [41], the predecessor of the present archbishop, the talk was all of brigands, werewolves and phantoms. To the great amusement of the women–and of the men too–marvellous tales of revenants were told, in the spirit of pure theatre. On the stage where the audience had reassembled, the narrators turned their tricks, as comedians say, pointing their fingers this way and that at the very fields that had served as scenery for their supernatural dramas.

The crowd, as always, included both believers and skeptics. Under the Restoration, the Faubourg Saint-Germain had its little philosophical corner, and we know of more than one marquis of that era whose life was spent in imitation of

---

[40] Like the other ancestral lists with which the novella is peppered, this one serves to emphasize the continuity between the aristocratic society of the early 19th century and the persons and events which had shaped European history during the preceding centuries. Féval, a Breton himself, had a particular fondness for the great families of that region. The list ends with the names of the last king of Brittany, François II (1435-1488) and his daughter Anne, who enjoyed a brief rule before the duchy was more fully absorbed into the rapidly-evolving French nation.

[41] François de Harlay de Champvallon (1625-1695) became Archbishop of Paris in 1671. Charles Maurice de Talleyrand-Périgord (1754-1838) was one of the foremost and most versatile Frenchmen of his era: a Churchman, a statesmen and a diplomat. He was a leading figure in the Revolution before helping Napoleon take power, but subsequently fell out with the Emperor and took a prominent part in the Bourbon Restoration before also taking a hand in the Revolution of 1830.

Monsieur de Voltaire. In the matter of werewolves, incredulity is understandable, as it is with regard to phantoms, but brigands! That requires explanation. The skeptics on the subject of *brigandage* took refuge in a question of chronology. According to them, the day of the authentic brigand–the romanesque, picturesque, dramatic brigand–was done. The present era only had mere thieves–by way of recompense, however, the same skeptics contended that it did have a truly remarkable quantity of them.

Now, I defy you to take a ring of secular trees, about two or three hundred yards from an old château, and to place thereabouts, on a dark and stormy night, an assembly of thirty people discussing horrific or mystical subjects, without a kind of vague fear leaching into the conversational mix. I shall make a significant concession, granting you two levels of incredulity–indeed, I will go even further, if you wish and grant you unanimity of skepticism, including the narrator himself, provided that he is skilful, and I will still bet against you, so certain am I of what I say: the *frisson* of fear will arrive.

The *frisson* always arrives. It is not necessary, in the final analysis, for anyone in a circle affected by such a spirit to be a believer or victim of superstition. The frisson requires nothing but a powerful imagination. At the appointed moment, while the ordinarily timid restrain a tremor, the strongly imaginative suffer nervous attacks and become faint. The "strongly imaginative" are typified by the brave boy who sings at the top of his voice in the darkness in order to allay his fears.

Among the more strongly imaginative members of the party on that evening at the Château de Conflans was a beautiful woman, very spiritual and very eloquent, whom we shall call the Princess de Montfort (because the actual names and titles of the persons in question must be protected; the Princess, having a leading role in our play, must be given the benefit of appearing incognito). She was there with her younger son, the Marquis de Lorgères, a tall, pale and handsome adolescent, who had been destined for the Church but had hesitated over his vocation. The Princess, who adored her younger son, affected a certain severity in her treatment of him, concealing her approval of the new route that he wished to take: the young marquis was ambitious to become a diplomat. The Princess was a slightly eccentric woman, but she was blessed with great intelligence and a good heart.

His Grace the Archbishop expressed no opinion on the matter of the supernatural or the persistence of *brigandage*, and seemed preoccupied with other matters. There were fors and againsts. His Lordship the Bishop Frayssinous of Hermopolis, who was then the Minister of Ecclesiastical Affairs, was an enthusiastic believer in the supernatural and had already recounted some fine tales. He was just beginning another when the Princess interrupted:

"It's becoming cold. Shouldn't we go back indoors?"

It would be inaccurate to speak of laughter bursting out. Laughter, especially of a mocking kind, does not "burst out" above a certain social level–but the Devil is everywhere and he never loses an opportunity. There was, in response to the words "it's becoming cold," a gentle murmur which tickled the ears of the Princess sufficiently to compel her to cry out: "Don't think that I'm afraid! Let's go!" The young and beautiful Comtesse de Maillé got up and came to drape a summer cloak over her aunt's shoulders.

"Auntie," she said, "let's tremble for a little longer–it's so nice!"

And everyone, in unison, cried: "Yes! Your story, My Lord Bishop!"

Instead of answering the general plea, the Bishop of Hermopolis remained silent for a moment. Then, in a restrained voice whose altered tone caused more than one heart to beat faster, he asked abruptly: "Are you not here, Monsieur von Altenheimer?"

There was another moment of silence. The moon displayed half her face between two storm-clouds that were as solid and heavy as slugs of lead. The Princess called her son to her side.

"Indeed I am," a deep baritone voice replied, profound and full of metallic vibrations. "I am here, My Lord."

The person who had spoken was unseen. His voice seemed to come from the trunk of a huge dead elm whose leafless branches took fantastic form in the sudden moonlight.

"Come closer, Baron, I beg you," the Bishop replied, "and relate to us, according to the Galland formula, one of those tales that you tell so well."

A man of tall and slender stature immediately moved into the middle of the circle. It seemed to the Princess, in the grip of her powerful imagination, that he had sprung from the earth, so sudden was his appearance. Nothing in the world could have renewed her determination to retreat to the château.

The light of the moon fell directly upon the newcomer, and it is a fact that everyone saw something extraordinary in him. That may also have been a result of the general predisposition. No one knew him; no one had seen him at dinner. He was doubtless one of those who had been invited purely for the after-dinner discussion; several other members of the audience were in the same situation. His costume, which was black from top to toe, was very formal, resembling that of the other laymen present. Why, then, use the word extraordinary? It was a mystery, quite inexplicable. Save for the pallor of his long Teutonic features, he was like all those who surrounded him, and yet the word was appropriate. The company was dumbstruck, as if a trapdoor had opened to allow the passage of a fantastic individual. The moon scarcely had time to illuminate him before it was hidden by a large cloud and obscurity enveloped him again.

"I am at His Lordship's disposal," said the baritone voice.

"That is most kind," replied the Bishop of Hermopolis, adding as he took the newcomer's hand: "Ladies, I have the honor of presenting to you the privy councilor Baron von Altenheimer, director general of the police of His Majesty the King of Wurtemburg...[42]" The privy councilor must have bowed, I suppose, but no one saw it.

"...And elder brother," the illustrious Bishop continued, "of Monsignor von Altenheimer, prelate of Rome, Chamberlain to Our Holy Father..."

"Here present," put in a tenor voice, as soft as a note from a flute. That tenor voice reassured the beautiful women a little.

"What kind of story does My Lord Bishop desire?" the baritone voice asked. "Phantoms or brigands? We have both of them in the Black Forest."

"Phantoms!" half the circle voted.

"Brigands!" opined the Princess, under the influence of her strong imagination.

The fearful, on the other hand, eager for a fine time of mortification by terror, demanded: "Vampires!"

Whereupon His Grace the Archbishop de Quélen, with a mildness in which a light note of irony was perceptible, said: "One could make an agreeable mixture out of all these good things."

"That's it! That's it!" cried the Bishop of Hermopolis, in the voice of a man who is certain of the virtue of what he has produced. "Baron, these ladies desire a tale to make their hair stand on end, in which there is a phantom, a brigand and a vampire all at the same time!"

"Hilarius," said the soft tenor voice, "The tale of the brothers Ténèbre is precisely that."

"Yes," the baritone replied, at the utmost depth of its range, "you're right, Benedict: the tale of the Ténèbre brothers!"

"The name is well-chosen!" murmured the Princess, suppressing a giggle while her hand closed convulsively upon the arm of her son, the Marquis de Lorgères.

"The name is not chosen at all!" replied the Monsignor, his tone a trifle piqued. "Everyone in Germany has heard of the Ténèbre brothers."

"And everyone in Paris will have heard of them soon," said the privy councilor quietly, as if he were speaking in spite of himself.

Even if the name had not been chosen for effect, one could nevertheless say that it was as appropriate as any that might have been invented. The circle drew closer. This was not included in the program of the soirée, which would culminate in a benefit concert, but it was worth ten times as much as the entire banquet. Chance gave to His Lordship's guests an unexpected performance, a delightful surprise–and, although no one could explain exactly why, it is certain

---

[42] Wurtemburg became a major European state in 1495, when the duchy was established, but it only became a kingdom after its conquest by Napoleon and it was gradually absorbed into the evolving German nation during the 19th century, exemplifying one aspect of the pattern of historical change to which Féval is calling attention.

that the hearts of our beautiful ladies were considerably stirred by emotion and alarm.

Baron von Altenheimer resumed an oratorical tone that served to emphasize his German accent. "Your excellencies, and most illustrious persons, my brother and I are strangers in the capital of France, and we are both charged with a difficult mission. We desire to be worthy of the generous welcome that has been extended to us, and of the protection that we have been promised. My brother Benedict will sing some traditional Westphalian songs for you this evening, and a few original Christmas ballads. I have a voice that is good enough for the chorus but not for solo performance, so I am glad to have found an opportunity to make myself equally agreeable. Historical legends and other traditional tales featuring the supernatural are so very abundant in our homeland that I would have had a thousand to choose from in attempting to satisfy your curiosity. I prefer, however, to set aside our popular tales and tell you a true story of the same kind, based on my personal experience and that of my brother. Here, a little while ago, I heard some very powerful people of both sexes discussing age-old controversies say: There are no more specters. A very illustrious lady exclaimed: There are no more authentic brigands; the times of Rob Roy, Schinderhannes, Zawn, Schubry, Mandrin and even Cartouche are gone. We no longer have anything but thieves [43]! I admit that we have an enormous number of thieves, but I am compelled to affirm that we also have brigands. Leaving aside the successors of Fra Diavolo [44] in southern Italy, Hungary, Bohemia and the southern provinces of Austria still produce bandits fully worthy of that name. On the other hand, specters continue to lift up the stones of their graves just as they did in the past: nothing changes in that sphere. I have seen vampires in the region of Belgrade and phantoms in our own cemetery at Tübingen."

---

[43]   Rob Roy was a famous Scottish outlaw of the early 18th century, immortalized by Sir Walter Scott's eponymous novel. Schinderhannes was the alias of the German brigand Johann Bückler, who was hanged at Mainz in 1803. Louis Mandrin was an 18th-century French brigand whose campaign against tax-collectors made him a folk hero; his name was often coupled with that of Louis Dominique Cartouche, the leader of another famous robber band; both were eventually captured and broken on the wheel. According to Charles Mackay's essay on "Popular Admiration of Great Thieves" in *Extraordinary Popular Delusions and the Madness of Crowds* (1852)–which Féval might have read and from which he might have taken some inspiration, Schubry was a Hungarian brigand, but Zawn is not mentioned there and I can find no other reference to him.

[44]   Fra Diavolo was the nickname of Michele Pezza, or Pozzo, an Italian robber turned Bourbon partisan, who was hanged in Naples in 1806 by General Hugo. Paul Féval gave the character a starring role in *Les Habits Noirs*.

We are relying here upon our memory, and we have made every effort to reproduce Baron von Altenheimer's preamble word for word. The manner of his delivery was remarkably well-suited to his style. To begin with, there was in both a depth of *naiveté*, which imparted an emphasis to certain expressions. On the surface, there were unequivocal signs of knowledge: a literary mixture of the philosophical and the scientific; the overall impression, however, was one of oratory pretension, with a distinct whiff of charlatanry, as serious as the black robe of a professor.

His Lordship the Bishop de Quélen leant towards the ear of his neighbor and said to him: "That's Germany [45]."

The judgement is not without profundity. That is Germany, indeed: that old wives' wisdom; that bourgeois philosophy; that naive predisposition to make a discourse of what Paillasse [46] called patter; all of it accompanied, supported and perhaps saved by a sort of nobility, which may deserve the name of truth. The ladies would not have made any such analysis, but the Baron's preface pleased them regardless. The session turned into a public lecture in the German manner, concerning phantoms and brigands—the two most frightful and interesting things in the world.

The propitious moon, as if to join the party, emerged in full from behind its cloud to muffle the dread that might have prevented us from paying full attention. The illuminated glade gained a sort of gaiety without losing its poetry.

The tall, black-clad German could be seen distinctly now, his two wide eyes shining in his long pale face. His younger brother, the monsignor, stood beside him; he was shorter and plumper, wearing a garment that was not quite a frock-coat and not quite a cassock, after the fashion of the priests of Rome.

The elder brother wore a badge of office as florid as that of any privy councilor in the tales of Hoffmann [47]. The younger wore no decoration at all, save for a long chain of polished steel, which passed around his neck above the

---

[45] This translation is taken from the Marabout paperback edition of 1972, which reprinted the text of the 1875 book. I do not know whether, or to what extent, that version varies from the original serial version of 1860, but it might be worth noting that the Franco-Prussian war of 1870 (in which Wurtemburg sided with Prussia) occurred in the interim. It would not be surprising if Féval had taken the opportunity to import a little extra anti-German sentiment into the book version, but neither would it have been unusual to find this kind of stereotyping in a French popular magazine in 1860.

[46] Paillasse is the French version of the Italian Pagliacci: the epitome of the sad clown.

[47] The German writer Ernst Theodor Amadeus Hoffmann (1776-1822) was the most significant pioneer of modern horror fiction, usually keeping a fine balance between psychological and supernatural interpretations of the grotesqueries featured in his tales.

dark collar of his coat and dangled by his right side. On the end of the chain was a rectangular object, also of polished steel, which seemed to contain a breviary or a missal.

All around them, the circle of listeners emerged from the shadows: heads handsome or venerable, foreheads furrowed, blonde tresses, avid eyes, mouths agape...

"Most illustrious friends," Baron von Altenheimer continued...

II. Chandor Castle

"In 1821, there was a Magyar family living in the ancient Chandor Castle near the banks of the river Tisza, not far from the city of Szeged–which is some seven leagues around and has eighty thousand inhabitants. All Magyars are aristocrats, but these were princes of the house of Baszin, whose founder had befriended Matthias Corvinus, the Charlemagne of the Danube nations [48].

"Chrétien Baszin, Prince Jacobyi, possessed an immense fortune, evidence of which was met throughout the land; he had thousands of peasant serfs, including Serbs, Czechs, Croats and Walachians. His estate was as big as a province and extended as far as that isle of vineyards surrounded by a sea of maize where the Turkeve harvest the amber liquid of their royal vintages.

"The massive walls of Chandor Castle, situated on the edge of an oak-forest, overlooked the Tisza. Its four large thickset towers bulged at the top like the turbans of the Turks who had constructed them in olden times. From the tops of the towers one could see the minarets of Szeged in the distance, beyond the vast cornfields. Its pasturelands fed eight hundred horses and twice as many cattle: proud Hungarian beasts with pearly hides and widespread white horns. The prince was as generous as he was magnificent: fifty places were always set at the enormous square table that was placed every day when the bell sounded noon on a silver dais in a cedarwood-paved courtyard beneath the open sky.

"You, ladies and gentlemen, are the happy citizens of the most civilized nation on the globe, but you probably do not have an accurate idea of the aristocratic life in certain other countries that you call barbarian. There, we did not have–I say we because I have spent many years with the prince in Chandor Castle–all the refinements of your spotless, white and dainty French dinner services, and perhaps we lacked the fine delicacies of the portable luxury, if I may call it that, that you carry in your luggage on your tours of Europe, but we lived in a grand and luxurious style nevertheless, among all the proud display of absolute power.

---

[48] Matthias I, Corvinus, a.k.a. "The Great" (1443-1490), the younger son of John Hunyadi (see note 12), was king of Hungary from 1458-90. He was perennially engaged in wars against the Turks, the Bohemians, the Poles and the Holy Roman Emperor.

"It is for such as they, the last high barons, that the purest juice of your Bordeaux grapes in carefully extracted; it is for them that the most piquant spirit of your champagnes is trapped. The American Indians, it is said, sell their gold for small quantities of whisky; you sell your nectars for small quantities of gold, and it is, alas, only rarely that a French gullet is permitted a taste of those astonishing ambrosias. To taste your wines you must go to Russia or the far shore of the Danube. Chevet sends his fresh vegetables and preserves, Lesage his pastries; we have everything that you have–and we have, in addition, the noble game of wild boars and your champagne whisked in the crushed pulp of our water-melons.

"Thus far, there is no hint of menace in my tale; but the sky is blue above our heads and the moon is bright–nevertheless, the storm is there, and it will break soon enough. Prince Jacobyi did not know the extent of his fortune. Once a month his stewards brought him their accounts, which he accumulated, unread, in his library. Vast as it was, his library gradually became cluttered, its tiled floor hidden beneath untidy heaps of paper. Each month he signed, unread, a warrant addressed to his banker in Pest, in order to obtain money by means of a mortgage.

" 'Such as they would have to rob me prodigiously,' he would say, 'if they were ever to get to the bottom of my inheritance!' And when he looked at his daughter Lenore, a sweet-natured golden-haired angel, he would exclaim: 'I defy anyone to prevent this one from being the richest heiress for a hundred leagues around!'

"That was what he said, and truer words were never spoken by any man alive; but he had two stewards in his house and a banker in the city of Pest. As the proverb says, one steward is enough to devour an estate.

"Lenore was fourteen years old. It was already obvious that she was as beautiful as her mother, whose smiling portrait illuminated the house. Her life was solely devoted to learning; in those barbarian lands young women are highly and extensively educated. She had only one friend in the entire world: a girl of her own age–also a Magyar and an aristocrat, but poor–with whom she had been raised. Lenore had recently experienced the first tragedy of her life: Efflam, her companion, had left her to visit her father and mother, who lived near the border, not far from Belgrade.

"One evening, two Walachian gypsies arrived at the castle. They belonged to a wandering tribe that had camped in the banate of Timisoara on the other side of the Tisza. They had rowed across the river–which flows as fast as the Rhone and is three times as wide as the Seine, although it is only a tributary of the royal Danube. The night was just like this one, and I remember that the setting moon was continually appearing and disappearing behind black clouds so thick that its gleam could not tint their fringes with silver. The tortuous mirror of the waters of the Tisza were soon to be plunged into the profoundest obscurity.

The storm was in the southeast, the direction from which the menacing clouds were moving. The two wretches asked for hospitality.

"Lenore had been sad since the departure of Efflam, and the prince–who adored her–said to her: 'These people know how to juggle and do conjuring tricks. Would you like them to come in to entertain you?'

"Lenore shook her head languidly to signal her refusal–but when a servant said that the tribe had come from Belgrade, her eyes lit up.

" 'Bring them in,' she instructed.

"They were two brothers, the older still young, the younger very young indeed. They gave their names as Mikhael and Solim. Mikhael was the taller, and his features gave every evidence of his origin among those lost children of a forgotten civilization who are strangers in every nation of the world, having neither law nor God: the Egyptians of Scotland, the bohemians of France, the *gitanos* of Spain, the *zingari* of Italy. Solim, by contrast, had a pale fresh face, blue eyes and blond hair.

"The prince ordered them to entertain Lenore. Solim sang the strange melodies of the Moldavian lands, accompanying himself on his rounded guitar with two steel strings. Mikhael performed the dances of Yataghan, and both of them juggled with wine-glasses, bottles and knives.

"Lenore only yawned, and the prince made a gesture of dismissal.

" 'Hospodar [49],' said Mikhael, instead of obeying, 'wouldn't your daughter like to hear a good story?'

"His impudent eyes were fixed upon Lenore, who blushed and seemed ill-at-ease. The prince knitted his brows and opened his mouth to call for his servants, but the gentle voice of Lenore stopped him.

" 'Father,' she said, 'I would like to know...'

"Mikhael immediately took a step towards the girl, threw his cap upon the floor and knelt upon it, while Solim remained standing in the middle of the room, his eyes lowered and his arms crossed upon his breast. Mikhael reached out, demanding Lenore's hand, which she offered to him in spite of herself. He examined it minutely for a long time, speaking periodically in an unknown language. These words were addressed to Solim, who still stood motionless in the middle of the room; they seemed to make an extraordinary impression on him. His limbs trembled, the veins in his forehead swelled up, and the hair on his head shook. It was as if the pythoness of old were on her tripod.

"Mikhael had examined the hand, but it was Solim who played the oracle, saying: 'Hospodar! Woe is mine, who must cry woe! I see through the night, in the distance, the vampire Ange whose eyes are upon your daughter...'

"The prince burst out laughing, while Lenore grew pale.

---

[49] Hospodar was a title originally borne by the princes or governors of Walachia and Moldavia when they were vassals of the Turkish Sultan; it was retained long afterwards by Lithuanian princes and Polish kings.

" 'Are there still vampires?' cried the prince, who was still amused.

"Mikhael returned to stand beside his brother and put his hand over Solim's mouth. The prince's face clouded over. Thumping the table with his hand, he said: 'For my part, I want to know! And remember that the Chief Magistrate of Szeged would not trouble himself at all about a couple of miscreants suspended from the trees in my park!'

" 'Lord,' Mikhael replied slowly, 'you have enough servants to guard your daughter, and you owe us some recompense for having warned you.'

" 'Who is this vampire Ange?' asked Lenore, all a-tremble.

"Solim replied, while wiping the sweat from his brow: 'It is the younger of the Ténèbre brothers.'

" 'And who are the Ténèbre brothers, knave?' cried the prince.

" 'You have the right to abuse me, Lord,' Mikhael replied, drawing himself up to his full height. 'You are strong and I am weak. You also have the right to chase me out into the gathering storm and to have me beaten by your Slovaks, but I have no desire to tell you anything but the truth: the Ténèbre brothers are two of the dead.'

"Lenore huddled close to her father, while Solim repeated, as if he were an echo: 'Two of the dead!'

"The prince took his daughter in his arms and said: 'Explain yourselves.'

" 'Hospodar,' Mikhael began, 'are they not dead, and thoroughly dead, who have swayed in the wind for three days and three nights on the gallows? We wander ceaselessly, as you know, in search of the bread that never satisfies our accursed hunger. Between Itèbe and Semlin the gallows of Magnate Karolyi, the High Lieutenant of the Banate of Timisoara, is to be found [50]. We passed close by it on the twenty-seventh of October of last year, three days before the feast of All Hallows. There were two men hanging there, one large and one small. We stripped them bare, and went on our way.

"'On the first of November, as we returned towards Itèbe, heading for Belgrade, we found the two executed men again, still stripped bare, surrounded by a

---

[50] The city of Semlin-Zimony in Hungarian–Zemun in Serbian–was situated on the bank of the Danube opposite to Belgrade; it was eventually swallowed up by its larger neighbor. The town which Féval calls Itèbe presumably suffered a similar fate as I have been unable to locate a likely candidate on modern maps. In general I have followed the policy of substituting the current names of the Hungarian and Rumanian geographical features for those that Féval uses–e.g. Tisza for his Theiss, Petrovaradin for his Peterwardein, Timisoara for his Temesvar– but where this proved impractical I have let his versions stand. I have used "the Great Hungarian Plain" (which is clearer than "the Great Alföld" or "Nagy Magyar Alföld") where Féval refers to the plain of "Grand-Waraden," since the province of Warasdin is long gone.

flock of crows. We made camp on the flat area between the gibbet and the Danube.

" 'At midnight, we were awakened by the sound of the crows, which were cawing plaintively. There was no moon, but there was another light, brighter and more vivid than moonlight. Where was it coming from? By means of that illumination we saw a huge cloud of fleeing crows. We saw, too, the gibbet, silhouetted in black against the strange aurora, with its two corpses slowly swinging.

" 'Two white horses with flowing manes ran right past us, bearing neither bridle nor saddle; they glided like arrows, but we heard not the slightest sound of their hoofbeats. They both halted beneath the gallows, one beneath the taller hanged man, the other beneath the shorter. We saw the four limbs of the executed men move, separating one from another.

" 'A sudden glare ripped through the cold November clouds like summer lightning; the two gallows-ropes broke at exactly the same moment and the two cadavers fell as one, legs apart, on to the two horses, which galloped away to the sound of a thunderclap...'

" 'See how feverishly my poor, dear Lenore is shivering,' said the prince. 'Take your tall stories to hell with you!'

"Solim lowered his arms, murmuring: 'My brother Mikhael has told the truth.'

"And Lenore, whose pretty white teeth were chattering, said: 'They are amusing me, Father–let them go on.'

" 'At Itèbe,' Mikhael continued, 'we asked the names of the two criminals, and were told that they were the Ténèbre brothers: Ténèbre the bandit and Ténèbre the vampire. Now, in the middle of the Great Hungarian Plain there are two graves that you can see for yourselves, one large and one small. Each is covered by a black stone, both of which carry inscriptions in the French language: on the larger one. Jean Ténèbre, *Chevalier*; on the smaller, Ange Ténèbre, *Prêtre*. Educated men say that they are the tombs of two French noblemen who came with many others to help the voivode John Hunyadi [51] defend Christendom against the Turks four hundred years ago. Men who are not educated affirm that for four centuries there has lain beneath these marble slabs an oupire and a vampire: one an eater of human flesh, the other a drinker of human blood.

" 'Hospodar, one thing is certain! On many occasions, during the four hundred years, those graves have opened, to the terror and the horror of the surrounding country. Sometimes, two corpses were found beneath the stones, one

---

[51] John Hunyadi (1407-1456) was the scion of a noble Hungarian family, who became voivode of Transylvania and Captain of Belgrade, in which capacity he waged war against the Turks. He won a famous victory over Mezid Bey in the last year of his life–the year in which Vlad the Impaler first became ruler of Walachia.

tall and one short, which gave every indication of recent death: eyes open and shining, blood liquid in the veins, tongues moist and lips red. At other times, the open graves displayed nothing but their emptiness: two black cavities from which the odor of death emerged. It is certain, moreover, that many attempts have been made to destroy these graves: the marble slabs have been broken, the rubble dispersed, the ground leveled–and invariably, when some time has passed, the two black stones resurface beneath the grass or the corn, intact once again, bearing the same funerary inscriptions.

" 'Lastly, it is certain–as the registers of the courts testify–that within the last twenty years alone, the brothers Ténèbre have been hanged in a dozen different places in Hungary, and seven times impaled in Turkish territory.

" 'But supernatural occurrences make little impact, unless they happened in the recent past. It is a story of the recent past that I want to tell you now. After having wandered for six months in the Turkish lands and traversed part of Serbia, our tribe returned towards Belgrade and camped once again on the banks of the Danube, below Semendria [52].

" 'At midnight, those of our kin who were keeping watch perceived two lights moving slowly downstream on the surface of the river. They went to investigate, and found two leather bags, one large and one small, drifting in the current, each one bearing a lamp and a placard headed The Pasha's Justice. The placard attached to the larger bag also bore the name Jean Ténèbre; that of the smaller, the name Ange Ténèbre.

" 'These two cadavers had been set afloat because the treasury of Belgrade had been looted three days previously and the daughter of the learned treasurer had been found dead in her bed, as white as an alabaster statue. We heard of the theft and the murder later–but when our sentinel came to wake us, we saw a long black boat that drifted by itself in the current with no one to steer it. The black boat came abreast of the two dying lights and, a moment later, had turned against the current as swiftly as a bird in flight, and was steered upriver by two men, one tall and one short.

" 'We arrived on the following day–the day beginning this very week–at the gates of the town of Petrovaradin in Slavonia...'

" 'Where my dear Efflam is, father,' murmured Lenore, offering her face to her father's kiss.

" 'It was morning,' Mikhael continued. "We pitched our tents in the place reserved for our tribes, under the ramparts of the town between the cemetery and the black ditch watered by the river Drave, into which the bodies of dead animals and executed criminals are carelessly thrown. We thought that there must be a festival in the town, because a great throng of peasants was pressing at the gates. When we were allowed to enter,we found that the festival was a public

---

[52] Although the modern name of this city is Smederevo, the old name still survives so I have let it stand.

execution by the sword. On the scaffold, we saw two condemned men, one tall and one short. And two names were on everyone's lips: the brothers Ténèbre! Hospodar, the heads fell: I saw it with my own eyes...'

" 'The heads fell,' Solim repeated, 'and they rolled across the planks of the scaffold.'

" 'And we returned to the camp,' continued Mikhael, 'behind the cart which carried the executioner's work. The two heads and the two bodies were thrown into the ditch in front of us while, on the far side of our tents, a poor child of fifteen years was carried to the cemetery.'

" 'Her name! The name of the dead girl!' cried Lenore, as if she had been seized by a heart-rending presentiment.

" 'Efflam,' replied Mikhael.

" 'Efflam!' repeated Solim, with lowered eyes and flared nostrils.

"Lenore put both hands to her breast and collapsed, deprived of her senses, into her father's arms..."

Baron von Altenheimer paused at this point, and Monsignor Benedict took the opportunity to say, in a very soft voice: "I admire the memory of my dear brother the privy councilor. While he was speaking, it seemed to me that he could still hear that rogue the Chevalier Ténèbre–for no one here can have failed to divine that Mikhael, the pretended gypsy, Mikhael the Romany, was none other than the elder of the brothers Ténèbre."

III. A Wedding in Venice

The Princess much preferred this tale to others, which might have featured French brigands or indigenous phantoms. The overall impression produced on us by a tale will, it must be admitted, depend on the involuntary response of the listeners themselves. This remark is particularly true with respect to fictions calculated to produce fear. No legend or fantastic tale will ever produce in a Parisian drawing-room the shivers that will find you out by a huge log fire, gathered around the enormous fireplace of an ancient château. Specters no longer come into Paris, as everyone knows. Listeners can be amused, but not frightened–but in cases like the present one, amusement can only be truly or fully obtained in being frightened.

Baron von Altenheimer's tale seemed curious, and that was all. All that it had contrived in its audience was that level of emotion that is so easily produced in the theatre, as soon as the curtain rises half-way and some unknown person crosses the darkened stage with his hat tilted over his eyes. Fear no longer exists. Parisians cannot be frightened–not top drawer Parisians, at any rate–by the vampires of the Drave and French cavaliers interred for four hundred years in the Great Hungarian Plain!

The Princess was so completely cured of her terror that she looked at her son the Marquis and laughed. She found that he was very pale, and was on the point of asking him whether he could take such solemn nonsense seriously–but everyone seems pale by moonlight. The Princess let go of the Marquis; she had no further need of his bodily protection.

"Monsieur le Baron," said the benevolent and courteous Archbishop of Paris, "we did not expect such good fortune. Permit me to thank the Bishop of Hermopolis for all the pleasure that you have given us this evening."

The audience chorused its approval. In high society, as our readers well know, the bravos are always polite, and triumphs are a thousand times sweeter.

But the Bishop of Hermopolis was not content. He had hoped for more than this. One expects a great deal from the virtuosos one has produced. Several signs of impatience had escaped His Lordship. "It must be admitted," he said, in his rich southern accent, "that Monsignor von Altenheimer has favored us with an unfortunate revelation! How can you expect us to be interested in the story, now that we know how it ends?"

"Does Your Excellency really know how it will end?" asked the hollow voice of the Baron.

That single sentence was sufficient to make everyone pay attention. The Bishop, already modifying his tone, said: "Seeing that we know that the two bohemians are none other than Jean and Ange Ténèbre in person, young Lenore will surely be devoured..."

"By no means!" cried the Princess, all her courage evaporating. "I certainly hope that we shall be able to save her... isn't that so, Monsieur le Baron?"

The privy councilor to His Majesty the King of Wurtemburg offered a respectful bow to the whole audience, and directed more specific ones at the Minister and the Princess. By the rays of the moon, one could see a satisfied expression upon his long face. He took from his pocket a big golden box, embellished with large sparkling diamonds, which sent scintillating reflections in all directions.

"Noble ladies and gentlemen," he replied soberly, playing with his royal snuff-box–which looked for all the world like a handful of pure light–"my brother Benedict has done no wrong. Nor has he, as His Excellency appears to believe, given away the punch-line of the joke–God grant that it were, in fact, a joke! Unhappily, in telling tales like these one can disdain such cleverness. There is no need to manage with due care the petty effects and little surprises that storytellers usually employ. I will give you further proof of this by telling you straight away that the Ténèbre brothers are now in Paris, and that I have come here in pursuit of them, at my own risk and peril."

This time, the majority of the audience-members started violently, while the remainder pricked up their ears. The Bishop of Hermopolis, who stubbornly insisted on seeing the matter from an artistic viewpoint, clapped his hands and cried bravo. The Princess recalled her son, the Marquis de Lorgères, to her side.

"That's some joke," she murmured.

Baron von Altenheimer slowly inhaled a pinch of snuff, then–just as slowly–he wiped the back of his hand on his black coat. It must be admitted that such a gesture is more effective at the *Comédie Française*; it really requires a frill. Even so, it wasn't bad, for a Westphalian.

"Now!" the Baron continued, in a deliberate tone. "I shall proceed as swiftly as I can to the matter of the crown jewels of Wurtemburg. Consider, noble ladies, the fact that in the 19th century, we live our lives surrounded by prodigious events that, for some reason, we neither see nor deny. Personally, I am a believer, because I have learned the truth to my cost. I believe in the Chevalier Ténèbre, the most audacious, the most improbable, the most authentically diabolical brigand who ever lived; I believe in Ange Ténèbre, the vampire. I have seen the pale remains of his victims, from which not a drop of blood could be recovered.

"What is the exact nature of beings like these, and where do they fit into the known categories of God's Creation? I don't know. A theory that could accommodate such monstrosities would have to extend much further than ordinary moral failings or deviations from the common mold. There must be prodigies within the order of created beings that are immediately superior to mankind and, in consequence, unknown to mankind. Seeing that the fraction of the work of God that is visible and tangible to us presents anomalies–since we encounter in our streets hunchbacks, hare-lips and idiots–it may be that death itself, or the mechanical organization of life, if you prefer, is similarly subject to deviations and *dérangements*. It may be that the clay of which we are formed is occasionally treated with other and more powerful reagents..."

"Monsieur Privy Councilor... brother," Monsignor Benedict interrupted at this point, "I beg you to drop this subject, lest you become enmeshed in the toils of sinful materialism."

This was said with gentle severity. Baron von Altenheimer extended his hand to his younger sibling and said: "I beg your pardon, brother."

"It could be explained, up to a point," Monsignor Frayssinous put in, "without any recourse to materialistic philosophy..."

"Of course, Excellency, of course," the Baron interrupted respectfully, "but it's entirely my concern. I have my reasons for believing, so I believe; that's quite sufficient. An objection of a different order has been put forward, which appears to me more serious, because it challenges my conduct. The question needs to be put to me: if you are a believer, as you affirm, how is it possible that you would compromise your good character by such vain speculations? You accept the reality of these two creatures of popular superstition, and you commit yourself to their pursuit! Why? To kill them, even though they are immortal? Ladies and gentlemen, in our German universities we call this a disputation. I believe that these creatures have existed for four centuries and more..."

At this point, the Baron was interrupted by a murmur mingled with a certain amount of politely-muffled laughter.

"He is superb," the Bishop of Hermopolis said, in a low voice. "He sets out these follies with such magnificent sang-froid."

"...For four centuries and more," repeated Baron von Altenheimer. "That is my utterly firm and very well-established opinion—but I do not believe that they are immortal. Tradition is definite upon this point. No oupire or vampire can resist combustion. As it will probably fall to me to defend France, I propose to put this theory—advocated by all ancient authors—to the test by taking the miscreants to Stuttgart, where they will be carefully burned, after which their ashes will be divided into small portions and transported in several different directions before they are scattered on the ground. If they rise again, after that, then will be the time to say that the privy councilor, Baron von Altenheimer, is nothing but a poor head without a brain!"

There were some in the audience who thought that the tall German gentleman with the *basso-profundo* voice was simply and deplorably mad. Others supposed that he was joking. The remainder, among whose ranks was the Princess, were inclined to concede that his was a rather ingenious method of exterminating oupires, vampires and the like.

"You will not be surprised to know," Baron von Altenheimer continued, "that misfortune was not long arriving in the house of Prince Jacobyi. His daughter was carried off that very same night. How vast the sums were that the brothers Ténèbre had appropriated by theft is unknown—but it is certain that they loved money. Some said that they had buried fabulous treasures in various different places in southern Germany.

"Prince Jacobyi was advised that his daughter Lenore would be returned safe and sound on payment of a ransom of half a million florins, but he was warned that if he made the slightest effort to recover her by force, or by recourse to the law, the child would be lost to him forever.

"He did not hesitate. Forty-eight hours later, he had the twelve hundred thousand francs—and Lenore, safe and sound, as promised, slept in her own bed that night. But it happened that the Chevalier Ténèbre and his brother Ange, the vampire, were not the only bandits who had dealings with the Magnate: his two stewards and his banker in Pest were also vampires, after their own fashion. They had been mining his fortune for a long time, and the loan of five hundred thousand florins caused an explosion.

"All his creditors demanded settlement of their mortgages at the same time, and in the full amount. The Chandor domain was put up for public auction. It was not so much an estate as a country; even in the depths of Hungary it was worth more than two million *louis*. The prince, once the sale was made, had only just enough to pay off his debts—but the two stewards and the banker in Pest were now as rich as lords.

"The Prince became an expatriate. He may be in England, or Italy, or perhaps in France. He lives, it is said, on what his daughter earns...

"My lords, the night would be entirely gone and the new day born before I could complete a detailed account of the horrors with which the voice of the public has charged the brothers Ténèbre. Their name, if spoken aloud in the regions through which the Danube flows, will not only put women and children to flight but strong men. Captain, or Chevalier Ténèbre, as he is variously known, has fought pitched battles against entire troops of Austrians and Turks; he has plundered tax-collectors and routed their protective escorts ten times over. Ange, his brother, is no soldier, but don't think him any less dangerous for that. He is a master of disguise, well able to play any role; the captain and he are on an absolutely equal footing. They amass their fortune ceaselessly, and I have often heard it said in Hungary, not only by the common people but in the reception-rooms of the Archduke in the Imperial Palace at Ofen, that if there were a kingdom for sale, the brothers Ténèbre would be kings.

"Last year in Venice, at the beginning of spring, the entire city was celebrating the marriage of the young Comtesse Barberini, the god-daughter of Her Royal and Imperial Majesty, to the scion of the Policeni family: it was the reunion of two of the greatest Lombardo-Venetian fortunes and from the dawn of the day the city wore the face of public celebration [53]. The poor people of Venice knew Pia Barberini as an angel of charity. It was said that Andrea Policeni--formerly a spirited young man, a king of patrician pleasures, the last of those mysterious Romans who slid under the Rialto in former times, behind the curtains of so many gondolas, when moonlight blanched the palace of the marble Venus risen from the crest of the wave–had divested himself of the dark mantle of the adventurer, cast it away and become a saint at her behest.

"I was in Venice, my lords, not on any political mission on this occasion, but merely to embrace my beloved brother, who was enrolled in the army of God, stationed in Rome with the Holy Father. Venice is half-way between Stuttgart and the Eternal City..."

As if each of the two brothers had yielded to an irresistible impulse of tenderness, their hands sought and clasped one another. The audience approved; the gesture was greeted with softened expressions, as a demonstration of the beautiful love that flourishes in families.

"We each made a journey, to meet one another at the half-way point," Baron von Altenheimer continued, in a slightly emotional voice. "At the wedding, in which we assisted, there were representatives of all the aristocracies in the world–but there were two strangers, in particular, who excited the curiosity of the entire city: John Stuart, Earl of Glasgow, the son of the pretender Charles

---

[53] As with the other ancestral lists, the family names employed here are real, but the particular individuals are not. The Barberinis were a notable Roman family who had become extinct in 1738. Féval used the Policenis in *Les Habits Noirs*.

196

Edward Stuart–and, in consequence, the legitimate heir to the English throne–and his younger brother Charles, the Duke of Richmond.

"The common opinion, to tell the truth, holds that the last Stuart died in Rome without issue; but even in Rome, as my brother Benedict can assure you, many eminent persons reserve doubts in that regard. The pretender, who had lived in fear of the combined intrigues of the House of Brunswick and his own brother, Henry Stuart, Cardinal Duke of York, had contracted a secret marriage and concealed the birth of his son, the supreme hope of a dynasty threatened on all sides [54]. The Earl of Glasgow was in possession of papers of the utmost importance. Certain titles, emanating from sources so respectable that to persist in doubting them is almost sacrilege, become unbelievable. The majority of the noblemen of Venice addressed the Earl of Glasgow as 'Majesty'.

"There was, moreover, the evidence of two particularly handsome faces–and, one might almost say, historic heads. John Stuart, who was a tall man, had a long and bilious face as similar to his father's as two drops of water on his coat of arms. His younger brother, by virtue of his curly blond hair and the delicate cut of his features, might easily have been mistaken for the subject of Van Dyck's portrait of Charles I–especially given his stature, for Charles was as short as his namesake.

"In the ancestral hall of the Barberini Palace there was a table of blue porphyry, supported by four massive silver feet. All the gems to be worn at the wedding had been assembled there; it was a jewel-case that a queen would have envied.

"There were the diamonds to be worn by the present Comtesse Policeni, who was a Howard, like the fifth wife of King Bluebeard, Henry VIII of England; those of the grandmother, Rose Gritti, and the great-grandmother, Ann Gradenigo; the ruby necklace in which Phébus of Lusignan had married Catherine Pépoli; the diadem of Catherine Cornaro, her mother, the Queen of Cyprus; and the sapphire *rivière* of Tranquille Paléologue, the wife of the last doge but one–and all of that on the bridegroom's side.

"On the bride's side could be seen the solitaire known as the Montserrat; the rose-cut diamond that the Dukes of Austria had carried in their crown; the seven brilliants of Pallas Comnène–the Pleiades; the bracelets of Antonia Doria

---

[54] Charles Edward Stuart the "Young Pretender," also known as Bonnie Prince Charlie, had settled in Italy in 1766 and died there–childless, so far as anyone knows–in 1788. Charles's younger brother Henry, who supported him during the Jacobite rebellion, styled himself Henry IX thereafter, until his own death in 1807. Henry was unlikely to have been involved in plotting against against Charles–although a man of Henry's conspicuous piety could hardly help disapproving of his brother's dissolute lifestyle–but if Charles had had a son, Henry's claim to be the rightful king of England from 1788-1809 would have been even falser than it actually was.

of Genoa, who became the wife of Nicolas Barberini in the denouement of that eternal drama whose principal roles are Romeo and Juliet; the ring of Cardinal Frégose–and outshining all that marvelous finery–the wedding-present sent to his god-daughter by His Majesty the Emperor of Austria.

One touching incident occurred that can be told in a few words: the king without a crown, that heir to such misfortune and such grandeur, the Earl of Glasgow, advanced towards the porphyry table, laden with all these treasures, and asked for permission to throw upon it a simple string of pearls that had been worn by the unfortunate Mary, Queen of Scots. I can still see his venerable figure and the nobly ingenuous air of his young brother, as the affianced couple offered their thanks to him.

"And I swear, on my honor, that I did not begin to recognize in them the two sordid gypsies of Chandor Castle...!"

There arose in the circle of listeners such a murmur of astonishment that the Baron's words were literally cut off.

"Bravo! Bravo! *Bravissimo!*" cried the Bishop of Hermopolis. "That's what I call, for the sake of delicacy, a sudden reversal of fortune!"

"What?" said His Grace the Archbishop de Quélen. "That's too bad...!"

"I've guessed it," murmured the Princess. "In placing the false pearls on the porphyry table, the King of England slipped some beautiful diamond up his sleeve..."

Baron von Altenheimer offered her a dignified bow, and replied: "Beautiful lady, nothing escapes the perspicacity of the French. Except that the Chevalier Ténèbre did not perform his conjuring trick with all the world looking on, nor were the pearls false–for, that very night, he took them back, along with everything else that was on the porphyry table.

"What?" the cry went up. "All of them?

"All of them," confirmed the soft voice of the Monsignor. "Including the silver legs of the table."

IV. Baron von Altenheimer

The windows of the château, visible between the trees, were illuminated one by one. The final preparations were being made for the Archbishop's charitable distribution.

"We shall soon be interrupted, Baron," said the Bishop of Hermopolis, "but in the meantime, the ladies would dearly like to hear the end of your story."

"In other words, Your Lordship, you want me to cut it short," replied the King of Wurtemburg's privy councilor. "Well, in the first place, I am at the disposal of Your Excellency, and that of His Grace and all the other eminent persons who have done me the honor of listening to me–and in the second, I really do have only a little left to tell.

198

"I have not yet told you that the family of King Wilhelm, my master, is the most numerous surrounding any throne in Europe [55]. His Majesty has four children by his two marriages; his very illustrious son, likewise has four children; his five very respectable uncles have an even greater wealth of descendants, and such an assortment of children, grandchildren, sons-in-law and daughters-in-law, that the five collateral branches boast no less than fifty princely heads. God, the protector of France, also seems to concern himself a little with the dynasty of Wurtemburg.

"Now, all this notwithstanding, until 1823 King Wilhelm did not have a direct heir of the male sex. There was, in consequence, great joy in Wurtemburg when, on the sixth of March, the birth of a prince royal was announced, who was privately baptized, according to the rites of the Lutheran church, Charles Frederick Alexander. The King wanted to postpone the definitive baptism ceremony, in order to express the full extent of his gladness, and so that all the friends of the court might gather for a feast that would be both a public and a family celebration.

"There is no time to contrive any petty surprises, and in any case, after everything that had gone before everyone will be able to guess that the Ténèbre brothers came to the feast–but under what pretext, and in what form?

"I beg you, my dear lords and ladies, not to gauge these two truly prodigious beings according to the measure of your timid impostors, your bird-brained brigands or those phantoms whose puerile roles are restricted to the gratuitous terrorization of female feebleness and the poltroonery of little children. My judgement, which I have not sought to hide from you, is that we are faced here with the supernatural, employing means which are beyond our comprehension to satisfy two purely human passions: Avarice and Lust. Interred beneath those two black stones, covering the two graves on the Great Hungarian Plain, are not two corpses but two deadly sins, incarnate since the beginning of the world...in other places, there must be other marble slabs covering those other vampires which are always dead and yet always alive: Ambition, Wrath, Hatred, Dishonesty and Pride.

"You, who are amazed by the petty comedy played out by your Comte Pontis de Sainte-Helène, should not be tempted to make comparisons. Don't say that there are difficulties, or impossibilities, in my story–or anything else that might be masked by that loose term, implausibility, which is the protestation of minds that are too narrow against truths that are too broad.

"Yes, certainly, there were difficulties involved in entering that court, to mingle with the princes and princesses whose alliances embraced all Europe like a familial net. Yes, certainly, there were what the vulgar call impossibilities standing in the way of their presentation, under some royal name–and how else

---

[55] King Wilhelm I was one of the longest-reigning monarchs of 19th-century Europe, occupying the throne from 1816-1864.

could they present themselves?–in that palace teeming with the guests and friends of all the real kings. Anyway, the brothers Ténèbre, as you would expect, chose their disguises and their roles with great care.

"This was not an occasion of the ingenuous phantasmagoria of Venice. Wurtemburg does not treat fallen royalty with such religious chivalry; it is a new and pragmatic realm, which has no fear of alloying its dynastic blood with that man who became your Emperor–and who, a mere four years ago, paid with his death on a desert island for the magical splendor of his victories. What was required here was, if you will permit me to express it thus, a solid emanation of an extant power. The occasion required someone living, not dead; it required, in a word, a personage that all the princes and all the princesses could call cousin, without creating a diplomatic incident or starting a war–a representative of a peaceful and relatively weak state.

"Where could that state be found? Not Russia, from which had come the late Queen, the daughter of Paul I, and whose armies were commanded by Prince Alexander, the King's uncle; nor Prussia, where Prince Auguste, the nephew of the King, served in the guards; nor Austria, where Princess Marie, the cousin of the King, bore the title of Archduchess; nor any part of Germany, where Nassau, Saxe-Altembourg, Bade, Stolberg, Waldeck, Hohenloe, Tour-et-Taxis were all sons-in-law or fathers-in-law; nor the Netherlands, where a betrothal had already been secured between the heir to the throne and Princess Sophie, who was still in her cradle; nor England, where Duke Louis, the father of the actual Queen, lived; nor even France, the adopted fatherland of Duke Frederick Philip. Where, then?

"There is a troubled land, one of the greatest in history, but which seems in our modern epoch to be hiding behind its mountainous wall, ashamed of its decadence. Germany no longer knows Spain, now that the house of Austria has ended its reign in Madrid. The noise of your last war, the heroism of your princes and your soldiers at the Trocadero [56], reached us as a muffled echo, too distant to be heard. Spain is a China in the middle of Europe–but you know what effect that the ambassadors of India had on the court of Louis XIV; a literal Chinese ambassador would have caused a stir throughout Europe. At the baptism of our prince royal, no one paid any attention to the son of the Spanish *infanta*.

"Were there, then, no official diplomatic links between Spain and Wurtemburg? Yes, there were–there was still a Spanish *chargé d'affaires* in Stuttgart, but he was tricked into becoming an accessory. Notes were exchanged between Madrid and Stuttgart; it was my responsibility to look at them, and I looked at them. I am not particularly intimate with most of that which surrounds me but I am, after all, a learned man; in my own country I am an accredited savant. I hold doctoral diplomas from four universities. My sight is good, my

---

[56] The French invaded Spain in 1823 and fought a crucial battle at the Trocadero which won them entry to Cadiz.

health has not deteriorated under the strain of mental labor, I am perfectly sane–and yet those documents seemed authentic to me!

"I am not afraid to say it: it was a veritable miracle! Anyone who has been admitted into a chancellery, whether by the humble door that I use or by that which opens to the knocking of Your Excellencies, knows what a mountain of impossibilities–I will use the word, this time–must be climbed in order to create false diplomatic correspondence. Each such dispatch passes through a hundred hands that must be corrupted, and before a hundred eyes that must be blinded; but the correspondence was manufactured. I have in my files here in Paris a letter signed by King Ferdinand, but written by the Chevalier Ténèbre or by Ange Ténèbre the vampire!

"That's not all, however. The court at Wurtemburg had issued real and authentic notes; the court of Spain had responded, that much is certain. Add the suppression of the real documents to the creation of the false ones and your minds may boggle at their leisure–for that, I repeat, is a miracle.

"What remains to be told re-enters the category of ordinary prestidigitation. Once the two creatures had been able to trick me, acting and speaking as they did before me–who has paid so dearly for their acquaintance–it was merely a question of artfulness. It must be admitted that they had had all the time in the world to become accomplished impostors and admirable comedians. But those papers...!"

Baron von Altenheimer fell silent, as if his retrospective astonishment had choked him, and Monsignor Benedict sighed as he shook his blond head. "Ah! Don't you see... the papers! The papers! There is the miracle!"

Archbishop de Quélen leaned over to whisper into the ear of the Bishop of Hermopolis. "Well, it's stunning, I must admit... but it's only an audacious phantasmagoria, isn't it?"

"It's the truth," Bishop Frayssinous replied. "The pure truth! I have seen the Baron's own letters of credit, in the company of the prefect of police. He is highly respected at court. Besides, there's his brother–Chamberlain to His Holiness...

"But how is it," murmured the Archbishop, "that we have never heard talk of any of this?"

"It only happened a few days ago, Your Grace! The baptism of the Prince Royal of Wurtemburg took place at the end of August, and September has just begun."

"It was exactly a fortnight ago," said the Baron, who appeared to have fully recovered his composure. "All Stuttgart took part in the celebration, whose like had never been seen in our homeland. Fifty princes and princesses of the German and Northern courts were received at the castle–who, together with the army of princes and princesses related by blood, formed a veritable royal crowd. His Majesty said, joyfully: 'I have waited two and a half years, but it is a complete success. There is not a single fairy missing from my son's cradle!'

"He certainly appreciated how much he owed to the courtesy of the states of Germany and the North, but that which flattered him even more was the unexpected tribute from the South; what made his success complete was the presence of Don François de Paule, *Infante* of Spain, and his august companion, Louise-Charlotte de Bourbon, daughter of François I, King of Sicily.

"The *Infante* was a man of twenty-three years, dark-skinned but seeming not a day older than his ostensible age. It would have taken a sorcerer to detect any trace of resemblance between that bold and taciturn young man and the pretended heir to the royal privilege of the Stuarts, a stiff and desiccated old man whose ravaged features were already crowned with white hair. As for the *Infanta* Louise-Charlotte, we all knew that she was born in 1804, and was in consequence twenty-one years of age–and noble, gracious and charming! The Chevalier Ténèbre could pass for the king of actors, but there is no greater comedian than brother Ange: that is a magician who could make you see the sun at midnight!

"It was the brothers Ténèbre, and their brilliant retinue was probably the same gypsy band that camped on the far bank of the Tisza in full view of Chandor Castle. And that royal farce–which, it must be said, was probably unique in the annals of the world–was paraded for three full days before the assembled houses of Europe!

"It was the brothers Ténèbre! The denouement you already know, in part: the crown jewels of Wurtemburg disappeared during the second day. On the third day, an angelic child died, the daughter of Chancellor Reinhardt, who had been placed with the infanta in the capacity of maid-of-honor. That same day there was a general clear-out so audacious that the astonishment which seemed exhausted was reborn. Everything had gone: the jeweled ornaments of the princes and princesses alike.

"The *Infante* and the *Infanta* had done a great deal of dancing that evening. As midnight approached, Monsieur Metternich [57], whose sister is the King's aunt, asked the Archduchess Marie, the older sister of the Queen, what had become of the eagle modeled in diamonds that she normally wore at her throat. The Archduchess searched and, while searching, said to Monsieur Metternich in her turn: 'Prince, where is your Golden Fleece necklace? Where is your Annunciation string? Where is your Danish brooch?' An immediate outcry went up,

---

[57] Prince Klemens von Metternich (1773-1859) was one of the leading statesmen of the early 19th century. He eventually became a leading opponent of Napoleon, having studied the Emperor carefully while he was Austrian minister to France in 1806-8. Metternich was the main architect of the Austrian Empire reconstructed after Napoleon's defeat, but his influence began to wane after 1825. There is considerable symbolic significance in this mutual recognition by key representatives of the old and new aristocracies of Europe that the symbols of their wealth and power have been stolen.

everyone perceiving at the same time that they had been robbed. The King–the King himself–had been stripped of the emblems of his identity! The doors of the palace were shut, but it was too late. The *Infante*, the *Infanta* and their retinue had already gone, carrying booty whose worth could not be estimated at less than a million gold crowns."

"At the very least," Monsignor Benedict added, equably.

A noise of carriage-wheels on the roadway, coming towards Conflans, was heard. The wind, which had begun to blow in gusts, carried vague sounds along the brilliantly-illuminated side of the château: fugitive instrumental notes groping in search of harmony. The Archbishop of Paris gave the signal to return, saying: "We can't be late arriving at our little concert!"

Everyone immediately stood up. The sensation of terror was utterly dispelled, for the very simple reason that the most recent episodes narrated by the baron had no trace of the diverse emotions that had previously agitated the assembly. The Venetian tale had been set in broad daylight; the adventure in Stuttgart had taken place by the bright light of a thousand candles; there had been no further return to the kind of dark and mysteriously moonlit night that surrounded the Archbishop's guests. Baron von Altenheimer's vampires and brigands had taken on the character of a comic opera.

The Princess took the arm of her son and bodyguard, the young Marquis de Lorgères. Pleased with herself because she was no longer trembling, she had just opened her mouth to reproach Baron von Altenheimer because she had not been sufficiently frightened, when she saw two eyes fixed upon her. They had that particular gleam that the eyes of animals of the feline genus take on in the darkness.

Madame de Montfort was an intelligent person, who knew perfectly well that vampires rarely interest themselves in princesses of a certain age; nevertheless, the gaze startled her. It belonged to Monsignor Benedict, who pointed a white and delicate finger, on which a magnificent solitaire sparkled, at the wide lawn in front of the château and said in a honeyed voice: "I would like to point out to Madame the Princess how easily even the simplest things can be reinvested with genuinely fantastic aspects by darkness."

In the middle of the lawn, a white object could be seen, which was moving slowly, cutting across the dark expanse of grass. It was a woman, but the way in which the diffuse rays of the moon fell upon her billowing dress really did give her the appearance of a ghost. She glided through the dark obscurity of the park like a hazy apparition. The arm of the young Marquis trembled beneath his mother's.

"Gaston! What is it?" she cried. "Are you trying to frighten me as well?"

"The wind is chilly," Gaston mumbled.

At that moment, the Archbishop said; "Do you see that phantom? It is my charming and angelic *protégée* Mademoiselle d'Arnheim, who will perform some beautiful classic masterpieces by the German masters for us. Ladies, I recommend her to you with all my heart, for she is a Christian Antigone who supports her father in his old age. The Opera is richer than we are, and has offered to pay two thousand *louis* a year for her unparalleled voice and admirable delivery. Mademoiselle d'Arnheim, who comes from a good family and is as pious as a prayer, would rather remain poor than risk her soul for gold; she is content to give lessons. I have promised to help her and would be very grateful to anyone who would like to second me in that good work."

The white form had disappeared behind the trees lining the avenue.

"Gaston," said the Princess, "you must go to see Monsieur Récamier about the beating of your heart. I can feel it against my arm; it's a veritable palpitation."

Baron von Altenheimer had drawn nearer to the Archbishop. "My Lord," he said, after a respectful hesitation, "perhaps I do not understand the French language well enough to express things very delicately. I am rich. Would it be possible for me do something, via Your Lordship, for the young lady who has the honor to be your *protégée*?" As he spoke, he took a pocket-book from inside his coat. The Archbishop looked at him and reached out a hand; it was only to clasp his, for he murmured: "Monsieur le Baron, you are a good-hearted man!" The Baron, however, pretending to have misunderstood him, deposited the wallet in the Archbishop's hand, bowed in an exaggerated fashion and disappeared into the crowd of guests.

The Princess came to a sudden halt at the foot of the steps and said to her son: "Gaston, I think I have left Madame de Maillé's cloak on the grass...

The Marquis immediately retraced his steps, and had no difficulty in finding the cloak. As he turned to leave the lawn again, he saw a brilliant rectangular object at his feet, glittering in the grass at the spot formerly occupied by Monsignor Benedict. He picked it up, in order to return it to its owner–it only required a single glance for him to recognize the roman prelate's velvet-bound steel-boxed missal.

By the time the Marquis got back to the château, everyone else had gone in. While crossing the entrance-hall, he shifted the missal in his hand and the box opened of its own accord between his fingers. He tried to close it again, but could not; it had a secret spring, whose mechanism had doubtless been released when it fell upon the ground.

While Gaston tried to readjust the catch, the pages of the missal opened, and he glanced down at the two exposed pages.

He stopped dead, as if thunderstruck, stifling the cry of amazement that rose unbidden from his breast...

V Conversational Trifles

The great hall of the Château de Conflans was arranged for the concert. The orchestra was set on a stage, before which a Nuremberg organ-chest had been placed. Five or six rows of chairs faced the stage, most of them occupied by women and children, in "the costume of the archdiocese," as it was known in the district at the time. These were not ball-gowns–most definitely not; there were chaste sleeveless jackets and decorous wimples everywhere–but nor was it everyday clothing. The dresses were smart and ornaments were worn. The male members of the assembly–priests, aristocrats and civil servants–were standing around the perimeter.

Immediately after entering, Princess de Montfort had sought out Doctor Récamier and laid hold of him, in order to talk to him about the palpitations suffered by her son the Marquis.

"He's a good boy, Doctor," she said, "and so different from his brother, Monsieur le Duc! That one will be the death of me, my nerves are so bad. Whereas Gaston, you know, is exactly the opposite. I don't know why he lost his religious vocation–to me, the boy certainly seems to be cut from clerical cloth. I can't see him in any other garb, and he'd suit a tonsure. The diplomatic corps! I ask you, does he look like a diplomat? But we lost you, Doctor–you weren't with us in the garden. We have been listening to a most original German storyteller, who immediately put us in mind of the Devil... wherever did you get to?"

Her gaze scanned the room and picked out Baron von Altenheimer, who was standing near the entrance door. In the candlelight, the fantastic aspects of his person seemed quite lost. He was probably thirty years of age, but his plainness made him seem older. He had, appropriately enough, one of those faces with which all our readers are familiar, which lasts from the twentieth year until old age and which common parlance calls ageless. He had long, pronounced features, rather pale and drawn, with bushy eyebrows over his sad eyes. His thick hair was brushed down over his forehead, with two thin and lobeless ears projecting from it. His unusually wide mouth wore an expression of naive placidity. His entire physiognomy, in sum, was emphatically bourgeois and common. His carriage was stiffly erect, and his black coat was as distressingly ill-fashioned as his trousers, which were cut several fingerbreadths too short, exposing silk socks of an extreme thinness. His shoes were robust, with pearly buckles.

The Princess noticed that his ankles looked like two knots on a stick.

"There, nevertheless, is the romantic unknown who made us feel an immediate shiver," she continued, laughing. "The moon and darkness are all that is required to play those kinds of tricks! After ten o'clock at night, my niece Madame de Maillé mistakes all the oak-stumps beside the highway for African lions escaped from menageries, and every post for the brigand Rinaldo Rinaldini, about whom she has read in tales of Italy. The gallant German has spoken a great deal about the Danube, but I'm sure that the Danube peasantry has less deplorable tailors. His brother is nice. There's the costume I'd like to see on Gaston!"

Doctor Récamier responded with an assortment of eloquent smiles, as appropriate. Women in general found him extraordinarily attentive. His awesome medical reputation was founded on the most basic of principles: he healed all maladies by prescribing no remedies.

The brother was, indeed, nice–although the word seemed a trifle familiar in the mouth of a princess as a description of a roman prelate in the hall of the Archbishop of Paris. He carried his clerical coat with a proper and perfect grace. His blond hair, smooth and fine, was pierced at the center by a microscopic tonsure; it fell upon his cheeks–which were slightly too rosy–in soft curls, giving him the appearance of a cherub. The Princess was not the cause of that blush; she had used the right word in spite of herself; Monsignor Benedict was nice.

"Hold on!" the Princess went on, touching the Doctor on the arm. "Look over there, at my mirror image!" Her smile, impregnated with that maternal mockery whose falsity always demands contradiction, indicated a tall young man, too slender but very handsome, who was leaning on a window-ledge. His eyes were lowered, perhaps because they had just encountered his mother's.

"Well!" said the Doctor, "I would never have recognized the Marquis de Lorgères. He's grown up into a remarkable cavalier!"

The Princess blushed with pleasure. "Don't you think he's rather too pale?"

"A nervous temperament... an affusion of cold water in a warm bath... a tonic regime without too much excitement... lots of healthy exercise... distraction... I would be honored to pay him a visit..." The Doctor bowed and tactfully withdrew, delicately disengaging his arm from hers.

The Princess fluttered her eyelashes at Gaston, and turned around.

As soon as the Princess had turned her back, Gaston lifted his own eyes again. His gaze, which certainly seemed a trifle feverish, fixed itself on a closed door half-hidden by the orchestra. The Marquis de Lorgères was evidently waiting for someone, and that someone would soon be coming through the door. But was it only anticipation that made his eyes seem hollow and put sweat upon his brow?

At the other end of the room, the Archbishop of Paris approached the Bishop of Hermopolis.

"Is the Baron von Altenheimer a personal acquaintance of yours, My Lord?" he asked.

"Not at all," replied Bishop Frayssinous. "He was presented to me by his brother, who brought me letters of introduction from Cardinals Pacca, Gaysruk and Riario Sforza, as well as a note signed by the prefect of the Congregation of Rites. I know that he has the ear of my colleague at the Ministry of the Interior and of the prefect of police..." He broke off and said: "But here comes the very man! We shall have more information now!"

The prefect of police had indeed come in, and the two prelates could see him exchanging a handshake with Baron von Altenheimer, who was still standing by the door.

"Many of the things he said to us," the Archbishop said, "suggested a mental state which was, to say the least, bizarre..."

"He's a German," Bishop Frayssinous put in, "and a storyteller–two halves of madness!"

"A generous madness–prodigal even," the Archbishop of Paris persisted. "Did you notice that he gave me his pocket-book for Mademoiselle d'Arnheim?"

"I thought I saw that–what was in the pocket-book?"

"A sum so large that I don't know whether it was a mistake on his part. Ten banknotes, a thousand francs each."

"Ten banknotes of a thousand francs!" repeated the astonished Bishop of Hermopolis, before adding, in a lower voice: "But we in France are poor, while these Teutons spend money like water."

The orchestra began playing a motet by Lesueur [58]. Baron von Altenheimer maintained his stiff and awkward posture through the first few bars, but as the French master's majestic and grandiose endeavor was further extended it seemed that the Baron's own stature matured in parallel. His pose altered as he drew himself up to his full height and his breast swelled, filling out the folds of his black coat. Little by little, his eyes lit up for all to see, and his nostrils dilated as if thrust aside by ardent breath. Once again he became the center of attention, instantly acquiring the reputation of an enthusiastic music-lover.

"I fear, your Lordship," the prefect of police replied, in the meantime, to the questions of the Archbishop, "that Wurtemburg has no *chargé d'affaires* in Paris at the moment; Austria is representing its interests for the time being. I will consult the ambassador tomorrow. Messieurs von Altenheimer seem to me to be eminent men and quite dependable. The Baron is a close friend of Prince Metternich–Prince Talleyrand has told me as much... as far as the authenticity of their mission is concerned, it is not my place to comment upon it, alas. The brothers Ténèbre are evildoers of the most dangerous kind, and we have the dubious honor of their presence in Paris. A bold, extraordinary and highly improbable theft was committed yesterday at the home of His Lordship the Duc de Bourbon–who is, in fact, one of Baron von Altenheimer's patrons. Antiques and jewelry worth more than fifty thousand crowns have been abstracted from his gallery, including three Isabey miniatures, five of Madame de Mirbel, two enamels by Petitot and three rapier-guards that the late prince brought back from

---

[58]   Jean-François Lesueur (1760-1837) was the outstanding French composer of religious music during the early 19th century and a famous teacher–Berlioz and Gounod were among his pupils.

Florence [59]... Her Majesty sent for me today; she desires to see Baron von Al-tenheimer."

"And is there any trace of your men?"

"My Lord, Baron von Altenheimer has a brigade of highly-skilled legal practitioners in his company–including, it is said, two detectives from Scotland Yard... yes, if you're not familiar with the English police, two sleuths chosen from the finest that London has to offer... The King seems to desire that the Bar-on has a certain freedom of action... I can only stand aside..."

The prefect of police made no attempt to conceal his bad humor; he was obviously a little jealous of the Baron, and thought it outrageous that anyone could dismiss his proven troops in favor of the militia of some petty country no bigger on the map than his thumb.

Whether something happens in the halls of a noble house or on the foot-path of a muddy street, rumor spreads with a magical rapidity. Within five minutes, the occupants of the best seats and the remotest recesses were equally acquainted with the circumstances of the audacious theft committed by the brothers Ténèbre. No one had the least doubt that it was the work of the brothers Ténèbre.

The awful celebrity of the brothers Ténèbre, however well its groundwork had been laid by the German's story, had been no more than a light hidden be-neath a bushel while the self-interest of the crowd had not been involved. There is a world of difference between a scourge that is only in the mind and a scourge that is alive, menacing and present. Do you remember the immense shock that ran through the social scale from one end of the Seine to the other, in conse-quence of the sudden fame of that other demon, cholera? Baron von Altenhei-mer had certainly said that "The brothers Ténèbre are in Paris," but words are worth far less than facts and a fire does not bring forth cries of terror when all one can see is smoke. The brothers Ténèbre had confirmed their presence by what the prefect of police himself had called a "highly improbable" theft. What timing! The German baron went up sharply in everyone's estimation. An imme-diate link was established between him and the superb bandits, whose Homer he had become. Henceforth, many of the ladies would find something interesting–and strange–in that pale and elongated face, unfortunately attached to those un-graceful shoulders.

The interest was soon further extended. While a circle formed around the two prelates chatting to the prefect of police, a servant came in and handed a let-ter to the Baron. The servant's livery was unfamiliar. The Baron discreetly ac-quainted himself with the contents of the letter, shaking his head in a concerned

[59] Jean-Baptiste Isabey (1767-1855) was a celebrated miniaturist, Madame de Mirbel was presumably the wife of Charles François Brisseau de Mirbel (1776-1854), a botanist. Jean Petitot (1607-1691) was a Swiss painter noted for his work in enamel.

manner and exchanging a few words with his brother; then he crossed the room, his steps determined and ponderous, to stand before the Archbishop of Paris.

"Your Grace," he said, "I had no need, in order to desire an introduction to Your Eminence, of any other motive than the admiration that I have expressed for your person–nevertheless, I did have another motive. I knew that the brothers Ténèbre would come to your episcopal château this evening."

There was a profound silence around the Archbishop, who paled visibly.

"They won't find the Condé gallery here," he murmured, with a smile [60].

"They will find someone that it is in their interest to approach," replied the Baron, "and they know, moreover, that His Lordship the Bishop of Hermopolis will deliver a sermon and raise a collection on behalf of the Christians of the Holy Land."

"That could be postponed," said Bishop Frayssinous.

"I humbly beseech Your Excellencies to do no such thing!" von Altenheimer exclaimed. "To begin with, I give you my word of honor that neither the illustrious master of this house, nor his guests, have anything at all to fear. I have my men all around the château, and twenty-five gendarmes from the Bercy precinct are awaiting His Grace's permission to enter its grounds..."

"It's news to me!" cried the prefect of police.

"They are operating according to the written orders of the Ministry of the Interior," said the Baron, half-withdrawing a large ministerial document from the side pocket of his jacket.

The prefect interrupted the gesture and said, not without a certain resentment: "That's fine... so much the better! They can do without me, for now."

"Illustrious colleague," von Altenheimer replied in a sincere voice, extending both hands towards him, "if I may employ that term with respect to a man such as you, we are joined in a desperate battle here, and I beg you not to withdraw your aid. If the brothers Ténèbre slip through our hands now, they will lose themselves in that Black Forest called London, and the pursuit will have to be handed over to another authority. Have I committed some offence against etiquette or neglected some formality of rank? Forgive me, dear sir–I am a foreigner; my King has charged me with a very difficult task; I am doing my best..."

The honest privy councilor's voice was almost tearful. The two prelates thought that it was their duty to address a few conciliatory words to the prefect. The audience, deeply moved by the idea of the drama that might well reach its climax before their very eyes, and beset by diverse sensations mingling fear, curiosity, expectation, whispered its opinions. That good and noble congregation discovered that it had been conscripted in its entirety–unknowingly, but not against its wishes–to serve as the bait in a rat-trap. That function has a name in the language of thieves which has also lent its color to the speech of honest men: a vile and detestable name which we need not write down because everyone

---

[60] Condé was the family name of the Ducs de Bourbon.

knows it. But what pleasure children take in playing the brigand beneath the great chestnut-trees of the Tuileries!

We all have a little of the child ingrained in us: witness the success, in recent years, of the revival of the innocent pleasures of farcical comedy. We know that everyone loves to dress up and that everyone loves to see others dressed up, the donkey always in the lion's skin and the lion sometimes in the donkey's skin... and then, there is the joy of becoming something else for a little while: the joy of quitting, if only for a moment, the abhorrent role of mere spectator! Think on it! There have been conspiracies–serious and terrible conspiracies–which have no other origin. We can credit to the same account that pure gladness which takes possession of the human being at the thought of a prank, and which grows in direct proportion to the social standing of those who plan the escapade. Does a king not derive a thousand times as much pleasure from playing truant than a schoolboy?

It would not be overly reckless to declare that everyone at the château of His Lordship the Archbishop of Paris that evening was something of a policeman–everyone, that is, with the exception of the prefect of police, who was thinking of handing in his resignation. Dukes and princesses, lovely wives and charming daughters, ordained priests, peers of the realm and cross-bred sons alike surprised themselves by throwing themselves wholeheartedly into a game of cops and robbers. The concert had a new twist, courtesy of a different kind of music. What disguise would the two bold villains have adopted to gain entry to the home of the Archbishop? Through what keyhole had they come? There were imaginative marquises who could already see the Chevalier Ténèbre in a cardinal and brother Ange the vampire in a young German canoness...

Baron von Altenheimer was certainly a clever man, for he sensed the common sentiment and immediately exploited it. "Illustrious people," he said, as if he were addressing a prayer to the whole gathering, "I can say that my fate is in our hands. I have let you in on my secret without being forced to do so. Join with me in an endeavor which is both important and noble, given that our victory could save the fortunes of many families and the lives of a great many Christians. Be on your guard! I can guarantee that the brothers Ténèbre will be here within the hour. Take account, therefore, of any unfamiliar face among those of your friends and acquaintances. Remember that the range of their disguises is limited by the nature of their physiques: one tall, one short, rather like the figurative relationship that exists between my beloved brother and myself. They could present themselves as an old man and a young one, a husband and his wife, or a father and his daughter..."

As he pronounced these last words, the sliding doors behind the orchestra opened. A young woman dressed in white, escorted by an old man of considerable stature, appeared on the stage.

The sight of them caused a shiver to run through the assembled audience...

VI. O Fount of Love!

The young woman was Mademoiselle d'Arnheim, the Archbishop's *protégée*, who had no wish to earn forty thousand francs in the theatre; the old man was her father. If the Princess had glanced at that moment towards the window-bay in which her son Gaston was standing she would certainly have been astonished by the change wrought in his features.

Gaston de Lorgères was, as we have said, a handsome young man, of an excessively timid and slightly faint appearance. His mother, who loved him madly, nevertheless entertained some doubts as to the scope of his intelligence. She still saw him as a child, and wondered why the spark of virility had not sprung forth within the peaceful adolescence which seemed to have lasted far beyond his twentieth year.

Many a noble husband, it is said, does not know the first thing about the heart of his wife; one might add that many a noble mother struggles in vain to fathom the mind of her son, even though the book lies open before her eyes. Noble mothers often have not the least gift for intellectual rapport; a working-class mother always knows her Charles or Jean-Marie, but Madame la Duchesse is often totally ignorant of Monsieur le Comte or Monsieur le Marquis.

What would have astonished the Princess de Montfort, at that moment, was that the spark in question was springing forth in a newly-conceived passion. He was still pale and his large black eyes had lost none of their timidity, but beneath his half-closed eyelids there was a gleam of brightness. He was a statue of flesh and bone, for the moment, but there was a soul within that marble. I doubt that even the affusions of cold water in a warm bath prescribed by Doctor Récamier could have calmed the beating of that heart. Although it is impossible to put the judgement to the test, I fear that palpitations of that sort require a different kind of remedy.

The flame that burned between Gaston's long eyelashes was directed towards a particular target. His gaze was riveted to the young girl in the white dress who had stepped forward on to the stage. The Archbishop of Paris had said, in speaking of her, "my angelic *protégée*." He had not exaggerated. The wonderful oval of her face, framed by shining blonde hair, did indeed resemble the delicate profiles which the imagination of great art has lent to celestial envoys. She seemed to be about eighteen years old at the very most. It was as if her clear and soft expression were veiled by melancholy. She was as beautiful as a dream of Raphael...

Now then! Fantasy has its limits, has it not? Could it really be the case that this seemingly seraphic head belonged to brother Ange Ténèbre, the vampire? We raise the issue because that thought had taken feverish possession of three-quarters of the assembly. Everyone had measured with a single glance the proportional relationship of the Baron von Altenheimer and his young brother,

Monsignor Benedict. It was certainly very close to that pertaining to the adorable young girl and the old man who accompanied her. The last words of the Baron, listing the possible disguises of the brothers Ténèbre, had been a father and his daughter and here, coming on the scene as if on cue, were a young girl and her father!

You must take due note of the fact that the brothers Ténèbre were capable of anything. Had not the vampire played the role of the Spanish *Infanta* in Stuttgart? Fifty gazes avidly interrogated Baron von Altenheimer, who had taken up his position beside the entrance door once again, and Monsignor Benedict, who was standing beside him–but the Baron remained impassive, and Monsignor Benedict maintained a honeyed smile upon his lips. Bear in mind, if you will, that this proved nothing: they were two artful men, and it was necessary that the brothers Ténèbre had no clue that their presence was suspected.

She was certainly beautiful, that young girl, but there were many among the assembled women who found, on due consideration, something intimidating about her. What was it? What caused those vague feelings of unease? It was neither the clear blue of her eyes, nor the delicate tint of her complexion, nor the virginal purity of her bearing, nor the halo of her blonde hair. No–it was nothing in particular, but rather the whole ensemble. That was it! She was simply too beautiful!

As regards the old man, the Chevalier Ténèbre had hidden his satanic brow well beneath that venerable mass of snowy hair. That hadn't happened overnight. What deep wrinkles! What a ravaged complexion! What strength of character! But what mortal sadness! One could go to the Great Hungarian Plain and search beneath the crop-fields for the black graves; one could lift up the stones which carried the mysterious inscriptions. There would be nothing there! One would have to look elsewhere for the Chevalier Ténèbre and the vampire priest.

The orchestra played two long chords, followed by a battery of arpeggios, to which accompaniment Mademoiselle d'Arnheim sang Haydn's *Fons Amoris*. She had a *mezzo-soprano* voice of magnificent integrity and incomparable worth. The women had expected a *contralto*, but they were no longer held back by the objections of rationality. What use is reason when it runs up against things that are irrational, mad, impossible, supernatural? In any other circumstances, they would have admired, perhaps passionately, the almost pious manner–expressive of asceticism, of divine candor even–in which Mademoiselle d'Arnheim interpreted the work of the Viennese master. They were connoisseurs; the tender majesty of style could not have escaped them, not the splendor of the voice–but, I ask you, what did all that signify when it was a matter of diabolical illusion? Were they even listening? I don't know. If they were listening to anything, it was the insistent and confused poetry of their fevered brains...

In his window-bay, Gaston drank deliriously from that enchanted cup; by the door, Monsignor Benedict put his open hand over his eyes, doubtless to hide his inquisitive expression. The latter was playing the dilettante, but the Princess, who was on the lookout, thought she saw a piercing gleam between the fingers. It was the Monsignor's eyes, fixed upon Mademoiselle d'Arnheim.

When the last note died within the throat of the *virtuosa*, and while the orchestra played its final chords, Baron von Altenheimer–who had remained until now as stiff as a bronze statue–gave a noisy lead to the applause. The women immediately followed his lead, thinking that they were playing their part. The two prelates–and, for the most part, the male half of the assembly–were entirely sincere in their long-drawn-out applause. It was a veritable triumph; the unanimity of the acclamation was broken by a single protestation. Gaston alone did not applaud, because his two hands were tightly clasped upon his heart.

It was not the custom in His Grace's salons to bestow noisy ovations upon the artistes, but everyone concurred in this instance in prolonging the tribute; feigned enthusiasm came to the aid of genuine enthusiasm, and one would have to look to the pits of theaters to obtain some idea of the din which lasted for several minutes in the Archbishop's hall.

There was one singular circumstance. At the first bravos, the tall figure of the old man, who had taken a seat to the left of the orchestra and slightly of the rear, came erect again. Painful surprise could be read in his eyes, like an expression of wounded pride; then his white head fell upon his breast again, and two large tears ran down his cheeks.

Mademoiselle d'Arnheim, blushing from her shoulders to her forehead, bowed deeply, took hold of her father's arms, and disappeared.

Archbishop de Quélen made a tour of the room, collecting opinions with paternal pleasure. Everywhere one heard the same things. How charming! Perfectly charming! An admirable voice! What spirit! Marvelous style! Those whose ears had played them false or rendered them deaf–the majority of those in the concert-hall–spoke more loudly than the sensitive, and those women who were putting their hearts and souls into their new profession made the warmest bids of all.

Baron von Altenheimer had become a statue once more. His expression, as mysterious as a closed book, made no response whatsoever to all the beautiful eyes that were fixed upon it. The moment had not yet arrived; it was necessary to be prudent.

There was, however, one curiosity that was closer to the boil and stronger than all the other impatiences. The Princess could not take it any longer. She turned towards her son, who was dreaming–God only knows of what–in his window-bay, and she beckoned to him urgently.

The Marquis de Lorgères roused himself, and obeyed.

"Gaston," the Princess said to him in a low and very mysterious voice, "do you understand what is happening here?"

"What is happening, Madame?" Gaston replied. "Yes, of course."

"Would you do me a favor?"

"With pleasure."

"Go strike up a conversation... discreetly, you understand... with Baron von Altenheimer, and..." She interrupted herself, somewhat discouraged. "But you're so timid, my poor boy." Then she added, presumably to herself: "And so simple!"

"What?" Gaston demanded, in a manner that his mother thought distinctly unappreciative.

"And ask him to tell you, in confidence," she went on, with a smile of renewed hopefulness, "whether those were they for whom we are looking out."

"They?" Gaston repeated. "Which they do you mean, Madame, if you please?"

The Princess tapped her foot and replied: "In God's name! The brothers Ténèbre!"

Gaston stared at her, utterly stupefied. The Princess saw immediately that hope had misled her. Gaston's hauteur had evaporated. "Go," she said, regardless, "and do what you can."

Gaston did not hesitate. He went immediately towards Baron von Altenheimer. His mother followed him with her eyes and said to herself: "His brother, the Duc, has matured perfectly well. Poor Gaston is obviously retarded. One must accept whatever one gets."

At that moment, Gaston resolutely set himself beside the Baron, who greeted him with the same fulsome gestures that he extended to everyone. Gaston did not seem disconcerted. A conversation was quickly established between himself and Baron von Altenheimer. Gaston spoke, in truth, very freely and made himself heard.

How happy his mother was! Doubly delighted–for she was witness to the progress of her son and her son was the bearer of her news–the happy mother triumphed in her heart and in her mind. Whatever one gets; the dictum of all mothers!

This, however, was how Gaston, Marquis of Lorgères, accomplished the highly confidential mission entrusted to him by the Princess.

"Monsieur le Baron," he said, "I have listened to you this evening with a good deal of pleasure and interest."

"I am grateful to Monsieur le Marquis..." the German began.

"And you will understand better," Gaston continued, "when you know that the remarkable subject of your tale is conjoined, for me, with a series of family considerations. We are, Monsieur le Baron, first cousins once removed of Field-Marshal Victor de Rohan, Prince de Guémenée, Duc de Rohan, de Bouillon and de Monbazon, who actually resides in Hungary..."

Von Altenheimer bowed.

"And as the heads of the family of the late duchess," the young Marquis continued, "who died childless, as you must know, we possess several properties there, near Debrecen, which are not let but are quite considerable..."

The Princess, meanwhile, was saying to herself: "What's this? What's he saying now? Monsieur le Baron seems to be paying very close attention to him!"

This was nothing less than the truth: Baron von Altenheimer was all ears. Gaston continued: "After certain digressions which added much, from my point of view, to the piquancy of your tale, I saw that you were pleased to conceal beneath the frivolous spirit of the storyteller a considerable depth of actual knowledge..."

"Ah, Monsieur de Marquis..."

"If you will permit me... This is not a compliment, but a matter of preparing the way to ask you a great favor."

"I am entirely at your disposal," the Baron said.

"A thousand thanks... it concerns our properties in Hungary... my brother, the Duc, was the victim of a certain youthful recklessness, and when he came into a part of his inheritance, he was able to mortgage the estate of Niszar. It is seven hundred leagues from Paris to Debrecen. Without making any accusation against German or Hungarian lawyers, I merely state the facts: the Niszar estate has been sold at public auction to pay the mortgagees..."

"How long ago was this?" the Baron asked, sharply.

"Three years ago, perhaps four..."

"You are sure that five years have not passed?"

"Perfectly sure. My brother, Monsieur le Duc, was only seventeen then."

"And he must have had time to squander the estate. That's right... I'm with you, Monsieur le Marquis."

"I have heard some report," Gaston continued, earnestly, "of the Hungarian laws regulating the right of repurchase after a forced sale, but no Magyar authors have been translated into French and their use of Latin idiom does not always seem clear to me... Mayruth fixed at four years the period of facultative redemption and the full right..."

"Mayreuth," said the Baron, correcting the spelling of the name, "is an obstinate pedant who is no longer read... the Austrian court, in giving Hungary the benefit of its ancient legislation, has codified the matter. The legal period of redemption and the automatic right of repurchase is five years and a day from the date of the public auction... and it is not without precedent for the period to be extended on the basis of a request submitted to the Chancellery, with supporting documents..."

Gaston bowed ceremoniously in his turn.

"Monsieur le Baron," he said, taking his leave, "I beg you to accept all my thanks."

"Now then, Marquis," his mother said to herself as he came back towards her, "do me the favor of giving me the three essential points of that sermon you preached to him?"

"Madame," Gaston replied, with a smile that the Princess had never seen before, "I have begun my diplomatic career. These privy councilors, it seems to me, are very difficult to get around."

"He did not want to answer your question?"

"Indeed he did."

"Tell me, then," the Princess said, petulantly. "Tell me immediately."

"Mother, Monsieur le Baron told me that the two men in question are here..."

"Oh! I was sure of it!"

"But no one," the young Marquis finished, calmly, "has recognized them: neither you, nor anyone here, has identified them as yet."

"Oh!" repeated the Princess, in a very different manner. "He's just making fun of you."

Gaston kissed her hand with a grace that made her think again. "Madame," he replied, with a slight hint of mockery that completed her discomfiture, "would you like me to do you a second and even better favor?"

"What, Gaston?"

"Would you like me to go into the next room, to talk to Monsieur d'Arnheim himself?"

"And ask him if he is the Chevalier Ténèbre?" The Princess laughed.

"To find out without asking him, Madame," Gaston corrected.

The Princess took him by the hand and put her mouth very close to his ear. "If you can do that, Gaston," she said, "I will give you a Tilbury carriage like the one your brother has."

"I would prefer something else, Madame," the young Marquis replied, gravely.

"What then? Tell me."

"Only promise," Gaston replied, "not to talk about me to my cousin Emerance for six weeks."

The Princess burst out laughing, showing her teeth–which were still quite beautiful.

"Monsieur le Marquis," she said, "I forbid you to fall in love! Someone must have waved a magic wand over you." She pointed a finger at him tenderly and added: "Go! And find out whether this Mademoiselle d'Arnheim is really an old priest dead for four hundred years!"

The young Marquis negotiated a passage towards Archbishop de Quélen and said to him: "My Lord, my mother has asked me to speak to Monsieur d'Arnheim about the possibility of taking lessons."

"Excellent!" murmured the Archbishop, who took Gaston by the hand, led him to the door situated behind the orchestra, and opened it. "My good Monsieur d'Arnheim," he said, raising his voice, "I bring you an ambassador. This is the beginning. If it pleases God, our dear child will soon be obliged to refuse lessons!" He closed the door behind Gaston.

There was no one in the room but the old man and the girl. Mademoiselle d'Arnheim, at the sight of the young Marquis, changed color two or three times. Her father lowered his eyes while the vivid blush showed on her cheeks.

Gaston, so eloquent a moment ago, stood before them with a pale face and silent lips.

VII. A Proposal of Marriage

On the other side of the door the concert continued. The Nuremberg organ warbled beneath the fingers of Monsignor Benedict, who was playing a charming ditty, the famous Bolognese Christmas carol *Jesu Bambino*.

As for our three individuals, the silence had not yet been broken and the unease was growing. Monsieur d'Arnheim finally made an effort to overcome the awkwardness, and began: "You came, Monsieur, to discuss with me the possibility of lessons to be given by my daughter...?"

He stopped. No words are adequate to describe the humiliated pride, the crushed nobility, the bitter regret, mingled with resignation, melancholy and love, with which the old man pronounced those few words.

Gaston took a step towards him.

"Prince," he said, in a low voice, "you are mistaken. That is not why I am here."

"Prince!" echoed Monsieur d'Arnheim, whose limbs had begun to tremble, while his daughter hid her tearful face between her hands. "Prince...!" Then, placing his tremulous wrists on the arms of his chair as he made ready to rise to his feet, he said: "Who do you think you are talking to, Monsieur?"

"I know," Gaston replied, his voice having hardened again, "that I am talking to Chrétien Baszin, Prince Jacobyi."

The old man slumped back in his seat. "Who told you that?" he demanded, darkly.

"Lenore, your daughter."

"Lenore! My daughter!" He turned towards Mademoiselle d'Arnheim, whose hands were clasped together as if in prayer, perhaps to implore Gaston to be quiet.

Monsieur d'Arnheim stood up. "Who are you?" he demanded.

"Gaston de Montfort, Marquis de Lorgères, second son of the Prince de Montfort."

"Ah!" said Monsieur d'Arnheim, his gaze moving back and forth between the young man and the girl. Then he asked one more time: "What do you want from me, Monsieur le Marquis de Lorgères?"

"I want to ask for the hand of your daughter. I love her, and she loves me." This was said in a distinct voice, with head held high and a steady gaze.

Mademoiselle d'Arnheim had closed her eyes and had let herself fall into a chair.

In the next room, the sweet voice of the Monsignor embellished another carol, harvesting at the end of every verse a rich crop of merited applause.

The old man looked once again at his daughter. It was not anger that was in his eyes; it was bleak despair. "You've deceived me!" he murmured.

Mademoiselle d'Arnheim threw herself towards him. He thrust her back, but not rudely, while he added, addressing himself to Gaston: "Monsieur de Marquis, to take the last possession of a ruined man is to steal from the altar!"

"Father!" cried the girl. "Good and noble father! I will never leave you, and I swear to you that I have never done anything deserving of reproach."

"In that case," said the old man, directing a scornful glance at Gaston, "this is a madman, who should go away!"

"Not before I have your answer, Prince," the young Marquis replied. "I have told the truth: I love your daughter; she loves me; and I ask for her hand."

"You have spoken to this man, Lenore?" Monsieur d'Arnheim demanded.

"Never, Father," she replied, in a faint voice.

"How, then, does he dare to boast...?"

"Father," the young girl interrupted, sliding to her knees, "he is not boasting... but if he knows it, his heart must have told him, for we have never exchanged a word."

"There is a mystery here..." began the old man, whose stern face had gone as white as snow.

His daughter interrupted again: "There is nothing, Father," she said, "but my love for you and our destiny. While you were ill, and after having sold everything that you possessed in the world, it fell to me one day to go in search of medicines without having the money to pay for them. I was refused credit. I sat down on the step of the shop, exhausted and discouraged."

"And you begged for alms, child!" cried Monsieur d'Arnheim, his eyes lighting up.

"I would have done, Father, if I had thought of it. But I was utterly lost, and I thought of nothing but coming back to you, and of dying with you. Monsieur le Marquis was passing by; he stopped before me; I did not see him. Mina had followed me; Mina went towards him..."

As the name Mina was spoken, a little black spaniel came out from beneath Monsieur d'Arnheim's armchair, in order to jump on to a chair and from there to the table next to which Gaston was standing. She began to lick Gaston's hand. The old man averted his eyes.

"I remember that in the depths of my distress I prayed fervently to God," Mademoiselle d'Arnheim continued. "I implored him to work a miracle and to send to my father that manna which the celestial birds had carried to those lost in the desert. When Mina returned, Monsieur le Marquis was no longer there, but Mina put her muzzle between my knees, and in the folds of my dress I saw the glitter of a gold piece..."

Monsieur d'Arnheim let out a groan. Mina leapt with one bound to the carpet and went to comfort him; he pushed her aside as gently and as sadly as he had pushed his daughter away.

"We are Baszins!" he murmured. Then he asked, his voice taking on a different tone: "How was the acquaintance renewed?"

"You have been ill for three months," the young woman replied. "That grand and luxurious residence which you are in the habit of admiring is the town house of the Princess de Montfort; I don't know how Mina knew the way. Whenever the gold piece was spent, Mina went out again, and always returned with manna."

"And you knew whence this manna came, did you not?"

"From God, whose help I had implored, Father."

"And you let Mina out! Had you no shame?"

The old man's lip quivered; his eyelids fluttered like those of a woman fighting to hold back tears.

"Father," said Mademoiselle d'Arnheim in a low voice, "I let Mina out because she brought the breath back to your lungs and the blood to your veins...and I had no shame because I already loved the hand of that God who sent us his manna."

"Thank you," murmured Gaston, his eyes moist.

"But what did you expect? What did you expect?" cried the old man, in anguish.

Mademoiselle d'Arnheim lifted her angelic gaze towards the heavens, and replied: "Father, I put my trust in God."

There was a momentary silence. Monsignor Benedict was still chanting his mild Italian devotions. Monsieur d'Arnheim looked Gaston in the face, then he offered his hand.

"Chrétien Baszin, Prince Jacobyi, as you have called him, and as I called him myself in former times, is indebted to you, Monsieur le Marquis," he said, slowly. "He sees that you are a noble and generous young man. Perhaps he would even have been flattered by your quest in happier times–but he cannot ignore the fact that the house of de Montfort is one of the richest in France. Chrétien Baszin could never permit his daughter to enter such a family as that unless the gate were opened wide; he possesses nothing but his pride. If the Princess de Montfort herself came in search of the Princess Jacobyi, then it might indeed be God's wish to contrive the union of two great houses."

"If that is what is required, that is what will be done," Gaston replied, without hesitation. "I give you my word."

But what, you may ask, of that cousin Emerance to whom the Princess had said too much about Gaston? Was not Monsieur le Marquis being much too forward, for a timid young man? We do not know, to tell the truth, whether his mother would have been delighted or desolated by his words. The chick, it

219

seems, had broken his shell with one blow of his beak and come out in his full plumage.

Gaston shook Monsieur d'Arnheim's hand and respectfully kissed the young woman's; it was a sort of conditional betrothal. Then, raising himself up again, he went on in a brisk tone: "Prince, would you recognize, if chance were to bring you face to face with them, the two gypsies who received hospitality at Chandor Castle, on the night when your daughter was kidnapped?"

Mademoiselle d'Arnheim started in surprise, and became as pale as an alabaster statue.

"How do you know...?" the old man stammered.

"There are many things I need to explain to you, Prince," the young Marquis interrupted, "but this is neither the time or the place. I beg you to be content with answering my question."

"I would recognize them," said Monsieur d'Arnheim, through gritted teeth, "ten years from now!"

Gaston cocked an ear. Monsignor Benedict had finished singing.

"Prince," he went on, "you are destined to find yourself, perhaps this very evening, face to face with those who have accomplished your ruination..."

"Rubbish!" cried the old man.

"We have mentioned God more than once in this interview," said Gaston gravely. "He moves in mysterious ways. A person who seems to me to know what he is talking about has predicted that the brothers Ténèbre will put in an appearance, this evening, in the Archbishop's house. When Mademoiselle d'Arnheim goes to perform again, you will doubtless accompany her. Look around, but be sure to hide your legitimate anger and rightful resentment. It is vitally important to you, to your daughter, and also to me, your future son-in-law, that no one except me penetrates your secret. We shall draw apart from one another, but there must be a signal. If you recognize the two evildoers, promise me two things: make this gesture openly, and no other; and abstain absolutely from taking any action." He touched his right hand to his brow, with all five fingers extended.

Monsieur d'Arnheim hesitated for a moment, then he said: "I trust you, young man, and I will do as you ask."

As soon as he had received that promise, the Marquis de Lorgères bowed twice, putting into the smile that he addressed to Lenore everything that he could not express in words. Then he moved rapidly towards the door opposite to that which had admitted him.

He crossed the hallway, descended the staircase, and went out into the gardens. It was not to calm his simmering blood, nor to refresh his bare head, that the Marquis de Lorgères made this nocturnal expedition. He looked around him attentively as he went, and paused from time to time in order to listen.

The night was black, but Paris was not asleep, and the noise of the city could still be heard in the distance. Above that muted din other sounds, closer and more distinct, were discernible: footsteps, whispers, muffled laughs. All around the château, the darkness was populated.

Gaston reached the park and found a wooded place. He pushed his way into the heart of a thicket, looked around once more, listened more carefully, and finished by secreting beneath the thickest foliage an object which he took from his bosom.

Then he retraced his steps to the château and went back into the salon by the main door...

Baron von Altenheimer, who seemed to have appointed himself as a concierge, so faithfully had he stuck to his post, gave a slight start of surprise at Gaston's appearance. It was only momentary; afterwards, his face resumed its placid expression.

"Monsieur le Marquis has not heard my brother Benedict, then?" he said.

"Yes indeed," Gaston replied. "Heard, and applauded."

The Monsignor thanked him, and the Baron added: "I did not see you go out, Marquis."

"A little fresh air," Gaston replied, as he went on into the room. "It's stifling in here."

"Monsieur le Marquis," the Princess said to him, in a tone intended to be most severe, "you have been gone thirty-five minutes, by the hands of the clock. Your conduct is extremely improper." But she added, pointing her finger at him: "I shall give you a penance, if you have not brought me a generous armful of news."

"Has nothing happened here?" Gaston asked.

"I have a stiff neck from looking this way and that," the Princess replied. "The Doctor pretends that it is all a huge practical joke. But these devotees of the profound wisdom know nothing, you know... now, Gaston, we are losing our heads. You are interrogating me and I have been good enough to reply—everything is upside-down!"

Gaston remained silent.

"How pale you are," his mother said, uneasily. "You should have brought some color back with you. You owe me an explanation, Gaston my boy. We have begun our first romance, have we not? Be honest! Poor Emerance! Speak, Gaston, I insist. What have you been doing since you left the room?"

"Madame," replied the young Marquis, forced to make the effort to save his dream, "I do not believe that this is a romance, but it is a strange story nevertheless. Tomorrow, if you will permit, I will submit to your levy: I have the greatest need to talk to you."

There is no word to express the passion for knowledge that mothers have. It would be unjust to give the name "curiosity" to such a profound desire. The Princess's astonishment was magnified. She no longer recognized in her son the child of old of whom she had said: "When will the man awaken in him?" The man had awakened, with a definite start! The Princess, completely overtaken, was still searching for the child and no longer understood.

Gaston would not have got away so lightly if there had not been a great stir in the salon. The Bishop of Hermopolis moved towards the stage, and an emotion that had no direct relationship to the sermon that he intended to give took hold of the audience. The appearance of the brothers Ténèbre had been anxiously anticipated since the quest for them had begun. The Archbishop's salon was beset by curious maladies, fears, desires and fevers–none of which, most assuredly, had anything to do with the unfortunate Christians of the Holy Land.

As the Bishop of Hermopolis took his position on the stage, the Princess only had time to say: "Will you tell me, at least, who these people are–the d'Arnheims?"

"You shall know tomorrow, Mother," Gaston replied, as he moved away. "It is for precisely that reason that I need to see you."

Bishop Frayssinous began to speak, commanding silence.

There are still many people alive who were personally acquainted with the illustrious author of the *Défense de la Religion*. All of them agree in saying that the public eloquence of the Bishop of Hermopolis was distinguished above all by measured argument, moderation and an abundance of proofs deduced with calm authority and certitude; but they add that his private eloquence was another thing entirely. He had a southern ardor in his blood and a lively impulse to charity in his heart. When he went into battle against the selfishness of worldly men for the purpose of extracting alms, he was not a regular soldier in the apostolic army but a lightly-armed sharpshooter: a *zouave* [61], if such an anachronism is permissible. He never retreated; he was prepared to make arrows from any kind of wood. One recalls what Monsieur de Talleyrand said of the sermon preached at the home of the Duchesse d'Angoulême on behalf of the widows and orphans of the war in Greece: "He had our charity by the throat!"

In this instance, his theme was just as real and even more urgent; it concerned those unhappy Christian families scattered throughout Palestine and groaning under Turkish domination. In more recent times, the Eastern war has educated us on that subject, and no one is ignorant of the lamentable barbarities which formerly cast a shadow on the light of the guiding stars of our century, but there was at that time an almost impassable barrier between Europe and

---

[61] The name *zouave* was borrowed from an Algerian tribe for application to members of French infantry regiments whose brightly-colored uniforms included baggy trousers, short jackets and tasseled caps. Although the regiments in question were originally made up of Algerians, they soon had a majority of Frenchmen. When he wrote the story Féval, would not have known that the uniform would be borrowed by some volunteer regiments on the Union side in the American Civil War, but he would have appreciated the absurdity.

those cries of agony. Their first harrowing echo was, however, heard that evening in the hall of the Château de Conflans.

Bishop Frayssinous had, moreover, to contend with a general inattention, for the fever that had gripped the crowd was a rude rival to his speech. After several minutes had passed, though, that inattention had been tamed, and every face took on an expression of intense concentration, directed towards a common focus: the orator.

All those previously-stifled moans; all those previously-unheard cries, all those groans extracted by long and intolerable torture, were reunited in one single voice to burst forth like a thousand simultaneous death-rattles in the bosom of that rich, brilliant and happy assembly. The discourse did not last long, but when it ended there was sweat on every brow and a tear in every eye.

The Bishop of Hermopolis came down from the stage then, and the Archbishop of Paris embraced him effusively before handing him the huge red velvet purse in which the collection was to be taken.

As soon as he took his first step, the prelate began to accumulate an abundant harvest of gold pieces and banknotes. The force of good example mingled with that desire to emulate which peevish philosophers call vanity. The Marsh apparatus extracts arsenic from the same soil that gives us wheat for outer bread [62]; in the moral order, as in the physical order, is there anything on Earth that is entirely pure? Having rendered the eternal negative in answer to that question, the point of great and good works is to ameliorate intoxication, to tame passion, and to direct impetuousness towards a noble end. The Princess donated her bracelet. From that moment on, jewelry rained into the increasingly-heavy and swollen purse. Ear-rings, brooches and strings of pearls hastened to join the Princess's bracelet. Charity also has its auctions.

"Monsieur le Baron," said the Bishop of Hermopolis, as he arrived at the entrance-door, "I know that you have already despoiled yourself on behalf of another unfortunate; I shall take care to ask nothing of you."

Baron von Altenheimer was in the process of making a little paper trumpet out of an envelope. He was doing his best, but his large clumsy hands were making rather a mess of it.

"Give, my dear brother Benedict," he said, after an interval when he paid no attention to His Excellency.

Monsignor Benedict removed from his finger the exceedingly beautiful solitaire which had excited the admiration of the assembly, and dropped it into the purse. It was a gift fit for a king. The Bishop of Hermopolis bowed and was about to pass on, when the Baron said to him: "If you would graciously permit it, Your Lordship, I would like to keep a little snuff–it is a distinctly tyrannical habit..."

---

[62]   The apparatus in question, invented in 1836, was the work of the English chemist James Marsh (1794-1846).

The bishop turned back. Into the little trumpet he had fabricated, rather awkwardly, Baron von Altenheimer was busy emptying the contents of his splendid gold snuff-box encrusted with diamonds the size of peas. Having achieved the transfer, he slipped the box into the purse, adding with perfect simplicity: "A thousand thanks, Your Lordship."

The box was worth three or four times as much as the ring. The gesture had a tremendous effect, especially the little trumpet and the thousand thanks. More than one person wondered whether the kingdom of Wurtemburg, which had the honor of harboring the Black Forest within its narrow bounds, might actually be Eldorado.

The brothers von Altenheimer had resumed their peaceful and modest attitudes, and the Bishop of Hermopolis continued his collection, which had already produced a fortune.

"Mademoiselle d'Arnheim, for the finale," said Archbishop de Quélen, signaling to the orchestra. One of the musicians went in search of the *virtuosa.*

Gaston had his offering in his hand at the moment when Monsieur d'Arnheim and his daughter reappeared on the stage. He saw the avid gaze of the old man make a rapid tour of the room and come to a halt, staring fixedly at the entrance-door, next to which the two brothers Altenheimer were standing in isolation.

The reaction experienced by Monsieur d'Arnheim was so violent that he staggered like a man about to fall backwards.

"Well, Marquis," said the Bishop, whose purse had been extended towards Gaston for several seconds.

"Well, Gaston," repeated the Princess, who was watching him. "He has given silver," she gasped, almost immediately afterwards, as she collapsed into an armchair. "Doctor, he has given silver! My son, to the collection of the Minister of Ecclesiastical Affairs! For the Christians of the Holy Land! Mademoiselle d'Arnheim must indeed be an ancient ecclesiastic! See! Gaston is mad! That's an enchantress in flesh and bone! He's twenty-three years old! Are there affusions of cold water administered in warm baths powerful enough to prevent young men from behaving like idiots? I have longed for him to assert himself a little, but not like this! Lord Above! The Duc has already tried to drive me mad. And can you imagine, to cap it all, that he does not want to hear talk of his cousin Emerance–a charming girl, in good standing at court?"

She aired her grievances as best she could, but we must admit to you, in confidence, that there was a smile beneath her anger.

The Bishop also laughed as he left the young Marquis, whose hand had let three forty-*sou* pieces fall into his collection: the only ones! He realized well enough that a mistake had been made.

But Gaston was not laughing; his entire being was in his eyes. I do not know whether he had even noticed the look of timid tenderness that Mademoiselle d'Arnheim had darted towards him while entering. He had eyes for no one but her father: her father, whose white hair quivered on his forehead.

Slowly, so very slowly, Monsieur d'Arnheim lifted his right hand to his forehead, on which the five trembling fingers rested for a moment, fully outstretched.

Gaston let out a deep sigh, and lost himself in the crowd.

VIII. The End of the Soirée

The brothers Ténèbre had not yet put in an appearance. The two prelates, the prefect of police and a few other important people were counting up the collection in a small room just off the hall, whose door stood open, while Mademoiselle d'Arnheim sang Mozart's *Ave Verum*, accompanied by the orchestra.

The admirable artiste surpassed herself in rendering the admirable work. The quiet crowd was all ears, when everyone was suddenly subjected to a violent shock. Baron von Altenheimer half-opened the entrance-door and shouted at the top of his voice: "Look out!"

At the same time, he threw himself into the neighboring room where their Lordships were.

From the other side of the half-open main door, several voices replied: "Yes!"

The Monsignor was already at a window, rapidly turning the handle that would release its lock. "Look out, everyone!" he cried, cupping his hands like a megaphone.

From all sides, distant voices replied from the park: "Yes! Yes! Yes!"

There is no need to add that the orchestra and the singer immediately fell silent.

There was a moment of indescribable tumult. The first woman's scream gave birth to a hundred, as is always the case. The men in the great hall launched themselves towards the small room, those in the little room raced back into the larger one.

Not one of them saw anything, search as he might, but everyone believed that others had seen something. By the time three minutes had gone by, two dozen women had fainted.

"Here! In the garden!" cried a voice from outside.

There was a sudden surge towards the window.

"Here, on the stairs!" shouted another voice.

The door was shut.

Gunshots were heard in the distance.

Baron von Altenheimer reappeared then, with his big black coat buttoned up. His head was held high and his eyes shone.

"I must beg your pardon," he said, calmly. "Come, brother Benedict... I will have them, or die trying!"

The Monsignor also had the bearing of a little hero. They hurled themselves through the door together and disappeared, amid the myriad pleas of women begging them not to expose themselves to any risk.

Once they had made their exit, the hue and cry faded into the distance, then died away.

When three more minutes had passed, a profound silence reigned in the hall of the Château de Conflans. No one said a word, save for two men half-hidden behind the orchestra, one of whom was struggling as hard as he could against the other.

"Why did you stop me?" Monsieur d'Arnheim demanded, exhausted by his efforts.

"Prince," replied Gaston, Marquis de Lorgères, "I give you my word of honor that they shall not escape!"

Others were coming out of their trance. Each one took hold of himself and looked at his neighbors. So little trace of the tempest remained all around them that it might all have been a dream. Besides, the von Altenheimers were gone. Everyone listened; no one felt obliged to speak. Everyone felt a vague apprehension growing in himself: an uneasy impression of having been duped.

There was no longer any noise of footsteps outside, nor of shouting, not of gunshots.

The Archbishop was the first to speak. "There is something inexplicable in this business."

"These conflicts of interest between the Minister of the Interior and the Prefecture are an outrage!" the prefect of police added, peevishly.

"Did you see something, Madame la Marquise?" the Princess asked her neighbor.

"Something, Madame? No, I cannot tell you what I have seen. I closed my eyes, as one does when gunshots ring out in the theatre... but I sensed... oh, I am sure that I smelled something burning..."

"Aunt," cried Madame de Maillé. "Leonie saw a man in black."

"I saw it too," said the doctor. "A huge hairy body..."

There was some laughter. Perhaps it only required a frank and well-chosen word to turn the whole thing into a joke, but the word was not forthcoming.

The Bishop of Hermopolis said: "Let's finish counting the collection." But he had hardly put a foot into the little room when he made an exclamation of amazement.

The jumpy nerves of the audience had settled a little; there was no renewal of the panic. But as His Excellency, rather than stepping back, hurled himself towards the table which occupied the center of the little room, he was followed across the threshold by several other men and a few women.

His Excellency, who stood before the table with his head lowered and all strength gone from his arms, was soon surrounded.

"Mercy!" cried Archbishop de Quélen, wringing his hands. "Our collection!" That was all that was said. The noble assembly fell into that particular species of silence which follows utter mystification.

The table was bare. Not one of the objects lately contained by the red velvet purse was to be seen.

"See!" said the prefect of police, eventually. "If the Minister of the Interior had only consulted my people..."

"Monsieur!" interrupted the Archbishop, with a wrath whose wellspring was the frustration of his charity. "There was not only the Ministry of the Interior in this, but the Court of Rome and the Chancellery of the Kingdom of Wurtemburg! We have lost the wealth of the poor, and someone is making a mockery of us!"

"One tall, and one short," murmured the Princess, repeating the words that Baron von Altenheimer had spoken for the first time in the verdant arena.

"It was them! It was them!" twenty voices cried at the same time.

"The Baron is the Chevalier Ténèbre..."

"And the Monsignor is brother Ange, the vampire!"

IX. An Essay on the Philosophy of Theft

All men whose trade is deception, or the foiling of deception–which is to say, all game and all hunters; for example, the admirable thieves of London, who learn their profession at a university, and the equally admirable detectives of Scotland Yard who are trained to follow their tracks across the pavements of that great Babylon–will tell you that there are two principal methods of rendering oneself invisible, not including Aladdin's lamp. One is to hide, the other to display oneself while covering one's face with a mask; to lurk in the shades of night, or to confront the light of the sun valiantly.

In two words: cunning and audacity.

Cunning is primarily associated with the old school; audacity is the *forté* of the modern movement. The majority of the gentlemen savants whose field of study is the art of thievery recommend audacity very highly, and do not scruple to say that wiliness has had its day. The honorable Josuah J. Marshall [63], the pride of the London criminal fraternity, who was sentenced to hang at the Old

---

[63] In view of the highly unlikely first name, it seems probable that this gentleman is an invention of Féval's, although it is not beyond the bounds of possibility that some such character might have been featured in the Newgate Calendar or the "broadside ballads" that chronicled the adventures of British criminals in the late 18th and early 19th centuries. It was, of course, the Newgate Calendar and its literary spin-off that made Jack Sheppard the most famous English thief of his era. Féval might have read William Harrison Ainsworth's *Jack Sheppard* (Bentley, 1839), a novel similar in spirit to Suesque *romans feuilletons*.

Bailey as the reign of King George neared its end, put it thus: "Tell the constable that you are Jack Sheppard and he will not believe you; prove to him, by means of your birth-certificate, that you are Jack Sheppard; steal his watch, his purse, his shirt and his truncheon, and he will laugh, saying: Get away! Jack Sheppard!"

In all good things, you can be certain, the spirit of the English will find the extreme; but there is a great deal of truth in the opinion of the honorable Josuah J. Marshall, and the fact that he was hanged does not disprove his theory. A true gentleman of the criminal fraternity accepts the inevitability of the noose philosophically, as the rest of us are forced to accept the inevitability of death. It is, in either case, a mere matter of time; that is a fact of life. The issue at hand is to live as well as one can, or to put off being hanged as long as possible. Josuah J. Marshall attained the ripe old age of eighty-three years before being hanged. He bequeathed his methods and his philosophy to his children and his children's children.

Now go into the prisons and ask the governors by what means their boarders most frequently escape. Their response will be unanimous: however they can. Do not be content with that overly vague reply; get to the bottom of the question. Establish the categories. It will not put the jailer in a good mood, of that you can be sure, because you will put your finger on some remembered wound, ancient or modern, but in the end you will know this: there are more escapes at noon than midnight, more by the main gate than by underground tunnels. The majority escape with heads held high, faces bare and a smile upon their lips, bowing politely to the concierge's wife and saying "Good-day, my friend" to the guard.

The human mind is made that way; it has a passion for contradiction. Precautions can, in the final analysis, only be excited or intensified by the affirmation: "I am not a thief." That is sufficient in itself to provide a constable or a gendarme with a motive to put you to the test in case you are a liar. But say to him "I am a thief" and he will feel a perfectly natural temptation to try and prove the opposite.

This is a serious matter. There was recently to be found in London, behind Drury Lane, a very respectable place where practitioners of the art demonstrated various ways of picking a lock without spoiling it. The course was open to the public, and we had the honor of being present–Rule Britannia! Whereas the preceding considerations were matters of university education, this was a primary school.

If Baron von Altenheimer and Monsignor Benedict really had been the brothers Ténèbre, they had obviously employed the Marshall procedure. Except that, as the German bandits were still studying their Plutarch, they had been obliged to build up their own reputation in the Archbishop's salon and sing their own epic. Then they had cried out, after the fashion of the honorable Josuah J. Marshall: "We are the brothers Ténèbre!"

And no one had believed them.

They had, to be sure, not said it in so many words, but they had arranged matters in such a way that the thought had occurred to everyone—and that thought had, indeed, occurred to everyone at the given moment; but everyone had said, like the constable to Josuah J. Marshall: "The brothers Ténèbre! Get away!"

Once a thought has come to knock at the door of the imagination, and has been refused its hospitality, everything is set: the blindfold is covering your eyes, tied in a triple knot. That is the real import of the calculation.

Now, gentlemen of the second rank have been seen to operate in this jolly manner by taking the name of Jack Sheppard. Had the von Altenheimers, then, stolen the identities of the brothers Ténèbre? Where did the falsehood end within their tale? Did the brothers Ténèbre actually exist, or was there not even an atom of truth at the bottom of their shameless lies?

The prefect of police climbed into the first available carriage and returned to Paris at full speed. The ability of that eminent magistrate is proverbial; undoubtedly, he must have put the battalions of his secret army into the field without delay. He found not the least trace, however, in the archives of the Prefecture, of the Chevalier Ténèbre or of brother Ange the vampire, nor the least trace of Baron von Altenheimer or Monsignor Benedict. It appeared that mounting a hunt for an oupire and a vampire was no trivial enterprise!

The remainder of His Lordship's guests withdrew sadly. The good Archbishop, on going to his room, kept one secret consolation in the depths of his heart. There remained to him, to lighten the burden of his misfortune very slightly, the certainty that the pocket-book destined for Mademoiselle d'Arnheim had never left his person. He wanted to count the banknotes again.

Alas, the pocket-book had vanished, along with His Lordship's magnificent pastoral cross!

X. The Missal

That evening the Princess de Montfort did not have the hand of her usual cavalier to help her down from her carriage. For the first time, the Marquis had left his mother in the lurch.

The Princess was a strong-minded woman, as we have observed, and the opinion of all strong minds is that the doors should be thrown wide open once youth has reached its end. But among women, especially strong-minded women, there is a world of difference between theory and practice. One paltry ghost story had brought the Princess's entire body out in gooseflesh, even though she did not believe in ghosts. Youth must come to an end, but the Princess was decidedly heartsick when she took the hand of Doctor Récamier as she mounted the steps of her townhouse.

"You have a touch of fever, my lady," the Doctor said to her, "and I'm not surprised, after everything that has happened. Take my advice: have a nice warm bath tomorrow morning, with a simple affusion of cold water."

"When I think, Doctor," the Princess sighed, "that I took that *demoiselle* d'Arnheim for... oh, the shameless villains! Leonie felt a hairy hand... she's a little mad, poor thing... but look at Gaston, with the bit between his teeth! Oh, I hope he's done the right thing, leaving the seminary! She's pretty, at least. There's nothing to be said. And poor Emerance has a slight squint... but not un-becoming, eh? What a party! It was too terrible, Doctor!"

The Doctor took his leave, saying: "In a nice warm bath, my lady, a simple affusion."

If anyone had asked the Princess where her son was at that moment, she would have replied without hesitation and with perfect confidence: "My son Gaston is prowling around Mademoiselle d'Arnheim." She might perhaps have added, in her capacity as a strong-minded woman: "At least the Duc never chas-es after angels!"

In spite of her long experience and ample powers of deduction, the Prin-cess would have been in error in this case. Gaston was not prowling around Mademoiselle d'Arnheim; Gaston was all alone, making his way on foot across the three leagues that separated the Château de Conflans from the Rue de l'Université.

Gaston had indeed escorted Monsieur d'Arnheim and his daughter as far as the humble carriage that awaited them at the gate of the château, but there he had left them, saying to the old man: "Whatever time it may be when I call on you tonight, you must see me; you will understand the reasons for my actions then." He had then gone back towards the château, but instead of going in to find his mother, who would have pestered him for news, he had circled the building and then gone back into the park.

The moon was hidden; the sky was still full of huge, heavy and slow-moving clouds, through which its light occasionally showed for brief intervals. Gaston retraced the route that he had followed during the soirée; he seemed very agitated. When he reached the patch of woodland the darkness was so deep that he hesitated, unsure of his path.

The mysterious noises that he had heard earlier within the park and its en-virons had ceased now. All was silent save for the distant murmur of the great city, whose presence also revealed itself by the red tint reflected from the low clouds that lay over it.

Such fears are childish! thought the Marquis de Lorgères. Even so, I have heard it said that the whole world is vulnerable to such effects, including the King... I am no exception.

He had passed into an elmwood, whose undergrowth was composed of thorn-bushes and privet, entwined with serpentine honeysuckle. It was here that he had come during the soirée; he remembered it well–but the elm-grove extended for more than an acre. How could he locate one particular spot in the midst of that profound obscurity?

He took advantage of one shaft of moonlight to move out of the wood, then he set himself to follow the edge of the stand, looking for the little footpath that he had already missed once. A second glimmer of light showed him a dozen petty paths winding into the undergrowth, all very similar. At the same time, he heard the sound of carriage-wheels on the driveway; the guests were going home and the doors would soon be closed. He had to make haste.

Gaston picked one of the footpaths at random and followed it for a hundred paces; it led him straight to an enormous stump surrounded by heaps of dead wood. He retraced his steps at a run and took another route, then another: they both took him deeper into the wood. The lights were being extinguished in the château. It would no longer be possible to leave by the gate.

An entire hour went by while he searched in vain, and Gaston had quite lost heart, when a shaft of moonlight lit a spark at his feet. Something flat and metallic glittered in the brushwood. He bent down, picked up the object that he had previously hidden there, buttoned his coat over his precious find, and made for the wall that enclosed the park.

A stone wall is a small obstacle to a twenty-year-old in good health. He climbed over it easily, without injury to anything but the knees of his trousers and the cuffs of his black coat. I dare say that His Grace's guard-dogs howled a little, but Gaston was already on his way along the highway.

There was an official on duty at the toll-gate, sleeping in that extraordinary fashion which does not prevent officials from seeing confusedly and moving slowly. There are barriers on every road into Paris, whose presence is vital to the taxation of wines and spirits. The somnambulist, seeing a bare-headed man whose trousers were ripped at the knees and whose coat was torn at the cuffs, leapt to the conclusion that he must be a smuggler intent on the fraudulent introduction of a vast quantity of wine, and sounded the alarm in order to rouse his five companions from the same magical sleep. The six functionaries, moved by the best of intentions, demanded that Gaston should either show them his import license or pay his duty.

When Gaston demanded to be allowed through, he was seized and searched, but released again because the officials had found nothing on him but a little missal bound in velvet and enclosed in polished steel, at the end of a length of chain, also made of steel. Gaston, when he saw the missal in the hands of these good men, fell into a chair and almost lost consciousness–but the unanimous opinion of the officials was that even if the object were hollow and full of proof spirit, its capacity was too small for any tax to be payable.

Gaston accepted the return of the missal as if he were taking possession of a treasure and hurried on his way, without bidding farewell to the men in green who had persecuted him while they were lost in a dream.

The missal was, as we have already established, bound in velvet and hermetically encased in steel, sealed by an antique lock; its solidity seemed proven. A large number of ecclesiastics possess breviaries of that sort, but we have no intention of laying a trap for the perspicacity of the reader. The little book was most certainly the one which had formerly hung, attached to a steel chain, around the neck of Monsignor Benedict. Gaston had found it on the ground and picked it up when the Archbishop's guests had left the lawn after the story-telling. But why had he not returned it to Monsignor Benedict? Why, instead, had he hidden it as if he were concealing a treasure? The young and handsome Marquis de Lorgères certainly did not look like a thief.

To tell the truth, it could hardly have been an object of very great importance, since Monsignor Benedict had not even noticed that it was missing during the three hours that the concert had lasted.

Or could it?

It was about two o'clock in the morning when the Marquis arrived at the end of the Rue de l'Université, in front of his mother's townhouse. The de Montfort residence was situated not far from the Bourbon Palace, close to the corner of the Rue de Courty. Gaston did not pause at the impressive gateway; he turned the corner of the Rue de Courty, still running, and rang the doorbell of a modest house which backed on to the rear garden of the mansion.

This simple topographical detail will perhaps explain to the reader the innocent and mute mystery of the sentiments of Gaston and Lenore. Lenore's bedroom window looked out upon the vast garden where Gaston had—for an entire month—been taking endless walks.

The door opened. Gaston went up to the second floor and was introduced by Monsieur d'Arnheim himself into a rather squalid apartment. The little spaniel, Mina, came to welcome her friend.

The silent and somber Monsieur d'Arnheim opened the door of his study and closed it behind them.

The clock on the Bourbon palace was sounding five o'clock when Monsieur d'Arnheim's study-door opened again to let Gaston out. Some agreement must have been reached between them, because they shook hands before parting.

XI. The Statement of Account

There was a large bowl of punch steaming on the table. It was already half-empty. They were both there: the tall one and the short one.

Baron von Altenheimer was pacing back and forth across the room, with an enormous Prussian pipe clenched in his teeth. His thatch of black hair was gone; this was a tall young man, nearly bald, and what hair he had was reddish-brown. His black coat had been replaced by a Turkish jacket crisscrossed and edged with gold embroidery.

Monsignor Benedict, wearing a crimson satin dressing-gown, was stretched out on an old sofa with a Havana cigar between his lips. Under the dressing-gown the black collar of his clerical garb was visible, the sluggard not having taken the trouble to get out of it. The room was large and high-ceilinged, but it was untidy and ill-furnished. It had two beds. A distinct odor of low-life was in the air.

They both gave every impression of being in a good mood, and there was a brotherly intimacy in their chatter.

"There'll be a big noise in the corridors of power in the morning," the tall one said, laughing.

"Better there than here," replied the short one. "I love the Rue de Richelieu. If I ever settle in Paris for good, I'll treat myself to a house on the corner of the Rue de Richelieu and the boulevard."

"Personally, I prefer that nice house that looks out on the Rue de la Paix," the Baron replied. "I think it's the Osmond house. I must pay my respects there some day...but think of the row we kicked up last night!" He went on laughing.

"You were superb," said the younger brother, insincerely.

"And you were very pretty," the older riposted, "but I must admit that when it comes to dupes, these Parisians are the cream."

"The most spiritual people in the world," Benedict murmured, yawning.

The Baron resumed his pacing. "There were a lot of trinkets in that collection," he went on, disdainfully. "Except for your ring and my snuff-box, I didn't see much apart from the Princess's bracelet..."

"You're telling me," Benedict replied. "Parisians have jewels specially made for collection days."

The Baron smiled and downed a glass of punch in a single draught. He filled up the Monsignor's glass, which had also been drained, albeit in smaller gulps. "We won't get as much as a thousand *louis* for the lot," he said. "Paris is a dump, I tell you."

"For work, certainly... but when one retires from the business..."

"All right then," the elder interrupted, depositing his immense porcelain pipe on the table. "You said it. Let's talk business. It's already one o'clock in the morning and it's scarcely worth going to bed–we have to be on the road to Boulogne by four."

"I'm tired," said the Monsignor, yawning for the second time and stretching lazily on his sofa.

"We have to, for safety's sake..."

"Leave off! Who the devil do you expect to winkle us out of here?"

"Stranger things have happened," the tall man said.

"There are two places made for hiding in," the shorter man replied. "Paris and the Black Forest–and Paris is ten times as good as the Black Forest!"

"But you agreed..." said the Baron reproachfully.

"I've changed my mind," Benedict said, dryly.

"You no longer want to leave?"

"Of course... but not tonight."

"Why not?"

"I have my reasons."

"It's foolishness," complained the elder, testily.

"Possibly," the younger replied, "but I'm my own master, and am at liberty to be foolish."

The Baron made an effort to contain the anger that was rumbling within him. "Look here," he said, abruptly but without losing his temper. "What mischief has Satan put into your head? Tell me!"

"Very well, Old William," the Monsignor replied. "I don't want us to fall out over this; there's probably a nice stroke or two to be pulled in London these days. I'll tell you my reasons, just as though you had the right to call me to account. To begin with, we have nothing to fear here; not one of our hirelings knows where we are. No one even knows that English is our mother tongue, since you had the honor of being raised within sight of the Tower of London and I was born in the parish of Saint Giles, not two steps from Oxford Street, where I did my earliest jobs. So, tomorrow morning, we get out of this slum; we go to Vincennes, clean ourselves up in the woods and we come back, arm in arm, to the toll-gate: William Staunton, bookseller of Ave Maria Lane and Mrs. Olivia Staunton, his young companion, both on their first trip to Paris, their pockets full of guineas and determined to have a jolly good time. We come down somewhere in the vicinity of the Palais-Royal–and who'll see what has become of the privy councilor to the King of Wurtemburg and the pope's chamberlain?

"It's absurd," said the older, coldly. "Is that all?"

"No. If you're absolutely determined to be gone, I'll go too–but not till tomorrow evening, and not without Mademoiselle d'Arnheim."

The Baron's pallor gave way to redness. "Do you know who that d'Arnheim girl is?" he murmured, through clenched teeth.

"Of course!" the younger man replied. "It's Lenore...I gave her up for twelve hundred thousand francs when we were poor, but today I'd pay two millions for her... I love her!"

"Imbecile!" said the elder, harshly. "You've risked your life ten times for a few *louis*..."

"I love her, d'you hear?" cried the blond man, raising himself up on his elbow. "I want to carry her off, and I shall! Don't shrug your shoulders like that! It's a long while since you were in command here, Old William. I'm no longer a child; my word counts for just as much as yours."

Old William–seeing that yet another name has been given to Baron von Altenheimer, we might as well use it–crossed his long arms over his breast and said: "You don't suppose, Bobby, that I'd help you to play that sort of game?"

Bobby–which was, perhaps, the Monsignor's true name–replied: "Didn't you help me with the blond girl in Itèbe? And pretty Efflam in Petrovaradin?

And the girl in Venice? And the one in Stuttgart? And the rest? Me, I've always helped you, like the minor player who feeds the cue to Kemble or Talma [64]. I'm as good an actor as you are, William, and you need me more than I need you."

Smiling scornfully, the tall man turned his back and went to refill his glass,

"Just listen," the short man went on, "and you'll see that we both know how to put together a plan of attack. When you donated your pocket-book with the thousand-franc notes—which wasn't bad, I admit—I thought of something better. I went to His Lordship in my turn and said to him: Your Highness, could you tell me where this respectable Monsieur d'Arnheim lives? What could His Highness think but that the fortune of his protégés would be made if we were to go there? I have the address: in the Rue de Courty, at the corner of the Rue de l'Université. Tomorrow, I'll spend half an hour making up my face in the image of a very respectable marquise, fifty or sixty years old. There was just such a one at the Archbishop's; I'll copy her perfectly. I shan't bother to mention the costume, which is a mere bagatelle. Thus transformed into a dowager, I arrive at Monsieur d'Arnheim's house at the hour when society ladies are wont to circulate, in mid-afternoon. Madame la Comtesse de Chastellux... or de Noailles... or de Mortemart... some irresistible name, at any rate... on behalf of the Archbishop of Paris. I go in; I explain that I heard the young and interesting *virtuosa* yesterday at the Château of Conflans. I have a niece... or the daughter of my poor eldest son, who is dead. I have found that she has a natural bent for music, which is not surprising, since her father had such a lovely voice! Would you like to get into my carriage, my dear child? I want to introduce you to my daughter-in-law... in spite of all your skepticism, you can't pretend that there's anything in the least difficult about it. The little one gets in..."

"And you take her all the way to London in one go?" the erstwhile Baron von Altenheimer interrupted, sarcastically.

"You'll allow me to suppose," Monsignor Bobby replied, acidly, "that a boy like me, transformed from a dowager into a great lord, could easily succeed in pleasing a young girl..."

"You'll allow me to suppose," the tall man interrupted again, "that a stupid act is the greatest stupidity of all! Even if it were supposed that a boy like you, a little less highly-born than my boot, is exactly what is required to play the role of Don Juan, I'd still say that it's absurd. Firstly, the Prince might recognize you. Secondly, I don't want to be inconvenienced on our travels by a woman."

The smaller man lay back on his pillow and sent a long plume of smoke spiraling towards the ceiling. "Ripe fruits that one hesitates to pick go bad," he muttered, clenching his teeth. "Between the two of us, I believe the pear is ripe; if we stay together, William, it will go so bad that we'll get it into our heads to cut one another's throats before long."

---

[64] Charles Kemble (1775-1854) was the leading British actor of the period; François-Joseph Talma (1763-1826) was his French counterpart.

"I've a mind to..." William began, his voice tremulous and menacing.

"There, you see!" Bobby said, coldly. "The pear's ripe–we must go our separate ways."

The tall man made a determined effort to contain his anger. He drank two glasses of punch in rapid succession, then he said: "All right, then–split us up!"

"The share-out won't be difficult," said Bobby, who seemed much less emotional than his elder partner. "It won't take long. The banknotes are in two lots in the missal. I anticipated that our association wouldn't last forever and I've always taken care to divide them up into wads of equal value."

"Oh, you anticipated that, did you?" William said. "When I found you so poor, and so ragged."

"Were you rich?" Bobby demanded, before adding: "Go on, Old William, we have nothing for which to reproach one another. If you've earned your share, I've deserved twice as much."

"Ungrateful spawn," murmured the tall man. "But you're right–it's time to part... where's the missal?"

Bobby put his cigar between his lips and patted his side beneath the dressing-gown. "Good accounts make good friends," he said. "You should have a statement listing the exact contents of the missal in your pocket-book."

"I have the pocket-book."

"Get it out, so that we can settle up." He was still rummaging among the ample folds of satin. He showed no obvious signs of anxiety.

"Right!" said the tall man.

"Right," Bobby echoed. "I must have put it under my pillow when I came in, as I usually do. Go see."

William crossed the room and snatched the pillow from one of the beds. "There's nothing here," he said. "You have it on you."

Bobby got up. His expression was seized by a vague dread. Instead of continuing to pat the satin of his dressing-gown, he tore it from his body, to gain better access to the costume which he had worn at the Archbishop's soirée. Both hands groped about his left side. He became very pale and his cigar fell from his lips. William, who was following him with a determined stare, was red in the face but he said not a word.

They moved towards one another, each now clutching an open blade produced from who knows where. They came face to face in the middle of the room, looking deep into one another's eyes as if to read the minds behind them, and they said with one voice, through gritted teeth: "You've stolen the missal!"

Bobby tried to duck under William's thrust, while William swayed backwards in the attempt to avoid Bobby's. Then they set themselves on guard again, standing toe to toe, the long face of the taller looming over the blond head of the smaller. Bobby's neck was bleeding and there was a red stain in William's armpit; both thrusts had struck home.

They paused for a moment thus, their left hands splayed before their breasts, ready to parry, while their right hands trembled as they gripped their daggers tightly. Both men obviously knew enough about the art of fencing to concentrate on protecting the head and the heart, leaving the limbs to take their chances–it doesn't matter much if one is wounded there, provided that one kills one's opponent. Each of them knew that he would have to sacrifice a little blood of his own to purchase a full measure of the other's.

Their eyes shone like four red-hot coals. Perhaps William seemed stronger, but Bobby was the more terrible. On seeing them both inflamed by rage and intent on murder, one would have bet on the knife of Ange the vampire against the dagger of the Chevalier Ténèbre.

William was the first to drop his weapon, having first taken a step back. Bobby lowered his arms, saying: "You're scared, and you're going to give back the missal!"

"I'm not scared," the tall man replied, "but I can see that the chain is still around your neck. You haven't stolen it–you've lost it!"

"Lost it!" cried Bobby. "The chain is pure steel. It would carry a hundred books."

"Yes," the other interrupted, while seizing a loose end of the chain. "It's broken!"

Bobby dropped his knife in his turn.

"Right by the rivet," he murmured. "But how was it that I didn't feel the absence of the weight? I know! I remember! On the lawn, I pulled on the chain and it resisted..." He jerked violently at the other end of the chain, which detached itself from the material of his vestment.

"A flaw," he stammered. "And the broken link was caught up in the fold of my costume."

William took the chain, while Bobby, who had froth at the corners of his mouth, closed his fist and said: "I bought that chain in Frankfurt, at number three the Zeil. I'll make an express trip to Frankfurt to tear that shopkeeper's heart out."

They knew only too well that they had both made a mistake. Neither could maintain their suspicions in the face of that mute witness, the broken chain. They were now entirely given over to consternation.

William took one end of the chain in each hand and pulled them apart with all his strength; the chain remained solid.

"It only had the one flaw," he murmured.

His pocket-book was on the table, ready to verify the count. He opened it and began to read in a faint voice: "Two banknotes of fifty thousand pounds... number one... two million five hundred thousand francs!"

"The Bank of England only took five impressions from the plate," Bobby sighed, "and we had two of them."

"Number two," the tall man went on, "two banknotes of a thousand pounds... Number three, two banknotes of a thousand pounds... Number four, two banknotes of a thousand pounds..."

"There were a hundred of them" Bobby interrupted him.

"Another two million five hundred thousand francs! Number one hundred and two, two banknotes of five thousand pounds... that was after the Venice job... Number one hundred and three, from the same job, two banknotes of four thousand pounds... Number one hundred and four..."

Bobby threw himself on the pocket-book, tearing it from William's grasp, and pressed it tightly between his hands.

"We had millions!" said the tall man, collapsing in a fit of tears. "Millions and millions and millions..."

"Millions and millions and millions!" echoed the small man, grinding his teeth like a tiger.

They were still looking at one another.

"Shall we kill one another?" Bobby said, coldly.

William picked up the punch-bowl in both hands and drank down its remaining contents in one draught. Then he drew himself proudly up to his full height and he too said: "Shall we kill one another?"

But Bobby had already put his blade away. He began to pace back and forth across the room. William let himself fall into a chair. There was a long silence.

"Brother," said the short man, in the end, "you said it a little while ago: we've often risked our lives for a few *louis*."

"Do you have a plan?" William asked, his eyes calm and clear now.

"There are two possibilities, brother. Either the missal is still on the lawn, in the place where it fell, or one of the Archbishop's guests picked it up."

"That's true."

"We must not forget that in either case the missal is secured by a secret catch that would defy the most skilful of locksmiths."

"I believe so."

"We have two more parts to play: one on the grassy stage, the other in the bedroom of the man–whoever it might be–who had the misfortune to find the missal."

They took one another by the hand and said in unison, in a low voice: "He's a dead man!"

XII. The Princess Gets Up

Shortly before dawn the dogs guarding the Château de Conflans began to howl. It is a matter of record that the Archbishop's guests got little sleep that night. At four o'clock in the morning, or thereabouts, two men–one tall and one short–climbed over the wall and went into the woods. They wore the costumes of working men, but they were both well-armed beneath their shirts.

Dawn, when it broke, found them in the clearing where the friends of the Archbishop of Paris had gathered as night fell on the previous evening. They were both crawling on the grass, searching the shadows with their eyes.

"We won't find it," said the tall one, abruptly rising to his feet.

"Why's that?" the shorter one demanded.

"Because someone got here before us."

"What makes you think...?"

"Get your bearings, now that it's not as dark," William replied. "I am on the exact spot where you were standing as I finished my story, and my foot is where the missal fell."

"Should have fallen."

"Did fall," the tall man insisted. He pointed a finger at the grass between his feet.

The smaller man approached, got down on his knees and leaned over the designated spot. He could clearly see the bruised grass–and beneath it, the imprint cut into the soil by the sudden arrest of a rectangular object. He immediately got to his feet.

The two brothers, without saying a word, redirected their steps towards the wall of the park. The first part had been played, and the game lost; the second had yet to begin.

As they approached the wall, William suddenly stopped, saying: "Someone else came this way last night."

Bobby's educated eyes were already examining a section of the wall whose tapestry of ivy had been disturbed. The broken shoots had not had time to go yellow, and the detached foliage was still fresh.

"A scrap of cloth!" he cried.

"Fine cloth," said William. "That never belonged to the clothing of some night-prowler. Look at these tracks!"

The footprints left by the Marquis were, indeed, visible on the dewy ground.

"Dancing-shoes," William went on. "A foot like a woman's!"

Bobby climbed in car-like fashion to the top of the wall, where something white was lodged.

"G. L. and the crown of a marquis!" he cried, throwing a handkerchief to William.

"Gaston de Lorgères!" murmured William. "Why didn't he leave the château by the main gate?" He climbed the wall in his turn.

The two of them took the road to Paris, pensively.

"Anything under your shirts?" asked the guard at the toll-gate.

William stopped, as an idea came into his head. Striking the pose, innocent and astute at the same time, of a concerned citizen, he said instead of answering the question: "Are you also responsible for arresting thieves?"

"Why do you ask?" the official countered, while patting the tall man's shirt in a tokenistic fashion.

"Because it's my opinion that our thief must have come this way."

The official, three-quarters awakened by curiosity, said: "What thief?"

"The sharp dresser who was carrying Monsieur le curé's brand-new breviary, that's who!"

"Well, I never!" exclaimed the man at the toll-gate. "There's a turn up!"

He said this in such a manner that sweat immediately sprang up on William's and Bobby's foreheads. Their hearts beat faster. They said, as one: "You got him!"

"He had no duty to pay," the official retorted, stoutly, "and I'm no gendarme."

"What time was it when he came through?" William asked, sadly.

"An hour after midnight... he'll be a long way off by now, if he's still running."

Later that morning, an impoverished old woman took up a position in the Rue de Courty, not far from the house where Monsieur d'Arnheim lived, while an unfamiliar beggar established himself on a step facing the house occupied by the Princess de Montfort.

This occurred some considerable time before the Princess, whose sleep was prolonged by the emotions and exertions of the previous night, was ready to face the new day. Her first words, after waking up. were an enquiry as to Gaston's whereabouts.

"Monsieur le Marquis," her chambermaid replied, "has already presented himself three times asking to speak to Madame la Princesse."

"It couldn't be helped, Justine. I feel weak, and I haven't the strength to get up to receive him. Tell him to come in."

An instant later, Gaston was introduced into his mother's bedroom.

"My dear child," the Princess said to him at once, "You know me, and you know that I don't like to scold. Today, when even I might be inclined to reprimand you, I shall abstain, because I want you to trust me, to trust me absolutely. Something extraordinary has happened to you; I know that. Would you like to make your confession to me?"

"With all my heart, mother," the young Marquis replied, kissing her hand tenderly. "It is precisely for the purpose of telling you what is happening to me that I have taken the liberty of demanding an interview with you this morning."

"Then I shall listen, Gaston, asking only one thing of you: that you are perfectly frank with the mother who loves you."

The Marquis blushed slightly, but he replied without hesitation: "You might well complain about me, Madame, but not of any lack of frankness. I want to marry."

The Princess reeled from the blow, taking cover beneath her bedclothes. The timid Gaston had gone for good, it seemed.

"I must point out," the lady replied, her eyebrows furrowing in spite of herself, "that you are a child, in love for the first time, and that you have gone mad."

It seemed that Gaston was prepared for that kind of reaction, for he lifted his mother's hand to his lips again.

"To marry a singer...!" the Princess began, angrily.

"Permit me, Madame," Gaston interrupted her, very softly. "I hope to furnish proof in the course of this conversation...I am in love, as you have done me the honor of observing, in the second place. I admit that much. As for having gone mad, it's said that such is the lot of lively minds illuminated by superabundant imagination; in my mind and my conscience I feel that I am out of reach of that danger–I am not at all well-endowed for going mad. If my cool, practical and prosaic character has no other advantage, it protects me from that..."

"Oh, get on with it!" the Princess cried, impatiently.

"Which brings us to the singer, Madame, and since you have asked me to be frank, I will admit, frankly, that I am astonished and wounded by that insinuation. I have long attained the age when such pranks are played, and I have noticed that the stubborn regularity of my conduct has occasioned a certain mockery among my friends. I believe I can even affirm that it has sometimes put a smile on my mother's lips..."

"Oh, Gaston...!"

"My God, Madame, youth which does not pass, as it is said, is entitled to raise a smile... I have been living like a little saint. On the other hand, no crisis or malady, chivalrous or romantic, has ever troubled my existence, which has been as peaceful as the lovely little stream that winds through your park at Chelles–which you yourself have bitterly reproached for having neither a waterfall nor a whirlpool... Were I not a de Montfort, I would say that I had good bourgeois blood in my veins, retaining from the first of January to Saint Sylvester's day [65] the moderate and calm temperature of mediocrity..."

"What case are you pleading now?" the Princess interrupted him, raising her eyes. "You're like a Norman lawyer this morning. Are you starting your diplomatic career with me?"

---

[65] The Roman Catholic Church celebrates St. Sylvester's Day, as might be deduced from the context, on the thirty-first of December. There is, however, a neat irony concealed in this mode of expression, because the Eastern Churches celebrate St. Sylvester's Day on the second of January.

"I have renounced diplomacy, Madame," Gaston replied, calmly. "My vocation is to make a rich marriage and to live on my estates."

"A rich marriage!" echoed the stupefied Princess. "Your cousin Emerance has fifty thousand francs a year."

"My mother might perhaps have been able to deduce," Gaston replied, lifting the Princess's hand to his lips for the third time, "that if I have not shown overmuch eagerness in the matter of that union, it is because I have another, more important, party in mind."

Madame de Montfort rubbed her eyes with her knuckles. She suspected that she was not yet fully awake.

"More important!" she repeated, perhaps more shocked by the manner of the expression than the idea itself. "Are you really there, my boy?"

"I believe that I have been unkindly judged thus far, Mother," Gaston replied, "and my preamble, which may have seemed overlong to you, can hardly have modified your opinion on that score. I can only do myself justice by telling you that I am a respectful son, obedient and loving–but marriage, Madame, is one's entire future!"

"I have never tried to force you..." the Princess began.

"Of course, Mother, of course–but do you imagine that you had not made it clear what path your maternal affection wished me to take? My cousin Emerance..."

"Say no more, I beg you, about your cousin Emerance, Gaston! Your cousin Emerance was not an accessory to the building of my beautiful castles in Spain. I don't even know if we would have been able to obtain her hand."

"I don't know either, Madame, and I don't care. It is in Hungary, not in Spain, that I have built my own imaginary castles." He stopped, as if a vision had suddenly taken hold of him.

The Princess looked at him, open-mouthed. "And what connection have you ever had with Hungary?" she asked, after a pause.

"You have forgotten, Madame," Gaston replied, "that you commissioned me, some time ago, to take steps to withdraw your interest from the property at Debrecen owned by my brother the Duc."

"And you met the daughter of some local magnate in the lawyer's office?"

"I implore you, Madame, not to make fun," the young Marquis said, seriously. "there was never a subject less suitable for joking... Do you remember the story told last night by the Baron von Altenheimer?"

The Princess clapped her hands together. "I knew that there was some extravagance under all this!" she cried. "I suppose it concerns the lovely Lenore, daughter of Prince Jacobyi."

"You are right, Madame," said Gaston, unblinkingly.

"What an evening!" the Princess went on. "I dreamed of those cunning scoundrels all night. I refused to believe their silly story as a matter of principle... Look, Gaston, all joking aside, I want to talk to you seriously..."

"Does the party not seem suitable to you, Mother?..." asked the young Marquis, his calmness put to the test.

"What party? Are we going back to the vampires of yesteryear and that stupid phantasmagoria? Don't talk to me about marrying the Sleeping Beauty or some other fairy tale. Stop now, Monsieur le Marquis, or you'll have me convinced that your mind is definitely unhinged."

"Madame," said Gaston, unhurriedly, "Hungary is not Fairyland. Our cousin Camille, Prince of Guéménée and de Rochefort, was married only last year to the Princess of Wertheim-Rosenberg, and we ourselves are descended from the ancient kings of Hungary through Charlotte de Croy d'Havré, my great-grandmother on my father's side."

The Princess took her flask, opened it, closed it again, then opened it again so that she could close it again. In every country where there are flasks, such gestures indicate the exhaustion of patience.

"I suppose," the Marquis continued, redoubling his persuasive efforts, "that any teller of fantastic tales, whether honest man or bandit, might take the name de Montfort–which you wear so well, Mother dear–and introduce it into his tale like the one we heard yesterday. Would that prevent you from being at the head of a noble French family? Madame, I beseech you to believe that the information I have does not come from Baron von Altenheimer–if that really is his name. I am speaking seriously of serious matters, and I have come to ask you whether you are willing to approach Prince Jacobyi on my behalf to ask for the hand of his daughter in marriage."

If the Princess had been standing up, she would have fallen down.

"This is too much, Monsieur le Marquis!" she said, sitting up straight again. Then she added, in a sarcastic tone: "And to what part of the world would it be necessary to address the letter to this Oedipus, soliciting the hand of his Antigone?"

"I would not have dared to compare the one that I love to the saintly figure bequeathed to us by antique poetry," Gaston replied, still perfectly placid. "The letter must be addressed to Chrétien Baszin, Prince Jacobyi, at Chandor Castle, near Szeged, Hungary."

The Princess opened her eyes wide. "Gaston," she murmured, "is there really something at the bottom of all this?"

"I don't know how to convince you of that elementary truth," the Marquis replied, "except to assure you that there is a young lady who will be your daughter-in-law and who will bring me a dowry of five or six hundred thousand francs a year."

"This is so extraordinary!" murmured the Princess. "You have said not a word to me before today!"

"I confess, Madame, that I have only been a man for twenty-four hours."

"You cannot hope, however," said Madame de Montfort, in a tone which was already much changed, "that I will embark upon an enterprise of this sort without explanations and proofs."

"Mother," replied Gaston, solemnly and sincerely, "I will give you clear and precise explanations–but as for proofs, it will be necessary to content yourself with the word of honor of a man who has never told a lie."

"Is it your own word of honor?"

"It is my own word of honor, Madame."

"I will listen, my son. Remember the name that you bear, and what indignity and cowardice there would be in deceiving your mother."

Gaston set out, briefly and clearly, the provisions of Hungarian legislation regarding matters of litigation.

All princesses have some understanding of the language of business. Let us not be deceived; only those possessed of considerable fortunes are elevated to such a condition, and that prose is the very soil in which the poetry of grandeur flourishes. The Princess de Montfort understood readily enough the mechanism by which feudal rights could be repurchased: a powerful instrument, which is not as insolently injurious to the idea of progress as the principle of inalienability or the right of primogeniture, but which works usefully and ceaselessly to consolidate great territorial domains.

"Chrétien Baszin, Prince Jacobyi," Gaston continued, "having been dispossessed at the end of 1821, has until the end of 1826 to buy back his estates, at the same price at which they were sold, without any regard to any further or partial sales which have taken place since then. That is the law. So much the worse for those who have taken advantage of the same law! Prince Jacobyi, profiting from the benevolence of the law, has bought back his castle and his lands, which are as vast as a province."

"Has bought back?" the Princess repeated. "The deal is done, and completed, is it not? You can assure me of that, under oath?"

"I assure you, under oath, Mother," the young Marquis replied, firmly, "that the magnate Jacobyi will receive your request at Chandor Castle, of which he will be the sole and sovereign master. I assure you, under oath, that if I introduce Lenore into your house, it will be as Princess Jacobyi, sole heir to her father's immense fortune."

Everything had now been said. The Princess remained silent and Gaston allowed her time to reflect. We shall take advantage of the pause to admit to the reader that, given the character of Madame de Montfort–who was otherwise a most excellent and charming princess–Gaston had chosen, with devastating tact, the only route which could possibly have won her consent. He had played the part of the money-lover so admirably that the first words his mother spoke were: "I fear, in truth–yes, my child, I fear–that the idea of a fortune... in marriage, believe me, a fortune is not everything!"

"I like a fortune, Madame."

"Undoubtedly, but the wife herself..."

"But I adore the wife, who is an angel!"

"Very well, Gaston. Ring for my chambermaid. I want to get up. We shall see... we shall think on it..."

Instead of ringing the bell, Gaston went to the sideboard to pick up one of those ornamental rosewood boxes called *papeteries*. He placed the charming object on the coverlet in front of his mother. It contained blue ink (which princesses and Doctor Récamier love, although I hate it myself), Surrey paper as glossy as satin, a steel pen–the first one, invented by Perry–and Spanish wax that exhaled a light and temperate perfume. Gaston opened the dainty desk, arranged the pad of paper and dipped the Perry pen into the blue ink.

"I have rivals," he murmured, "and time is pressing."

If he had done as others do; if he had put his head upon his mother's bosom, saying only: "I love..." Who knows? Perhaps it would have worked as well. We are describing what actually happened.

The Princess, who was a woman of style, wrote a dignified and concise letter, perfectly polite but getting straight to the point. She was paid in full, for Gaston hugged her as if she were some poor woman of the suburbs and as if he, the Marquis, were wearing the shirt of some Parisian urchin. Such extravagant gestures of affection, proscribed by etiquette, are nevertheless well worth having.

Gaston fled with his prey. We cannot say for sure whether he noticed the beggar sitting on the step facing the main gate of the de Montfort house, or the poor old lady stationed across from the house where Monsieur and Mademoiselle d'Arnheim were living. He could have seen both of them, for he went directly from the grand gate to the humble door on the Rue de Courty. What cannot be doubted is that the beggar and the poor old lady saw him; they abandoned their posts instantly, meeting at the corner of the two streets and exchanging several words in a low tone.

Gaston did not stay more than a quarter of an hour in Monsieur d'Arnheim's house. He came out, his face radiant, and went on foot towards the Rue de Lille. The beggar walked behind him, while the poor woman went back to her sentry-duty. The beggar returned an hour later and said to the old woman: "He's ordered a carriage."

"When for?"

"I don't know... let's wait for nightfall."

At five o'clock, Gaston returned to the townhouse in a cab. As he passed the threshold of the gateway, the beggar went towards the old woman and said: "He's going in to dinner. We have an hour to do likewise."

They went off together. They were gone for no more than five minutes, but it was too much.

Every sentinel knows that he must have a very good reason to abandon his post. The Marquis had not, in fact, gone in to dinner. He could have been seen coming out again a few moments later, on horseback, and turning once again into the Rue de Courty. A carriage and horses drew up before Monsieur d'Arnheim's house, and Monsieur d'Arnheim came out in his travelling clothes to take his place in the carriage. The driver whipped his horses into motion and Gaston galloped alongside.

The carriage went right through Paris and made its exit through the toll-gate at La Villette, then took the Strasbourg Road. Gaston maintained his escort over a considerable distance; darkness had fallen when he turned back.

In the meantime, the beggar and the old woman had taken up their posts again and continued their vigil. At about six o'clock, the old woman went to find the beggar. "The Devil with this!" she said.

"Wait," the other replied. patiently, in a deep baritone voice. "The time will come and the place suits our purpose. There's not so much as a stray cat in the Rue de l'Université. We can sit down now on either side of the door."

Scarcely had they taken their places on benches of the kind which are set at the entrances of a great many townhouses in the Faubourg Saint-Germain than the hoofbeats of a horse were heard in the distance. The ragged couple paid no attention to the noise; it was not a horseman that they were waiting for.

The horseman approached and stopped directly in front of the closed gate. The beggar and the old woman stayed in their corners until the moment when the horseman cried out, in an imperious voice: "The gate!" Then they started, both as one.

They leapt to their feet, and a second bound carried each of them to one side of the horse. Gaston was seized by both legs, dragged to the ground, stabbed and searched from head to toe within the blink of an eye.

"Nothing!" said the beggar.

"Nothing," echoed the old woman, with a curse.

The gate opened. The old woman and the beggar took to their heels and, while still in full flight, threw off their rags. One could then have seen, under the next street-lamp, two men running with equal rapidity: one tall, one short.

As for Gaston, the servants who came to open the gate found him bathed in his own blood beside his motionless horse. His breast had been pierced by two thrusts of a dagger.

XIII. The Black Graves

The Marquis de Lorgères was confined to his bed for four months by his wounds. The thrusts had been masterly; either might have been fatal, and Dupuytren [66] was able to boast for many years afterwards of that particular cure.

---

[66] Baron Guillaume Dupuytren (1777-1835) was the leading French surgeon and anatomist of his day. Although surgery was a nasty business in the days before effective anesthetics, when cauterization was the only effective ward

In the meantime, Prince Jacobyi's reply arrived in Paris–bearing the address of Chandor Castle–and was favorable.

As one would expect, the Princess, although she trusted the Marquis's word completely, had not been deterred from obtaining information from her cousins the de Rohans, who were established in Hungary. It was, after all, part of her duty as a mother. The information thus transmitted was, like the Prince's reply, favorable.

The Prince had bought back his lands. The Prince was, as before, one of the greatest lords of the Austrian Empire.

The marriage of the Marquis de Lorgères to Princess Lenore took place in Szeged, at the beginning of March 1826.

Early in April that same year, a little old man with a pleasant face and an easy-gong manner was trudging along the high road from Pest to Szeged, pulling a hand-cart containing a poor creature who looked like a living corpse and who had, moreover, lost his reason. Not far from Szeged, upstream of Morzau, there is a spring whose water is clear, protected by a little minaret from the dust of the road. The water of that spring was blessed by Saint Miklos, and has the power to cure madness. The little old man was a good father who had come from the region of Ofen, dragging his unfortunate son every step of the way.

Since that era, our French engineers have laid four parallel iron bars all the way from Pest to Belgrade, via Szeged. It only requires a few hours to cross that vast plain. The last time I saw Szeged, that strange town which contains as many bells as the entire district of Beauce [67], it had an old pupil of our *Ecole Polytechnique* for its king. He was in the process of building a four thousand-feet bridge across the Tisza: a magnificent bridge to carry the railway. Austrian engineers came to study the work, carried out by a human ant-hive in which one could identify twenty races and whose members spoke fifteen languages.

I realized then that the confusion of languages had counted for nothing in preventing the erection of the Tower of Babel. The bridge marched upon the waters, so to speak, supported by great tubular columns, and I saw a daguerreotype machine with the round eye of its black chamber already focused on its arches. This is our future civilization–but on that same voyage I saw accused and condemned men, stretched out entirely naked on the damp earth in the cellars of Turkish forts: forts whose walls, flanked by corpulent towers, looked over that same Parisian bridge. We have, however, already raised the possibility that men

---

against infection, surgeons usually did more good than physicians, most of whose remedies were impotent or dangerous. Féval's sarcastic treatment of Doctor Récamier's favored panacea of "cold affusions taken in warm baths"–i.e., pouring cold water over a patient sitting in a warm bath–is reasonably good-humored because he knew well enough that the "treatments" favored by most quacks were likely to make matters worse.

[67] The French district which includes Chartres.

might break out of prisons, even those whose stones have been set permanently in place.

In 1826, the high road entered the city via a lake of mud in winter, a sea of dust in summer. The dust of Szeged is famous in Hungary, and the mud too. Ingenious Magyars set planks end to end in order that these precipices may be crossed, but the regulations require carriages to pass alongside them lest they be rendered useless, and the trusting pedestrian who dares to set foot upon them is almost certain to fall off.

The pious father, the hand-cart and the son arrived two hours before sunset at the horribly churned-up plain called the Place Joseph II, in the shadow of the beautiful Byzantine Church of Saint Job. The hand-cart stopped in front of a sort of caravanserail, bearing a sign depicting a saint clad in red, whose interior courtyard, as large as one of our public squares, was bordered by worm-eaten wooden arcades. The little old man asked politely for the least expensive room in the inn, deposited his son there and went out to get his papers stamped by a government official. His passport bore the name Petroz Aszuth, leather-merchant of Kaiserbad.

The servants in Hungarian inns are usually Slavs and, in consequence, almost as garrulous as the staff of French taverns. Before dinner was served, everyone knew the whole story of little Petroz Aszuth, who was taking his idiot son to the spring of Saint Miklos. The poor *lumpen* boy was certainly in great need of the spring. The innkeeper's daughter who took him his food was kind enough to strike up a conversation with him to relieve his boredom slightly, but she returned saying: "One might as well talk to Schwartz, the guard-dog!"

The night was already well-advanced when the little old man came back. He did not want any supper and immediately went up to his room. As soon as he was inside, he locked the door and drew the curtains over the window.

The idiot leapt from his bed and put on a blond wig. You would have immediately recognized the long lean figure of Baron von Altenheimer. "Do you know something, Bobby?" he asked, animatedly.

Bobby removed his dirty beard, which was making his rosy cheeks itch, and plunged his face into a basin of fresh water, displaying the pretty face of Monsignor Benedict.

"Well," he said, "this place hasn't changed–they still chatter like magpies. I know the story from beginning to end."

Tall William sat down on the foot of his bed to smoke his porcelain pipe. "Go on," he said.

"It was the Marquis all right," Bobby replied, lighting his cigar. "He's given the missal to old Jacobyi, who's bought his hovel back..."

"Then they're thieves like us!" William cried. "The missal only had five hundred thousand florins of his, from Lenore's ransom, and he'd have needed six times that to buy his estates back!"

Bobby shrugged his shoulders. "If they'd kept the lot," he replied, "I could almost have forgiven them–after all, it's every man for himself, isn't it? But since old Baszin got back his castle, his forests, his lakes and his fields, he's taken out all his mortgages again and borrowed exactly the same sum as the excess he took from the missal. Even before he celebrated the marriage of his daughter, he had delivered our cash into the hands of the Primate of Hungary, the Archbishop of Graz. The fact has been advertised in Vienna, Venice, Stuttgart, Paris and everywhere else, and all the sheep that we have fleeced have turned up, demanding their wool! Pillaged, all of it! Not a single florin of our little hoard remains–and if there were anything left, the rogues would still be queuing up!"

"Wretches!" William groaned.

"Let me tell you," Bobby went on, "everyone is talking about us here. Since we've done what we came to do, we'd best be on our way. They know everything! The story of our Paris venture has become legendary. The tale of the Archbishop's collection is all the rage. And the missal itself... but it's the story of the missal that I want to tell you. The Marquis was running an errand for his mother when he picked up the missal. His intention was to return it to me, but the missal had fallen so unluckily that the secret catch had been sprung. Nothing was broken, but the steel casement could be opened as easily as one might open a book. The Marquis did exactly that, perhaps by chance, and the two fifty-thousand-pound banknotes leapt to his eyes. He understands English, and you had taken care to acquaint him, a few minutes earlier, with the story of the father of Lenore, with whom he was already in love even though he had never spoken to her..."

"I remember!" murmured William. "He had the nerve to ask me for information about rights of repurchase, on the pretext that his brother had property in Debrecen..."

"When he asked you for that information, his plan was conceived," Bobby went on. "He's a smart fellow and I won't regret the bullet that smashes his head."

William took a flat square bottle from his overcoat, which contained brandy. He took a big gulp. "Ever since that business," he said, "we've been unable to get back on our feet. All our capers have gone wrong, in London, in Berlin, in Vienna–he's the cause of all our misfortune!" He passed the bottle to Bobby, who drank before repeating: "He's the cause of all our misfortune!"

"When we've bled him dry, he must die!"

"He must die!" Bobby echoed, again. "I have all the necessary information. They talk of little else in Szeged, because of the story of the missal, which has been on everyone's lips. He's spending his honeymoon at Chandor. He hunts and he fishes. A big hunt is planned for tomorrow."

"We'll be there!" snarled William.

"We'll be there. We must be up early–let's get some sleep, Old William."

The next morning, before daybreak, the little old man from Kaiserbad hitched himself up to his vehicle and carted his maniac son off towards the welcoming spring. The staff of the inn were most impressed by the conduct of the little old man; they pointed him in the right direction and wished him good luck.

The way to the spring was the road to Chandor Castle. After an hour's march, at the moment when dawn silvered the horizon, the hand-cart reached the vast forests of the Baszin domain.

The old man left the main road and pushed the hand-cart into a dense wood. The invalid son, suddenly recovering the agility appropriate to one of his age, leapt on to the moss and opened the false bottom of the cart, from which he extracted two double-barreled shotguns and two costumes of the kind worn by Czech peasants. The change of clothes was affected in no time, and the cart hidden under a bush.

It was not a moment too soon. In the distance, the sound of horns could already be heard.

That day, the Marquis de Lorgères heard several gunshots fired from cover while he was chasing a wild boar. One shot hissed past his ear, and so that he might be certain that he had not been the victim of an illusion, another bullet lodged itself in the material of his hunting-jacket.

But William and Bobby had said it: fortune was against them.

They were found and recognized, and had to show their pursuers a clean pair of heels. When they came to recover their hand-cart and their disguises, they found that the cache had been looted. The road of retreat was closed to them; they could not resume their roles in Szeged.

They spent the night in the woods, resolved to flee; their enterprise had failed. They knew that by the following day the news of their presence would spread throughout the land with lightning rapidity. As soon as they could, they had to put the Tisza between themselves and the crusade that their old misdeeds would launch against them.

"We'll come back later!" William said.

"There'll be a time when Lenore is alone in the castle," Bobby added.

Arriving at the edge of the forest, they saw shadows moving along the river-bank. They had presumed too much in thinking that they had a night to spare; the crusade had already taken up its arms.

They were two determined and tireless individuals, a small army in their own right. They were both fit and they knew the territory well. They conferred for a few minutes and decided to take on the hunt while darkness could provide cover for their flight. The choice of direction was vital; now that the Tisza crossing was closed to them, they could either retrace their steps towards Szeged, then push on towards Kolocza and the Danube, or go upstream to Czongrad, where there was a pontoon bridge.

They decided on the latter course and dived straight into the forest. The night was very dark, which was in their favor.

At two o'clock in the morning, they arrived at the Czongrad bridge, at the moment when the moon–which was in its last quarter–showed its pale and narrow crescent above the horizon.

While they were crossing the bridge unhindered, already congratulating themselves at this first success, they saw boats coming swiftly up the watercourse; at the same time, they heard the muffled sound of hoofbeats made by horses coming along the bank they had just quit.

Was it the Devil himself who had put their enemies on their track?

The moon illuminated them, and their path was discovered.

"Fire!" cried a voice, which came from the nearest boat. They realized immediately that it was old Baszin in person.

They ducked down just in time to avoid a volley of shots which passed over their heads.

The horses on the bank took to the gallop and their hooves were soon drumming on the planks of the bridge.

William and Bobby, desperately accelerating their pace, had reached the other bank. They threw themselves into the cornfields which covered the whole plain between the Tisza and Turkeve. There, they cowered like two partridges in a furrow, getting their breath back.

The cavalcade was already in the field and the cornstalks rattled, shaken by the passage of the horses. There was one moment when the two fugitives had pursuers to the right and left of them, in front of them and behind–but then the hunt passed by.

The foot of the rearmost horse touched William's head, but he stifled a gasp and kept silent. Its rider was Chrétien Baszin, Prince Jacobyi, who had disembarked on the bank and rejoined his galloping horsemen. "Form up in fours!" he cried to those who were ahead of him. "The wretches have made two attempts to assassinate my son-in-law! They shall not escape! Close ranks and beat thoroughly!"

The sounds gradually retreated into the northeast, in the direction of Turkeve. William and Bobby recovered and took a new course, this time heading towards Timisoara, whose wild landscape was almost certain to provide them with adequate shelter. But the horsemen were beating the fields in a zigzag fashion and from time to time our fugitives were obliged to turn aside from their path. Day broke when they were crossing a second river at a ford, below the town of Ghila, which was situated on an island. There was no further shelter thereafter but the tall cornfields of the Great Hungarian Plain.

They were tortured by fatigue, and it was necessary for them to cross a large open space, but chance had put some distance between themselves and the hunt for the time being.

"We must make the most of the last few minutes of darkness," William said. "One last effort!"

They hurled themselves forward, running in a straight line towards the cornfields. On attaining the edge of that ocean of verdure, they looked back in order to scan the ground they had covered. No one was in sight: the hunters had lost their trail. They ran on into the young cornstalks like stags plunging into a forest. After taking a few paces more, they threw themselves on the ground, utterly exhausted, pressing their burning faces to the fresh earth.

"I couldn't have taken another step to save my life!" said Bobby, in a choked voice.

William consulted his watch. "We've been on the run for eleven hours," he said, "and we've covered more than twenty leagues [68]."

"Do we have time to rest?"

"The sun's coming up. In broad daylight they'll soon pick up our trail."

"You're very calm," murmured Bobby.

"Because I'm certain that I can still save myself," William replied.

"How's that?"

"In ten minutes, we can be back in the graves!"

"The graves!" cried Bobby, leaping triumphantly to his feet, no longer feeling fatigued.

The day brightened and the hunters found their trail again. They followed the fresh tracks which cut across the fields of the Great Hungarian Plain at the gallop. They were certain now of their quarry. For the Chevalier Ténèbre and brother Ange, the vampire, to escape it would be necessary for the earth to open beneath them and swallow them!

The hunters went on and on, guided by their master, Prince Jacobyi. At a certain place, though, the tracks became confused, tangled like a ball of string–and then there was nothing.

The earth had indeed opened up and swallowed them. There was no doubt about it.

XIV. The Tall One and the Short One

September came again. One stormy day, the sun shone on the flat country to the east of Paris, near the confluence of the Marne and the Seine, where two or three more factory-chimneys were smoking.

A train of bundled wooden logs and barges laden with barrels drifted sadly down the river, bound for Bercy, as gloomy as a wine-cellar–but one which contained, in its casks and bottles, novels, sword-thrusts and vaudevilles, Regency rendezvous and songs in honor of the God of good souls, the poetry of the boudoir and the barrier, spirits of every quality, the laughter and smiles of old age for the young and of youth for the old, extravagances for everyone; in sum, all the joy–true and false, sincere and adulterated–which maintains for three hun-

---

[68] Eighty kilometers, or fifty miles.

dred and sixty days of every year the chronic folly of the Parisian Carnival! Jean Raisin, elder son of Suresnes, licensed inhabitant of Courtille, has dethroned Bacchus, who is too gentlemanly a god [69].

I once had a nightmare in which I saw Homer revived, with scarlet pimples on the end of his nose. I asked him for news of Achilles, Hector and Agamemnon; he replied that Bordeaux, Mâcon, Epernay, Beaune, Lunel, Cognac and Montpellier had disputed one day the honor of having shown him the light, and that he had written, between two barrelfuls, the twenty-four songs of the Berciad.

This is the repulsive underside of our century: this insulting odor of bad wine, mingled with the noxious fumes of poetic tobacco-smoke, which is all the rage.

When evening came, white dresses were again to be seen here and there on the lawns of the Conflans park beside the Seine, grouped as if in flower-beds. As on the day on which our story began, Archbishop de Quélen was holding a charitable soirée, and the exact parity of circumstance spares us the necessity of elaborate description. The scenery was the same and the guest-list was almost identical. The Bishop of Hermopolis, now as before, was to deliver a short speech, and the same singer—yes, the very same, although she had changed her name to Madame la Marquise Lenore de Lorgères—had been engaged to perform at the concert. She was there, as lovely as youth and happiness, under the wing of the Princess de Montfort, her mother-in-law.

You must certainly have seen, at some time in your life, some pretty little girl, excited by her love for some brand new doll. There is nothing offensive in the comparison; that is exactly how the Princess was in respect of her charming daughter-in-law—quite mad, in effect, with all the liveliness and joyousness that

---

[69] "Jean Raisin" can be translated as "John Grape"—an imaginary character of a lower social class, as well as a more urban disposition, than the Classical god of the Bacchanal. The Seine town of Bercy, as the first chapter of the story also pointed out, was the site of the warehouses where wood and wine bound for Paris was stored. Suresnes was the neighboring wine-producing region, formerly famed for its quality but notorious by the time at which Féval was writing for vintages so poor that the first (1872) edition of Larousse described them as "*très-laxatif et très-médiocre.*" The reference to Courtille has to be seen in the context of the previous sarcastic reference to a 360-day Carnival. (Properly speaking, of course, Carnival—derived from the Latin "farewell to meat"—refers to the last few days before the beginning of the Lenten fast, especially to the final *Mardi Gras*, or "fat Tuesday," when the last remaining meat-products had to be consumed.) One of the more remarkable and less salubrious manifestations of the Paris Carnival in the mid-19th century was the so-called "*descente de la Courtille*," a procession through that district of Paris, which was then notorious for its cabarets and dance halls.

kind of madness brings. She was ten years old again; she had a constant need to smile and caress. The pretty Madame de Maillé let slip at one point: "If that were not my aunt, who has the authority of a princess, I would say that her wheedling ways were in very bad taste." But that was unjust; it is always necessary that good taste should permit good humor.

At dusk, a few drops of rain put all the dresses, white or not, to flight. They took refuge in the hall, where the chairs were already set out for the concert.

It would have been impossible, given the place, the people and the similitude of the setting, to prevent memories resurfacing.

"I hope," said the Doctor, who was still enthusiastically prescribing affusions of cold water taken in warm baths, "that His Lordship the Bishop of Hermopolis will put the produce of his collection in a safe place this time."

"Oh!" the cry went up. "The brothers Ténèbre are not here this evening!"

I cannot deny that a slight shiver of apprehension was manifest here and there in the audience. More than one gaze turned involuntarily towards the entrance-door, beside which Baron von Altenheimer, with his long pale face, and Monsignor Benedict—one tall and one short, the oupire and the vampire—had installed themselves on that eventful night so long ago.

"I wonder what became of those two bold adventurers?" said the Bishop of Hermopolis.

Marquise Lenore turned pale.

"She had one of her migraines yesterday!" exclaimed the Princess. "Ask Gaston about that, when he comes, Your Lordship."

"Is the story so very terrible?" asked the Archbishop.

"Yes, it is very terrible... let it be... you'll make me ill!"

It was like throwing a cup of water on a raging fire. A hundred voices were raised—among which, to tell the truth, those of the two prelates were included.

"There's a story here!"

"Oh, Madame la Marquise, please! Do tell!"

Lenore smiled sadly. "Mother," she said to the Princess, "I can't refuse these women the finale of a drama in which they have played a role—but the denouement is horrible; I ask your permission to cut the story short."

"Not too short!" they implored. The word horrible is not nearly as intimidating as it is believed to be.

The charming Marquise de Lorgères collected herself for a moment, then began: "Did the person who took the name of Baron von Altenheimer, in relating the incident that caused the ruination of my father, happen to mention a young girl named Efflam, who was my friend and companion?"

"Yes indeed," came the reply from all sides. "Efflam, the young Magyar girl, whose parents lived at the Turkish border: one of the vampire's victims!"

"A poor angel who has her rightful place in Heaven," Lenore replied, in a melancholy tone. "Efflam's father left Petrovaradin after his daughter's death;

his wife did not survive her grief. He went to live in an isolated cabin in the middle of the Great Hungarian Plain. He was in great distress.

"He had heard tell of the two black graves that were sometimes occupied by the bodies of the Chevalier Ténèbre and his brother Ange, the vampire, who were forced to return at least once a year to their mortuary domicile. He had heard, too, that if it were possible to take them by surprise and burn their hearts with a red-hot iron, the world would be freed forever from those two monsters.

"He waited for his opportunity. He went out every morning to lift up the black marble slabs which covered the two graves..."

"So these two graves actually exist?" Archbishop de Quélen asked.

"Certainly," the Princess replied. "I saw them myself while I was there for the wedding... one great and one small, with the inscriptions you know."

"One day last April," Lenore went on, "during a hunting-party in the Chandor forest, two assassination attempts were made against the person of the Marquis de Lorgères, and that same evening my father was told that the brothers Ténèbre were in the vicinity. It is necessary to tell you, at the risk of diminishing the interest of the story somewhat, that the Chevalier Ténèbre is an old employee of the London police, and that his brother Ange, the vampire, came straight from Botany Bay, whence he had been transported as a common thief. The chevalier was named William Moore and the vampire Bob or Bobby Bobson. A few weeks after the adventure I want to relate to you, Szeged was full of police officers from London, following the trail of our two phantoms.

"My father put the whole household on horseback, arming the entire force, in order to search the area. The chase began as night was falling. At two o'clock in the morning, the fugitives were recognized, but they slipped out of sight until morning, when their tracks were found and followed. The trail led my father and his troop into the middle of the Great Hungarian Plain, more than twenty leagues from Chandor. There, it ended. One might have thought that the two fugitives had vanished into thin air. My father and his men returned to the castle on the following day, after a day of futile searching.

"That night, however, when our men had gone, David Kuntz, the father of my poor Efflam, went, as was his custom, to lift the marble tombstones.

"Under the first, he saw a sleeping man; under the second, another in the same state. He sharpened a plowshare in order that he might heat it up and plunge it, as was their due, into the hearts of the oupire and the vampire, but his courage failed him. Instead, he went to find huge and heavy rocks, which he deposited on the slabs of black marble in such a fashion that no human force would be able to disturb them again. Afterwards, he spent several days collecting bits of wood, dry vegetation and straw, an enormous quantity of which he piled up above and around the two graves.

"Each time that he returned, he heard voices coming from the ground, asking him for mercy, but he paid them no heed.

"The voices gradually became fainter. The one which came from the larger grave fell silent first, then the other faded in its turn. They had pleaded for twenty-eight hours each.

"The pile of combustible material was now as high as a two-story house. David Kuntz set it alight. It burned, and continued smoldering for three days. It took a further three days for the tombstones and the surrounding earth to cool down again. It was, in consequence, not until the seventh day after the fire that David Kuntz was able to take the rocks away and lift the marble tombstones. He found beneath them two human corpses—one tall and one short—which had kept their shape, but were now the color of charcoal. When he put out his hands to touch them, the two corpses fell into dust..."

"And since that moment," added the Princess, "you will understand that nothing more has been heard of the brothers Ténèbre."

As she finished, the prefect of police came in, followed by Gaston and his father-in-law, Prince Jacobyi. The Prince seemed anxious; Gaston's face had a mortal pallor.

"My Ladies," asked the prefect of police, "do you remember those two audacious bandits who robbed our *protégés* in the Holy Land, at this very same event last year?"

The question sounded so strange, after the tale told by Lenore, that it was met by a profound silence.

"Their exploits are following the same course," the prefect continued, in a light tone. "Here is a newspaper from The Hague, which tells of their latest tour de force. Anna Paulowna, the Princess Royal and Princess of Orange, was robbed of her diamonds in broad daylight, and in their place in the jewel-case was a visiting card: an old Flemish woodcut depicting two men, one tall and one short, the tall one wearing armor and the short one costumed as a priest. Under the former were the words Le Chevalier Ténèbre; under the latter Brother Ange, the Vampire..."

There was a protracted murmur in the hall, which covered the voice of Prince Jacobyi asking of his son-in-law: "Will you let me see that letter?"

Gaston, without replying, unfolded a piece of paper that he had crumpled in his hand. The Prince took it and read:

See you soon!

And by way of signature:

The tall one and the short one.

Léon Gozlan: *The Vampire of the Val-De-Grâce*

Le Vampire du Val-de-Grâce *by Léon Gozlan was originally published in book form in Paris by E. Dentu in 1861. It comprised one volume of a two-volume set collectively entitled* Le Faubourg mystérieux *[The Mysterious Neighborhood]. The set comprises a series of tales narrated by the same character, Monsieur Morel, an aged male nurse in a sanitarium in the Faubourg Saint-Denis.*

As Monsieur Morel observes in his preamble, one sometimes looks for the fantastic in the wrong place, and Le Vampire du Val-de-Grâce *is, in essence, a story about looking for the fantastic in the wrong place: the world of objective events rather than the world of the human imagination. The novel is primarily a horror story, but, like many feuilletons of the two distinct periods in which they were written—before and after the revolution of 1848 and the coup d'état of 1851—it also tries to be other things as else as well, in the hope of engaging all reading tastes.* Le Vampire du Val-de-Grâce *is also a love story, a mystery, a comedy and, at least marginally, a scientific romance. Perhaps, as a result, it is a trifle confused, but that very confusion is productive of more than mere eccentricity.* Le Vampire du Val-de-Grâce *is unique in its excess and its bizarre absurdity, and that gives it a certain precious verve as well as a certain capacity to make the jaw drop.*

Léon Gozlan (1803-1866) was a writer fond of occasional excess, who was not entirely a stranger to extreme experiences himself. In the brief memoir he wrote of Gozlan, Eugène de Mirecourt records the actual incident that Gozlan used as the launching-pad for the best and most bizarre of all his novels, Les Émotions de Polydore Marasquin *(1857; tr. as The Emotions of Polydore Marasquin, A Man Among the Monkeys and Monkey Island), which tells the story of a castaway on an island prolifically inhabited by dangerously intelligent apes. As a young man wanting to follow in his father's footsteps as a successful entrepreneur, Gozlan had charted a ship to take a cargo of champagne to the African colonies. The trouble that he ran into when the bottles had all been smashed in a violent storm and the ship had to make a forced landing on an unknown shore, was not as ludicrously bizarre as Polydore Marasquin's adventure among the apes, but it was fantastic and horrifying nevertheless, and nearly cost him his life—at least in the way that Gozlan told the story to his friends in Paris, when he had decided that the life of a writer was preferable to that of an adventurer.*

It is, of course, entirely possible that Gozlan's anecdotal account of being trapped by an African horde and having to fight his way out, using his rifle as a club, after failing to placate his captors by giving them all his gunpowder and bullets, was slightly exaggerated, as travelers' tales often are, but it was not as exaggerated as the second-hand versions of the tale that were peddled in Paris, growing as they spread. The rumor finally assumed such proportions that Gozlan was said to have murdered his ship's captain and turned pirate—and the true measure of the man is that, according to Mirecourt, when this suggestion was put to him, he simply shrugged his shoulders and pointed out that the story-teller had forgotten to add the necessary detail that, after having killed the captain, he had eaten him.

That was not the kind of additional detail that Gozlan was ever likely to overlook in his own works, as Le Vampire du Val-de-Grâce *eventually proves, in some style. Although no modern reader is likely to be unable to penetrate the mystery element of the novel's plot as soon as it is formulated, the point of the story is not the mere revelation of that solution, but the extra detail piled upon it in the climactic chapters, which do not hesitate to go over the top and keep on going, ever further into the wilderness of absurdity. Although the principal substance of the story is clearly descended from the* romans noirs *produced in France in imitation of German and English "Gothic novels" in the early decades of the century, it obviously belongs to a later and more sophisticated period, in which it had been generally realized that horror and farce are closely akin, and that there is considerable narrative currency to be gained from dancing on the thin tightrope that separates the two.*

Insofar as it makes use of the vampire folklore originally introduced to France in Dom Augustine Calmet's Dissertations sur les apparitions des anges, des démons et sur les revenants et vampires de Hongrie, de Bohème, de Moravie et Silesie *(1746; tr. as The Phantom World) and repopularized by the oft-reprinted* Infernaliana *(1822), incorrectly attributed to Charles Nodier,* Le Vampire du Val-de-Grâce, *belongs to the cynical and somewhat tongue-in-cheek tradition of Pierre-Alexis Ponson du Terrail's* La Baronne trépassée *(1853)[70] and Paul Féval's* Le Chevalier Ténèbre *(1860), which teasingly refuse explicitly to confirm or deny the real existence of vampires, but play extravagantly with the idea, while merrily exploiting the sinister fascination and appeal of anecdotes of that sort.*

Modern readers are, of course, thoroughly accustomed to horror-comedy of various shades of ambiguity, but in Gozlan's day such hybridization was still relatively new, and ripe for innovative literary exploitation. No matter how fantastic Le Vampire du Val-de-Grâce *ultimately becomes, however, it remains based on real terror and real experience; the one fate that all his characters somehow contrive to avoid—that of actually falling prey to the cholera epidemic that ravaged Paris in 1849—Gozlan suffered, and although he did not die of the disease (and managed to avoid the various crazy treatments that were then ap-*

---

[70] Published by Black Coat Press as *The Vampire and the Devil's Son* (ISBN 9781932983555).

plied in cases thought to be desperate), it scared him sufficiently to drive him out of Paris following his recovery, in order to seek temporary refuge in Brussels. There is an echo of that real terror in the construction of the novel's climax, just as there had been an echo of Gozlan's actual experience in Africa in his account of Polydore Marasquin's tribulations.

The manifest element of scientific romance in Le Vampire du Val-de-Grâce *is restrained, in that it refers not to a speculative discovery that might be made in the future, but to the rediscovery, albeit in a somewhat exaggerated form, of an invention supposedly made in the past. Modern readers might think the subject of embalming a rather odd choice for a speculative novel, but it must be remembered that our thorough familiarity with the practice is relatively new. Not only had the art not been mastered in 1861, but its potential still remained inestimable. If Dr. Kanali's hopes for his method seem exaggerated, it is worth considering the subsidiary use of the same theme in Hippolyte Mettais'* L'An 5865 *(1865)[71], which imagines a future society in which the practices of interment and cremation are regarded as repulsively primitive, and civilized societies use improved embalming techniques to keep all their dead permanently available for contemplation, after the fashion of Jeremy Bentham—and, at a later date, Lenin.*

In Dr. Kanali's view, in fact, competent embalming is merely a significant step on the road to resurrection, a long-term project in which he is playing the role of a modern alchemist rather than a physician—but that too seemed not entirely impossible in 1861, when alchemical dreams still had a certain currency, in aspiration as well as anecdote. That element of the plot is its clearest echo of the work of Honoré de Balzac, whom Gozlan had once served as secretary, and about whom he wrote three memoirs, most famously Balzac en pantoufles *(1856; tr. as* Balzac in Slippers*). It is arguable, however, that the more intriguing aspect of scientific romance in the novel is the attitude of its narrator and the story's construction as a psychological "case study."*

As is typical of feuilletons of the period, Le Vampire du Val-de-Grâce *is rather repetitive, in the interests of reminding readers forced to absorb the story over a period of weeks what has gone before, and—equally typically—was not revised for book publication in such a way as to remove repetitions unnecessary in that context. It helps to remember, in suffering such mild annoyances, that writers routinely made such serials up as they went along, never knowing whether they might suddenly receive orders to cut the story short or expand it indefinitely. They often indulged in blatant padding if they ran short of inspiration, but rarely did so quite as blatantly as Gozlan does the entirely gratuitous Montmartre-set passage in* Le Vampire du Val-de-Grâce, *into which he drops a short play that has nothing whatsoever to do with the plot. The play is not without an interest of its own, however, in terms of its somewhat avant-gardist meth-*

---

[71] Published by Black Coat Press as *The Year 5865* (ISBN 9781612271002).

od; it is, in effect, a radio play written three generations before there was any such thing as radio.

Like most 19th century writers, Gozlan began his career as a poet, arriving in Paris in 1828 from Marseilles with the manuscripts of his early verses. Like his peers, however—and with the assistance of his fellow-Marseillais Joseph Méry—he soon switched to journalism, which offered the only real hope of making a living from his pen at the time. Although he was fortunate enough to start more-or-less at the top, working for Le Figaro, and later the Revue de Paris, even that career proved difficult, and although he branched out into novels with some success in the 1840s, the work he did for Balzac at that time must have provided him with a useful steady supplement. Gozlan probably did not achieve any substantial financial security until he began writing plays in considerable quantities, eventually becoming one of the leading Parisian producers of dramas and comedies in the early days of the Second Empire—but that too must have had its tribulations, especially during the direly difficult years following the 1848 Revolution and Louis-Napoléon's coup.

Like Méry, but unlike many of his other literary friends and acquaintances, Gozlan was indifferent to the Revolution; Mirecourt records with some amazement that Gozlan never seemed unduly bitter about the fact that Louis-Philippe appeared to loathe him, and routinely struck his name off any list of candidates for honors offered for his approval, but that he was equally unmoved when wooed by Republicans. By virtue of being politically uncommitted, he was able to stay in Paris and keep working during the awkward interval of turmoil, but he must have had a difficult time; it is not entirely surprising, therefore, that he would take time out in 1861, while writing a novel set in 1849, to reminisce about the tribulations that men of his stripe had to endure even before he came down with cholera, nor that he should take the opportunity to publish a play that he would never have been able to put on the stage, in 1849, 1861, or any other phase of his career, because it was simply too eccentric. It would, at any rate, be a trifle inappropriate to hold the self-indulgence against him.

It is worth noting, too, that Gozlan's talent for the baroque stayed with him to the end, and beyond. He had regarded himself throughout his life as Jewish, like his highly successful father, and had been regarded as Jewish by everyone who knew him, but when his funeral was in the process of being conducted by a rabbi, one of his relatives on his mother's side appeared waving a certificate of Christian baptism, referring to a ceremony apparently carried out in his infancy—thus bringing the funeral to an abrupt halt and requiring a substitution of clergy and place of interment. Gozlan was in no position to laugh about it, but he would surely have appreciated the irony of having gone through his entire life without ever knowing that he was a Christian.

B.S.

I

One often looks for the fantastic in places where it is not, and one then forgets to ask where it arises naturally, like grass in the plains of sand on the shores of the sea. The staff of sanitaria knew that a long time before the somber Prussian Hoffmann and the American Edgar Poe, who both deserve, for so many reasons, a place of honor in those establishments designed for the treatment of mental aberrations.

Where else in the world, in fact, gathers together in the same place so many varieties of maniacs, lunatics, dreamers, neuralgics, bizarre individuals, madwomen and madmen?—and madwomen and madmen of all species and all nuances: men mad with pride; women mad with love; men mad with ambition? And by virtue of a special privilege, sanitaria, the true fatherland of the fantastic, have the beginning and the end of all the insanities in the world. It is there that they are placed when there is still some hope of a cure; it is there that they are taken when their cure is not complete; whereas hospitals specializing in madness, like Bicêtre and Charenton, only receive the mentally ill when they have, so to speak, lost their classification number in life, when they no longer count, when there is no more to do than treat them as things and not as intelligences.

There will only be question here of human eccentricities and singularities, but of rare and precious singularities, which it would be difficult to offer as fireside tales during the most exciting winter evenings. That vanity is perhaps permissible to me. I do not create my stories; I offer them as they come to me. I am not an author, but a simple historiographer.

We are at the beginning of the year 1849, a year with a very jaundiced complexion. Cholera and political anarchy held sway; Paris was not a very cheerful place to reside, in spite of the comedies that certain legislators enacted every day.

In that era, therefore, which will be characterized more clearly in the course of the story, we see the arrival in Paris, on a warm day in May—and May 1849 was a very hot month—a foreign family composed of a father, mother and young daughter. It was the Kanali family.

The mother had come to seek treatment for a nervous affliction, the daughter for a chlorosis; the father was in very good health, but it seemed natural that he should accompany his wife and daughter into an establishment in which they were going to follow a rather long course of treatment. All three of them were accommodated here.

It was a strange time they had chosen to come here! The epidemic was taking on an apparent development that was not at all reassuring, and was still far from reaching its end; on the contrary, it was soon to extend to redoubtable proportions. Why, under such a threat, did these foreigners come to an establishment like ours, which had been obliged to put more than five hundred beds at the disposal of the sick? Why come here when their situation permitted them to take refuge elsewhere, at less expense and without exposing them to the dangers of such a residence? Did our great city not offer safer places, if they were absolutely obliged to remain in it for some time?

Besides which, the mother's malady, and that of the daughter, did not seem to me to be very grave—not sufficiently difficult to require treatment here and nowhere else. Salubrious country air, in particular, would have hastened their recovery. Never, it might be mentioned in passing, had the countryside been more beautiful, richer, and more apt to attract those who did not have the liberty to go any further from the nucleus of the epidemic.

The choice of our establishment by the family Kanali was, therefore, a veritable enigma for me—an enigma all the more obscure because our new lodgers visibly enjoyed a genuine ease, a well-being that authorized them to live where they pleased. I was entitled to be astonished by that determination, on the part of a family in which I saw a mother very susceptible, by virtue of her highly-strung nerves, to contracting all imaginable illnesses, and a young woman of such rare beauty that it was, so to speak, a crime to expose her to the risks of a scourge that has no pity on anyone—but I was even more astonished, if that were possible, when I learned that the Kanali family, before coming to us, had been resident in the Hôpital du Val-de-Grâce, where the malady had claimed, and was still claiming, as many victims as it had during its first appearance in 1832. That was veritably astounding. What was wrong with that family, who could cohabit with such peril?

That requires explanation. I shall provide it.

Monsieur Fabricius Kanali, the head of the family of that name, had obtained authorization, on the official recommendation of the Austrian government, to study the nature of the epidemic in Paris. His temerity had that medical and philosophical goal. It would be better to say that it had that pretext—I will reveal in due course the real motive for which he exposed himself, as well as his family, to the afflictions of an almost-inevitable disease, by lodging with them in our midst.

Dr. Kanali was an unusual man, and I believe that he merits our taking the trouble to pause, in passing, in order to describe him, albeit briefly. He was then about fifty years of age, but it was very easy to mistake his age, so rosy-cheeked and youthful did he seem sometimes, and so supple and lithe in his movements. I say *sometimes* because Fabricius Kanali, whom we sometimes called Dr. Kanali, changed character and expression with inconceivable rapidity. Sometimes he appeared cheerful, amusing, sprightly, full of zest and passion, making witty quips; at other times he was reflective and grave, slow in his gaze and his speech. He went with tempestuous violence from aphorisms to puns to the most amazing cock-and-bull stories—and he often concluded a Greek or Latin citation with a pirouette on his heels or an entrechat. The professor would suddenly depart from repose to become a clown; quitting the armchair where he was holding forth to bound on to the table like a charlatan in a public square.

It was not easy to tell what country Monsieur Kanali came from; he had no accent—neither English pronunciation, nor German, much less that Italian that it would have seemed most natural for him to have.

He dressed with care, but, for a serious man charged with a very serious mission, he was a little too fond, in my opinion, of bright and sprightly colors, suggestive of a provincial actor. I saw him wear waistcoats with yellow and white stripes, pearl-gray trousers and cravats of every spring-like shade. Because of that frivolity of costume, I often called him Doctor Lindor.[72] He was not annoyed by that; on the contrary, he encouraged the joke by singing: "I'm Lindor, of common birth!" But when he finished the song, he always took a large golden snuff-box from his pocket, on which the portrait of an old white-bearded scholar—Galen or Hippocrates—was visible, and solemnly took a pinch.

At other times, stopping in the middle of a scientific conversation, after having taken a pinch of tobacco, he would close his snuff-box abruptly with his elbow, after the grotesque fashion of a second-rate comic, and sing: *I have good tobacco in my snuff-box.*

In the beginning, these extraordinarily dissimilar habits surprised me to the point of making me doubt our guest's sanity; later, having got used to them, I paid much less attention to them. Besides, those eccentricities were explained to me by the individual's past—or, rather, pasts. Like the earth that bore him, of which he was kneaded like everyone else, he revealed, by means of his prismatic humor and character, various epochs of transition; he bore within him the traces of his primitive terrain and those of his tertiary train. His life had been clownish and reflective, studious and powdered. The inconsistent and variegated man described himself in those terms. He was fundamentally excellent by nature, generous and sympathetic, doubtless well-to-do, but allowing golden coins of bounty to slip through his cracks.

Madame Bela Kanali, much younger than her husband, was not at all similar in character. She was a calm person, one of those women resigned to misfortune, thoughtful in temperament; to make her known at a stroke, she had one of those faces detached from a painting on wood by Memling or van Eyck, the master painters of saintly immobility, the great poets of ecstasy.

I shall now relate what happened during my first interview with the Kanalis, a few days after their installation in the sanitarium. Their domestic came to ask me to go up to the apartment they were occupying, at the western extremity of the large interior courtyard, in a corner of the building from which one could see the chestnut-trees and catalpas of several large gardens that have been entire-

---

[72] There are several characters named Lindor in French literature, including two eponymous ones, but this reference is presumably to the Lindor in Pierre Lemonnier's comic opera *Le Maître en droit* (1760).

ly destroyed since the last upheavals that occurred when the new boulevards were opened. The three windows of the drawing-room in which they spent part of the day and all their evenings were open.

It was more than gloomy in the room; the lamps had been extinguished, doubtless to permit the discreet light of the moon, whose rise was truly magnificent that evening, to illuminate the drawing room alone. The noises of the house hardly every reached it. At other times I would have regarded it as the most agreeable place to reside—as was the rest of the apartment—but the epoch in which we were living altered its value completely. The infirmary was located directly opposite, and invalids were already populating it in large numbers. That long gallery, with its sinister façade, its uniformly white curtains and these casements that, when open, always allowed the sight in the background of a bed, the head of a patient or a nurse, did not present a very enviable horizon to the people lodged opposite, especially in 1849, when dramas of dolor were being completed and renewed at every moment behind the curtains.

We had, in all honesty, warned the Kanalis about the inconveniences of the location. The heard of the family had received the information in a very singular fashion; I will ever say that there was almost a satisfaction in the tone with which he replied. I was so surprised that the thought occurred to me—yes, it went back that far—that perhaps he had expressly arranged an accommodation facing the large infirmary.

Mademoiselle Marthe Kanali did not express any opinion when she was informed as to the neighbors she would have. Only her mother seemed troubled; a forceful frisson rather through her limbs; she paled all the way to her hands; but when the alarm had passed, she manifested a metallic calm, as if fatality had passed that way.

When I went into the drawing-room, Monsieur Kanali, clad in a white dimity jacket, was lying on the divan in the Oriental style, savoring a cigar. Happiness had never favored his digestion so well. The smoke that he was blowing out in long silvery spirals from his lazy lips, having played momentarily in the moonlight diagonally designed by the heavens on the parquet, faded away into the air, flocculating in little waves above the head of his daughter, who was sitting next to the window.

Mademoiselle Marthe had abandoned on her knees the book that she had been reading while the daylight permitted it. A bitter melancholy immobilized her visage, three-quarters lit by the star of amorous sorrows—and those two melancholies seemed, in fact, to be confiding matters of amour and regret to one another.

Mademoiselle Marthe Kanali combined in her features, and fused with considerable charm and originality, Italian pride, German solidity and French grace. The last nuance, to make use of an expression derived from the vocabulary of painters, *chilled* the other two, and poeticized them with an adorable harmony. Her dark eyes lit up a solidly pale face with a Southern vivacity, emphasizing the origin of her mother's father, an Italian from Dalmatia, and that of her mother, a Hungarian. Fabricius Kanali had cast a varnish of French grace over the whole.

It was obviously the suffering of love that had paled that lovely face, and the chlorosis that had come to reinforce the dullness of her pallor was nothing more than the suffering of repressed amour.

Marthe Kanali had to be in love—very much in love. We, who study all maladies—of which we are, so to speak, the turnkeys—also divine that gentle and dangerous malady, but we can never cure it, and never do. Yes, Marthe was in love; everything proclaimed it on her behalf: her hair, negligently disposed about her head; her head, inclined in the luminous vapor in which she was plunged; her neck, leaning toward the profound infinity that attracts all passion, because all passion is a vertigo drawing sufferers toward the abyss; and her hands, slackly abandoned on her knees.

She resembled her mother a great deal, but as the dawn resembles the evening twilight; there is no greater analogy, and no greater difference.

Madame Kanali owed her expression to a youth with no resemblance to her daughter's; she had habituated her life to aspirations other than love; her languor came from the depths of the soul and not the temporary disturbances of the heart. It was a very long meditation that had shadowed that forehead with gray hair long before time. Only the face remained young; the head had lived more than the face, because her thought was three times as old as her body. That thought was not one of those that real life wearies and bends over: it had searched other worlds, and brought back many doubts and fears, particularities only learned with time. That is why I speak of it with such certainty in anticipation.

I do not claim to have divined anything; the characteristics I am describing were familiar to me long before the pen for depicting them in the corner of a page. I am limiting myself to introducing the reader who is following me into the astonishment into which I entered myself in those first moments of my meeting with the members of the Kanali family.

Above the armchair in which Madame Kanali was sitting perched a bird, of which she seemed very fond. The bird was an owl, with yellow and melancholy eyes and a white beak terminated by a black point. A strange choice, such a bird! From time to time, the owl opened its wrinkled eyelids, and then its eyes of fire, surrounded by black circles, were unmasked—and its immobile gaze, red and lugubrious, stared into the gloom.

"Monsieur Morel," Madame Kanali said to me, with an accent slightly tinted with Italian, but sometimes a little more guttural than Italian, "I called you in order to ask you what time the sanitarium closes."

"It never closes, Madame."

My reply brought a great and painful annoyance to Madame Kanali's face.

"What? Never!" said Monsieur Kanali, for his part, sitting up.

"Let's be clear," I added, rapidly. "What I mean by that is that its doors remain open to all those who present themselves, at whatever hour of the night—but the gates are locked at ten o'clock, nine in winter."

"Good!" said Madame Kanali, slightly more reassured, and looking at the sky, where the moon was still rising, larger and brighter.

"Good!" said Monsieur Kanali, in a much less solemn tone: that of a good bourgeois who does not disdain locks. He resumed smoking.

"And once the gates are locked, no one can get in?" Madame Kanali continued her enquiry.

"No, Madame; no one can any longer get in without ringing the bell."

"Nor without identifying himself?"

"Nor without identifying himself."

Madame Kanali went on: "And not everyone who wishes to can enter, even by making himself known? It depends, does it not, Monsieur?"

"Of course, Madame, of course it depends..."

Mademoiselle Marthe smiled constantly, with an air of sight disdain, at all these questions addressed with various degrees of dread by her parents.

Madame Kanali resumed her inquisition: "And the walls that surround the house—are they very high? The exterior walls, that is?"

"Oh, yes, Madame—very high, I assure you."

"That's good to know," murmured Madame Kanali.

"Very good to know," repeated Monsieur Kanali, checking to see whether his cigar had gone out.

"However," Madame Kanali continued, "from those big trees that I can see from here, someone could jump over the top of the wall, and introduce himself by that means..."

"Madame, those trees, which seem to you to be so close because it's dark, are in reality some distance away, and I assure you once again that no thief, no matter how bold, would dare..."

"Oh, it's not thieves we fear," Madame Kanali interjected, with the same slowness of speech, and while a fearful expression ran through her eyes, above which the owl, for several minutes had been opening and closing its own eyes with a sinister gravity.

"With regard to thieves," Monsieur Kanali repeated, in his turn, "we have indeed no anxieties. Madame Kanali is right."

And Monsieur Kanali, without changing his horizontal pose, emitted a burst of laughter, followed by another puff of tobacco-smoke, which filled the apartment, and in the midst of which nothing could any longer be seen but the two fiery roundels that indicated the location of the eyes of the nocturnal bird.

II

Well, what do they fear, then, I wondered, *if it isn't thieves?*

After a period of reflection, during which I thought I had guessed, I continued in a low voice, placing myself as much as possible between Monsieur and Madame Kanali, speaking to both of them: "I don't think that lovers are in the habit of climbing over walls to get close to those they love."

"No, Monsieur Morel!" interjected Madame Kanali again, putting her hand forcefully on my arm and without lowering her voice—a precaution that I had thought it appropriate to make for fear of being overheard by her daughter—"It's not thieves and lovers that are to be feared, in these times of terrible proof that we're going through, by the will of God." Then, as if the gesture completed her thought, she looked at the dark row of windows of the large infirmary, where so many lives were being snuffed out in the midst of that darkness, so beautiful and limpid outside.

"Oh, my word, yes!" said Monsieur Kanali. "It is indeed lovers that it's necessary to fear. But we're alert, and if ever..."

"Fabricius!" Madame Kanali went on, solemnly. "You know full well that it's not them that are to be feared."

After letting these last words fall from her lips, Madame Kanali ran to embrace her daughter; with a surge of affection, she hugged her to her heart, the muffled palpitations of which I could hear.

During that effusion, the owl, perhaps jealous of that evidence of affection, which was not for itself, gave voice to its usual cry—the cry that is so unpleasant to hear emerging by night from some ruined monument: *crou! crou! crou!*—and the double speckled tuft on its head ruffled noisily, with strange feathery frictions.

While surrounding her daughter with a maternal embrace and caresses, Madame Kanali did not stop gazing at the pale walls of the infirmary. Her fear settled on one place after another, as if on one lighted lamp to another, behind the curtains.

What connection is there, I asked myself during that scene of tenderness and alarm, *between the fearful dread of that mother for her child—a dread to which I no longer know what motive to attribute, since it does not involve thieves or lovers—and that gallery of the dying in front of us?*

Mademoiselle Marthe sometimes looked at her mother, with an interest mingled with an obscure anxiety, and sometimes at her father, with a sentiment imprinted with resolute determination.

I was definitely beginning to sense a species of malaise, verging on fear, on the part of the three individuals—I might say four individuals, for the night-owl certainly counted as one of them, so important was the place it occupied in the Kanali family.

My presence having become unnecessary once I had assured them, as I had been able to do, as to the security of the sanitarium, I judged it appropriate to withdraw.

I left the apartment.

Monsieur Kanali followed me out. He stopped me a few steps from the door, and said to me, in such a way as not to be overheard by his wife or daughter: "You're not used to having guests like us in your house, I'll wager."

"I confess," I replied, "that at first sight you don't much resemble..."

"We don't resemble anyone," Monsieur Kanali interjected, with a serious expression—but suddenly corrected that serious statement by clapping me on the shoulder in a familiar manner. "We don't resemble anyone," he went on, "although we haven't the slightest intention of being eccentric. In life, however, there are origins, situations and events that give individuals incredible appearances. Have you ever gone into a theater after the play has begun? Yes? Well, you've seen around you people who were laughing or weeping as they listened to the play, while you didn't understand a word of it, and you were tempted to say: 'But these people are crazy to laugh or be moved by these things that make no sense!' Well, the life of every family is a drama or a comedy in progress; you don't understand that drama or comedy because, my dear Monsieur, you've come in a long time after the curtain has gone up. Everything about us seems to you to be incoherent, monstrous and extravagant. How I would like to redeem you from your error! If I were to explain to you what you don't know...but for the moment, pay no attention, my dear Monsieur Morel, to the slightly bizarre things you just heard inside. Let's talk rationally for a moment."

"Gladly, doctor."

"Let's not bother with the 'doctor,' I beg you."

"As you wish."

"You see to me to be a jolly fellow."

That beginning was original. "At present," I replied, slightly surprised by the epithet, "jolly fellows are at risk of losing their jollity completely in a matter of hours."

"No, no," Monsieur Kanali continued. "You have a good face."

"What? A good face?"

"Yes—a face admirably made for the theater: shiny little eyes, full of fire..."

"Everyone has them, from time to time," I said, with a certain irritation. "The description seems rather odd to me."

"You have a nose like a gimlet."

"Monsieur!" I exclaimed.

"Don't get upset! Noses like gimlets are excellent, precious. They inspire gaiety, expansion, joy; one laughs even before the mouth such noses crown has spoken. Tiercelin, the great actor, had a nose like a gimlet; Rébard, who recently died, had a nose like a gimlet—the finest gimlet-like nose that every embellished a face. And not only do you have a nose like a gimlet, but, like them, one of superb perfection! You have a ridiculously pointed chin."

"Permit me…permit me, Monsieur; this description…"

"You could have played Sainville and Arnal roles with an assured superiority."

"Well!" I said, forced to take it as a joke. "Are you trying to persuade me to become an actor?"

"Oh, Monsieur Morel—acting! Do you know anything in the world more excellent than performance? What an art! What a profession! I don't put any above that of the actor. The public! The stage! The sound of the orchestra! The emotion of seeing people listening to you, applauding you, loving you! I've seen Potier, I've seen Brunet, I've seen Baptiste; I've followed them; I've studied them. Well, I'd rather be Brunet or Potier than…"[73]

He stopped. Had he been about to inform me, at the end of his surge of enthusiasm, that he too had once been an actor? He resumed, in a less personal tone: "Are the theaters of Paris flourishing at present? It's nearly twenty years since I left France, and I'm no longer up to date…"

"I rarely go to the theater; my occupations keep me away. But I can assure you nevertheless, without any fear of being mistaken, that they're not getting rich, placed as they are between the political crisis from which we haven't yet emerged, and the epidemic crisis that we've just entered."

"The Palais-Royal, for existence, such a popular theater in my day?"

"I've heard it said that it's playing to empty halls."

"The Varietés?"

"Closed."

"The Vaudeville?"

"Its last director is running a café."

"And the Gymnase?"

"No better off than the others."

"I saw them in their heyday!"

"You must have gone to them very frequently back then, to take such a sincere interest in their fortunes?"

Monsieur Kanali replied in a discreet fashion: "Oh, very frequently! Looking upwards, addressing a sigh to the heavens that must have gone up to the

---

[73] It is worth noting that the author uses the terms "*acteur*" and "*comédien*" as if they were synonymous, and that I have routinely translated the latter as "actor" because "comedian" has the wrong implication in English. All the actors whose names Kanali cites would have played dramatic roles as well as comic ones, but were all better known for the latter. The comparison that Kanali is drawing between famous *farceurs* he has known and Monsieur Morel thus offers a hint that perhaps Morel ought not to be taken as seriously, either as a psychologist or a narrator, as he wants to be.

topmost floor of the house, he added: "Oh, those were good times! Those were good times!"

I thought that I ought to respect the long silence with which he followed that expression of regret. Monsieur Kanali broke it abruptly with a question that had the effect on me of a cannon-shot fired next to one's ear when one least expects it.

"Can you tell me, Monsieur Morel," he asked, "where the gravediggers meet up after finishing work?"

I was nonplussed; I thought I had misunderstood the question.

He began again: "I'm asking you whether you know the location in Paris to which the gravediggers go to take their common meal."

This time, I had understood—but, because of the tone in which it had been asked and the subject about which we had just been talking, I took it as a joke, and only replied in a dilatory fashion: "I'll tell you later." And I started going downstairs.

Monsieur Kanali caught me up on the third step. "But I'm quite serious," he said, "in asking you that question."

What a diabolical man! I thought. *Why is he so keen to know where the gravediggers gather? What is this monstrous curiosity, this extravagant fantasy?*

"Do you have the intention of employing them on your own account?" I asked Monsieur Kanali.

"Perhaps, Monsieur Morel, perhaps—but not in the way that you mean."

"There aren't two ways of meaning it."

"Do you think so, Monsieur Morel?"

"For my part, I only know one. When one employs them, it's for..."

"Shush, Monsieur Morel, shush! Let's not darken the present; it's dark enough as it is. As for me..." Monsieur Kanali concluded by murmuring a refrain borrowed from Béranger: 'I'm alive, truly alive, very much alive!'[74] Come on, tell me where I can find the gentlemen in question. I have the greatest need and the greatest desire to see them."

I knew perfectly well where the 'gentlemen,' as Monsieur Kanali called them, gathered, but once again, still assuming that, in spite of his protestations, he was intent on joking and was making fun of me, I avoided his question, which remained devoid of any precise response.

You shall see, in due course, that he was not joking.

I confess, to the shame of my curiosity, that I was very keen to discover why the Kanali family had exchanged the pompous abode of the Val-de-Grâce—a veritable palace—for that of our sanitarium, a meager and bourgeois residence by comparison. There are princely apartments at the Val-de-Grâce, service worthy of a royal house, and an immense garden where one can stroll

---

[74] The line is from "Le Mort vivant" [The Living Corpse], one of many popular songs written by Pierre-Jean Béranger (1780-1857)

amid beautiful hornbeams trimmed in the fashion of those of Saint-Cloud, with view extending as far as they eye can reach in every direction. It passes like a bird in flight above the great city to soar, wings deployed, westwards over the woods of Meudon and Versailles, southwards over green and cheerful countryside.

What did that exchange, devoid of any plausible reason, hide? And take note that, in order to study the epidemic, Dr. Kanali had been much better placed at the Val-de-Grâce, where there were always two thousand invalids, than in our establishment, which was a long way from attaining that impressive figure.

It is probable that I would never have found out the reason that had caused him to preferred him to prefer one residence to the other had it not been for a hazard of circumstance, which I shall report.

A physician at the Val-de-Grâce, who had once been attached to the medical service of our establishment, came to pay us a visit one day. It was a good opportunity for me to satisfy my curiosity. The physician's name was Sainson.

I interrogated him, and my desire was satisfied beyond my expectations. Monsieur Sainson told me, in a low voice, that there had been "love and magic" in the motive that had obliged Dr. Kanali to leave the Val-de-Grâce suddenly one morning. Love and magic! That was more than enough to make an obscure medical orderly like me, unspoiled by the surprises of life, listen with all ears. Love and magic! I had never been to such a feast.

"Monsieur Kanali," Dr. Sainson told me, "with whose character you are now familiar, took care, on his arrival at the Val-de-Grâce—which was preceded by the finest recommendations from the great medical organizations of Vienna—to ingratiate himself with all the servants in the establishment. He's rich; he distributed little gifts in profusion and multiplied his largesse in all directions. The apartment in which he was lodged permitted him to receive guests, and he hosted dinners twice a week for his friends from outside, mostly consisting of foreign doctors who had come, like him, to study the epidemic, who were joined by the principal interns of the hospital.[75]

---

[75] In French texts of this period, the dash signaling the opening of direct speech is only placed at the beginning of the first paragraph of the speech, and there is no signal to mark the end of the speech-act. It is thus unclear whether Dr. Sainson is speaking verbatim during the next few pages, or whether what he has told Monsieur Morel is being reported indirectly and paraphrased. I have opted for the former representation until part-way through the next chapter, because the text periodically employs "*vous*" as if a listener were actually being addressed, until a point in the narration comes at which there seems to be an explicit reversion to indirect reportage. Further confusion is added by the fact that it is difficult to believe that Sainson could be party to much of the information that Morel supposedly obtains from him.

"These meetings offered all the more charm because the fear of contagion had broken all the established connections of intimacy with the outside world. That's the usual effect; people flee, isolating themselves, afraid of one another. If a few pleasant meeting-places remain, those who have the good fortune to be admitted to them and brought closer together, becoming equals, or more than that, and put into that party, which might at any moment be their last, everything precious that they have in their heart and mind, like a wager. That's why, at those perilous hours, imperishable friendships are formed between survivors, and alliances of souls more vivid than friendships. It has been observed that one never sees more marriages than in epochs that succeed great calamities of this sort.

"Among the guests at Dr. Fabricius Kanali's gatherings was a young intern who had been at the Val-de-Grâce for two years: an intelligent young man, carved like an Apollo: and like the Apollo of fable, he cultivated the arts in a superior manner—a good painter, a good musician, a good singer. His name was César Caseneuve. Caseneuve would have been perfect, save for one defect that I shall tell you about shortly—a very great defect, in his position.

"Mademoiselle Marthe had singled him out among all the external and internal French and foreign doctors admitted to her father's gatherings, and quite frankly, that passion was nothing very extraordinary, and nothing very criminal. She was eighteen, he was twenty-eight. Add to the attraction that young people of their ages exercise upon one another the privilege of being able to meet during this sad year of 1849.

"So, they fell in love, with all the affection that scarcely exists any more at the present moment. It was, so to speak, bequeathed to them by everything, to be shared by them alone. They subsequently recommenced the beautiful poem of love, which was born with the world and will only end with it. They went through that divine book by way of a strange and difficult path, on order, one could say, that it might seem more bitter and sweeter at the same time, and that each passage would be marked more memorably in the heart for having been traversed in the midst of dangers.

"Those dangers, for them, were Death in all its forms, since they lived in its domain. Unlike Boccaccio's young patricians and gracious Italian women during the plague in Florence, they did not have the egotistical joy of saying to one another: 'People are dying all around us, but we, life's fortunate privileged, are braving the danger behind several uncrossable rivers, and two or three dense forests, in the middle of a circle of flowers, birds, sunlight, bubbling springs, cool shade, salubrious perfumes and vivifying emanations.' No, they did not have the right to say that. Marthe and César Caseneuve loved one another with the abandon of the last hours, for each of those hours might, indeed, have been their last.

"You may judge for yourself whether the expression is exaggerated. In Dr. Kanali's study a kind of counter had been placed, which announced, by a chime, every death that occurred in the wards. Well, for merely two months, that sinister clock had been chiming every five minutes. The calculation is not difficult to make; nearly three hundred voids were produced every day at the Val-de-Grâce. Only great battles produce such a deficit, so frequently renewed.

"Monsieur Kanali, who had not failed to notice Caseneuve's liking for his daughter Marthe and his daughter's tender penchant for him, did not raise any obstacle to the mutual sympathy of the two young people. Far from it—he sought, on the contrary, to take every opportunity to make his home more agreeable to the young physician. He lavished attentions upon him based on a great cordiality—perhaps too great for the short time that they had known one another, although the doctor's expansive nature explains a great deal with respect to that excessive intimacy. The prospective father-in-law had already got under the slightly immature plumage of the friend of a matter of days.

"Madame Kanali put much less effort into attracting and retaining César, but without raising any opposition to the welcoming provisions her husband made in his regard. There was a conflict within her treatment of the young intern. It was, for instance, impossible for her to hide the suffering and apprehension that she felt when he arrived, when he came into the drawing-room—a painful impression that often extended as far as terror, and which sometimes obliged her to withdraw for a few minutes—but it was also rare for her, annoyed with herself for having behaved thus, not to seek thereafter, during dinner or the soirée, an opportunity to make the excellent young man forget the less-than-benevolent welcome.

"Unfortunately, it was always repeated. The next day and on the days that followed, there was the same terrible welcome, the same affable and cordial revisions. Is it necessary to conclude that Caseneuve reminded Madame Kanali of someone she abhorred, whom she dreaded, and that it was quite impossible for her to overcome the horror caused by that resemblance? That is what events will doubtless tell us."

III

"In the presence of these annoyances, to which he ended up no longer paying any attention, Caseneuve remained the most radiant lover on earth. The epidemic, which reduced the happy intern to rarely going out by day, and never by night, rendered his prison very gentle and very dear to him. For him, it would not have been merely the Val-de-Grâce, it would also have been the Val de Bonheur,[76] without the fault that I mentioned to you—a veritable imperfection, a

---

[76] The name of the famous hospital can be translated in various ways, including "vale of mercy" and "vale of redemption," either of which would lend them-

real defect in a young man destined, like him, to exercise the profession of medicine.

"That fault was that César had a terrible fear of catching the redoubtable disease that was running riot, the disease that he was responsible for treating in others: a limitless, bottomless, indescribable fear. That fear wounded him, alarmed him, and terrified him. It gave him cold sweats, shivers and cerebral deliria, almost continuously.

"The mere name of the Indian epidemic—the epidemic that was filling the wards under his surveillance—paralyzed him from head to toe. At every moment he thought he had been infected, mortally afflicted and doomed. The young man, who had fought with the energy of an old soldier during the month of June in the previous year, in the ranks of the valiant Garde Mobile, in the Place du Panthéon,[77] trembled like a leaf whenever it was necessary to approach the bed of an invalid.

"He had only stayed at the Val-de-Grâce when the epidemic erupted in its full violence because he had been forced to submit to that harsh obligation by a rich uncle on whom he depended. That uncle, a former army doctor, would not hear of his nephew being afraid of anything whatsoever. In spite of that, and even though César was due to be his heir, César would surely have ended up quitting his internship at the Val-de-Grâce and running away, if he had not made the acquaintance of Mademoiselle Marthe Kanali just when he was on the point of fleeing.

"When that love—a first love—penetrated the soul of César Caseneuve, although it had not exactly dispelled the fear, it had at least reduced the space that it occupied. There were even moments when he seemed to escape from the vertigo of that colossal fear—and God knows, the epidemic did not decrease around him! However, he waited with such great impatience for the night to return on which he was to go to Dr. Kanali's apartment that the days because less difficult to get through.

"As soon as the night arrived, he ran there, and beside the young and charming Martha his terrors were forgotten. There were card games or games of chess, there was music, there was conversation about sciences, travels and literature, there was laughter; in sum, there was much amusement in Marthe's father's

---

selves to this play of words, where it is contrasted with "vale of joy" or "vale of happiness." It is worth bearing in mind, however, both here and in respect of subsequent episodes, that a *coup-de-grâce* is a death-blow.

[77] During the June insurrection that followed the February Revolution in 1848, the Place du Panthéon, which was fortified with barricades by 1500 insurgents, was the site of one of the bloodiest battles, which took place on June 24. The Garde Mobile, a volunteer force hastily assembled by the new government to support the Garde Républicaine, assisted in that and other assaults.

drawing-rooms—except that every night, at a given time, the laughter, the joyful chatter and the music suddenly stopped; the wagons were arriving.

"The interruption took place regularly, at eleven o'clock. As you know, it's at that rather late hour that the wagons do their work."

Monsieur Sainson made use of a specific term that designates a particular kind of long vehicle. I don't know why I shouldn't make use of the same term—which is to say, the word *tapissière*.[78] The function of these tapissières was to collect from all the hospitals in Paris a certain number of victims struck and carried off during the day by the pitiless breath of the epidemic.

"When the tapissières had unloaded their burden," he continued, "those guests who were not on duty resumed the momentarily-interrupted thread of their distractions, and stayed until daylight drinking punch or tea, or playing various card games.

"It was also then that Dr. Kanali spread around the waves of his verve and gaiety. He had constructed a little puppet-theater, of which he was simultaneously the director and the cast. He placed his dolls on the tips of his fingers, the exceptional thinness and intelligent suppleness you've doubtless observed, and made them speak on the stage of his theater with all the comic loquacity and exaggerated buffoonery of the Italian clowns he had had the opportunity to see and study in Italy. Any subject would do; people suggested them to him, and he improvised scenes that were often excellent, imitating the accents and gestures of the ridiculous actors and actresses he had heard marvelously.

"I was much less surprised by all those eccentricities later, when I found out—we all knew, eventually—that Kanali had once been an actor, under the name of Belleville. He'd been part of a troupe of French actors in Italy."

"What!" I exclaimed. "Dr. Fabricius—Monsieur Kanali—was once..." Astonishment choked the end of my sentence in the back of my throat.

"He had been a comic actor in a traveling troupe," Dr. Sainson went on, "but I won't dwell on that detail because I'm in haste to arrive at what you're doubtless most eager to know—which is to say, by virtue of what fatality of love and magic he had been forced to leave the Val-de-Grâce, in order to take up residence with you.

"I'll tell you how it happened—but it's necessary for that to listen to the story of little Colombe.

"Every morning, at four o'clock—five in winter—little Colombe Val-de-Grâce brought to the hospital little loaves of milk-bread that the hungry interns—which is to say, all of them—awaited impatiently. Since Dr. Kanali's gatherings had begun, the young portress had not failed to be introduced, with her little basket on her shoulder, into the middle of the drawing-room, where she

---

[78] A literal translation of this term, which normally refers to upholstery, would make no sense in English, and there does not seem to be a readily-comprehensible alternative.

had the joy of setting down her burden. People broke the bread standing up and devoured the delicious little loaves, still perfumed with the savory warmth of the oven, while chatting.

"Colombe Val-de-Grâce was an extremely remarkable girl, for her beauty and the elegance of her stature, in the fashion of the svelte caryatids of Jean Goujon, the Greek of Paris. She spread a blessing of grace and perfection around her. It would be necessary to go back to Raphael's *Fornarina*[79] to find anything as charming, as delicate and as sweetly beautiful as Colombe. She would have merited another Raphael modeling another Fornarina upon her. The double miracle of art and beauty would have been complete. That second Raphael has not appeared.

"Colombe owed her pretty name to the hazard of her birth, which had not been announced to the world beneath the gilded paneling of the Louvre, nor the silk curtains of Versailles. One winter night, some frozen leather-workers who were passing through the Faubourg Saint-Jacques observed, huddled beneath the gate of the Val-de-Grâce, a woman who was writhing, groaning and suffering mightily. They asked the cause of her complaints, and a few minutes later they rang the bell, rudely, had the gate opened, and carried the young woman into one of the wards. They were just in time; at that very moment a pretty little girl came into the world—a poor child who would have been destined, but for the providential help that she received, to die of cold on the icy paving-stones of the street.

"They took care of the child, as well as the mother, but the latter astonished everyone when, three days later, she clandestinely quit her bed and disappeared, leaving the infant to whoever cared to take responsibility for her. As you can imagine, the child was not sent away; she stayed where she had arrived. As for the fugitive, no one paid any heed to her beyond the curiosity and surprise of such an observation; no one bothered to run after a mother who cared so little for her daughter.

"A few days later, the child of the street, the orphan of the gate, was baptized in the name of Colombe Val-de-Grâce, because her mother had identified herself as a birdseed-seller when she had been asked for information about herself. From the nourishment of birds, one leapt, by natural analogy, to the name of a bird, and settled on that of Colombe for the child's name. Nothing was simpler thereafter than to add to the winged name in question that of Val-de-Grâce, which constituted thereafter a family name—and what a family! Val-de-Grâce!

"The baptized Colombe Val-de-Grâce grew up as desired beneath her blonde hair, living in the hospital exactly as she would have lived in her father's house. She came and went as she pleased through the courtyards, the linen-room, the chapel, the corridors, the wards and the garden. At first she was like a

---

[79] *La Fornarina* means "female baker"—hence the connection with the baker's assistant Colombe [Dove].

little green and pink caterpillar dragging herself around in the sunlight, without yet having the strength to walk; then she was like a fluttering butterfly, appearing and disappearing everywhere instantaneously. That nobody's child became, over the years, everybody's child, adored by all. The nurses taught her to read, the interns to write and the consultants to dance. Her dancing did not always have a sacred character, or the purest correctness, but Colombe was never more graceful than when she danced and fluttered in the style of the popular dance-halls of the barrières. People allowed themselves to feel a veritable gaiety before the deliberate poses of that little five-year-old fairy. As I said, everyone adored her.

"Her happiness grew with her; on feast-days she was given either a little pink headscarf, or a pretty tarlatan dress, or coral earrings, or an embroidered Nancy collar. When she had made her first communion at the church of Saint-Étienne-du-Mont, the curé demanded, with sound common sense, that she adopt a profession outside the Val-de-Grâce, or that she be give a job to do within the establishment, the profession being much preferable than the employment.

"The advice was taken. Colombe Val-de-Grâce was placed with an honest baker in the Faubourg Saint-Jacques in the capacity of bread-portress—a rather vulgar profession, no doubt, but the one she chose among many others that would have suited her protectors better. She said that she liked walking, going up and down stairs, from one house to another, getting up early and carrying a bread-basket on her shoulder. It was a marvel reminiscent of the prettiest frescoes in Pompeii to see her set forth from her employer's shop on a winter morning, with her basket wedged proudly on her left shoulder, displaying her pink nose, her pretty teeth, like those of a young lioness, her blue eyes and her blonde hair, through the violet November fog and the vapor exhaled by her excellent milk-loaves. They were genuinely superior to those of all the other bakers in the neighborhood; they were praised everywhere, and she was much in vogue.

"The baker in whose service Colombe was, a clever man, took advantage of the porter's fashionability to add fashionability to his products. That added to their value, so he had made a great deal of money and renown by the time that Colombe Val-de-Grâce informed him, with all imaginable circumlocutions, that she was going to marry a young painter-and-decorator of the Maçons-Sorbonne quarter, and that, in consequence, she would soon cease to be his bread-portress.

"The marriage became the talk of the Faubourg Saint-Jacques, from the Rue de l'Abbé-de-l'Épée to the Rue des Bourguignons, and all the way to the Gobelins. Everyone offered the most sincere and generous good wishes to the seductive and every-virtuous little bread-portress, now arrived very sweetly at her sixteenth year.

"Everyone offered her good wishes for happiness, as I said—except for César Caseneuve. The motive for that abstention is that César had experienced a great commencement to love for Colombe, whom he had known and appreciated for three years, since he had become an intern at the Val-de-Grâce.[80] He had not made any declaration, however, not daring to unite himself by marriage to a person of such obscure and dubious birth. He had waited, and had let the opportunity pass, and in the end, what always happens had happened, the chance he had not taken was lost. It is not impossible that Colombe would have been glad to be his wife; I was assured in the quarter that she had not been indifferent to the intern's tender assiduity—but all that remained vague and indecisive on both sides.

"Things having taken a different turn, as the frank vulgar saying puts it, Colombe Val-de-Grace made another choice. Her marriage-plans made rapid progress. Until the last moment, however, faithful to the establishment that had always been such a good mother to her, she wanted to bring the little loaves to her protectors.

"For the last time, therefore, she went into the Val-de-Grâce, whose pretty name she was about to abandon forever with a joyful sadness, with her basket laden as usual, to make her morning visit to Monsieur Kanali's guests.

"I've told you what a cordial welcome always greeted her there; imagine how she was received, with marks of amity, this time tinged with regret, when she told Dr. Kanali and all his friends that it was her last day for brining the bread. She was surrounded and embraced, and showered with the warmest farewells.

"Madame Kanali took from her jewel-box a garnet brooch she had bought in Carlsbad, the stones of which were mounted with superior skill, and gave it to Colombe Val-de-Grâce. Not wishing to be outdone in generosity by her mother, Mademoiselle Marthe took two golden bracelets from her wrists, surmounted by two beautiful pear-shaped topazes, and offered them to the delightful little bride.

"The poor child could no longer breathe; she trembled and quivered, weeping with happiness and timidity, joy and confusion. The excess of emotion got the better of her; she was obliged to sit down on the divan.

"A few minutes' rest did not calm her disturbance; she was seen to grow pale, turn white, and then to complain of a great oppression in her stomach, and to look around her with cavernous astonishment. She began coughing: a harsh, dolorous, incessant coughing.

"What was wrong? My God! The whites of her eyes became blue-tinted; a great chill overtook her; soon, her teeth were chattering. But what was it?

---

[80] The author inserts a footnote here: "Monsieur Morel, the author of these memoirs, was therefore mistaken when he said the César Caseneuve's love for Mademoiselle Marthe Kanali was his first love." Actually, it was Sainson who said it, and then contradicted himself, so it would make more sense to credit the note to Morel. (Presumably it was too late simply to alter the earlier passage in the serial version of the story, which must already have gone to press.)

"'It's cholera,' said the celebrated Dr. Desroches to his colleagues, taking Colombe's hand in order to make sure that he was not mistaken. 'Yes it is,' he confirmed. 'She's doomed.'

"Colombe was immediately transported into one of the neighboring rooms; she already had, on her cheeks, her neck and her arms, which were as rigid and cold as ice, the well-known signs of decomposition. Four hours later, she was finished. The Indian demon had forced itself between her jaundiced arms and choked her. It was over. The Dove was dead.

"Turning toward César Caseneuve and pointing at the icy body of the poor little bread-portress, Dr. Kanali whispered in his ear: 'Finally, I have what I need!'

"Great God! What did such words—'I have what I need?'—signify in the presence of such a scene and such grief.

"Then the doctor added: 'It's six o'clock. Be in the same place this evening at eleven. I need you for a great operation.'"

Before recounting that great operation, we shall say something—or, rather, Dr. Sainson will once again tell us—about Madame Kanali, because Madame Kanali plays an important role in this story, to which it is now time to pay heed, in the general interest of the story, and which is strangely connected with what Dr. Kanali meant when he referred to "a great operation" in speaking to the astonished César Caseneuve.

Madame Kanali, Marthe's mother, was the daughter of the famous chemist Salomon Kanali, whose name she had kept when marrying a man who bore no resemblance at all to him. Salomon Kanali had been born in Dalmatia, and after having carried out successful studies of various kinds in the savant universities of Italy and Germany, he had obtained the chair of chemistry and natural history at the Archigymnasium of Presburg in Austria.

A man combining imagination and science, like the majority of Dalmatians, and having been appointed a professor in a land much given to exalted beliefs, he had devoted himself wholeheartedly to alchemy, that admirable distraction of great minds. He had even gone beyond the frontiers of alchemy, for he had not sought to make gold, but to do something much more extraordinary than the fabrication of that precious metal. Step by step, through the caverns of meditation and the calm of long nights of reading, he had pursued a much greater work, the most temeritous and formidable of all.

Convinced, like all the impious, although he was not impious himself, that the saints and prophets had only carried out resurrections with the aid of scientific methods unknown to the vulgar and carefully hidden from the crowd, he had tried to resuscitate the dead.

He even believed that the problem of resurrection had already been solved by a few scientists who were too wise to say anything, for fear of being burned as sorcerers. In his eyes, that miracle, since it was called a miracle, extraordinarily difficult as it might be, was not much more difficult to achieve than certain operations of chemistry that had similarly passed for monstrosities, sacrileges, and impossibilities before chemistry had resounding proved that wrong. He did not rank the problem of resurrection, as a difficulty to overcome, above the efforts of genius that Columbus had required to discover America or Newton to affirm gravitation—and he set out from there to immerse himself in the most ardent research, the most bizarre and boldest experiments and trials.

Was he mad, or merely deluded? Who can say? But Salomon Kanali thought he had succeeded in bringing back from oblivion, among others, a young man who had been dead for a moment. It was an unusual story, of which we shall find the trace and the echo in more than place in the life of his daughter, who not only shared with him that belief in the resurrection of humans by humans, but committed herself to beliefs more audacious still, if that is possible.

IV

Even if Salomon Kanali, the celebrated professor of the Archigymnasium of Presburg, never brought anyone back to life, it is certain that, while searching day and night for the means of brining about the phenomenon of resurrection, he obtained prodigious results—and, above all, prodigiously unexpected results. Thus, by submitting an individual who was no longer alive to a combination of chemical agents with whose properties he as experimenting for the first time, he encountered the secret of Ruysch, the famous Dutch anatomist.[81]

Ruysch's secret consisted of rendering to a subject completely protected from disorganization any age one desired, provided that the subject had reached it during life. Ruysch could render to the subject either the freshness of youth, the notable gravity of maturity, or the serenity of old age. What an advantage! How superior that method was to all the procedures known and practiced since the Egyptians!

He alone, therefore, Salomon Kanali, had recovered Ruysch's secret while trying to uncover God's.

"It is known that Ruysch," says the *Dictionary of Medical Sciences*, "possessed a means of conserving in our tissues, after life, the softness and the ma-

---

[81] The Dutch botanist and anatomist Frederik Ruysch (1638-1731), immortalized in Jan van Neck's famous painting of "The Anatomy Lesson of Dr. Frederik Ruysh" (1683) used a "*liquor balsamicum*," whose composition he refused to disclose, to preserve specimens; he was probably the first person to replace blood with an embalming fluid as a mean of preservation. He amassed a prodigious "cabinet of curiosities," which he sold to the Russian Tsar Peter the Great, along with his secret formula.

jority of the properties that are their attributes. When the Dutch anatomist sold his cabinet to Tsar Peter I, he gave him a manuscript at the same time in which he made known the composition of the preservative liquid of which he made use, and declared expressly, in that manuscript, that the liquid was thing other than spirit of wine, brewer's spirit, to which was added, during distillation, a handful of white pepper. It appears, however, that Ruysch had not given the true composition of his liquid. Afterwards, it was thought that his means of conservation had been found. Geoffroy,[82] in 1731, was commissioned to carry out experiments, but the results did not live up to the hopes that had been conceived."

Hazard, that other great inventor, who is not a native of Holland but of everywhere, having delivered Ruysch's secret to Salomon Kanali, the latter made marvelously fecund use of it for his renown and his fortune, although he always regretted in the depths of his soul not being able to devote all his time and all his celebrity to the work of resurrection that he was pursuing so ardently. Those who have seen bodies embalmed by his enchanted hands proclaim loudly that nothing but the soul is missing from those beautiful creations of his genius. The Egyptians, much too highly praised, profaned the most sacred parts of a human being, the heart and the brain, in order to conserve the less noble parts. The moderns, under the pretext of embalming, make a white man delivered to them into a veritable negro of the African coast, a being of pure jacaranda wood or true mahogany.

The glory of Salomon Kanali was no more sheltered from the bites of envy than that of other men. His enemies objected that his means of conservation, perhaps good in certain climatic conditions in ordinary circumstances, could not prevail against the venom of the Indian cholera, whose invasion was then threatening Hungary. He would never succeed, they said, in neutralizing the effects of the transcangenetic[83] scourge, the most rapid and most disruptive of all scourges, the most skillful at ravaging from top to bottom, in a matter of minutes, the sublime face that humans have received from their divine creator.

In every true scientist there is a hero; when it is not Pliny the Elder, devoured by Vesuvius, it is Pilastre de Rosier, falling from his balloon on the shore of the English Channel. Salomon Kanali accepted the challenge. He had only to wait for the epidemic, and he did not have to wait long. It ran with every wind that it encountered in its passage. The crisis of the decisive proof was getting closer by the hour.

---

[32] Claude-Joseph Geoffroy (1685-1752), often known as "Geoffroy the Younger" to distinguish him from his brother Étienne-François, who was also a chemist, although that sometimes led to confusion with his son Claude-Francois Geoffroy, who became known as "Claude Geoffroy the Younger"

[83] I have Anglicized the original text's *transcangénétique*, although I can find no trace of any such word in French or English; if it is a misprint, I cannot determine what the intended word might have been.

Unfortunately, just as he was about to respond to the accepted challenge, Salomon Kanali suffered a deplorable setback. Having learned one day from a peasant passing through the vicinity that a traveler had been murdered some distance from the city, on the edge of a forest known as Ulmenbaum, he immediately thought about his secret of recalling the dead to life. That idea, which never left him, distracted him from any other idea, and even from any fear of the senior clergy of Presburg, who had threatened him with the heaviest of thunderbolts, the most frightful of anathemas and the darkest of their cells if he did not resolutely renounce that abominable impiety.

When night fell, he headed by way of sinuous paths for the forest of Ulmenbaum, where he did indeed discover, by the edge of a pond, a man killed several hours before by bandits. He believed that he had not been seen. He embarked upon his work—work judged to be diabolical, and further complicated by the duration of a long dark night.

Had he been followed, having always been watched? Had his informant set a trap for him? In either case, he was surprised by a nocturnal patrol of the local police, at the very moment when he was plunging a steel blade into the wound of the murdered man, doubtless in order to introduce some chemical substance thereinto. He was captured. He was accused of being the murderer.

There was a criminal trial. In vain he cited his official position, his irreproachable morals. As he dared not admit to the law, for fear of making his position worse, that he had gone to find the body of the man in the forest not to kill him but, on the contrary, to bring him back to life, he was considered to be the true guilty party. He would go to the scaffold, nothing less. He was regarded as already doomed.

A few young people from noble families of Buda and Pest, however, who were former pupils of the doctor, succeeded by means of maneuvers and gold to get him out of prison and obtain a pardon. He made honorable amends, swore that he would no occupy himself any further with either resurrection or alchemy, and, in order to give a certain guarantee with regard to the regular existence into which he promised henceforth to enter, he got married.

He married a young woman from Agram, who had also had a rather extraordinary event in her life, which we shall relate.

Before marrying Dr. Salomon Kanali, the young woman had been due to marry the Graf von Markfeld. The Graf von Markfeld had already been married twice, both times to charming daughters of Agram, a Hungarian town renowned for the fine aristocratic beauty of its women. After two years of marriage they had died, both of languor, it was said; others sought a more precise cause for those sudden deaths, but did not find any. Beautiful as those women had been, however, they were far from equaling him in bodily and facial perfection. Without the strange whiteness of his face—a matt whiteness without any analogy to known pallors—he would have had no reason to fear any comparison with antique marble statues. One very peculiar thing was that, although he was marrying for the third time, one would have thought that he had not aged a year, or a month, since his first marriage. He looked to be between thirty and thirty-five years old.

In addition to these details, from which his self-regard had the right to draw some pride, he exhibited two others of an even more personal character. A red spot, of such a vivid red that it was easily mistaken for a drop of blood, always pearled in the left corner of his lip; many people contended that it really was a droplet of blood. In that case, it must have been impossible to staunch, for it was always visible in the same place, to which the Graf von Markfeld continually put the tip of one of his fingers, as if he wanted to efface it.

He was, therefore, going to marry the woman who was destined one day to become the first Madame Kanali, wife of the celebrated chemist, when his bride-to-be observed, at first with curiosity, then with a certain anxiety, and finally fearfully, that her fiancé only ever offered her his left hand, whether at a dance or out walking. That intrigued and troubled her all the more because she had also noticed that the Graf von Markfeld was not left-handed. At table or at play, he made use of his right hand. However cleverly the young woman attempted to take hold of the Graf's right hand, she never succeeded in doing so. The hand incessantly escaped her. That was the second of the two singularities that remained to be mentioned.

However, the period of betrothal had passed, and the day chosen for the celebration of the marriage at the metropolitan church of Saint Martin approached. It arrived, with all its pomp. Saint Martin's was illuminated, the organs were playing their most beautiful psalms in the odorous fog of incense. The wedding procession had entered the sanctuary. The young spouses were already under the dais. How astonished everyone was when, at the very foot of the nuptial altar, the husband, or the man who was about to receive that title, the Graf von Markfeld, instead of offering his right hand to his young bride, again presented his left to her!

It was too much; the bride could not stand it any longer; she swiveled round abruptly, and grabbed that right hand, which was still concealed.

Horror! It was as hard and cold as ice.

"Beware," said a voice to her at the same time—that of a woman she could not see. "Beware, Mademoiselle; you are about to marry a brucolaque; you are about to marry a dead man; you are about to marry the vampire Bem Strombold."

The bride—who, from that moment on, was no longer the bride—uttered a scream of terror that cut through the church from end to end, and fainted beneath the golden dais extended over her head. She was taken to her father's house.

The metropolitan church of Saint Martin, considered to have been soiled by the presence of the vampire, remained closed for forty days, at the end of which it was purified by holy water and the appropriate prayers.

As for Bem Strombold, with the aid of one of those pretexts that one always has in the wake of a failed marriage, he was challenged to a duel by one of the young woman's brothers a killed by a sword-thrust—but they did not take the precaution of burying him with a stake through his stomach: an omission for which they paid dear. The brucolaque came back among the living several times, and caused great misfortunes in local families. We shall see the proof of that frightful assertion later, in what happened to the daughter of the woman who, by a providential stroke of luck, had avoided becoming the wife of the vampire Bem Strombold, and married Dr. Salomon Kanali instead.

While living alone with her father, who had been widowed at an early age, that daughter, who was Marthe's mother, formed a character strongly mingled with penetration and reverie, profundity and mysticism. Her father, although he had promised, and although he had sworn, had not renounced either alchemy or his research on the resurrection of humans by humans.

Well, the eternal preoccupation with another world within that young head, which followed in its flight all the deviations of her father—an ideal, unknown, apocalyptic world in which she lived far more than in the real world—had gradually drawn her to believe, quite naturally, in supernatural things: firstly, to believe, with her father in resurrection by human means; and secondly, to believe in vampirism, because of her mother's history of being loved by and having come to the point of being married to the famous vampire Bem Strombold, and also because of her own history, she having being born, like her mother, in Hungary, the fatherland of redivivi, brucolaques and vampires.

It was among her father's pupils that she met the young Hermann von Rosenthal. How and why did they fall in love? That is a question to which one can only reply with another question: why should they not have fallen in love? Both young and both charming, they were only waiting for an opportunity to come together, and the opportunity came of its own accord. They saw one another three times a week at Dr. Salomon Kanali's lessons, and Dr. Salomon Kanali, like all imaginable fathers, only perceived that a young man adored his daughter, and was adored in his turn, on the day when he came to make an official request for her hand in marriage.

Although Herr von Rosenthal was not of the highest nobility of the kingdom, the aristocracy of gold, he belonged to a family sufficiently well-titled and rich enough to alarm the doctor, who had imagined a more modest position for his daughter. He gave his consent nevertheless, even though he would have preferred some honest scholar for a son-in-law, brilliant in physics and mathematics and capable of aiding him in his research.

Rosenthal was not much of a scholar himself; he much preferred hunting chamois in the mountains to assiduous work in the depths of a library. Moreover, he bore all the signs of his resolute temperament; he was a sturdy fellow, hewn in the heart of oak of all true Hungarian hunters. That firmness, however, did not go as far as making him very bold in the presence of the woman he had chosen as his future companion. Even in the presence of her father, he had never dared to kiss her hand.

His comrades were astonished by that reserve—a reserve so excessive that a few of them sought bizarre and impossible explanations for it. The doctor's daughter, however, saw it as nothing but an honesty of soul, on which she counted, and which made her love him more. For others, it was indifference, coldness toward Dr. Salomon Kanali's daughter. His only true love, they said, was the hunt.

Even he seemed to be trying to prove them right. He often absented himself for a fortnight in order to follow, breathlessly, some young lord's hunt through lakes, marshes and bogs.

His blue eyes, of a savage limpidity, open in the oval of his colorless face, gave him an exceptional expression in the midst of the familiar types of the Slavic race. He therefore lacked the vigor of complexion with which tradition leads us, habitually, to redden the faces of hunters. He did not have that. Like the Black Hunstman of the German ballad,[84] his skin was as uniform and white as if he had only ever pursued deer by the wan light of the moon.

That great passion for hunting was to prove fatal.

His marriage to the only daughter of Dr. Salomon Kanali was about to take place when, during a hunt on the shores of the Danube at the castle of Graf von Stork, he was killed while emerging from a thicket by one of his friends, who doubtless mistook him for a roebuck breaking cover.

His death struck the woman he was to have married a few days later in the heart. She fell from despair into resignation, and from resignation into a long melancholy in which her health faded away. She was visibly perishing, in spite of the care she received and all the curative means invented by her father—as expert a physician as he was a chemist—in order to halt that rapid consumption.

There was something peculiar about that state of languor, in which she was soon seen to melt like a candle in the heat of a fire, taking on a joyful serenity as she became increasingly thinner. She was transfigured; her eyes lit up, more vivid and sparkling; her cheeks blazed momentarily against their profound pallor; and she often leaned over as if to listen to someone talking to her. By contrast with other invalids, she waited for the return of darkness with and anxious and agitated impatience.

One day, when the wasting process had brought her to an extreme of weakness, she told her father, with a reluctant confidence, as if long suppressed, that she had a great desire to make him a confession and wanted him to do something for her. Encouraged very affectionately to speak, she then told Dr. Salomon Kanali that since the still-present and still-dolorous loss of Hermann

---

[84] The folk legend on which Carl Maria von Weber's opera *Der Freischütz* (1821) is based.

von Rosenthal, she saw the latter every night in a dream, and in the following manner:

The dark background of her room opened and was illuminated by a gray and vaporous light; then, at the extremity of a pathway prolonged into the far distance, she saw Hermann heading slowly toward her. He advanced silently to the side of the bed, and then, parting the curtains in the same silence, he leaned over her.

Although she was very glad to see him again, she felt a mortal, insurmountable terror on feeling his lips settle upon her. Sometimes they were applied to her arm, sometimes to her neck. They remained stuck to her flesh for a time she could not measure, she said, but which seemed to her to be very long. That mouth was icy, and all the time that it remained attached, she thought she could hear her blood falling, drop by drop, and leaving her.

"It's a dream, like all dreams," her father said. "To search it for a meaning would be folly." *All the more reason to expel it from her mind*, he added, privately, *if it gradually leads her to believe, like her mother, that she is the victim of the dogged and pitiless domination of a vampire—but such dreams are meaningless.*

Not entirely sharing her father's opinion that she was merely under the yoke of a dream, Marthe's future mother continued her confidence in a low voice, as she had begun it, although there was no one there to hear. She told Salomon Kanali what service it was she expected from his constant and benevolent affection. Since his enlightenment, he claimed, had led him to communicate a second existence to those who had lost it, it ought to be much easier for him to render it to one who had only partly lost it, like Hermann. The young man was only partly lost, one could say, because he returned every night and only disappeared at daybreak, at cock-crow.

Although he cherished his daughter, Dr. Salomon Kanali was painfully affected on learning the kind of service she expected of him. It was only by a miracle, it will be remembered, that he had escaped the rigors of the law for having attempted the resurrection of a murdered traveler. To expose himself again…nothing would save him if he were caught. However, paternal affection overcame the dread. He promised to make the most violent and reckless efforts of science to grant his daughter's wish. He began work immediately, and his daughter began to hope.

Before attempting anything against oblivion, it was necessary to assure himself of the state of conservation of his former pupil in the monument that had been erected for him by his comrades. The night for that preliminary inspection was chosen.

Having left the town very late, and alone, after several quarters of an hour walking across country, Dr. Salomon Kanali reached the desired spot. No spy had followed him. With the aid of an iron bar that he had brought, he loosened one of the marble slabs that formed the base of the monument and went down several steps. Having arrived at the last one, he lit a torch; the vault was illuminated.

To his great astonishment, the cavity was empty—utterly empty! There was no one there!

V

Its inhabitant had gone. There was no longer anything there but the branch of box-wood that he had held between his interlaced fingers—for all eternity, it had been thought.

It was certainly here, though, Dr. Salomon Kanali said to himself, with a mental surprise equal to the most formidable fear, *that Herr von Rosenthal was deposited*. He had seen him deposited with his own eyes. To what could such a phenomenon be attributed?

Pensive, his features distraught, he went home, and in the morning he hastened to tell his daughter everything. She was momentarily struck by the same amazement, but, preferring to think that her father was mistaken to admitting that her Hermann was not resting a few leagues away from her, and going further still, in suspecting that her father, for fear of compromising himself once again with the magistrates, had made use of the pretext he had given for not undertaking his task, she pretended to accept his story—or rather, in her view, his lie—and went herself in the morning to the place where her Hermann was sleeping peacefully beneath the trees.

There she searched for the stone that her father said that he had loosened, sure that it would not be there. The stone had been detached from the others that retained it!

Courageously, she went down the steps, into the crypt. She looked...

Her Hermann was still there. His beautiful hands were still crossed over his bosom, and between them was the branch of blessed box-wood that she had placed there three months ago, when she had been taken into that calm, cold vault.

After a fervent prayer, she went back up to the ground, went home, and said to her father, with the bitter discontentment of a heart brushed by a lie, that he had deceived her. Herr von Rosenthal had not budged. She had seen him; she had just seen him.

Convinced that he would have fulfilled his promise to his daughter, although it would have cost his scruples dearly, which he had confessed to her without hesitation, Monsieur Kanali swore on the Bible that he had not deceived her, and, to prove his veracity, offered to return with her to the same place the following night. He believed with all his heart that he could demonstrate, his daughter being with him, that he had not made an error in his expedition.

287

His daughter accepted. They went out of the city gate by night, went into the country, and arrived silently at the designated spot.

Before going down, Monsieur Kanali lit a torch—something that he had only done the first time when he had descended into the interior, but which he did in advance this time, for fear that his daughter might slip on the steps. They both went into the vault thereafter.

They did not stay for long. A few moments later, the father and daughter reappeared, terrified, trembling and white-faced, as if they themselves had been pale inhabitants of the subterranean dwelling from which they were escaping.

Why that terror? Because the tomb was empty.

Their double terror is self-explanatory, if one has followed the events that preceded it. A man appears every night to the doctor's daughter; he is not found during the night in his tomb. She finds him there by day. The following night, neither of them find him. There is, therefore, no longer any doubt: Hermann too is a vampire, a vampire like Bem Strombold. He is the same vampire, who is attacking the daughter as he attacked the other twenty years earlier, and who, instead of having the icy hand that he had twenty years ago, now has icy lips.

To complete the unfortunate annoyances, the light of the torch lit in the open air by Dr. Kanali attracted attention, betraying his presence, and that of his daughter, at a superstitious hour of the night and in a very suspicious location. They had been seen, recognized and denounced; they only just had time to escape. Rapid horses transported them over the Julian Alps. They took refuge in Italy.

For the doctor, accustomed to the studious and calm life of the lamp, such a displacement was a dire revolution in his life. Thus, after a few years of bitterness and incurable discouragement, he died in Zara, his birthplace. Science lost a star. It was to his daughter that he left his numerous manuscripts, including his great *Treatise on Resurrection*, which contained a supplementary account of the conversation of bodies by the rediscovered method of the celebrated Dutch anatomist Ruysch.

A year after the doctor's death, a victim of his genius and his paternal devotion, his daughter, in order not to succumb herself beneath the weight of so many various ordeals, summoned up a few distractions, in response to the solicitations of her friends. Among those that she created, there was one whose consequences were most unexpected.

A troupe of French actors, chased from town to town by their unlucky star, had come to give a few performances. There, as elsewhere, they collected nothing but poverty. Touched by the plight of those poor people, the ladies of the town opened a subscription on their behalf, and at the head of that good work, to manage it, they set the daughter of the late Dr. Salomon Kanali. For that reason, she made the acquaintance of the director of the wayward and disorganized troupe.

That director, an actor himself, was an intelligent young man, full of fire and very personable. He was called Belleville, although that might not have been his real name. Perhaps he had performed in Belleville, a locality on the outskirts of Paris, and owed his topographical name thereto. Belleville and Mademoiselle Kanali thus found themselves connected. They met frequently, and felt disposed to love one another.

One day, Belleville dared to propose himself as a potential husband; the offer was not judged too bold. The doctor's daughter, free to dispose of her hand and her fortune, accepted. She consented to become the wife of the actor, but on the express condition that, on becoming her husband, he would take the name of Kanali, a tribute that she thought she owed to the memory of her father, the illustrious Salomon Kanali. The marriage took place.

In the leisure of his new position, Kanali, the second of that name, began one day to read the manuscripts left by his father-in-law, and it was in consequence of that reading that the idea occurred to him of profiting on his own account from some of the great discoveries mentioned therein. That of embalming seemed to him to be the least problematic; he settled on that, studied it in depth, and got to the bottom of it. He remained convinced that his fortune was there—or, rather, the indefinite increase of his fortune, for he had entered into possession of a considerable income by marrying the daughter of the celebrated chemist.

Many years after his marriage to her—about eighteen years—the Indian epidemic having revealed itself for the third or fourth time in Europe, it then being 1849, he thought seriously about exploiting he admirable method of conservation of bodies developed by his father-in-law. However, he avoided with the greatest care putting it into practice either in Hungary, where he dreaded meeting the same fate as Salomon Kanali, or in Italy, where it was no less dangerous.

All liberty loves France. He therefore came to Paris in 1849, in the epoch of the reappearance of the Asiatic scourge in that capital, and he went, as has been reported at the beginning of this story, to take up residence in the Val-de-Grâce with his wife and daughter, the young Marthe Kanali.

An account has also been rendered of the lavish and distinguished manner, thanks to letters of recommendation from Austria, doubtless obtained by his wife's credit, in which he was welcomed among us. He was treated as a colleague, and he merited that favor, for during twenty years of residence in Dalmatia, Italy and Austria, he had applied himself to the study of medicine and the serious sciences connected therewith—but without ever losing entirely, in contact with that elevated endeavor, either the enjoyment or the blithe philosophical insouciance of his original profession as an actor. He loved that profession in the depths of his heart, although he was not gratified when people talked to him about it without some precaution, out of respect for the gravity of his new position.

Kanali, who was counting a great deal, as we have just explained, one the advantages that he anticipated receiving from posthumous embalmings and rejuvenations, had thus only entered the Val-de-Grâce with the hidden but unique objective of carrying out experiments on bodies damaged by the afflictions of the devastating scourge.

Installed in his apartment, he occupied himself relentlessly with his project. He needed, above all, an intelligent, special, discreet, zealous and devoted assistant who belonged to the establishment, who could procure him bodies and make them available for his experiments. César Caseneuve seemed to him to fit the bill marvelously. By degrees, therefore, he attracted the young man to his home, encouraged his assiduities with regard to his daughter, and when he was sure of holding him by means of the love that Marthe had inspired in him, he judged the moment favorable for making him his accomplice—and, of course, associating him with his glory and fortune.

After the indispensable voyage that we have just made with our reader through the past of our characters, let us now return to the point at which we deviated—which is to say, to the rendezvous arranged by Dr. Kanali with César Caseneuve beside the bed of Colombe Val-de-Grâce, struck down in a matter of hours by the epidemic. They were to meet, it will be remembered, at eleven o'clock.

They did indeed meet at the indicated hour, which was the most convenient time for the endeavor meditated for a long time by the doctor. People were coming and going in the wards; the physicians, interns, consultants and service staff were crossing one another's paths in all directions in order to get everything done, and they were scarcely sufficient for the formidable demands of that difficult moment, when the patients from outside came in quantity and in disorder to take the still-warm places of those who had died and would be taken away by the long wagons that have been mentioned.

In response to a few words whispered by the doctor in the still-bewildered ear of César Caseneuve, the latter swiftly rolled up the delicate and charming body of Colombe Val-de-Grâce in her bedclothes and put it over his shoulder. No one on the ward paid any attention to that movement, and, if they had noticed it, would never have guessed the objective with which it was executed.

Preceded by the doctor, César, who still had no precise idea of the project with which Kanali was associating him, silently went down the steps leading from the ward in which Colombe had been deposited to the garden, and with the same contained discretion, they continued their nocturnal expedition, with a muffled tread, on the mute sand of the paths through the dormant hornbeams.

After a certain distance, César, perceiving with astonishment the direction in which the doctor was heading, stopped and turned toward him.

"But doctor," he said, "one would think that we were going to my lodgings."

"Of course—that is where we're going. Walk."

"But why? Why are we going there?"

"You'll soon find out. Keep walking."

"But..."

"Just keep walking," repeated the doctor, in the tone of a man who has no time to waste on the meager pleasures of argument.

César Caseneuve continued walking behind the doctor, but he experienced an anxiety that did not quit him as he felt the light and gentle body of little Colombe swaying gently and trembling on his shoulder: Colombe Val-de-Grâce, his first love; a love undoubtedly replaced, but not effaced; a rosy love that had appeared momentarily in the pale and monotonous sky of his early student days spent in the depths of the Saint-Jacques quarter—the quarter of poverty, science, resignation and love.

The sweat that streamed in an inexhaustible flood from his forehead, as if he were walking in bright sunlight—the night, it is true, was as hot as midday— added to the anxiety, the uncertainty and the unknown of such a situation in the midst of silence. Add to that, too, César's incurable fear of the yellow invasion and you will have some idea of the mental state of his tormented being. Half past eleven having chimed on the little clock in the lofty dome, he was gripped, as that drop of iron fell upon him, by such a sudden nervous tremor that he almost dropped his burden before they arrived at the building.

A few words about that isolated building, lost at the extremity of the garden, adjacent to the wall of the long Rue des Charbonniers: it had been ceded to Caseneuve; he had been relegated to it when his room was taken over to increase the space available for the invalids who had become too numerous. Now, let us explain the intention with which the doctor had thought it appropriate to put into action when he had exclaimed, beside the dying Colombe: "Finally, I have what I need."

What he needed her for was his experiment in embalming. To carry it out, he not only needed to procure a body, although that presented enough significant difficulties, but also, and above all, a distraction that would win him some notoriety in the quarter, and the city, in order that everyone, seeing the features of the individual seemingly recalled to life and beauty, would exclaim: "It's her! It really is! It's marvelous! It's a prodigy! She's smiling at us! She's going to speak!" Renown, fame and fortune were there, infallibly there, for previous so-called embalming processes, as Kanali and many others had said, were nothing but a ridiculous and hideous masquerade, to the profit of mahogany and ebony. Only the ebonists were able to guarantee a resemblance.

Let us continue. Once a body marked in the neighborhood by that indispensable notoriety had been found, it was still necessary to ensure a place where the experiment could be carried out without being seen by anyone; that was a condition of the greatest importance. Senior physicians and administrators do not readily lend themselves to the temerities of innovators. But what place could be chosen for the successful completion of the operation of which Kanali had dreamed for so many years and was finally about to attempt? It was not easy to find a house with the facilities, the space and the isolation necessary for the operation. Kanali thought of César's pavilion.

We could now describe the whole of that important operation, but are not indicate exactly the various chemical elements that entered into the savant composition employed by the doctor, following his illustrious father-in-law.

It has been supposed that Ruysch, whose secret Kanali possessed, put into that composition, in strictly calculated proportions, myrrh, aloes, cardamom, rosemary, styrax, benzoin, cypress, mace, imperatoire, tacamahaca, cassia lignea, germander, spikenard, oregano and enula campana, but Salomon Kanali dissolved these mostly-oriental products in a liquid that was neither spirit-of-wine nor brewer's spirit, as the Dutch anatomist had indicated in his memoir to Peter the Great, in order to deceive posterity. It was another liquid, and the composition of that other liquid—the one that Ruysch had not consented to reveal—Fabricius Kanali, the son-in-law of the great Kanali, knew, protecting it under three impenetrable seals.

He was ready to make use of it that night: that night full of feverish and nameless anxieties for César Caseneuve.

Although we shall not divulge Kanali's secret here, we can at least reveal the result that he expected, with a certainty guaranteed by abundant probabilities already obtained.

Of all embalming processes, the most complete, in Kanali's view, was the one called, in specialist treatises, "the embalming of the mummy of the sands"—which is to say, the conservation procured by the sands of the desert, a conservation due to the dryness with which those privileged sands grip bodies. Now add to that dryness produced by the sun the gleam of rediscovered color and you will have conquered both the eternity of duration and the eternity of youth and beauty.

"In the countries of Africa situated beyond the Nile," says Père Kircher,[85] "is a desert of sand whose immense waves appear in a limitless horizon similar to those of the sea. Stirred by the wind, these sands produce such frightful tempests that they bury travelers, beasts of burden and merchandise beneath their enormous mass. The bodies thus buried are desiccated after long years by the ardor of the sun's rays and the virtue of the burning sand. They are desiccated to the point of becoming as light as if they were made of straw."

---

[85] Athanasius Kircher (c.1601-1680), best known for his studies in Egyptology and geology, was also an early microscopist, who hypothesized in consequence a version of the germ theory of disease, with specific reference to the plague, and suggested corollary methods of preventing infection, but he failed to convince his contemporaries.

But what Père Kircher also says is that bodies thus calcinated become as black as Ethiopians—a disadvantage that cancels out all the benefits of the desiccation.

The new and admirable aspect of the sublime discovery of the great Salomon Kanali is, therefore, that one obtains by that means the incorruptibility produced by the sun and the desert sand, without deterioration of the tissues—on the contrary, while retaining its original paleness and coloration. Now comes the astonishing part of the discovery.

Understandably, not having the centuries to come and the sands of Africa at his disposal, it was necessary for the inventor to substitute chemical agents for them. They were substituted. It was necessary to pass the body through a rapid current of flames. That was not a slow combustion but a simple ballast of fire, rapid, radiant and overwhelming, which, by opening the pores, permitted the substance created by the great Kanali to fill and color the veins and the entire mucous network, the source of human coloration. That operation thus summarized and concentrated within itself, admirably, the effects of time and heat, the sunlight of several centuries.

Once they had arrived at the pavilion, where the doctor, having procured the key, had prepared everything necessary for the experiment, he and César went in. Kanali immediately locked the door and the windows and drew the curtains.

VI

César then deposited Colombe on a large, perfectly-horizontal sheet of burnished metal. When she was laid out on the plate in question, the doctor picked up a brass vase full of the special composition from a corner and spread it over Colombe's face, breast, arms and legs, which were already coal-black by virtue of the well-known effect of disorganization that arrives instantaneously in the wake of the infernal malady by which she had been struck. After handing the brass vase to César, he occupied himself with anointing the young woman's body with the liquid, initially deposited in patches.

When that was done, he set fire to the edges of the liquid at the extremities of the feet and the top of the head, in order that, in meeting up, the two flames would envelop the entire body.

Immediately, the blaze occurred in the anticipated conditions, and immediately, Colombe's youth, her complexion, rosy flesh and frank ingenuous smile— all of her, in sum—appeared and blossomed in the dazzle of that magical light.

It was a complete success. The process had produced the consequences of which the doctor had dreamed for so long with such pride—for the entire quarter would testify the following day, on seeing Colombe resuscitated in youth and beauty, to Dr. Kanali's victory over oblivion.

César ruined everything. Delighted to the point of fear by the spectacle displayed before him, and doubtless also emotional at seeing the child almost alive once again whom he had carried to his lodgings in a condition so far from life, lost his head. He became disturbed, and with a nervous movement that it is not difficult to understand, he brought the liquid that he was holding in his trembling right hand—a liquid more flammable than gunpowder—too close to the lamp that he was carrying in his right hand, and the entire pavilion went up in flames.

Never had a more violent blaze burst out in such a restricted space. The pavilion, saturated with gas to the ceiling, cracked and split; the roof was blown into the air, while part of the walls collapsed with a detonation similar to that of a mine-explosion.

The deflagration was followed by a broad and continuous jet of flames, which rose straight up to the level of the cupola of the Val-de-Grâce, lighting up the smallest architectural details for all the people of the faubourg, easily woken up by that enormous noise and immense glare. It was all the easier because in that epoch, in 1849, people were prompt to pay attention to anything, and to be irritated by anything, seeing hostile intentions in the slightest incident. Suppositions were therefore ignited in the four corners of the vast quarter, and made rapid progress.

"That's coming from the Val-de-Grâce," was murmured on the streets and crossroads, from one back alley to the next. "What's happening there?"

"What's happening is that they're burning the sick," said someone who had already looked over the wall and into the blazing crater of the pavilion."

"That's it—they're burning the sick, to be more quickly rid of the embarrassment they're causing."

That malevolent, venomous, deadly rumor ran around, and grew as it propagated. It soon became a cry, general howl; "They're burning the sick! They're burning the sick!"

An angry group joined the malevolent group; it became a mob; it became a tempest; the garden wall in the Rue des Charbonniers was scaled and the boldest went in. Guided by the flames, they reached Caseneuve's pavilion.

What a spectacle! Their rage no longer knew any bounds; they had perceived in the midst of the diabolical fire the body of a young woman, half-burned—a young woman they recognized: the love, the grace, the joy, the delight and the idol of the quarter: Colombe Val-de-Grâce, devoured by the flames. They had not even known that she was ill! The least they wanted was to massacre Caseneuve and Dr. Kanali, to burn them on the pyre to which it was impossible for them to attach any significance at all, except that of the commission of an abominable crime.

Fortunately for the two individuals, so close to being thrown on to the fire, the staff of the establishment came to their rescue. The police followed. In sum, they were saved.

The mob was told that the fire had been started by accident in César Caseneuve's lodgings while he was busy studying the character of the malady that had afflicted the body of Colombe, who had died several hours before. The mob withdrew, grumbling, but there had been a great excitement. It goes without saying that a profound silence was recommended and observed concerning the event.

The next day, the intern César was sacked, and Dr. Kanali, for his part, was requested to find other accommodation.

And that that is how the doctor came to our establishment, where no unfavorable rumor preceded him or followed him, since all rumor had been prudently stifled.

From now on, I shall no longer be recounting what others have told me—it is Monsieur Morel who is speaking—but what I witnessed myself.

To begin with, I was witness to the somber melancholy that Mademoiselle Marthe Kanali brought in settling among us, a universal languor of which I shall reveal the cause straight away, although I only discovered it sometime after the family's installation.

Monsieur Kanali, who had only allowed César Caseneuve to establish himself within his familiarity, and to build up hopes of becoming his son-in-law, because he needed him, as an intelligent aide and devoted accomplice in his experiments, no longer wished to hear any mention of him in the deplorable wake of the success in the pavilion. As he held César Caseneuve solely responsible for everything disastrous that had happened to him on that memorable night—the fire, the invasion of the local people, his dismissal from the Val-de-Grâce; in sum, the complete ruination of his endeavor, on the brink of victory—he banned him from his home, conceived an aversion akin to hatred for him, and forbade his wife and daughter not only to continue to see him but even to pronounce his name. There is nothing like ambition to engender those black antipathies, those savage hatreds toward those who have upset the apple-cart in some way.

Marthe bowed her head in order to let the storm pass, but she promised herself not to forget her love, and such a promise is far-reaching. The ardent Italian woman drew upon her German firmness and her French mental resources to triumph over momentary ill-fortune.

As for her mother, Madame Kanali, the latter wondered whether she ought not to thank Heaven for having removed that young man from the threshold of their house forever—she assumed that it was forever. Never having vanquished the frisson that ran in icy threads through all her limbs at the sight of Caseneuve, who was evidently afflicted in her eyes with a unfortunate resemblance to some profoundly antipathetic individual, she had seen him depart with pleasure. With pleasure for herself, that is, albeit with some grief for her daughter, although the grief in question was still relative—for she had said several times to the divine confidant, in her prayers, that the day when Marthe married Caseneuve, if it were written in the stars that she would marry him, she would die at that very instant, of dolor.

We shall soon know what the reason was for Madame Kanali's insurmountable repulsion for César Caseneuve, whose remarkable intelligence, great honesty and well acquired science she did not deny—not to mention the other advantages that she did not refuse him either: an attractive face full of nobility, a distinguished stature and charming manners.

It remains to say now what César's situation was after the fatal misadventure of the pavilion, that shipwreck of all his hopes. It was not good. He was so explicitly banished by the doctor, the day after they had both been expelled from the Val-de-Grâce, that he did not have the courage, imperious as his love was, to present himself again at the Kanali family's new lodgings. It was one of those dismissals after which no hope remains, except for exalted lovers: supreme heroes such as the Des Grieux, the Werthers, the Saint-Preux,[86] and perhaps also for the César Caseneuves.

In any case, this explains perfectly the reason for the prudence with which Monsieur and Madame Kanali, with different motives, both asked me, with so much precision, during the first days of their residence, what time the gates of the sanitarium were closed, about the height of the walls, etc.

I have said that Mademoiselle Marthe Kanali's passion was combined with a great finesse; I do not know whether, in advancing that character trait, I have sufficiently characterized her new mental situation. After all, where is the young woman who does not have finesse at the moment when passion grips her? She acquires finesse because there is danger, and there is danger because there is an enemy.

An enemy rises up against every love; that enemy is either the family, or society, or the entire world. An impenetrable enigma! Marriage is made a necessity—the most obligatory of the necessities of life, for a woman—and yet there is no act in life to which more obstacles are raised for a woman. How many reasons there are for opposing it! Reasons sometimes based on the disproportion of ages, sometimes on the inequality of fortunes, sometimes on the difference of status. People are astonished to see so many old women on the sidewalk of celibacy; what astonishes me is to see so many other young women marry, when I think that it only requires two mouths to say "I do" in front of the Maire, where-

---

[86] The Chevalier Des Grieux is the hero of Abbé Prévost's *Manon Lescaut* (1731); Werther is the hero of J. W. Goethe's *Die Lieden des jungen Werthers* (1774; tr. as *The Sorrows of Young Werther*); Saint-Preux is the hero of Jean-Jacques Rousseau's *La Nouvelle Héloise* (1761). It is worth noting that none of those classic love stories has a happy ending.

as there are thousands and thousands who have no other desire and no other function than always to be saying: "No, no, no."

Having reached this point in the road mapped out for them, the story of the Kanali family finds its characters in the following disposition:

Madame Kanali believed more than ever in vampires, which was easy to see in the questions that she had addressed to me since her arrival in the sanitarium. The reflection that she had made in front of her husband, intended for him—"Oh, it's not thieves we fear"—sufficiently emphasizes the continual pre-occupation of her redoubtable belief in those creatures from beyond the grave.

That same credence explains to us the general panic that had invaded her at the sight of César Caseneuve and her terror when she discovered that he bore— like the vampire Bem Strombold, who had been on the point of marrying her mother, the wife of the great Salomon Kanali—a kind of little blood-red mark in the corner of his mouth. Except that Bem Strombold never offered his right hand, and César never refused it. No matter! Madame Kanali, because of that bloody sign, had shivered in all the delicate fibers of her heart on seeing César approach her daughter and fall in love with her; she thought that Marthe would be the victim of the third apparition of the same vampire in their twice-tested family, and that poor Marthe would die of that obsession for the very reason that her grandmother, the wife of the first Kanali, and herself, her mother, had escaped it.

Marthe would not have the same good fortune. A young victim was absolutely necessary to that great accursed creature; Marthe offered all the signs of the deadly predilection. A vampire is always preceded by languor, and Marthe's languor was evident to every eye; consumption accompanies him, and consumption was corroding Marthe pitilessly; he is surrounded by an aureole of pale colors, and pale colors covered Marthe's face. Therefore, Marthe would belong to him!

Now, add that Madame Kanali had only attached her attention with so much fixity to the windows of our long gallery of invalids because of vampires, that it is the recognized tradition in their stirring history never to appear in such great numbers as in times of major epidemics—and that we were, unfortunately, in one of those epochs.

Thus are explained the terror and anguish of Madame Kanali for her daughter, whom her eyes no longer quit. Marthe was followed and spied on by her with neither respite nor mercy. And that tyrannical surveillance of Marthe, born of excess maternal love, did not exclude that of Monsieur Kanali, whose anger against César Caseneuve had not weakened in the least. Far from it; it was one of those colossal scholarly hatreds, one of those hatreds compared to which the hatreds of the rest of humankind are almost amity.

All the incessant pressures exerted upon the love of César and Marthe, however, instead of cooling it, had only serve to exalt it to the point of delirium, to fever pitch. Having become, in one as in the other, the unique aliment of their thought, the inextinguishable flame of their brains, and their only reason for living, it rendered them incapable of anything else except loving one another.

The world was entirely contained within their love; there was nothing in the world except them and their love: it was a sublime egoism, a holy madness, that only those who have passed through that inferno of felicity once in their life have any possibility of understanding.

Here, naturally, arises the long sequence of difficulties, obstacles and dangers that Marthe and César would encounter before them whenever they sought to communicate their sensations.

César tried to write to Marthe; his letters were diverted and taken to the father and mother, whose surveillance and mistrust were augmented. He tried to climb over the garden walls; he was caught by the warders and risked being arrested as a thief. He renounced those means. Let us say right away that no means was successful for him, but that his multiple failures irritated instead of extinguishing the love of the two young people.

We have just seen that the love in question produced disappointments in Caseneuve; in Marthe it led from one discouragement to another, to a kind of dreamy idiocy, of one finds examples in young women tormented, as she was, by their most tender penchant. Her life became more distant by the hour from her connections with everything surrounding her, gradually isolating her within herself.

Mademoiselle Kanali walled herself up inside her love as if in a cloister, and from there, she no longer gazed upon the world, the sun and the living with anything but indifference. Her pallor increased further in the silent retreat of her love into the depths of her soul. Marthe was no longer anything but an earthly shade.

Before saying by what means, of which it is utterly impossible to form an idea coolly, Caseneuve final introduced himself into the sanitarium, it remains for me to describe he personal conduct of Dr. Kanali since he had been in our midst.

The doctor had not abandoned, and one would have been wrong to think otherwise, his project of embalming and rejuvenation, in spite of the serious check he had received at the Val-de-Grâce. He had come to our house in the Faubourg Saint-Denis with the sole objective of taking a triumphant revenge. My readers will not conserve any doubt in that regard when I have conducted them, in due course, to a certain establishment that I pointed out myself to Dr. Kanali, fatigued as I was in the end by always being asked the same question: "Monsieur Morel, can you tell me where the grave-diggers congregate?"—a question that he had asked me, as you will perhaps remember, during our first conversation.

Let us get back to the love of Marthe and César.

Marthe's melancholy soon became, by virtue of an effect often observed in young women afflicted with thwarted love, an exaggerated piety. Mademoiselle

Kanali did not even stop at the exaggeration that takes the form of spending nights in prayer and taking communion on Saturday; she wanted to be a nun, and, in order to sanctify her novitiate, declared that she wanted to share with the sisters of St. Vincent de Paul the mission of caring for the sick.

Her frightened mother protested; her father revolted at the idea. What did such a determination signify? Was it destiny, the vocation of a young woman brought up for society, rich and celebrated by virtue of her grandfather and father?

Marthe was inflexible. She would let herself die, she said, if she were not allowed to devote herself entirely to the salvation of the sick. Arguments and pleas were futile. Nothing would make her renounce her resolution—a very imprudent resolution, I said to myself, as the indirect witness of these family disputes.

I would never have allowed her to prevail if I had been in her father's place, because it was doubtful that forbidding her to become a sister of charity would have caused her to die, while it was almost certain that she would fall victim to her devotion by going to breathe the subtle poisons of the epidemic at the bedsides of its victims. Already, out of ten sisters of St. Vincent de Paul who had come to care for out patients, seven had disappeared forever, and they were women accustomed to fatigue, hardened to long vigils, immune to any repugnance and whose morale was certainly sheltered from dread, for it was precisely the danger they were braving that they sought, and loved more than anything else.

It became futile to oppose Marthe's desire any longer, so firmly decided was she to devote herself, in a religious sentiment, to caring for the sick. She was abandoned to her recklessness. She went down into the wards and began her service. She made her debut at an exceedingly perilous moment.

Developed by the excessive heat of the month of June, the malady suddenly took on a more sinister character. We saw the black days of 1832 again. Already much weakened by the political situation, commerce disappeared completely. The shops scarcely opened; they were briefly opened to answer the demands of material life and closed again as soon as night fell.

The nights were hard to traverse. At distant intervals, red lanterns indicated the ambulance stations where one could go in search of first aid. Silent and deserted, the streets were furrowed in all directions by long files of stretchers, and toward midnight, when the inhabitants were imagined to be asleep—and they slept very little in that epoch—the carriages whose usage has already been mentioned outlined the exaggerated grimace of their shadows on walls shivering with fear: phantom carriages laden with phantoms. In order not to strike fear into the depths of houses that were always nervously on edge, the wheels were wrapped in thick cloth. It was a wasted precaution; fear always extends; it extends when there is nothing to be afraid of and it extends far more when there is something. There was a lot.

It was on one of those lamentable nights, impossible to forget, when our wards had no more room for anyone, that I saw a young man arrive, supported by two of his friends. His eyes were half-closed, his face anxious, his body arched by painful contractions, his breath halting and brief. His incoherent speech left no doubt as to the redoubtable name that had to be given to the disease by which he had just been struck down.

VII

Strangely enough, however—although I was perhaps the only one to notice it—he appeared, on entering our wards, to be at least as frightened by the scene displayed to his right and his left as by his own situation. I believe, in fact, that he forgot his own situation—which is not ordinarily the action of any sick person—in order to abandon himself immeasurably to the impression of superhuman terror that froze him at the sights he perceived.

His lips suddenly became violet, almost black; his eyes retreated beneath the somber arcade of his pale forehead; his hair stood on end—a phenomenon in which I had never really believed—like steely needles; and he murmured between his teeth, which were chattering as if with extreme cold: "No, I don't want to stay here! Oh, staying here is too horrible. All these people are specters; they scare me; in a little while, I'll be a specter like them. Take me away! Take me away!"

We succeeded in calming him down, though, or he succeeded in mastering himself, and when he was a little less agitated, his friends asked me for a separate room.

Coincidentally, alas—I do not say fortunately—the patient occupying the cabinet placed in the middle of the room, near the chapel, the only one that was vacant that night, had bid farewell ten minutes before, even though she had only come in that evening. People passed on so quickly then! We put the newcomer in that room, and his friends confided him to our care. They left immediately; people did not like to stay among us long in those days, so pernicious in character. The customary treatment was about to commence for their protégé.

God only knows what that treatment would have been! There were so many! Would they work on him with fire or with ice? The intern summoned to give him primary care declared that he would not last the night, that any effort to save him would be futile, and that the best thing to do, instead of seeking to martyrize him at will, was to subscribe to the latest and ultimate expression of his will, which was that a sister might come to sit beside his bed, charitably, to recite a few final prayers.

Mademoiselle Marthe happened to be there; she heard what the intern said, and immediately offered to be that pious reader.

The offer was accepted all the more readily because no other sister was in a position, at that moment, to dispute the precious task with her. They were occupied elsewhere, in medical services that claimed them without respite—for, in spite of their number, zeal and devotion, they were far from sufficient for their courageous and sublime mission.

Mademoiselle Marthe, therefore, went in to the new patient's room. The entrance to the cabinet—set, as we have said, in the middle of the huge gallery—was masked by the double fall of the large pleats of a long white curtain. Mademoiselle Marthe went in by herself, and remained alone with the patient.

She was enclosed in that refuge of silence and pious prayer for about three hours, and it was two hours after midnight—you will see that I have a reason for specifying the time with such exactitude—when a storm that had long been brooding beneath heavy, warm and stifling clouds broke over Paris, unleashing all the meteorological horrors into the atmosphere as it did so.

I shall never forget the disastrous effect of that storm on our poor invalids, and that is why the occasion is fixed in my mind. A poison—even prussic acid—could not have had more immediate or more frightful results on their organism. Each of them was snuffed out in turn, like a series of candles over which a horizontal wind has passed.

The rainwater was streaming in cataracts over the window-panes and livid flashes of lightning rain through the wards from one end to the other; the thunder never ceased to rumble and break forth in strident blasts. I had never seen anything like it in my life, but I was far from having seen everything.

At that moment, I saw Dr. Kanali and his wife arrive at the end of the ward at a precipitate pace, looking around anxiously. I deduced their intention; they were looking for their daughter. By means of a gesture I drew them to my station.

"What a night!" Madame Kanali said, as she drew near. "What a night!"

"Hard to bear, Madame—oh yes, very hard!"

"And my daughter?"

"There," I replied, pointing to the cabinet veiled by the white curtains. "Praying beside a patient."

"But that's intolerable!" said Monsieur Kanali, containing his rage, although, at that moment, he could have spoken as loudly as he wished; the storm had not diminished and its racket overwhelmed all other sounds. "It's intolerable! I don't want her to stay in this terrible place any longer. She could perish here in a matter of minutes. Let's snatch our child away from this poisoned gulf."

"But she's praying," I repeated, in a voice that I moderated because of a momentary pause that had just been produced in the patchier release of the tempest.

"Praying or not, I'm getting her out of here," retorted the doctor, also lowering his voice, as if he were seeking to reconcile his habits as a physician with his paternal wrath.

Then I saw him advance toward the cabinet with the white curtain; his wife went with him; I followed both of them.

The doctor lifted the curtain. What astonishment! What a surprise! What a circumstance!

Marthe was not praying; her hands were in those of the invalid, who seemed to me to be far less imperiled than I would have imagined, given the condition in which I had seen him when he arrived. They were not a moribund and a charitable angel helping him to pass peacefully from this life to a better one, but two lovers ecstatically delighted to find themselves together, fusing the surges of their soul in the same happiness.

The noise of the storm having prevented them from hearing our approach, they retained the same attitude before us. Sitting next to the bed, Marthe had placed her head on the pillow where that of César Caseneuve rested—for I shall not make you wait any longer to tell you that it was him, César Caseneuve, who was there with Marthe. And just imagine how they were praying together!

Many words of love must have been spoken in that sad space during the three hours that that tête-à-tête on the same pillow had lasted. Words of love! What power that love of the springtime of life must have had, in order for that young man to have braved a malady that no one in the world feared more than him! To have given him the miraculous strength to spend, in such a place, a night that might have been his last, as it was for so many others! No, I would never have attributed so much determination and valor to the sentiment in question. I had thought ambition alone capable of that heroic scorn for danger. I was mistaken.

The danger to which the two lovers had exposed themselves, which they had both prepared at leisure—for Marthe had only demanded to care for the sick in order to get closer to César Caseneuve—rendered them more interesting in my eyes that it would be possible for me to say. Courage, which changes everything, rendered their aberration very excusable: the sin of loving one another, of seeing one another, in spite of the will of their parents, in spite of the world entire. Who would not have been disarmed by so much heroism in passion, so much abnegation in the midst of so many dangers? Who would not have pardoned that love, if only because one might have thought it the last love remaining on earth, at that moment when the material world seemed to be plunged into physical distress, the moral world into the confusion of political opinions, and both were nearing their end? Who, we ask ourselves, would not have pardoned them?

Two people, however, did not pardon them—but one of them represented wounded pride, and the other fanaticism, which are equally pitiless. They were Dr. Kanali and his wife. The spectacle of their daughter, delivered to Caseneuve, awoke all Madame Kanali's superstitions and reignited her believe in redivivi, brucolaques, vampires and all those supernatural beings in which so many peoples of the Orient have believed, still believe and perhaps always will believe.

"Yes, it's him," murmured Madame Kanali, in a low voice, squeezing her husband's arm with a visible tremor. "It's him; recognize him, now; it's him, the imperishable, eternal persecutor of our family, the demon who has waged war successively against my mother and against me; against my mother under the fatal name of Bem Strombold, against me under that of Rosenthal. He is now pursuing our dear daughter in France, under the name of César Caseneuve. Yes, now it's our child's turn; and it's here, in the circumstances I which we find ourselves, in the place where we are, that he had to reappear—and has reappeared!"

What gave Madame Kanali's words a quasi-prophetic quality, and led to the denouement of the scene, were those of the two lovers. I shall report them as I heard them:

"Marthe, is this truly determined in your mind and your will?"

"Yes, my friend."

"You consent, then, to follow me, dear Marthe?"

"Yes, anywhere it pleases you to take me."

"Anywhere?"

"Anywhere."

"Think hard—you won't regret it one day?"

"No."

"Whatever happens, you'll never curse me?"

"Never."

"Well, then, let our destiny be accomplished; under cover of the tempest we'll quit this house; we'll go way from Paris toward the storm and the darkness, and we'll be together forever."

"Let's be together forever," Marthe repeated. "Death alone can separate us."

"Even death will not separate us," said Caseneuve, hugging the doctor's daughter in his arms with passionate effusion.

It was on hearing that vow, so solemnly expressed by Caseneuve, that Madame Kanali uttered a cry of maternal terror and revealed herself to her daughter and the man who spoke of remaining attached to her beyond the grave.

Deeply troubled, but fundamentally less convinced than his wife about the existence of vampires, the doctor took his daughter by the arm and dragged her back to his apartment, saying to her that he finally knew why she desired so much to be a sister of charity and nurse. Madame Kanali followed them.

I have no need to tell you that César Caseneuve did not present any symptom, however slight, of the disease that he had usurped as a pretext for introducing himself to Mademoiselle Marthe's presence—no symptom, except for an immeasurable desire to see where she was. It was that fear and the absence of any malady that gave the punishment that he was about to receive from Marthe's father an originality as burlesque as it was moving.

This is what the punishment in question was.

When Monsieur Kanali had taken his daughter back to her apartment—which only took a minute—he came back to where he had left Caseneuve stupefied by surprise, and where I was still suffering the effects of astonishment myself. Adopting the tone and authority of a doctor attached to the house, even though, if he was a doctor, he was not attached to the establishment, he told two interns who were accompanying him: "This young man is very ill. Examine him."

"Monsieur!" protested the astonished Caseneuve. "There's been a mistake. I came here to..."

"He's very ill, as you can see, Already, his disturbed mind no longer has any real consciousness of what he has done..."

"I tell you, Messieurs, that I'm not ill at all, and that I came here..."

"Terminal cholera!" continued the doctor, placing his hand on Caseneuve's bed. "Terminal cholera!"

"But Monsieur!" cried Caseneuve, again, very agitated by the threat that attributed a disease to him of which he was so terrified. "I repeat to you that I'm here for..."

"Incessant cramp!" the doctor continued, obstinately. "You see—his body is entirely contorted."

"But Monsieur, I'm not experiencing any cramp, and in truth..."

"Hippocratic face—see!"

"Me, I have a Hippocratic face?"

"Exceedingly Hippocratic—so called because Hippocrates was the first to describe its characteristics. Observe those characteristics on his face."

"What, this face!"

"On his face: the skin of the forehead taut..."

"My skin is taut?"

"Don't interrupt the definition of the father of medicine!"

"Even if he were the grandfather, you couldn't prove to me..."

Kanali resumed, authoritatively: "Skin of forehead taut, dry or covered in cold sweat; eyes sunken in their orbits; nose pointed."

"But my nose..."

"One more, don't interrupt the divine Hippocrates. Nose pointed, temples hollow, cheekbones protruding, ears cold and drawn back, lips discolored, livid and slack. Hippocrates has spoken."

"I too will speak!"

"Shut up!" Dr. Kanali continued, addressing the two interns. "Notice, too—a magnificent diagnostic—that he has opaque corneas."

"Me?"

"You have opaque corneas..."

"Yes, he has opaque corneas," the intern repeated, in order to agree with the master.

"I affirm to you, Messieurs..."

"He will soon be overtaken by lipothymia."

Exasperated, Caseneuve raised his arms to the heavens, murmuring in a sigh: "Lipothymia!"

"Lipothymia!" Kanali repeated. "Weakness, lipothymia; *deliquium animi*: lack of soul and courage; instantaneous loss of movement and sentiment, although respiration and circulation still continue—until, in syncope, the latter two functions are suspended. The invalid is lying there before our eyes, and is therefore struck with lipothymia, since sentiment is extinct within him, and he is still breathing."

"Of course I'm still breathing!"

"Yes, you're still breathing a little," said Kanali, "but soon, accidents such as respiration will..."

"What will happen?" demanded Caseneuve, becoming desperate and making efforts to leap out of bed.

"Syncopes, carphologias, spasms of the tendons," Kanali replied.

"But for the hundredth time..." Caseneuve said, howling with rage—or, rather, tried to say, for again he was interrupted and held down in his bed by the doctor.

"See how agitated he is! That's the spasms of the tendons. He's passed through the algid phase, the cyanic or blue period; he's approaching the most serious phase, the asphyxiant phase. It's a superb case!"

Fear finally succeeded anger in Caseneuve's soul. After having denied, then doubted, he now believed, in the face of the doctor's persistence, that he had contracted the Indian plague, by coming to breathe the air of one of its most active nuclei.

The doctor did not surrender his ascendancy.

"Look, Messieurs," he went on. "See how the glacial chill is gripping him; he's shivering; his limbs are stiffening. Observe!"

On hearing these last words, Caseneuve thought that he was about to perish—and he no longer had the slightest doubt when Marthe's father had terminated his anatomical description by saying: "He's doomed."

"Doomed?" demanded César, his eyes, mouth and entire body lurching forward. "Doomed!"

"However," the pitiless and ironic doctor went on, "We're going to attempt an energetic, desperate treatment on the subject."

"I don't want it!" César Caseneuve still had the strength to cry, beneath the weight of the denomination, so familiar to him, which eliminated a person from the number of the living: *subject!* He was no longer anything but a subject!

Without paying any heed to César's resistance, the doctor immediately began his prescription.

"First, frictions on the breast, all the way to the quick."

Moans from Caseneuve.

"Vesicatories on the epigastrum."

Lamentations from Caseneuve.

"Copious sanguine emission."

Louder lamentations from César.

"Vomitives."

Choking sounds from César.

"Quicklime around the body."

At the thought of that last treatment by quicklime, youth got the better of fear in Caseneuve. He bounded out of bed. He was determined to put an end to those threats, which he believed to be on the point of turning into deadly realities for him.

He was about to react against the evil by smashing the doctor's skull with the aid of the first object that came to hand, when someone was brought into the room, with a movement multiplied by footsteps and words, for whom the cabinet we were in was required. The cabinet was demanded in such a fashion that I believed that César Caseneuve would have been thrown out even if he had really been ill, in order to take unceremonious possession of his bed—but he was not there; he had taken advantage of the confusion caused by the newcomer's noisy entourage to get dressed in haste, so far as he could, and run away as fast as his legs could carry him.

There was only me, I'm sure, who heard the words that he darted behind him as he fled: "I wasn't able to steal her away while alive; I'll come and steal her away when I'm dead."

Then I saw him reach the far end of the ward and, by way of the stairs, which he went down in three bounds, take flight into the courtyard and the street—where, one may suppose without difficulty, he was very glad to exercise the liberty granted to his entire person.

What significance can now be attributed to that unexpected threat uttered by César Caseneuve—"I'll come and steal her away when I'm dead"—unless, like Madame Kanali, one believes in vampires?

VIII

The sick man who had come to take the place of César Caseneuve was brought in on a stretcher by a crowd of anxious, extremely agitated people, as distressed as if a member of the family had been struck by the disease. Their great number astonished me at first. How, at such an hour of the night, and on such a night, had so many people been gathered together? My second astonishment arose from the no less singular detail that all the people knew one another.

The commotion produced by their mass entrance into the ward having settled down somewhat, I attempted to obtain some enlightenment from one of them. I learned that the person—or, rather, the personage—who had just been transported into our midst, escorted by so much sympathy, was a celebrated club-member of the Salle Martel; he was the orator with the largest following, the most influential and the most popular.

You will not know the exact significance of the words *orator, club-member* and *Salle Martel* if you have forgotten that we were, in 1849, a Republic, or very nearly a Republic, in an epoch in which clubs were much in vogue, and when, by consequence, orators attracted universal attention, with their success, their clientele and their influence—an influence often greatly redoubted.

Among these clubs, much the most famous at the time—the only one still remembered today—was the club at the Salle Martel, placed less than a quarter of an hour's walk from our sanitarium. There, people agitated and discussed the most burning questions of politics and social philosophy; people agitated so strongly that there were sometimes fisticuffs beneath the speaker's podium—but an understanding was often reached, and at the end the session, fellow feeling was manifested in the street by the hymns of Pierre Dupont,[87] which were sung in chorus, to the great patriotic alarm of the inhabitants of the Faubourg Poissonnière and the Faubourg Saint-Denis.

Now, our personage had been touched by the wind of the epidemic during one of those oratory nights in question, in the very midst of his admirers in the Salle Martel; he had been very seriously afflicted. It was not a repetition of César Caseneuve's performance. Felled in the midst of his triumph, his friends had hastened to bring him to our establishment, where he arrived in a very serious condition. The effervescence of passions produced cases that were almost invariably incurable, and I was told, in fact, that it was during a debate in which the orator had abused his strength, pushing the heat of his words to the extent of enthusiasm, that he had felt wounded in his entrails. The blade steeped in the Indian poison had traversed him while he was launching an inflamed reply at his adversaries.

Save for the remarkable face of Caseneuve, I had not seen a specimen as correct and handsome as that of the orator of the Salle Martel. He was a man of about thirty-five or forty. His black hair, which was very long—as it was then the Republican fashion to wear it—descended like black velvet gauze over his superbly white neck: a striking contrast, easy to grasp because of the other fashion reigning in that epoch of wearing the short-collar broadly turned back over the shoulders. His beard, similarly pure black in color, terminated in a point, in

---

[87] Pierre Dupont (1821-1870) was a song-writer who performed many of the fervent works he composed during the Second Republic at working men's concerts in the Salle de la Fraternité in the Faubourg Saint-Denis.

the manner of the kings of Babylon, over his athletically-developed breast—and, in fact, are not orators also athletes?

One might have thought that one were looking at one of the young satraps of the colossal Biblical city, a city emerged from its ashes expressly in order to show us a greater beauty than Greece, a greater elegance than Athens, closer still to the ideal grandeur of demigods. There was nothing as simultaneously mild and majestic as his gaze, although it was already considerably weakened by the disease whose atrocious grip he was supporting so heroically. His portrait has remained in the memory of some of his contemporaries. He enjoyed the popularity, unfortunately very ephemeral, of the photography of circumstance.

Although the memory of his name has faded somewhat today, like the memory of his face, into the violet mist of a distance soon destined to be nothing more than vapor, colorless air, I shall not describe him in all his integrity. Everyone knows that one can wound someone even by praising them, when one touches on the still-dolorous past of our civil discords. I shall only hint at his identity; let us say that he was called Jean-Paul Désormeaux; that slight alteration of his name will not go so far, evidently, as silence regarding his noble origin, which he did not conceal—a frankness that had not harmed his popularity.

With his immense oratorical talent he combined, let us add, personal qualities of an exquisite humanity. Possessed of a fairly large fortune, he only retained what he needed to live in a small room in the Faubourg Saint-Martin. The rest went to the poor, for whose health he also cared, for he was a qualified physician, and he had practiced in Brazil—to which, I believe, he had followed the little phalansterian colony of Fourier.[88] That leads me to tell you that he harbored no illusions as soon as he was afflicted by the murderous breath of the epidemic, and he proved that to us with an admirable calmness as soon as he could pay attention to his situation without distressing the brave men who had accompanied him to our sanitarium.

When they had gone—and God knows how many times they looked back in order to see him again before leaving him—he said to Dr. Nivière, who was interrogating the rate of his pulse with his infallible experience and simultaneously examining the contraction of his pupils: "Nothing will save me, Doctor, but if you will permit, I can suffer less than one usually suffers in my condition. Put me in a bath, and ask that I be left in peace to write my last thoughts in favor of the people."

His wish was immediately satisfied. He was placed in a bath-tub and he wrote for two hours as if he were experiencing no pain. It was Roman fortitude.

---

[88] The utopian philosopher Charles Fourier (1772-1837) proposed that the ideal egalitarian society ought to be organized on the basis of communal dwellings called *phalanstères* [phalansteries]; his works inspired numerous experimental communities, including one established in the Sai region of Brazil in 1841.

Underneath, agonies was racking him cruelly; by the third hour they were the stronger. Sometimes, the cramps were so violent, so intolerable, that the paper fell outside the bath-tub and the pencil into the water. Several times he was restored to a sitting position, and with great efforts of will he tried to resume work, but toward first light his head slumped; weak and fainting, it rested on the edge of the tub, while his extended arms and the whole of his inert body were under the water. The orator of the Salle Martel, the thunderous Jupiter of the clubs, had passed on.

It was at that indecisive moment between light and darkness that I saw Dr. Kanali coming toward me.

He immediately drew me into the cabinet where the great clubman Désormeaux had just expired. Without having needed to take me to one side, for there was no one around us within earshot, he said: "Do you know, Monsieur Morel, that you have a heavy task on your hands in this house, especially in infernal times like those we're going through."

"Oh, very heavy," I replied. "But that's life; it isn't easy for anyone. Habit and resignation..."

"And you're suitably rewarded?"

"Not exactly in the manner of a Maréchal de France..."

"But all in all...?"

"A drab existence," I continued, smiling, having no idea where that dialogue, growing almost devoid of roots, was leading us. "Very drab—but the satisfaction of serving honest folk..."

"It's necessary, however, not to neglect an opportunity to be useful to oneself, and you aren't rich, I can see, judging by what you've told me, Monsieur Morel. Be careful!"

The warning of such a danger made me smile. "Oh, certainly not—I'm not rich, and probably never will be. But what can one do?"

"Perhaps you don't like money anyway? In which case..."

"On the contrary, I like it well enough—but it doesn't like me, and that's why we're never seen together." Once again, I wondered where the conversation as leading.

Monsieur Kanali began to speak to me in an even lower tone. "You could have ten thousand francs, if you wanted."

"What do you mean, if I wanted? Who doesn't want ten thousand francs? With ten thousand francs and the little nest-egg I inherited from my father, I could go to live like a little lord in Normandy, in a corner of the beautiful valley of the Auge, near Lisieux. Oh, how I'd like to have ten thousand francs!"

"That depends on you, Monsieur Morel."

"To have them?"

"To earn them."

"That's just it. It depends what one has to do to earn them."

"Easily—oh, very easily."

Diminishing the range of his voice, and drawing me next to the bed on which I had deposited Jean-Paul Désormeaux, he said: "You don't doubt," he went on, pointing to the famous clubman, "the universal impression of regret and grief that the unexpected death of such a man, so popular in Paris, will create?"

"The grief and regret caused by his loss, I agree, will be immense in Paris, but it's an irremediable misfortune."

"Oh, not entirely irremediable."

I looked at Monsieur Kanali with the same sentiment of close discretion that he had put into the final sentence.

"Not entirely irremediable," he repeated, meeting my interrogative gaze.

"I don't understand," I told him, finally, "the singular restriction that you seem to be bringing to the affirmation of the most evident and most irreparable fact in the world. That is a life utterly extinct, and you can't reanimate him."

"Perhaps, I tell you again, Monsieur Morel."

"There's no perhaps about it, and great doctor though you are..."

"I beg your pardon; if you mean that I can't resuscitate the man who is lying there before our eyes, as motionless as a stone, then you're right, although ambitious men have appeared on earth, temeritous rivals of God, who have claimed...but that's not what concerns us."

"Not in the least," I agreed. "You mentioned my earning ten thousand francs."

"Precisely—and I'm getting there," said Monsieur Kanali, his voice taking on something of the emphasis of the charlatans of the public square, to the point at which I thought I saw the apparatus of a vanishing-trick between his fingers and his suit turning into the red multi-pocketed apron of a trickster. "No, I don't have the ability to resurrect that man," he said, "but I can render him the physical superiority with which he was endowed before he was as he is now—which is to say, unrecognizable, thanks to the fatal hand of destruction. I have the ability to restore his rich complexion, his solid and ardent pallor, his eyes full of genius and rebellion, his mouth armed with irony, like those of all popular orators, from Demosthenes to him, via Mirabeau.

"And what renown would ensue, what a triumph that would be, for the man who brought about that transformation, who contrived that embalming, a great work with no resemblance, thank God, to the imperfect and infamous work of those pretended conservers with patents, whose art consists of rendering the subjects delivered into their maleficent hands ever uglier, more disfigured and more unrecognizable than they were before being entrusted to them.

"That man's glory would be marvelous, enviable among all the glories of the present and all time; people would clap their hands and cry miracle when they see him pass by; they will come from afar to see him. The State would not remain indifferent; it would be eager to reward the creator of that prodigy. He would be showered with distinctions, honors, medals.

"If positions and rewards have been heaped upon a clever man for having said that there is one star more in some distant crossroads of the sky, as if that star had not been there before him and would not always remain when he is dead, what would not be given to a man who had discovered something very different from a useless star, to a man who had given human beings a means of only making a partial exit from life when their hour comes to quit it?

"That man's glory would be as immeasurable as the service rendered—and that glory will perhaps be mine."

"Well, what's preventing it from being yours, Doctor? What's stopping you?"

"One thing, Monsieur Morel, just one."

"That's not very many."

"It's up to you to decide it," the doctor continued, putting his arm around me with the familiarity of one colleague to another. "I need this man to be left entirely at my disposal for forty-eight hours."

"This one?"

"This one."

"Forty-eight hours!" I protested. "When the authorities demand, imperiously, that he be disposed of within twelve hours, because of the excessive elevation of the temperature, and because...of many reasons. It's impossible!"

"The authorities, the authorities!" Monsieur Kanali murmured, impatiently, but with a great deal of suspicion in his disdain. "Of course, the authorities... however, if the man were hidden from the authorities, and another substituted for him... anyone at all... there are so many here at present..."

He cast a significant glance over the gallery, where all was silence—sufficient to permit the doctor to carry out the substitution that he planned without exciting the slightest protest. He concluded: "In that case, what would the authorities say? What would the authorities see?"

When he had finished, I said in my turn: "Who would dare to carry out that substitution?"

"You."

"Me!"

"I've told you the rather handsome price; I believe that I can count on your condescension."

"You mean my complicity."

"Complicity, condescension—what does it matter? Words are just words. Say yes, and in exchange for these banknotes"—he opened his wallet—"you'll deliver to me that man, whom, in a few days, when all his enthusiastic partisans think that he is gone forever, I shall cause to reappear in the light, strikingly handsome, real and superb in expression, almost alive. Do you accept the bargain?"

I confess that I hesitated momentarily. It seemed to me at first glance that I would not be committing any reprehensible act by accepting—but reflection, that conscience of the intelligence, immediately intervened, and I understood that putting one body in place of another was a grave contravention of the authorities' orders—orders which, respectable at any time, become sacred in times that are hazardous to public health. I told myself that it was bad, from the religious point of view, to summon on behalf of one individual the prayers destined for another. I thought, as well, about the moral censure that I would bring to the house when the substitution became known, as was bound to happen with a man like Monsieur Kanali, a hero of fanfares and acclamations.

I told myself all that, without forgetting that it was after a experiment similar to the one that he was proposing to me that the doctor had been expelled from the Val-de-Grâce. I therefore refused my tempter's proposition pointblank, and rejected it in such a way to leave him no desire to renew it.

He was about to go away, for daylight was invading the wards, but he retraced his steps to say to me: "Since you have the deplorable weakness of not consenting to earn ten thousand francs, I beg you to do two things."

I listened.

"The first is that you keep the conversation we've just had secret."

"I can promise you secrecy. What's the other?"

"To tell me immediately what you didn't want to tell me the first time I asked you: the location, which must exist in Paris, of the place where the gravediggers habitually meet up."

"I didn't answer the question the first time you asked because I didn't think it was serious, but I see that I was mistaken," I said to the doctor, who was all ears. "The gentlemen in question meet every day at six o'clock in the Rue Myrrha in Montmartre, at the Crémerie Myrrha, where they eat together."

"Well," Dr. Kanali told me, laughing, "I shall dine at the Crémerie Myrrha this very day. You were wrong not to accept my offer, Monsieur Morel."

And he went away, humming a vaudeville tune: "It's so good to get rich when you're in love..."

IX

The Rue Myrrha is in Montmartre; it begins at the Rue Chaussée-Clignancourt and changes the name of Myrrha to that of Constantine in the very middle. To tell the truth, neither the Rue Myrrha nor the Rue Constantine gives rise to any idea of beauty; the two halves are as bad as one another; the beginning is as ugly as the end.

No other street in Paris is as incorrect, tortuous, bumpy, ill-constructed, badly paved, deformed and deplorable to the feet and gaze as the long Rue Myrrha. It is reminiscent of those absurd provincial streets that are named the Rue de Paris to honor Paris, but do that honor great disservice. Descending, or, more accurately, falling from the backbone of the Chaussée Clignancourt, the Rue Myrrha resembles a horse's saddle whose girth-strap has broken; it slips.

What a street! Oh, what a street! Here, the tall, thin houses rise up, stretching as far as they can, so to speak, as if to say: look at us, passers-by! Then, beside those houses run to seed, a steep gap suddenly opens up, only stopping at the flat roofs of another row of houses, with a single story. After these single-story houses, hanging on the flanks of the larger ones, other houses spring up, even taller, but much uglier. The latter are overburdened with balconies: balconies on the first, second, third and fourth floors. The Rue Myrrha is crazy about balconies. In the final analysis, all those big houses stiffly all the small houses, the former pumping the air and light from the latter.

It is the same throughout the street; one continually sees observatory towers on Eskimo huts and Eskimo huts on observatory towers. Sometimes, one encounters something even better though. There are groups of houses gathered into heaps and decorated with the name of "cities." A gate denounces their presence on the street; an avenue of rickety trees leads to them. One has before one a development of walls pierced with holes, like a bottle-rack. Those holes are windows. And as those windows have not shutters, they look as if they have been stripped after an attack, a looting or a gust of wind.

It's crazy and sinister. Summer there is horrible; one sees sweaty men with bare arms, children more than half-naked, and women with unkempt hair and dresses gaping, floating in rags and tatters, all going up and down, appearing and disappearing all day long through the spirals of these houses; urchins slide down the banisters of the stairways in order to get down more rapidly, and the wooly heads of workers stick out here and there through the snuff-box roofs, opening their mouths to breathe. Higher still, finally, there is nothing—the sky and the swallows.

At the foot of these houses, more unequal than—or, if you prefer, as unequal as—their human inhabitants, shops offers you, as in the center of Paris, everything that desire and need could wish, but with a particular character of accumulation, bad taste, abandonment and impropriety. The clothes-merchants seem to be selling clothes already worn, the cobblers shoes that have long lost their freshness, the hatters headgear that has already been introduced to water and has retained dust, the furnishers beds that have taken the road to the auction-house more than once, the grocers comestibles saved from a shipwreck, the milliners hats beneath which one imagines that one can see the vile heads that have worn them out, the clockmakers pendulum-clocks three days behind time and pocket-watches that emit the gleams of saucepans.

This is not an effect produced by bad taste and bad maintenance, but is reality itself and not appearance; it is the pitiful proximity and antipathetic cohabitation of all those shops: the coal merchant's dust blackens the ice-cream seller's wares; the plaster-merchant's whitens the butcher's cutlets; the cake-merchant is haplessly perfumed by the scented soap-water that the barber eternally squirts outside his door; the barber, in his turn, is overwhelmed and obscured by the resinous smoke of the bakery; the midwife's sign, unhooked, hangs down over the umbrella-merchant's sign, while the tinsmith's serves as a visor for the stationer, who, in his turn, extends is display into the midst of the apricots and salsify of his neighbor the fruiterer.

A charming street, the Rue Myrrha in Montmartre.

We have said that it changes its name in the middle; the middle in question is indicated by its intersection with the Rue Lévisse, which cuts the Rue Myrrha perpendicularly. It is shortly before the Rue Lévisse, still in the Rue Myrrha, that the creamery of that name flourishes, about which we are going to talk.

The Crémerie Myrrha offers its friends, and its enemies, a surface development that consists, to the right and left of its entrance door, of a system of shelves in sheets of coarse crystal, defended by a glass case. The shelves are poorly defended, the crystal being of a slightly bottle-green shade, but they are numerous and have an agreeable variety of products. That variety is astonishing and intimidating at first, for the term "creamery," strictly speaking, indicates an establishment where one can buy milk, eggs, butter and cheese.

Could anyone, even Herodotus, have described everything sold, found and encountered in that singular creamery?

For instance, through the dubious purity of the right-hand display-window, one perceives a metal-plate bowl, ornamented with a ladle in the same metal, a double utensil indicating sufficiently that punch is sometimes drunk in the establishment falsely dedicated to dairy produce. One is gripped by regret on seeing it that time has devoured the shallow layer of silver extended over the bowl's flanks; the copper has vanquished the silver. Half a dozen large cups in fake porcelain, around which run a double pale-blue stripe, are arranged next to the bowl. None of them is intact; this one is scuffed, that one chipped, a third cracked from top to bottom like the tower of Coucy-le-Château. Let us not dwell on the injuries of the others. So one can take coffee as well as punch at the Crémerie Myrrha?

One can even get milk there, for here is a varnished earthenware jug full of milk. The milk in question is half-covered with flies, which would cover it entirely if their caresses were not shared with another chipped jug in which prunes are floating. These charming insects go from the milk to the prunes without anything troubling their pleasures. It's marvelous to behold the traces of their sojourn in the Crémerie Myrrha. Everything is embroidered by their feet and ingenious mouth-parts: the mirrors, the window-panes, the woodwork, the chairs, the wallpaper, the curtains and the ceilings have suffered to such a degree from their incrustation that one can say without exaggeration that the windows are already crystal and flies, the paneling wood and flies, the ceilings plaster and flies, on their way to being nothing but flies.

The second floor of the creamery shows to passers-by another enormous bowl full to the brim, and sometimes brimming over, with chocolate à la crème;

the cream has disappeared, the chocolate can be deduced. The place of honor between that yellow-tinted lake and a sort of faience pyramid from which seasoned pipes emerge, stuck in by their shafts, is occupied by a bright red piece of veal enveloped in excessively-developed loins—loins that could become, in time of war, artillery ammunition. On Sunday, an oval is designed with carrot slices round the master morsel, but the piece of veal is often replaced itself by a rabbit placed on the tray in a picturesque pose; one might think that it were about to run away.

That rabbit forms a ridge; over that ridge an ingenious hand usually scatters, instead of carrot slices, slices of onion, culinary hieroglyphics signifying that the rabbit will be "*aux petit oignons*"—which is to say, delicious—and to prove that there is no error of natural history on the part of the cook, a live cat, of a russet hue particular to cats in suburban restaurants, is asleep on the shelf next to the rabbit.

Beyond the veal and the rabbit one sees bottles of beeswax, an ungilded tea-caddy, a bottle of cherries and a plaster bust of Béranger, all dotted and disfigured by little fly-specks.

At the top—right at the top, on the uppermost shelf—one can make out commemorative porcelain mugs, two vases with artificial roses, and a basket, similarly in porcelain, but pierced with diamond-shaped holes. Sometimes, one can see tufts of packing-material sticking out through these diamonds. Why? Because one puts eggs that one wishes to conserve therein.

The wall against which these shelves are backed was once painted with coarse frescoes representing subjects drawn from cynegetic pleasures relevant to the table. Half way up there was a boar-hunt; above it, a deer-hunt. That eloquent painting has disappeared; it had too much irony built into it for the regulars ever to request its restoration. What possible connection was there between their meals and roebucks or wild boar?

What, then, is eaten at the creamery on the Rue Myrrha?

The shelves placed to the left of the main doorway emphasize that one can also drink there.

On the first, unequal in size but densely-packed, stand bottles of cognac, old rum and cheap brandy, of which people seem to be extremely fond in the Rue Myrrha. Liqueurs flourish here too; the ladies are not forgotten. On illustrious labels one can read *Walnut Elixir; Jasmine Flower; Tears of Adonis, Spirit of Béranger, Lip Dew, Cream of Cassis, Angel Water* and *Milk of Love*. No, the ladies are not forgotten, for beside a slab of Gruyère, in summer, one can see half-price tickets for the Bal du Château-Rouge scattered in a soup-bowl, in winter, tickets for balls at the Opéra, and in all seasons, reduced-price tickets for concerts and other amusements.

The shelf-unit that overhangs that one belongs more particularly to fruits and the *toilette* of the fair sex. I have seen a corset on that shelf, with all its whalebone bristling, displayed between a basket of nuts and a basket of lady-apples; the apples seemed to have become effeminate by gazing at the upper part of that ornament, which bore an inscription pricked with a pin, in which one could read: *Bargain.*[89]

In the second part of the same set of shelves, there is a stuffed partridge, as if to prove that game is not entirely unknown in the Crémerie Myrrha. That small masterpiece of taxidermy rubs elbows with a hunk of lard stood on end, a symbol much truer than that of the partridge, larded soup being far more readily available all year long in the establishment than partridge with cabbage. The end of the shelf is devoted to the exhibition of a superb calf's head destined to be adored *à la poulette, à la vinaigrette* or in its shell. It awaits its fate in a melancholy fashion, with a sprig of parsley in its nostrils.

As for the third shelf-unit, it is entirely taken up by printed squares stuck to the glass itself. On these rarely-renewed squares one can read *Beef Broth, Fried Eggs, Breaded Cutlets, Beef with Cabbage, Soup of the Day, Tripe, Dumplings, Prunes* and *Raspail Tonic Liqueur.*[90]

But half past five is about to chime on the telegraphic clock of the Église de Montmartre.

Dr. Kanali stopped outside the scarcely-monumental entrance to the Crémerie Myrrha. He had arrived. Before going in, he sought to make sure that this really was the establishment that I had indicated to him that morning, without having had the time to describe its features with an engraver's precision, to the point that he would recognize it without hesitation. He had imagined it much less grand. Thus, on going in, he was quite surprised by the sight of the interminable rows of tables that one encounters, along with the equally-extensive rows of whitewashed joists supporting the ceiling. He was disturbed by it; he thought he was confronted by the refectory of an entire population—and there was some truth in that.

He went forward, and then saw that the depth was terminated by a high glass partition, behind which he saw other benches and tables. Finally, he saw beyond those two gigantic rooms, in the far distance, a large blazing fire, a Hellish kitchen, a Gargantuan fireplace, in which torrents of flame were steaming upwards, in which crackling and spitting armfuls of dry wood were incessantly being fed to the flames, and in which six pairs of skewers were rotating—a cheerful, noisy spectacle, as lively as could be, which would certainly have mer-

---

[89] I have translated *Occasion* as "bargain," as that preserves something of the intended double meaning; the word could also be translated as "opportunity."

[90] François-Vincent Raspail, a leading figure in the 1848 Revolution and a candidate for the Presidency of the Second Republic, was a chemist and physician; in 1845 he published *Histoire naturelle de la santé et de la maladie*, which contained a recipe for a famous antiseptic "elixir." He was another anticipator of the germ theory of disease who failed to win over his contemporaries.

ited being seen were it not for an excessively strong odor of food and boldly buttery cooking not gripped you in the throat and eyes.

At the sight of that sumptuous space, Dr. Kanali permitted himself more than one reflection, and, in going to stand in the middle of the creamery, into which the diners were already flowing, he thought that he would never have supposed that men of the particular species of which he was in search were so numerous in Paris. His astonishment, already great, was doubled by an even greater astonishment when he saw quantities of women coming in at least equal to those of men.

The majority of these women were unaccompanied. They took their places around tables unceremoniously. Many of them immediately started chatting to the men in terms of the broadest familiarity. Who were they? In his corner, Kanali racked his brains for an answer, and especially for a means of explaining satisfactorily how gravediggers came to have such easy and expansive manners, and to mingle in this way with the society of women—who, in general, whatever their status, are not very disposed to welcome and treat kindly people of the unattractive profession to which he supposed the entire assembly to belong. He was destined to go from one surprise to another, as you shall see.

Who did he recognize in many of these diners, arriving at the Crémerie Myrrha in groups with every passing minute and taking possession of the tables. Former comrades of the theater! Yes, actors! Actors with whom he had once played comedy. Like him, of course, they were twenty years older, but they had aged well; he discovered them in his memory—which made him fear, for the same reason, being recognized by them. He huddled close to the pillar on to which his table backed, and enveloped himself in the fumes of his soup. We shall see that the precaution was no great help to him. But what a strange thing! Actors there, where he had come in search of gravediggers.

Had he mistaken the place? No...he really was in the Crémerie Myrrha. Did both categories gather there? Was that plausible? Laughter and tears together, at the same time, over the same tablecloth? No—it was impossible to admit. Besides which, where were the tears? He could certainly see the laughter, but he saw nothing that betrayed dolor, even official, even obligatory, even habitual. All these people, without being models of elegance, were very gaily dressed. They wore straw hats, creole waistcoats, white trousers...

There must, therefore, be an error in his presence, he reverted to thinking—and he thought that perhaps I had intended to made fun of him...

While he was ruminating these reflections, however, someone came to sit down at his table, and that someone looked at him intently. He tried in vain not to notice that he was the object of persistent attention; hat gaze made him impatient, and he became so impatient that he saw that he would either be obliged to leave the table or to ask the ill-bred individual why he was staring at him in that way.

"It seems to me, Monsieur..." Monsieur Kanali said to him.

"It seems to me," said the impertinent fellow, interrupting him, "that I'm Saint-Aimable and you're Belleville."

"I'm not Belleville."

"What! You aren't Belleville? You're definitely Belleville. I recognize you; we've appeared on stage together. First, begging your pardon, at the Luxembourg, at twenty francs a month; then at the Folies-Dramatiques, under Père Mourriez, who similarly paid us very little, but treated us very badly; then at the Gaîeté; then..."

"I haven't appeared on stage anywhere, Monsieur, I tell you!" exclaimed the doctor, ashamed and happy at the same time about the encounter, wounded in his pride but charmed in his memory, ready to strangle Monsieur Saint-Aimable, whom he wanted simultaneously to hug with all his strength.

"You've never been on stage anywhere, you say?"

"No, Monsieur, and the unwonted familiarity with which you're addressing me..."[91]

Kanali made as if to get to his feet; Saint-Aimable held him back by the arm.

"The proof," he said to the doctor, "is that you're acting right now—a little better, admittedly, than you used to do..."

"Monsieur! Put an end to this!"

"It isn't the end yet—we're only in the prologue, my dear Belleville."

"Monsieur! This gross importunity..."

"Will you accept a glass of Madeira in honor of your return to our midst?"

"To your midst? To whose midst?"

"To whose midst, he asks, O immortal gods! Our midst: actors, hams, bohemians, anything you like, who come every day to take our meals here, when we have the consideration and bounty of payment. For we're not well-off, Belleville, since the recent revolution, which was not—oh no!—made in our favor. But tell me, will you accept the dry Madeira that I'm offering you?"

"No, Monsieur," said Kanali, who was nevertheless yearning to clink glasses with the old comrade of his youth.

"Oh, that's too bad, Belleville, that's too bad. You could have told us about your Italian campaign, which wasn't as fortunate as General Bonaparte's. Michelin, the juvenile lead of that traveling company of which you were a part, is the only one who returned alive to Paris."

"Michelin isn't dead! He's here!"

"You know him, then? Ah, you know him!"

The doctor had given himself away. He stammered: "No...there are so may Michelins... I knew a Michelin once...a surgeon...that's why..."

"See how you've unmasked yourself! Waiter, Madeira!"

---

[91] The actor is addressing Kanali as "tu" rather than "vous," as an old friend would.

Kanali, utterly defeated and realizing that he was compromised, got up resolutely this time and half-turned in order to go. He felt himself forcefully retained by two arms and held against a voluminous chest. He gazed into the enormous mouth of a comedy financier, which said to him, face to face, while laughing and stifling him with his embrace: "Michelin! To whom you fed lines so long ago! Little Michelin—now big Michelin."

Emotion got the better of pride. Softening, the doctor embraced Michelin in his turn—and then all three of them embraced.

"But don't give me away," the doctor said to them. "I'm no longer an actor."

"What are you then, wretch?"

"I'm rich."

"You're rich!"

"I'm famous."

"Famous!"

"I'm a physician."

"A physician!"

"I'm even German."

"And German!"

"German."

"Is   that   all?   Then   tell   us,   milord,   by   what   miracle…?"[92]

---

[92] It is truly remarkable the Monsieur Morel can quote this conversation, not to mention the play featured in the next two chapters, word for word, when he was not present. One might almost think that he were making it up. At any rate, it seems highly likely that the introduction to this chapter, as well as much of the next two, was originally a separate work that had nothing to do with Morel at all.

"Not just now. You first, I beg you—tell me where I am, for I confess to you that everything I've seen here in the last hour has confused me to the point that I'm no longer conscious of myself."

"But you're in the famous Crémerie Myrrha."

"All well and good—but I expected to find in that creamery..."

"What? What were you expecting?"

"No...once again, you talk...you wouldn't believe me if you knew why I came here...and how far I am from finding what I sought. I beg you, Saint-Aimable, tell me all about this place...in order that I know..."

"A superb place!" said Saint-Aimable, while the doctor ordered the best wines in the house—which could not be said to be the finest vintages. "Let's begin, if you please, with the mistress of the establishment.

"The person that you see sitting at the counter is Mademoiselle Zélie Patri-arche, who has run it for ten years. She has, so to speak, conquered it, for before being the sovereign of the Crémerie Myrrha she was, a long time ago, a modest client, its subject. One day, as her charms were declining and her savings had reached an elevated level, she bought the creamery. That's how she mounted that mahogany throne, which is sometimes a podium and sometimes a confessional. It's from the height of the counter, when it's also a throne, that she commands, giving her orders to her employers—kitchen-staff, waiters and waitresses; it's there that she receives complaints, and then it's a podium, from the guests who pay and want to be treated in accordance with their money; finally, it's there that she listens to the avowals of those who don't pay much and the sighs of those who can no longer pay; then the counter changes into a confessional.

"Zélie Patriarche loved and she was beautiful, my dear Belleville. One can still see the superb ruins that her back reflects in the tall mirror behind her. She still has magnificent blonde hair and richly arched shoulders. In society, she could still make two or three conquests of much younger men if she experienced a belated pride in making use of her beautiful debris, but she prefers to conserve them for the sake of the dignity of her house. It is generally unknown, moreover, how much more complete and sincere renunciations of society are among women like her than women who lead an honest and conventional life. They retire much more rapidly and resolutely from the stage to go back into the wings. Their philosophy is profound; the excessive rigidity of their mores becomes evident when the time comes for them to convert to good. Then it's more than a change of mores that takes place in these great sinners; it's almost a change of sex; they become men by virtue of the elevated maturity of their intelligence."

"But I wasn't familiar with that world."

"Know it thoroughly then, my dear Belleville." Saint-Amiable continued: "Without having attained that final perfection, Mademoiselle Zélie Patriarche had already been able to acquire the good sense to put herself in a position to sustain the battle against the evil days of old age. She has built this fortress, from which she can see them approach without fear. She paid twelve thousand francs cash for this creamery, which has increased in value to thirty thousand since she bought it, and she has lived and paid off many old debts on top of that.

"Few people, it's true, would have been in a position, as she was, to increase the value of the establishment. She knew so many people and so many professions before retiring here! Those were the people she attracted; they are her true clientele. That clientele came to add itself to the one she had bought in buying the establishment, and those two populations of regulars offer an exceedingly varied physiognomy. You have before you type-specimens taken from the two sexes that sit down at these tables every day: look and listen.

"Over there are dried-up petty clerks earning between twelve and fifteen hundred francs a year; over there are widows whose husbands left no more trace behind them that Captain Franklin; over there are chronic debtors pursued through Paris from street to street, house to house and roof to roof, who have finally taken refuge in the impenetrable fissures of Montmartre and Batignolles; over there are petty landladies of the Rue des Martyrs, the Rue Rochechouart and a hundred other streets of the same family, who never dine at home because they dread kitchen odors and are not cooks; over there are shady, crooked and fraudulent businessmen who buy merchandise in the morning on credit and sell them for cash an hour later at a fifty-per-cent loss; their names are well-known in the Place du Palais de Justice; over there are aged female players of the stock-market, who offered their charms as guarantees when they had charms.

"Over there, near the window, are painters misunderstood for forty years, who have not even succeeded in becoming sign-painters, because being a sign-painter in Paris required a certain talent and special aptitude; over by the other window in the corner are promising writers; there beside them are writers who are no good; to their right are actors who are starting out and actresses who are finished; over there, between two poets, young actresses who still don't put on rouge in order to go on, and, further away, old actresses who put on more than ever because they no longer go on; there are juvenile leads with the chimerical dream of an engagement with the Palais-Royal or the Variétés; great coquettes whom the directors of the Porte-Saint-Martin or the Vaudeville always promise to come and hear their debuts at the Tour-d'Auvergne but have never been heard and never will be; young girls who claim to be pupils of the Conservatoire and who really are, unfortunately for the Conservatoire; and finally, over there, the directors who are always in the process of putting together companies for next season, a false pretext by dint of which they dine on credit throughout the time that precedes the famous season in question, which has never been indicated on any calendar.

321

"And then, further away—much further—there are hundreds of other characters, demi-characters, walk-on parts, human profiles, all of which I would tell you about, my dear Belleville, if we were not in such a hurry, my comrade Michelin and I, to know whether, among all the categories of people, man, women and professions that I have just caused to pass before your eyes, there is the one you came here to find."

"No, it's not there," replied the doctor, slightly stunned by the list reeled off by his old comrade without drawing breath.

"What! Not there!" cried Saint-Aimable and Michelin in chorus. "Who the devil are you looking for, then?"

"It's unnecessary to say, for the moment..." Kanali replied.

"No, it's not unnecessary. Come on, talk..."

"Once again, my good friend..."

"Once again, talk, if we're your friends."

"Well..."

"Well?"

"I came here in search of a gravedigger..."

"They're here."

"What! They're here?"

"Yes. There are as many gravediggers here as actors."

"Then I haven't been deceived?"

"Not at all, since you have two of them in front of you."

"Two what?"

"Two gravediggers, of course."

"Two gravediggers? I can only see two..."

"Well, Michelin and I are two gravediggers."

"Get away! You're two actors."

"That doesn't alter the fact. Thus, in the theater, I'm the second lead Saint-Aimable, and in the city, the gravedigger Piquelard."

"Can I believe my ears?"

"And I," said Michelin, "am the utility player Michelin in the city, and the gravedigger Fleur-des-Champs in the city."

"Good God! You don't say? To begin with, I'm heartily glad of it, in the interests of the motive that brings me here, but I can't help being surprised by its strangeness."

"There's nothing very strange in it, and when you know...anyway, you'll know right away why Michelin and I, and many others who are here, are actors and gravediggers."

"Ah! I'm listening with a double interest, my good friends."

But it was completely impossible, at that moment, to listen. The Crémerie Myrrha was in motion and abuzz, seething over its entire surface.

"What is it?" demanded the doctor. "What's happening."

"It's the custom of the creamery," Saint-Aimable replied, "that between dessert and the moment when coffee is served, the habitués enjoy a local diversion, a kind of improvisation. The dessert is finished and we're awaiting the coffee, so it's the moment when the scene in question is staged. We're therefore forced, if we want to hear one another, my dear Belleville, to delay for a few minutes the explanation you desire to have from Michelin and myself regarding our double profession of actor and gravedigger, and for you to tell us with why—for we're excessively eager to know—you came here in search of gravediggers."

"Messieurs et Mesdames," said a rich and sonorous voice—the voice of a stage-manager, which must surely be that of an unemployed stage-manager—"we have the honor, myself and my comrade Tavel de Saint-Georges, of enabling you to hear today, if you care to do so, *The Echoes of the Damned City*. Let everyone, in consequence, retake their seats in order that silence can be established."

"What does he mean by *The Echoes of the Damned City*?" Dr. Kanali demanded, immediately.

"That's right," replied comrade Saint-Aimable to comrade Belleville. "Having been absent from Paris for more than twenty years, it's quite impossible for you to divine the significance of the words *The Echoes of the Damned City*."

"Educate me, then."

"I'll do so briefly, for the play's about to begin. Draw a line from the Faubourg Poissonnière to the Madeleine; from the two extremities of that line draw two others that converge here, where we are, in Montmartre, and you will have outlined an area vast enough to contain a city at least as big as Toulouse. That city, whose contours you've just traced, has a distinct population: a population classified since its origin under the heading of fallen women."

"Oh yes—I've heard mention of...*lorettes*."[93]

"Shh! Fool...you're in their territory here, you're surrounded by them...don't get yourself into trouble...let's speak in whispers. There is, therefore, in Paris, as I've just explained—in the very heart of Paris, at the center of the boulevards, theaters and railways, an immense city uniquely populated, from north to south and east to west by the women in question. They have an entire city to themselves. Anyone who wishes can see it. You could see it; you could see these ladies' little cardboard town houses, the apartments constructed for their use; you could also see their markets, their fountains, their theaters, their promenades—and you would know the physiognomy of the *Damned City*."

"I've beginning to divine it from your description."

---

[93] An argot term approximately equivalent to the Anglo-Saxon "slut" in meaning, but with an inevitable French euphony that dignifies it somewhat.

"A few more details of mores and you'll comprehend, like all of us, the setting of the *Echoes*, which is about to be performed before you.

"People get up very late in the damned city, because they also go to bed very late. When the Paris on the other side of the Boulevard Montmartre, the Boulevard des Panoramas and the Boulevard des Italiens already has its shops open, its cafés awake, its circulation established, everything is still closed, barricaded and asleep in the idle quarter—the Rues Bréda, des Martyrs, Rochechouart and, generally, all the daughter and granddaughter streets of those districts. No café is open in that zone, no fiacre is clattering along the road, no shop has yet exposed its widow-displays. Only the milk-sellers, the eternal milk-sellers who have been in the same places since Julian the Apostate, since the foundation of Paris, are stationed in their corners at the thresholds of doorways.

"The moment comes, however, when all the door on the streets I've just named open slightly, and then one sees appear, here in profile, there only represented by a hand sliding between the two battens of a door, there in a short skirt, there in furtive slippers, there in sparse tresses, there in a bonnet still rumpled by the tempests of the nights, there in a headscarf, there is a simple checkered peignoir and bare legs, the same women that were seen the previous night, only a few hours ago, coming home in delivery carts, in fiacres, in cabriolets, in phaetons, in américaines, getting down therefrom in elegant costumes, with big bouquets collected in the corridors of the Opéra and the greenhouses of the Galeries Jouffroy.

"They're the same women; one sees them in the evening in the Bois de Boulogne, at the Bal d'Asnières, the Château des Fleurs—all the spectacles of Paris; and one sees them in the morning coming in person, for want of a domestic, to buy their milk modestly at their door. Many among those ladies, so rapidly metamorphosed, venture as far as the end of the street to go in search, at the baker's and the grocer's, of the complement of the first meal of the day. And that bizarre merry-go-round, scarcely credible if one has not witnessed it, is repeated every day with the same contrast of sumptuousness and poverty.

"Now, my dear Belleville, suppose, on a clear and silent night, that you were floating high in the sky over the *Damned City* with us, all of us who lend ourselves to that fiction; suppose too that, like a new Asmodeus, you remain suspended in that manner until morning—and you will have the key to the *Echoes*, and a depiction much more exact and much more colorful of that double existence of supreme glamour and profound misery that I have just described to you."

A final call for silence was hurled over the assembly, and the two actors charged with playing the scene of the *Echoes* began.

Attention! Attention!

Nocturnal Echoes of the Rue Pigalle.

"Charming evening, Alphonse!"

"Delightful, Florentine!"

"Not so delightful for me—I lost ten louis at baccarat."

"Florentine, I'll give you double hat sum if you tell me with whom you lost it."

Nocturnal Echoes of the Rue Saint-Georges.

"Could I eat crayfish *à la bordelaise!* I've got a craving for them. Suppose we go get something else to eat, Gontran?"

"Do you think so, at two o'clock in the morning?"

"Why not? Crayfish are timeless."

Nocturnal Echoes of the Rue Turgot.

"The face of that Russian haunts me. He's ugly, but completely lacking in elegance."

"Pass me a cigar, Marquis."

"Paquita, you've already smoked five."

Nocturnal Echoes of the Rue La Bruyère.

"I want to go back to the cascade!"

"Me too; shall we go back to the cascade?"

"But my dears, the horses are exhausted."

"To the cascade! To the cascade!"

"Coachman, return to the cascade."

Nocturnal Echoes of the Rue d'Aumale.

"God! I could gladly swallow a maraschino ice-cream!"

"And me half a dozen sardines!"

"What if we went to supper?"

"Bonvallet's is closed now, Mesdames; what do you have in mind?"

"He'll open up for us. To Bonvallet's!"

"To Bonvallet's!"

Nocturnal Echoes of the Rue de La Tour-d'Auvergne.

"Mabille has definitely become too upmarket."

"What do you expect, Zoé?—everything in this world comes to an end."

"What happened on the Bourse today?"

"Please let me go to sleep."

325

Nocturnal Echoes of the Rue de Douai.

"Here we are at last, thank God!"
"Who's taken my shoe?"
"It was the stockbroker who lifted the foot this morning."
"No jokes—give me my shoe and stocking."
"Good! It's not just her shoe, it's her stocking now."

Nocturnal Echoes of the Rue de Navarin.

"James, you'll restock my window-box tomorrow?"
"Yes, my dear, I thought of that."
"And you'll send me fifty bottles of Ermitage-Bergier?"
"I sent you fifty bottles the day before yesterday."
"That's all right then—and six of Chartreuse?"
"Green or white?"
"Six green and six white."
"But that makes twelve of Chartreuse?"
"I won't say no."

Nocturnal Echoes of the Avenue Frochot.

"How do you like my mantilla, Delphine?"
"Admirable. How much?"
"Not dear."
"But from the shop?"
"From the shop, three thousand francs."

Nocturnal Echoes of the Rue Fontaine.

"Gaston, you'll get me a box at the Vaudeville?"
"You'll have it at midday, my darling."
"Not number thirty-three, you hear?"
"Why not? There's a perfectly good view from there."
"Yes, but one isn't seen."
"That's true."

Nocturnal Echoes of the Rue de la Tour-des-Dames.

"Who has a chambermaid to give me?"
"What have you done with yours?"
"She quit last night."

"Bah!"

"Word of honor! To go to work right away for a Brazilian widow."

Nocturnal Echoes of the Rue Blanche.

"Gentlemen, you're going to come up and take tea with me."

"It's very late, Mathilde."

"Pure *caravane*, as yellow as amber."[94]

"There! Coachman, stop!"

Nocturnal Echoes of the Place Bréda.

"Jules?"

"What?"

"You're not going, are you?"

"Why not?"

"You want to go to the Club."

"So what?"

"You're going to gamble."

"No, to read the *Moniteur*."

"Leave me my money, or you're not going."

Mesdames and Messieurs, the echoes of the night being exhausted, we shall pass on to the echoes of the morning.

XI

Matinal Echoes of the Rue Pigalle.

"Quickly, three sous' worth of milk."

"There you are. Do you need eggs, Madame?"

"How much are they?"

"Two sous each."

"Give me six—I'll pay you tomorrow."

"Then I'll sell them to you tomorrow."

---

[94] "Caravan tea," and its equivalents in various European languages, was once a general term referring to a range of aromatic Chinese and Russian teas, but this reference is more likely to be to a specific kind of Moroccan tea, sometimes known as "gunpowder."

Matinal Echoes of the Rue Saint-Georges.

"Where've you been, Rosine?"

"To the butcher's. I've brought this leg of mutton."

"And you paid?"

"Ten francs."

"Ten francs! It's made of solid gold, then?"

"It's on solid credit."

"I understand. It's like me—I paid forty sous for these cutlets."

"You got them on credit too?"

"Not entirely. My butcher sells me one on credit, the other for cash."

"And he steals twenty sous from you on each of them—he's much smarter than mine."

Matinal Echoes of the Rue Turgot.

"How much will you give me for this bracelet, Monsieur Munich? It cost three hundred francs."

"I'd be mad to give you fifty francs for it."[95]

"But that's armed robbery."

"Not a liard more."

"Oh, thanks a lot. You'll give me fifty francs?"

"Not so fast! Before giving you that, I have to accompany you home, and ask your porter whether you really live in the house you take me to. The police require it. There are thieves around here!"

"That's out of the question! You want me to let my porter know that I'm selling my jewels? That's atrocious."

"Complain to the police."

"Come on, isn't there a way?"

"There is a way, yes, one way."

"Ah! What is it?"

"One alone. Instead of giving you fifty francs for your bracelet, to cover the risk I'm running in buying from you without knowing you, I'll only give you forty francs. That's good of me, eh?"

"You're taking another ten francs off me?"

"Yes, yet—only ten francs for not going to make enquiries of your porter."

"Give me the forty francs and let's have done with it."

"There, in beautiful brand new five franc pieces."

"It's a hundred sous short! Brigand!"

---

[95] The pawnbroker's speech is rendered in a tortuous eye-dialect intended to represent the accent of a German Jew speaking French. I have not attempted to reproduce it.

"That's right. You're very pretty, you know."
"What are you saying? Oh, it'd have to be a lot shorter than that!"

Matinal Echoes of the Rue de La Bruyere.

"Restaurateur?"
"What can I do for you, Madame?"
"At six o'clock today, I need a superstitious diner: trout, fillet mignon *à la maître-d'hôtel*, *ris de veau* with truffles, chicken *à la financière*, artichokes *à la barigoule*, potato fritters, charlotte russe, a brie and two plums. For wines: Romanée, Conti, Médoc, Château-la-rose, Bouzy. The rest goes without saying: coffee, liqueurs..."
"Very good, but what doesn't go without saying is the money. The dinner in question will cost eighty francs, at least. You already owe me two hundred and twenty, and you've owed the since last carnival; if we add another eighty francs..."
"That will make three hundred francs."
"I don't know about that!"
"Do you know why I'm giving this dinner?"
"To have a good time, I presume."
"In order to pay you, you ingrate!"
"What?"
"At the moment, I have a young Moldo-Wallachian prince hitched up. He's already galloping quite well, but he sometimes bolts when he feels the bit. One more dinner and I'll have him broken in. Will you or won't you help me to tame the Moldo-Wallachian?"
"What time's the feast?"
"Six o'clock for quarter past."
"You'll be served on the dot by my waiters."
"One more thing, Restaurateur."
"What, Madame?"
"I need your silverware; mine's a bit short."
"The Ruolz?"[96]
"No, your silverware—the genuine article."
"So be it—but it'll be me, then, who has the honor of serving you."
"What a good opinion you have of me."
"Of you, no...but of Moldo-Wallachian princes..."

Matinal Echoes of the Rue d'Aumale.

---

[96] Ruolz is an alloy of copper, nickel and silver, named after a French comte of that name, extensively used in ersatz silverware.

"A four-livre loaf, Baker."

"There—that's sixteen sous."

"I'll pay you later."

"Certainly not!"

"Just four hours' credit."

"None. Pay, or do without the bread."

"Take this eighty-franc batiste handkerchief; I'll come and get it back at four o'clock and give you your sixteen sous. I'm taking the bread."

The improvised scenes of the *Echoes* ended there.

It was during the supreme moment consecrated to the delectation of the coffee that Saint-Aimable said to his former colleague Belleville: "It's time to tell you why Michelin, myself and fifty other castaways here combine the functions of actor and gravedigger. The '48 Republic has killed the theaters; they've been dead for more than a year, and will be for a long time yet. The Opéra takes two hundred francs in receipts, the Théâtre-Français between fifty and sixty. Where can we go? What can we do? To whom can we turn?

"There's a shortage of arms to meet the demands of the epidemic; we've offered ours; the funeral directors have accepted them gladly. *Saved! Saved!* as one says on stage in the boulevards. We were put to work immediately; we make fifty francs per day—I mean per night, given that we only work at night. Otherwise, we dispose of our time in the following manner: from six to eleven in the evening we perform on stage; from eleven until eleven in the morning we do what I said; as soon as eleven o'clock chimes we take off our prince- or shepherd-costumes, cast aside our wigs, wipe off our rouge and run gaily to the funeral director, who dresses us in black coats and all the conventional accessories.

"Now you know, my dear Belleville, the motive that has led us to become carrion-beetles, like the majority of the brave artistes that you see assembled here. Now it's your turn to tell us what motive, no less strange, brings you here in search of gravediggers."

Kanali told his two rediscovered colleagues about the scientific goal that he had been pursuing for years, through the difficulties raised up everywhere against him by ignorance and fanaticism, and confided to them that the goal might be obtained in the following manner: "You're not unaware, either of you, of the death of Jean-Paul Désormeaux, the adored, venerated clubman mourned by all the fanatics of the Salle Martel?"

"How could we be unaware of it? It's us—Michelin and myself—who will inevitably be charged with burying him tomorrow."

"You! That's my fortune, then!"

"Why is it your fortune?"

"And my imperishable glory!"

330

"Your glory? Always your glory...your fortune. What connection...what significance...?"

"Yes, it's my fortune and my glory, and a thousand-franc note for each of you."

"A thousand-franc note! Oh, Belleville don't give us false joy—we'll die of it."

"You know as well as I do, both of you," Dr. Kanali replied, who was about to make Michelin and Saint-Aimable the same offer that I had rejected, "the universal and fanatical regret aroused in Paris by the Republican party's irreparable loss. In Paul Désormeaux it lost a god. Well, I can give him back."

"You, Belleville?"

"Me, the celebrated Doctor Fabricius Kanali. Yes, I can give him back, if you'll consent to lent me your assistance."

"We're with you—talk."

Kanali talked.

After having explained to his two former comrades what the reader already knows—which is to say, the preservative superiority of his method of embalming by comparison with all known and knowable methods—the doctor said to them more intimately: "Listen to me; since it's you who will lower the body of the illustrious clubman into the grave, will you consent to raise him up again three days later, in order to deliver him to the great and sublime operation about which I've just told you, and delighted you."

Kanali's two friends consulted one another with their gazes, and were both of the same opinion, which Saint-Aimable took responsibility for communicating to the doctor immediately.

"What you're proposing isn't without danger."

"I know, but that's why..."

"That's why friendship makes its demand beneath the graceful features of a thousand-franc note," Saint-Aimable added.

"In sum, you accept?"

"We accept."

"Ah!"

"But..."

"There's a but?"

"There's only one."

"Let's have it, quickly!"

"The place where the great clubman, the Republican of the Salle Martel, is being laid to rest tomorrow," Saint-Aimable went on, "was only consecrated to the designation assigned to it a short time ago; it's still frequented by crowds. It won't be possible, at any hour of the day or night, to carry out the removal with which you want to associate ourselves without the risk of being discovered, and being discovered would ruin everything—the operation, you and us."

"That objection has some weight," said the doctor, "but how long do you think it will be before the terrain you mention is free, returned to its original solitude?"

"At the rate things are going, I estimate that it will be about twenty days."

"Yes, twenty days," Michelin agreed, swallowing the last drop of his cognac.

"Well, let's not hurry; let's postpone the execution of the project for twenty days," said Kanali. "On that condition, are you with me?"

"Oh, entirely."

The doctor opened his wallet and handed each of his old comrades a hundred-franc note, by way of an advance, as a guarantee of good faith.

"So I can count on you both?"

"For life and until death," replied Saint-Aimable. "It's agreed, to be done twenty days hence." He rose to his feet. "I beg your pardon, but we need to bid you farewell; we're performing this evening at the Palais-Royal at the benefit of an artiste's widow, and we're in the first piece."

"Go, my friends. How lucky you are to be on the stage!"

"Yes, but at eleven o'clock we quit the stage for the other music; it's not as cheerful."

"I know, but you also know that Boileau, the legislator of Parnassus, said: 'Happy is the poet who can pass with light veneer/from grave to smooth, from pleasant to severe.'"

"What if we were to have, on Boileau's advice, another glass of smooth?"

"To the theater, Fleur-de-Champs!"

Saint-Aimable and Michelin left the room, followed by their old comrade. The session had ended anyway; the diners of the Crémerie Myrrha, men and women alike, where flowing out into the streets and alleyways of Montmartre, some to play comedy, some to sing, some to dance, but all to exercise, by gaslight or in shadow, some meager industry that would bring in what was needed for the next day's dinner.

I could tell, by the way Dr. Kanali treated me, that he was no longer counting on my collaboration to bring his project to a successful conclusion. He did not mention the clubman or the Salle Martel to me again, nor the clandestine substitution of one body for another, nor embalming, nor any of what he had said so much about on the memorable night of the great storm. He devoted all his attention to his daughter Marthe, whose mental condition required all his concern. The discouragement and chagrin of having been thwarted in her beautiful temerity of love had severely disrupted her health.

What had she hoped to result from that action, daring among the most daring? Does passion see anything else but the moment, though? Is not the moment everything to it? Her happiness had been destroyed—and it had been quite sufficient—by snatching away the veil of her tenderly hypocritical devotion to all the sick, when she was only preoccupied with one, and one who was not sick as yet. That hypocrisy had not succeeded, and how many deceptions were enclosed within that one!

For the time being, Marthe declined, without being able to stop herself, toward the dreamy melancholy into which her mother had once descended when Herr von Rosenthal was struck dead on the Hungarian plain while hunting. That also darkened the grief of Madame Kanali, frightened by the many points of resemblance between her daughter's love and her own. What more redoubtable confirmation could that resemblance require than the little red spot that César Caseneuve had in the corner of his mouth, like Bem Strombold the Vampire?

Besides which, for Madame Kanali, Bem Strombold and César Caseneuve were but one and the same apparition, permanent within her family, within her race, perhaps destined to march side-by-side with her race and her family until the end of time. What a frightful predestination!

However, Madame Kanali said to herself, *since my mother and I were both saved from the persecutions of the evil genius that reproduces itself incessantly in our house, why should Marthe, thanks to my perennial daily and hourly surveillance of her threatened life, not escape it?*

Madame Kanali forgot that there is one moment among all moments by means of which the love of a young woman escapes, whatever surveillance is mounted around her; that moment is not marked on any clock-face; it is not called a minute, or a second, or a fraction of a second; it is nameless; but it chimes, it vibrates in the brains of the amorous like the most sonorous bell. Marthe was on the lookout for that moment, and when one is stubbornly in the desire for just one thing, one obtains it—that is the great power of inventors and lovers!

How did Marthe obtain it? You will doubtless recall the bizarre bird of which Madame Kanali was fond: the bird of ill-omen that you have seen, one evening, perched on the back of an armchair; the sinister owl with the round, plaintive yellow eyes. Marthe appeared smitten in her turn by a great passion for the owl, and the owl, for its part, a bird as gentle and faithful as sadness, followed Marthe anywhere that Marthe desired. Sometimes it posed on her wrist like a falcon, sometimes on her shoulder like a parrot; and in the evening, when the young woman went to sit down, at dusk, on one of the most isolated benches in the depths of the garden, she then set the owl free—which took advantage of it to take flight, with the heaviness characteristic of birds of that sort.

Once, however, I noticed that it flew up rather high into one of the linden-trees that formed a curtain at the back of the garden, and that it assumed a attitude of attentive meditation on one of the branches nearest to the wall.

The accentuated physiognomy of those birds is familiar; not only do they seem to be thinking, but also reflecting, pondering, meditation with profundity. They are the philosophers and metaphysicians of the ornithological race. It is impossible not to notice their preoccupation. They have eyes in the form of headlights, which beckon like the radiance of lighthouses. Those of Marthe's owl stopped me that evening with a singular tenacity of expression. They forced me to look at it. It tilted its head to one side, also one does when listening with strict attention, and its gaze also seemed to be listening, so oblique was its direction.

For what was the owl listening. What was it trying to grasp in the tranquil immobility of the air? Strongly intrigued, in order to see better without being seen, I took up a position some distance from the bench on which the doctor's daughter was sitting, her eyes turned toward her bird, which seemed to be covering her with its wings, while Marthe seemed to be trying to fascinate the bid with her gaze. Add the fixity of mine, poised between Marthe and the funereal bird, and you have a tableau of the most magnetic coloration, something in the dark manner of a drawing by Albrecht Dürer, the Michelangelo of witchcraft.

At the moment when this was happening, the guttural cry of an owl sounded in the air some thirty or forty meters from the spot from which I was observing, and the owl I was watching above Marthe's head immediately replied to that cry. Evidently, I thought at first, it's some owlish love-affair that I'm witnessing. Why shouldn't owls love one another?

I was confirmed in the opinion that I was witness to a tender affair of the heart between two birds of mourning when, following the raucous cry that I had just heard, I saw Marthe's owl rise ponderously from branch to branch and hurl itself from the last one to pass over the wall of the garden, which it left behind. It disappeared. I was about to go away when, remembering my Buffon, I recalled that the month of June, which we were then in, is not the mating season for owls. My petty erudition as a naturalist held me in place. It was not, in fact, a matter of love.

Having heard a few *crou crous* and a few *pou pous* through the branches, I saw the owl return from its expedition. It did not pause in its original position; it descended from the topmost to the lowest branch, only stopping at the bench where Marthe was sitting. She welcomed it and set it on her knees. Thanks to the lipid clarity of the night, I could distinguish the young woman's hands; they were occupied; I had seen them make anxious searching movements at the bird's neck. She detached therefrom something white, doubtless a piece of paper, some note.

It was a note, which she unfolded and read—assuredly some message of love, for Mademoiselle Marthe, while reading the note brought from the other side of the trees, kissed the great tufted head of the night-bird, evidently trained by the patience of the two lovers to perform that trick.

If it was a love-letter, though, who else but César Caseneuve could have written it? Had love, therefore not perished in the night when the two young people had been caught by a father wounded in his diabolical pride as a scholar and an inventor, and by a mother crazed by superstitious terrors? Was it really César Caseneuve who was on the other side of the wall? How I admire love in those insane individuals given to other things than our prejudices, who overturn everything in order to reach their goal—and get there!

Thus, it was in a hospital, and in a hospital cruelly tested at the hour at which I am writing these lines, that love joined two hearts, exiled from one another, pining for one another; and it was an owl, the redoubtable osprey of the ancients, that was bearing the messages of love exchanged by those two your hearts in turmoil, around its neck!

Having become party to the secret of that aerial correspondence between the two young people, I asked myself whether I ought to betray them to Marthe's parents. My internal response was that morality did not demand that severe intervention from me, for the simple reason that the day after I had revealed it, they would have devised, I was sure—who could have doubted it?—another means of exchanging their thoughts. To whose advantage, then, and for whose benefit, would I be playing the ever-equivocal role of informer? Besides which, I did not have the leisure to worry for long about the question of whether, in the circumstances, I had a moral obligation to remain silent or to speak; a most unexpected event came to cut everything to the quick.

I shall describe that event.

XII

Shortly after the scene in the garden, one morning when I was fetching ice from the cellar situated under the window of the Kanali family's apartment, I heard the murmur of heated words, punctuated by intervals of moaning. I listened; the words were being spoken by Monsieur Kanali; the moans were being exhaled by Mademoiselle Marthe. Over both floated confused exhortations, confused for me, but which I nevertheless recognized as emerging from her mother's mouth. The sum of the words and plaints indicated that some unfortunate incident had recently occurred.

Having carried my blocks of ice to the little pharmacy where they would be distributed according to the exigencies of service, I ran to the Kanalis' to discover the cause of the plaints and lamentations that I had heard under the window. I did so with my customary discretion; I found a plausible pretext for introducing myself into their apartment at a time when I was not in the habit of going there.

The pretext was, in fact, unnecessary. Scarcely had I gone into the drawing-room than Monsieur Kanali, who was very animated and red in the face, pacing back and forth, said to me: "Don't be surprised, Monsieur Morel, by the state of agitation in which you find us. This newspaper"—he handed me *La Ré-*

publique, a paper much in favor then with the Montagnard[97] party—"has informed us this morning of the death of a person…of a young man we knew in the early days of our arrival in Paris…a young physician attached to the service of the Val-de-Grâce. We liked him…we liked him a great deal. But what can you expect in the accursed days that we're enduring? It's necessary to expect anything. Today one, tomorrow another…"

With the same hesitancy of ideas and expression, not knowing whether he ought to be mortified or to talk about the accident with indifference, the doctor continued: "Certainly, he was a fellow who didn't lack knowledge… quality… a veritable aptitude for medicine. It's regrettable… very unfortunate. One doesn't know, word of honor, whether one will be alive tomorrow…this evening… in an hour's time. Eh? My God, after all… it's destiny... At the end of the day, one has to resign oneself… yes, resign oneself…"

"And what was the young man's name?" I asked the doctor.

He replied to me while setting his watch to the hour that he could hear chiming at Saint-Laurent: "César Caseneuve."

On hearing that name pronounced by her father, Mademoiselle Marthe experienced an involuntary and violent nervous movement in her hand, which was clutched in Madame Kanai's. She withdrew it; her mother tried to retain it; my attention was summoned in that direction. Mademoiselle Marthe had hidden her face in a white handkerchief thrown over her head, which was tilted backwards on one of the cushions of the sofa.

On seeing her thus veiled, I was reminded in an entirely personal manner of the intention of the painter Timanthes, who, in my opinion, was not so much seeking to mask a dolor that he recognized, so it was said, that he was unable to reproduce with his paintbrush, but to render human suffering in a new way, taken to its culminating degree of exaltation.[98]

That white handkerchief did not mask anything: neither Marthe's eyes, very apparent under the fabric and swollen with tears; nor the ridge of her nose, outlined like that of a corpse beneath its shroud; nor her cheeks, to which that pale veil was stuck and over which it stretched; nor her lips, whose edges lifted it up by virtue of their moist and staccato palpitation. Uncovered, hr face could not have expressed as distinctly the ill-contained ravages of her soul.

Madame Kanali completely lost sight, in sharing her daughter's immense affliction unrestrainedly, of what César Caseneuve's sudden end had rid her. She

---

[97] In the Convention established after the 1789 Revolution the "parti de la Montagne" was a group occupying the highest-places benches in the Chamber, which always voted for the most violent measures. Just as the Jacobin "clubs" made a comeback after the 1848 Revolution, so did the Montagnards.

[98] Timanthes of Cythnus, who flourished in the fourth century B.C., was famous for a painting of the sacrifice of Iphigenia, in which Agamemon is shown veiling his face, supposedly because the artist despaired of his ability to depict his grief.

forgot that she was freed from the perpetual dread that he had imposed on her, as a vampire—although it is true that vampires die repeatedly, since they come back to earth repeatedly.

I have forgotten to report the content of the newspaper, in which the doctor invited me to read the lines relating to Caseneuve's death. I read them, and this is the text of that necrological paragraph:

The ranks of young physicians, already so cruelly decimated, have experienced another sensible loss in the person of an intern full of talent named César Caseneuve. He died, we may boldly say, a martyr of science, for it is recognized that young Caseneuve, wishing to prove the non-contagious character of the reigning malady, dared to introduce himself into a Paris hospital and lie down in the still-warm bed of a victim of the Asiatic scourge. He had made use of a ruse to enter and have himself admitted to the hospital; he had been able to imitate to a surprising degree of verity the particular symptoms of the disease. The physicians and employees were duped for several hours by that heroic act, but after he had been there for a certain time, accepting with a stoic firmness the energetic treatment meted out in such circumstances, one doctor more clearsighed than his colleagues perceived that César Caseneuve was not afflicted by the infection whose tortures he was feigning, and he was immediately discharged. The interesting intern thought that he had remained exposed to the peril long enough, however, and spent sufficient time on the battlefield, no longer to have any doubt about his medical theory—which is to say, to sustain unshakably henceforth that the scourge was not contagious. A fatal error!— literally fatal! On arriving home the young doctor was struck in a pitiless manner by the same disease that he claimed to have vanquished. He had breathed in the deadly germ[99] in our wards. He expired in the night. César Caseneuve, the new Empedocles, who precipitated himself into the abyss of the Indian disease in order to make its acquaintance, and who, like Empedocles, was devoured by it, had not yet reached is thirtieth year.[100]

I handed the newspaper back to Dr. Kanali, and immediately withdrew in order not to disturb a grief to which I could only bring embarrassment by my

---

[99] It was not until 1864, some years after the publication of this novel, and long after 1849, that Lois Pasteur made the speech in a debate at the Académie des Sciences that is nowadays viewed, in retrospect, as the crucial landmark in the establishment of the germ theory of disease attributing infectious diseases to tiny organisms rather than "miasmas" or some other vague source, but it had been proposed several times previously and the author was presumably aware of it, as he mentions two of its earlier proponents in his text.

[100] The pre-Socratic philosopher Empedocles was said to have vanished, leaving only a sandal on the rim of the volcano Etna, thus implying—rightly or wrongly—that he had jumped into the fiery crater for some unknown reason.

presence. I should not omit to report, however, a highly characteristic remark that I heard emerging from the doctor's mouth as I drew away.

"Come, come, my child," he said to his daughter, gripped by a new nervous crisis. "Don't distress yourself so. *I'll embalm him.*"

A fine consolation, you see, for a young woman who had just lost the man she loved madly! What magnificent egoism! What scientific egoism!

That family scene had moved me considerably—me, to whom Mademoiselle Marthe was nothing—but, distressed as I was, I could not help a few reflections occurring to me relative to the young man's death. The newspaper had told the truth in writing that César Caseneuve had dared to brave a formidable danger when he came to us—for it was here, in the sanitarium, as the newspaper had not said, that he had put his life at risk for the sake of his experiment...oh, not for his experiment, but his love, if you please. It had also told the truth when it added that Caseneuve manifested no symptoms of the disease that he had braved when he was sent home—but what appeared to me to be less evident in the paper's story was what came after the incontestable assertion of those two facts. It added, however, that the reckless young man had expired the following night at home. That seemed to me to be impossible, since eight or ten days after that night he had come to correspond with Mademoiselle Marthe at the end of the garden via the intermediary of the owl. Unless he was not the one who had been exchanging love-letters with the doctor's daughter over the garden wall...but who, then...?

These reflections, I alone was in a position to make, for Marthe's parents were completely ignorant about the nocturnal rendezvous of the young woman and Caseneuve—if, that is, I repeat, it really was him who kept those amorous rendezvous. On the other hand, though, if it was not him, why that desolation; why were Marthe's tears so hot and abundant at the news of his death? She could not have been subject to two passions at the same time, conducting two intrigues...that was an absurd supposition.

These preoccupations troubled me for two days; after those two days they left me—I had others to bear! Augmented by the political overexcitement to an alarming degree, the sick imposed an impossible task on the staff. We did not have enough arms to service wards that were never less than full. I shall pass over days and nights whose scenes, if they were recalled to my memory, would render me mad or idiotic. Thirty years of experience had not yet hardened me to the point of considering coolly what my eyes have seen.

And with that, an exquisite temperature! There was never a more radiant summer than that of forty-nine; nights worthy of Sicily or Naples. It was scarcely for a few hours of those beautiful Oriental nights that I allowed myself the rare leisure of a little stroll in the gardens.

It was during one of those nocturnal relaxations, which I only permitted myself between midnight and two a.m., that I had the opportunity, which I had desired for a long time, of a deep conversation with Madame Kanali regarding her belief in the existence of vampires.

If anyone is astonished to find Madame Kanali awake so late and wandering around at those advanced hours of the night, they have forgotten the excessive heat of the summer of 1849—a summer during which staying in a apartment had become a scourge; they have forgotten the impossibility of sleeping under the fearsome burden of those asphyxiating nights; they have forgotten the vigilant character of Madame Kanali, born for the night, born for insomnia as for meditation, like all the great thinkers of ancient and modern times. She was a woman similar to those Rembrandt painted, her chin sunk into the pensive hollow of her hand, her elbow leaning on the window-sill, her gaze endlessly searching the limitless mystery of the stars and the immensity of space.

On the night in question, Madame Kanali, lying back in an armchair, enveloped in a peignoir with green and gold stripes, entirely adapted to Dalmatian tastes, was dreaming between the little basin and copse of the Jambe-de-Bois. One day, I will tell the story of the man with the wooden leg who gave his name to the basin.

The circumstance was favorable. I approached Madame Kanali and said to her, with the familiarity that her natural generosity authorized: "I'll wager, Madame, that at this moment, you're thinking about vampires."

"In which you doubtless don't believe?"

"I'd like to see one—just one—in order to believe in them."

"Oh, don't make such a wish! Never see one! But you Frenchmen don't believe in anything; you're the sons of Don Juan, who only believed that two and two are four. Will you even go as far as that? I'm afraid that you might have surpassed Don Juan! A strange contradiction! You admit without reluctance phenomena much more surprising and much more extraordinary than vampires, but that of vampires leaves you incredulous. In your country, incredulity is in the blood. One mystery more frightens you, as if everything around us—around you—were not a mystery, from birth until death. The sun that returns every morning, the stars that appear every night..."

"Oh, I beg your pardon, Madame, that's science; it's astronomy. The sun and the stars return quite simply by virtue of the movement of the earth."

"Quite simply! Since it's as simple as you say, go on. Tell me, Monsieur Morel, who gave this movement to the earth, which it certainly did not adopt of its own accord? If you have faith, you will reply: it was God; if you don't; you don't have any reply to make to me—but the earth turns nevertheless; I defy you to deny it. Well, it's exactly the same with the existence of vampires; if you believe, you'll reply that they exit because God..."

I interrupted Madame Kanali at that point in her statement, not wishing to embark upon a debate with a woman ready to confuse her faith in vampires with her faith in religion. "So you, Madame," I said to her, in a tone that did not stray far from the line of a mere doubt, "firmly believe that there are men dead for many years, who escape from the tomb and come to apply themselves by night to the living, in order to aspire their blood drop by drop, and of whom the living can only be rid by piercing their hearts after cutting off their heads?"

"Yes, Monsieur, I firmly believe it."

"Are these men—these vampires—really dead?"

"Yes. God permits them to resume their original form in order torment certain persons condemned to their persecution, with an intention whose motive he keeps to himself."

"So you admit, Madame, that, although dead, they return as they were during their lives?"

"Oh, certainly I admit it, since, when they are killed, their blood runs as bright and crimson as when they were wounded in life."

"And there are many examples of such resurrections?"

"Many, especially in Hungary, Moravia, Poland and Greece, where they are called brucolaques. Do you suppose that intelligent and learned people like those of the countries I cite would profess belief in vampires if there were no truth underlying that belief?"

This time I refrained from making the slightest objection to Madame Kanali's argument. She continued thus: "If you had read a book entitled *Magia posthuma* by Carl-Ferdinand von Schertz, published in Olmütz in 1706,[101] you would know that four days after a woman had died, an extraordinary noise was heard at the extremity of the district in which she lived. It was eleven o'clock and the ground as covered with snow. At that unaccustomed noise, the inhabitants emerged from their doors, and they saw a white specter, which sometimes attacked a man and sometimes and animal, grasping their throats to choke them.

"Then there was a Bohemian shepherd who emerged every night from his tomb to cal to people under their windows, and who predicted the day and hour of their death. When his heart was transpierced with stakes, he uttered loud screams, but he was still living; it was necessary to burn him.

"And there was Arnold Paul—listen to this story—who, after having been killed by the weight of a hay-cart under which he was crushed, came back a month later and caused the death, pumping the blood by slow suction from beneath the left breast, of four people who happened to be on the road with him when he was killed. People in Madreiga—that was the Hungarian name of the town where Arnold Paul was born—trembled, but they remembered that it had often been said that Cassova-Kachau, a sizeable town, as you know, on the frontier of Serbia had been tormented by a Turkish vampire. Had that one's vampir-

---

[101] This book is frequently mentioned in dissertations on vampirism, but all the references seem to be based on a citation in Dom Augustin Calmet's famous treatise; the details of the Paul case also seem to be taken directly from Calmet, as they contain numerous details not reproduced in *Infernaliana*.

ism, then, passed like a venom into the blood of Arnold Paul? They determined to verify the matter.

"Arnold was exhumed, and it was found that his body was indeed intact. His fingernails, his hair and his beard had grown, his eyes were open—evident signs that he was a vampire, and a vampire of the most redoubtable species, for, shortly hereafter, four people weakened by him and annihilated by a consumption that carried them away became vampires. Those four new vampires aspired the blood of seventeen young women, who, after having also died of an incurable languor, emerged after a few months from the ancient cloister in which they had been buried and committed frightful ravages in their turn in the unfortunate village of Madreiga, which it as necessary to commit to the flames in order to finish once and for all with the legion of vampires.

"All these facts were examined carefully and attested publicly and in due form by the surgeon-majors of the regiments garrisoned at Cassova-Kachau and the principal inhabitants of the area. That legal document was then sent to the Imperial Council of War in Vienna, which appointed a commission to examine the fats again. After a scrupulous check, the commission determined them to be quite true, quite real, and confirmed them formally with the attestation and signature of its members, who were Battuer, first lieutenant of the regiment of Alexander of Wurtemburg, Clickstenger, surgeon-major of the regiment of Furstemburg, and Guoichitz, captain at Stallatz."

"Those are doubtless authorities," I said to Madame Kanali, "but I would prefer another to all those, respectable as they are."

"What other authority do you need? I've cited villages, towns, earnest witnesses, public officials, names belonging to great Hungarian families whose descendants still exist..."

"I'd ask for yours, Madame—your authority."

My reply was not merely a simple courtesy; it forced Madame Kanali, indirectly, to tell me what I had already heard from Dr. Sainson of the Val-de-Grâce. I was anxious to obtain that repetition, firstly in order to have absolute confirmation of facts that seemed to me to be very difficult to believe, and secondly to persuade Madame Kanali to tell me whether she really put César Caseneuve in the rank of vampires—and whether, if she did, she feared that he would come back, since he had not been pierced with a stake after his death, as is the custom with redivivi, oupires, vampires and brucolaques, in order to prevent them from ever returning among the living.

I only obtained half of what I wanted, in consequence of an event that interrupted our conversation, which I shall relate in a moment.

Madame Kanali began by confiding to me, point by point, everything that I had already learned from Dr. Sainson's mouth, firstly, concerning the vampire dogged in his pursuit of her mother, the daughter of the great Salomon Kanali, the one named Bem Strombold, who only made use of his left hand, and secondly, concerning the vampire Rosenthal, the successor of the preceding one, if he was not the same, who had a little bloody spot in the corner of his mouth. When she was on the point of replying to me on the question in which I was most interested, however: whether she feared seeing Caseneuve return to attach himself to the existence of her daughter Marthe, César not having been subjected after his decease either to perforation of the heart by a long stake or cremation—which is to say, destruction by fire—she suddenly stopped speaking.

I looked for the cause of that untimely silence. Madame Kanali was staring straight ahead; she was trying to make out an object in the white and powdery mist that the moon, on the point of setting, was amassing in the depths of the pathways. With a gesture of her hand and a furtive glance she commanded me not to disturb her attention.

"But it's not a single object that is coming toward us," I said, in a low voice. "It's a group—there are two people."

"I think so too," said Madame Kanali—and she added: "Look, Monsieur Morel; doesn't it seem to you that…?"

XIII

She stopped speaking. I finished: "Yes, one would think it were a young woman and a young man…an officer. I can see epaulettes shining."

Although the sanitarium was frequented at night by many more people than in ordinary times, I was nevertheless very surprised to see that couple strolling at an hour when no one came into the garden, especially strangers.

Madame Kanali resumed: "If my daughter had not gone to bed two hours ago, and if we knew an officer, I would say, in truth…"

"Indeed, Madame, there is a resemblance between the slim figure, and the gait…the sway of Mademoiselle Marthe and the appearance of the young lady who is on the soldier's arm."

"They're coming this way; we'll see at closer range whether the resemblance is as great as it appears to us at our present distance—although, in the increasing darkness in which the moon's setting is leaving us, it will be hard to distinguish…"

It was not only the disposition of the moon that threatened to take away any means of observing ore clearly the analogy by which Madame Kanali and I had been struck. Instead of taking that path at the end of which we were seated, the two nocturnal strollers turned right, entering a parallel path, and from then on it was only possible to catch glimpses of them through the tightly packed tee-trunks and the curtain of branches that separated that path from ours.

It was the end of June; the foliage is very thick at that time of year. There were moments when we could see very little of our young people: a patch of white dress, the glided line of the peak of a kepi.

By the time they had reached a point parallel to our position, we could no longer see them at all. On the other hand, we were briefly able to hear Marthe's voice—for it was her—saying to the young officer, who was doubtless very attentive to her slightest words: "What you're proposing to me for our next meeting is, you say, very bold and perilous, and you fear that I won't accept—but when one loves as we love one another, I don't believe one has the right to hesitate over what you're proposing without giving you reason to think that my love for you is weaker than yours for me."

That was the only sentence that we caught, the two lovers not ceasing to walk straight ahead, and, in consequence, to draw away from the position that Madame Kanali and I occupied. That unique sentence was, however, clear enough to leave us in no doubt as to the nature of the sentiment that Mademoiselle Marthe experienced for the young officer who was accompanying her, whose uniform I recognized as that of a captain in the Garde Mobile—a body of volunteers formed in 1848, you will recall, to maintain the order that was furiously imperiled.

Although I was momentarily astonished to see that uniform again in 1849, the Garde Mobile having been dissolved some months earlier, I immediately reflected that the officers had been given the right to wear it until the moment of their incorporation into the line.

What happened at that moment before my eyes confirmed the opinion that I had initially rejected with all my strength: that Mademoiselle Marthe had already replaced the unfortunate Caseneuve in her heart. How could there be any doubt of that henceforth? Marthe was there, hanging on the arm of a new lover, and at a nocturnal hour that one normally refuses as a meeting time at anyone's request. I expected some movement of just maternal anger on the part of Madame Kanali; I expected her sudden and threatening appearance before her daughter, and a scene of the most furious violence, to the extent that I was preparing arguments in my head to calm her down; but she spared me those pleas for clemency and moderation.

"I'm the happiest of mothers," Madame Kanali whispered to me, having difficulty containing the excess of her joy.

I looked at her with an astonishment that must have seemed imbecilic.

"Yes, the happiest of mothers: my daughter is saved!"

I sank even further into my amazement.

"She's in love!" she went on. "She's in love! She has forgotten, praise God, hat fatal César Caseneuve, who has henceforth lost his deadly ascendancy over her. Nothing but a new love was capable of extinguishing within her the love that consumed her night and day for the man whose presence, whose phantom, will no longer return to desiccate her youth and her intelligence, to deprive her of sleep and happiness, and slowly consume her life. She has been returned to me forever, when I thought her lost forever. The vampire Caseneuve has been driven back to the deepest of his caverns, to which he was returned for the first time when my mother escaped his icy clutch by marrying my father, and again when I rid myself of him in my turn by marrying the doctor. Now she is free too, returned to the pure air, to the healthy light, to liberty—in sum, to life. The spell is broken."

It was not only the unlimited joy of having recovered her daughter that was shining in Madame Kanali's flame-filled gaze as she expressed her gratitude to God in the most enthusiastic tones; it was also the fanatical intoxication of a woman of conviction who has triumphed over obsession with the evil spirit. Her whole face was radiant; she was floating in the mystic light of a redemption. It was as if I were dazzled by it, and I felt in spite of myself the force that was lifting her up and carrying her away. It overwhelmed me.

I had never understood so well until that moment how the intoxication of faith causes intoxications similar to its own, and how easy it is to make others believe when one beliefs so energetically oneself. Humankind is merely an electrical circuit extended by divine power from one end of the world to the other.

I will not venture to say that Madame Kanali forced me to share her exalted opinion about the existence of extrahuman creations; I confess, however, that she reduced me to no longer knowing what to say to her about the strange conduct of her daughter. Moreover, all of that—individuals and surroundings—vanished like a veritable apparition.

While Madame Kanali was talking to me about her happiness and I was listening to her, the two young strollers were eclipsed in the violet shade of the pathways; the moon had descended below the horizon; the harden, darkened by the obscurity, no longer offered the uncertain sight of any graspable form; and I could hear the unspeakable cart bearing away the day's funereal harvest passing by, grating beneath the arch of the sanitarium and rolling away with dolorous jolts over the roadways of the Faubourg Saint-Denis.

I went to get a few hours' rest.

Let us pass on immediately to the following day.

I was still utterly stunned by the previous night's adventure, and I was wondering how Mademoiselle Marthe's meeting with the young officer might be explicable when Dr. Kanali took me aside mid-morning and drew me along with him into a deserted pathway in the garden. I feared that he might be about to talk to me about embalming again, but it was nothing of the sort.

"Monsieur Morel," he said to me, "my wife told me at breakfast what you both saw, last night, here in the garden, and I assure you that I intend, at any price, to get to the bottom of that singular event. She mentioned a young officer...a young woman...but I won't believe anything, or admit anything, until I've heard from you."

"My God! I'm ready to tell you everything I know, Monsieur le Docteur, but I warn you..."

The doctor did not let me finish. "First, is there any officer being treated in the establishment?"

"None. Last year, in the same epoch, after the events of June, we received several, but since then..."

"So you can affirm that there is none in the sanitarium?" he continued, in a tone of anxiety and ill-humor.

"None, I assure you."

"Could one introduce himself clandestinely?"

"You know better than anyone," I told the doctor, "that no one can get in here without permission. By trickery, it's impossible. In the early days of your installation in the house you examined the height of the walls with me—a sufficiently reassuring height—and you observed all the other material impossibilities of getting in. Although, in the disastrous epoch that we're undergoing, the orders are sometimes relaxed slightly during the day—how can we argue with all the visitors who flock here to see their sick friends and relatives, about the authenticity of their entitlement to pass through the gate?—by night, I defy any anyone to get in without being seen and identified. It's as impossible as any impossibility in the world."

"But then, how do you explain the presence of the young officer you saw? You did see him, didn't you?"

"Oh, certainly."

"As you see me?"

Oh no, of course not! Not at such close range, or in broad daylight, as I see you."

"My wife had not caused you to enter into the chimera of her hallucinations? She has in imagination sufficiently extraordinary to do that."

"Madame Kanali might evaluate a fact mentally in a manner different from a man as positive as me, but I cannot grant her the faculty to make me see someone when there is no one there."

Without appearing to be entirely convinced by my reasoning, the doctor, still very agitated in spite of the efforts he as making not to let it show, to the point of forgetting, in his anxiety, that he had not thus mentioned the name of his daughter, for propriety's sake, said: "I love my daughter Marthe very much; I agree with her mother that she could only have made the choice of a man worthy of her—but still, it is my duty to find out who this young man is."

That paternal pretention would doubtless have appeared eminently reasonable to anyone in the world—except that the doctor brought to the manifestation of his incontestable authority a hidden agenda that was suddenly revealed in its full breadth at that moment of our conversation, without, however, showing itself as yet in its entirety. What, then, did that dull anger mask? What object of hatred was at the bottom of that seething anxiety?

"However," he went on, "we're not in an enchanted palace here. No one descends into it in a balloon. No one insinuates himself through the cement of the walls. And since it's a house like any other, a means surely exists of discovering who the man is whom you saw—the man who must have been here before and will come again."

"Certainly that means exists, and you've just indicated it yourself/"

"Let's have it, right away."

"It's a matter of hiding yourself in the place where Madame Kanali and I were at midnight yesterday, and waiting. If the young officer appears, you can reveal yourself to him immediately, and that way you'll know..."

"I've thought of that, so natural and so facile for me not to have thought of it immediately—but I'm afraid, and more than afraid, that in doing that..."

"Of what are you afraid?"

"Of getting carried away when I come face to face with a man who has not acted honestly, in loving my daughter thus without first introducing himself to us; I'm afraid, in that explanation from which moderation will necessarily be excluded, of offending, wounding or killing my daughter's affection for the young man—and it's to that affection that I don't hesitate to attribute, with her mother, her unexpected return to life.

"There's more: that passion once broken by my action, by the anticipated action of a legitimate violence, I'm afraid of similarly annihilating—and this is my greatest fear—the only reason that my wife has for not dreading that her daughter is still thinking about that accursed César Caseneuve; a dead which even his death has not tranquilized. Oh, far from it! Thus, since his death— you're doubtless aware of Madame Kanali's bizarre opinions...outré beliefs...superstitions...call them what you will, insanities, if you wish—all of that has returned to her mind, darker and stronger than ever.

"Well, this new love of her daughter has been a rainbow suddenly raised above the storm...it's over... entirely concluded, since yesterday...a few hours were sufficient. She's calm again, reassured, confident, happy. To reopen within her the immeasurable source of terrors and fears would be a crime on my part, an abominable cruelty...

"However, I shall pass with a firm tread over all the scruples, all these dreads, if necessary! There is beneath it, you see, Monsieur Morel...what is there? I can't guess, but surely...that sudden change in my daughter's heart...I must have an explanation! What I'm going to attempt is dangerous...but I'll master myself...I shall see this young man. Your advice will be followed, Monsieur Morel. I'll be there, in the place where you saw him last night."

"At the same time," I added.

"At the same time," the doctor repeated.

"There it is," I concluded, pointing into the depths of the garden."

"Very good! Until tonight!"

"Until tonight!"

The doctor left me. When I was alone, I became anxious, for different reasons than Dr. Kanali, about the presence in the sanitarium, in the middle of the night, of that young officer, who, as the doctor had said himself, had indeed not fallen from the clouds into a garden path in order to adore his daughter. But what route had he taken? I had no inkling. Although it occurred to me that he had corrupted the fidelity of one of our domestics, the possibility seemed too implausible to be admitted, even for a moment. Nevertheless, to soothe my conscience, I questioned the employees responsible for manning the gate. None of them gave rise, in his responses, to the slightest suspicion. It was therefore necessary for me to renounce for the time being any further attempt to explain the phenomenon on the fantastic introduction of the handsome nocturnal officer.

My resignation on that point did not, however go as far as permitting me to remain indifferent to circumstances that might give me some clue. I was so far from that resolution that I stuck firmly to my intention to lie in ambush for the young officer with Dr. Kanali and his wife, the following night, in the depths of the garden.

At the agreed hour, midnight, I therefore went to the place fixed that morning by the doctor and myself I order that we would find ourselves in the path of the lovers if their unlucky star led them to a repeat performance of the previous night's rendezvous.

It was not only curiosity, nor simply my desire to render myself agreeable to the doctor, that decided me to get mixed up in that adventure, with which, strictly speaking, I had nothing to do. My position in the house—a position already long-held in 1849—obliged me to keep close track of events therein, in order not to allow any bad publicity emerge into the light of day.

Monsieur Kanali and his wife had reached the rendezvous ahead of me; they were occupying the location I had indicated to them. The doctor's face had the same expression of umbrageous anxiety that I had seen imprinted upon it in the morning, while his wife was even more radiant with joy, if that were possible, than the preceding night. As soon as she perceived me, she hastened to assure me that she could now answer for the health and life of her daughter, to whom she intended to say, after the surprise that she and the doctor were about to give her in a few minutes, that she had been wrong not to confide her new affection to her parents. They were rich enough not to refuse her the right to chose a husband of modest means, if, in fact, it were the mediocrity of the fortune of the man she loved that was the cause of the absolute silence she had maintained.

"Isn't that your opinion?" she said to the doctor.

"Undoubtedly, undoubtedly—unless Marthe has other reasons for concealing this love from us."

"What other reason could there be, my love, to fear the slightest opposition on our part to a young man about whom she surely has no reason to blush?"

"I don't know, but..."

"Then why create one at will?"

"There might nevertheless be a reason..."

"That I deny."

"In that case, I'll say to you in my turn: why is Marthe so suspicious of us?"

"Firstly, because of the perfectly adequate reason that I've already told you, and secondly because, you see, my love, young women experience a kind of need for secrecy, for discretion...dissimulation, I might say...in order to give love a bitter and stimulating aroma of dread and dolor. And finally, remember too that Marthe, who was so madly in love with César Caseneuve such a short time ago is, so to speak, ashamed to expose another passion, born yesterday, immediately to the full light of day—an admissible passion, I repeat, which she will confide to you, I'm convinced, once that modesty has vanished. Do you understand a little better now?"

"Yes, yes," the doctor replied. "Nevertheless, I'm curious, and increasingly impatient, to see the man who has extinguished in a breath the love that was consuming her, and immediately ignited another in her heart."

As on the preceding night, the June moonlight was illuminating the immense cupola of the heavens with its dreamy light. The great silence of midnight floated over the great city. The hospital gate, which had just opened, as had been its habit for two months, to let the sinister cart pass through, had furtively closed behind it. Nothing, at that moment, troubled the universal calm extended over the old faubourg, through which the suburban market-gardeners were not yet passing, over the sanitarium and the garden where we were waiting for something to happen.

The event was not long delayed in occurring; the two shadows that had appeared the previous day were vaguely outlined at the extremity of the double pathway that has already been mentioned, and it was then a question of seeing which one they would take.

The idea occurred to me that, having taken the other path the previous night, this time, the two phantoms would take the path where we were waiting for them. On that inspiration, I suggested to Monsieur and Madame Kanali that we ought to move to the other.

They followed my advice, and all three of us immediately went into the neighboring path, where we did our best to make ourselves invisible.

My presentiment was justified. We soon saw the two shadows go into the path we had quit, advance slowly, with their arms linked, and then sit down on the bench we had abandoned, placed there expressly for lovers, and excessively propitious for sweet conversations by starlight.

Hazard determined that the young officer of the Garde Mobile had his back toward us, while Mademoiselle Marthe was placed in such a manner as to show us her full face—which permitted me to observe that, as her mother had said so delightedly, her new passion had indeed wrought fortunate changes in her entire person. I had never seen her so youthful or so lovely; nothing was as charming to contemplate as her complexion in the pale and delicate light of that radiant summer night.

As their confidences were being made in hushed tones—everything de-manded that: their situation, and the silence of the night, which invites discre-tion—it was fairly easy for us to be able to hear them, but for the same reason, it would have been very difficult to recognize, by the sound of his voice, who the young man sitting next to Marthe was, if by chance he had already been known to us, for words have the same anonymous character when emitted without em-phasis as when they are very faint; one is, so to speak, speaking in pencil.

"So, then," the young officer said to Marthe, "you firmly believe that your father will never consent to grant me your hand?"

"I'm convinced of it by virtue of his character, his ambition—in sum, by virtue of everything that he is."

"You see! You see!" whispered Madame Kanali to her husband. "I was right. Marthe is sure that you would never consent to give her hand to a mere officer, whose épée is probably his entire wealth and entire future."

"Listen," he doctor relied, dismissing his wife's reflection with a gesture of his agitated hand in the shadows. "Please, listen..."

"In that case," the officer said, "let's hope that my plan succeeds, my dear Marthe."

"And what is this plan, my love, which you mentioned to me last night and which I've been thinking about all day?"

"A plan as old as the world, but which is still the best one offered to poor hearts thwarted on earth. My plan is to abduct you."

At these words the doctor made a movement as if to pass from one path to the other. He was prevented from doing so by his wife.

"All this," she told him, "ought to appear to us as what it is, and that's mere childishness—pure childishness, given that we have, ourselves, the inten-tion of marrying them, have we not? Look—the young officer seems to have a graceful and noble figure..."

"You're not replying, Marthe," the young officer went on. "You assured me last night, however, that you would consent to anything, not wanting to let me believe that you did not love me as much as I love you."

"Of course I said that, my love...but where will you take me when you car-ry me off?"

"A few steps away from here, to the house of one of my relatives, where we shall write to your father that we're already far away—very far away—and that we're going to leave for Russia is he persist in refusing us his consent."

"You hear that," Madame Kanali continued whispering to the doctor. "You hear that—it's still a romance. Oh no, dear child, no one will carry you off; you won't leave here without us, for you'll leave married, and married to the man you love, to the young officer to whom we owe it that you're alive and have been returned to us."

"And how will you abduct me?" Marthe went on. "It's not easy to get out of this place; by day my mother never leaves me alone and by night the gate is locked. We'd be seen, and then..."

"We won't be seen, my dear Marthe; we'll simply go out the way I came in. Has anyone seen me come in? No! For five nights running, however, I've got in."

Five nights running! I said to myself. *But how? How?* I resumed listening immediately, though.

"How did you get in?" the doctor's daughter persisted. "How do you get in, the gate always being locked?"

We were all asking ourselves the same question at the same time, waiting with extraordinary attention for the young officer's reply.

"Don't ask me that," he replied.

"Do you climb over the wall? It's very high."

"Oh no! How, in that case, would I get you over it, in order to get out of here?"

"Do you disguise yourself, and does some employee of the house whom you have bribed let you in by a secret door?"

"I haven't bribed anyone."

"It's the Devil, then," said Marthe, laughing. "It's the Devil who gives you the means to get in."

"If only it were the Devil!"

"So what is it, then?" said Marthe, astonished.

"So what is it?" murmured the mother, simultaneously, with a quiver in her voice, addressing her question to the more-than-attentive ears of the doctor, who had at that moment the face, the neck, the gaze and the tense attitude of a lion pausing, a wild beast that has just scented the suspicion of a prey in the air.

"Don't interrogate me any further, Marthe," the young officer replied—and I noticed that after that recommendation addressed to the doctor's daughter, he wiped his brow incessantly; one might have that his nerves, contained with difficulty by an effort of will, were being racked by an internal terror. Sweat was inundating him.

"No, I need to know how you get in here at night," Marthe insisted.

"If I told you, you wouldn't want to go with me."

"That's impossible!"

"I repeat to you that, in spite of your love for me, you wouldn't want to go with me if I told you what means I'm going to employ to abduct you, and which I've used until now to get in."

Again the young officer passed his handkerchief over his forehead.

Convulsively, the doctor gripped the two large branches forming the screen that concealed him, and Madame Kanali, whom I was observing, went suddenly pale, as if all her blood had been drawn away to her feet.

Marthe continued, taking the young officer's hand affectionately.

"It's very dangerous then, your means of getting me out of here?"

"It's...terrible."

"Terrible?"

"Yes."

"Tell me immediately, then."

"There'll still be time to tell you, at the moment of execution."

"And what if I don't want to go with you then?"

"You will, I know," said the adventurous young man, putting his arms around Marthe's lovely head.

"If that's so, why make me wait?"

The young man drew even closer to Marthe, whom her mother never quit with her gaze, looking at her with an indefinable emotion.

"Why? Because the fright I'd cause you now by revealing my means of escape wouldn't diminish the fright you'll feel when the moment comes. I'd rather only give it to you once."

"But my God, what is it, then?"

"Stop, Marthe—don't ask me about it anymore."

"César, I beg you, in the name of our love, tell me…"

"César!" cried the doctor, forcefully parting the branches that he was holding in order to launch himself from one path to the other. "César!"

And he launched himself.

Caseneuve, on hearing his name pronounced behind him, turned round abruptly. Madame Kanali saw his face then.

"The dead man has returned!" she screamed. "Oh, this time it can no longer be denied: It's Bem Strombold! It's Müller von Rosenthal! It's César! It's the Vampire attached to our family, to the blood of our house, vowed to his murderous lips. Death to him! A stake in the heart! A stake in the heart!"

Madame Kanali seemed terrible to me, veritably frightful at that moment, pale beneath her gray hair, crazy with maternal dread, crazy with magical terror, crazy on behalf of her entire family, as somber and unhinged as the redoubtable figures of German witchcraft, who danced barefoot by moonlight in the Harz mountains, when she cried for a second time: "A stake in the heart! A stake in the heart!" and looked wildly around as if to discover an actual stake to plunge into Caseneuve's heart. The latter, not having waited for the stake, had set off along the path at a run, at a phantasmal pace.

Someone else, however, was gathering speed in that hectic flight: it was the doctor, whom I also followed at a run, but at a much less rapid gallop. His intention was obvious to me; when he saw that César was heading for the arch of the main entrance, evidently to get out through the gate, which he supposed to be open, he got ahead of him by taking a short cut, and ran to place himself between the two halves of the gate—which was closed.

Now, as I was a few paces behind César, it was impossible for him to get away from us. Suddenly, however, I could no longer see him and judged that he had gone under the vault, where Monsieur Kanali was waiting for him. So I lessened my pace as I ran breathlessly toward the doctor, who was even more breathless than me.

"Well?" he said, on seeing me. "Did you get him? Where is he? Give him to me!"

"No—it's you who caught him."

"What, me? But he was there, in front of you…"

"Yes, but he was coming toward you."

"Undoubtedly…"

"Well, then," I said, "what's become of him?"

"What? You're not bringing him to me?" said the bewildered doctor, intoxicated by exasperation, replying to my question with the same question.

"No, I'm not bringing you to him, since it's you who…"

"Ah!" he said. "He's got away from us!" The doctor was choking with anger.

The fact was that César had got away from both of us.

"Has he gone underground, then?" said the doctor, flabbergasted by that strange and inexplicable disappearance. "Is there another floor underneath the house?"

Our doubt and colossal astonishment would have lasted several minutes more in front of that iron grille, through the bars of which César could not have passed, and where the doctor had mounted on stopping him, if someone had not suddenly moved us out of the way in order to open it—and to open it for something less poetic and, more particularly, less alive than our amorous fugitive: the *tapissière*, drawn by two strong horses.

This evening, the *tapissière* was creaking under the weight of its heavy load.

"In that case," said the doctor, two-thirds in despair but still sustained by a rage that took hold of him in a final third of hope, "he's gone back to the garden…let's search for him in the garden. Let's track him down…he mustn't get out…he shan't get out!"

After the scene that you have just read, I truly did not know what to think the next day when, by means of reflection, I sought to explain it to myself. I said to myself: *So here's César, who was dead but has come back in perfect health, more amorous than before, and more resolute than ever, since he's talking about abducting the doctor's daughter.*

Less bowed down beneath the heavy realities of his world, in truth, I might perhaps have yielded myself to the stirring superstition of vampires—which, all things considered, at least explains the extraordinary by the extraordinary, which didn't seem so false a form of reasoning now. As I wasn't entirely ready, however, and, rightly or wrongly, could scarcely believe what everyone in the world had previously believed, I did not feel that I had the strength, in spite of the marvelous aspect of the event and Madame Kanali's fanaticism, to accept the lady's convictions, any more than I had admitted them two nights earlier, when she had obligingly recounted to me at such length the facts relating to the vampires unleashed against her and her mother, which I shall willingly call vampires of the first and second kinds.

They were not my beliefs, and I promised myself to get to the bottom of the intrigue, in which, unromantic as I am by nature, I was progressively drawn to take an interest, and which I was eager to see through to its denouement.

You can imagine how glad I was, animated by such sentiments of research and curiosity, to accept the invitation that Dr. Kanali extended to me a few days later—an invitation that, in any other circumstances, I would have declined, as much out of modesty as propriety. He asked me to sit in on a kind of family council that would examine, from the viewpoint of resolutions to be made in everyone's interests, the facts concerning the night marked by the reappearance of César Caseneuve, fundamentally quite extraordinary whether he was a vampire or not. I stammered a few insignificant reasons to excuse myself for not being able to accept the invitation, but in the end, I did accept it and I went.

The three individuals comprising the family were gathered: the doctor, his wife and their daughter.

The owl was asleep on the mantelpiece.

I have no memory of any face more expressive in its desolation than Madame Kanali's. Cruelly put to the proof, it appeared, by virtue of the emotions of the still-recent night on which she had seen César again, that she retained in her terror-petrified features the surprise produced by that apparition. Distress hollowed out an infinite depth in her eyes, and her mouth seemed torn by the cries of anathema she had uttered. When I went in, she was leaning back on the sofa, tightly wrapped in a big black shawl that hung down to her knees.

Only mental excitement can bring about these somber ecstasies, which the greatest material dolors do not attain, because they break the body and in this case, the impact had gone beyond physical harm to strike squarely at the sensibility, the reason—in sum, everything that God alone has the secret of healing. The return of that young man, after the official certification of his death, had reminded her too dolorously of the return of the other two phantoms, which it had been so difficult to drive back into the caves of oblivion, not to trouble Marthe's mother, exasperating her to the extent of rendering her such as I saw her before my eyes.

Her own eyes only quit their meditative immobility to search her surroundings with the wild anxiety of monomania, as if she were expecting to see César Caseneuve emerge at any moment from the thickness of the walls. That dread was so powerful within her that she was holding her daughter's hands in the position of someone who is holding up a person fallen over the edge of a precipice or into a fire, striving energetically to pull her up in order to save her.

"What!" she began by saying to her daughter, plunging her gaze like twin épées into Marthe's astonished eyes. "You haven't guessed that you have been the victim of a deadly lie, when you have seen César Caseneuve appear before you again?"

The word *deadly* was not the least surprising to Marthe among those that had just opened fire upon her. Why deadly? Besides why, she was also wondering what lie there was in the presence of César—an extraordinarily unexpected presence, to be sure, but very real.

"Let's leave aside the question of apparitions, which we can discuss later if you still insist," said the doctor, "and ask Marthe how she explains the return of César Caseneuve to this world, when it had been publicly alleged that he had quit it on a particular hour of a particular day..."

"Isn't that what I'm asking?" Madame Kanali retorted, without letting go of her daughter's hands.

"Of course, but you set the question on the vaporous terrain of magic, while I'm putting it in the much more solid ground of reality."

"Reality!" said Madame Kanali, ironically. "Reality! But that's what I've seen—it's what all of us have seen that is the reality: an apparition escaped from the world of darkness."

Although habituated since infancy to her mother's mysterious ways, Marthe, to whom Madame Kanali had never talked about her superstitious doctrines for fear of frightening her and awakening presentiments within her that she supposed to be only too disposed to gather and develop, did not understand her agitation or her language. She found it very difficult to understand the bizarrerie of her mother's conduct toward her. One day, she had given her to understand that she knew that she had a new love in her heart, and had appeared very happy about it; the next, she had heaped her with reproaches because she had discovered that she had faithfully returned to the returned Caseneuve. Why?

Marthe, however, had never noticed an absolute repulsion against the young man on her mother's part. Marthe's reasoning was accurate on all points except one, which is that her mother had always had considerable apprehensions in seeing César courting her daughter, but had only confided the secret of her alarm to her husband.

"All right," the doctor continued, "your reality is the right one—but I've already told you that we'll examine that side of the question later. I'll ask Marthe once again to answer me: Marthe, how do you explain the return of César Caseneuve naturally?"

"I'll explain it," Marthe replied, increasing disturbed by the ceremonious questions and her mother's increasingly haggard expression, "as Monsieur Caseneuve explained it to me himself. His physicians had left him so ill the last time they saw him that they thought him domed, to the extent that when they left his house they said to the concierge: 'Your young tenant is a dead man,' and the concierge immediately ran to make his declaration at the Mairie. Monsieur Caseneuve was not dead, and was so far from it that he got up the next day, went out the following day, and came here to the rendezvous that he had arranged with me."

"All that is, indeed, possible," said the doctor, when his daughter had given her explanation. I admit it without difficulty, but I intend..."

"Possible! Possible!" groaned Madame Kanali. "You admit it, you say, without difficulty. But it's insane! Just think..."

"Undoubtedly, it's quite possible," the doctor repeated, sensing the approach of a storm that he wanted to avoid at all costs. "I'll make Monsieur Morel the judge of it."

"My opinion is yours," I replied. "In times like this, declarations at the Mairie are not rigorously checked; names are inscribed on the list of the deceased more or less as one pleases. It's easy. It's a ready-made pretext for disappearing at will and reappearing when one deems it appropriate."

"Very good!" replied Madame Kanali energetically. "But consider, then, that the accursed creatures of whom you want to prevent me from speaking, always choose the best pretexts for reappearing on earth: they make use of the most natural in order to deceive the living more fully—and it's precisely because the pretext employed by César Caseneuve is natural that it's all the more necessary to be suspicious of it.

Madame Kanai raised her voice. "Besides which," she continued, "who has interrogated the physicians who said to the concierge: *Your young tenant is a dead man*? No one! Which of you has questioned the concierge who confirmed the judgment? No one! And furthermore, why was he, César, the man of the night, who has so easily advanced all these impostures, unable to say how he had introduced himself into this establishment? It's because pretexts were lacking on that point. The walls? He told you himself, when questioned: insurmountable. The employees? He said it himself: incorruptible. How then, did he get in? He made no reply; he had no reply to make. That's because, in order to get into the sanitarium, it's necessary to say what one is, and that is what he cannot say. Well, I'll say it: he's a vampire, a vampire, a vampire!"

XV

As we have just said, Marthe had always been kept distant by her mother from any precise confidence regarding the dangers run by the descendants of her family by virtue of contact with tenebrous beings in which, as we have just seen once again, Madame Kanali had a blind faith, incarnated in her by way of personal experience and natural prejudice. One can imagine, therefore, how her mother's final exclamation struck her with alarm and distress. Her blood froze in her veins, her nerves quivered, as if a detonation had suddenly occurred beneath her feet and hurled her into the air.

Horror! The man she loved, César, had suddenly passed, on the sacred authority of her mother, from the possible world, the everyday world of humankind, into that of magic, that of subterranean beings, vile and outcast creatures. She had mingled her young, innocent, delicate love with that of a being lower than a demon—for demons, at least, are in possession of the violent life of damnation; they enter into creation on a warrant from God; they are the persecutory genii commissioned by him for the punishment of human beings—but vampires do not enter into any order, any class or any calculation of creation. They belong neither to life nor death, neither oblivion nor Hell; they are the dead-alive, the dead that affect life; or, rather, they are the frightful grimace of one and the other. The dead reject them with the terror of the night, and the living fear them no less.

As Marthe only knew about them what she had read in books, she had never debated with herself from the viewpoint of their real possibility, had never found herself in a state of mind to deny them with the firmness of reason. On the contrary, her reason, taken by surprise, gripped, enveloped and carried away by the rapid whirlwind of fire emerged from her mother's fanaticized mouth, was lost, plunged into a crazed intoxication, into an immeasurable terror, and it surrendered her to her mother—a strange but not unique phenomenon—frisson for frisson, swoon for swoon, pallor for pallor.

Taking advantage of the bridgehead established, so to speak, by her frenetic verve, Madame Kanali passed over it to go directly to questions that, in any other circumstances, I would have found extraordinary coming from her mouth. It is true, as Molière has proved sufficiently in his *École des femmes*, that fear sometimes approaches naivety.

"When that monster spoke to you, Daughter, did you not feel invaded by an earthy vapor, which stifled you?"

"I don't know," Marthe stammered, confusedly. "I don't know...I felt so many things...it's possible...but no, no...no earthy vapor."

"That's because you wouldn't have noticed it," Madame Kanali went on, without letting go of her daughter's hands, which she squeezed even more energetically instead. "And when he took you by the hands, didn't you feel that his were horribly icy?"

"His hands...?"

"Yes."

"Wait while I try to remember...no, Mother, no...I even believe I remember having told him several times that they were hot."

"It's not general, in fact," Madame Kanali continued. "There are vampires who dissimulate that chill in several ways. Let's pass on. Tell me, Marthe...but I don't know myself how to tell you…it's necessary, though…I'm obliged to ask you…"

Madame Kanali was very hesitant to explain herself with regard to one final point, which she judged most essential, but also very delicate, as is evident. There was a conflict within her between her respect for her daughter and the need to convince her nevertheless with the most incisive precision that she ought not to doubt for a single second that she had shared her love with a vampire.

"Marthe," she resumed, making an extreme effort, as if resolutely decided, no matter what the cost, to put the question to her daughter. In a faint voice, she continued: "Marthe, when the accursed one's lips touched you.…"

Dr. Kanai interrupted. "Enough!" he said. "Enough! For the third time, I don't want you to stimulate the imagination of our child to the point of delirium, when it's quite simply a matter of telling her that the love she has experienced for this young man is a love that can have no result, no goal, no future for her, because I, her father, will never consent to her marrying a man that I have already refused—never! Since that, Madame Kanali, is where you want to get to, I've got there immediately, saving a great deal of time and unnecessary terrors."

"Unnecessary terrors!" cried Madame Kanali. "Unnecessary terrors! But if I hadn't led Marthe to the edge of the gulf, in order to unveil all its black profundity to her, she would never have had the salutary vertigo that she is experiencing; she would never have recoiled; she would never have know why her hand has been refused to a young man that she loved and whom she will now hate, execrate and curse as much as she loved him."

"I could never hate him," said Marthe.

"What! You don't detest him?" demanded Madame Kanali, astonished to see the approval of what she had just said and affirmed to the doctor vanish in that singular manner.

"Oh, on the contrary."

"Then," Madame Kanali continued in the same tone of naïve stupefaction, "you won't promise us not to lend yourself any longer to the attempts he will dare to risk in order to renew his relationship with you?"

"I can't promise that," Marthe replied, in spite of the fear that was still blanching her lips.

"But such a love will be the death of you!"

"Then it will be the death of me," replied Marthe, trembling.

"A slow death."

"Then I'll be happy for longer."

"But he'll take you with him!"

"Then I'll be happy forever."

"Well then, I'll kill him myself, I swear! I swear!"

"Then I'll be happy sooner, for I'll die with him," said the inflexible young woman, still in spite of the terror from which she had not emerged.

"Oh!" cried Madame Kanali. "Oh! That's how all these unfortunate young women fall under the influence of these abominable reptiles, who begin by fascinating them, in order to damn them thereafter and finally steal them away from the affection of their parents, from the eye of God, from the salvation of their soul."

After the final word of that last sortie against the vampires, Madame Kanali, sibyl and mother, somber and in tears, excited and in despair, wrapped her shoulders and head in the upper folds of her Indian shawl, and allowed herself to yield meekly to fatality—without, however, forgetting the oath she had just sworn: the fanatical oath to kill César Caseneuve, and to kill him as one defeats those of his species when one wants to make them die for good and all.

"You've employed all the means in your power," said Dr. Kanali, putting his hand on his wife to calm her down, "and nothing's come of it. Here's mine."

The doctor turned to me. "Monsieur Morel," he said, "you will draw up an account of our expenses in the house, which we shall be leaving in a few days' time in order to go to America. We'll see whether vampires can cross the Ocean."

Twenty days having gone by since Dr. Kanali's bizarre encounter with the actors Saint-Aimable and Michelin at the Crémerie Myrrha, the moment had therefore come when the two part-time gravediggers had undertaken to deliver Jean-Paul Désormeaux, the popular orator of the Club Martel, to him.

The doctor awaited the hour of this delivery with the most anxious impatience, in order to proceed with the embalming of that magnificent subject. He was all the more eager to take possession of it, and to enjoy the success of the operation—a certain, immense, infallible success—because he had decided, with an infallible determination, to leave France immediately after his triumph. As he had told me, he intended to go to America with his daughter Marthe, whom he intended, at any price, to extract from her fatal love for César Caseneuve—a love that had become, by virtue of a combination of natural or supernatural circumstances, the trouble and delirium of the family. Marthe, as we have seen, was under his spell; Madame Kanali had discovered in that a divine malediction, in a horrible form, and the doctor himself had ended up regarding it as an outrageous challenge to his authority as a scientist and a father.

There are such duels to the death in many families, between the desires of children and the demands of parents. Such conflicts are marked by a final day, a final catastrophe in which the bonds of affection, respect and blood, long stretched, break under the shock of a passion unjustly conceived or unjustly suppressed. Well, that final day, that final catastrophe, had sounded for the Kanali family.

Five days after the almost-magical appearance and disappearance of Caseneuve, Monsieur Kanali came toward me via the pathway of the Convalescents; he appeared, from one moment to the next, upset and radiant. I had just taken the

Journal des Débats to the director and was about to take *La Presse* to the chaplain. I had paused at the circus around the large basin, where I was busy scraping away the moss and grass that had blocked the grating.

On Dr. Kanali's contracted features, usually much calmer, sudden joys burst forth and flared up at intervals. Evidently, sentiments of equal strength, but different in nature, were diving his heart; sometimes one submerged the other, sometimes they collided—and then, as in eclipses, light and darkness cut across his face, lending it a bizarre appearance. The pathway of the Convalescents being sufficiently long, I had the leisure to observe that picturesque conflagration on his physiognomy.

I went to meet him, for I had to talk to him about his own interests—and surely one of the two powerful preoccupations that he had as he came toward me, without having yet perceived me in the place near the basin that I had just quit. He was talking loudly and gesticulating a great deal, smiling to himself, threatening, increasing his pace, suddenly slowing down, and then becoming excited again; again he rubbed his hands with satisfaction, only to recommence his threats against an absent enemy further on.

"Well," I said to him, at a distance, "nothing new, Doctor. I haven't learned anything."

I pulled him out of his waking nightmare.

"Oh, it's you, Monsieur Morel. Nothing new about the young man, that is?"

"Nothing."

"However, since the night when we chased him so hotly and let him get away from us so easily—which is to say, five days ago—he's been back four times."[102]

"Yes, he's come here four times—and in spite of my vigilance, prepared for any ruse he might employ, it's impossible, Doctor, still impossible, to find out how he gets in and how he gets out."

"Four times," the doctor repeated, with an ager full of irritation. "Four times! He hasn't seen my daughter again, to be sure, for we don't let her go down to the garden by night or leave her alone in her room. Her mother has moved her into hers. Nevertheless, he's come, and come four times; I have the proof of it. The first time, he attached a bouquet under her widow, from which I took a note in which these words were written: *Hope, dear Marthe; in four days we shall be reunited.* Do you understand than audacity? In four days they'll be reunited! The next day, another note, this time attached to the neck of the owl,

---

[102] The chronology of events has become slightly confused, and will remain so. If, as César said on the occasion of his last reported dialogue the Marthe, he had already got into the sanitarium five times, Dr. Kanali's current calculation would make a total of nine, with a tenth still to come; as the reader will see, however, that figure does not correspond with the arithmetic offered hereafter.

which, unable to get into Marthe's room, since Marthe is no longer resident in that room—a circumstance unknown outside—ended up by returning to Madame Kanali's room. Madame Kanali saw, took hold of and has obviously read that second note and the words it contained. Those words were: *Continue to hope, dear Marthe; only three more days.*"

The doctor interrupted himself to say: "He persists, as you see, he persists, the wretch! What plan has he made? I'll go on: the next day, which was yesterday, a third note, slid under the door of the room when her mother was assumed to be asleep, and these words: *Always hope, always, dear Marthe, two more days to hope.* Well, what do you think, Monsieur Morel, of that impertinent security, that certainty, which renews its affirmation every day? Ah! Finally, this morning, a fourth and final note, which I found just now, pinned under the chair in which my daughter sits in the sanitarium chapel—here it is; I still have it in my hand, having just discovered it under the chair."

And the doctor read the fourth note, of which I will tell you the approximate contents: *Hope more than ever, dear Marthe; tonight we shall be reunited; the chloroform that I enclose in the ring hidden in this letter will put your mother to sleep for a few minutes, during which you can get out of her room without running the risk of waking her. Until this evening, then, where we usually meet, at the usual time. You have told me that in order to follow me you will not recoil before any means of getting out of the house; the moment has come to fulfill your dear promise, but I won't hide it from you that the method is terrible. Will you have the courage?*

"With the result that if I hadn't found this note," the doctor continued, "this evening, when my wife had been put to sleep by the chloroform, my daughter would have escaped, would have come here to the garden to join Caseneuve, and they would have left together." The doctor stamped his foot on the ground and struck a tree with his fist. "But it's enough to make one believe, like my wife, in black magic and white magic, in brucolaques and vampires, when one sees this indefatigable pursuit of my daughter, this persecutor of our repose insinuating himself into this house without anyone ever being able to figure out by what superhuman means, what unknown path, what fantastic breach in the wall, what door or what ruse—for you've discovered nothing in the last five days?"

"Nothing, I repeat—and yet, I affirm to you on my honor that I've put a guard on all the places by which it might be possible for someone to get in: the garden, the courtyard, the cellars, the grain-lofts..."

"And yet, he's not a spirit, a flame or a flash of lightning, is he, Monsieur Morel?"

"No, but he's ungraspable."

"Oh, not to be able to lay a hand on him! How glad I would be, how much pleasure I would obtain from catching him here and making him pay, drop by drop, for all the anger and all the rage that he has been igniting within me for far too long!"

"Dare I ask, Dr. Kanali, why, overcoming a certain reluctance, which I admit, but which I have difficulty admitting to be eternal in a man of great sense like yourself, you won't give your daughter to this young man, whose intelligence and honorability you have praised to me, who is due to be the heir one day, if I'm not mistaken, of a rich uncle—a young man who is a doctor like yourself?"

Monsieur Kanali did not let me finish.

"Why don't I want him for a son-in-law, you ask me? Why? I don't want him precisely because he is a physician, or, rather, because, having the title and the science of a physician, he does not have the qualities, because he does not have the most important of all: courage. A physician is a soldier; on many occasions that soldier is bound to rise as far as heroism. Danger is a part of our noble profession.

"On the battlefield, the physician runs through a hail of bullets, traverses webs of cannonballs, guides himself by the light of bombs, in order to bandage the wounded and pick up the dying. In our cities, he plunges continually into the atmosphere of the most murderous fevers; he breathes them in; he inoculates himself with them by contact. From the poisoned arms of the patient he is treating, a mortal drop often springs forth, which might kill him by landing on his hand or in the corner of his eye. And in our hospitals, Monsieur Morel, as no one knows better than you, is not the peril immediate, constant in all forms and all places?

"You see, in times of epidemics such as the one that God is inflicting upon us at this evil moment, it is almost certain loss of life for the physician within a given interval. Whoever recoils or hesitates before those conditions imposed on our profession is not worthy to exercise it, to wear the title."

The doctor continued, drawn to make allusion—I saw it coming—to his attempted embalming at the Val-de-Grâce, when, I knew, Caseneuve has lost his head. "Well, that young men about whom you are talking, whom you are astonished that I don't want for a son-in-law, does not have the courage that the profession of medicine demands; he is a poor soldier; he is afraid of the bullets of disease and the cannonballs of death. I would not want him in our ranks; I do not want him for my daughter. Let him tremble elsewhere. Don't speak of him to me again as a possible son-in-law—don't mention him to me at all! Rather than see my daughter Marthe in his arms, I would rather see her leave here this evening in one of those sinister carriages that I never see myself without an invincible shudder, wholehearted physician though I am."

Dr. Kanali stopped, astonished to see me take several steps backwards and go pale at the last words he had pronounced. "What's the matter?" he asked. "Are you feeling ill?"

"Nothing, nothing," I told him. "What I'm experiencing is all in the mind. Look, while I pull myself together—which won't take long—read this newspaper on that bench. I'll talk to you afterwards...I need to think for a few minutes."

XVI

Although the doctor did not understand my sudden weakness, he suspected that it had something to do with the disparate threads of the conversation that we had been having with regard to his daughter. He examined me, and then sat down on the bench near the basin to read the newspaper I had just handed to him, while I delivered myself to my reflections.

"Oh, great God, what am I reading?" cried Monsieur Kanali. "No, never has disappointment fallen so cruelly upon anyone!"

"What is it?"

"It done for me! Abomination!"

"But what is it?" I asked the doctor for a second time. "You seem overwhelmed by the weight of some terrible news. What have you learned from the paper?"

"I'm in despair, more than one can say—despair!"

"If I knew why..."

The doctor was choking. He paused momentarily to breathe. With difficulty, he went on: "You know that man from the Salle Martel, the political orator who was brought here one evening, dying, about a month ago...on the night of the storm?"

"Jean-Paul Désormeaux, I believe..."

"Yes, Jean-Paul Désormeaux. I had made plans to give him a second immortality by embalming him according to a procedure that would have returned him to the eyes of his partisans as handsome as ever. I'll pass over the details regarding the various trials of that sort that I've already attempted successfully, and which promised me an immense success."

Details which I know, I thought.

"This evening—this very evening," the doctor continued, "I was to bring about the miraculous transformation; everything was ready: location, isolation, chemical agents."

"Well? Has the newspaper warned you of some unexpected difficulty?"

"If it were only a difficulty!" cried the doctor, angrily crumpling the newspaper in his hands. "It's an impossibility: a radical, insurmountable impossibility. What a scoundrel!"

"Who's a scoundrel?"

"Him!"

"Who's him? Indignation is obscuring your ideas, and your words..."

"Him, I tell you!"

"Jean-Paul Désormeaux?"

"Listen to this article in the paper."

After having smoothed the creases out of the newspaper with his still-agitated hands, the doctor read in a voice trembling with passion the following article, to which I listened with all my overexcited attention:

"To the profound astonishment of the Republican party, it has just been discovered that one of the most popular orators of the club of the Salle Martel, the famous Jean-Paul Désormeaux, the virtuous, incorruptible Jean-Paul Désormeaux, was in daily communication with the police, to which he had always belonged. Convicted at the age of twenty for forgery, he had spent five years in Melun, where his first-rate education, his facile eloquence and rare aptitude for all mental exercises had distinguished him from the other inmates. When his punishment was concluded the police selected him out as a subject of whom they could make the best use. First, he was given a new name—an exchange by which he had nothing to lose—and under his new name he was able, without giving offense to the justly-suspicious Republican party, to make useful daily reports on the members and intentions of that party to the Paris police.

"Thus, it is claimed that he rendered great services to the administration of the Rue de Jérusalem in recent times. He was responsible for the arrest of several section-leaders, who are sailing for Nouka-Hiva at this very moment.[103] The Salle Martel was the field in which he labored with great success, to the profit of those whose gratitude was shown in the generous form of two thousand francs a month. It was there that he built an intimate rapport with the red party, which never suspected that a wolf had slipped into the fold, if it is permissible to make use of that rural comparison with regard to the gentlemen of the red party. Imagine their furious indignation during the two days in which the news has been circulating.

"There is talk of nothing less than exhuming Jean-Paul Désormeaux and plunging him into the sewer of the Faubourg Poissonnière. Although we disapprove of that excessive gesture of vengeance, we fully understand the horror that a traitor must inspire, whichever party he is selling. The silence of scorn is the only punishment that it is necessary to inflict upon him, especially when death has already removed him from the range of his enemies' blows.

"At any rate, Jean-Paul Désormeaux has passed in an instant from the luminous Capitol of popularity to the Tarpeian Rock of insult. We remain Roman in relation to this violent contrast in our manner of conducting ourselves with those who deceive us during great political upheavals, the touchstone of individuals as well as the masses."

---

[103] France took possession of Nouka-Hiva, nowadays known as Nuku Hiva, in the Marquesas Islands in 1842, after the U.S.A. and England, which had earlier fought over its possession, failed to make their claims stick. Its use as a venue of transportation was brief, and the French abandoned it in 1859.

Dr. Kanali's voice had altered when he resumed, and it was in a tone of despondency that he spoke. "And now, how can I be expected to embalm a traitor? Oh, the fine plan of rendering animation, expression and the coloration of life to a spy, an informer! The project is sunk, the affair gone up in flames!"

As Dr. Kanali concluded, I admired the quality of his oration while stifling a strong desire to laugh. "You see, Monsieur Morel, it's necessary never to let forty-eight hours go by between the death of a man and his resurrection. Three days later, it's already too late; the great man has become a bandit, recognized as a spy or a wastrel, exposed as a traitor or a thief, confirmed as a forger or a scoundrel. But what am I going to do now?"

The doctor answered himself, while trying to tear apart the bench on which he was sitting with his bare hands: "There's nothing more to be done. That's twice I've been thwarted in the same attempt. There's a fatality in it; I won't recommence my struggle against it. This country is against me. For me, then, it's another country, another fatality! I'm leaving France! And I'm leaving immediately. My decision is made. It's noon—I'll catch the three o-clock train to Dieppe. I'll go to London, which is where my family and I will be tomorrow. The day after, I'll embark at Southampton for New York."

Driven by excitement, the doctor stood up. He was about to go away, to carry out his project immediately.

I stopped him. "Doctor," I said, "give me until tomorrow."

"Until tomorrow? What for?"

"Just until tomorrow."

"But again, what for, when my destiny is forcing me to go?"

"I have a presentiment," I replied, "that a decisive fact will present itself here tomorrow which will change it."

"To my advantage?"

"I wouldn't ask you otherwise."

"No, it's impossible that anything that might happen here tomorrow will improve a situation even further aggravated by the acute family chagrin with which you're familiar. The only possible consolation that I might have had in the confusion into which I've been plunged by what has happened, my only consolation, my daughter, is afflicting me like all the rest—more than the rest, in afflicting her mother too. It's a family shipwreck. No, believe me, don't ask for a futile delay. Let me go."

"You won't experience that shipwreck—at least, I hope so—if you consent to what I ask."

"What plan have you got in mind? You have in your voice, in your gaze, in the hand that's shaking mine so cordially, preoccupations, sentiments…things of which you offered no glimpse when I arrived here a little while ago."

"Something you said, Doctor," I replied, "was a flash of enlightenment for me, a ray of fire in the darkness, Trust me, give me until tomorrow."

"All right—I'll give you until tomorrow."

"That's not all—I can't do it all alone."

"Speak! What more do you expect from me?"

"Go back to the chapel, from which you brought the note written by César Caseneuve to your daughter, and replace it under the chair. It's probable that your daughter will find it, read it and, by means of some sign of intelligence for which we need to be on the lookout, will reply to it in the course of the day. Her response is a foregone conclusion; she'll accept. Tonight, therefore, she'll be at the rendezvous given to her by the writer of the note. We'll be there too: you, Madame Kanali, and me. The denouement of this intrigue, obscure but not impenetrable, will burst forth immediately.

"It will be a denouement for everyone: for you, for your wife, for Mademoiselle Marthe and for the man whose influence over the fascinated heart and dominated will of your daughter have become a persecution that Madame Kanali shares and which is increasing, every hour of every day, the personal terrors of her beliefs. Be ready, therefore, tonight. The 'usual time' of which César Caseneuve speaks is about half past midnight I'll come to find you a quarter of an hour earlier. During the day, you'll alert Madame Kanali, and the three of us will go down to the garden in silence. The rest is up to the course of events."

After these final arrangements, the doctor went to do as we had agreed: replace the note he had taken and bring his wife into the secret of the ambush set for the two young people.

I had much on which to reflect after his departure.

I had taken a great responsibility on myself by making a promise to bring enlightenment and peace into that family tormented by so many various passions, but it interested me to the highest degree, and I had a sincere conviction that this affair, like all those in which people lose their heads, required more common sense and reflection than effort to avert misfortune. Those who are drowning do not require a continent beneath their feet; much less will suffice; it is often on a piece of wreckage that one survives a shipwreck.

That item of debris, for me, was César Caseneuve; he was destined, in my thinking, to bring the olive-branch into the house. But where was César Caseneuve? Would he come, as he had promised? Might not the ruse that he employed to get into the house, which I believed I had finally discovered, and which was the cornerstone of all my hopes, fail on the very day when it was important to the success of my calculations that it achieve the great result for which it had been imagined?

Let us admit that the ruse would not fail, vanquished by ill-luck, and that César would get into the house, as he had promised. Was that all? What other means did I have thereafter of making him acceptable as a son-in-law to a father and mother set against him, exciting one another to a peak of irritation? The events that will follow, from which we are separated by a matter of hours, will tell whether my method was sound, and whether the prophetic opening created in my brain by the involuntary remark that Dr. Kanali had made was or was not a hallucination.

Circumstances presented themselves in the best conditions imaginable, as I had foreseen, and as I would have arranged them myself had I been the invisible order of the world.

We allowed Marthe to administer the chloroform to her mother—who, forewarned of the occurrence, took care not to breathe in while the phial was placed under her nostrils. Then we allowed the young woman to go down into the garden in complete confidence—two characteristic facts that permit us to have no doubt that she had found and read the letter pinned to the wickerwork of her chair.

We went down to the garden in our turn, and, the moon no longer illuminating the last nights of the month, were able to reach, without being seen or our presence suspected, the bushy location where the two lovers' last conversation had take place, and from which they were planning to depart forever.

After due reflection, I decided to tell Monsieur Kanali and his wife the reason why I had brought them; it was not appropriate for me to maintain the mystery any longer.

"Your daughter is there," I said to them. "In a few moments, César Caseneuve, whom she is expecting, will be with her, and this time, if I'm not mistaken about the means that he has contrived to get in, it will be easy for us to catch him, no matter how clever he is in eclipsing himself or how nimble he is in fleeing.

"The means that I attribute to him, which I don't want to keep secret any longer, is this: in order to slip into the sanitarium, César must be taking the place of the cart-driver who brings the *tapissière* here every night. There is no other supposition to make, and I have made it. Yes, underneath the smock of that nocturnal carter, whose function he purchases for a few hours—I don't know at what price—he wears the costume of the Garde Mobile in which he have seen him. Once he's inside, he folds up the smock, throws it over his arm in the guise of a cloak, and, after his meeting, with your daughter, he puts it on again and takes his place at the head of his horses. Search for the officer; he has disappeared.

"That's the skillful game he has played every time he has got in here by fraud, and it's with the aid of that rapid change of clothes that he's escaped us. He won't escape us this evening, but let's be prudent. Let's allow him to accomplish half his transformation, then allow him to come this far, where we are, costumed as an officer in the Garde Mobile—and when he's on the point of withdrawing with your daughter, of getting out of the house by the means that I suspect, catch him…and everything will be settled."

When I had finished speaking the doctor looked at me with the phenomenal astonishment that I had experienced myself when the thought of the means employed by Caseneuve to slip furtively into our midst had occurred to me. He was all the more astonished because he knew better than anyone what immeasurable fears the young man had in that regard. What love! What passion! What a folly of passion and love César must therefore experience for his daughter Marthe, since, in spite of that infinitely boundless fear, he made himself into a personification of fear: the fearful man became a conductor of shades and a collector of phantoms in order to get close to her!

"The struggle with such a fear," the doctor murmured, "is almost courage!"

Madame Kanali did not say anything; she was awaiting events for the last word on that legend of the Middles Ages. For her, Caseneuve remained what she had always said he was: a vampire.

The half hour after midnight chimed on Saint-Laurent, and on that warning of the imminence of the crisis, the doctor and I imitated the granitic immobility of the eccentric woman, with her dark and distant superstitions.

A few seconds after the last vibrations, we heard the gate of the sanitarium open, and over that noise passed another: that of the wheels of the tapissière rolling under the arch.

After a few minutes, footsteps caused the sand of the pathway where Marthe was waiting to rustle.

"However impatient you are," I whispered to the doctor and his wife, "restrain yourselves. Listen, and don't move. Let it suffice for now to be sure that he can't escape you, if it's him that we can hear coming."

It was him.

He was wearing the costume of the preceding nights, that of an officer.

After thanking Marthe for coming to a rendezvous that would by unlike any other, he said to her: "My dear Marthe, we have ten minutes to spend together; listen to me solemnly, for what I have to say to you is solemn."

"I'm listening," Marthe replied, slightly surprised by the authority in César's words; he had been more amorous than grave in his speech thus far.

"I've already warned you," he went on, "that you'll only be able to get out of here by accepting the means that I use myself to come in."

"Haven't I already said, for my part, that I would consent to anything in order to go with you. Why go over it again?"

"Yes, you've told me, and that's good."

"It's neither good nor bad, my love; it's because I love you," said Marthe, whose voice, less confident than during preceding meetings without being less tender, testified to an emotion surely due to the influence recently exercised upon her by her mother. The traces of Madame Kanali's conversation were still fuming—the conversation in which, you will remember, she had forced her daughter almost to allow herself to be convinced that César belonged to the frightful family of beings rejected both from the bosom of creation and that of oblivion. Drawing all her energy from the finest sentiments of the heart, although Marthe continued to love Caseneuve in spite of what her mother had said, she nevertheless could not entirely pass over what her mother had said. At her age, there are no two ways of receiving the impressions of the external world. She believed César because she loved him; she believed her mother because she loved her—but that hesitation in her voice had much to do with the similarly hesitant utterance that escaped César, which he had perhaps been holding back on previous occasions, or which, even better, he had thought of not pronouncing at all.

"Well," Caseneuve resumed, after Marthe's protest, imprinted with devotion, that she was ready to accompany him, "I still doubt it."

"What do you doubt?" she asked.

"That you have the strength to fulfill your promise."

"But I've told you that I will have the strength to follow you anywhere it pleases you to take me."

"Anywhere?"

"Anywhere."

"Even into the tomb?"

On any other occasion, that outré expression of hackneyed vocabulary—but always new to lovers—would only have been an image for Marthe, beyond which she would have gone in search of César's true meaning. On this occasion, however, remembering her mother's attack upon him, she was, in spite of the natural solidity of her constitution, gripped in the heart by a sudden, nervous, involuntary fear; she saw in César what that fear made her see: a different being, a different creature. His pallor seemed to her to be dull, verging on the immobility of marble; his eyes, stuck by a supernatural fixity; his hands, which held hers, as cold as those that her mother attributed to vampires.

"Oh, it's not into the tomb, exactly, that I want to take you," Caseneuve went on, smiling, "but it resembles it strongly."

To that response from César, which had just confirmed his nature and his intentions in Madame Kanali's eyes, the latter made a movement as if to precipitate herself into the other pathway. I held her back and, at the same time, stifled a cry on her lips with a hand that prevented its explosion.

Caseneuve continued: "If you knew, Marthe, if you even suspected the means by which I have come..."

"It's time—tell me," Marthe replied, in a curt and choked voice.

At that moment, in the air the enveloped us all, actors in and witnessed to that scene, there was a particular fluid of excitement that gripped and twisted our nerves to breaking-point. We were like sappers waiting avidly for the ignition and explosion of a mine stuffed to the brim.

"Yes, it's time, my dear Marthe," Caseneuve continued, "to tell you by what means I've come, and, in consequence, by what means we'll go."

We listened.

Then Caseneuve told her the strange things you are about to read.

"After having been chased out of here as a fake invalid," said César Case-neuve, "I didn't know how to get in again. Desperate, mad with discouragement, I prowled around the house incessantly, going back and forth past the gate by day and night.

"The other evening, at midnight, when I was standing near the gate, I saw that fatal vehicle with which you're familiar going in...the sinister *tapissière*. Immediately, the idea occurred to me—why hadn't it occurred to me before?—of sneaking in by sliding unobtrusively behind it. I thought the idea triumphant, and immediately put it into execution, walking stealthily behind the two men who were following the vehicle, my shadow overlaid and hidden by theirs. I didn't get far. As soon as I was under the arch I was seen, identified, thrust back and expelled by I don't know whom, and the gate closed in my face, with its ironic grating sounds and all its iron bars. I was pushed back into the street. It was then, however, when all seem lost for me, that I conceived the plan that I'll tell you, and whose boldness will doubtless leave you incredulous at first, but which, in the final count, you'll be obliged to believe."

That project, I thought, *really is the one I attributed to him; what he's jut said confirms my opinion. Yes, that idea occurred to him in the street—the vehicle, the gate...so my anticipations were just...in order to get in here, he took the costume and the place of the driver of the tapissière.*

"First," César went on, "in order that no one would any longer pay any attention to me, I passed myself off as dead. Nothing is easier at present. I went to the Mairie myself, where no one knows me, to inscribe myself in the list of the deceased. Then, in order to put any enquiries off the track, although no one had any great interest in making any about me, I put on the uniform of a officer in the Garde Mobile, lent to me by a friend by whose side I fought against the insurgents last year at the Place du Panthéon and the Barrière d'Italie.

"By virtue of that uniform, still respected, I was able to circulate in the vicinity of the Val-du-Grâce, where you shall see how important it was for me to be, and it was easy for me to get into all the courtyards, in the guise of an officer from the nearby guard-post, charged with maintaining order in the quarter. Once that was done—that, alas, was not the difficult part—I thought of carrying out the plan in question, the idea that had lit up like a torch in my brain, like an inspiration, in front of the very gate of the sanitarium. It's time to tell you what it was.

"Paris has an organized service of special vehicles, which depart between ten and eleven o'clock in the evening, from various points of the barriers, to come to relieve the capital's hospices, over-full of a certain population—that which has definitively settled its accounts with life. My period of service at the

Val-de-Grâce had informed me in detail of the itinerary followed each night by those necrological carriages. I knew, for example, that the one serving, among other establishments, the sanitarium in the Faubourg Saint-Denis, departs from Bicêtre at ten o'clock and goes to the Val-de-Grâce to take on its first cargo. That's where I waited the first time for eight hours. I saw it arriving cautiously from the Barrière Saint-Jacques. It came through the gate of the Val-de-Grâce and stopped at the steps in the interior courtyard.

"It was at that moment that I had hoped to see, as usual, the driver and the two men charged with walking behind the vehicle by way of an escort go into the Val and leave me a free hand for a few minutes. My expectation was disappointed; instead of going into the monument, as usual, to help their comrades in their work, the three men stayed outside, two on guard behind the vehicle, at the very opening of the kind of double-batten door by means of which the phantom passengers are introduced horizontally, and which the two guards close thereafter with the aid of a strong iron crossbar. The other one, the driver, took up a position at the head of his horses, and did not budge.

"That change astonished me as much as it frustrated me. I could not restrain myself from asking the driver why it had been made. He told me that the previous evening, the horses, left to their own devices, had taken it into their heads to go out of the courtyard, go calmly back along the faubourg and go into the country by way of the Barrière Saint-Jacques, not stopping until they got home, to the village of Ivry where they had produced a rather disagreeable surprise by arriving, with their characteristic rig, into the midst of a local fête. Such was the explanation I received from the driver, which did not modify my situation at all. My hopes sank to the bottom, like a man falling into the sea with a lead weight attacked to his feet."

These statements by César no longer fit in with my initial supposition. It was not a matter of borrowing the cart-driver costume and taking his place. What, then, was the plan that he had formulated? What was the one he had put into execution? How had he got in?

"With its cargo loaded," César continued, "the long vehicle draws away from the Val-de-Grâce to complete it at other points. It resumes its route. It goes down the Faubourg Saint-Jacques, still making as little noise as possible, in order not to reveal its passing to the inhabitants, whose ears are pricked, kept alert by well-founded dread for themselves or their families. And I follow it, mechanically and pointlessly—pointlessly, because my plan seemed to have failed from the moment the three men could no longer leave their positions of surveillance around their depot.

"I knew that the long carriage was following that road to go to the Hôtel-Dieu, where it took on its second load. Now we're taken by surprise at the corner of the Rue Soufflot, directly opposite the Panthéon, by patriotic songs intoned in ferocious voices by drunken socialists, up late, who are emerging like a tempest from the famous club in the Rue de Grès. They're singing *Die for the*

Fatherland! at the top of their voices. They come toward us, still singing, but while they're arriving from the Rue de Grès, other socialists, who reply to them with the acclamation: *Long live the democratic and social Republic!* are coming upon us from behind, from the Rue Saint-Hyacinthe. They're both interrupted, like two torrents that find a rock in their course, by the obstacle of the tapissière. As soon as they've recognized the moving destination, all of them, as if compressed by the effect of a spring, fall silent and open up a passage for us; we pass through the somber, murmuring, rippling, noisily silent swarm. I've never experienced such an immediate contrast in my life. They flow into the shadows in black waves, and we continue going down the old Parisian faubourg.

"Having arrived at the Quai Saint-Michel, the rig I'm following, still shaving the tortuous walls, takes the Petit-Pont and goes into the Rue Neuve-Notre-Dame, which leads, as you know, to the Hôtel-Dieu, into the Place du Parvis itself. There, I hesitate as to whether I should go back to my hotel in the Passage Dauphiné, where I've been living since being sacked from the Val-de-Grâce, or whether I should cross the bridges to exhaust myself further in impotent means with the illusory goal of getting into the sanitarium. I still don't go away, however, in the midst of that indecision, and in that I act very judiciously without knowing it, for I soon see the cart-driver say a few words in the ears of the two escorts placed behind the vehicle.

"Those few words having been said, they head toward a wine merchant's shop in the Rue des Trois-Canettes, where all three of them go in. I'm mistaken—the third one only goes half way in; he's the driver. Standing in the doorway, he stays on watch, his attention divided between his duty and his pleasure. He has one eye on the counter, the other on the tapissière, in order to be quite sure that the horses are behaving themselves, that they aren't going to the local fête at Ivry again, or any other fête. That accursed surveillance, so fundamentally praiseworthy, renders my plan as impossible to execute in the Place du Parvis as in the courtyard of the Val-de-Grâce. I'm beginning to despair again. How can that importunate eye be distracted?

"A young woman passes by, emerging from the hideous Rue des Trois-Canettes with a cracked and sniveling guitar under her arm. She's just been delighting the cut-throats of the local taverns with the delightful strains of her lyre. I call to her; she comes over. I tell her to go place herself in front of the wine merchant's shop and sing her most beautiful ballads there in her finest voice.

"'Sing them with gusto,' I tell her, 'so as to make the peasants gather round.'

"'I only know one,' she relies, but I know it, of course, in the finest perfection. It's *Black-eyed girl.*'

"'Here's thirty *sous* for you—go sing that one.'

"The young Sappho of the Trois-Canettes accepts, and runs to fulfill the conditions of our hasty bargain. She sings, she scrapes her strings, inspired by the money I've given her and a crowd assembles. My cart-driver already seems distracted. The distraction turns to delight; already, his redoubtable eye is no longer gazing at his horses; he leans over the young singer in a melancholy fashion and I see him give her something, doubtless an obol of admiration; Polyphemus is vanquished.

"I take advantage of the fine moment of generosity that has absorbed him, and slip into the vast tapissière, whose two battens have, as usual, remained open for the requirements of the service."

"You got into the tapissière!" exclaimed Marthe. "You shut yourself in with the corpses!"

I uttered the same cry inwardly, with an astonishment that rooted me to the spot, on hearing about that act of redoubtable temerity, of unparalleled imprudence, of unprecedented passion—an action whose folly of which, it must be admitted, only a vampire, in a fit or violent crisis, would be strong enough to carry through to the end.

You can imagine how, in listening to César, the ever-present idea of the vampire crossed the fanaticized mind of Madame Kanali, how the word *vampire* came to her agitated lips, and that I had had once again to beg her, tremulously, to restrain herself lest she give us away.

"Scarcely am I in the moving coffin," César continued, "the swaying, convulsive, ill-suspended grave, than I'm gripped by a nervous tremor, as if I'd fallen into a well of icy water. My hair stands on end with the chill; my chest contracts with the chill; I rebel, however; I want to struggle: a violent combat, ardent, then desperate, between the terror increasingly oppressing me, which is making my teeth clench and pushing me outside, and my love for you, Marthe, the love that makes me ashamed of my fear, which holds me in place and retains me. I don't know yet, at that moment, I confess, whether it is my love that will conclusively hold sway over my fear, or my fear over my love; but just when I am perhaps about to hurl myself, recklessly, outside the sinister cart, no longer being able to stand it, I hear someone open the door at the back.

"I only just have time to throw myself backwards and to imitate, by lying flat, the rigid immobility of the bodies that form, by their superimposition, a kind of wall on the side opposite the door that has just opened. Through that gap, I see the introduction, repeated several times, of objects similar to those I've just mentioned. The force of impulsion that shoves them from the outside to the inside pushes them up against me, but I dare not push them away for fear of giving myself away, although I'm fearful of their contact, of dying on the spot.

"The operation complete, the doors close again; the iron bar seals the entrance, and the carriage moves off again toward the Grève, via the Pont Notre-Dame. From the Grève it goes into the Rue Saint-Antoine, but quietly, moderating the rotations of its wheels on the roadway; I've told you why; it's so as not to frighten the houses situated on its route.

"Can you imagine my situation, my dear Marthe? I was in complete darkness and only able to move with great difficulty in the midst of those and badly-stowed inert masses. I could hear the beating of my heart, as one hears the swinging of a pendulum by night. A sickening, stifling situation.

"Wanting, at any price, to see, to breathe, to live, I decided, with the aid of a knife that I was fortunate enough to have on me, to make a hole in the thin wall of the carriage. The task wouldn't have taken as long or been so difficult if I hadn't been restricted in my movements. However, after a few minutes, the opening was pierced, and I was then able to distinguish the reddish blinking of lights distributed here and there at the level of the shops we were passing by that were still open, and passers-by who were fleeing from us with signs of revulsion when they recognized the particular character of our conveyance.

"Toward the middle of the Rue Saint-Antoine, at the corner of the Rue Percée, it stopped, and I wondered why, knowing that we were still a long way from the Hôpital Saint-Antoine, which was probably our next stop. This was the reason—or, more accurately, the pretext—for that halt, which prolonged my intolerable sequestration so cruelly: I saw the driver confide the care of his horses to one of his companions and draw away in a casual and contented fashion; he went a little way along the Rue Percée and tapped on the window of a shop, which, from its grayish façade, I deduced must be that of a laundress. A young woman, sprightly and cheerful, appeared on the threshold in a white under-bodice, with a thousand creases in the sleeves and the basques, with the fine figure of an eighteenth-century marquise, an intelligent forehead and an oval face, carved and creased by Coustou.[104]

"The muleteer went in unceremoniously, and the door remained ajar, which permitted me to see from my strange observatory that it was nothing less than an amorous assignation. What a well-chosen moment! As soon as they were in the shop, the gallant fellow took a large bouquet of wild flowers from beneath his smock, with a movement of his arm worthy of Céladon,[105] and handed it to his lady. That tribute appeared to obtain the highest approval for the one to whom it was addressed. The pretty laundress put the bouquet to her lips and kissed it for a long time, half-closing her eyes—a voluptuous sign of gratitude. I was, therefore, resolutely witness to an amorous episode: Charon quitting his ferry-boat to meet the laundresses of the Styx. Charming!

"Yes, but me, I was in the boat, waiting...still waiting...what a wait! I cursed that ill-timed love from the bottom of my soul. Had I really the right to do so, though? Was it not also love that had led me to my situation? And was it

---

[104] It is unclear whether the reference is to Nicolas Coustou (1658-1733), his brother Guillaume (1677-1746) or the latter's similarly-named son (1716-1777), all of whom were noted sculptors.

[105] The shepherd lover in Honoré d'Urfé's immensely long pastoral romance *L'Astrée* (1607-27), which was completed by other hands after the former's death. The love of Céladon and Astrée was cited by the utopian Charles Fourier as the spiritual ideal of the emotion.

not thanks to the charioteer who was here that I was going to see you, Marthe, in a matter of minutes? No matter—the fellow irritated me. If I had dared, I would have shouted through my loophole, in a manner to put a redoubtable end to his tenderness: 'Hey! When are we going?' I didn't do it, firstly because I no longer had any courage, any idea or any voice, and secondly because all my vital energy was concentrated in the gaze that I was directing at him, as if to pull him away from his laundress.

"My magnetism didn't work. The wretched muleteer sat down, and sat his lover down next to him; once they were both seated, he took a crumpled, blue-tinted piece of paper from inside his felt hat; then, putting his arm around the neck of his enchantress, he began reading the piece of paper with her. What was it? I couldn't guess. Ah! I was about to find out...two voices started singing. It was the ballad performed on the parvis of Notre-Dame, in front of the wine-merchant's, by the little Bohemian songstress of the Rue des Trois-Canettes: *Black-Eyed Girl*. All the verses went by; there was not a word of that abominable ballad that did not enter into the quick of my flesh like a red-hot nail.

"Finally, the sentimental scene came to an end; the funereal Lovelace, whose name was Fromentin—which I knew by virtue of the tender farewell addressed to him by the laundress from her doorway: 'Adieu, my Fromentin!'—rallied his two comrades, and, to compensate them for the tedium of a halt that had not had the same charm for them as for him, took them to the wine merchant's placed at the other corner of the Rue Percée! Always wine merchants!

"I would not have been able to witness that feast from the tortuous position that I occupied if the handsome Fromentin had not turned the heads of his horses toward the Place de la Bastille instead of leaving them immobile, as they had been in the Rue Percée for a good half hour. Great God, how all three of them took advantage of that infernal station, which added ten further minutes to the torture, the fire, the rack, the pincers—to all the tortures that I had already endured. What they drank in those ten minutes, what they swilled, is incalculable. If it had only been wine! But I saw all the shades of the rainbow mingled in their glasses, although the yellow returned most frequently. I concluded that cognac played a leading role in the party.

"In sum, they drank prodigiously. They drank too much, for, when we set off for the Bastille, in order to go into the Faubourg Saint-Antoine, they went from right to left, from side to side, as if they were being tossed by waves. The vehicle, left to its own devices, no longer following the good side of the road, also experienced that frightful pitching, and all of its human cargo poured over me. My arms were insufficient to ward off the avalanche. How is it that all my hair did not turn white? I say all, for the next day, the temple were blanched, for a long time, forever. You can see that, Marthe.

"However, by dint of gong right and left, and a little forwards, we reached the Place de la Bastille. There, the two men representing the rearguard drew closer to Fromentin and said to him, without fear of being overheard in that vast space, where passers-by were becoming less numerous, and where, for reasons already deduced, they had little apprehension of their indiscreet contact: 'Fromentin, there's a superb coup to bring off if you wish, which would give us a good time for the rest of the night.'

"'What superb coup? Where's the superb coup?'

"'Don't shout!'

"'As if anyone were likely to hear us in this basket!'

"'All the same, keep your voice down!'

"'I'll keep my voice down—let's hear this coup, quickly!'

"The three men huddled together to the right of the shafts, almost edge to edge to the planks that separated me from them.

"'This is the coup. Well, instead of us killing the mood by going all the way to the Hospice Saint-Antoine, and from there to the Saint-Louis, then from there to the house in the faubourg, then from there to—damned if I know where—let's not go anywhere!'

"'What's that?' Fromentin interrupted. 'How do we do that?'

"'Let's go along the Canal Saint-Martin, which is right in front of us, close to the edge. We break the chain, that's all, and then throw all the merchandise— rat-a-tat!—into the water: goodnight all! Tomorrow we say that we were asleep, that the cabriolet tipped over. How does that suit you, Fromentin?' Choffar asked. Choffar was the name of the man who'd just finished talking.

"Continue to imagine, my dear Marthe, my new situation. Already the horses, avoiding the entrance to the Faubourg Saint-Antoine, were taking the road down to the Canal Saint-Martin, along the Rue de Charonne.

"The entire cargo was about to be tipped into the canal, and me with it."

XVIII

"The driver had consented, then?" Marthe asked.

"Perhaps it seems to you," César continued, "that nothing would have been easier than to cry out, to get out, to escape…but first of all, I couldn't get out; the iron bar was securing the two battens of the door. Cry out? It was half past eleven; no one would come to my aid; and after all those cries and all those movements, if I hadn't succeeded in getting myself out of it—and I wouldn't have got out of it—what would have happened? I'd have found myself in the presence of three vigorous fellows who would have roughed me up right away. They were drunk…one corpse more or less wouldn't have made much difference to them. I therefore had good reason to reflect profoundly on the originality of my situation.

"The cart was still going down, unsteadily, toward the canal. It wasn't until we were level with the Rue du Chemin-Vert that Fromentin appeared to hesitate, for his part, to carry out the abominable project of the mass drowning. Had love rendered him, that evening, better than his accomplices? I don't know…but I saw, through the fog of his drunkenness, a calculation of prudence glimmering.

"Afraid of opposing the opinion of his comrades, two muscular fellows who might well by-pass his assent if necessary, he told them that their plan pleased him enormously, and that he was all for it, but that it was still too early to carry it out without considerable risk. Plenty of people coming out of the theaters were still crossing the bridges to go home, either to the Barrières or the La Roquette and Ménilmontant quarters.

"It would be better, he went on, to go straight to the Hospice Saint-Antoine first, take on the usual cargo there, and then come back to the canal as if to go to the Hôpital Saint-Louis, one of their destinations, and to which, of course, they wouldn't go. That was what Fromentin said, in his semi-common sense. There might have been some resistance to his proposal, but, the fear he had put into them having weighed upon them, they took the Rue du Chemin-Vert and turned right by way of the Rue de Popincourt toward the Faubourg Saint-Antoine, in order to end up directly in front of the hospice.

"After a lot of jolting and pitching in the potholes of the atrocious Rue Popincourt, the most uneven of all the bad roads in Paris, a kind of communal route—which says enough about how rarely it is repaired—we reached the Faubourg Saint-Antoine.

"The concierge who came to open the gate of the hospice was astonished, and complained about the lateness of the vehicle. They were careful to keep quiet about the reason for the delay, but he deduced it easily from the unsteady gait and strongly alcoholic ambient atmosphere of the three men. Closing the two sides of the gate behind them, he muttered: 'It seems someone's been having a party this evening.' They made no reply, and followed him into the ground-floor rooms.

"In order to get the work done more rapidly when they came back, before leaving the tapissière they had removed the iron crossbar sealing the two battens of the door, so that the door was open and nothing as any longer preventing my escape. The facility was all the greater because the abominable somersaults of the Rue Popincourt had upset the carriage's container to the point of opening gaps large enough to pass through by dragging oneself through with one's hands and knees.

"I therefore had the opportunity to escape, to put an end to the unspeakable tortures—and it is permissible to say 'unspeakable,' this time, with less banality—of one of the most frightful nights ever, and above all to spare myself the almost infallible chance of dying, drowned at the bottom of the muddy Canal Saint-Martin. I could doubtless have done that—but to give in to that idea would be to renounce forever penetrating into the sanitarium, seeing you again, my dear Marthe, who had been forewarned of my arrival.

"You were waiting for me, perhaps at the cost of great difficulties, for, with the aid of the owl, you had not left me in ignorance of the combined and coalesced sentiments of hatred and anger with which your father and mother had viewed my indefatigable obstinacy in returning to you in spite of their disapproval and prohibition. That you should expose to yourself to those risks while I…I might recoil before peril—any peril whatsoever! No! A thousand times no!"

"Then again, you see, Marthe I have proved that there is a fatality in passion. It is no longer you who acts when it is true, when it is strong; it is passion that leads you. It triumphs over everything, over the individual will, and that of others, over reason, self-interest, honor—often fear itself… yes, fear. I am the proof of it, and the example.

"To describe to you the black terrors, the mortal palpitations, the frights the horripilations, the superhuman swoons that I went through during that nocturnal expedition, without parallel, I believe, in human life, is impossible. I shall not try. To support myself, in order not to expire in place, I had but one means—that of thinking constantly of you, Marthe, of constantly pronouncing your name: Marthe; of saying to myself: *One more ordeal, and I shall be with Marthe! Behold the work of love!* That alone, I repeat, that alone, perhaps with maternal love, is capable of giving birth to that beautiful, rare and powerful miracle of determination over fear.

"My determination, therefore, defeated my nervous tremors. I stayed.

"The same reproaches that had greeted the three men, my companions, in the course of that night, so memorable for me, escorted them when they were on the point of setting off again, the loading operation having been completed. One of the hospital administrators had even joined the concierge at the gate, and threatened them with destitution if they took it into their heads to be late again.

"They left.

"I attributed the abandonment of their plan to go down to the Canal Saint-Martin, into which they had intended to unload the deposit entrusted to them, to those severe words on the part of the administrator. That salutary terror, to which I owe my life, made such an impact on their resolution that they avoided taking, in order to go the Hôpital Saint-Louis, the road they had taken in coming, in order—that as visible—not to expose themselves to the risk of changing their minds in the presence of the great temptation of the water.

"Taking the longer route, they climbed the Faubourg Saint-Antoine as far as the Rue Saint-Maur, which would take them to Saint-Louis without any deviation, for the Rue Saint-Maur, the most desperately extensive street in Paris, the dorsal spine of the mastodon, ends at the foundation of the pious king, whose name it has taken and preserved. I had, therefore, the right to count, after the various accents of the night, on a relative calm until the end of my journey.

"Vain hope! At a certain point of the Rue Saint-Maur, a difficult point to specify exactly, in view of the small number of poor disreputable lanterns placed

377

out of pity on that immeasurable extent of terrain, but, to judge by the surroundings, somewhere between the Rue des Trois-Couronnes and the Rue de l'Orillon, in the dense obscurity in which I was curled up, in a space made even narrower by the addition made at the Hôpital Saint-Antoine, I felt a hand place itself on my jaw. A hand!"

"A hand? A hand, you say?"

"Yes, Marthe, a hand."

"Oh my God!"

Madame Kanali extended her head through the branches of the hedge of bushes that extended between the trees in places, listening with shivers of terror. I could hear her breath, noisy within her taut breast.

"That hand... it's distressing," said the doctor. "I've been through many situations in my life... but that one... oh, that one!"

"Yes, it's frightful," I said, "but let's listen."

"My blood," Caseneuve continued, "retreated *en masse* to my heart, which seemed to want to burst out of my breast, and rose into my throat. The cold of that hand entered into me like five talons of ice, so profoundly that I thought that one of those five terrible fingers had penetrate and was digging into my skull.

"Momentarily, the situation raised me to the vertiginous summit of madness. I saw red; I heard something akin to a monotonous sound of bells in both ears—that was the blood surging to my brain and erupting therein."

Marthe threw her arms around César's neck and looked at him, eye to eye and heart to soul, with the immense, indescribable interest that one feels for a beloved individual narrating a perilous ordeal—so perilous that it seems to be still present.

Another interest was combined with that one in Marthe's heart, that one very serious, very consoling, which gave birth to a conviction that she had now acquired forever: her mother was fanatically mistaken in classifying that poor young man, so brave by force of love, in the category of those who deceive the tomb in order to come to the earth to light to satisfy filthy appetites at the expense of the living. It was him, her beloved Caseneuve, who was threatened, at this point in his terrible poem, of becoming the victim of some brucolaque, of some vampire!

Hugging Marthe, entirely happy and shivering all over, to his bosom, César continued.

"What should have followed in servile fashion the chromatic scale of the old novels you read, my dear Marthe, is that I ought to have screamed at the icy contact of that hand. In fact, one does not scream in the situation in which I found myself trapped; on the contrary, the voice falls into the cavities of the breast, and the throat closes over it. One can no longer breathe; one can no longer see. My ears continued to run, to groan, to buzz around my head.

"However, as I did not want to die, I imparted a desperate, outré shock to myself, like that of a drowning man touching the bottom, and, raising myself up—for you will not have forgotten that I was still lying on my back—I pulled away the marble hand stuck to my cheek; I shoved it far away from me, with horror.

"But the hand immediately returned, this time applying itself to my breast, which it seized and dug into with a force at least equal to that I had put into shoving it away. Then, I passed my own arm beneath the arm that was gripping my clothing and my flesh, and seized the elbow that was compressing my breast.

"What a struggle! What a struggle in the darkness, in the suffocation, in the silence! With whom, then, was I contending in that darkness? A breath passed through my hair, ran over my face, preceding words that had the appearance of emerging from somewhere nearby I could not locate: 'Are you dead or alive?'

"I had the strength to reply: 'Alive!'

"'Good! I too am alive—but tell me, how the devil did you get into this gracious phaeton?

"'It's a long story,' I stammered, still asphyxiated by the unexpectedness of the occurrence.

"'You weren't put in here by mistake, I suppose...?'

"'No, not by mistake.'

"'It's just that in Paris at present,' my funereal interlocutor went on, 'there are kindly relatives and worthy heirs who are profiting from the rapidity with which people are exiting from life to make you exit a little sooner, in order to inherit more quickly. But in that case, why are you in this boudoir? Forgive me for my curiosity, but truly, when one doesn't have a motive like mine for cramming oneself in here... I don't know... I can't see any other motive...

"'Anyway, mine is... damn it, I can tell you. It's one young man to another, isn't it? For I divine from your voice that you're still a the fortunate age of billiards games, dominoes, card games, parties at Pinson's, idling, cigar in mouth, at the Brasserie du Luxembourg, balls at the Capucins and the Prado. Monsieur, I've just come out of the Prado—what about you?'

"'I haven't come out of it.'

"'Too bad! *It's a jolly place*, Monsieur Prudhomme[106] would say. *One drinks there between laughter and love*. So, I've come out of the Prado and I'm going back to the Hôpital Saint-Louis, where I'm an intern. You can see how I'm interned. This gracious vehicle is taking me back to my hôtel...Dieu. Joking apart, let's talk seriously. Who are you? One likes to know down here with whom one is traveling.'

"'I'm an intern like you,' I replied.

"'You're an intern! And to what royal establishment are you attached?'

"'I was most recently an intern at the Val-de-Grâce.'

---

[106] The archetype of self-satisfied banality in the work of Henry Monnier; the speaker must have encountered him in *Scènes populaires* (1830) rather than the definitive *Les Mémoires de Joseph Prudhomme* (1857).

"'I'm very glad to meet you! I'll go on then, I'll continue and conclude: at Saint-Louis, the interns only go out once a fortnight, and for myself, it's necessary that I get some air every evening. I have a sentiment in the Rue des Boucheries-Saint-Germain. How do I reconcile my duties as an intern with my tenderness as a lover? The amphitheater and the polka? This is how: I escape in the evening before the gates of the hospice are closed; I go down into Paris; I go to the café, the ballroom, as the mood takes me; finally, at eleven o'clock, to get back in…ah, but getting back in is a little more difficult—impossible, even. So what do I do?

"'Having observed that this jolly tapissière, before stopping at Saint-Louis, stopped, in its journey, at Saint-Antoine, and that during that stop it's entirely unmonitored for about six minutes, I acted in consequence of those fortunate observations. Taking advantage of the temporary absence of the three men commissioned to guard it, I climb in at the rear, lie down—and it takes me to Saint-Louis every night.

"'At Saint-Louis, I seize the moment when the three men are drinking in the wine merchant's shop located opposite the gate; I emerge from my brilliant carriage and climb up to my intern's bedroom, to descended therefrom at two hours after midnight and do my duty until dawn. That, my dear and admirable companion, is the cause of my absences and the reason for my presence among these shades.

"'Well,' I said, somewhat reassured by my young comrade and colleague, 'your story is much the same as mine.'

"'Impossible! Surely not!'

"'It's true,' I went on, 'except that you're making use of the vehicle to return from your amorous rendezvous and I'm making use of it to go to mine.'

"'Where is it, then?'

"'On the other side of the canal, at the sanitarium in the Faubourg Saint-Denis.'

"'I understand. Oh, admirable! So, we've both had the idea of having recourse to the same strange means, unprecedented since the world's beginning, to see our beloveds. O love and surgery!' After that exclamation, he resumed, with an adorable naivety: 'And who knows… perhaps there's a third young man with us in this space, so poorly designed to receive…'

"We did not have time to verify the fact; the necrological carriage went into the first courtyard of the Hôpital Saint-Louis, rolling over the poor gray sand and the sad yellow lawn that enamel the pavement there. What my joyful intern had told me was realized, to the letter.

"Once the carriage had stopped, the three men hastened, before any consignment of new passengers took their place, to go make their habitual maneuvers, belatedly, in the establishment of the wine merchant, whose shop was no longer open at that hour of the night save for once entrance, which was for them. While they were filling their glasses, my traveling companion bid me farewell;

he shook my hand with the hand that fear had caused me to find icy, and he slid from shadow to shadow projected in the pavement by the old walls of the ancient establishment of Saint-Louis, all the way to a door, by means of which he went up quietly, as he had said, to this intern's bedroom, into which he slipped in such a manner as to let the house believe that he had never left the attics all night long.

"One other and final event marked my journey from the construction of the pious King Saint Louis. We crossed over the Canal Saint-Martin without the slightest accident reminding my three men of the intention they had manifested earlier in the evening of getting rid of their load in the black depths of those stagnant waters. In the old Rue des Récollets, however, between the Faubourg Saint-Martin and the Faubourg Saint-Denis, I almost lost within an instant, by my own fault, the fruit of my constancy, my firmness and, perhaps I have the right to say, my heroism, in spite of my mortal anxieties."

"What happened, then?" asked Marthe, who thought that she was emerging forever from a terrible dream.

"I have the habit," César concluded, "when I find myself in darkness and I want to know the time, of activating the chimes on my watch. That night, I did not reflect on the consequences of that action, so insignificant in other circumstances. I pushed the button of my watch, and at the third tinkling stroke sounded by the bell, the driver suddenly reined in his horses and I heard him say to his acolytes: 'Did you hear something?'

"'What? No.'

"'There's a repeating watch in there—a gold watch, for sure... people are in such a hurry nowadays... someone's forgotten to take his watch off. We're not going much further—let's take a look... it's worth the trouble...'

"'No, keep going,' said one of the two confidants to whom the carter was speaking. 'There's no more a watch in there than a pendulum clock.'

"'You're scared!'

"'No I'm not!'

"'Yes you are!'

"'Let's see—how many chimes did you hear sound?'

"'Three, I think.'

"'Well, that proves you were sleep and dreaming, because it's midnight. You'd have heard twelve strokes.'

"'That's true, damn it,' murmured Fromentin.

"'And then, think about it,' the other went on, 'repeating watches don't chime on their own hereabouts. If you heard one chimes inside, there'd have to be someone there inside...someone alive...'

"'That's true too, damn it'

"'You were dreaming a clock, that's all.'

"The dialogue stopped there—but I'd still run a terrible risk! If Fromentin had only heard three strokes out of twelve, it was because, realizing my silly imprudence, I'd put my watch into my mouth after the third stroke, in order to stifle the sound."

César paused momentary, and then went on: "I've told you, dear Marthe, about my first night with the shades; the four other nights that followed were marked by events that were scarcely calm, as you may suppose, but none was as tragically eventful as the first, which honesty obliged me to relate to you."

"What!" Marthe cried. "Five nights!" She put her hand over her eyes in order no longer to see, even in memory, the scenes of that narrative. Involuntarily, her pale lips murmured, repeatedly: "Five nights! Five nights!"

"Yes, five nights," César Caseneuve repeated in his turn, "on which I used the same means, the same ruse, to get in here, to see you, to tell you the sweetest thing in the world: *I love you*; and the best thing in the world: *I will love you all my life*; and finally, to say to you, this evening, that we shall never be parted again, never be parted again... Shh! Shh! Listen!"

"It's the quarter hour sounding," Marthe said.

"Then it's time to go," said Caseneuve, getting to his feet.

Marthe got up too.

"Do you have the courage," César said to her, "the immense courage, to be free? To be yourself, to be mine, to climb into that same... that same... thing that brought me here, and which is presently unguarded... oh, I've calculated my time well... and remain enclosed with me all the way to the barrière?"

Marthe was unsteady on her feet. Her hand, which was leaning on Caseneuve's shoulder, prevented her from falling over.

"At the barrière," César continued, "it stops one last time—and one last time, the three men escorting it go to drink at the tavern on the Butte Montmartre. It's left alone for a few minutes more on the exterior boulevard. We take advantage of that moment, we escape, we're free! Once free, you write to your father... but we don't have a minute, a second, to lose. We have to go. You have to go with me... it's now or never—will you? Oh, you're hesitating... well, don't hesitate, Marthe—do better. Refuse. It's a horrible means, it's horrible, a thousand times, horrible!"

"Let's go!" said Marthe, taking Caseneuve's arm. "Let's go!"

They went.

They did not get far.

Between the end of the pathway along which they were running and the gate of the house, the doctor, more on his guard this time that on the previous occasion, stopped the two young fugitives. They were caught.

But then, while Madame Kanali embraced Marthe, for whom she no longer had to fear the murderous affections of a vampire, the doctor told César, hugging him in his arms, that he would give him his daughter, since he had demonstrated, by his rare and sterling courage that he was worthy to be his son-in-law, and a physician like himself.

A few days later, all four of them left Paris and France to go to America, where Dr. Kanali intended, with a joy slightly colored by hatred of France, to embalm the President of the United States.

www.ingramcontent.com/pod-product-compliance
Lightning Source LLC
Chambersburg PA
CBHW020258030726
47499CB00001B/242